SEVEN COME ELEVEN

Also by Charles Deemer

SCREENWRIGHT: THE CRAFT OF SCREENWRITING

THE DEADLY DOOWOP

TEN SONNETS

CHRISTMAS AT THE JUNIPER TAVERN

Seven
Come
Eleven

Stories and Plays
1969-1999

Charles Deemer

Writers Club Press
San Jose · New York · Lincoln · Shanghai

These stories first appeared in the following periodicals: "The First Stoplight in Wallowa County" in *Northwest*, September 4, 1988; "The Man Who Shot Elvis" in *Prism International*, Fall, 1977; "The Epistemological Uncle" in *Whirlwind*, May, 1994; "The Thing at 34-03-15N, 118-15-23W" in *The Colorado Quarterly*, Spring, 1969; "Lessons from the Cockroach Graveyard" in *Expression*, Volume 3, 1991; "The Idaho Jacket" in *Prism International*, Spring, 1973; "Fragments Before the Fall" in *The Literary Review*, Summer, 1971.

Christmas at the Juniper Tavern was originally published by Arrowood Books, 1985.

Published by Writer's Club Press, an imprint of iUniverse.com, Inc.

For information address:
iUniverse.com, Inc.
620 North 48th Street
Suite 201
Lincoln, NE 68504-3467
www.iuniverse.com

URL: http://www.writersclub.com

IN MEMORY OF:

Richard Crooks
friend, storyteller, mentor, soul brother

who said, above all else,
"Pay attention!"

And with special thanks to five directors
Steve Smith, Gary O'Brien, Peter Fornara, Julie Akers,
Diana Callihan

and one songwriter
Lynne Fuqua

and five editors
Joe Bianco, Ralph Salisbury, Jacob Zilber, Paul J. Carter,
Charles Angoff

and one teacher
Bob Trevor

for their encouragement and support

Contents

Introduction

THIS MUST HAVE HAPPENED around the summer of 1950. I would have been ten.

Deemers on my father's side gathered at our home in Pasadena, California, for a reunion. This was unusual in several respects. Many Deemers tend to be more solitary than social, so any gathering of the clan always took considerable planning, effort and good fortune.

But this reunion was helped by a timely accident: the relevant Deemers were all living in Southern California, far from their roots along the Delaware Valley in New Jersey, where such gatherings were apt to be called in small river-front towns like Milford.

My father had been the first to escape west, settling in Pasadena after retiring from the Navy (he was still under forty, so retirement really meant the search for a new career, something that would not be easy for him). Apparently his report on Southern California had been glowing enough to convince his brothers and sisters to pack up their families and follow him, and on this summer day our house was filled with them all, including my father's two brothers and two sisters, Uncles Don and Bert, and Aunts Hilda and Dot. They soon would return east, scared off by earthquakes and freeways, but for this rare reunion they all gathered at our home.

My mother put up with these affairs more than she embraced them. She had only a sister, Aunt Billie (who also was there this summer day), and was not comfortable with the loud chaos that was so much a part of these rare Deemer reunions. I'm sure she kept her sanity by staying out of the way, doing the routines of a good hostess, which had the advantage of keeping her on the move and therefore spared, as much as possible, the joke-telling, trick-playing brouhaha of the Deemer clan.

I imagine it was during one such flight that my mother entered the den to find me, Uncle Don and Uncle Bert on our knees, thoroughly engaged in the fate of two dice rolling across the carpet. Or maybe she entered a moment sooner. She would have found me with both hands shaking the dice, as I softly pleaded, "Seven come eleven!," the magical new incantation I was learning as part of what my uncles called "the old Army game."

Mother would not have approved of this scene but she wouldn't have stopped it either. Surely she continued through the room as if she hadn't see us, on her busy way to whatever real or invented errand was at hand.

The trouble started later. I found her in the kitchen and asked if I could borrow a quarter — in pennies. She wanted to know what had happened to my allowance, which I'd received only yesterday, on Friday. Well, I explained, Uncle Don and Uncle Bert taught me how to play this old Army game and, well, I lost it.

Mother imploded when she hit the roof. She put together the pieces of the puzzle very quickly: Uncles Don and Bert had invited me into a game of craps and had the audacity to let me wager with my allowance – and lose! There was, however, no confrontation on this point, at least not immediately, because when I followed her to the den, the room was empty. Uncles Don and Bert, who knew my mother well, already had fled the scene of the crime.

"Come on seven, come on eleven! Seven come eleven!" — it was one of the great lessons of my childhood. I learned that games can be real, you could lose an allowance in them. My mother may have been horrified at my uncles for teaching me this, but I'm forever grateful. I also am grateful to have been exposed to the magic of possibility, the realization that sometimes you win as well as lose, the shaking and throwing of the dice can reverse one's fortune in an instant.

The seven short stories and eleven plays in this collection map my throwing of the dice over a period of three decades. Not everyone will agree that the dice come up seven or eleven here. In fact, these stories and plays do not include all of my most "successful" work, measured either critically or financially (for example, two of my three *Best American Short Stories* "Roll of Honor" selections are not included), but instead are the stories that still resonate with me. At this point in my life, this is the work that still interests me. This is the work I stand by.

I also am in that wonderful moment of life when, to use Raymond Carver's perfect phrase, everything is gravy. Uncles Don and Bert taught me how to throw the dice in a game without mercy, but they also taught me that every now and again, with a little magical incantation – "Seven come eleven!" – the dice come up winners. Despite often being my own worst enemy, I've had my share of good fortune in this life. Some of that good fortune is represented here.

All things considered, that's mighty thick and rich gravy.

Charles Deemer
Portland, Oregon
June 13, 1999

Better to write for yourself
and have no public
than to write for the public
and have no self.

—*Cyril Connolly*

You have to decide
whether you are going to make money
or make sense.

—*Buckminster Fuller*

Part One

SEVEN SHORT STORIES

The First Stoplight in Wallowa County
"Portland was a city that commissioned Beauty and got Portlandia, a copper statue of a scantily-clad lady holding a pitchfork."

The Man Who Shot Elvis
"They stole my song. It would have been a hit for me but it was a hit for them instead. They stole it."

The Epistemological Uncle
"Do you really knoooooooooooooooooow?"

The Thing at 34-03-15N, 118-15-23W
"Remember the hay rides? Or the campfires, roasting wieners and marshmallows, and later singing, *The bear went over the mountain to see what he could see?*"

Lessons from the Cockroach Graveyard
"The older I get, the less I understand women."

The Idaho Jacket
"Do I have the family madness, Richard? Is this the beginning?"

Fragments Before the Fall
"Everything is a manifestation of the search for the appropriate parting gesture. Everyone wants to be valedictorian."

The First Stoplight in Wallowa County

Northwest (September 4)

FLETCH HAD WOKEN UP without an alarm clock at 5:30 a.m., give or take ten minutes, for so many years that neither Sunday off nor a bad hangover could keep him in bed past six. On this Sunday the hangover was worse than usual because he had been lucky playing cards last night at Mel's Tavern, putting together a rare string of winning poker strategies. Twice he drew successfully to an inside straight. At stud, in the largest pot of the evening, he bluffed Jensen into folding three visible kings in deference to his own two aces up, even though he had only a junk deuce down. And more often than not, he folded the two pairs on which he habitually raised — and lost. When the game was over, Fletch walked away from the table almost $50 richer, most of which he spent setting up whiskey at the Cowboy Bar down Main Street.

Fletch rarely drank hard liquor, which made his first gesture this morning tentative — but right on time. Or so he thought.

The first hint that something was wrong was that the clock read four, not five-thirty. The second was that he could read the time at all. His Big Ben came from a preluminous era when clocks had big hands and little hands instead of radiant numerical displays. Fletch's big hand had not reached the bed lamp yet, and so he shouldn't have been able to read the time. But read it he did.

Fletch's room was located above the selfsame Mel's Tavern responsible for his hangover — or at least that had financed it. Looking out the window to Main Street, Fletch saw the one thing in the world that should not have been there: a stoplight. A genuine traffic light, swinging lightly in the summer breeze, showing him a devilish green even as it showed Swede's Tavern across the corner a diabolical red. As anyone in northeastern Oregon could tell you, there wasn't a single stoplight in all Wallowa County. Since Joseph was in the county, Fletch must be looking at some alcohol-induced mirage.

Moving in the green glow to the window, he leaned on the windowsill and stared out at the light. He scratched his belly and stared for a long time

5

— until suddenly, impossibly, the green light turned yellow, and the yellow light turned red.

Fletch moved quickly then. He hurried back to bed and pulled the single sheet up over his head. He swore to quit whiskey forever, even to give up drinking beer — and this time for real.

NOT AN HOUR had passed before Renford was shaking him. Fletch never locked his door — in Joseph, locked doors were as rare as stoplights.

"You're not gonna believe this," Renford began.

By his usual waking time, Fletch had followed Renford into a growing crowd of men on Main Street, each man staring up at the stoplight with something between outrage and wonder. These were the early risers who started off the day with coffee at Tony's Cafe when it opened at six, workday or not. Each turned silent, as if standing before an inexplicable disaster. The speculation didn't begin until Tony's opened, where coffee cleared the mind.

"It's gotta be Divorak who done it," Fletch suggested, referring to the mayor.

In Joseph, being mayor is not really a job — at least not a full-time, paying one — and in the most recent election Divorak had won easily by garnering the write-in, sympathy vote. Election Day fell a few weeks after his stroke, and everyone knew that only makeshift work such as politics could keep Divorak out of the fields and away from the hard work now forbidden by his doctor.

To everyone's surprise, Divorak took an immediate liking to the job. He started hanging around City Hall even when there was nothing to do, which was most of the time. Moreover, lately he had been ending rare meetings of city business by yelping like a coyote, as if aiming to outdo the infamous "whoop whoop!" of Portland's mayor, Bud Clark. While no one actually believed that Divorak was trying to get on the Johnny Carson show, as Clark had done, nonetheless a man who yelped like a coyote wasn't entirely to be trusted.

Divorak, for example, stood fully behind the summer re-enactment of the Great Joseph Bank Robbery. At first, this idea for luring tourists from the Wallowa Lake campgrounds into town had been scoffed at, almost universally. The very idea that working farmers and ranchers would volunteer an hour or more in the middle of the day to playact at robbing the First State Bank building, long home to the historic museum, was ridiculous. So ridiculous, in fact, that no one was quite sure how such an idea had actually come to pass, so that all summer — on Wednesdays, Fridays and Saturdays — grown men quit work to dress up like cowboy outlaws, much to the delight of hundreds of tourists (during Chief Joseph Days, thousands) who lined Main Street to watch the five-minute performance. The Great Joseph Bank Robbery was the promotional coup of the summer, and Mayor Divorak had been behind it from the beginning. Such a man was fully capable of putting up a traffic light for the tourists as well.

Such was Fletch's reasoning, and he was close to calling for a vigilante march on City Hall when someone pointed out that City Hall was rarely open — and never on Sunday. Before a consensus was reached on an alternative plan, the mayor himself walked into the cafe, beet-red and looking like another stroke was in progress.

Everyone started talking at once. The mayor was getting redder and redder, and Fletch worried that soon he would be yelping like a coyote, so he yelled for the crowd to give Divorak its full attention.

The mayor explained that he knew no more about the origin of the stoplight than anyone else. In fact, he had rousted his son-in-law, who worked for Power and Light, to get his truck over here right away so they could take the damn thing down. His son-in-law pointed out that it might be the county's doing, in which case the mayor of Joseph was powerless. Because it was Sunday, there was nothing to do but wait until morning, call the county, and find out what was going on. There followed considerable discussion about proper governmental chains of command, all of it speculative.

Fletch was never a man to trade action for discussion, and so he put his own plan to work. Gradually, with knowing nods, men began to slip out of the cafe, climbing into their pickups and driving home. Thirty minutes later the mayor was still holding court, mainly to tourists who eavesdropped over their breakfasts and wondered what all the fuss was about.

Suddenly a gunshot was heard — but too loud and resonant to have come from a single weapon. Mayor Divorak, Peg the waitress, Jimbo the cook, a handful of residents and a multitude of tourists, all rushed out onto Main Street to see what had happened.

Although the early morning breeze had died down, the stoplight was swinging wildly, all of its signals shattered. Below it a large crowd had formed; women stood beside their children, and in front of them was a foreboding circle of men, Fletch and Renford among them — men who, except for the different colors of their billed caps, could not have been told apart, they looked so much alike, cradling their smoking rifles and sporting their wide grins.

IT TOOK THREE red beers before Fletch figured out what had happened. Without a hangover, he would have figured it our immediately;

under this morning's affliction, he couldn't think clearly until Vitamin C was back in his system.

"Renford," he said from a bar stool at Swede's. "You know who was responsible for that? Enterprise."

Of course! Having heard it, no one doubted it. No one doubted in at Swede's, or later across the street at Mel's, or at the Cowboy Bar, or at Tony's, where the dinner special was chicken-fried steak. It had to be Enterprise, the county seat, and the motive had to be jealousy.

The Great Joseph Bank Robbery must have had something to do with it as well. The re-enactment was based on an actual robbery on October 1, 1896, when three men held up the Old Joseph Bank. The leader of the gang had escaped with $2,000, but one compatriot had been killed and the other, a local boy named Tucker, had been captured and sent to prison. After getting out, Tucker returned to Joseph to become a successful sheep rancher and, eventually, vice-president of the very same bank he had helped rob. Of such stuff the West was made, and Enterprise had no story — not even a lie — that could match it.

If this were not humiliating enough, it was the year of two local centennials, and Joseph had raised its blue city banners three days before Enterprise had raised the red county ones. Rivalry between the two towns, which were only six miles apart, was always fierce, but this summer, with all the additional tourists coming for the centennial activities, competition was especially aggressive. Because Joseph clearly was winning the tourist sweepstakes, it would be just like someone from Enterprise to try and downplay the victory by creating a diversion. No one wanted to be stuck with the first stoplight in Wallowa County.

By evening, Fletch had sworn in a posse of sorts to take responsibility for the retaliation. They all agreed they would have to erect a stoplight in Enterprise — and that very night. The trouble began over where to put it.

Fletch wanted to erect it at the corner by the courthouse, across from where all the fancy new shops had gone in. Enterprise had become so gentrified that one could buy a cup of espresso, a cone of frozen yogurt, a scented candle, computer software, a salad with sprouts, a bamboo beach mat, any number of ridiculous T-shirts and strange greeting cards, and who knew what else, all without walking two blocks.

Renford wanted to attack more directly. He had a cousin camping at the lake, he explained, a cousin from California. Let his cousin hang around the taverns in Enterprise for a few days and learn who did it.

"We'll string the stoplight over his driveway," said Renford.

No, no, insisted a sheepman named Hancock. What is it that really separates Enterprise from Joseph? What most symbolizes Enterprise's departure from Wallowa traditions in order to enter the mainstream of progress? Clearly one thing. Enterprise has a Safeway store. Put the damn thing up in front of Safeway, was Hancock's idea.

Too much beer had brought out the intransigence in Fletch's posse, and for the next several hours little progress was made. In fact, they didn't get back on track until the bartender at the Cowboy Bar yelled last call. Then they quickly decided to draw straws among the six sites that had been suggested, and Fletch was drawing up the slips when Mayor Divorak walked in for a nightcap.

"Can you believe these tourists?" the mayor said, grinning. "As soon as my son-in-law got that stoplight down, some joker in a Winnebago pulled over and offered 50 bucks for it. He said his son wanted to put it up in his dorm room back in Portland."

If there was one place worse than Enterprise, it was Portland. By the time the bartender had shooed Fletch and his posse out onto Main Street, the focus of their insults had changed considerably.

"Look at Portland's crime rate," said Fletch. "You can't leave home without locking your door."

"They got drugs worse than L.A.," said Renford.

"Streets full of whores and winos," said the mayor, and he yelped like a coyote.

Others pointed out the lack of mountain-clear water and clean air in Portland, no fresh beef available, all that big city red tape, new freeways opening all the time, traffic you wouldn't believe, and no real beauty, certainly nothing like the Wallowas. Portland was a city that commissioned Beauty and got Portlandia, a copper statue of a scantily-clad lady holding a pitchfork.

They continued the litany of insults while ambling to their separate pickups. Compared to Portland, Enterprise was downright appealing, and so no one objected when Fletch suggested the six-mile drive to Toma's Restaurant, the only place short of La Grande where a fellow could get breakfast on a Sunday night.

The next morning, a working day, Fletch woke up at 5:30 on the money, rolled over and switched on the bed lamp. He was at Tony's shortly after 6, where he joined a table with Renford and others, and over many cups of coffee not one word was spoken about the strange and short life of the first stoplight in Wallowa County.

1977

The Man Who Shot Elvis

Prism International (Fall)

SO HERE HE WAS, in the casino with hundreds of other tourists,
waiting in line two hours before showtime, bored, drink in hand, watching
his wife shoot craps. Mary was losing and angry but all the more striking
for it, her blue eyes intense as she shook the dice in a fist near one ear. She
brushed aside a strand of blonde hair that had fallen across her face, still
shaking the dice, softly demanding of them *five, five* — she reminded him
of a mad Scandinavian queen who had one roll to win or lose a kingdom.
For a moment, he looked away, attracted by the ringing payoff of a slot
machine, and when he turned back the blonde queen was coming toward
him, dethroned and pouting.

"I hate that game, I just hate it," Mary said.

"You love it," said Lester.

"I don't have the luck I have on the machines." She took a sip of his
drink. "If you'd loan me five dollars ..."

He gave her twenty, and she was off to get change. It was true, her
luck on the dollar slots was phenomenal, more than once her winnings had
paid for their weekend in Las Vegas. The only reason she had gone to the
craps table at all was because their place in line had brought them next to
it. As a businessman, Lester admired the savvy of the hotel's manage-
ment: make the customers line up for the show in the casino, where they
would have things to do while passing time and would spend money
passing it. The line stretched past slot machines, twisted around roulette
tables to games of craps and twenty-one, then extended back across the
red carpet to the slots, a long traffic jam whose little order was imposed by
three young hotel employees, who reminded people that they were in line
and therefore should have someone keep their place before drifting away
to gamble. Lester was spending money without gambling, on dollar-and-
a-quarter drinks before the show began and the price went up to five
dollars. More savvy: admission was disguised as a two-drink minimum.

He lost Mary in the crowd. Everywhere he looked — hanging from
the ceiling, posted on walls and pillars — were photographs of Elvis and

11

banners with his name. It had been Lester's idea to spend the weekend in Las Vegas, Mary's to see the show at the International Hotel.

THEY ESPECIALLY NEEDED this vacation since the night he had been robbed. This had happened two months ago, in the parking lot of the bank as Lester walked to his car. He was tired after working late and oblivious to the shadows in the still night. Someone was suddenly in his way, a gun-like protrusion pointing from a pocket, and Lester heard, "Your wallet, man." It was that simple. "Your wallet, man," no more. Lester was about to reply with something automatic, "Good evening," when the sight of the pistol, out of the pocket and real, made him understand what was happening. He quickly handed over his wallet, his gaze never leaving the gun, the authority of which was absolute although the pistol itself seemed fragile in the way it reflected light from a streetlamp. When the man ran off, Lester got in his car and drove home. He had two drinks before telling Mary, who could not understand why he wouldn't call the police. "I had less than twenty dollars on me," Lester explained. "I'll notify the credit card people tomorrow. I won't be liable. Maybe he needed the money. He was black. If he'd been white, I don't think I'd have given him a dime. He would've had to shoot me first. But he was black."

He could not forget the absolute authority of the gun. A few days after the robbery he went into a pawn shop and purchased a pistol and shoulder holster, which he began to wear everywhere. He felt unmolestable with a weapon. He would feel its weight near his heart and think, I am safe.

THEY CHOSE A MOTEL on the strip. As Lester mixed drinks in their room, Mary looked through the brochures and coupons which the woman at the front desk had given them. They had the weekend to relax and see a show or two. Mainly they wanted to escape Los Angeles with its robberies.

Mary said excitedly, "Elvis is at the International!"

"Who?" Lester's back was to her, hiding a grin.

"Who! Elvis Presley, you nerd."

"Oh, him. I think B. B. King is supposed to be in town, too. Where's B. B. playing at?"

He turned and gave Mary her drink.

"I simply have to see Elvis while we're here."

"You've already seen him."

"But that was, god, how long ago?"

In 1956 or thereabouts, as Lester recalled the story. Mary, fifteen, had waited in line for five hours to get a front seat in a Miami moviehouse. She had screamed through the entire show, almost close enough to touch him.

Mary said, "I can go alone tomorrow and we can meet afterwards for dinner."

"If you really want to see that clown, I'll take you myself."

"We can see him, really?"

"There's probably nothing more amusing in town."

"Oh you," and she threw one arm around him, almost spilling their drinks. He could feel the pistol between them, and so could Mary.

"I'm going to take that off," she said.

"Don't stop there," said Lester.

LESTER LOOKED AROUND for a waiter from whom to order another drink. Unable to find one, he began to stare at Mary, hoping to catch her eye and beckon her over to save their place in line while he went to the bar. Mary was playing three slot machines simultaneously, engrossed.

"Can I get you a drink?"

It was the man in line behind him. Earlier he had nodded at Lester, who had nodded back; his wife had smiled and Lester had smiled in return. He was expecting them to start a conversation.

"I'm going to the bar anyway," the man told him.

"Thanks," said Lester, reaching for his wallet. "Scotch and water."

"Let me buy." The man had turned to go before Lester could pretend to object.

The woman introduced herself.

"I'm Nancy Waterby. My husband's name is Ralph. We drove down from Medford just to see Elvis."

"Medford."

"It's in Oregon."

She offered her hand, and Lester gently shook it.

"I'm Lester Williams, and that blonde fanatic over there, the one hogging the winning machines, is Mary, who belongs to me."

The woman smiled. Lester wondered at which moviehouse she had seen Elvis in the fifties.

"This is an unbelievable crowd, isn't it?" Nancy said. "I wish we'd gotten in line much earlier. I don't think we'll be seated on the main floor."

"The dude's not hurting for fans," Lester agreed.

He turned away, pretending to be interested in the craps game. Ralph Waterby returned with the drinks.

"I forgot to ask if your wife wanted anything," Ralph said.

"Oh, I more or less do it heavy for both of us."

Ralph laughed. Nancy laughed. Lester looked at his watch and, as if on command, someone across the casino shouted, "We're moving in!" Lester called Mary, who brought news that she was twenty-four dollars ahead. Their cover-charge was covered, Lester noted. Counting Mary's drinks, he would have four to get him through the show. He was no longer sure he'd be able to handle that many.

THEY WERE SEATED at a long table in the first balcony with the Waterbys and two couples who were together and remained aloof. Mary was very excited, squeezing Lester's arm and standing up from the table to get a better view of the massive ballroom into which her idol would descend, perhaps from heaven itself. Lester, too, was impressed: the stage covered the entire width of the ballroom, and a golden curtain just as wide dropped in front of the stage from a height above the second balcony. Naked cherubs flew among clouds on the side walls, above paintings of Greek ruins and imposing figures from some forgotten French court. A waitress handed Lester a souvenir menu with Elvis' photograph on the cover and informed him that the minimum number of drinks had to be ordered at once. Soon there were four glasses lined up in front of him.

Ralph was telling him what a great show it would be.

"What a fantastic comeback he made! After all those lousy movies, what? about three a year through the sixties?, and now this, it's just spectacular. That curtain alone must be worth thousands. This show will be unbelievable. I wonder when it starts. How can they expect us to sit here waiting?"

Business savvy, Lester knew. And just as he expected, not Elvis but a comedian opened the show, doing his routine in front of the golden curtain. "Folks, they gave me this job tonight because Colonel Parker figured the show needed a sex symbol." The crowd laughed and waited for Elvis. But when the curtain finally rose, the stage revealed a trio of black women, The Sweet Inspirations, who sang a medley of Aretha Franklin songs as photographs of Aretha flashed onto a screen behind them. Yes, somebody sure knows what they're doing, Lester thought. The delay only increased the excitement, and Mary couldn't stop squeezing his arm. Lester slid away one empty glass and moved three full glasses forward, one by one, like customers advancing to his window at the bank. Since being robbed, he greeted customers with an apprehensive glance, trying to discern their motives.

When the curtain dropped again, the crowd hushed. "Oh God, this is it," Mary whispered to him. Without introduction an orchestra began to play, and Lester recognized the theme from the movie, *2001*. The music seemed to come out of every wall. Scattered cheers and shrieks identified those who were no longer able to contain themselves; "This is it!" Mary said again. The movie theme was picked up by a chorus, which like the orchestra was hidden behind the golden curtain unless the voices be-

14

longed to cherubs, to French royalty. The crowd floated like a frail bubble. Then the curtain began to rise slowly, the bubble was burst by the quick rhythm of a drum, by heartbeats, and Mary began to scream. Elvis ran onto the stage and came forward to the very edge of it, arms outstretched to his fans as he walked up and down the width of the ballroom for everyone to see. He was dressed entirely in white, his clothes sparkling with jewels. What can that dude be thinking now? Lester wondered. *I am Elvis, this is my body.*

WHEN LESTER WAS SIXTEEN, he decided to become a rhythm-n-blues star. Three friends agreed that this was a great idea, and they immediately formed a group called The Woodpeckers. They spent most of the summer learning songs, rehearsing, building a repertoire, and by the time school started they could imitate a number of popular groups, singing "Sincerely" like The Moonglows and "Gee" like The Crows, "Earth Angel" like The Penguins and "Sh-Boom" like The Chords. They changed their name to The Blackbirds and began to sing at high school dances and talked of cutting a record soon. Lester wrote a song called "Shoo-Do-Be, You Need Me," which everyone agreed was their best number. They recorded this song and a few others on tape, which they left with the secretary of a record company. They would hear from the company soon, they were told.

The record company never contacted them, and graduation ended their dream. One of The Blackbirds went to college on a track scholarship, another joined the Army to flee a pregnant girlfriend, a third disappeared from the neighborhood. Lester, who had kept remarkably good grades for the little time he spent studying, enrolled in Los Angeles Junior College.

Two years later he heard "Shoo-Do-Be, You Need Me" on the radio, sung by a group called The O'Brien Sisters. He knew he had been robbed but it didn't matter, his dream now was to make money in business. He wanted to make a lot of money because his father, a mailman, earned barely enough to support a wife and six children. Lester was determined to do better than this. For a beginning, he wouldn't make the mistake of having a large family.

He graduated from Junior College and transferred to Business School at UCLA, supporting himself with a night janitorial job. He met Mary in his senior year, and they fell quickly in love and were secretly engaged. Anticipating the objections of both sets of parents, they stretched their secret to include marriage in Las Vegas as soon as Mary came of age. Lester still planned to make a lot of money in business, but while waiting for more specific intentions to occur to him he decided to get his Army obligation out of the way. Mary accompanied him overseas, and from Germany she wrote her parents that she had decided not to be an airline stewardess after all, as a matter of fact she had gotten married instead, and she and her husband were in the Army now, an ocean's length from home. She was sorry to be so sudden and late with the announcement but she knew they would understand and would like Lester because she loved him very much and had never been happier.

IT OCCURRED TO LESTER that it would be the easiest thing in the world to shoot Elvis Presley through the head. He saw no visible security precautions. If an assassin were willing to wait four hours in line instead of two, a front table would put the target within easy range. Even from the first balcony, even from the second, Elvis was closer than President Kennedy had been to that window in the warehouse.

But shooting from a balcony, an assassin would have to be an excellent shot because Elvis never kept still. He sang while doing splits and leaps and karate chops. Using the whole stage, Elvis worked himself into such a sweat that he had to stop after several songs to wipe himself dry with a red silk scarf, which he then threw to the screaming crowd. A flunky brought Elvis a blue scarf, and after three or four songs it, too, was thrown to the fans, and the flunky raced forward with a purple. Lester wondered, What is that man's salary?

He pictured Elvis writhing in pain. Elvis was singing a hit, "Hound Dog" or "Heartbreak Hotel," when the bullet struck him below the navel, above the thigh. He grabbed himself like a man with a hernia, sinking to his knees when he knew he should be making a flying leap, rolling onto his side as the drummer awaited a karate chop to punctuate, blood flowing readily but soaking only the crotch of his white pants before the advancing crowd, panicked and furious, had them pulled off, then his diamond-studded shirt torn to shreds, his hair portioned out from the roots. Lester quietly slipped out an exit, unnoticed. He waited for the press in the casino but the reporters were skeptical. "I tell you, I did it! I did it because a long time ago they stole my song. They stole my song. It would have been a hit for me but it was a hit for them instead. They stole it."

HE WORKED IN PAYROLL in the Army and this, with his degree, landed him a job with a Los Angeles bank after discharge. Lester was soon well-liked as one who paid attention to details: he changed his white shirt daily, he wore only black socks, he never wore a loud tie, when there was extra work to do he worked nights without having to be asked, he learned the first names of the right customers and was formal with the right customers. After two years Lester felt secure in the job, and only then did he tell Mary that she could look for a house to buy. By 1967 no one could say

Lester was not a success. He was even successful enough to exercise some independence, wearing wide and colorful ties before his boss began to wear them. At a party his boss told him, in the presence of others, "Lester, you wouldn't have gotten away with dressing like that before you became such a credit to the bank." Lester shocked everyone by replying, "Don't ever call me a credit to anything again. I do my job, period."

AS ELVIS SANG "Love Me Tender," Mary softly wept.

Ralph asked Lester, "Why doesn't he play the guitar?" After the first two songs, the flunky had taken the instrument away. "I wanted to hear him play some more. Play your guitar, Elvis!"

Lester stared at the last drink in front of him. It was going to be a horse race.

BEFORE LEAVING THE MOTEL to see Elvis (and she had insisted they go early), Mary called her sister in Los Angeles to check on the children. They had waited six years before starting a family, and Krista, the oldest, was now five. Krista wanted to speak to her daddy on the phone.

"What's up, sugar?" Lester asked. "You behaving yourself?"

"Yes. Will you bring me a pitchur."

"What kind of picture? Want a pretty postcard?"

"A pitchur of Elvis."

"Elvis! Where'd you find out about Elvis?"

"Mommy said you are going to see Elvis. I want a pitchur."

"Okay, sweetheart."

As soon as Mary had hung up, he asked, "How did she find out about Elvis?"

"We listen to him all the time."

"You do?"

"Well, you ought to know that."

"Stop brain-washing my daughter."

"Don't be silly. We listen to your records, too."

HE WAS SO DRUNK that he had missed everything, and Mary had to explain.

"There were two of them," she said. "They just jumped up onto the stage and ran at Elvis and before you knew it, pow!, he did a couple karate chops on them. It was fantastic. Police came out from everywhere and hauled the guys off."

Lester, moving along with the crowd, felt like a leaf floating down the gutter. He couldn't remember finishing the last drink or seeing the end of the show.

"At least they didn't try it earlier. Elvis was doing his last song, so nobody missed anything. I don't think that'll be tried again once people find out he can do karate. It was fantastic."

They emerged from the ballroom, and Lester stopped to take a deep breath.

"Are you okay?" Mary asked.

"I just need a minute. Little dizzy."

"You didn't have to drink mine. We could have left them."

"I'll be okay in a minute."

He concentrated on breathing until his head began to clear.

"I'm exhausted," said Mary. "I've never been to a show like that in my life. I'm just exhausted."

"Yeah, you scream a lot."

"Oh, you. Are you sure you're alright?"

"Much better. Let's go."

But he had to stop again outside on the sidewalk. A universe of blue lights towered above them, silhouetting the International Hotel against the desert sky. He recognized the Waterbys coming toward them.

"Would you folks join us for a nightcap?" Ralph asked.

Lester said, "I've had it."

Nancy suggested coffee.

"We have an early start in the morning," said Lester, stretching the truth.

"Well, it's been great," said Ralph. "What a great show. Here, I'd like to give you my card. If you're ever in Medford, look us up."

"We'd be so delighted," said Nancy.

Ralph said, "I don't quite know how to say this but Medford, you see, is a little backward in some ways and we've never had the opportunity or pleasure before to — well, what I mean, what I'm trying to say is, we enjoyed being with you. You're excellent company."

"You mean I'm a credit to my race," said Lester.

"Now I didn't mean to —"

"Then I'm not a credit to my race."

"You are! I mean, I didn't think of it that way."

Lester slapped him on the arm.

"We had a ball," he told the Waterbys. "Have a safe trip home."

"You, too," said Ralph.

The two couples shook hands before walking off in opposite directions. At the car, Lester asked Mary to drive.

THE MORNING NEWSPAPER explained that the two men merely had wanted to shake Elvis' hand. They were unarmed and a little drunk and intended to shake hands on a bet. Elvis wasn't pressing charges, so the police let the men go.

Getting into the car after breakfast, Lester asked Mary if she believed that's all the men wanted to do.

"I think so. Why?"

"Because it would've been easy if they'd wanted to shoot him."

"What kind of hypothetical situation is that?"

"It's not so hypothetical."

"Who would want to shoot Elvis in the first place?"

"Lots of people."

As the car idled, Lester looked for something to play on the tape deck.

"Who?" Mary wanted to know.

"Jealous husbands."

"Oh God, Les, you're not going to tell me you were jealous last night."

"Because you turned into a thirty-two-year-old teenager? Not me, baby."

"You're being stupid. Nobody wants to shoot Elvis."

"It would be easy to do. I had a gun in there, didn't I? Who would've stopped me?"

"I don't want to talk about it."

He put on a tape of old rhythm-n-blues songs and turned the car toward Los Angeles. He sped across the desert at ninety miles an hour, listening to *his* music as Mary slept, and Elvis was not mentioned again until they were home and Krista ran to him for her pitchur.

1994

The Epistemological Uncle

Whirlwind (May)

IN THE CAREFREE IDYLL of my youth, when Appletons twenty strong gathered at my grandparents' house each Thanksgiving Day, Uncle Buck always drank too much and never failed to do something that would embarrass Aunt Betty. He would return from the bathroom with his fly open, or belch during grace, or tell a very dirty story, or dribble giblet gravy on the tie he wore only on holidays, before grumbling, "I knew the goddamn thing was good for something. Kept the shirt clean, didn't it?"

Aunt Betty, who was my mother's sister, would begin the process of coaxing him home then, and she usually succeeded before the pumpkin and mincemeat and apple and pecan pies were passed around the table.

A bit later, after grandfather began to fidget prior to suggesting that the men retire to the basement, where whiskey and cigars awaited them, the loud backfiring of Uncle Buck's ancient pickup could be heard outside and soon thereafter the slamming of the pickup door in the driveway and then the idiosyncratic howling that was my uncle's habit whenever he had too much to drink, which was often:

"Do you really knooooooooooow?," he howled.

Everyone knew that Uncle Buck was back.

After shooting a stern glance at me and my cousins, daring us to laugh out loud (though cousin Judy, Buck's daughter, always looked close to tears), grandfather would ask grandmother if there were clean sheets in the guest room, knowing full well that she never let anyone in the front door unless there were fresh sheets in all the bedrooms and fresh towels in all the bathrooms.

As Uncle Buck continued to howl outside, grandfather would make the habitual suggestion to retire, and so the men would rise in unison to head for the stairs to the basement, where they would let Uncle Buck in through the outside entrance.

Before long Uncle Buck wouldn't be the only intoxicated relative in the house, nor the only one howling.

This routine was so attached to Thanksgiving that I looked forward to it and was disappointed to learn, the holiday of my freshman year in high school, that Uncle Buck had stopped drinking.

Sober, he proved to be as quiet as a zombie. Although he didn't do anything to embarrass Aunt Betty, he also failed to entertain me and my cousins, who didn't realize how much we enjoyed Uncle Buck's antics until we were deprived of them. As far as we were concerned, he had been the life of the holiday.

Cousin Judy was the exception to our disappointment: her father's new silence seemed to give her a feminine radiance I'd never noticed before. She was, I decided, the most beautiful relative I had.

FOUR YEARS PASSED before Uncle Buck started howling again. It was near the end of summer, and I was getting nervous about going off to college.

One afternoon, cousin Judy phoned and told me, "Dad's drinking and being crazy again. Can you come over? He's howling in the back yard right now."

Judy and I were the same age but had ignored one another until high school. About the time I discovered she was beautiful, we discovered together that we could be good friends. Soon we were calling ourselves Mutually Adopted Siblings, since neither of us had one still at home. We delighted in the fact that most of our classmates didn't know what we were talking about, "sibling" being no part of standard teenage vocabulary in the small farming town of Adam in the Idaho Palousse.

I told her I was on my way.

Judy was outside waiting for me and quickly led me to the backyard. In the distance was the barn, which had seen better days, and acres of grainland stretched around us to every horizon.

Uncle Buck was clearly drunk, staggering around and groping at a pile of canvas that, in steadier hands, would easily have risen to form a tent. With every yank, he had a bigger mess and harder task than ever, which frustrated him into loud swearing at the universe in general. Empty beer cans were scattered across the lawn, and a pint whiskey bottle stuck out of the back pocket of his coveralls.

"Mom said she wouldn't stay in the house as long as he's drinking," Judy explained. "She went to spend the night with Aunt Milly, and Dad came out here. He says if she doesn't want him in the house, he'll just spend the rest of his life in a tent."

"Not by the looks of it," I said. "Should we help him?"

"I don't know what to do. He started drinking this morning, Mom said."

I touched Judy's arm and gave her a squeeze, then moved across the lawn.

"You want some help, Uncle Buck?," I called on my way.

He swore without turning around, another obscene remark for the universe at large.

I reached him as he was pulling the bottle from his pocket.

"I wish you wouldn't drink any more," I said.

I reached him and stopped. Uncle Buck took a swig without acknowledging my presence.

"What are you going to accomplish by drinking?," I asked.

When he turned my way, I held out my hand for the bottle. He glared at me before saying gruffly, "Accomplish! What the hell do you think you're accomplishing by minding other people's business, Mr. Wise Ass?"

Uncle Buck took a step backward, almost falling over. Then he cocked his head to the sky and bellowed, "Do you really knoooooooooow?" Finally losing his balance from the exertion, he fell flat on his back.

Judy screamed and came racing across the lawn. I was already on my knees beside him when she arrived.

"Is he all right?"

"He's breathing," I said. "I think he passed out."

"We can't leave him out here."

Uncle Buck was a big man, and I wasn't sure we could handle him by ourselves. Judy had the same notion.

"He's too heavy for the two of us," she said. "Would your dad help us?"

"Maybe it'd be good for him if he woke up out here," I suggested.

I spotted a wheel barrow near the fence that defined where lawn ended and farmland began. Without saying a word, I moved off toward it.

"Why did he have to start drinking again?," Judy asked, catching up with me.

I hesitated before replying, "I don't know." I'd come close to saying, "Do you really knoooooooooow?"

It took some effort for the two of us to get Uncle Buck into the wheel barrow. He was as heavy as a sack of potatoes and just as awkward to handle. We wheeled him to the back door before realizing that our problems were just beginning.

"Mom would have a cow if we tracked up the carpet," said Judy.

"How about making a bed for him on the patio?"

Patio was an exaggeration: a small square of concrete, just big enough for the gas barbecue set, stood alongside the house like an ambitious project long abandoned.

"I think we should put him in the tent," said Judy. "He was going to sleep outside anyway."

We left Uncle Buck sprawled awkwardly in and on top of the wheel barrow while we set up the tent. Then we wheeled him back across the lawn, dumping him, as gently as possible, inside before folding down the canvas door flap.

Moving to return to the house, we both turned into one another, brushing slightly together, chest to chest. I could smell her perfume and felt a sudden urge to kiss her, which she must have realized, maybe even feeling a similar urge herself, because she blushed blood red.

I could hear myself breathing heavily and wondered if Judy could. I knew I had an erection, which made me feel conspicuous and embarrassed.

"I wish we weren't cousins," she said softly.

I swallowed and said, "So do I."

The silence was unbearable. Finally she said, "You'd better go. I mean, I have some chores to do and everything."

"Right. I think he'll be okay out here."

"He was going to sleep in the tent anyway."

"Right. Spend the rest of his life out here."

"Why did he have to start again?," she asked.

"I don't think anybody knows." I grinned and said, "Do you really knoooooooooow?"

Her transformation was so sudden, at first I thought she was playacting: she glared at me and said, "I hate it when you do that."

"That's the problem," she went on, "people like you always laughed at him when he was drinking . You just inspired him to keep acting crazy. You don't know what it was really like to be around him."

But before I could find out, Judy was running into the house, crying. I had no idea what had just transpired or what I had done to upset her so suddenly and so strongly. I gave up the thought of following her inside and went home.

I ONLY SAW JUDY one other time before I left for college. Although I telephoned her that same night, and a few times after that, Aunt Betty always answered the phone to tell me Judy wasn't home, and she never returned my calls. My aunt also told me that Uncle Buck was "in treatment now."

"What exactly is treatment?," I asked Dad at dinner.

He gave the question some thought before saying, "If you're referring to Buck, ask your mother."

"It means he's in the hospital to get well," Mom quickly said.

"What's the matter with him?"

"He can't drink," she said.

I wasn't sure what she was getting at. After all, Dad drank and I'd heard him howling in the basement on more than one Thanksgiving. I knew Uncle Buck drank too much but I didn't think he was an alcoholic, like the bums I'd seen in Lewiston. But I also knew the matter was put to rest because my parents were staring down at their plates, so I looked down at mine as well.

One afternoon I came outside to find Judy standing in front of my house. I couldn't be sure, but she appeared to have been crying. She would look at me, then away, as I walked toward her.

"Are you all right?," I asked.

"I came by to see if you want to come with me to visit Dad. I guess you already were going someplace."

"Just to the store. Where's he at?"

"Serenity Villa. He checked in the day after we put him in the tent."

"It's a long walk," I said. She hadn't brought the family car.

"I was hoping you could get the car."

"I can." I reached into a pocket and brought out my own set of keys to Mom's Toyota, dangling them proudly. "You want to go right now?"

"Sure."

We were awkwardly silent during the drive to Serenity Villa, which was near the hospital some thirty miles away. Neither of us mentioned that it had been almost a month since we'd talked, which was a very long silence for us. I didn't know how to broach the subject of our falling out since I still wasn't sure what had happened. I vaguely hoped she would apologize for being unreasonable, and everything could go back to the way it had been between us, cousins, good friends and Mutually Adopted Siblings. But we remained silent during the drive through golden fields almost ready to harvest, which made the ride intolerably long. By the time we were there, I was sorry I had come.

Although I'd seen television ads for Serenity Villa, I knew nothing about it. It looked more like a resort than a hospital, and its sprawling size surprised me. I didn't know there were that many alcoholics in Idaho, but the full parking lot gave the impression that they were doing a thriving business.

Judy led the way and knew where she was going. I followed her in the front entrance, down a long hallway, and out onto a patio graced with shade trees and flower beds. From out of one of the trees came recorded "easy listening" music.

Uncle Buck sat at a picnic table, waiting for us. After he and Judy embraced, he offered his hand to me, grinning broadly. He looked good, amazingly good, maybe ten or fifteen pounds lighter than I remembered him. But the eyes were the real difference, they looked at me with such clarity, in such attentive focus, that it made me wonder if Uncle Buck had ever really looked at me before.

"How you doing, Bobby boy?," he said. "About ready to head out on the great adventure, aren't you?"

"I leave next week."

"Glad I got to see you before you go."

"Me, too."

There were other families on the large patio, all speaking in hushed voices, trying to maintain a sense of privacy. Although Uncle Buck was in pajamas and a robe, he was in the minority, and at most of the picnic tables across the large patio it was impossible to tell the patients from the visitors. No one looked like an alcoholic to me — not even Uncle Buck. Alcoholics looked like bums living on skid row.

Only when Judy excused herself to use the bathroom did Uncle Buck reveal a bit of his old self: suddenly he grabbed my arm, leaned over the table and said, softly but ominously, "Do you really knoooooooooow?"

He was grinning and staring at me so intensely I had to look away.

"You know the best thing about this place?," he asked out of nowhere. I shook my head. "I learned I can be crazy and sober at the same time."

Then again: "Do you really knoooooooooow?"

He slapped the wooden table and said, "So maybe I don't know, huh? But I think I do. I feel like I do. But you can never be too sure about these things, huh? What do you know that you know, Bobby boy?"

I laughed, more out of nervousness than anything else. I felt like I was being tricked into going along with some kind of practical joke in which I would prove to be the butt.

"Life is very, very, very short," Uncle Buck said. Again, the remark seemed to come out of nowhere. "I know it's hard to tell that to a young hotshot like yourself. I think I know that. Pretty sure, anyway. You're going to do what you're going to do. But I hope you keep away from the booze, Bobby boy, though I know you'll have your keggers or whatever the hell it is you call them today. I had a year of college myself, you know. Bet you didn't know that, did you?"

"No," I said, my voice involuntarily cracking. One of the family stories repeated *ad nauseam* was how Uncle Buck became a successful farmer despite having only a sixth grade education. I noticed the story was always forgotten when one of my cousins wanted to drop out of school.

"Didn't think so," said Uncle Buck.

I coughed and smiled, trying to hide how on edge I felt, still wondering where all this was heading.

"Drank my way through one of the best freshman curriculums in the country. Make that curricula. The University in Moscow. Wasn't always a farmer, no siree. Actually fancied myself an engineer way back in the Middle Ages. But I liked my toddy, and that cost money, and to a youngster, working always looks better than an education. You're different, I suspect. You got a good head on your shoulders. Probably become a teacher or something. Know what you want to be, Bobby boy?"

"I've been thinking of teaching," I admitted.

"Honorable career. Just keep your options open. Now tell me about Judy."

The last remark landed like a grenade from left field.

"What about her?," I asked.

"I see how you two look at each other. Too bad you're first cousins, right? Or does it matter any more? I mean, we're in the Age of Condoms, you get them right there in the high school nurse's office, don't you?"

I could feel myself blushing.

"I think I said the wrong thing," said Uncle Buck. "I talk too much, don't I? The thing is, I never realized I could talk sober before. Been a very long time since I did that. So I sort of indulge myself. The point I was trying to make is, don't let life pass you by, Bobby boy. You've got to make your own mistakes, I realize that, but maybe when you look at an old codger like me, drinking most of his life away, probably end up with more drunk days than sober days even if I live to be eighty, which I doubt — look at yourself in the mirror real hard, boy, and always try to do what you really want, what's really in your gut. And if that means pretending Judy isn't your cousin — well, talk to a doctor, I don't know all that much about it, maybe they got pills to take now so you don't end up with Mongoloid kids or whatever happens, I'm not sure what the exact problem is with cousins marrying, I've just heard the kids don't come out right, but I also know it's real important to find the right kind of better half in this life, the right kind of partner of the opposite sex, and you and Judy sure do seem to get along good. I think I know that. Of course, one can never be sure. Do you really knoooooooooow?"

And then he suddenly asked, "Bobby boy, are you still a virgin?"

I stood up quickly, as if I'd just sat on a pin. I saw Judy heading back from the bathroom and, mumbling my departure, I headed her way.

"He's acting really weird," I said. "Can we go soon?"

"Weird how?"

"I'll explain later."

I continued on to the bathroom.

Judy was alone at the patio table when I returned.

"What happened?," she said right off.

"Where is he?"

"He said it was time for his nap. He seemed upset about something. What happened between you two?"

"He did all the talking."

"What did he say?"

"Nothing that made much sense. You ready to go?"

She stood up.

"I want to know what happened."

I tried to tell her indirectly, both on the drive back and then in her kitchen, where she made us iced tea. A note on the refrigerator announced that Aunt Betty was away until dinner time, giving us a couple hours alone. But no matter how closely I circumvented the truth, Judy didn't catch my meaning. Finally, out of frustration from her persistence, I spat out, "He wanted to know if we were sleeping together."

As soon as I saw the look on her face, I regretted saying it. She looked stunned, as if this was the last thing in the world she expected to hear.

Finally she said, "In just so many words or what?"

"No, more round about."

"Damn it, what did he say!"

She took a deep breath and said, "I'm sorry. I just want to know what he said. As close as you can remember."

"He said we made a neat couple."

"About us sleeping together."

"He asked if I was a virgin."

She gave me an odd look, as if trying to figure out if I was serious.

She said, "You said he asked if we were sleeping together."

"That was the meaning I got. I mean, he didn't ask in so many words, but he went on and on about how good we were together, and how important it was for a guy to find the right girl and all, and then he wanted to know if I was a virgin and if you could get rubbers at school. It all added up to the same thing. I didn't mean to upset you."

Judy took another deep breath and asked, "Are you?"

"What?"

"Are you a virgin?"

"Jesus, Judy, what a thing to ask."

"I'm not," she said.

"What? I don't believe you."

She stood up and at first I thought she was going to refill our glasses. But she only moved a few steps from the table and stopped. Her back was to me as she cocked her head up and howled, but softly, strangely, like a lyric in a dream, "Do you really knoooooooooow?"

She laughed and howled softly again. I didn't know what was going on. If this was a joke, I didn't like it. This was a side of Judy I had never seen before. She kept up the eerie howling while turning slowly around to face me.

Her gaze seemed to cut right through to my very core, forcing me to look away, forcing me to look at the naked breasts that dropped between the edges of her unbuttoned blouse. Then, as if moving despite myself, despite fear, despite any sense of what was the right or wrong thing to do, I rose to my feet and moved to her, and so we were in one another's arms, kissing passionately, and then going upstairs, and then undressing to lie naked together — though within the hour I was being told I'd better leave, and then was hearing the click of the front door behind me as I hurried to my mother's car, still scrambling to finish dressing, all the while wondering what the hell had just happened.

JUDY DID NOT come to see me off at the train station. If she phoned me, she hung up before anyone answered — as I had done numerous times.

And so — as the train pulled away past the encouraging and energetic waving of my parents, leaving Judy and the carefree idyll of my youth somewhere behind in the vast stretch of harvest-ripe golden grainland, and moved forward into the wind to begin the long journey to college — I settled into my seat, closed my eyes and for the first time began to realize how little I knew and how uncertain would be the knowing yet to come; so that by the time the train announced its departure from Adam, sounding like the howling of my Uncle Buck, "Do you really knoooooooooow?," I knew I didn't know what had really happened between Judy and me, or why Uncle Buck drank, or what was waiting for me at college.

I didn't know much of anything, though I didn't yet know that this itself was knowing.

1969

The Thing at 34-03-15N, 118-15-23W

The Colorado Quarterly (Spring)

Falling into the generation gap, I miss Willie Mays' home run

I CAN HEAR THEM out there. They are, to ignore the language's index of elasticity, *dancing*. And they are dancing with each other, I am asked to believe, although the fact of the matter is that when I left the patio they were exhibiting their individual spasms of ecstasy over a separation of six to twelve feet. Now I ask you: is that dancing *together*? I will admit that they are — for lack of a better word — *involved*. Yes, they are involved. They are so involved that they neglect to admire the new patio, the excuse for this party in the first place. I finished it last Wednesday, designing and building the whole thing myself, setting it into a three-colored form of a navigator's compass, at the center of which a brass plate marks the exact location of the patio: 34 degrees, 3 minutes, 15 seconds north, 118 degrees, 15 minutes, 23 seconds west. Having been a navigator in the Navy during the war, I made that measurement precisely. Myself.

I retreated thirty minutes ago. I did not leave for the specific purpose of watching the ballgame. This I would have sacrificed in order to be an attentive host, but frankly it is impossible to be any kind of host, attentive or indifferent, unless one has *guests*. Whatever these kids today may be, delinquents, revolutionaries, or spoiled *nouveaux riches* (Jim tends toward the latter), they certainly are not guests. They rather are like some of my bloodsucking relatives, who expect everything they ask for immediately and for nothing. No, they need no host out there. Whatever they need, they need no host.

You might say I retreated in self-defense. In time the eardrums begin to ache, no doubt in sympathetic vibration with the trembling sycamores and quivering rose bushes, which in turn get their motion from the vibrating phonograph. In the living room the music still can be heard but it is bearable. I cannot hear the ballgame, of course, but since Dizzy Dean left the air no announcer is worth listening to anyway. I used to sit through ballgames just to hear old Diz sing *The Wabash Cannonball* during the seventh inning stretch. Well, times have changed. Today I watch the Giants and Dodgers to the screeches of Bob Dylan, who has the honor (if it is that) of being Jim's and everyone else's favorite — I should say, *thing* — this afternoon. Over and over it's Dylan, Dylan, Dylan. Spasms, spasms, spasms. And Mary is out there with them, which must say something about the maternal instinct. She is fortunate to have the hearing aid, however: a flip of a switch brings silence, peace.

Willie McCovey is at the plate when Jim comes in. He asks, "Dad, has Frank called up?" I wave the question away until McCovey strikes out, stirring up a tornado with his last swing. Once I saw him swing, miss, and dislocate a shoulder. McCovey out, I reply to Jim's inquiry negatively.

"Let me know if he does, okay?"

I nod. Frank is Jim's best friend and is supposed to be here eventually, bringing over more records, I think. Frank was a pretty fair athlete (track, a quarter-mile man) until this, his senior, year when he gave it up to grow his hair long. Jim's hair remains respectably short, I would hope in deference to the wishes of his parents, although it seems to lengthen suspiciously between haircuts. Now what barber would cooperate in such a conspiracy?

I trail behind Jim to check on the progress of the party. Progress heads linearly to dinner, at which time I may have a brief opportunity to play host in my chef's apron. In an hour or so they'll be wanting hamburgers out there. A funny thing — they come close to using decent manners when they want something badly. Food.

But at the moment they are still doing their *thing*. Spasms. Mary is sitting at the picnic table, lost behind that sweet matronly smile of hers, lost as well in silence, I suspect. For me there is no switch to flip, and the racket is unbearable. From two six-inch speakers Bob Dylan is screeching garbled lyrics while electric guitars explode. The lyrics, could they be understood, would prove to be arrogant in the manner in which a young man dumps his girlfriend after getting from her what he was after. Wham, bam, thank you, mam. I read some of Dylan's lyrics once, in *Life*. *You just sort of wasted my precious time*, he tells his girl. He's as spoiled as the rest of his generation. At times I think another depression would be healthy for this country.

"Do you want to dance, Mr. Simpson?" Jim's girl, Sue, calls to me from across the patio. It is not unusual for her to flirt with me. Initially I am fooled into thinking she is being polite, being a *guest*. Initially I give her the benefit of the doubt, waving and grinning and yelling back, over the racket, "It's not my cup of tea!" She does a sexy little dancestep just for me and then joins whichever of the three near boys, none of whom is Jim, is her partner for the dance. Perhaps they all are.

Sue's offer is the sole gesture made in recognition of my presence. Mary dreams away, a nursing mother's smile on her lips, ignoring me. I quickly tire of so much self-centered behavior and again retreat to the living room. I enter just in time to see "Say Hey!" Willie Mays round third after hitting a home run which, typically, I missed.

I quote Marshall McLuhan and keep cool

BEER ON THE ROCKS is my drink, and soon I am sipping my fourth glass. I have acquaintances who frown at the idea of drinking beer over ice — it's unusual enough a practice to demand an explicit spelling out when ordering the drink in a bar — but my motives are simple, honorable and certainly not eccentric. I drink beer for the taste and, unlike Europeans, I find the flavor heightened by cooling. In addition, I prefer not to get drunk when I drink, and ice cubes dilute beer enough to make possible a certain length of sober indulgence. I've started drinking late today, as Saturday beer drinking goes, but I make up for lost time with three quick glasses and then pour a fourth, which presently I sip. I keep my wits about me. I still have them when Sue enters the house.

Now have no doubt about it, Nabokov was right. If anything, he understated the facts of the matter. The nymphets are everywhere and my patio is no exception. Yet I am no Humbert and pay no attention to Sue's entrance, which at first I presume is for the use of the toilet. Instead of turning into the hallway, however, she comes directly into the living room and, so help me Nabokov, joins me on the divan.

"Is the game almost over?" she asks.

She smiles more broadly than necessary for such an inquiry, showing off her good teeth. She is thin and slight-breasted, as this Nymphetic Age demands, but her hair, instead of being blonde, is a very ordinary brownish "hair color," though typically it also is straight and drops past her shoulders. Sue always works very hard at being charming.

When I reply that it is the seventh inning, Sue says, "I like your patio. You did a beautiful job."

Aware of this thrust at my weakness, I finish my glass of beer quickly and move unannounced into the kitchen for another. When I return, Sue is gone. I have a brief moment of regret until Jim's entrance returns me to more sober reflections.

"How long are you going to watch TV?" he wants to know.

"Depends on the ballgame." I catch myself sounding grouchy. *Keep cool*, I am alerted.

"I thought you volunteered to be the chef."

"Is everybody ready?"

"Well, no. I just thought maybe you were going to spend the day in here. Hey, you don't think we're putting you down or something, do you?

Everybody really digs the patio. But, I mean, just because we do our thing doesn't mean you are banished from society or anything. Everybody really digs the compass bit."

"I'm glad you like it."

"You're sure you're not put off?"

"Put off?" I have to laugh. "My friend, I happen to be participating in the electric environment as much as the rest of you. A phonograph, a television set, what's the difference? Marshall McLuhan would be happy with us both."

"If you say so," Jim shrugs. "No big thing."

As he starts away, I swallow a more aggressive reply to say, "Let me know when you kids are hungry."

"Yeah," Jim yells back and the screen door slams. It has never been clearer to me that his generation is characterized by arrogance.

Mary turns on.

NO DREAMS are quite like dreams that originate in front of a television set and that are nurtured on beer. Frequently these dreams take place with a slight awareness: the eyes are open if heavy, the hands are numb but function well enough to grasp a glass, the mind is listless yet omnipresent. Thoughts, the dream content of this state, are never remembered in context but their existence is profoundly impressed upon every breath, every yawn. Who cares what the thoughts are? They are there, thought-dreams, and they are more relaxing than a snooze in the country. *Cogito, ergo sum*, as the philosopher said. An interruption, therefore, is an intrusion into existential bliss and when it takes for form of, "A penny for your thoughts," it is presumptuous as well since it intimates that such private euphoria can be shared.

Although my eyes have not been closed, it takes me a moment to focus on Mary in the room. Her silhouette comes in first, by the sheer bulk of it, and then slowly her smile, matronly and inquisitive. I expect her to ask me if I would like lunch — cookies and Kool-aid — but the fantasy is temporary. She asks, "Why don't you go out and join the fun? They love the patio. You should be out there."

Mary is forty-five and admits to thirty-five. Like Sue, she has "hair color" hair; unlike a nymphet's, her hair drops nowhere but rather just seems *to be there*, short and plain and ordinary. A mother's hair. She is wearing shorts and the veins run up her legs like water lines.

"We'll be ready to eat in an hour," she goes on. "It takes that long to get the coals going, doesn't it?"

On television a movie has replaced the ballgame. Who won? I recognize the scene in *On the Waterfront* in which the priest asks Brando, *Why do you do these things?* Mary says, "I'll make a salad and lemonade." She wanders into the kitchen.

I am taking a beer from the refrigerator when she asks, "Will a big salad be enough? Should we have pork and beans, too?"

"They'll eat anything. We might as well make it as least damaging to the cupboards as possible."

"Frank is due yet," Mary says. "I'd better have beans, too."

"You spoil them." I pour, and over ice cubes the head rises like lather.

"I made up the hamburgers this morning," she says. "Do you think thirty will be enough? Everything's on the bottom shelf of the refrigerator when you need it. I sliced the tomatoes and onions."

"I'm going to have them shut that music off for a while. You can't expect a guy to cook if he can't hear himself think. They've been playing that brat Dylan all afternoon."

"Do you think anyone will want milk?" Mary has moved to the refrigerator and stands gazing into it. In the silence lyrics enter intelligibly from the patio, *Do you, Mr. Jones?* Mary says, "I didn't think to get any more. There's only a half-gallon left. Roger —" She considers the request and changes her mind. "Oh, lemonade ought to be enough to hold them." She laughs as though amused that for a moment she could have considered any beverage other than lemonade.

"I suggest straight whiskey. It might untangle their nerve ends and put them into a quiet, peaceful stupor." I have to laugh aloud.

"If Frank hasn't arrived by the time you put the meat on, save three patties for him in the refrigerator. He has a big appetite. And don't forget to save him some trimmings." Mary fetches three heads of lettuce and a handful of tomatoes, which she takes to the sink.

"You spoil them," I say. When Mary ignores me, I repeat more loudly, "You wait on them hand and foot. You spoil them. Make Jim slice the tomatoes. Or at least Sue. How's she going to learn to cook?"

I count to ten, finish off the beer, and move to the sink, standing just behind Mary. Into her left ear I say firmly, "You haven't heard a word I've said. Turn your cheater on."

Grinning with some embarrassment, Mary flips the switch.

Can Bob Dylan feel pity?

WHEN FRANK ARRIVES, it is to a fanfare deserving of General MacArthur. With typical arrogance he anticipated no less enthusiastic a welcome, having waited at the edge of the patio until he was noticed. I saw him first from the barbecue spit but said nothing. Soon, over the electric screeches, the greetings thundered, "Frank!" "Where have you been?" "Hey, man!" "You bring the record?"

The odor of glowing charcoal, which twists visibly to the sycamore branches, is ignored by these teenagers; they are insensitive. How much of the beauty of growing up has been lost! The family picnics, the golden evening's trout, the barn dances, the seasons as they ... Well, it's too late for them. Their habits are formed and inflexible, the habits of the *nouveaux riches*, which presently gather them into a circle around Frank, asking, "Can I see the record?," demanding, "Come on, let's put it on."

Bob Dylan has come out with a new record, and Frank possesses it. He is the first of Jim's friends to get it, the reason being that he works in the album department at Martin's Music downtown. No one has heard the album yet and all demand to. Bob Dylan has a new record! The first one since the motorcycle accident, Sue informs me. The first in over a year.

A solemn moment. Sue leaves me to join the others, strutting away with an anatomical rustle. I am taken aback, expecting her to begin the dance spasms of before, seeing her turn solemn. Frank handles the album as though it was his first rosary, and everyone watches silently as he places the record on the turntable. I catch Sue's eye — with tongue and lip she sultrily twists the moment into something heinous. Then she is solemn again. I feel smoke rising into my face, stinging my eyes.

I make a special point of ignoring both the record and its mesmerized audience. I prod the coals, poking them into a little pyramid to burn faster. I am hungry. The kids, however, have only one appetite, which surprisingly is not gluttonous: they huddle around the phonograph and strain their collective expressions for *deeper meanings* whenever Frank raises an index finger, nods his head, brushes aside a strand of hair that has reached his nose, or says, just above a whisper, "Catch this part."

I bet Mary is fixing pork and beans after all. Holding onto the thought, I can ignore the music. It is important that I will the music out of existence: an honest opinion on my part could ruin the afternoon. We must have peaceful coexistence here. Here, at 34-03-15N, 118-15-23W, peace at all costs!

But in time I sneak a listen. Not to do so is impossible since I have no switch to turn off. Listening, I am again astonished by the unexpected: Bob Dylan is not accompanied by electric screeches. No charged guitars, ionized organs, the electric bombardment of violated musical scales. I catch a line, *I pity the poor immigrant* ... Pity? No wham, bam, thank you, mam? Does Bob Dylan have a new *thing*? Well, there also is a verb of the times, which stretches out beyond the language's elastic limit — *to put on.*

By the third playing of the album, the congregation loosens up enough to sway gently, like a sapling. A few begin to dance. The rest impress each other arrogantly.

"Man, that album's weird," says Jim. "You know what I mean?"

Frank does. He nods superciliously, a gesture which suddenly is more than I can stand. The coals glow, waiting to prepare meat for these aristocrats *democratically*, without preferring one man's patty to another's. These kids are spoiled. I intrude, asking, "What happened to the electric environment? Marshall McLuhan would have a fit."

"It's the electricity in the phonograph that counts," Franks says. He has that self-righteous attitude of a few of my Basic Government students at the high school, the ones who bring to my office their rehearsed diatribe about the sanctity of dialectical materialism. I grant that a teacher's job in part is to elicit open discussion, but this is easier to do in the classroom than on the patio, standing over the twisting odor of charcoal, a mere compass's length from the sultry Sue. Dylan interrupts, ... *and turns his back on me.* I step up the attack with, "But the electric dimension is singular there, whereas with electric guitars and organs ..."

"You're not in the classroom, Dad!" Jim intrudes, feigning amusement. He immediately continues, "Frank, did you notice the compass? It gives our exact location. Dad figured it out with the sextant and some math tables." They move in one motion and kneel before the brass plate.

"You figured this out yourself?" Frank asks, pointing at the inscription on the plate.

"It's not as difficult as you may think to determine the coordinates of your location," I admit. "The sextant measures the angle of elevation of the North Star, for example, which is not really at the celestial pole, and from there you ..."

"Hey, let's eat!" Jim exclaims.

Mary exits from the house with salad and, of course, pork and beans, and I am submerged in a roaring ocean of hunger tantrums.

Doing my thing

REMEMBER THE HAYRIDES? Or the campfires, roasting wieners and marshmallows, and later singing, *The bear went over the mountain to see what he could see*? Sneaking a kiss in the shadows of the night? The autumn moon, as large as a grapefruit? The leaves whispering before the thunderstorm and the special smell of morning the next day? Today such pleasures are buried treasure, and we have only a few maps by which to remember them. After dinner the kids listen to Bob Dylan some more, and in the misty twilight they huddle around the phonograph trying to decide which drive-in movie to go to. I discover that Jim and Sue are holding hands.

Mary gathers the plates, silverware, and glasses, cleans up the patio without assistance, and returns in time to learn that the kids have decided to see *Beach Blanket Bingo*, although it is a rerun that they've seen before. I toss the keys to the T-bird to Jim, who one-hands them silently. Tonight he gets to leave his '65 Chevy in the garage.

Naturally they offer little thanks. Sue tells me, "The hamburgers were swell," and the others nod like a chorus of school children. They are off soon. Mary, who spoils them, volunteers to put away Jim's phonograph and records so the kids will be sure to get to the theater on time. Frank picks up his new Bob Dylan album and guards it. Then they are off. The sun is sinking rapidly; perhaps they are late already.

Leaving Mary to her devices, I go to the den, where I have my work desk. I try to grade Friday's test, one hundred true-false questions on the Constitution, but my interest soon fades. The arrogant mood of the evening returns, creeping up on me like indigestion. Bob Dylan's voice echoes like a bad dream, neither wholly remembered nor forgotten. A mood torments me. Listlessly I move to the living room, where Mary is watching television.

She turns, presents a short welcome, and returns her attention to the tube. The Saturday Night Movie. I don't recognize it.

When is the last time Mary and I made love before sunset? The question erupts without prelude. I consider leading her into the bedroom right now, while the twilight lingers and we can see without lights. Does Mary read my mind? Before I reach a decision she gets up and turns on the television lamp. It is official now — the night has begun.

In the kitchen I pour beer on the rocks. I sit alone in the near darkness, sipping. Mary comes in during a commercial. Switching on the light, she asks, "What are you doing in here? Aren't you going to come watch the movie?"

I go to her. The light makes me squint for a moment. Mary draws a glass of water, and I reach from behind her, my hand grazing one breast as I reach for her stomach. She is too big down there.

"Is something bothering you?" she asks, taking my hand and turning. I step back.

"Those kids wore me out," I say. The remark is exhaled like a sigh. "That music drives me nuts."

"Well, we were as bad, if you remember." She smiles at this reminiscence. "Remember when Dad broke your Tommy Dorsey records and you challenged him to a duel?" She giggles. "Maybe we were worse."

"It's not the same. We didn't drive a T-bird somewhere to be entertained. We didn't *have* to be entertained. We amused ourselves. We ..."

"Thank God kids today don't have to go through everything we went through, though." She turns and starts toward the living room. Habitually I follow.

At the next commercial I say, "I'm going to Sammy's. You want to come?"

"I'll be along after the movie."

Sammy's Tavern is only two blocks from the house. I walk over, enter, take an end stool. John, the bartender, draws me a beer over ice, and I slap a quarter onto the bar.

Pleasantries are exchanged with the regulars: Eddie and Judy, who are playing pool with Ralph and a girl I don't know, who's stacked; old Joe, who watches them; the Nelsons, dancing to the juke box. It's a busy night, with a couple dozen customers I've never seen before. Some are good lookers. The two best, one a blonde, don't look like they could be twenty-one.

"Where's Mary?" old Joe asks me from down the bar. He's retired and always high. I point to the television screen on the wall, on which the scenes of the Saturday Night Movie pass silently, noticed only by a few men along the bar. Joe chuckles and coughs, then buys me a beer.

"Where's Mary?" It's Ralph, who introduces me to his latest, Betty somebody. I lose the last name in the perusal of her anatomy, which is no less than staggering. Ralph really picks them.

I explain to Eddie and Judy, who come over next, that Mary will be along as soon as the movie ends at eleven, about an hour from now. "I expected you'd drop by earlier," Eddie says. "We needed you. That Betty is hotter than blazes with a cue stick." He laughs uproariously, winking to make sure I catch the dirty suggestion. Judy joins in.

I tell them about the barbecue and the kids. "I went crazy listening to that music they play."

"We know what you mean," says Judy. "Who was it? The Rolling Stones or the Beatles?"

"They're both out this year," Eddie informs us. "It's the — what is it? The Drawers? The Doors?" He laughs.

"It was Bob Dylan at the house."

Judy admits that she can't tell one group from another.

Ralph and Betty are dancing now and we watch, particularly noticing how Betty presses herself against him. "That's indecent," Eddie happily notes. "Why don't you dance like that?" he kids his wife.

"Well, one thing about those new dances the kids do, you don't see them crawling all over each other," Judy says. Then she drags Eddie onto the dancefloor.

Ann Nelson asks me to dance and I accept. She is blonde, bleached I think, and trim for her age. She hinted at a proposition once, cornering me in the kitchen at a New Year's Eve party. I hinted back at a raincheck, and we've been close ever since. I enjoy the dance for several reasons, not the least of which is the close range it brings me to the young, the authentic, blonde. I predict she's not a day over twenty.

After the dance I concentrate on drinking. For a change I feel like getting smashed. Although I drink constantly, I am seldom drunk. I stick to beer on the rocks and a sipping pace. I feel a constant glow, usually euphoric but tonight dismal, depressing, dreadful for some reason. One of my occasional philosophical moments, I decide. Another beer and I'll be spouting epigrams. The gang will laugh and jokingly call me The Professor. I don't mind — I have a sense of humor and can laugh even at myself. I'm over thirty, so you can't call me arrogant. My dad, in fact, would take a belt to me at the slightest hint of arrogance; he beat it out of me early, I tell you. He was a good fellow, too, though with his faults. So who's perfect? But he taught me responsibility and proper humility. Will Jim ever learn the same? I hope to Christ he does. I can't understand today's kids. How do you communicate with them? If you're over thirty, they clam up or *suspect* you. They're spoiled, is the thing. They have whatever they want. They know nothing about suffering, struggling, striving. They are spoiled. The *nouveaux riches*.

I spin to the pool table. Betty is leaning forward, leaning toward me for a shot, and the position swells up her blouse. My stare is interrupted when the authentic young blonde passes by on her way to the restroom. Her perfume stays behind her, caressing me like skin.

A chorus of greeting rises, "Mary, Mary." Slowly, I turn toward the doorway.

1991

Lessons from the Cockroach Graveyard

Expression (Volume Three)

THE OLDER I GET, the less I understand women. Their sense of cause and effect, for example. I am opening a beer in the kitchen, prior to preparing tonight's stir-fry, and as I do a cockroach appears on the wall over the faucet. I see it, I probably even see it first, but for the moment I do nothing because the critter is still too close to the faucet to ambush — one move by me and it'll be scurrying into the plumbing. I know this because I've tried it before: cause and effect. And Maggie was there when I tried it, too, screaming as if she'd just spotted a ten-pound rat.

This evening she doesn't scream. When she sees the cockroach, she says, "You're doing this on purpose, aren't you?"

"What?" I reply.

"You know what. Jesus."

Even though my back is to her, I can sense Maggie moving slowly toward the refrigerator, reaching for the can of Raid we keep up there. I buy Raid because it was the great poet Lew Welch who wrote, "Raid Kills Bugs Dead!" I raise the bottle of Full Sail and tip my head back, drinking deeply, taking in a third of the brew. Then I belch.

"Ahhhh!" screams Maggie, charging forward like a mad bee, spraying Raid at me and the cockroach, though I'm not sure which of us is the primary target. I cuss under my breath and get the hell out of the kitchen, grabbing a full beer from the fridge on my way.

In a couple minutes Maggie joins me in the studio's largest space, the bed-living-dining-room. She looks exhausted. She is as dark as a Mediterranean gypsy but is proud to be Irish and doesn't like it when I start talking about gypsies in the woodpile.

"Any luck?" I ask.

"He got away into the plumbing." She always refers to cockroaches in the masculine.

I don't get it. Will my beer bottle hit the ceiling if I drop it? Don't women know anything?

EVENING. The stir-fry was average, conversation at dinner non-existent. We've been living together almost three years and haven't talked of marriage for the last two. We still have sex, which is about all we have.

I'm still drinking beer, Maggie has poured another glass of Chablis, and we stare silently at the small black-and-white TV that sits on my trunk. It's one of those television magazine shows, full of scandal and gossip.

My mind is adrift, trying to remember the closing lines of Lew Welch's "Chicago Poem," which for some reason has been on my mind lately. I no longer have a book of Welch's poems. I no longer have books. I met Maggie three years ago after a bad divorce and have been traveling light ever since.

Trying to recall Welch's lines, I don't see it at first. But Maggie does. She has eyes like a hawk. Suddenly she throws her wine glass against the wall, and I jump.

"What the hell's the matter with you?" I ask.

"You drive me crazy, pretending you don't see it."

"See what?"

"On the screen!"

She's on her feet, going for the Raid, when I see the dark speck moving across the belly of a woman in her underwear. At first I'm confused, wondering what scandal I've missed, but then I understand that it's a Maidenform ad.

Maggie is a wasteful cockroach hunter, she's spraying the Raid when she's still six feet from the screen, not only wasting spray but warning the cockroach, which now hurries down a thigh to try and escape under a tuning panel. But Maggie is on the critter before it gets to the woman's foot, spraying like crazy, until the room is filled with a mist of Raid.

"All right already!" I shout, standing up. "You don't have to waste the whole can on the thing."

Maggie stops spraying. She turns to me and gently, like a father pitching the first softball to his son, tosses me the can of Raid. Then she grabs her coat and leaves.

I fetch another beer, sit down, stare at the television and try to remember Welch's lines. "Chicago Poem" is a wonderful poem about Welch finally refusing to contribute anything more to the stinking polluted mess that is Chicago. But I can't remember his phrasing.

I'M IN BED when Maggie gets home. She's brought her girlfriend, Martha, to help her move out.

At first I pretend to be sleeping. I'm not surprised, really, I'm just angry she chose to do it this way, at this hour. I keep my eyes closed under the bare lightbulb and listen to them gathering her things in the closet, taking her spices from the kitchen, sorting through the mess that is everywhere for what belongs to her. It's all as clear as day, even with my eyes closed.

Then there is a silence that confuses me. Facing the wall, I open my eyes and see a cockroach not two feet from my nose. I slowly, quietly, roll over and can make out whispered conversation at the small table off the kitchen. I reach for my robe on the floor, slip it on and make my appearance.

Martha quickly gets up and says to Maggie, "I'll wait in the car." Passing me, she gives me a stare that would give Raid competition.

I sit down and Maggie pours another glass of wine.

"I'm sorry," she says, "I just can't take it any more."

"Take what?"

"Oh, Raymond."

"You could have warned me," I say.

"I don't believe you haven't seen this coming."

"We could've talked about it."

"You don't talk, that's part of the problem. Maybe that's all of the problem. You stopped talking when you stopped playing."

I play jazz guitar, or used to. Everything left me about a year after my divorce. You don't explain these things, you just go with the flow. If a riff doesn't occur to you, it doesn't occur to you.

"For the past year, even longer, we've both just been going through the motions," Maggie says. "I need more than that. So do you."

"Don't tell me what I need," I mumble.

"What?"

"Nothing."

Maggie drinks her wine and stands up. She starts toward the door.

"What if we talk more?" I ask.

She turns long enough to say, "Oh, Raymond," then moves toward the door again. I stand up and follow her.

When she opens the door, I say, "I don't get it. I don't understand you. No warning, nothing."

Maggie turns and starts to say something but stops. She's looking at the wall near the door, where the cockroach I saw earlier is hovering near the mattress on the floor.

When I understand what is happening, I say, "Want me to get you the Raid? One last shot?"

"That's not funny. This is as hard for me as it is for you."

"Is it?"

"Yes, it is!"

I feel bad for making her angry. Maggie takes a deep breath, starts to go, and changes her mind. She takes one step into the room.

"I don't know what you're going to do about it," she begins, "but I know what I'm going to do about it. I'm just going to walk away from it. Maybe some of it will die if I'm not around feeding it any more. Lew Welch, remember?"

I correct her paraphrasing of "Chicago Poem," saying, "Maybe *a small part* of it will die. *Small part.*"

"Goodbye, Raymond." She turns and gently closes the door behind her.

I look at the wall. The cockroach is still, as if daring me to go for the Raid.

WE MAKE an undeclared pact, the cockroaches and I. I lay off the Raid, and they don't show up as often any more. I even come to admire them in a way. Somewhere I read that cockroaches would be the sole survivors of a nuclear war. A guy could have a worse role model, if he's interested in surviving.

A couple weeks later I run into Maggie in a bar. She's leaning over a small table, leering at a guy who dresses like a banker. I can't believe it. I can't resist going to the table either.

"Well, looky here," I say.

Maggie sits up stiffly. "Hello, Raymond," she says. "Harold, this is Raymond."

"Hi, Harry!"

Maggie gives me the smile that says, Go away! I grab a chair from the next table but before I sit down an amazing thing happens, Maggie brings out a can of Raid from her purse and points it at me. I start laughing. Then she starts spraying.

I squint, moving forward to grab the can away from her. The banker, Harold, is on his feet, ready to protect the fair maiden or something.

"You can't do that to me," I tell Maggie.

"Raymond, you're even bringing them in on your clothes now. Look, he's dead on the table."

Sure enough, there's a dead cockroach next to the ashtray. I glance at Maggie, who looks as if she's about to cry. I turn and go.

NOW IT'S all-out war. I complain to the manager and tell him if he doesn't get the building sprayed I'm moving, which is a lie, there isn't a cheaper studio in the city.

So I have to do it myself. Me and Welch. I buy cans of Raid a half dozen at a time, attack the critters with a can in each hand, going for broke.

I wear a red bandanna over the lower half of my face, looking like a bank robber, spraying behind the refrigerator, spraying under the sink, spraying where the pipes come out of the wall, spraying around the toilet and tub.

The more I spray, the more of them that appear. Finally, I run out of Raid. Then I run out of money.

IT'S A DUMB GIG, playing popular songs in a seafood restaurant, accompanying a bad pianist, but it pays the rent, it pays for the Raid. Then one night Maggie wanders in. She's alone, which surprises me. She looks great, which doesn't.

I try not to look at her but during the break the cocktail waitress tells me that the pretty girl with the dark features has bought me a drink.

"Long time," I say, sitting down.

"Yes, it has been."

"So how are you doing?"

"Terrible. I miss you."

This takes me by surprise, and I almost choke on my beer.

"Didn't you get my letters?" she asks.

There were three of them, long handwritten analyses of our relationship, the pros and cons, and an indirect inquiry if I'd be interested in sitting down across the table from her to analyze the relationship together. I never answered one. I didn't know what to say.

I reply, "Of course, I got them."

"Had nothing to say, right?"

I shrug.

"I've forgotten how well you play."

I force a smile. "It's embarrassing to be here, really."

"No, I think it's good for you to be here. It's better than not playing at all."

Actually she's right, but I don't respond.

"I've got to get back to work," I say and finish the beer in a long gulp.

THROUGH THE LAST SET, I can't help but wonder why she's still hanging around. Is she trying to tell me something? Maybe she's horny. We managed to do that right most of the time. But as it turns out, she still wants to sit across the table from me.

"I think in a different context we can be very good for one another," she says. "I know that I love you."

Love. Do I love her? The Greeks had three words for it, *eros*, *fidelia* and *agape*. We'd had the first from the beginning, the second most of the time — and the third? I'm not sure if I could love a woman the way I love my music.

"I've learned a lot from living alone," she says. "I think I can bend for you if you can bend for me. I realize how important your music is to you. Not just as a profession, but as a way to communicate. When we fight in the future, I think you should start whistling jazz to me."

I have to laugh, and as I do she reaches across the table and takes my hand.

"Can you bend at all, Raymond? I don't think I'm asking for much."

"I never did understand what you were asking for," I admit.

"Respect."

The word astonishes me because I've always respected her.

"That surprises you, doesn't it?"

"Frankly, yes."

"I can't live in a hovel," Maggie says. "I'm affected too much by my environment. I know you thought it was all we could afford, since you were out of work, but we could've cut corners and rented a better place, a cleaner place."

"No cockroaches? Good luck. Not in this city."

"Someplace where they spray the building regularly. It's important to do things like that on schedule, you know? Just like it's important to do the dishes every day before they start piling up in the sink. If you ignore little things like that, before you know it everything gets out of hand. Then it's a major project to clean up. Do you understand what I'm saying?"

"Neither one of us are great housekeepers."

"I'm not saying it's all your fault. I'm saying your environment can affect how you feel, how you behave, your attitude, everything. I never want to live in a place like that again."

I admit that I've been looking around for another place, now that I have a regular paycheck again.

"Maybe we can talk about your moving in with me," she says. "I have a one bedroom."

I say, "Maybe we can go there tonight."

She squeezes my hand, lets it go and smiles.

"Not tonight. I don't want us to get back together for the wrong reasons. I love you, Raymond. I want us to work. I want us to sit down soon and talk about the things that went wrong. And why."

"I was hoping you were ..." I finish the sentence by raising my eyebrows in the way that once was a signal between us.

"I am, Raymond, believe me." She stands up. "I don't know what you're going to do about it, but I know what I'm going to do about it."

She comes around the table, bends down and kisses me on the lips.

"I'll call you tomorrow morning, okay?" she says.

"I'd like that."

"Oh, Raymond."

I don't even close down the bar. Even with money in my pocket I don't buy a new can of Raid. Something has changed. I'm hearing riffs again. I celebrate by taking a cab, not the bus, to a hotel and renting a room. By the time a lone cockroach crawls out from the bathroom plumbing, the room is dark and I'm enjoying the soundest sleep I've had in months.

1973

The Idaho Jacket

Prism International (Spring)

Roll of Honor, Best American Short Stories 1974

RICHARD, realize one thing: I am beginning to wear the Idaho jacket comfortably now. Perhaps I'm not wearing it as comfortably as you would have, had genetics not played its tricks on us all and given the second son, and not the first, the bulky characteristics of the father. To Buck, I gather, biology remains so much scientific claptrap and when he gave you the jacket he did so knowing it was not your size. But you had asked for the jacket as a kid, the story goes, and so when you turned twenty-one, Buck gave it to you. And I have no quarrel with any of this past history, Richard, not even as I wear the jacket today. Frankly for a long time I did not understand why you gave me the jacket, particularly with the gesture by which it became mine. Not understanding, I was unable to wear the jacket comfortably. I wore it, yes, but rather with the self-consciousness with which a timid boy will wear a Halloween costume. That soon may be history, too.

I'm as ignorant about Idaho as I ever was. The memories I have before Mother took me with her to Los Angeles remain vague, like those hazy events subsequent to an accident which one experiences while conscious but later cannot recall. I cannot say whether or not I thought it was strange to be going on a long trip without you and Buck. Mother must have answered satisfactorily whatever questions I asked, for my mind unleashes no ghosts of a home and boyhood lost in Idaho. To tell the truth, I have no memory of the Idaho jacket before references to it began to appear in your letters.

When did we begin to correspond? By the time I was a teenager your letters had become my text, a text wiser than the dull books I was expected to read at school. Well, I shudder to think what Dr. Jefferson would make of that remark! Mother, God rest her soul, retained one idiosyncrasy which irritated me to the very moment of her death — her addiction to psycho-analysis. I must have told you what her last words to me were. "Tell Dr. Jefferson I have no more repressions." If I didn't know better, I'd think she said that for my benefit, hoping to get a grin out of me before passing

49

away. Richard, something is grossly unethical about the way that head-shrinker catered to Mother's obsession to be "normal." We all know she was a bit mad — madness was a large part of her charm, wasn't it? She was very kind. Eccentric and unpredictable, yes, but kind to the end. Could her last words have been for me after all?

At any rate, your letters have always meant something special to me. When so much space in them came to anticipate your twenty-first birth-day, the day on which you'd receive Buck's jacket, I found myself growing excited with you. I was excited even though none of your reasons for wanting the jacket made sense to me. You wrote me so many stories about your northern Idaho, the land, and about something called "the high lone-some" and how the Idaho jacket was part of each, but not once did you say that you wanted the jacket simply because it had belonged to Buck. Reading your tales, I decided you were an incurable romantic. But my fingers were crossed for you all the same.

Then you mailed me a photograph and in it you were wearing a green and black plaid jacket several sizes too large for you. Buck's Idaho jacket, I presumed. I put the photograph in my wallet, often taking it out to look at it. Do you see a physical resemblance between us? I fail to. Nonetheless the photograph, whatever lack of family similarity it documented, brought me closer to you. Looking at it, I began to want more and more to see you, I should say to meet you, to sit across the room from you, to talk to you, Richard. To talk to you. I don't know why I felt this way about you but didn't have the same strong desire to get to know Buck. I'm sure Dr. Jefferson could come up with something! Well, he wouldn't necessarily be right. I just know I wanted very much to meet you. I wanted to know my brother. But although I was fourteen, and older in many ways, when alone with Mother I couldn't bring myself to broach the subject of a visit. I don't know why.

I feel foolish admitting this. It should have been easy to visit. Do you know how far it is to Orofino from Los Angeles? Something over a thou-sand miles. Then why did we all wait until Mother died before meeting? We essentially were strangers, you, Buck and I. If Mother hadn't willed to be buried in Orofino, would we remain strangers today? What was hold-ing us back from each other?

So Mother died and I took her home to Idaho. What do we ever know about death, Richard? Or even about dying? So many questions! The coffin was on the train, fortunately out of my sight, and I thought a lot about death on the trip north, thought about it while drinking myself into maudlin reverie. Death happens to each of us, we decide, but can this really be the end of our journey? I doubt that my young man's theories about this will last out middle age. Well, I'm not sure I have any theories.

I drank my way to Idaho. And because I was drunk when the train pulled into Orofino, I can't recall whether you were wearing the jacket at the station or not. To tell the truth, I have only a fuzzy recollection of events up to and including the funeral. Too much happened at once for all of us, I think you would agree. Mother was dead; we were meeting. Vaguely I recall that you and Buck shared my anxiety drink for drink. What a sorry lot we must have been for the relatives, husband and two sons staggering under liquor instead of under a more dignified grief. I met lots of relatives at the funeral, didn't I?

I do remember the poker game. It began two or three days after we buried her, I think, at the instigation of Buck's Indian friend, Gib Hill. You must realize, Richard, what a city boy I am and that the trip to bury Mother provided the occasion for my first encounter with — shall I call it the wilderness? The funeral seems longer ago than a year, doubtless because so much of its presence was drowned in sorrow, in liquored mourning for Mother. Yet there may be no more dignified way to suffer, Richard. There may be no dignified way to suffer at all.

I'm a city boy and the poker game fits right into the romantic Idaho landscape. When I set Orofino against Los Angeles, I can't comprehend Buck's complaints that Idaho is getting too "civilized," that Idaho isn't the same country in which he grew up, that the hills have been stripped of timber. To my eye, the hills around Orofino are covered with more trees than I could find in all of Southern California. And the Clearwater River is getting polluted, Buck complained, and yet the Clearwater is, yes, the clearest river I've ever seen. Too many people moving in? Into Orofino! How many could even find it on a map? For me, Richard, to enter Orofino was to step into a page from the journal of Lewis and Clark.

And as if towering trees, as if foaming rivers and a vast unpopulated landscape weren't enough, you had to show me Indians and poker games! For a while, cynically, I thought the whole affair was a sham. Indians, hard-drinking lumberjacks, two-day poker games — it was all part of a skit you had arranged to impress your city boy of a brother. What is it the cowboys say in the westerns? "Let's pull one on the dude," or something close.

Endings have a way of defining what passed before them, and of course I have no doubts about events now, not about those events I can recall. We were at home, two or three days after the funeral, drinking coffee at last although it was well into evening. I felt out of place, the son who was a stranger, who didn't know his father or his brother. I wanted to know you both, certainly, and had stayed over in order to get to know you. But so far I remained a stranger and I was worried, the way things were going, that I'd return to Los Angeles one.

Then Gib Hill arrived. His appearance was reason enough to doubt the authenticity of what followed. Los Angeles is the home of the world's weirdest sects, Richard, and Gib's attire reminded me of one of the many costumes a native comes to accept as being part of Southern California's natural landscape. Gib, by dressing the way he did, gave himself away: he was not a "real person." Add together the black cowboy hat, with a red rose in its band; the dark glasses, never removed; the fringed jacket, the faded jeans and the wide black belt with its silver dollar buckle; the black cowboy boots, winged with red eagles on its sides — add them together and you have an actor, a ham, a mere surrogate of an "authentic personality": a Marlon Brando motorcycle-riding cowboy. This judgment was Mother's legacy to me: that damned analyst's point of view!

"Poker game is hatching at The Lumberman's," Gib told Buck. Well, at least The Lumberman's was authentic, I had learned that. Buck had owned the bar and hotel in the forties and Mother, those old Idaho stories went, had dealt black jack there. My mother? The old photographs and stories aside, the woman who raised me in Los Angeles, the woman who gave what little money she could spare to an analyst because she wanted to be "normal," this woman was different from your card-dealer. Yet not as different as I used to think.

We followed Gib to The Lumberman's, where at a back table the poker chips were already up for sale. You were wearing the Idaho jacket, I recall, and its cuffs dropped to your knuckles. The men sitting at the bar were kidding you about the jacket's not fitting as soon as we entered, and I gathered it was an old joke between you. As a matter of fact, you did look a little silly in the jacket. It is one thing for a boy to stomp around the house in his father's slippers, quite another for an adult to do something very nearly the same. You must have been 25 then, for I had just turned 21. And yet our ages seemed to be reversed, Richard, and I acted like the more mature brother. You answered one old man's kidding by picking him up and carrying him around the room on your shoulders while the others laughed and hooted. To be honest, I was embarrassed. Embarrassed for us both, perhaps.

Buck bought into the game and you wanted in, too, but when you learned that I didn't know how to play poker (I still can see your disbelief), you stayed out, despite my objections, in order to keep me company. We took a table near the game and began what turned into a marathon of drinking. Or at least it was a marathon for some of you.

The poker game intrigued me from the beginning. It was played so theatrically, like a scene in the lowest grade western, which only increased my doubts about the authenticity of the entire affair. Talk about cool characters, the likes of Paul Newman or Steve McQueen! Buck and Gib seemed to be having a contest to see who could push forward the most chips with the least concern. I expected to see money change hands, yes, but I did not expect to see poker pots worth hundreds of dollars. I did not watch in awe for long: I concluded that the game was a sham, just as I had suspected. No one except Hollywood actors can bet a hundred dollars on two pair (I've since played poker myself, Richard) without a flutter of emotion. At any moment I expected the fraud to get the best of Buck, Gib and the others, at which time they would break into hysterics, the joke revealed and on me. I watched the game silently, waiting for the punch line.

You had warned me that poker games at The Lumberman's had been known to run for days on end but I doubted this, too, since I doubted the legitimacy of the game itself. But the game went on, while the bar filled with boisterous spectators who looked as though they were willing to wait for the outcome, no matter how long it took. By the time I drank myself into drowsiness — it must have been three in the morning by then — the game's end was nowhere in sight. Perhaps I then decided that the punch line was more subtle, that the laughing at me wouldn't begin until morning. You excused yourself to talk to the bartender and returned with a key: we had rooms upstairs. "You're sleeping in Nellie's old room," you told me, grinning. "Nellie was the best looking whore on this side of the Clearwater." Nellie, the prostitute, of course. Of course, Richard. I'm sure I shook my head. You were carrying the joke too far, making it much too melodramatic.

In the morning the game was still in progress. No one had dropped out, though it was evident by the distribution of chips around the table that Buck and Gib were winning. Many spectators had retired. Buck waved as I entered the room. I went to the bar, where soon you joined me. We drank "red dogs," beer with tomato juice in it. After several drinks, you suggested breakfast.

On full stomachs we hiked through the hills behind Orofino. Once, when we had to crawl through a barbed-wire fence, I warned that we might be trespassing. You laughed and went on. You led me to a place with the improbable name of Crazy Man's Gulch, a hollow to which (the story went) Buck escaped as a young man whenever the "high lonesome" got the best of him. I listened as though to a foreign language as you went on to tell me about the gallon jug of whiskey that accompanied him, about the Idaho jacket that was his bed, about the young wife (our mother) left behind. When I suggested that perhaps Buck needed psychiatric help more than Mother ever did, you said, "Hell, we're all nuts. Only Buck likes being crazy. Relishes it." I was not prepared to believe you, Richard. There is no

Crazy Man's Gulch in Los Angeles and gallon jugs are filled with Gallo or Italian Swiss Colony. Young wives left behind commit adultery.

Returning after the hike, we began drinking again. The poker game went on, and spectators returned in large numbers, watching with an enthusiasm more proper to a horse race. Slowly players began to drop out, as much from exhaustion as from lack of funds, until only three were left, Buck and Gib included.

Buck was the first of the three to hit a losing streak. After dinner he asked you, "How much money you got?"

"A hundred. Maybe more."

I looked for a sign that you were kidding. But you weren't, for soon you passed him the money.

"Give me the jacket," Buck said.

You took it off and handed it to him.

Richard, what was I supposed to make of all this? Although by then I was beginning to believe that the game was legitimate, only legitimacy being able to sustain itself to the very brink of boredom, as I watched you take off the jacket I found myself with doubts all over again. As before, the scene was lifted from the worst western I could imagine — the passing of the rabbit's foot, the lucky silver dollar, the magic spur, after which the winning streak would follow. Buck put on the jacket and kidded Gib, "Watch out, redskin, I'm wearing the luckiest coat in Idaho." Gib said, "Deal." Was I supposed to believe such dialogue? We don't have similar melodrama in Los Angeles.

Your own reaction puzzled me. You seemed offended that Buck wanted to wear the jacket. Was he an Indian giver, was that it? For Christ's sake, Richard, enough was enough! That's why I begged my departure and went upstairs. You were carrying the joke too far. If you wanted your dude, you were going to have to come upstairs to catch him.

And later, hearing the knock on the door, I prepared for the punch line. Finally! You stood in the doorway, carrying a bottle of whiskey and looking morose.

"Buck dropped out," you told me. "He lost big." Was this the last parcel of bait? Who was hiding in the hallway?

You came in, sat on the bed, opened the bottle and drank from it. I turned down a swig. No Hollywood gestures for me.

"How much is losing big?" I asked.

"He lost what cash we had between us. Big enough. He lost in the jacket, that's what surprises me. He always bragged about never losing in the jacket."

Who could miss this melodramatic springing of the trap? I waited silently and soon there was another knock on the door. Buck let himself in.

54

"Here's your jacket," he said and tossed the Idaho jacket into your lap. He stopped just inside the doorway, looking ill at ease. You handed him the bottle, he drank.

"What's the matter with you two?" he finally asked. "I'm the guy who lost the silver, I'm the one who should look gloomy. Smile, why don't you?" He turned and walked away.

"Where's he going?"

You replied with an expression that said, Don't you know? Then you remembered that Buck and I were strangers.

"He's going down to get drunk. Gib won, so Gib buys the drinks." You stood up, carrying the jacket. "You coming?"

"Downstairs?" I could hear the festivity below.

"You don't think Buck came all the way up here just to give me the jacket, do you? He wants us down there to amuse him so he doesn't have to think about losing."

I said, "He took Mother's death hard, didn't he?"

You shrugged. "He's got losing to worry about now."

Without further word you tossed me the jacket. I followed you downstairs, Richard, where we would conclude our last drunk together, but it wasn't until the next afternoon, while I was packing, that you explained to me that the gesture of tossing me the Idaho jacket had meant it was mine.

I'M LEARNING TO WEAR the jacket comfortably. Other coats appear on campus — letterman's sweaters, Army fatigue jackets, leather jackets — but none rivals the Idaho jacket. It's been in every whorehouse and drunk tank in northern Idaho, Buck claims. Is it then too romantic to insist that the jacket is special?

I've changed since wearing the jacket, Richard, that's what I must make clear. Take today, for example. I stopped on my way home from campus to watch the construction that is going on down the block. Another high-rise apartment building is going up, something quick to meet the demands of increasing enrollment, and all day long the clamor and rumble of construction makes studying impossible. Passing by on the way home, I sometimes stop to watch.

Putting up an apartment building is a rather straightforward procedure, I think, one without your Idaho melodrama. There is no mystery about what is going on, even if to a casual observer the purposes of the workmen appear to be random. There are blueprints and guidelines and specifications to follow, and everything is figured out ahead of time on paper.

I'm not sure why I stopped to watch today, or any other day for that matter. I think the building going up is ugly.

But today as I was watching, a middle-aged man joined me. He was a businessman by appearance, or perhaps a professor since we were so close to campus. He watched the men drive nails, a crane lift boards, workers scan blueprints and then he said, but not really to me, "Terrible." He seemed embarrassed to have attracted my attention and, perhaps for this reason, he quickly added, "I'm afraid I'm old-fashioned. I prefer the old homes that used to be here. But you can't argue with progress, can you?" he laughed. And he went along his way, whistling.

I don't know, Richard. I get scared. Is it normal to be twenty-two and scared? Shouldn't I be charging out into the world, lance confidently poised, eager and willing to carve out my niche of stability? I graduate this year! Sometimes I wish the Idaho jacket fitted me like it fits you. I'd hunch myself down into it and hide.

Am I making any sense? I can't think of "sense" without thinking of Dr. Jefferson and *his* kind of sense. I abhor it, Richard. I'd rather be scared. I'd rather be mad! Today, as the man departed whistling, I turned to the rising building and looked at it as I had never looked at it before. "Terrible," he had said, but so what? Who among us had any control of its going up?

But what if I *took* control? Not by myself really, for I'm quite sure — I can't explain it rationally — that if I hadn't been wearing the Idaho jacket, I'd never have done what I did next. Somehow wearing the jacket justified what followed.

The construction area, of course, is fenced off. A number of doors provide entrances into the working area but above each of them is a sign which reads, DANGER AREA! CLOSED TO PUBLIC. NO ADMITTANCE. AUTHORIZED PERSONNEL ONLY. In the evening, after the workmen go home, children climb the fence and play in the area but during the day both adults and children heed the warning. I always have. But today, Richard, I didn't.

I entered one of the plywood doors and began to traverse the corner of the lot, which would bring me to another door exiting onto the street near my apartment. I bothered no one and entered no area where a board might have fallen on my head, or where I was in any danger whatsoever. I merely walked across the corner of the lot, where building material was stacked, then exited and crossed the street to go home.

A workman was shouting at me before I was thirty feet onto the property. "Hey! This is a limited area!" Others quickly picked up the protest, "This area's off limits!" "Get on the other side of the fence!" "Can't you read the signs?" I walked on my way without turning around and soon heard a voice behind me, which was getting closer. It wasn't until I was out of the area and crossing the street that the workman caught up.

56

He yelled, "What's the big idea?" I turned, found him standing in the plywood doorway just behind me, smiled and nodded. Then I went on my way, Richard, turning up the collar of the Idaho jacket as I left.

Already my imagination is running wild, and this small incident expands into the following:

I was walking across the lot under a shower of boards and debris, walking under cranes which swung their metal necks menacingly above me, passing by jackhammers which tore the ground from my feet and steamrollers which tried to make me a corner of a parking lot, I was walking through it all, Richard, and I kept walking, walked through it all in the Idaho jacket, through all the bellowing workmen and protesting machines, the clamor and rumble, the violated signs screaming DANGER AREA!, I continued home without a glance behind me, without a remark, I continued nonchalantly on my way.

Do I have the family madness, Richard? Is this the beginning?

Fragments Before the Fall

The Literary Review (Summer)

I WALK a tightrope between two mountain tops over the Valley of the Waters of Fire. The waters are rising and all too soon the flames will disengage the embracing strands of fiber which hold me up, casting me to my fate below — incineration. I stand very still. To move would be to lose my balance and become cinder too soon.

I RECOGNIZE the voice: "Mummy, can I take this magazine to school? It has a story in it that is full of symbols, and Mr. Walker just loves symbols."

YOU, my friend, have not believed me from the beginning. But you say you do. And that makes you a phony.

THE MOUNTAIN from which I come is called the Mountain of the Sun. There I lived for many years, happy in my employment as an Accountant, happy with my wife Rose and with our two children, Fred (the boy) and Sally (the girl). My specialty in Accounting was figures. I added them, subtracted them and strung them in long columns in ledger books. It was as a result of such figuring, especially the adding of figures (and the figuring of adding), that I decided to begin the journey to the Mountain of the Moon across the valley. Whence the present.

IF YOU must think of me as a character in a work of fiction, I wish you would stop reading immediately. Ditto if you think of yourself as a reader of anything but the most literal truth.

WE, of course, had knowledge of the Mountain of the Moon. On clear days we could see it. Although I personally knew no one who had been across the valley, my analyst claimed to have a number of patients who had made the journey. They returned insane. In this context my analyst's reasons for discouraging my own journey become clear enough.

Yet the figures pointed the way, and I obeyed them. My respect for mathematics, I must admit, is greater than my respect for psychology. As disciplines, you understand. As disciplines.

I MUST rest now. I'm allowed as much from time to time. Five minutes should do it. Keep your eyes fixed here.

(WELL, if you're reading this before the five minutes are up, then I simply cannot trust you. Please stop reading. Call me what you like, but stop).

THE HARD PART was telling Rose. Although she is an attractive women, she had an adolescent complexion problem the camouflage of which gave her the habit of putting the flesh of her face behind a measurable thickness of powder, upon which she then could draw eyebrows, eyes, nose, lips and facial shadows in an attempt to pass herself off as being real. I anticipated Rose's anger upon hearing of my plans, and when she is angry her face cracks like putty or, in cases of rage, shatters like pottery. In either instance I do not enjoy witnessing what occurs. It rather would be like watching Van Gogh cut off his ear. Watching self-inflicted pain and so on. I mean, no one had to cut off Van Gogh's ear for him. He did it himself. And Rose powders her own face.

IF AT this very moment you took out a match and burned this page, do you think I would turn to cinder? But I know I shall become cinder. Though not quite yet. And under different circumstances.

ON HANDS and knees we picked up the pieces of her face and talked.
"Why?"
"I could make a joke and say, Because it is there."
"Is that why?"
"No. No, it is because the figures lead there. Because the net profit totals $131,515.14, which is 13-15-15-14, which is M-O-O-N if the letters of the alphabet are counted in order."
"That's no reason."
"It is the reason."

ROSE FAVORED my hospitalization, my analyst favored hospitalization but the children were against it and they won.

IT IS difficult to breathe, only to breathe. Breath is the movement of the lungs, the movement of the lungs is the movement of the body, whence

60

the swaying, the slipping of rope underfoot, and the ensuing fall to the flames below, which consume.

ONE NEEDS special equipment for the journey. Special shoes. Special food. Special ability to keep one's balance and to sleep on one's feet. Soon I could use special heat-resistant fabrics with which to insulate my smoldering body but they neglected to tell me this while there still was time.

THE PROBLEM, which my analyst claims is mine and not his, is that I do not relate to reality. Hence my fabrications, as he calls them. Hence the situation I presently find myself in, which is called a story by readers I do not trust.

WHEN I am immobile, my mind wanders. And my present situation, I suppose, is the final immobility, the immobility before the fall. It is appropriate, under the circumstances, to think of a parting gesture, something to suit the occasion. A valedictorian for every class.

I TOLD my analyst, Nothing relates to anything that doesn't relate to anything that doesn't relate to something. In other words, reality doesn't relate to me.

I HAD a big sendoff the day I set out. Rose and the children waved, my analyst looked glum, and strangers gathered the way they are prone to when they discover a man sitting atop a flagpole or a young woman standing on a window ledge. When I reached the tightrope, I stepped forward uneasily. The sudden cheers behind me were so deafening that I bolted, almost managing to tumble to an end before I had begun. But farther along the way the noise no longer bothered me, and for some time now I haven't been able to hear it at all. The conditioning of an athlete, it's been called.

IF YOU still are with me, then there is hope. Trust me and keep the faith.

IT WAS late on my second day on the rope when I discovered the Valley of the Waters of Fire. Of course, we already had our own name for it, the Valley of Green Pastures, for from the Mountain of the Sun the view below is pastoral, heavenly. But midway across the valley, at the first point at which it becomes more economical to continue ahead than to return, the scene below changes. Greens become reds, and the cooling pastures of heaven become the very blast furnaces of hell. For the first time the volcanoes are visible, erupting like simultaneous wars and filling the valley with the molten rage destined to consume me.

MY POINT is that it is impolite to laugh. You could have stopped reading or, if you insisted on going on, have given me the benefit of the doubt. But you shouldn't have laughed. (To hell with your point).

I RATHER expected the television cameras to appear. Rescue, of course, was out of the question from the beginning but I confess I expected more interest in my journey than what I've received, which recently has become no interest at all. They cheer no longer. There are no cameras. There are no witnesses except yourself, which is why I am taking you so seriously.

ONE BEGINS to long for the good old days. The pre-perspiration days, as I am tempted to call them now. The office in which I worked was cool, modernly air-conditioned. On the Mountain of the Sun it frequently gets very hot but in my office it was pleasant and cool. Not so cool at home, however, and Rose often complained. I am beginning to understand what she was getting at.

HOW LONG can you hold your breath? Not until I am finished, I'll wager. I, on the other hand, have been holding my breath for several hours. The motivation is considerable, of course. That's how my analyst would put it. But I'd just say I'm damn good at holding my breath and let it go at that.

WHAT to do?

THERE IS a lot of propaganda on the market claiming that to die is easy. You'll find it in churches, in literature, on television, in ledger books, everywhere. Don't believe any of it, my friend.

DOES ROSE miss me or does she have a lover already?

IN TIME one gets impatient for the end. The mind can play its games only for so long before it, too, begins to get bored. Hence the more frequent changes of subject. Everything is a manifestation of the search for the appropriate parting gesture. Everyone wants to be valedictorian. I see that clearly enough now. (Now that it's too late and I sweat, wait, wonder if skin pops as it burns and if burning flesh can hear itself).

AND ONE gets angry. Somehow you seem to be involved in my predicament. The ones who stopped reading earlier, too, play their part. I get the impression that there are cameras here after all, only the cameras are hidden or mounted with super-lenses capable of focusing on me from the Mountain of the Sun. And are there spies on the Mountain of the Moon, too?

YOU'LL get yours.

I HAVE gone out of my way to surprise my analyst. I can admit that now. When he prompted me to admit I hated my mother, I said I loved her. When he suggested a carnal attraction to my daughter, I denied it. But when he concluded I must be sane, I gave him the works.

THERE IS, finally, at long last, nothing to do. I am done. Sshh.

AND YOU? You will follow. You must, for I have a parting gesture in mind but it depends on your following in order to make sense, and I give no value (absolutely none!) to gestures which do not make sense. You will follow and so I say, Welcome, my friend, Welcome to the Valley of the Waters of Fire, where you will be consumed. And sooner than you think, even as I will be consumed sooner than I think, since we all get tired of waiting and jump from the rope in the end. As we fall our hands trail over our heads, making the hand the last organ to go and the appropriate vehicle for whatever parting gesture can be mustered by flesh heated in agony. What do you think it will be, my friend? An erect middle finger? Perhaps you'll be surprised. I may give you the flat palm of my hand, raised horizontally to cushion your own fall, which so quickly follows mine. But hurry! For I am burning.

Part Two

ELEVEN PLAYS

Christmas at the Juniper Tavern
"Mill workers drink beer, swamis meditate. It's the nature of things."

The Half-Life Conspiracy
"The Pacific Northwest! The land of lumberjacks and fishermen and cowboys! That's why I nuked it, you're so close to the mythological center of things."

Waitresses
"Waiting for something is better than waiting for nothing."

Varmints
"Nations die, Paddy, but gold is eternal. And why? Because man's nature is greed. Greed!"

Famililly
"We hold these truths to be self-evident, that all children are created equal..."

Sad Laughter
"My life is a dress rehearsal for a play."

Bedrooms and Bars
"What the hell's wrong with being a romantic?"

The Stiff
"What the people expect, they deserve. What they deserve, they get. Always."

Country Northwestern
"You don't earn a goddamn thing in the music business, Red. You either kiss ass or you don't kiss ass."

The Pardon
"There was a war. There was a war but there were no heroes. Perhaps you remember."

Who Forgives?
"My name's Ed, and I'm a perp."

1984

Christmas at the Juniper Tavern
a play in two acts

First performed at the Wilson Center for the Performing Arts in Portland, Oregon, on January 5, 1984. Directed by Steve Smith.

Produced for public television, winner of ACE award.

THE CAST (4M, 5W):

Stella, *owner of the Juniper Tavern, a no-nonsense woman.*

Frank, *an unemployed mill worker, a Korean vet, a little lost.*

Rex, *an unemployed log truck driver, imaginative, a little crazy.*

Margie, *his wife, not too smart.*

Sheriff Billy *of Juniper County, more heart than brain.*

Ann, *a young woman, searching.*

Joy, *her mother, a college professor, bright and cynical.*

Swami Kree, *guru of the Kree cult.*

Ma Prama Rama Kree, *his personal secretary, protective, suspicious.*

THE TIME:

Christmas, 1979.

THE SET:

The Juniper tavern. A bar, tables. A jukebox. A Christmas tree with presents under it. Stage right to restrooms. A telephone on the wall. A door behind the bar leads to a storage area.

Two other areas must be defined: a neutral playing area; area for car interiors.

"Song of the Swami" by Lynne Fuqua.

Logging poems by Fred Ross.

ACT ONE

Scene One

(AT RISE: Frank and Stella are waltzing to an instrumental version of "Silent Night" on the jukebox. The mood is romantic; it could be Saturday night, they could be dancing to "Waltz Across Texas." The music stops.)

FRANK: Want me to put in some more quarters?
STELLA: Sit down a minute. You look antsy.

(Frank sits down at the bar. Stella goes behind it.)

FRANK: Not enough sleep.
STELLA: You look antsy and you dance antsy. What's on your mind, Frank?
FRANK: *(to change the subject)* You mad I woke you?
STELLA: I thought maybe you had something important to talk about.
FRANK: I'm hardly awake. You pouring yet?

(She pours him a beer.)

FRANK: Seems like I sleep less when I'm laid off than when I'm working.
STELLA: I wonder why.
FRANK: Maybe I am antsy.
STELLA: So it's just being out of work that's bothering you?
FRANK: Hell, I don't know. What do you mean, I dance antsy?
STELLA: All stiff, like you don't want to be here.
FRANK: Why'd I wake you if I don't want to be here?
STELLA: That's what I'm asking, Frank.

(He doesn't reply. A pause.)

FRANK: You want to exchange gifts before you open?
STELLA: You oughtn't've gotten me anything, being out of work.
FRANK: Hell, it's nothing like I wanted to get.

STELLA: You want to exchange presents or you want to tell me what's bothering you?

FRANK: You sure are persistent this morning.

STELLA: Whichever you want, Frank.

FRANK: I came by, Stella because — hell, it's Christmas.

STELLA: Let's open presents.

(As Stella starts for the tree, there's a loud banging on the front door of the tavern.)

REX: *(off stage)* Stella! Merry Christmas in there! Hey, open up, will you?

(Frank tips his baseball cap knowingly to Stella, then goes to answer the door. Stella comes downstage, the lights change to a spotlight on her and she speaks to the audience.)

STELLA: Some folks say it's a sin to open up on Christmas Day. Whoever thinks that can take a flying you-know-what at the moon.

You see, we got people here in Juniper, the tavern's the only home they know. Or it's the only place they can really relax and have a little fun. This is especially true with the mill closed like it is. Half the men in Juniper work at the mill, or depend on the mill being open, which means most ain't been working for almost a year now, and there's nothing to do at home but stare at the bills piling up.

I lowered my beer prices when the mill closed down. It's the least I could do. Just like that sign I put up outside. There's folks who think I did that for the publicity but I didn't ask no reporter to come snooping around about it. I put up that sign because it was needed. Ever since that religious cult took over the old Thompson spread, 15 miles out on Old Ranch Road, tourists speed by here like Juniper's as worthless as a eunuch in a whore house. They just want to hurry out to the ranch so they can stare at all the blue shirts and at that Swami's 26 Rolls-Royces. The only reason I put up that sign was to protect my customers:

SLOW DOWN, GODDAMN IT! DRUNKS CROSS HERE!

(LIGHTS UP on tavern, with Rex and Margie entering.)

REX: This a private party?

STELLA: Not any more. What's your poison?

MARGIE: Beer and tomato juice for me. Rex?

REX: Frank and I will be right back.

69

MARGIE: Don't you go running out on me on Christmas morning!
REX: I gotta get your present. Be back in a jiff.

(Frank and Rex start out.)

MARGIE: *(after them)* What're you talking about, present? Rex!

(They exit.)

MARGIE: We can't afford no presents. The Sage Tavern isn't open this early, is it?
STELLA: We got the only drink in town today.

(Stella gives Margie her beer and tomato juice.)

MARGIE: Bet he's got a bottle hid in the pickup. He's been drinking for three days. Didn't get in til five this morning.

(A pause.)

MARGIE: Frank spend the night upstairs?
STELLA: No, he woke me a couple hours ago.
MARGIE: Did he ask you?
STELLA: Even if he was fixing to, I don't think he'd pop the question this early in the morning.
MARGIE: Rex gets romantic after drinking all night. I'll bet they was together last night.
STELLA: May be.
MARGIE: He's gonna ask you one of these days. You know you got your bags packed.
STELLA: I think Frank's too set in his ways to marry.
MARGIE: The engagement can't last forever, Stella. You either get hitched or break up. Something's gotta break the monotony.
STELLA: We're not engaged.
MARGIE: Time he spends upstairs, it's the same difference.
STELLA: We have a nice arrangement.
MARGIE: For him.
STELLA: For me, too. We both need a little room.
MARGIE: That's what Rex says. Then he stays out drinking all night.
STELLA: You know how men get when the mill's closed. Happens every recession. But the mill's gotta open up sooner or later. It always

does.

MARGIE: I don't know how much longer I can stand it. Our benefits end next month. We're already dipping into savings.

STELLA: Don't fret about it on Christmas. Have one on me.

(She turns a glass upside down in front of Margie, marking her for another drink.)

MARGIE: I wonder if he really got me a present. We made a deal not to exchange gifts this year. That son-of-a-bitch.

STELLA: If he got you something, you tell him he has fifteen dollars on credit right here — a gift certificate.

MARGIE: You don't have to do that.

STELLA: I know. Come on, cheer up. I'm feeling Christmasy. Look here, a card from Fred Ross came yesterday.

(She hands Margie a Christmas card.)

MARGIE: Didn't he go to the valley looking for work? Rex heard he ended up in Junction City.

STELLA: The postmark don't show through too good.

MARGIE: Postmark doesn't mean a thing any more. My sister in Rock Springs? I got a card from her, the postmark said Gopher.

STELLA: Maybe she mailed it in Gopher.

MARGIE: She can't stand Gopher. If she needs a bigger store than Rock Springs, she drives to one of the malls in Eugene. The post office just took away Rock Springs' postmark and gave them Gopher. Post office don't give a damn if folks don't want a Gopher postmark on their letters. Criminy.

STELLA: If it's more efficient that way, maybe the price of stamps won't go up.

MARGIE: My sister hates Gopher!

STELLA: Fred sent a poem with the card.

MARGIE: That's Fred.

STELLA: It was published in *Logger's World*.

MARGIE: Fred Ross got published in a magazine?

(SHERIFF BILLY enters. He is in uniform.)

BILLY: Merry Christmas, all.

STELLA: Merry Christmas, Billy.

MARGIE: Fred Ross published a poem.

BILLY: So?

MARGIE: So whoever expected Fred Ross to publish a poem in a magazine?

STELLA: Right here in *Logger's World.*

BILLY: Let me see that.

(Stella gives Billy the poem.)

BILLY: I'll be damned.

MARGIE: Think he got paid?

BILLY: Respectable magazine like *Logger's World*? He's a damn fool if he let them have it for nothing.

STELLA: Read it out loud.

BILLY: There here is one of my favorites:

(reading) There's an empty seat on the crummy,
Where used to sit Hook Jack.
In a little bungalow in the suburbs,
There's a new widow dressed in black.

It happened last Thursday afternoon;
There was nothing anyone could do.
The puncher ran into a hang-up
And jerked the mainline in two.

So Old Jack is in Logger's Heaven,
And many stories have been told
About the cold brooks that trickle by the wayside,
And the streets are paved with gold.

We know when at last we join him,
He'll have the layout made,
And with his coffee jug beside him,
He'll be sitting in the shade.

Then Old Jack will rise,
This logger big and strong;
"I been through a whole pot of coffee!
What took you guys so long?

Up here they only fly one choker
And there's four men on the crew.
You don't have to wear your hard cats,
And your cork boots are shiny and new.

The crummies are all air-conditioned,
The side rods never come round.
The yarders all have mufflers
And never make a sound.

There's no such thing as Monday
And you'll all get paid every day.
The cookshack door is always open
To feed each and every stray.

Sometimes I think it's almost too easy
For a high-ball logging man,
Who gave all those years of his life
In pursuit of the silver strands."

(A pause.)

BILLY: I can almost hear Fred reciting it himself.
STELLA: Fred must be doing good enough.
MARGIE: Bet he didn't get paid enough to get drunk on.
BILLY: *(reciting from memory)* His hickory shirt was glazed with
dirt
As he stepped up to the bar.
"Gimme a shot of your rotgut whiskey
And the butt of an old cigar.

I'm in from the cold where the vine maples grow
And the dogwoods bloom in the spring.
I've been in the woods for thirty years
And I haven't accomplished a thing."

Jesus, Fred Ross can write! *(He raises his glass to make s toast.)*
Merry Christmas, Fred, wherever you are.
STELLA: It was a nice present, seeing Fred get a poem published. I
miss him around here.
BILLY: I got a present for you myself.

(He hands her his ticket book.)

STELLA: I know it's easy to get your quota of speeders these days.
BILLY: This ain't just another speeder. Look at the car make.

STELLA: A Rolls-Royce. You mean ... ?

BILLY: Nailed the Swami himself!

STELLA: You mean he was driving?

BILLY: He's such a con-man, he don't have to do diddly-squat. One of his blue shirts was driving. They was pushing eighty.

MARGIE: You can't touch the Swami if he wasn't driving.

BILLY: I still nailed him with a fat fine.

MARGIE: Big deal. If he can afford twenty-two Rolls-Royces —

STELLA: Twenty-six. He got four for his birthday last month.

MARGIE: He can damn well afford a speeding ticket.

BILLY: Twenty-five Rolls-Royces. That's why he was speeding, trying to catch a car thief.

STELLA: Somebody stole one of his cars?

BILLY: Ain't that something? *(Toasting)* Merry Christmas!

STELLA: Merry Christmas!

BILLY: I stopped by to enjoy it while I can. I'm the poor son-of-a-bitch who's supposed to find it. Hell of a deal.

MARGIE: Since when it is your job to chase car thieves?

BILLY: This county is my jurisdiction and if it happens in Juniper County, then yours truly is on the case. I chased rustlers, I can damn well chase car thieves.

MARGIE: Rustlers, hell.

BILLY: You take a man's goat, that's rustling, same as a cow — makes no difference if Rex was drunk or sober.

MARGIE: Rex won that damn goat at cards.

BILLY: That's not what Luke said.

MARGIE: One man's word against another. You can't question the damn goat.

BILLY: If he won it at cards, why'd he give it back so easy?

MARGIE: Because I don't need no goat chewing up my lawn!

BILLY: Anyway, I imagine they're halfway to Portland by now. You can't hide a Rolls-Royce around here. I'll check out the countryside and that ought to take care of it as far as I'm concerned. I got to play Santa Claus at the hospital later anyway.

MARGIE: Don't you get tired of doing that every year?

BILLY: I like it. Hell, I can play Santa with my eyes shut.

STELLA: Billy being Santa Claus is practically an institution.

(Frank enters.)

MARGIE: *(quickly)* Where's Rex?

74

FRANK: *(avoiding the question)* Billy ... thought they'd give you the day off.

BILLY: I get off pretty quick now. Gotta put on my Santa suit.

MARGIE: Where the hell is he, Frank?

FRANK: Stella, I'm buying the house a Christmas drink.

BILLY: I'll take a rain check. Frank, would you believe I have to look for a Rolls-Royce? That poor damn Swami, somebody took one of his Rollses and now the poor son-of-a-bitch is down to twenty-five. Some folks carry bad luck in their pocket.

(He exits.)

MARGIE: Where's Rex, Frank? I don't like the look on your face.

FRANK: He's ... outside.

MARGIE: Why don't he come in? He got a present for me out there?

FRANK: Sort of.

MARGIE: That son-of-a-bitch. We made a deal.

(Billy returns and makes a slow cross to the bar. All eyes are on him. He leans on the end of the bar.)

BILLY: You think that Swami plays cards? I hope so. Rex is out front, relieving himself on the front fender of a Rolls-Royce. Now, Frank, if you know anything about this, I'd be obliged to listen.

FRANK: Don't know what to tell you, Billy.

BILLY: The way I figure it, you were playing poker over in that ashram. And the Swami, being a foreigner, it was duck soup, right? Ain't that what happened, Billy?

FRANK: Sure, Billy, you got it exactly.

BILLY: That's what I figured.

(BLACKOUT.)

Scene Two

(LIGHTS RISE on MA in the neutral area. She wears the blue clothing of the Kree cult and speaks to the audience. Her accent is from India.)

MA: You Americans are full of contradictions. I was educated in your country and know something about you. On the one hand, you represent the ideal of freedom in the Western world. And then you come in droves to stare at the Kree because we are different from you.

What has happened to this country? The United States is the land of religious freedom. This is what I was taught at your great University, UCLA. America was founded by men who fled religious persecution in England. Then why are the Kree being persecuted?

There are so many rumors about us. No, we are not fanatics out to take over the world. We wear blue for religious reasons, not military or political ones. Blue is the color of the holy sky and the immortal ocean.

No, we do not have sex orgies on the ranch. We are building an ashram, which means we work hard for twelve and fifteen hours a day. Who has energy left over for a sex orgy?

As the Swami's personal secretary and PR officer for the Kree, I have to deal with questions like this all the time. For example, I'm often asked, Why does the Swami have so many Rolls-Royces? What kind of a question is this? Why did your Hollywood star Joan Crawford have so many pairs of shoes? And why did Elizabeth Taylor have so many husbands?

Let me explain about the Rolls-Royces once and for all. The Kree do not dismiss the material world. It's not the ultimate reality but it is something we pass through according to our karma. So we believe in having a good time while visiting in this incarnation.

We have a great need for vehicles on the ashram and so what better investment can we make than a Rolls-Royce? You Americans, who gave the world capitalism, should understand this. We bought Swami four new cars for his birthday, to celebrate the end of his one-year vow of silence.

(LIGHTS RISE on Rex in a Rolls-Royce.)

FRANK: *(voice off)* Rex? We'd better get while the gettin's good.
REX: Hang on, partner!

(Frank enters.)

REX: You're not gonna believe this. Which hand?
FRANK: You counted the cars. Let's get out of here.
REX: He's got twenty-six of them Rollses, Frank. And look here —
each one has the keys in it. Ain't that a Christian for you?

(The focus returns to Ma.)

76

MA: Oh yes, I saw them steal the car. They were too drunk to be very careful. As it happens, I was working on the books upstairs. We had bought two more Rolls-Royces for Swami for Christmas. Of course, Christmas is not a religious holiday for the Kree. We celebrate Swami's birthday, not Christ's, but we realize that Christmas is the most important American holiday, the time when you give the most expensive gifts, so we wanted to be good neighbors by recognizing Christmas ourselves. We knew we could surprise Swami with two more cars. He wouldn't even be celebrating Christmas, except maybe to eat fruitcake. Swami loves fruitcake.

(Focus on Frank and Rex.)

FRANK: Twenty-six Rolls-Royces. Why do you suppose he has so many?

REX: Pussy. He can't drive but one himself, can he? I hear it's a regular sex orgy out here. It ain't nothing but twenty-five ladies he's trying to keep happy with them cars, Frank. Goddamn, if I knew religion was like this, I'd've gone to Sunday school.

FRANK: You counted the cars. Let's get the hell out of here.

REX: You take the pickup. I'll be right behind you.

FRANK: What do you mean, you'll be right behind me?

REX: Look at them — twenty-six Rolls-Royces! It's better than harps and angels, Frank. I may never get this close to heaven again.

FRANK: Now don't do something crazy, Rex. You're in enough trouble at home as it is.

REX: This is going to get me out of trouble at home, good buddy.

FRANK: What is?

REX: When I drive up in one of these here Rolls-Royces.

FRANK: That's car theft.

REX: I'm not stealing it. I'm borrowing it. I'm going to let Margie take a ride in it. That'll be her Christmas present.

FRANK: She don't want to ride in a stolen car.

REX: Listen, I know Margie. Hell, the day I drove up in my pickup — when it was new, I mean — Margie can turn into quite a woman when she wants to. We did it in the drive-in in that new pickup not ten hours after I put down the payment.

FRANK: That was a long time ago.

REX: That's what I'm saying. Margie ain't done nothing crazy since then.

FRANK: You wake up Margie at this time of the morning, she ain't gonna be interested in no car ride.

REX: We'll hide the sum-bitch in the garage at Steve's Texaco. I still got the keys from when I was working on Margie's Chevy. Then when Stella opens at seven, we'll drive it over to the tavern and give everybody a ride.

FRANK: I don't think this is gonna help you with Margie, Rex. It's gonna make things worse, is what it's gonna do.

REX: You don't know what a new car does to that woman. And a Rolls-Royce — goddamn!

(LIGHTS FADE on them and RISE on Ma.)

MA: When I saw they were taking the car, I phoned Swami. "We'll give them a head start," he said. "This is only sporting. Then we'll catch them. It'll be like the Grand Prix."

(BLACKOUT.)

Scene Three

(LIGHTS RISE in the tavern. Stella is behind the bar. Frank and Margie sit on stools, Rex standing near Margie. Billy sits at a table.)

REX: At least go out there and sit in the goddamn thing.

MARGIE: I have no desire to sit in a "hot car."

REX: It's Christmas, for Christ's sake.

MARGIE: I don't see what Christmas has to do with it. I hope you're not implying that's my present.

REX: Come on, Margie — it's the season to be merry. When else are you gonna have a chance to ride in a Rolls-Royce?

BILLY: Whatever you two plan to do, ride or sit, I can't get off duty til I wrap this little deal up.

REX: She'll ride in it, just give me a minute.

MARGIE: I'm not gonna take a ride.

REX: You're getting old, Margie.

MARGIE: You're a fine one to talk — Mr. Limp.

REX: Now you just shut up about that!

MARGIE: There is nothing in this world that's gonna get me into that car.

(Ann enters. She is a young woman, hesitant, perhaps shy.)

78

ANN: Excuse me. Isn't that Swami Kree's car outside? The license plate says BLUE 7 ... blue for the Kree.

REX: You a friend of his?

ANN: I came to join the ashram.

BILLY: *(getting up)* I'll phone and see if they can get somebody over here for the car.

(He goes to the phone and will call.)

STELLA: You want something to drink?

ANN: Then Swami Kree isn't here?

STELLA: No, honey. One of his cars broke down outside and Billy's trying to get a blue shirt to come for it now. If you hang around, maybe you can follow them back to the ranch.

ANN: I'll have a seven-up.

(Ann sits at a table. Rex joins her.)

REX: So you're gonna join the Kree ...

ANN: If they'll take me.

REX: Why wouldn't they take you?

ANN: To live on the ashram, I mean. It's pretty competitive. Especially now, when they're still building.

REX: So you have to get on the Swami's good side to live on the ranch or what?

ANN: You have to demonstrate your faith.

REX: How do you do that?

ANN: *(reluctantly)* Lots of ways.

REX: Hey, Swami hangs around here all the time. That's why his car's outside. You're among friends.

ANN: I wrote him a song. "The Ballad of the Swami."

(Stella brings the seven-up to the table.)

STELLA: That's fifty cents, honey.

(Ann pays. Rex notices that she has an impressive bankroll of cash.)

REX: I thought you might be a songwriter. I'm a songwriter myself. One can always spot another, you know?

ANN: It's the only song I've ever written. I'm not even sure I wrote it — I sort of found it in my head and put it down on paper.

REX: No kidding?

ANN: Is the ladies' room through there?

STELLA: That's why it says restrooms on the door.

ANN: Excuse me.

(She goes to the ladies room.)

REX: You catch her roll of bills?

STELLA: Sure did.

REX: A little weird to boot.

MARGIE: If she wants to join the Kree, why isn't she wearing blue?

STELLA: I think you have to be accepted first.

MARGIE: I haven't worn jeans since they took over the ranch.

STELLA: That's going a little too far, don't you think?

MARGIE: I don't want no tourists thinking I'm a Kree.

BILLY: *(returning from phone)* The Swami's still looking for his car. If he ain't here in an hour, they'll send a blue shirt over.

STELLA: He's coming here?

BILLY: They think he drove over to Madras. He'll see the car outside if he comes back this way.

REX: Maybe he'll buy the house a round. After all, we found his car. Right, Frank?

FRANK: Say what?

REX: We were out cruising, enjoying a little whiskey, when we ran into those kids joy-riding in his Rolls. We sent them home to Redmond where they belong. Hell, I'd be grateful as hell if I was the Swami. I'd give us a reward, is what I'd do.

FRANK: I don't think he's interested in giving us no reward.

REX: Why not? We returned the car and reported it to Billy first thing, just like the law says we should do. Right, Billy?

BILLY: I agree with Frank. You take a rich man, he's twice as stingy as you or me who ain't got shit.

REX: Hey, what's a little reward to the Swami? His followers are giving him money all the time. That girl has a bankroll on her that won't quit. Stella saw it.

STELLA: She's not poor.

REX: All you have to do, Billy, is say Frank and me reported the stolen car to you. Maybe you can add that in Juniper County a reward is usually appropriate under the circumstances.

MARGIE: What circumstances? That you're flat-ass broke because you've been on a three-day binge? And the house payment's due in a week. And you ain't working.

REX: Hey, did I close down the mill? Am I volunteering to go off benefits next month?

BILLY: I don't know, Rex.

REX: It'd be like the Swami giving us a Christmas present.

MARGIE: More like you getting one.

REX: Giving, getting, what's the difference? It's still Christmas.

(A pause.)

REX: Ain't it still Christmas?

(BLACKOUT.)

Scene Four

(LIGHTS RISE on Swami Kree in the neutral area. He is wearing a blue robe and a blue cowboy hat. He clears his throat.)

SWAMI: *(to audience, with accent from India)* Excuse me. Speaking still feels strange to me. It's not easy to talk after a full year of silence. Not the least problem is — what to say?

How do you like my hat? It was a special gift for my birthday. To tell the truth, I prefer it to the four Rolls-Royces I received. If you've ridden in one Rolls, you've ridden in them all.

This is my first cowboy hat. Where we are building the new ashram, this was once a big ranch, full of horses and cattle and working cowboys. So naturally it is appropriate for me to wear a cowboy hat myself. When in Oregon, do as the Oregonians do.

I want to be a good neighbor. For the past year I had nothing to say, I didn't speak a single syllable to anyone. What a good neighbor I was then! Now it's more difficult. Speech is so complicated.

I realize there are many questions in your mind about me. Who am I to have attracted so many thousands of followers around the world? Why am I building my new ashram in Oregon? Why do I let my students buy me so many new Rolls-Royces? Why did I take a vow of silence for an entire year? Who do I like in the Super Bowl?

Perhaps some of these questions can be addressed in time. For now, I must rest my voice. I wanted to show you my new cowboy hat. It makes me feel very good, wearing it. I feel like an Oregonian. I feel like a good neighbor.

(BLACKOUT.)

Scene Five

(LIGHTS RISE in tavern. Ann returns from the ladies room and takes a table. Rex joins her.)

REX: Like I told you, I write songs myself.

ANN: I'm really not a songwriter. "The Ballad of the Swami" just happened.

REX: You must've been inspired.

ANN: What kind of songs do you write?

REX: *(on the spot)* Oh, you name it ... country songs, love songs ...

MARGIE: *(to trap him)* Why don't you sing us one?

REX: I don't think the lady is interested in no —

ANN: I'd love to hear one.

MARGIE: The lady would love to hear one.

REX: Course, I usually have my band behind me ...

ANN: You play guitar?

REX: Oh, sure.

MARGIE: You still have that old clunker upstairs, don't you, Stella? Maybe he'll play the guitar for us.

STELLA: Sure do. You want it, Rex?

REX: If I'm gonna sing, I'll sing acapeller.

MARGIE: I can't wait to hear one. You know, we've been married eight years and he's never sung to me once.

REX: Not without the band, she means.

ANN: Will you sing one of your songs?

REX: Sure. Let's see ...

(Stella comes over to serve the table and slips Rex the published poem by Fred Ross.)

BILLY: Hard to get inspired this early in the morning.

REX: Actually, I'm the songwriter, not the lead singer.

MARGIE: We'll make allowances.

(Rex looks at the poem.)

82

REX: This one here got published. *(He starts singing, making up a country tune as he goes, a sad, maudlin ballad.)*

There's an empty seat on the crummy,
Where used to sit Hooker Jack.
In a little bungalow in the suburbs,
There's a new widow dressed in black.

(He stops.) Hell, that's too sad for Christmas. I'd rather hear your song about the Swami.

ANN: I'd be embarrassed ...

REX: Hey, you're among friends. Really. The Swami has lunch here all the time. He loves Stella's chili.

ANN: I thought people around here resented the Kree.

REX: Who told you that?

ANN: That's the impression I got from the TV.

REX: You know how they exaggerate. Doesn't make a good story unless it's negative. We'd love to hear your song about the Swami. *(To the others)* Well, wouldn't we?

BILLY: I'm all ears.

STELLA: You don't have to sing unless you feel like it, honey.

REX: Frank'll even play piano. *(Looking around)* Where's the piano?

STELLA: I sold it last summer.

REX: I didn't know that. You know that, Frank?

FRANK: She sold it on June 17th.

STELLA: Are you still mad at me about that?

FRANK: I'm the only one ever played it.

REX: *(to Ann)* Guess you have to sing acapeller. Unless you want Stella's guitar.

ANN: No. Only place I've ever sung it is in the shower.

REX: Any time you're ready ...

ANN: It's just about how I feel about the Swami. I think I must've written it in a previous incarnation.

REX: Never wrote one like that myself.

ANN: Well ... *(closing her eyes, singing)*

Blue is the sky
Blue is the sea
Blue is the color
Of eternity

Deep blue the night
Pale blue the morn
Clothed in this hue
I'll be reborn

(*Chorus:*) Swami, please hear my plea
I know my path
Lies with the Kree
Swami, I'll give all I own
To live in your light
Never alone
(New verse:) You come from a land—

(Rex interrupts with applause.)

REX: That was great! Wasn't that great? He'll love it.

ANN: I hope so. I'm pretty nervous about singing it to him, actually.

REX: For a song like that, you should get a whole suite in that ashram.

ANN: I just want a room like anybody else.

BILLY: Sort of like a dormitory, is it?

ANN: It was in India. My sister lived in Swami's ashram in Bombay. I visited her just before she passed into her other life.

REX: Her other life?

ANN: Her incarnation in Bombay ended when she was hit by a car.

(A pause.)

MARGIE: How many people are fixing to live on that ashram out there?

ANN: Lots, eventually. Maybe five thousand.

STELLA: Five thousand! The population of Juniper ain't but fifteen hundred.

BILLY: If they all drank, you'd do a hell of a business.

ANN: Oh, the Kree can drink. It's not against Swami's teachings.

REX: Then how about a beer on me?

(Margie, disgusted with Rex's flirting, storms to the ladies room.)

ANN: When do you think Swami'll be here?

REX: You said in about an hour, didn't you, Billy?

BILLY: That or a blue shirt will come by to pick up the car.

REX: You got time for a beer then.

ANN: I prefer white wine.

REX: You got it. On my tab, Stella.

STELLA: *("What tab?")* Merry Christmas.

REX: I'm Rex.

ANN: I'm Ann. I don't have my Kree name yet.

REX: I noticed you all had funny names. Well, I don't mean funny. Just different.

ANN: When we embrace Swami's teachings, we get a new name and a new birthday. It's starting a whole new life, actually.

(Frank starts slowly toward the men's room.)

STELLA: How long was your sister in India?

ANN: Almost a year. She loved it there but I think she'd've liked it here better. It's exciting to be at the beginning of something. If they accept me ...

REX: I think the Swami will love your song.

FRANK: *(singing)*Swami!

How I love ya!

How I love ya!

My dear old Swami!

(He exits to men's room.)

REX: Great sense of humor.

ANN: Humor is very central in Swami's teachings.

BILLY: Twenty-six Rolls-Royces shows one hell of a sense of humor.

(Ann's mother, JOY, enters the tavern. She looks weary.)

JOY: Hello, Annie.

ANN: Oh, God ...

JOY: I'd like a beer, please.

STELLA: Henry's?

JOY: Fine.

(A pause.)

JOY: I saw your car outside.

ANN: Mother, there's nothing to talk about. I know what I'm doing.

JOY: We can still visit, can't we? When I looked at the calendar this morning, it said Christmas.

(A pause.)

JOY: Merry Christmas.

(BLACKOUT.)

Scene Six

(LIGHTS RISE on Swami and Ma in the back seat of the Rolls-Royce.)

MA: They must've lost us.
SWAMI: I'm not lost, Ma.
MA: Shall I tell Shrivaroma to turn back?
SWAMI: We're almost to Madras. I like that truck stop with the vegetarian omelet.
MA: *(to the "driver")* We're continuing to Madras, Shrivaroma! *(To Swami)* I should've called security as soon as I saw them.
SWAMI: No matter. Everything flushes through the toilet.
MA: Which reminds me: the plumbing in the main hall should be operative next week.
SWAMI: And the printing presses?
MA: This has been the greatest challenge, getting water for the printing presses.
SWAMI: Dig wells.
MA: We are.
SWAMI: Where there's a well, there's a way. *(He chuckles.)* I'll have to remember that for my lecture tonight.

(We hear SIRENS, a police car behind them. The cars stop and Billy walks up.)

BILLY: *(to imaginary driver)* Your license ...

(He sees who is in the back seat.)

BILLY: Well, looky here. A little early for joy riding, ain't it, Swami?
MA: It is never too early to be joyous.

86

BILLY: That may be so, ma'am, but the fact of the matter is, this here stretch of road is posted at fifty-five and I clocked you doing almost eighty. That means I'm gonna have to write your driver here up with a ticket. I know it's early and there ain't no more traffic than jobs in a lumber mill, but the law's the law.

MA: Give me the ticket.

(Swami puts on a blue nose plug.)

BILLY: Swami, I hope that there nose plug ain't supposed to imply how you feel about an officer of the law doing his duty.

MA: Swami is very sensitive to scent. He has several allergies. Nothing personal, but it's your after-shave. Please write the ticket.

(Billy begins to do so.)

BILLY: He don't talk for himself?

MA: He's resting his voice.

BILLY: Maybe it's none of my business, ma'am, but when I found the Swami here stuck in a ditch last month, sitting in the back seat all by himself, and I asked him if he needed any help, it would only have been neighborly to reply.

MA: I don't know the incident you mean.

SWAMI: We did get stuck in a ditch, Ma. The others went for help.

BILLY: You remember me coming by?

SWAMI: Of course. But I was on a vow of silence at the time.

BILLY: You remember me banging on your window, trying to get your attention?

SWAMI: Of course.

BILLY: Waving my arms around?

SWAMI: Yes.

MA: A vow of silence is very strict.

BILLY: You made a face at me. You stuck out your tongue.

SWAMI: I wanted you to leave. It was embarrassing, the way you were carrying on.

MA: Officer, all this is beside the point. We were speeding because we were chasing a car thief. Someone stole one of Swami's Rolls-Royces.

BILLY: Why didn't you speak up?

MA: It was taken about thirty minutes ago. The license number is BLUE-7.

BILLY: They probably headed for Portland, ma'am, but I'll see what I can do. Here's your ticket.

MA: Can I write you a check?

BILLY: You have to mail it to the courthouse. I'll do my best to find your car, Swami. Well, Merry Christmas.

(He leaves.)

MA: Still to Madras?

SWAMI: Of course. I want to wear my new cowboy hat into the truck stop.

MA: On to Madras, Shrivaroma! And watch your speed!

(BLACKOUT.)

Scene Seven

(LIGHTS RISE in tavern. Frank has returned from the rest room.)

ANN: Can I use your ladies' room to change clothes?

STELLA: You can use it for anything your little heart desires, as long as you clean up after yourself.

(Ann starts for the exit.)

JOY: Annie?

ANN: There's nothing to talk about.

JOY: I'm not here to change your mind.

ANN: You tried to change Cindy's.

JOY: I thought we could spend some time together on Christmas.

ANN: Swami is coming here to pick up his car. I have to change clothes.

JOY: They're going to let you live on the ashram?

ANN: I don't know.

(She exits to fetch a suitcase from her car outside.)

JOY: You have another Henry's?

STELLA: Kegs and cases.

(Margie returns from the rest room.)

MARGIE: Your girlfriend leave?

REX: *(to Joy)* My wife has a great sense of humor. Margie, this is Ann's mother.

MARGIE: You joining the blue shirts, too?

JOY: No. Just came to say goodbye.

MARGIE: That bad, huh?

JOY: That bad.

STELLA: I can sympathize with you, lady. Must be tough.

JOY: I lost Cindy and now I lose Annie. There's nobody else to lose.

FRANK: Maybe she'll be happy.

JOY: I think the word is ecstatic. You walk around grinning like an idiot all day. You've been saved!

FRANK: I had a cousin converted to a Catholic. Didn't change a hair on his head that I could tell.

JOY: This is different. They even give you a new name, a new birthday. My first daughter, Cindy, lived in an ashram in India run by this same Swami Kree. This guru. Swami Cretin. She died over there.

STELLA: I'm sorry.

JOY: You have your own problems. They'll control the town before they're through. They'll move in until they outnumber you. They'll take over city hall. They'll make it so you're glad to sell out and leave.

FRANK: Ain't much worth saving, with the mill closed down.

JOY: They'll buy the mill and manufacture small statuettes of the Swami, suitable for attaching to the dashboard of a Rolls-Royce.

(Ann enters with her suitcase and crosses to the rest room as the others silently watch.)

JOY: The Swami is really coming here?

REX: Within the hour. Right, Billy?

BILLY: Him or one of his blue shirts, to pick up the Rolls.

JOY: What's it doing out there?

REX: I stole it, ma'am.

JOY: You're kidding.

REX: Nope. I was a little under the influence.

JOY: You just went out there and drove off with it?

REX: We're gonna tell the Swami some kids took it. Maybe we'll get a reward out of the deal.

JOY: I love it.

REX: You ever been in a Rolls-Royce?

JOY: Never.

REX: Billy, I'm gonna take the lady for a spin around the block. If you want to ...

JOY: I'd love to.

BILLY: I don't know, Rex.

REX: I won't be but five minutes.

BILLY: I don't want to have to come looking for you.

MARGIE: Is this an open invitation?

REX: I didn't think you wanted a ride.

MARGIE: Well, I have changed my mind.

REX: Anybody else?

BILLY: Five minutes, I mean it.

REX: Word of honor, buddy.

(Rex, Joy and Margie exit. A pause.)

FRANK: I don't think I ever asked you. How much did you get for the piano?

STELLA: You ask me once a month, Frank. If I'd've known you liked it so much, I wouldn't have sold it. You should've spoke up.

FRANK: I hardly ever played it.

BILLY: I remember one night you got drunk and played boogie woogie. I liked it.

STELLA: Frank, you should've spoke up.

FRANK: No big deal.

BILLY: You played nice piano that night. You remember, don't you, Stella?

STELLA: Frank, goddamn it!

(BLACKOUT.)

Scene Eight

(LIGHTS RISE on Ann in the neutral area, now wearing her blue clothing.)

ANN: Blue is the color of life. Life came out of the ocean, which is blue. The air we breathe comes from the sky, which is blue. Blue attracts more good vibrations than any other color. Blue is the root color of existence.

You can't explain any of this to your mother. It's impossible.

Cindy tried. She's five years older than me and in another incarnation now. It was just an accident in India, getting hit by a car, but I lost my best friend.

I didn't know very much about the Kree when I went to India, I just wanted to visit with Cindy. But when I saw how happy she was and when Cindy started telling me about her life there, and what she believed in, I was really impressed. I wanted to meet Swami Kree myself but, of course, he's so sensitive to odor and everything else, I couldn't get past his guards. I still smelled like an American.

The song was an inspiration. I think I must have dreamed it, or maybe I wrote it in a previous incarnation, because the words and melody just came to me all at once and it was like being a medium for this spiritual essence that was outside me somehow. I wrote down the song in a single afternoon.

For months I kept the song to myself, singing it in the shower, when suddenly I realized that the song wasn't mine at all, it was his, and somehow I had been chosen to receive it and write it down and now I must find Swami Kree and sing it to him.

That was really scary to think about. It still is.

(LIGHTS RISE FULL in tavern.)

Scene Nine

(CONTINUOUS: Ann joins Stella, Frank and Billy in the tavern, coming from the rest room. Frank and Billy are into some serious drinking.)

STELLA: Well, don't you look nice.

ANN: Did my mother leave?

STELLA: Her, Rex and Margie went for a ride. She'll be right back. Another white wine?

ANN: I'd better switch to seven-up.

STELLA: I noticed you and your mother don't see eye-to-eye.

ANN: Which is totally ridiculous. There's supposed to be religious freedom in this country.

STELLA: I got the impression she wasn't really criticizing your beliefs, just sort of, you know, missing you moving away from home.

ANN: People think we're brainwashed. It's so ridiculous. I have two years of college. I worked as a bookkeeper after that. I'm not some drugged-out weirdo or something.

(Stella serves her the seven-up.)

STELLA: Lot of misunderstanding in the world, I'll grant you that.

ANN: I think people are jealous because the Kree are so happy. People are so miserable with all their extra-marital affairs and divorces and careers and taxes and doctor bills, they go into a rage whenever they meet someone who is perfectly happy and content.

STELLA: Are you perfectly happy and content? You look a little nervous, to be honest.

ANN: I'm nervous about singing the song. What if Swami doesn't like it?

STELLA: You must want into that ashram pretty bad. Couldn't you rent an apartment and still go worship there?

ANN: It's the honor of living so close to him. His love is so powerful. They're building a new ashram from the ground up, and people will be coming from all over the world to live there. It's just incredible to think that I could be part of something like that.

STELLA: You must've left Portland pretty early in the morning to get here when you did.

ANN: We had a fight last night. I can't believe she followed me.

STELLA: I'm not choosing sides, understand, but I think your mother's more tolerant than you give her credit for. She just doesn't want to lose you.

ANN: She's not losing me. That's another stupid thing people are always bringing up, that the ashram is a prison or something. The Kree spend lots of time outside the ashram. There's tea to sell, books and bread to sell, lots of things.

STELLA: You need to raise money in any religion. I read where the Kree even opened a nightclub in Portland. That surprised me, to be honest.

ANN: We like to have a good time, just like anybody else.

STELLA: Nightclub seemed a little wild for a religious group.

ANN: It's just a place to have fun. We dance to the Kree rock band — the Blue Bliss.

STELLA: Why not? The Salvation Army does it.

ANN: We're not like the Salvation Army.

STELLA: Drumming up business with music, I mean.

(BLACKOUT.)

Scene Ten

(LIGHTS RISE on Frank in neutral area.)

FRANK: Nobody in my family was musical at all. Only music in the house was Hank Williams and such on the radio. But they had a piano in the little school I went to. That wasn't here in Juniper but out in the desert, past Fossil. It was one of them little school houses that teach all the grades in there together, and they had a piano. The teacher would play it when we sung hymns.

I learned about honky-tonk in the Army, in Korea, from a fellow named B.J. He was a colored man and he played honky-tonk piano himself. Right away I liked that ol' music better than just about anything I'd ever heard before. B.J. kept teaching me little bits and pieces of it but, of course, pianos were hard to come by in Korea, about the only place to find one was in the NCO Club and it wasn't very often that it was empty enough for a beginner like myself to sit down and practice. B.J. taught me a couple of nice licks, though. Then he found himself on the wrong end of a commie mortar and that was the end of my honky-tonk lessons.

I used to play Stella's piano every once in a while when I was drinking but, to tell the truth, I never did remember too well how it turned out. But people seemed to like it. Then when the mill shut down, I figured I might start practicing regular and surprise myself. There was nothing else to do. Flirting with Stella, that's about it. Then I got the idea she was taking me more serious than I intended and even flirting stopped being fun.

So, I told myself, why not take up the piano again? I was just about to get off my butt, too. Then Stella went and sold it out from under me. It was June 17th.

(BLACKOUT.)

Scene Eleven

(LIGHTS RISE on the Rolls-Royce. Rex is driving, the two women in the back seat.)

MARGIE: Don't you go getting us no speeding ticket we can't afford.

REX: Who's going to stop us? Billy's getting himself into some serious drinking. Damn, would I love to own one of these. Rides as smooth as silk, don't she?

(A pause.)

MARGIE: You live around here?

JOY: Portland.

MARGIE: Too bad about your daughter joining them blue shirts. I don't see why anybody would do that, personally. They say he has twenty-six of these cars. How can you feel religious about somebody with so many expensive cars?

REX: I feel like I'm in heaven!

JOY: It's called brainwashing.

MARGIE: You think they hypnotized your daughter or something?

JOY: It's more subtle than that. Some very talented con-men take advantage of young people who are searching for answers.

MARGIE: *(sincerely)* Answers to what?

(A pause.)

REX: What do you do in Portland?

JOY: I teach.

MARGIE: I got a cousin who teaches kindergarten.

JOY: I teach at the University.

REX: A professor?

JOY: Yes.

REX: Your daughter must have a pretty good job herself. When she bought her seven-up, she flashed a bankroll that wouldn't quit.

JOY: She just received an inheritance from my late husband. I take it she plans to give it all to Swami Cretin.

REX: She's pretty interested in him, alright. Even wrote a song about him.

JOY: A song?

REX: About how much she needs him and all.

JOY: The Kree practice a sophisticated form of brainwashing, I swear they do. What I should have done with Cindy is hire a deprogrammer before she left the country. Maybe that's what I should do with Annie.

REX: She ain't a kid.

JOY: Her mind is somewhere in the sixth grade.

MARGIE: I saw something on TV about how they do that. I think if I was in your shoes, I'd've done it.

(A pause.)

REX: Want me to kidnap your daughter for you?

MARGIE: Rex!

94

REX: Me and Frank could do it easy. We'd drive her back to Portland and you could hire yourself a deprogrammer.

MARGIE: Don't listen to him, he gets crazy ideas all the time.

REX: Be easy to do.

MARGIE: He's just bored from not working.

REX: What do you say?

JOY: What would you charge?

MARGIE: Rex! Criminy!

REX: To be honest, I'm not sure what the going rates are. I'd trust you to be fair.

JOY: All I'd ask you to do is drive her to Portland. I could handle it from there. Two hundred dollars?

REX: Sounds fair to me. Do we have a deal?

MARGIE: You two are talking about a crime here.

JOY: You said it's what you would've done.

MARGIE: But when Rex gets involved, nothing turns out right.

REX: Thanks a hell of a lot for the vote of confidence.

MARGIE: You'll wind up behind bars and then where will you be?

REX: In jail, Margie! Hang on, I'm gonna see how fast this ol' Rolls will go ...

(BLACKOUT.)

Scene Twelve

(LIGHTS RISE on the tavern. Billy heads for the men's room.)

BILLY: I was afraid this would happen. Rex is dangerous when he's not working.

STELLA: He'll be back.

(When Billy is gone, Ma enters.)

MA: Pardon me. Do you have a phone I can use?

STELLA: Right through there.

MA: Thank you.

(She goes to the phone and will make a call.)

ANN: That's Ma Prama Rama Kree! She's the Swami's personal secretary.

STELLA: I've seen her on television.
ANN: But the car isn't here. She must've come for the car.

(Swami enters. He wears his cowboy hat and nose plug. He surveys the tavern, saying nothing. Finally he chooses a table and sits down.)

(Frank enters from the men's room. He passes Ma on the phone. When he spots Swami, he stops. He then heads straight for the exit and is out of there.)

(Ma returns and goes to Swami.)

MA: They found the car. It's at the Juniper Tavern.
STELLA: This is the place. We got a man out road-testing it right now.
MA: What happened to the car?
STELLA: Nothing Rex can't fix. He'll have it in better shape than when you lost it. Can I get you folks anything while you're waiting?
MA: Do you have herb tea?
STELLA: No, but I think I've got some Lipton around here somewhere. Used to be a mill worker who drank tea. What the hell was his name? Must've been three or four years ago.
MA: I'll have a glass of water.
STELLA: And you ... sir?
MA: Swami will have water as well.

(Billy enters from the men's room and goes to Swami.)

BILLY: Found your car.
MA: We know.
BILLY: Should be back any minute.

(No reply. Billy hesitates, then heads for the exit.)

STELLA: You leaving?
BILLY: Think I better see what Rex is up to before I put on my Santa suit.

(He exits. Ma takes out her knitting, something blue. Ann makes a slow approach to Swami.)

MA: Yes?

ANN: I believe.

MA: You wear blue. But no medallion.

ANN: I haven't been accepted yet. But I want to belong. I really do.

MA: And you want to live on the new ashram.

ANN: Oh, I do very much!

MA: You and thousands of our followers around the world.

(Disappointed, Ann turns to go.)

SWAMI: Please sit down. Please ...

(Ann sits.)

SWAMI: What is it you want to tell me? I can feel the energy of your question but I don't know what it is.

ANN: I wrote a song. Or maybe it was just given to me. It's about the Kree, about you.

SWAMI: Then sing it.

(Ann closes her eyes and begins to sing.)

ANN: *(singing)* You came from a land
So far away
To teach us the Truth
And show us the Way

You've always possessed
What we hope to find
The secrets of life
True peace of mine

(Chorus) Swami, please hear my plea
I know my path
Lies with the Kree
Swami, I'll give all I own
To live in your light
Never alone

(Joy has entered and approaches the table.)

JOY: *(to Swami, interrupting)* We met briefly in Bombay.

(Ann stops singing.)

JOY: I said, we've met before. My daughter was in your ashram in Bombay. Her name was Cindy. She got hit by a car over there. She died. I'd come over to get her body but she was cremated before I arrived. Her ashes were thrown in the river. I made an appointment to see you but could never pass your odor test. Apparently I stunk, no matter how many showers I took. Finally I saw you walking across the ashram grounds. I ran up to you and our eyes met before your guards pulled me away. Do you remember that? I'm sure we made eye contact.

(A pause. Swami doesn't reply. The moment is tense. No one moves.)

JOY: I'M TALKING TO YOU!

(BLACKOUT. End of Act One.)

ACT TWO

Scene One

(LIGHTS RISE on Rex in the neutral area.)

REX: The bottom line is, You gotta eat. I don't know what Margie expects me to do. You won't find a harder working sumbitch than yours truly but I can't open up the mill if the company don't want it open. If the mill ain't open, I can't haul logs. It's that simple.

There was a time when I'd've hit the road by now. But, damn it, I love this part of the country. I love Central Oregon. I love Juniper, the home I'm buying, my neighbors, the kind of life we share. I wake up in the morning, look out my kitchen window, and see nothing but snow-capped mountains. A rich man can't see anything prettier.

But you gotta eat, is what I was saying. And if there ain't work in the woods, that means you gotta find something else. You gotta use your imagination.

Like winning Luke's goat at poker. Hell, he didn't have the cash to match my raise and that means I could've raked in the pot right then. But he said, Can I put up my goat? Everybody thought that was funnier'n hell but I started thinking, Well, why not? I read in the paper that them blue shirts are health nuts, so maybe I could sell them a little goat's milk on the side. Course, this was too good an idea to share with the rest, so I joked about needing a new lawn mower anyway and let Luke put up his goat — which I won.

Then Margie wouldn't have a damn thing to do with that goat anyway, so I just gave it back to Luke. The point is, I was thinking, I was using my imagination, always looking for a way to make a buck on the side.

This is why I thought maybe the Swami would give us a reward for his car. This is why I offered to kidnap that lady's daughter. The jobs that come down the pike may not be the jobs you're used to having. You gotta be flexible. Because there's no way on God's green earth you're ever gonna change the bottom line — you gotta eat. You don't eat, you deal yourself right out of the ball game.

(BLACKOUT.)

Scene Two

(LIGHTS RISE in the tavern. It's the moment immediately after the end of Act One.)

JOY: I said, I'm talking to you. I know what you're about. I know what's going on in that ashram of yours. And you know I know.

(No reply. Ma knits. Ann sits frozen. Swami sits benevolently. A pause. Joy turns and goes to the bar. Frank, Rex and Margie enter.)

ANN: I'm sorry.
SWAMI: Don't worry. Everything will be fine.
ANN: She doesn't understand anything.
SWAMI: She's not alone.

REX: Excuse me, Swami. I'm happy to report that I found your Rolls-Royce.

MA: He and the other are the ones who stole it. I'm sure of it.

REX: No, ma'am, that's not true.

MA: I was working upstairs and saw you in the parking lot.

REX: Well, you must not've been there an hour earlier or you would've seen those kids from Redmond tampering with the engine. Christ, when me and Frank saw them doing that, I didn't know what to expect. I thought maybe they were rigging it with a bomb or something. The more I considered that possibility, the more pissed off I got. Pardon my language, ma'am, but I was damn mad. We like to be good neighbors here in Juniper, and the last thing we need is some punks from Redmond coming up here to assassinate the Swami. I mean, that's what went through my mind. So that's why I took the car, to give it a road test and make sure it was safe to drive. They could've pulled a pin somewhere, any damn thing. I wanted to make sure it was safe for the Swami to drive. That's the truth, ma'am. I'm a Christian like yourself.

MA: I'm not a Christian, I'm a Kree.

REX: Well, I'm sure neither religion permits lying.

SWAMI: Thank you for road testing the car.

REX: We just try to be good neighbors.

(A pause. Rex is waiting for his reward.)

REX: Well, Merry Christmas to you.

(A pause. Rex finally moves to the bar.)

MA: Shall we go?

SWAMI: Not yet, Ma. *(To Ann)* You really wrote that song yourself?

ANN: It just came to me.

SWAMI: I think it's beautiful.

ANN: You do?

SWAMI: Very much so. What's your name?

(Joy, unable to take any more, exits into the ladies' room. Rex follows, waiting for her near the door.)

SWAMI: Don't worry. What's your name?

ANN: Ann. My sister Cindy was in your ashram in Bombay.

SWAMI: I remember Cindy very well. She told me about you. I'm sorry we didn't have a chance to meet in Bombay.

ANN: I heard you speak several times. I was so impressed.

SWAMI: And now you want to live on the ashram, don't you?

ANN: Very much!

SWAMI: Why?

ANN: To seek the truth.

SWAMI: You think you have to come to the ashram to seek truth?

ANN: I have so much to learn. Please teach me.

SWAMI: I have only one message: the truth is inside you.

ANN: I want to meditate with you. I want to belong to the Kree.

SWAMI: I am not the truth. You are the truth.

ANN: Yes, I want to learn that.

SWAMI: Then look inside yourself!

ANN: I want to learn everything you have to teach me. I'd do anything to live on the ashram.

SWAMI: I must meditate on this, Ma.

(Ma reaches into her blue knitting bag and brings out a roll of blue toilet paper, which she hands to Swami. Swami carries it to the men's room.)

(Joy exits the ladies' room, meeting Rex.)

REX: You still want your daughter kidnapped to Portland?

JOY: I'm not sure ...

REX: With him in the bathroom, it may be now or never. Frank and I can do it. It's up to you.

JOY: Oh Christ ...

REX: She's your daughter.

JOY: If you think you can ...

REX: Wait here for Swami and keep him occupied.

(Rex returns to the tavern proper.)

REX: *(To Ma)* Want me to drive the other Rolls back to your ashram, ma'am? I could give Ann a lift.

MA: Our driver is outside, and Swami can drive the other one himself.

REX: Just trying to be neighborly.

(A pause.)

REX: *(To Ann)* That's not your VW bug outside, is it?

ANN: Yes. Why?

REX: I told you it was hers, Frank. You got a flat and it's locked. I was going to change it for you but couldn't get the spare.

ANN: I'm sure it's not locked.

REX: I tried both doors.

ANN: I don't understand.

(Ann heads for the door. Rex follows, gesturing to Frank to come along.)

REX: I'll be glad to change it for you. Won't we, Frank?

MARGIE: Rex ...

REX: She has a flat, for Christ's sake.

(Ann exits with Rex hustling Frank out behind her.)

MARGIE: Rex!

(Joy, impatient, now comes back into the tavern.)

MARGIE: *(To Joy)* They're going through with that crazy plan, aren't they?

JOY: I don't know what you're talking about.

(Margie exits to see what is going on.)

STELLA: *(To Ma)* Why's he wear a nose plug?

JOY: He thinks we stink.

(Margie returns.)

MARGIE: They're going through with it! They're kidnapping her back to Portland!

(Joy exits.)

MARGIE: Stella, they're kidnapping that girl.

STELLA: Come on, Margie. Frank and Rex ain't kidnappers.

MARGIE: They're going to take her to a deprogrammer.

MA: And they accuse us of brainwashing ...

STELLA: If they ain't back in thirty minutes, I'll phone Billy myself.

(Swami returns from the men's room. Before he arrives, Stella fetches a clothespin from behind the bar and puts it on her nose. She faces Swami, one nose plug against the other.)

SWAMI: I like your sense of humor!
STELLA: Nothing personal, understand, but I'm allergic to the smell of curry powder.

(Swami removes his nose plug.)

SWAMI: Of course I understand!

(BLACKOUT.)

Scene Three

(LIGHTS RISE on Rex, Frank and Ann in the pickup. Rex drives, Ann is wedged between the men.)

REX: She ain't behind us, Frank. She should be right behind us.
ANN: My mother drinks too much. She'll stay in there til they kick her out.
REX: I don't know why she ain't behind us. What do you think, Frank?
FRANK: She ain't behind us?
REX: I don't see her.
FRANK: Then maybe she ain't coming. This is a crazy idea anyway.
REX: She's got to come. How do we know where to go in Portland?
ANN: Is that where we're going? I'll just leave and come right back. This is all so stupid.
REX: Maybe I'd better pull into the station and call the tavern. What do you think?
FRANK: No point in going to Portland if we don't know where to go.
REX: I'll call the tavern.
ANN: She's paying you to do this, isn't she?

(The truck stops. Rex gets out.)

REX: Keep an eye on her, good buddy.

(He exits.)

ANN: They can put you in jail for doing this. She's not going to help you. You'll be left holding the bag alone. She's going to stay at the tavern and drink herself into a stupor.

(A pause.)

ANN: I have to go to the bathroom.
FRANK: Better wait til Rex gets back.
ANN: I have to go now. Want me to wet my pants?
FRANK: It dries out.
ANN: I don't believe you guys. She must be paying you pretty good. She's going to hire a deprogrammer, isn't she? It won't work. I know what I'm doing. I know what I believe in!

(A pause.)

ANN: How much is she paying you?

(A pause.)

ANN: I'll pay what she did, plus a hundred dollars — if you drive me to the ashram.
FRANK: This is Rex's deal. You have to talk to him.
ANN: What do you do, go along with everything he says?
FRANK: Rex is my guru, you might say.

(A pause. Ann makes a move to scoot out Rex's side but Frank grabs her.)

ANN: You're hurting me!
FRANK: You gonna behave?
ANN: Yes.
FRANK: I don't like this any more than you do. Just go along with it.

(He lets go.)

ANN: This is so stupid. No one can deprogram me.

FRANK: Look, I'm just looking out for Rex. If it was me, I'd move you out to the ashram myself. For nothing.

ANN: They can still put you in jail. You're a co-conspirator.

(Joy enters, standing beside the truck.)

JOY: Hello, Annie.

ANN: Mother, this won't work! You're just getting yourself in trouble!

JOY: *(To Frank)* I want to be alone with her for a minute.

FRANK: I'll tell Rex you're here.

JOY: Tell him we're not going through with it.

(Frank nods and exits. Joy gets into the pickup beside Ann. A pause.)

JOY: Can we talk?

ANN: There's nothing to say.

JOY: I realize that. You're a very strong-minded young woman. So was Cindy. I don't think a deprogrammer would've had luck with either of you.

ANN: Thank you.

JOY: You both take after your mother.

ANN: If we have anything at all in common, you know you can't change my mind.

JOY: Is Swami Cretin that important to you?

ANN: His name is Swami Kree!

JOY: What happened to you in India?

ANN: I become enlightened.

JOY: I hardly recognized you when you got back.

ANN: Mother, there's no point in this ...

JOY: India's so pathetic. How can anyone find enlightenment in a country with so many problems?

ANN: I think India's beautiful.

JOY: Beautiful! With the streets packed with beggars? You did see the maimed children begging in the streets, didn't you?

ANN: I saw people in their karma.

JOY: In their karma ...

ANN: I saw Being.

JOY: Then perhaps we don't have anything to talk about.

ANN: I'm sure we don't. Goodbye, mother.

JOY: Annie!

ANN: *(leaving)* You can't change my mind!

JOY: *(after her)* When you change it yourself ... you always have a home ...

(Ann is gone. Joy exits.)

(Rex and Frank return and get into the pickup. Rex fetches a bottle from under the seat, which they'll share.)

REX: No guts. No imagination.

FRANK: Lady has a right to change her mind.

REX: Two hundred dollars! For a round-trip to Portland ...

FRANK: I don't think a deprogrammer would've had much luck. This probably saves everyone a lot of trouble.

REX: Shit, Frank, I sure miss driving my truck, I'll tell you that.

FRANK: I hear you.

REX: I don't know if logging will ever be the same. Maybe Fred Ross had the right idea — chuck the whole deal and start over.

FRANK: Hard to say.

REX: Sometimes I get so damn frustrated. I'm a working man, for Christ's sake. If I'm not working, I go crazy. I drink too damn much.

(They drink.)

REX: I'm not big on patience, you know?

FRANK: I hear you. Neither was your dad.

REX: I guess not.

FRANK: In the old days, when your dad and I got laid off, the town wasn't safe. I was a little crazy then myself.

REX: You still do pretty good.

FRANK: You should've seen me in the old days.

REX: Dad raise more hell than I do?

FRANK: I'd call it even. Like father, like son.

REX: Shit ...

FRANK: You want to head back?

REX: I want to scream.

FRANK: So scream.

(A pause.)

REX: Shit, Frank. Where's it all end?

FRANK: Your guess is as good as mine.

REX: Goddamn it to hell anyway!
FRANK: I hear you, buddy. Hear you loud and clear.

(They drink. BLACKOUT.)

Scene Four

(LIGHTS RISE on Joy in the neutral area.)

JOY: When Annie told me she was going to visit Cindy in India, I thought, Yes, maybe Annie can talk sense to her in a way that I can't. Cindy was her father's daughter but Annie was more like me — more deliberate and practical in her view of the world. If anyone could talk sense to Cindy, it would be Annie.

Needless to say, I was wrong. The power those people have over young minds! When Annie returned, I saw in an instant that something had happened to her over there. She had this look in her eye, a look divorced from intelligence and self-awareness. She looked like a blissful zombie. She couldn't be talked to, a conversation was quite beyond her power. All she could speak were platitudes about Swami Cretin.

Then Cindy was hit by a car. I went to India immediately.

India was a nightmare. The heat and humidity were insufferable, the streets of Bombay were filthy and the air stank with smoke from the crematorium. It was like going to another planet. Everywhere you turned there were beggars, old men and women and even children, some of them maimed, all of them pathetic and filthy, pleading for handouts with shrill cries of "Ma, Ma!"

The weeks and months after returning were the worst in my life. I was drinking too much, my teaching suffered. And then Swami Cretin came to Oregon. Well, there's karma for you.

I knew we'd have our confrontation. I didn't know when or how, but I knew it was going to happen.

(LIGHTS RISE full on tavern, as Swami approaches Joy. Ma is knitting. Stella is behind the bar. Margie sits.)

SWAMI: At last we can talk.
JOY: I've tried talking to you.
SWAMI: There is a time for silence. And a time for language.
JOY: There's a time for exposing what you're really about.
SWAMI: I know how you feel. I used to feel that way myself.

JOY: You know nothing about how I feel.

SWAMI: I was not always a guru. I used to teach at University, like you do.

JOY: How do you know that?

SWAMI: Cindy told me. She was very fond of you. She wanted you to understand her.

JOY: What I understand is that you brainwashed her.

SWAMI: You think I did that?

JOY: It's not an opinion. It's a fact.

SWAMI: When I taught at University, I also looked at the gurus in my country as fakes, as tricksters out to prey on the gullible lost souls who are everywhere. I was a blind skeptic like yourself. But then a marvelous thing happened. I woke up one morning with eyesight! I quit University the same day.

JOY: I know what you're about, Swami Cretin.

SWAMI: You feel so much anger.

JOY: Of course I'm angry! I lost both my daughters to your lies.

SWAMI: You think you feel anger because your daughters are gone. But no one is gone. The form of life changes only. The reality is immortal.

JOY: Your mystical mumbo-jumbo won't work with me. Cindy is dead.

SWAMI: Cindy's karma took her on many journeys, as it continues to do now and in the future, and in one of those journeys you were blessed to play the role of her mother. You should celebrate your good fortune, not grieve for what was inevitable.

JOY: Don't mock my grief! Cindy would be alive today except for you.

SWAMI: You don't feel grief for Cindy.

JOY: Cindy is dead! Of course I feel grief.

SWAMI: The grief you feel is for yourself. And why should you grieve for yourself? Because you didn't love your daughter fully when it was possible to. If you'd loved her fully, unconditionally, during the accident of your role as mother, then all your energies would have been dissipated in that great total love.

JOY: You know nothing about love. You don't even respect human life.

MA: They don't understand, Swami. Let's return to the ashram.

SWAMI: Not yet, Ma.

JOY: The only thing I regret is not stopping you from brainwashing anyone else.

SWAMI: I've been thinking about our meeting. First Cindy comes to India and then I meet you and Ann here. This is significant.

JOY: I'm going to expose your mystical mumbo-jumbo for the crap it really is. There is no karma. There is no spiritual journey. There is life — right here and now. Breath! Heart beat! When it ends, we are dead. We are gone from the earth forever. Period.

SWAMI: You have such a small mind. You think in a prison.

JOY: It's impossible to talk to you, isn't it? You think you have a monopoly on the truth.

SWAMI: The truth is not in me. The truth is in you.

JOY: Then why do you have so many disciples kissing your feet?

SWAMI: I have nothing to do with this. For the past month, I've been telling my followers the truth every day. I say, "You are going in the wrong direction when you come to me. Go inward, into yourself. Go home!" I tell them this, and they all nod. But no one goes home! It usually takes many months for them to understand the truth. Then they leave and tell people that I am a fraud. At last, they aren't using me for a crutch! They've made a beginning! This makes me very happy.

JOY: You stand there and expect me to believe you want your followers to go home? You are so goddamn clever ...

SWAMI: I tell them they can stay on the ashram for as long as they like. But this is a vacation on the spiritual journey.

JOY: I'll agree with you on one thing. I knew we were going to meet again. And when we did, I was going to silence you once and for all.

SWAMI: I just ended a vow of silence.

JOY: You goddamn charlatan. As long as you didn't talk, no one could show you up.

SWAMI: There is a time for silence. And a time for language.

JOY: You talk in circles.

SWAMI: See? The truth *is* in you!

JOY: You know why I wanted to see you again? To shoot you. I have a gun in my purse.

SWAMI: Then use it.

JOY: You think I won't?

SWAMI: It's irrelevant whether you do or not.

STELLA: I don't allow threats like that in my tavern, lady. Now sit down and behave yourself.

(Joy sits. Billy enters, dressed as Santa Claus but not wearing his beard.)

BILLY: If you promise not to tell anyone, Santa can use a drink. Where's Rex? I see he brought the car back.

STELLA: I'm not sure what's going on.

(Ma gathers her things to leave.)

SWAMI: Sit down, Ma.
MA: They understand nothing.
SWAMI: But now I understand ...

(Swami approaches Joy again.)

JOY: Don't you know when to leave well enough alone?
SWAMI: Another thing they don't understand at the ashram is that I'm not their guru. It's not for the student to pick the teacher. How can the student know what he needs? The guru chooses the disciple and not vice-versa. This is always the way.
JOY: Don't press your luck ...
SWAMI: Yet gurus do not consciously choose their students either. Events reveal their students to them. This is my revelation just now. This is why Cindy came to India and talked so much about you. This is why Ann came here today, so that you would follow her. Everything is happening according to its karma. Everything has been arranged for this moment of revelation.

(A pause.)

SWAMI: I am *your* guru!
JOY: You! ... are not! ... my guru!
SWAMI: I don't like it any better than you do. But I'm your guru.
JOY: You are no one's guru! You, Swami Cretin, are a fake, and if I'm the only one in this room who knows it, at least there is someone — me! — who isn't being brainwashed.
SWAMI: It's incredible, Ma. I'm this lady's guru! But why me? Life is such a joke!

(BLACKOUT.)

Scene Five

(LIGHTS RISE on Margie in neutral area.)
MARGIE: All of a sudden everybody's worried about the meaning of life. I don't understand it. You're supposed to live life, not try to

110

figure it out.

Course, I believe the way I was brought up to believe, same as my parents.

The meaning of life? I'll tell you a little meaning of life ...

Rex comes in this morning at five, smelling like a brewery and full of romance. My first impulse was to kick him out of the house. But Rex has my number, I'll hand that to him, he sure knows how to sweet-talk ol' Margie.

So his sweet-talking finally gets me interested and then the son-of-a-bitch is too damn drunk to get it up!

Now there's some goddamn meaning of life!

(BLACKOUT.)

Scene Six

(LIGHTS RISE in the tavern. We hear the closing chorus of "Rudolph, the Red-Nosed Reindeer" on the jukebox.)

(Joy goes to the ladies' room. Swami sits cross-legged on the floor, meditating. Ma is knitting. Stella is behind the bar. Billy and Margie sit at the bar.)

(The song ends.)

BILLY: Guy who wrote that is a millionaire.

(Ann, Rex and Frank enter.)

ANN: Is my mother here?
STELLA: She's in the can.
REX: *(about Swami)* What's he doing?
STELLA: I think he's meditating.
REX: What for?
STELLA: Mill workers drink beer, swamis meditate. It's the nature of things.
MARGIE: Have a nice time in Portland?
REX: I'm in no mood for wisecracks, Margie.
ANN: Is there a motel around here?
STELLA: Down the highway about two miles.
ANN: Do you think they have a vacancy?

STELLA: They haven't been full up in years.

(Rex approaches Swami, stares at him, then takes the Swami's blue cowboy hat and puts it on his head, trading his baseball cap for it. He goes back to the bar.)

ANN: Why did you do that?
REX: Just being neighborly. I don't take just anybody's hat.
BILLY: No trouble, Rex.
REX: I don't know, Sheriff Billy — I've never been arrested by Santa Claus before.

(Frank goes to Rex and removes the cowboy hat.)

REX: What do you think you're doing?

(A stand off: then Frank removes his baseball cap and puts it on Rex. A tense pause.)

REX: *(laughing)* Get asshole here a beer on me.

(Frank goes to Swami and puts the cowboy hat back on him. He puts on Rex's baseball cap.)

(Joy returns from the rest room.)

JOY: I wasn't sure you were coming back.
ANN: Just long enough to find a motel. Goodbye, mother.
JOY: Annie! Let's enjoy a little bit of Christmas together.
ANN: We have nothing to talk about.

(She starts out.)

JOY: Annie!
ANN: We can't talk until you accept me as I am. Goodbye, mother.

(She moves again to leave but is stopped by:)

SWAMI:
AHHHHHHHHHHHHHHHHHHHHHHHHHHHHHHHHHHHHHHH!
BILLY: What's the problem here?
REX: What the hell's the matter with you?

SWAMI:
AHHHHHHHHHHHHHHHHHHHHHHHHHHHHHHHHHH!
  Everything is foolishness!
  Everything is pride!
  Everything is ego!
  Everything is blindness!
  The eyes do not see!
  The ears do not hear!
  The nose does not smell!
  The tongue does not taste!
  The mouth only is alive with speaking!
  Everything is speaking, speaking, speaking!
  Speaking and pride and ego and foolishness!
  AHHHHHHHHHHHHHHHHHHHHHHHHHHHHHHHHHHHHH!

(Ma has approached Swami with a glass of water, which she now throws in his face. Swami is immediately silent. He looks around. He slowly gets up. All eyes are fixed on him.)

SWAMI: I feel like the center of attention!
  You are asking yourself, What was that all about? I'll be expounding on the significance of what you've just witnessed in my lecture tonight. Usually we charge outsiders two dollars and fifty cents — but all of you can come free. A Christmas present from Swami Kree!
  (To Joy) And you — it would make my job so much easier if you came to stay at the ashram.
  JOY: You're insane.
  ANN: If there's a vacancy, I could make much better use of it than she can.
  SWAMI: Ann, I cannot choose my students. Events choose them for me.
  ANN: She doesn't even believe in you.
  SWAMI: If you want to live on the ashram, Ann, then come. Perhaps this is the only way you'll understand that I am not the truth. You are the truth.
  JOY: You goddamn charlatan!
  SWAMI: It is common for the student to reject the guru. This is further proof of the guru's obligation.
  JOY: You are not my guru!
  SWAMI: We'll see. Good people, I've enjoyed meeting you all. We're neighbors! I hope to see you at my lecture tonight. Shall I make reservations?

113

(No reply.)

SWAMI: No reservations? Good! There are enough fools listening to me already. The truth is not in me. The truth is in you.

JOY: If the truth's in me, Swami Cretin, I'm here to tell everyone you're a fake!

SWAMI: *(ignoring this)* Ann, you can ride with me to the ashram if you like.

ANN: I have my car. I'll follow you.

SWAMI: Good people, Merry Christmas to all!

(Swami, Ma and Ann exit. Joy follows quickly behind. At the doorway, she takes a gun from her purse and fires once, outside. A scream from Ma.)

STELLA: *(hurrying to Joy)* Why don't you give me the gun, honey? I'll give you a nice cold beer on the house.

BILLY: You just sit down and relax, lady. Stella, get her that beer.

(Swami, Ma and Ann return. Swami is wounded in the arm.)

MA: Swami, please ...

SWAMI: Relax, Ma. This has to be done.

MA: We have to get you to a hospital.

SWAMI: JOY!? Where did you get such a ridiculous name? When you join the Kree, I am going to name you Smoldering Volcano.

BILLY: No trouble, Swami.

SWAMI: You're shooting in the wrong direction. The anger you feel is really for yourself.

BILLY: You'd better get that looked at.

REX: I can drive him to the hospital in the Rolls.

BILLY: Better do it.

SWAMI: Maybe "Merry Christmas" was the wrong thing to say, Ma. I need a new exit line.

(They start out.)

SWAMI: "Have a good day."
"See you around."
"Regards to the family."
"Don't do anything I wouldn't do."

114

(Swami, Ma and Rex are gone.)

ANN: I don't believe this, mother. *(To Billy)* What are you going to do with her?

BILLY: Gonna have to book her.

ANN: I just can't believe you did that.

(Ann is comforted by Margie and both exit.)

BILLY: We're gonna have to go into town, ma'am.

JOY: Can I have another beer?

BILLY: I have a Christmas show to do.

JOY: Very well.

(Billy starts off with Joy.)

STELLA: You take care of yourself, Joy. Do a good Christmas show, Billy.

BILLY: I'll be back later.

(Billy and Joy exit.)

STELLA: I need a drink.

FRANK: I can't believe she did that.

STELLA: He didn't help, egging her on like he did.

FRANK: Don't defend what she done, Stella. She could've killed him.

STELLA: When he started yelling like a lunatic, I thought of shooting him myself.

FRANK: Thinking and doing are two different things.

STELLA: He was asking for trouble.

FRANK: I think I know why he started yelling.

STELLA: I knew from the beginning — it was a stunt to get us to one of his talks.

FRANK: No, I think he has a point.

STELLA: What point is that?

FRANK: "Ahhhh!" I've felt the same way myself more than once.

STELLA: So what the hell's "ahhhh!" supposed to mean?

FRANK: It means you've got something to say but just don't know how to say it, so you say "ahhhh!" instead.

STELLA: Go play some music.

(Frank goes to the jukebox. Christmas music will play.)

STELLA: I can still sympathize with what that lady done. I'm not saying she should've shot him but, hell, there's something about that man that mixes you all up. People are so lost any more, they believe anything just for the security of it. What kind of answer is "ahhhh!"? God help us if we end up with five thousand people out on the ranch, all screaming "ahhhh!"

FRANK: You get this place full of loggers and what do you hear? Nothing but hollering. "Yahoo!" "Yehee!" "Timber!" Same difference.

STELLA: Well, if you're looking for a blue shirt, Frank, the big sales start tomorrow.

FRANK: I'm not joining up with anybody.

STELLA: And here I thought you had an ulterior motive, waking me up so early this morning.

FRANK: What motive is that?

STELLA: Think about it, Frank.

(A pause.)

STELLA: Frank, are you going to ask me to marry you or not?

FRANK: I don't know what to tell you.

STELLA: I just want to know where I stand.

FRANK: I can understand that, Stella, and I did give it some thought.

STELLA: And you decided, "ahhhh!"

FRANK: I'm too fixed in my ways. I got more bad habits than you can shake a stick at. I wake up in the morning coughing so bad I'm not fit to be near.

STELLA: I've woken up with you in the morning, Frank.

FRANK: Now and again ain't bad but regular I'd drive you crazy. You know how much I care for you, Stella, but I'm already upstairs more often than I've got a right to be.

STELLA: That's my decision, not yours.

FRANK: I'm too set in my ways. I'm a lone wolf and a born bachelor.

STELLA: Well, you finally said it! What the hell took you so long?

(She fetches Frank's Christmas present.)

STELLA: Merry Christmas, Frank. Well, open it.

FRANK: Sometimes it's hard to keep up with you ...
(He opens the present. It's a book, and he reads the title.)

FRANK: "The Confirmed Bachelor's Book of Drinkery, Cookery, and Housekeepery."
STELLA: I know you too goddamn well, Frank. It's Margie that keeps wanting us to get hitched. I like our arrangement just fine.

(Frank fetches Stella's gift.)

FRANK: Merry Christmas, Stella.
STELLA: You oughtn't've done that, being out of work.

(She opens it. A blue see-through nightie.)

STELLA: Oh my word!
FRANK: Try it on.
STELLA: Later, Frank. Come with me ...

(She leads him behind the bar.)

FRANK: You need a keg changed?
STELLA: Just go in.

(Frank enters a door behind the bar. Then we hear a chord on a piano. Stella is delighted. Frank returns.)

FRANK: Always did play better when I was drunk.
STELLA: You ought to practice sober once in a while.
FRANK: I hope you didn't pay more than you sold it for.
STELLA: I want to see you in here practicing every day.

(A pause.)

STELLA: You like it, don't you?
FRANK: Of course I do. I just don't know what to say.
STELLA: I thought that meant you were supposed to say "ahhhh!"
FRANK: Listen ... you want to dance or something?
STELLA: I'd love to dance.

(LIGHTS FADE TO HALF and RISE on Billy in the neutral area, dressed as Santa Claus.)

BILLY: And there were in the same country shepherds abiding in the field, keeping watch over their flock by night.

And lo, the angel of the Lord came upon them, and the glory of the Lord shone round about them: and they were sore afraid.

And the angel said unto them, Fear not: for, behold, I bring you good tidings of great joy, which shall be to all people.

For unto you is born this day in the city of David a Savior, which is Christ the Lord.

(Focus changes.)

FRANK: Ahhhhhhhh!

STELLA: Maybe you should start your own cult and give the Swami a little competition.

FRANK: I'm a lone wolf. I belong in the woods with the rest of the wild animals.

(Focus changes.)

BILLY: And this shall be a sign unto you: Ye shall find the babe wrapped in swaddling clothes, lying in a manger.

And suddenly there was with the angel a multitude of the heavenly host praising God, and saying,

Glory to God in the highest, and on earth peace, good will toward men.

(Focus changes.)

FRANK: But we've already logged the woods out of wild animals and practically out of trees. Who the hell knows where it's gonna end?

STELLA: Sshh — it's Christmas.

(Focus changes.)

BILLY: And it came to pass, as the angels were gone away from them into heaven, the shepherds said one to another, Let us now go even unto Bethlehem, and see this thing which is come to pass, which the Lord hath made known to us.

And they came with haste, and found Mary, and Joseph, and the babe lying in a manger.

(LIGHTS OFF neutral area, FULL in tavern.)

FRANK: Fred Ross hit it right on the money:

I'm in from the cold where the vine maples grow
And the dogwoods bloom in the spring.
I've been in the woods for thirty years
And I haven't accomplished a thing.

(Billy enters, still in part of his Santa costume. Frank and Stella stop dancing.)

STELLA: How'd the Christmas show go, Billy?
BILLY: Terrible. I kept thinking about that Swami. What the hell makes a guy like that tick?
STELLA: Ask Frank. He's the convert.
FRANK: I'm a lone wolf.
BILLY: Listening to him got me all mixed up. When he started yelling, I felt like yelling back at him.
FRANK: Like this? Ahhhhh!
BILLY: Ahhhhhhhhhhh!
FRANK & BILLY: AHHHHHHHHHHHHHHHH!
STELLA: Frank? Billy?
FRANK & BILLY:
AHHHHHHHHHHHHHHHHHHHHHHHHHHHHHHHHHH!
STELLA: *(under the yelling)* God help us all!

(LIGHTS FADE TO BLACKOUT as the yelling continues. The play is over.)

For royalties information:
contact Charles Deemer
1-800-294-7176
cdeemer@teleport.com

1983

The Half-Life Conspiracy
a play in two acts

First performed at the New Rose Theatre in Portland, Oregon, on February 25, 1983. Directed by Gary O'Brien.

THE CAST (3M, 3F, in order of appearance):
Cynthia Moore, *a director with the Portland Community Players*;
Joe Barge, *President of the Players*;
Ann Barton, *an actress with the Players and Cynthia's lovemate*;
Robert Olson (Todd Westlake), *a playwright and TV writer, Cynthia's ex-husband*;
Bill Stevens, *an actor with the Players*;
Willow Stevens, *his wife, an actress with the Players.*

THE TIME:
The present (an election year), summer:
Act I: FRIDAY. i: *The Reception* (6 p.m.); ii: *"Half-Life," a one-act play by Robert Olson*
Act II: SATURDAY. i: *The Cast Party* (1 a.m.) ii: *Fallout* (3:30 a.m.)

THE SET:
The deck of Joe Barton's home in the west hills area of Portland, Oregon, overlooking the skyline of the city. For *I, ii*: the stage of the Portland Community Players.

ACT ONE

1/ The Reception (Friday, 6 p.m.)

(AT RISE: CYNTHIA is alone on the deck, pacing. Inside, beyond the sliding door, we hear the vague sounds of a party going on. CYNTHIA is visibly nervous about something. The sliding door opens and JOE appears long enough to say:)

JOE: He's here!

(He leaves. ANN comes out onto the deck.)

ANN: It might help if you screamed at me.

CYNTHIA: And why would I want to do that?

ANN: To clear the air between us before you meet him.

CYNTHIA: Ann, what difference does it make now? You and your activist friends have made your decision and who gives a damn what the director has to say about it?

ANN: No one's going to disrupt the play. We're just after support.

CYNTHIA: It politicizes everything. It's like adding a political prologue to the play, taking a position—

ANN: You can always make an announcement before curtain: "The demonstration outside the theater blah blah in no way reflects the opinion of the Portland Community Players blah blah."

CYNTHIA: I may ask Joe to do exactly that.

ANN: I think you're being paranoid over nothing.

CYNTHIA: You didn't clear it with me, and you certainly didn't clear it with Robert Olson. He may not appreciate his play being used that way.

ANN: We're not "using the play." It's like passing out leaflets at a supermarket.

CYNTHIA: I know goddamn well what you're doing. It's not as if we haven't argued about this before. You can't leave well enough alone.

ANN: Well enough?

CYNTHIA: You know what I mean.

ANN: Cynthia, there are a significant number of misguided people in this community who want to pass a law that affects the way I live my life and—

CYNTHIA: This isn't the time or place. He may come out here any minute.

ANN: You're nervous about meeting him.

CYNTHIA: I've never had to deal with the playwright being around before. What if he doesn't like it?

ANN: He'll love what you've done. By the cast party, you'll be higher than a kite.

CYNTHIA: After you get done with our image, I may never be allowed to direct for the Players again.

ANN: We've been in a rut. If what I'm doing is controversial, maybe it's good for us.

CYNTHIA: The play's controversial enough without all your bleeding hearts out there—

ANN: Your life will be affected as much as anyone's if this—

CYNTHIA: I said I don't want to discuss it.

ANN: Which makes you an ostrich with your head in the sand.

(At the tail end of this, JOE enters with OLSON. There is an immediate shocked moment of recognition between CYNTHIA and OLSON before each quickly recovers; the audience doesn't have to see this, it will learn soon enough.).

JOE: I'd like you to meet Cynthia Moore and Ann Barton. Robert Olson.

OLSON: Hello.

JOE: Ann plays Mary, and Cynthia's your director.

ANN: I've been looking forward to meeting you.

CYNTHIA: Yes, so have I.

OLSON: I've been looking forward to seeing the play.

CYNTHIA: I hope you like what we've done with it.

JOE: Can I get you a drink, Robert?

OLSON: Bourbon and water, if you have it.

CYNTHIA: *(quickly)* I'll get it.

(CYNTHIA leaves and ANN quickly follows behind her.)

ANN: I need a refill myself. So nice to have you here.

OLSON: Thank you.

(And the women are gone.)

JOE: *(not sure what has happened)* You'll have to excuse us. We're all pretty nervous about having you here.

OLSON: I'm pretty nervous myself. So — how long have you been having the contest?

JOE: This is actually our first year.

OLSON: Really? The way you advertised, I thought it had been around for a while.

JOE: We advertised more than we should have. We were flooded with scripts.

OLSON: I can imagine. Frankly, I'm surprised you chose "Half-Life." Community theaters usually favor bedroom comedies and musicals.

JOE: We usually do ourselves. But we're more adventurous in the summer: it finally stops raining, and everyone stays outside anyway. Who cares what the hell we do?

OLSON: I'm delighted to be here. Thank you for choosing my play.

JOE: I wasn't on the selection committee. I play the newscaster voice at the end.

OLSON: Then you get the last word.

JOE: My first curtain line.

(There's an awkward silence.)

JOE: You write for television.

OLSON: Pays the rent.

JOE: What show?

OLSON: "Heart Song".

JOE: I don't know it.

OLSON: It's a soap.

JOE: Fascinating.

OLSON: What is?

JOE: The pressure. Having to write every day like that.

OLSON: There're five of us. I write the Tuesdays.

JOE: I'll watch next Tuesday then.

(CYNTHIA returns with OLSON's drink.)

CYNTHIA: One bourbon and water.

OLSON: Thanks.

CYNTHIA: More arrivals, Joe.

JOE: Time to play host.

OLSON: This is your place?

JOE: Mine and the bank's.

OLSON: I like your view. I didn't realize Portland had a skyline.

(Joe exits.)

CYNTHIA: Jesus Christ.

OLSON: That was my line.

CYNTHIA: Todd, what is this? I disqualified you. I thought I did.

OLSON: I'm not sure what you mean.

CYNTHIA: "Roses for the Road."

OLSON: You have "Roses"?

CYNTHIA: How many scripts did you enter, under how many pseudonyms? Didn't you read the rules — only one script per playwright?

OLSON: I only sent "Half-Life." My agent must've sent "Roses." I'm impressed, he's usually lazier than that.

CYNTHIA: The committee wanted to do "Roses for the Road" and once I saw your byline — Todd Westlake's byline — I had a hell of a time talking them out of it. The last thing I needed was seeing you again. So how many pseudonyms do you have?

OLSON: Only Robert Olson. But if you think I would've sent anything, knowing you were involved. I thought you were still in San Francisco with what's-her-face. What was her name?

(No reply.)

OLSON: What'd you do, break up?

(No reply.)

OLSON: Cheers. Charming way to spend a weekend, winning a play contest. Travel expenses, room and board, a small honorarium. Not to mention all the fascinating people you meet.

CYNTHIA: We'll just have to get through the weekend as best we can.

OLSON: You really wanted to do "Roses"? I told my agent to burn it. It was so bad I started writing under Robert Olson. Start all over, more or less. Cheers.

CYNTHIA: Obviously your agent didn't burn it.

OLSON: Doesn't say much for your taste, wanting to do "Roses." But then there's no accounting for taste, is there?

CYNTHIA: *(distracted)* What?

124

OLSON: I said, there's no accounting for taste. I was referring to "Roses for the Road."

CYNTHIA: I know what you're referring to.

OLSON: Though it's a principle one can apply more widely. To more personal matters. To sexual preference, and so on.

CYNTHIA: I get the reference, Todd, and I'm not going to talk about the past with you.

OLSON: When I asked if you'd broken up, I was referring to the present — to your happiness.

CYNTHIA: I'm goddamn happy!

OLSON: Good. Cheers. So how do you two like Portland after San Francisco? It must be quite a change. Isn't this where they have that ballot measure against gay rights and —?

CYNTHIA: Todd, we have to—

OLSON: Robert Olson. I mean, if we're going to go through with this little charade, then you have to remember your lines. I'm not Todd Westlake. I'm Robert Olson.

CYNTHIA: I just don't want to argue about anything.

OLSON: I was referring to you calling me Todd.

CYNTHIA: So I'm sorry!

OLSON: Accepted. Cheers.

CYNTHIA: I don't believe this. Five minutes with you — after five years — and suddenly I feel like everything's my fault. I haven't done anything!

OLSON: I have an idea. Let's start over.

(A pause.)

OLSON: Hello, I'm Robert Olson. You must be the one directing my play. I'm so much looking forward to seeing it.

CYNTHIA: Shut up. Just pretend you've never seen me before.

OLSON: There's no invisible lady like an ex-wife. Excuse me — invisible *person*.

CYNTHIA: Just cut the crap.

(BILL and WILLOW enter.)

BILL: Bobby, I'd like you to meet the wife. Willow, Robert Olson. She plays Heather.

WILLOW: I'm so excited to meet you!

OLSON: You play Heather? How interesting.

WILLOW: "Interesting" usually means disapproval.

OLSON: No, not at all. I just didn't think of Heather being so attractive. Nice casting.

CYNTHIA: Thank you.

WILLOW: And I thought I was nervous before.

CYNTHIA: Will you be coming inside soon? People are anxious to meet you.

OLSON: In a bit.

CYNTHIA: If you'll excuse me...

(CYNTHIA exits.)

WILLOW: Bill told me you write for a soap opera.

OLSON: "Heart Song."

WILLOW: You're kidding! I watch it every day.

OLSON: I just write the Tuesdays.

WILLOW: I know it's not fair to ask — but is Priscilla going to get a divorce?

OLSON: Not on Tuesday.

WILLOW: I love the actor who plays Morgan. He's so evil and sexy.

OLSON: He gets killed in a car accident.

WILLOW: Oh, no!

OLSON: He got cast in another series, so we have to kill him off. On Tuesday, I hope.

BILL: I meant to ask you on the ride from the airport, but there's actually a lot of ad-libbing and improv on the soaps, isn't there?

OLSON: Mostly when actors forget their lines. Actually we develop a lot of the scenes with some theater games we play.

(Joe enters.)

JOE: There are some folks who are anxious to meet you, Robert.

OLSON: And I need a refill. Stay put, I can find it.

(He goes.)

JOE: He seems like a regular guy.

BILL: The first thing he asked at the airport was why wasn't it raining. Then he wanted to know if St. Helens was likely to erupt while he was here. How the hell am I supposed to answer that?

WILLOW: Did you get to tell him about your script?

BILL: I couldn't get a word in. You know what else he said — he'd never been to the Northwest before. He sets a play in Portland and has never been here.

WILLOW: The setting isn't all that central to the action.

BILL: That's the under-statement of the year. Nothing's central to the action. The situation in "Half-Life" is phony from top to bottom. We should've stuck with "Roses for the Road."

JOE: It's good for us to do something avant-garde.

BILL: Avant-garde is a synonym for "it stinks." Who can believe the premise? Even if Iraq did get a bomb, even if it used it, who can believe all the rest of that crap?

WILLOW: I can imagine it happening just the way he wrote it.

BILL: Come on, if Portland was being evacuated, would you hang around to play a parlor game? No way.

JOE: He's here, the play opens tonight, and the audience will tell us what they think soon enough.

BILL: Pardon the pun, but it's going to be one hell of a bomb.

WILLOW: I certainly hope you don't take that attitude on stage with you.

BILL: Don't worry about me, I'm a pro. You want some coldcuts or something?

WILLOW: I'm too nervous to eat.

BILL: Glass of punch?

WILLOW: Nothing, thanks.

(BILL exits.)

JOE: *(cautious)* I hope we can agree that I deserve an explanation.

WILLOW: Something came up. I couldn't get away.

JOE: You might have phoned. A quick trip to the market, a coin in the phone slot.

WILLOW: I didn't think of it.

JOE: I don't think that's the reason.

WILLOW: You're right.

JOE: Well?

WILLOW: I didn't come because I feel guilty as hell.

JOE: You've felt guilty from the beginning.

WILLOW: It's getting worse. That's why I'm not seeing you any more.

JOE: I don't believe that.

WILLOW: You will.

JOE: You're involved as deeply as I am. And as voluntarily, I might add.

WILLOW: You aren't married, and you don't have children.

JOE: Oh yes, let's not forget the children. We ought to bring Olson out here, this sounds like an audition for his soap opera.

WILLOW: That doesn't make what I'm telling you false.

JOE: Willow, I know how much you care for me.

WILLOW: No. You don't know me at all.

JOE: I see. Then whose fault is that? I haven't been dreaming these past few months. When I'm told something, I believe it. You have told me some very sweet things.

WILLOW: Joe, I'm still fond of you but—

JOE: "Fond" of me? Jesus.

WILLOW: It was a bad time for me. I needed to feel wanted.

JOE: How the hell am I supposed to react to that?

WILLOW: We'll always be special friends.

JOE: That's fucked, Willow. That's really fucked.

(OLSON returns.)

OLSON: Someone asked me for an autograph. I feel like a celebrity.

JOE: If you think it's bad now, wait til the cast party.

OLSON: By then I'll be drunk enough to handle it. Cheers.

(ANN enters.)

ANN: I see you escaped your admirers.

OLSON: Caught in the act.

WILLOW: If you'll excuse me, I have some errands to run before call. I hope we've done your play justice.

OLSON: In your case, I'm sure I have nothing to worry about.

JOE: Excuse me.

(WILLOW and JOE exit.)

ANN: They're having an affair. Everyone knows but poor Bill.

OLSON: I'll bet he knows.

ANN: No, he thinks she's having an affair with Dean Pill. Pill's the drama critic for the paper.

OLSON: Her reviews must be spectacular.

ANN: She even deserves some of them.

OLSON: Adultery's become the norm, hasn't it? That may make soap opera the dramatic form for our times.

ANN: Is that Robert Olson speaking — or Todd Westlake?

OLSON: Oh my. You're an investigative reporter disguised as an actress. I take it Cynthia told you.

ANN: No, I recognized you myself as soon as you walked out onto the deck.

OLSON: Have we met before?

ANN: No. I'm the dyke from San Francisco.

OLSON: The dyke. I remember.

ANN: You've changed since then. Your play shows it. To tell the truth, I'm as shocked as Cynthia that you're here. That you wrote "Half-Life."

OLSON: I thought all of you preferred "Roses for the Road."

ANN: I didn't. But it was the first round favorite. Cynthia vetoed it, and I led the charge for "Half-Life." I still can't believe you wrote it. You didn't seem to be in that kind of space five years ago.

OLSON: Well, I had this extraordinary experience, you see — my wife left me for a dyke in San Francisco.

ANN: You've recovered nicely. Better than Cynthia has, actually.

OLSON: Don't tell me: she still has a soft spot in her heart for me.

ANN: She's still afraid of herself.

OLSON: I don't remember seeing any fear when she moved out.

ANN: She still hasn't really "come out," you know. Not in Portland. She didn't like the San Francisco scene; she prefers being "discreet," as she puts it. She's afraid being openly gay will lose the business clients.

OLSON: Still in Public Relations?

ANN: Oh yes. And I doubt if anyone in Portland has the slightest suspicion that she's gay. Which is becoming a problem, to tell the truth. You've heard about our Ballot Measure 13?

OLSON: The anti-gay legislation.

ANN: Exactly, though the backers don't call it that. Cynthia's afraid to take a public stand against it. She gets angry when I do.

OLSON: I'd really love to exchange Cynthia stories with you but it feels too much like being at work.

ANN: She's living two lives.

OLSON: I live at least that many. Don't you?

ANN: I live in a community of growing homophobia. I see no advantage to burying my head in the sand.

OLSON: Then everybody here knows you're gay?

ANN: No, they don't. So far I've gone along with her. I'm not sure I can for much longer.

OLSON: Maybe she has a point about your clients.

ANN: Then we should be more selective.

OLSON: Does Cynthia know you're telling me all of this?

ANN: No.

OLSON: Why are you?

ANN: Why not? We're here.

OLSON: That sounds a little macho, like mountain-climbing or foreign policy.

ANN: I love Cynthia very much. It hurts me to see her denying who she is.

OLSON: If you got rid of your homophobic clients, maybe you'd go broke.

ANN: I've never understood why gay fidelity should raise eyebrows when heterosexual infidelity in the business world is commonplace.

OLSON: That sounds so logical it *has* to be wrong.

ANN: I wish there was something constructive that we could all get out of this.

OLSON: Our conversation?

ANN: The surprise of your appearance.

OLSON: If you're asking me to help you get Cynthia out of the closet, no thanks.

ANN: You might at least become friends again.

OLSON: Takes two to tango, and I don't think she's interested.

ANN: There's a rally against Measure 13 tomorrow. Maybe if you'd come, she'd see you've changed and would come as well.

OLSON: Going to a rally with a hangover is a little much — and I plan to have a hangover.

(CYNTHIA enters.)

CYNTHIA: It's getting close to call, Ann.

OLSON: I've just been invited to a rally tomorrow.

CYNTHIA: My, haven't we been busy?

ANN: He knows who I am.

CYNTHIA: And how on earth could he have learned that?

ANN: *(to Olson)* Think about it .

(ANN exits. OLSON is grinning.)

CYNTHIA: I fail to see what's so amusing.

OLSON: Opening night jitters. We used to spat every opening night, remember? And now you two are spatting.

CYNTHIA: We are not spatting.

OLSON: Could've fooled me.

CYNTHIA: It has nothing to do with opening night.

OLSON: Damn.

CYNTHIA: I beg your pardon?

OLSON: I was hoping marriage had nothing to do with gender.

CYNTHIA: What did she tell you?

OLSON: That coming out is bad for business.

CYNTHIA: Christ.

OLSON: Exactly — look where it got him.

CYNTHIA: As far as the weekend is concerned, you don't know either of us. I wish I could trust you.

OLSON: You can.

CYNTHIA: Even when you're drinking?

(OLSON looks at his watch.)

OLSON: I was wondering how long it would take you to bring up my drinking. I think you just set a record. Congratulations. Cheers.

CYNTHIA: Just be Robert Olson, who has never seen us before.

OLSON: Olson in the flesh. So how do you like the play?

CYNTHIA: I liked it better before I found out you wrote it.

OLSON: That's the "biographical fallacy" — that's what the whatchamacallits would say. What are they called? The assholes with all the answers?

CYNTHIA: The reviewers?

OLSON: Ah, the reviewers. The critics! They'd say, Don't confuse art with life.

CYNTHIA: There are certain parallels, Todd — Robert!

OLSON: And differences as well. You left me before the planet gets nuked. Gets nuked again, I mean. Funny how we forget we've already nuked it.

CYNTHIA: Then the play isn't about our marriage?

OLSON: No.

CYNTHIA: What's the source of all the anger?

OLSON: You sound like a critic.

CYNTHIA: Then questions aren't allowed? How convenient for you.

OLSON: If you don't know the source of the anger, then why the hell are you directing the play?

CYNTHIA: I do know the source of the anger.

(JOE and BILL enter.)

131

JOE: Time to get to the theater.

CYNTHIA: We're on our way.

(She exits. As OLSON starts out, he is stopped by BILL. JOE waits behind.)

BILL: Bobby, wait a minute. Let me run a scenario by you before it gets too crazy. There's this alcoholic, right? He's really into the hard stuff but he never touches a drop until after five. Then he'll do a fifth a night, practically. During the day he's a well-respected high school principal. His wife is head of the PTA, the whole shot. A real Jekyll and Hyde situation. A high school principal by day but by night, when he's been drinking, he can go after the old lady in a way that makes "Virginia Woolf" look like a romance. Now it turns out the wife is having an affair with the guy's best friend. The principal doesn't suspect a thing but it does let us sympathize with him despite the booze and violence because, you know, she's really doing a number on him. And with his best friend.

OLSON: We sympathize with him.

BILL: You got it! That's really important. Maybe he also had a leg shot off in the war or something. Whatever. Anyway, it's a night when the principal is having some teachers over for a party and naturally the best friend is there, too.

JOE: We're running late, Bill.

BILL: Don't worry, I'm giving Olson a lift. So it's late in the party and most of the teachers have gone home. The principal's hitting the sauce heavy. Meanwhile his wife and best friend are out on the deck alone. Nothing heavy, just a little touchy-feely. And the principal decides to go out for some fresh air, not knowing they're out there

(They have exited, lights fade to BLACKOUT.)

2/ "Half-Life," a one-act play by Robert Olson (8 p.m.)

(The set is an interior. With the house lights still up, JOE comes forward to speak to the audience.)

JOE: Good evening. If you've read your paper at all this week, then you know that the setting for tonight's play is a terrorist act leading to a limited nuclear war that requires an emergency evacuation of Portland

— and that in this tense moment, a man's wife admits that she has taken another woman as a lover. In this context, you might suppose that the picketing against Ballot Measure 13 going on outside the theater tonight is somehow connected to and even endorsed by the Portland Community Players. This is not the case. What happens outside on a public sidewalk is their business, and what happens here inside the theater is our business — and, I might add, our only business. Thank you.

(A pause.)

JOE: "Half-Life" by Robert Olson is the winner of the first annual one-act play competition sponsored by the Portland Community Players. When he isn't writing prize-winning plays, Mr. Olson is a writer for the daytime television series, "Heart Song." He has informed me that he writes each Tuesday episode. We've very excited about sharing this original and provocative new play with you, and we have the pleasure of having the playwright in the audience as our guest of honor. Robert, would you stand up and take a bow?...Are you out there, Robert?...I guess he's still back stage with the cast. At any rate, Robert Olson — along with our cast and director — will be available right after the play to respond to your questions about "Half-Life." I think you'll find that this is very different material for the Players, and we think that's good. Without further ado, then — oh yes, I want to remind you that our regular season continues next weekend with a brand new production of Neil Simon's *The Odd Couple*. This is the fifth time we've had the pleasure of bringing you this masterpiece by the master of comedy, and we have an all-new cast for you. So don't forget *The Odd Couple*, opening next weekend and continuing for ten weeks. And I should add that "Half-Life" will also be performed tomorrow and Sunday. And now, without further ado, the world premier of "Half-Life" by Robert Olson. Thank you.

(BLACKOUT.)

(LIGHTS UP on HEATHER. She is waiting, nervous. Three scripts rest on a coffee table. Heather's purse leans against a leg of the table. MARY rushes into the room.)

MARY: *(played by ANN)* What are you doing here? Didn't you hear the news?
HEATHER *(played by WILLOW)* I heard it.

MARY: It's a zoo out there.

HEATHER: I know. Where's your husband?

MARY: In the garage. He's loading the camp gear.

HEATHER: Get him.

MARY: You can't be serious. Are you all right?

HEATHER: What a fucking question. Are you?

MARY: I don't know how I am. It's so crazy out there.

HEATHER: You expect to go camping?

MARY: Everyone's evacuating. Haven't you been listening to the radio?

HEATHER: You saw the traffic. You expect to go somewhere? We're going to retaliate and this thing will escalate until . . .

MARY: But it's safer south. Isn't it?

HEATHER: The winds have been east out of Seattle.

MARY: There was an announcement to evacuate. Everyone's going south. We have to do something, for Christ's sake.

HEATHER: I know. That's why I'm here.

MARY: Why *are* you here?

HEATHER: To find out if you've told him yet. You haven't, have you?

MARY: Heather, this is hardly the time to discuss it.

HEATHER: I can think of no better time. It's rather a last chance to do anything, don't you think? Surely we've retaliated by now — whoever the hell did this has allies who have retaliated in kind — this is the grand final escalation we've all been waiting for. I should think today is the most existential moment in human history. It's now or never, love.

MARY: You're right. I haven't told him.

HEATHER: Will you tell him now?

MARY: You mean — *now*?

HEATHER: The most existential moment in human history: now.

MARY: He's packing the camp gear. I'm supposed to be packing clothes and getting our — toothbrushes.

HEATHER: Your fucking toothbrushes.

MARY: One can't give up. It's not necessarily the end.

HEATHER: Mary, the proverbial button has been pushed. So much for the end of the Cold War, hey? Welcome to the New Holocaust, where everybody gets to play.

MARY: So what do you think we should do?

HEATHER: I'll kill myself before I let this madness kill me. It would be considerably more dignified.

MARY: It's not necessarily the end.

HEATHER: Do you think we're not retaliating? Do you expect North Korea to stay out of this, and all those republics in Russia with names no one can pronounce — who are sitting on tons of nuclear weapons? Look at history. Look at how any world war starts. Face it, the game's over, Mary. The dinosaurs have won. Male aggression has won. They're taking the planet with them.

MARY: It's just so hard to comprehend.

HEATHER: On the contrary, extinction is the logical conclusion of the male way of doing things. You read *Power and Patriarchy*.

MARY: It all seemed so theoretical.

HEATHER: When the theory's right, the consequences are predictable. The miracle is that it took men so long to blow us all up.

MARY: Don't you have an instinct to survive? Despite everything?

HEATHER: My instinct is to die with dignity. Get your husband.

MARY: Why?

HEATHER: I brought some scripts for us to read.

MARY: What are you talking about?

HEATHER: Male consciousness raising. Have you forgotten already?

MARY: You actually wrote some scripts?

HEATHER: We did talk about it.

MARY: But that was just — thinking aloud and fantasizing. I didn't expect you to go through with it.

HEATHER: But I did — even before the shit hit the fan. It's now or never, love.

MARY: John will never go along with something like that.

HEATHER: With proper persuasion he will.

(She takes a pistol from her purse.)

MARY: This is crazy.

HEATHER: I didn't nuke Seattle, love. Get John.

MARY: I don't see the point of this.

HEATHER: The point is doing it.

MARY: You're serious.

HEATHER: Very. I also have the gun. The power of the male archetype. Get your husband.

MARY: Is the point to embarrass him?

HEATHER: He won't be embarrassed. He'll be outraged.

MARY: So we read the script. Then what?

HEATHER: Then I'm on my way to find dignity. I hope you'll come with me.

MARY: I don't think I can do that. Not like this.

HEATHER: I love you, Mary.

MARY: I'm — very confused about how I feel about you.

HEATHER: Get him.

MARY: Can I talk to him alone first?

HEATHER: I don't think I can trust you. Call him from here. Then you can talk where I can see you.

MARY: Fine. You have the gun.

HEATHER: Incredible, isn't it? With the male archetype, you can get anything you want. Except what matters.

MARY: You're not acting like anything matters.

HEATHER: Death with dignity matters.

(JOHN enters and stops as soon as he sees HEATHER with the gun.)

JOHN: *(played by BILL)* Give her what she wants, Mary. We don't want any trouble.

HEATHER: Give him a script.

(MARY hands JOHN a script.)

JOHN: What the hell is this?

MARY: Please do as she says. It won't take long.

JOHN: You know her?

MARY: She's a friend from school.

JOHN: *(to Heather)* You do know what's going on out there, don't you?

HEATHER: You'll read the part of Wifey.

JOHN: I'll do what?

HEATHER: We're going to stage a reading, and you're playing the role of Wifey. Mary is Hubby, and I'm the Narrator. Shall we begin?

JOHN: Look, I know it's hard to handle, but what's happening out there is real.

MARY: Do as she says, John.

JOHN: Iraq or somedamnbody has nuked Seattle and it's time to get the hell out of Portland!

HEATHER: The sooner we begin, the sooner you can join the lemmings rushing south.

JOHN: Get fucking serious.

HEATHER: I am very serious.

JOHN: She's a friend of yours?

MARY: Please. It won't take long.

136

JOHN: You want me to read a play? A fucking play!

(HEATHER fires a round from the pistol up in the air.)

JOHN: *(quickly)* So what do you want me to do?
HEATHER: Read the part of Wifey. I'll begin the narration. "The Habits of Hubby," a skit in search of peace, in endless movements *ad nauseam*. The First Habit: Hubby is Horny."

(A pause.)

HEATHER: The next line is yours.
JOHN: I don't understand the point of this.
HEATHER: Read your line.
JOHN: Why are we doing this?

(HEATHER gestures with the pistol.)

JOHN: Okay, just point that thing the other way.
HEATHER: "The First Habit: Hubby is Horny."
JOHN: *(as Wifey)* "Please, dear, I just put on my face."
HEATHER: Use a high voice.
JOHN: What?
HEATHER: I want you to sound like a woman. Use a falsetto.
JOHN: For Christ's sake— . . . okay, okay. Can we start over?
HEATHER: "Hubby is Horny."
JOHN: *(in falsetto, which continues below)* "Please, dear, I just put on my face."
MARY: *(as Hubby, in a deep voice)* "I'm not interested in your face."
JOHN: "We'll be late to the party."
MARY: "I won't take a minute."
JOHN: "You never take a minute, dear."
MARY: "Fastest gun in the west."
JOHN: "Maybe when we get back."
MARY: "I'm in the mood now."
JOHN: "But I'm not."
MARY: "Just a quicky, for Christ's sake."
JOHN: "I'm dressed, I just put on my face—"
MARY: "You're never in the mood."
JOHN: "You know that's not true."

MARY: "Who the hell brings home the bacon around here? Who works his goddamn ass to the grindstone while you sit around watching soap operas? I can't even get a little satisfaction around here."

JOHN: "We can put out some candles when we get home. Make it romantic."

MARY: "Candles in July? Are you crazy? Frigid bitch."

HEATHER: "The Second Habit: Hubby Needs Understanding."

JOHN: *(normal voice)* Can I say something?

HEATHER No. "Hubby Needs Understanding."

MARY: *(deep voice)* "Hi, Carol. Enjoying the party?"

JOHN: *(high voice)* "Frankly, no. How about you?"

MARY: "I've been better."

JOHN: "Where's Nancy?"

MARY: "Around. Is that a new dress?"

JOHN: "Just something I picked up on sale."

MARY: "Dynamite. Really. Mike is a lucky guy."

JOHN: "Tell him that."

MARY: "You always look so sharp."

JOHN: "Keep talking, I love it."

MARY: "Really. You always have a certain aura. A certain presence. A certain—. .. oh, I can't explain it. I think you're great!"

JOHN: "Thanks, I needed that."

MARY: "It's so easy to talk to you. Nancy hasn't the foggiest notion who I am. Not really. It's like living in a vacuum."

JOHN: "I didn't know. You two always seem so happy."

MARY: "The mask we put on. I guess I'm bending your ear."

JOHN: "I don't mind."

MARY: "Do you find it stuffy in here?"

JOHN: "A little."

MARY: "Let's go out on the deck."

HEATHER: "The Third Habit: Hubby Makes His Move."

MARY: "It's great to be with someone you can talk to."

JOHN: "I know what you mean."

MARY: "That dress is a knockout. You have an incredible figure."

JOHN: "I work at it in the gym."

MARY: "It pays off."

HEATHER: Now he tries to feel your left breast. You fight him off.

JOHN: *(normal voice)* How long does this go on?

HEATHER: He tries to feel your left breast.

JOHN: We have an emergency going on out there!

HEATHER: Your line, Mary.

MARY: "Your breasts are incredible."

138

JOHN: *(high voice)* "Please don't . . ."

MARY: "You don't know how lonely I've been."

JOHN: "Stop it, please."

MARY: "You turn me on."

JOHN: "Let's go back inside."

HEATHER Finally he reaches inside your dress and feels your left breast.

MARY: "My God."

JOHN: "I had cancer."

MARY: "Jesus, I didn't realize, I—"

JOHN: "I had an operation."

HEATHER "The Fourth Habit: Hubby Helps With The Housework."

JOHN: *(normal voice)* Look here.

HEATHER "Hubby Helps With The Housework."

JOHN: I want to say something! Would you please point that somewhere else?

HEATHER "Hubby Helps With The Housework."

MARY: *(normal voice)* Please read your lines.

JOHN: I won't put up with this.

HEATHER "Hubby Helps With The Housework."

JOHN: What do you, hate men?

HEATHER I'm not going to wait forever.

JOHN: So how many habits do we have to go through? If you expect me to take this personally, you're full of shit. I help with the housework! Tell her, Mary. I help with the housework all the time.

MARY: You seldom help with the housework, John.,

JOHN: I take out the garbage! We're in a goddamn war out there! Who has time for housework?

HEATHER "Hubby Helps With The Housework."

JOHN: I'll tell you this, you won't see any women on the front lines out there. Put that in your pipe and smoke it.

HEATHER "Hubby Helps With The Housework."

MARY: Maybe we can move on.

HEATHER "The Fifth Habit: Hubby Would've Won The Game If He'd Been Coach."

JOHN: So pull the trigger. I dare you.

MARY: *(to Heather)* I think you've made your point.

HEATHER "Hubby Would've Won The Game If He'd Been Coach."

MARY: *(prompting)* The Sixth Habit . . .

HEATHER "Hubby Is Laid Flat By A Mild Cold."

JOHN: *(to Mary)* Will you get her to stop this?

HEATHER "Hubby Goes On The Wagon For Three Days."

JOHN: Goddamn it!

HEATHER "Hubby Should've Known Better Than To Let A Woman Balance The Checkbook." "Hubby Taught Her How To Boil An Egg." "Hubby Could've Predicted It."

JOHN: I quit!

HEATHER "The Tenth Habit: Hubby Could've Predicted It." "Hubby Could've Predicted It." "Hubby Could've—"

JOHN: Predicted what?

MARY: *(deep voice)* "I knew the Cowboys would blow it." "I know the sonofabitch would back off his campaign promises." "I knew he had his hands in the till." "I knew that marriage would never last."

JOHN: What is the point of all this?

(No reply.)

JOHN: WHAT IS THE POINT OF ALL THIS?

MARY: *(to Heather)* I think it's time for us to go.

HEATHER *(aiming the pistol at John)* "Hubby Could've Predicted It…"

MARY: Heather, no!

(Mary grabs the gun: a struggle, which John joins in — and he ends up with the pistol.)

JOHN: Now!

MARY: John, please— . . .

JOHN: Now, goddamn it, it's my turn!

MARY: Try to understand.

JOHN: Understand?! Who is she? What kind of power does she have over you?

MARY: She had the gun.

JOHN: Yeah, well, you seemed to be enjoying yourself. So what the hell are you trying to prove? That men are assholes?

HEATHER: How perceptive of you.

JOHN: Are you fucking serious? Do you think all that shit, all those clichés about how men are the assholes of the universe, has anything to do with what's going on out there? Seattle's been nuked! Do you comprehend that? We're in a nuclear war out there! We're talking about the survival of this country here! Try doing that without men.

HEATHER: Yes, survival is precisely what we're talking about.

140

JOHN: *(getting crazier)* The shrinks predicted this. The human mind can handle only so much — and then it cracks. Goddamn women, you think the world is all rainbows and roses. You don't perceive reality.

HEATHER: I know what reality is.

JOHN: Then you should know what's happening out there!

HEATHER: Masculinity.

JOHN: What?

HEATHER: Masculinity is happening out there.

JOHN: I don't see any cunts volunteering for the front lines, I'll grant you that.

MARY: I'm not a cunt, John!

JOHN: Let me put it this way: you have strange friends.

HEATHER: At least I accept reality — meaning, that the game's over.

JOHN: The hell it is. We recovered after Pearl Harbor and we'll recover again. Whoever did this, we'll bomb them back to the Stone Age!

HEATHER: How masculine of us.

JOHN: Who the fuck are you?

HEATHER: Someone who is leaving. It's been swell.

(She starts away.)

JOHN: Like hell, you're leaving.

MARY: I'm leaving, too, John.

JOHN: I have more to say here!

MARY: There's no point in saying anything. I'm leaving you. I've been trying to get the nerve to tell you for weeks. Don't pretend you're surprised.

JOHN: She did this?

MARY: Not really.

JOHN: It's those classes you've been taking, isn't it? All that anti-male propaganda you've been reading? Give an inch and they take a mile.

HEATHER: Woman as nigger: perfect.

JOHN: I paid for those fucking courses you're taking, sweetheart.

MARY: There's nothing to discuss, John. Good luck to you.

(The women start away.)

JOHN: So that's it. How long has this been going on?

(No reply.)

JOHN: *(after them)* I asked how long you've been a dyke! How long have you been queer?!

MARY: I don't want to talk about it, John. Goodbye.

JOHN: I'm not afraid to use this!

(Mary is the first to exit.)

HEATHER: Don't act like a self-fulfilling prophecy.

(She exits.)

JOHN: *(after them)* Mary, you get your ass back here!

(He holds the pistol out with both arms, G-man style.)

JOHN: I'M NOT AFRAID TO USE THIS!

(He fires. A scream. He fires again, repeatedly, until the chamber is empty. He looks at the gun. He drops it.)

JOHN: Jesus Christ . . .

(He goes to a radio and turns it on. He finds the news. He listens as the lights start down.)

NEWSCASTER: *(voice of Joe)* . . .Iraq taking credit for the strike, and North Korea claims to have sent missiles into Europe. Retaliation by the United States has been immediate with missile attacks on Iraq, Siberia and North Korea. Unless the U.S. accepts an immediate cease fire, Moscow has threatened to . . .

(BLACKOUT.)

(A pause. The STAGE AND HOUSE LIGHTS COME UP together. All the actors, as well as JOE, CYNTHIA and OLSON, are sitting casually about the set.)

JOE: *(to audience)* Any other questions?

(A beat.)

BILL: *(responding to question)* Let me tackle that one. That's something that went through my mind as well. He blows his wife away — I mean, I do — because, you know, she's been cheating on me — with a woman, no less. She's gay, and this is real, real hard for me to take.

CYNTHIA: He *believes* she's gay, is the point.

JOE: In the back row . . .?

(A beat.)

ANN: Oh, maybe I've gone to bed with her once. I really haven't come out or anything. I'm in a process of deep personal change. Obviously I've been influenced by Heather, and by the courses I've been taking. But suddenly the unthinkable has happened, it may really be the end of the world — the most existential moment in human history, as it's put — and obviously I have to go through changes quicker than I would otherwise.

JOE: Your question, sir?

(A beat.)

OLSON: I don't know how to respond to that. I don't think of it as a political play. I think it's very realistic, that it can literally happen that way. I think the end of the Cold War makes for a more dangerous world, not a safer one, because now enemies are more invisible. It's nothing I can prove. It's just how I feel about things. There's no accounting for taste.

CYNTHIA: The context is what's important, like Ann said. What's happening outside makes the rules of ordinary behavior irrelevant. Everybody is acting through a crisis.

OLSON: I don't think you need any special context to explain their behavior. The context is on the front page of the newspaper every day. The world's as dangerous as ever — every day, every minute. We live on borrowed time.

JOE: The woman in the corner?

(A beat.)

OLSON: Sure, I'll answer that. I'm not gay. Why should it make a difference?

JOE: The lady in the hat . . .

(A beat.)

OLSON: I hear you — you don't like the "f-word." Again, what can I say? That's the way people talk.

JOE: Go ahead, ma'am.

(A beat.)

OLSON: But consider my point of view. I mean, here's a play set in a nuclear crisis, the beginning of a nuclear war, that tries to speak to the dynamics of why such things happen, and you're worried about a very popular if maligned little four-letter word pronounced "fuck." What the hell kind of hierarchy of obscenity is that, lady?

CYNTHIA: Robert, I think she's only suggesting that you could have made your point without using — the "f-word."

ANN: Fuck. Are we all afraid to say fuck here?

OLSON: *(to Ann)* Thank you. *(To the audience)* The point is: war is more obscene than saying "fuck." But here we are . . .

JOE: *(to woman in audience)* Go on.

(A beat.)

OLSON: I think that's a rationalization. If you don't like the play, fine, but don't give me that crap about f-words and melodrama and contrived situations. You dislike the play for the same reason you dislike turnips or horseradish or oral sex or whatever the hell it is you dislike. It's a matter of taste, not of reason, it's—

JOE: The gentleman in front . . .

OLSON: Wait, I'm not done yet! This is important. Reason isn't calling the shots out there. Anything can happen out there. Your so-called reason, looking at the world for motivations and causes, builds an edifice that hides what's really happening. It's pretty hairy out there, you know? I mean, we're going to end up blowing up the planet over an obsolete myth!

JOE: The gentleman in front . . .

(A beat.)

WILLOW: My character is definitely gay and radical. How would Heather make sense otherwise?

OLSON: She doesn't have to be gay and radical to make sense. Sense of what? Heather could be a conservative heterosexual and still pull off something crazy like that. Are you telling me you've never met a weird conservative heterosexual? The point is, all these labels and categories don't work. They hide what's really going on. People are more mind-boggling than we give them credit for. We fall victim to our own categories.

CYNTHIA: The masculine style that's brought up in the play — is this one of the things we fall victim to?

OLSON: Of course. But, hell, that's just a part of it. We fall victim to our mode of thinking rationally. We fall victim to language itself. You know, in Zen, language isn't supposed to say anything. In Zen, language is a bulldozer one uses to push all the garbage out of the way. Reality's between the lines, in the silence.

BILL: I was going to say something, but . . . .

OLSON: The language is insufficient to express the feeling.

BILL: You must love being a writer!

JOE: Anyone else?

OLSON: One more thing, and I'll shut up. Sure, we want answers. But what's to be done out there? Kierkegaard said that there are two ways: to suffer; or to be a professor of the fact that someone else suffers. In my humble opinion, we've got too many fucking professors. Sorry for the f-word, lady.

(He quickly exits as Joe tries to cover with:)

JOE: I'd like to thank Robert Olson for . . . being with us tonight . . . .

(Joe applauds, the others join in, as lights come down to BLACKOUT.)

ACT TWO

145

1/ The Cast Party (1 a.m.)

(Party sounds. AT RISE: OLSON and WILLOW are alone on the deck, dancing to a country song that OLSON is making up on the spot. He sings with an exaggerated twang and is pretty high.)

OLSON: *(singing)* He's cheatin' on she
And she's cheatin' on he
And you're cheatin' on me
And I'm cheatin' on thee
So it's plain, don't you see
Since she's cheatin' on he
And he's cheatin' on she
That we're cheatin' on we

(He does a very bad country yodel.)

OLSON: Yodel-lay-he-oh A-lay-he-oh A-lay-he
WILLOW: *(stopping the dance)* I hate country music.
OLSON: Run that by me again.
WILLOW: I like Bach. I hate country music.
OLSON: A Bach freak? You live in Oregon and you're a Bach freak?
WILLOW: Where do you think you are? West Gulch?
OLSON: The Pacific Northwest! The land of lumberjacks and fishermen and cowboys! That's why I nuked it, you're so close to the mythological center of things. But look there: you have a skyline. The skyline of a city. Almost.
WILLOW: There was a letter in "Dear Abby" recently—
OLSON: You watch "Heart Song" and read "Dear Abby" — my kind of girl.
WILLOW: A couple from the Midwest had moved to Portland and was surprised at how progressive the city is. For example, the woman met a lesbian at work who was very open about who she was. That had never happened to her in Ohio.
OLSON: All things are relative. To dear Albert. Einstein. Cheers.
WILLOW: For the first time in her life, she found herself being friends with a lesbian.
OLSON: Well, election day will take care of that . . .
WILLOW: You mean Measure 13? Oregonians aren't behind that. It's all the people moving in from out of state.

146

OLSON: Really?

WILLOW: California. Utah. Lots of Mormons are moving here.

OLSON: Well, let's put another Measure on the ballot and keep those fascists out.

WILLOW: I didn't say they were fascists. It's a very confusing issue when you study it. Bill's probably voting Yes but I'm not sure how I'm voting yet.

OLSON: You don't want to vote No and cancel his vote, do you?

WILLOW: I can make up my own mind, thank you very much.

OLSON: My kind of woman.

WILLOW: You confuse me. On the one hand, there's something very cynical about you. But other times you seem to be having so much fun.

OLSON: I have a theory. Behold the stars!, twinkling happily away. More than we can see in L.A., as a matter of fact.

WILLOW: Aren't they lovely?

OLSON: They don't exist.

WILLOW: Well, I certainly see them up there.

OLSON: They are not shining. Poof!, the stars have vanished, to the twinkle. However: since, to toast dear Albert once again, since their little twinkles take so long to get to our own untwinkling hunk of hot rock, we don't know they're dead yet. So here we are, writing love songs and poetry and fascist ballot measures in a universe that no longer exists. Cheers.

WILLOW: I see what you mean — some cosmic explosion may already have happened, for all we know.

OLSON: Precisely! In fact, there are no more stars anywhere, in any firmament. All gone! And like you say, we won't find out that cosmic fact for thousands of years. Or until tomorrow.

WILLOW: That's very pessimistic.

OLSON: On the contrary, I toast stars that don't exist! I'd say there's a bit of good will there.

WILLOW: Your play is pessimistic.

OLSON: Neutral. Ironic but neutral.

WILLOW: Ironic how?

OLSON: We have the audacity to blow up a universe when we're the only pigeon-hole left who hasn't gotten word of the Grand Cosmic Finale. I told you, the stars are gone. Poof! Not a twinkle left in the sky — we're just very late getting the word. Ironic, yes? But a far greater irony would be to keep on living in the universe as if it still existed! That would give us the last laugh.

WILLOW: You're pulling my leg.

OLSON: Literally, that would be a pleasure.

(BILL and JOE enter.)

OLSON: "The Twelfth Habit: Hubby Runs Off With The Leading Lady."

(He rather whisks Willow away.)

JOE: I'd say he's taken quite an interest in her.
BILL: He's not the only one.
JOE: If you brought me out here to recite your litany about Pill—
BILL: I didn't.
JOE: It's your fifth drink obsession.
BILL: I've finally got it figured out. It's not Pill.
JOE: How can you believe Willow's having an affair with anyone?
BILL: I live with her. I know.
JOE: So if it's not our renowned drama critic, who is it?
BILL: I have a very clear idea about that.
JOE: The suspense is killing me.
BILL: Think about it. Joe.
JOE: This is all your active imagination inspired by alcohol.
BILL: Really think about it. It's so goddamn obvious. It hit me when I was telling Olson the plot of my script. It's like I knew subconsciously all the time and was writing it down, while consciously I suspected Pill.
JOE: So who is it?
BILL: As soon as you hear the name, you'll know I'm right.
JOE: Did you drag me out here to tell me or not?
BILL: I want to be sure I'm right. I'm going to confront her with it.
JOE: And when does this little soap opera take place?
BILL: Soon.
JOE: Not here, I hope.
BILL: The culprit's here.
JOE: This is still my castle, buddy, and a little scene like that is something I can very well do without. I'm telling you, she's not having an affair. I'd give odds.
BILL: She is, but it ain't with Dean Pill.
JOE: I don't want a scene. I mean it.
BILL: Don't worry about it.

(He starts off.)

JOE: Where are you going?
BILL: To find Willow.

(ANN and CYNTHIA meet BILL at the sliding door.)

BILL: Help yourself, I was just leaving.
JOE: *(following Bill)* Great party!

(The men are gone.)

CYNTHIA: Well?
ANN: I can't do this any more.
CYNTHIA: Good. Then stop. What did all that marching around really accomplish tonight? Nothing. You lost as many votes as you may've gained.
ANN: I don't mean that. The opposite, in fact. I feel like Mary in the play. I can't avoid looking in the mirror any longer.
CYNTHIA: So what is it you feel like doing?
ANN: Being who I am. Telling everybody here who I am. Telling everybody here who we are together.
CYNTHIA: Looking in the mirror means you have to play show-and-tell?
ANN: I think it does, yes. Otherwise I'm living a lie.
CYNTHIA: Everybody makes compromises. Suddenly you tell everybody here and . . .
ANN: And what?
CYNTHIA: I can't believe we're talking about this. Ever since Todd got here, I feel like I'm in a soap opera.
ANN: *(hamming it up)* "I can't be discrete a minute longer. I have to drop the mask. I have to show the world who I really am: Ann Barton, Diesel Dyke!"
CYNTHIA: That's not funny.
ANN: We've become very different, haven't we?
CYNTHIA: Perhaps so. I thought we'd resolved this in San Francisco.
ANN: To your satisfaction, not mine.
CYNTHIA: You chose to come to Portland with me.
ANN: Because I love you. I'm just not sure how much I love myself any more. There are people out there who want to burn us at the stake, Cynthia — how can you just let that happen?
CYNTHIA: I think that's political paranoia. No one wants to burn anyone at the stake.

ANN: It starts with something like this, a harmless sounding law, a little restriction here and there, no gays in public office, no this, no that, the next thing you know—

CYNTHIA: Ann, somebody can come out here any minute.

ANN: What are you afraid of?

CYNTHIA: What about our livelihood? The business world is a very conservative environment.

ANN: We've been through this a hundred times. Who needs clients who are bigots?

(OLSON enters.)

OLSON: Ta da!

CYNTHIA: You look polluted.

OLSON: Scorn rolls off my back — because, for a brief moment, I've been in love with Willow. Unfortunately, her husband has just claimed squatter's rights. Robert Olson is crushed. But don't worry, my ex! I feel a second wind coming. For one quick private moment, Todd Westlake breathes deeply . . . and I'm quickly back into my disguise.

CYNTHIA: Please stay in it this time.

OLSON: Are you two spatting again?

ANN: We were, as a matter of fact.

CYNTHIA: Jesus Christ . . .

OLSON: We share heroes! To J.C. Cheers.

ANN: I think the play went very well. Don't you?

OLSON: Except for those idiotic questions at the end.

ANN: You made it clear enough you didn't like them.

OLSON: I was hoping I did.

CYNTHIA: Joe tells me you're leaving tomorrow.

OLSON: "Heart Song" calls.

ANN: When does your plane leave? I was hoping you'd speak at the rally.

CYNTHIA: By all means, speak at the rally. I'm sure you and Ann have much in common.

(She starts away.)

OLSON: Fetch the cast! I want to toast the cast.

ANN: A splendid idea. I'll get them.

(She exits. OLSON and CYNTHIA are alone.)

150

OLSON: Don't say it. You think I'm drunk. But I'm not! I'm the guest of honor. I'm the author of "Half-Life." And I am merely — high.

CYNTHIA: I hope you—

OLSON: Sshh! Mum's the word. You thought I forgot. Mum's the word! From now til the end . . .

CYNTHIA: And what's the end?

OLSON: Sleep.

CYNTHIA: Passing out.

OLSON: Same difference. The end justifies the means. *(saluting, singing)* "Oh, say can you see? By the dawn's early light…"

CYNTHIA: I'm sincerely sorry to see you like this. You have a talent that deserves better. "Half-Life" is a thought-provoking play. I'm glad we did it. Too bad you had to make such an ass of yourself afterwards.

OLSON: *(toasting)* The Seventeenth Habit: Hubby Is An Asshole.

(The others come out onto the deck: ANN, BILL, WILLOW, JOE.)

OLSON: The invasion of the body snatchers! I fabricate from the swills of my insomnia a family of friends to whom you, and you alone, give flesh and bone. A toast to my cast! To actors! To body snatchers everywhere!

BILL: Hear-hear!

(They all drink.)

OLSON: *(mock seriousness)* I suppose you all wonder why I asked you here tonight.

BILL: It's morning, Bobby.

OLSON: To play a game! We all love games, don't we? Why else are we in theater but to play games? Well, this is the "Heart Song" game. This is one of the games we play in Hollywood. I don't play it, the actors play it. I watch it. All the writers watch it. The actors play it and then we steal their best lines and rush to the office and plagiarize.

ANN: It's a theater game?

OLSON: It's the "Heart Song" game. It's a game for soap operas. What is soap opera? A drama of deceit. Therefore, it is the purest form of drama in our time. This is a game about deceit, and at the studio we call it, "The Truth, the Whole Truth and Nothing But." I think it would be fun to play it. Anybody too chickenshit?

CYNTHIA: Perhaps some of us have had too much to drink.

OLSON: Don't be a goddamn mother hen. You're going to play, and they're going to play, and even I'm going to play. I've never played it before. I only watch and steal lines.

JOE: So what are the rules?

OLSON: Let me illustrate. I am "it" and I pick someone. Eenie meenie miney moe. Willow!

WILLOW: What do I do?

OLSON: I'm trying to explain. I'm "it" and I pick you. I then make up a sentence that begins with "If ..." I put in everything before the comma and you complete the rest of the sentence. You can do so truthfully or falsefully. We try to figure out which. That's the point of the game.

JOE: We'd better have a dry run.

OLSON: I am "it." Willow: "If I were to commit adultery . . ." By "I", I mean you. "If I were to commit adultery . . ." You finish the sentence.

ANN: This could get pretty heavy.

OLSON: A game of deceit. "The Truth, the Whole Truth and Nothing But."

WILLOW: I can complete the sentence any way I want?

OLSON: The human imagination is limitless.

WILLOW: Okay. "I'd commit adultery with—"

OLSON: Repeat the whole sentence.

WILLOW: "If I were to commit adultery, I'd commit it with Tom Cruise."

OLSON: Do any of you body snatchers want to challenge that?

BILL: Yeah. What if Cruise isn't willing to go along?

WILLOW: I was stating a preference.

OLSON: Anyone else? Then we believe her? It's Willow's turn to be "it."

CYNTHIA: This is very exciting, isn't it?

OLSON: It depends.

ANN: On how honest we're willing to be.

OLSON: Thank you. Willow?

WILLOW: I can ask anyone?

OLSON: Anyone.

WILLOW: Ann: "If I were to play Mary again in another production of 'Half-Life' . . ."

ANN: That's easy. If I were to play Mary again, I'd play her the same way — as a woman embracing her true self for the first time.

BILL: I have a question. If everyone tells the truth, how does anything happen?

OLSON: It doesn't. Interest in this game is based on deceit.

ANN: I'm "it." Cynthia.

CYNTHIA: Since we're all going to tell the truth, and nothing happens when we do, why don't we play something else?

ANN: I need a second to phrase it right.

CYNTHIA: I think we should be mixing with the others. They'll think we're hogging the guest of honor to ourselves.

ANN: Cynthia: "If I were to marry . . ."

CYNTHIA: If I were to marry . . .?

ANN: Right.

CYNTHIA: If I were to marry, I wouldn't marry you.

BILL: That's great! You're it.

ANN: I challenge that.

BILL: How the hell can you challenge? She'd have to be queer.

OLSON: Ann challenges you.

CYNTHIA: So how am I supposed to defend myself? Whom I marry is my business and if you don't believe me, what can I possibly say that would change anyone's mind?

JOE: *(to Ann)* She has a point. She'd have to be gay to marry you.

CYNTHIA: And even if I was gay, I certainly wouldn't marry my business partner. You know what they say about business and pleasure.

OLSON: Nicely done! Ann?

ANN: I guess that answers my challenge. Nice job.

OLSON: Cynthia is "it."

CYNTHIA: Robert: "If you were to rewrite 'Half-Life' . . ."

OLSON: If I was to rewrite "Half-Life" . . . that's heavier than it sounds.

BILL: I'd set it in Los Angeles! Sorry.

OLSON: If I were to rewrite "Half-Life," I'd try to think of an ending that was less of a self-fulfilling prophecy. I'd try to think of something so he wouldn't blow them away. I don't know if I could find anything I could believe but at least I'd look harder for it.

CYNTHIA: Challenges?

OLSON: Then I'm "it." Ann.

ANN: Yes?

OLSON: "If I were gay . . ."

BILL: Oh boy.

OLSON: You'd be surprised at the insights into their characters that the actors come up with. After we play the game, we improv situations and they come to that with more depth, more dimension, as a result of the game. Makes for a goddamn tidy script.

ANN: And you like tidy scripts.

OLSON: The tidier the better.

ANN: If I were gay . . .?

BILL: You wouldn't marry Cynthia either!

CYNTHIA: I'm going to get a drink.

(She exits.)

ANN: It's really not fair to pass in this game, is it?

OLSON: There's no need to pass. When in doubt, lie.

ANN: I see. Okay: "If I were gay, then I'd be who I already am."

(A pause.)

BILL: Well, I challenge.

OLSON: Ann?

ANN: Don't challenge, Bill.

BILL: "When in doubt, lie."

ANN: But it's the truth. I'm gay.

JOE: You're not serious?

ANN: I am very serious. Hey, lighten up, it's okay, I don't bite. I've been gay for as long as I can remember. 'Bout time I 'fessed up, don't you think? Why are you all looking at me like that?

BILL: I think you're pulling our leg.

ANN: Fine. Think whatever you want.

OLSON: I believe you.

ANN: Thank you, Robert. It's nice to be accepted for who I am.

WILLOW: I believe you, too.

BILL: Come on!

(CYNTHIA returns. An awkward pause.)

CYNTHIA: Did I miss something?

ANN: Robert Olson's little game has inspired me to admit that I'm gay. I hope this won't jeopardize our business relationship.

CYNTHIA: No, of course not.

BILL: I still think you're putting us on.

WILLOW: That's because you're homophobic. I'm getting a drink.

(She exits.)

BILL: *(after her)* Hey, I have a couple friends who are queer!

ANN: I think I can use a drink myself.

OLSON: Let me escort you.

154

ANN: I'd like that.

(OLSON and ANN exit.)

CYNTHIA: *(nervous)* Why should it affect our business relationship? But what a surprise! Aren't you surprised?

BILL: I still think she's putting us on. She's always had a weird sense of humor.

CYNTHIA: Who can say? If you'll excuse me . . . .

(She exits.)

BILL: No way. I've acted with her for two or three years now. She flirts with me.

JOE: I think I believe her.

BILL: I acted with her in *I Do, I Do*. I kept wishing I did, I did. If she's queer, what a waste.

JOE: Ready for a drink?

BILL: In a minute. I have an apology to make.

JOE: Oh?

BILL: It's Pill, after all. I mean, it was. Willow confessed everything.

JOE: She did?

BILL: She and Pill have been doing their little number for about three months but she broke it off last week. She's been trying to get the courage to tell me.

JOE: But you were so sure it wasn't Pill.

BILL: I guess because I'd been sure it was him from the beginning and couldn't stand living with it any longer. The truth is, I'd decided it was you.

JOE: You've got to be kidding.

BILL: In my script, it's the guy's best friend. Maybe I started confusing art and reality. Sorry about that.

JOE: Well, forget it. Did you tell Willow you thought it was me?

BILL: Didn't get a chance to. I told her I knew she was having an affair, and that for a long time I thought it was with Pill, and she just came out and confessed everything. Anyway, it's out and it's over. We can pick up the pieces.

JOE: I'm happy for you.

BILL: How about that drink?

(They exit. A pause. ANN and OLSON enter.)

ANN: You don't like any rough edges, do you?

OLSON: "The truth shall set us free." Which is probably a crock.

ANN: I feel relieved. Free, if you will.

OLSON: I feel sorry for Cynthia.

ANN: Yes.

OLSON: Discretion has its place.

ANN: So does honesty.

OLSON: There's a book that's a favorite of mine. *Pygmies and Dream Giants* by Kilton Stewart. Stewart lived with a tribe on some island, in the South Pacific as I recall, and the tribe had never experienced war in their society. Besides being an anthropologist, Stewart was something of an amateur shrink, so he tried to find out just what it was about their society that negated war. To make a long story short, he discovered that these pygmies believed their dreams.

ANN: I'm not sure I follow.

OLSON: Literally. If they dreamed it, it happened. It literally happened. Dreams were just as real as action. Dreams *were* an action. For example, if one pygmy dreamed of seducing another pygmy's wife, it was as real as committing adultery. It *was* adultery. So he'd wake up feeling guilty as hell, and get his ass over to the other pygmy's hut and say, Look, man, last night I made it with your old lady, and I'm sorry as hell about that, so here's my fattest pig and three chickens and a couple gallons of home brew, so let's call it even, okay? In their dreams they did any damn thing they wanted but always woke up guilty as hell, so instead of war you had all these pigs and possessions being passed around all over hell, and nobody blew anybody away.

ANN: When women had dreams like that, did they also give away family property?

OLSON: I don't remember if Stewart recorded any dreams by women.

ANN: We do dream.

OLSON: As I recall, he concentrated on male dreams.

ANN: Same old patriarchy.

OLSON: It's interesting reading, all the same. I've always wanted to mention that book in a play.

ANN: Why haven't you?

OLSON: The critics would kill me. They'd say, "Book reviews are not dramatic. Book reviews are boring." Ideas aren't supposed to be interesting in their own right. Least of all, to a playwright.

ANN: I take it the critics aren't kind to you.

OLSON: They used to love me, when I wrote fluff like "Roses for the Road." A columnist once called me "one of L.A.'s most precious natural resources." Three years later I didn't even make his list of the 200 most interesting writers in town.

ANN: What does it matter what the critics think?

OLSON: Spoken like a woman who just came out of the closet.

ANN: Thanks for inspiring me to do that.

OLSON: Maybe I can thank you for something some day.

ANN: You already can.

OLSON: Then, thanks.

ANN: "Half-Life" didn't win the contest.

OLSON: Against my better judgment, I'll say, "go on."

ANN: There's no way a community theater would take a chance with material like that. After Cynthia vetoed "Roses for the Road," the committee wanted to do another piece of mush. So I took it upon myself to write you that you'd won — and then all I had to do was convince Cynthia to convince the committee.

OLSON: You made the decision alone?

ANN: The theater was in a rut. I thought your play had something important to say about masculinity. Fortunately, you wrote back so enthusiastically about winning that no one had the heart to take the prize away. So here you are.

OLSON: And Cynthia went along with you?

ANN: She made all the difference in the world. For a while, it looked like the committee was going to disown both of us. She really got behind the play in the end. Of course, she didn't know you were Robert Olson.

OLSON: Hubby Plays Guinea Pig . . . I wish you hadn't told me.

ANN: "The truth shall set us free."

OLSON: "Don't take any wooden nickels." Or something.

ANN: Let's go inside and dance.

OLSON: You expect to find a partner?

ANN: I want to dance with you.

OLSON: You do?

ANN: That's why I asked you.

OLSON: Won't Cynthia be jealous?

ANN: She has to live her own life.

OLSON: I'm a lousy dancer.

ANN: You really do wish I hadn't told you.

OLSON: Delusions of grandeur are so invigorating.

ANN: You're still a hero to everybody else. Only Cynthia and I know the truth.

OLSON: And, alas, myself.

ANN: Consider it grist for the mill. You can write a play about all this.

OLSON: I wouldn't know where to begin.

ANN: A playwright wins a contest . . . he comes to a strange city to see the premiere only to discover that his play is directed by his ex-wife . . . who left him for a San Francisco dyke . . .

OLSON: No, for a most interesting woman indeed. But later to discover that actually he didn't win the contest at all.

ANN: See? Sounds like Hitchcock already.

OLSON: I don't like it.

ANN: I'm serious, I think this material has real possibilities.

OLSON: There's no accounting for taste.

(They exit to BLACKOUT.)

2/ Fallout (3:30 a.m.)

(JOE and CYNTHIA are alone on the deck. The background noise of the party is gone now. We hear a car driving away below.)

CYNTHIA: I hope Bill's not driving.

JOE: Willow, I think.

CYNTHIA: They should be fine then.

JOE: Yes, they'll be fine.

(A pause.)

JOE: We were having an affair.

CYNTHIA: I know. You said "were."

JOE: We ended it tonight.

CYNTHIA: I'm sorry. Or is that condoning adultery?

JOE: You know how these little theater flings go.

CYNTHIA: You still care for her.

JOE: Yes.

CYNTHIA: Then I am sorry.

JOE: I guess you have your own problems. Ann.

CYNTHIA: Ann? Well, that's hardly my problem.

JOE: A thing like that can hurt your business.

CYNTHIA: Then we'll have to find more tolerant clients.

JOE: I was surprised but then when I thought about it, it made perfect sense. I don't recall ever seeing her with a man. In a dating situation, I mean.

(A pause.)

JOE: Nor you.

CYNTHIA: I'm a workaholic. You've been directed by me enough to know that.

JOE: You never suspected, sharing a house with her and all?

CYNTHIA: Never. I don't see much of her other than at work. We each have our own floor.

JOE: That's good.

CYNTHIA: Actually I've been thinking of moving closer in. The drive is getting to me.

JOE: I don't blame you. I've never liked the suburbs.

(A pause.)

JOE: May I ask you a personal question?

CYNTHIA: The answer is no, I'm not gay.

JOE: Wouldn't matter if you were.

CYNTHIA: The real answer, of course, is that it's none of your damn business. And I do date men, as a matter of fact.

JOE: Anyone in particular?

CYNTHIA: A pilot for United. Given both of our schedules, we don't get to see one another more than once or twice a month. But then I've always believed in quality in a relationship, not quantity. Anything else you want to know?

JOE: Sorry, I was curious.

CYNTHIA: Being in business with Ann, I'm sure I'll be asked that question quite often now that she's come out of the closet, so to speak. People are so damn nosy.

(ANN enters.)

ANN: Cynthia, can I speak to you a minute?

JOE: I was just leaving. Where's Olson?

ANN: Stretched out on the floor in front of the stereo. He found your dixieland tapes.

JOE: Pretty drunk out tonight.

(He exits.)

ANN: I'll move out right away.

CYNTHIA: No, I'm moving out. I want to live closer in.

ANN: I don't mind if—

CYNTHIA: I mind.

ANN: Whatever you want.

CYNTHIA: I want that you take the car home. I'll get Joe to give me a lift later.

ANN: You're spending the night here?

CYNTHIA: Please don't say you fear for my safety. Alone with a man and all that.

ANN: I don't feel like I owe you an apology, Cynthia. I did what I had to do.

(A pause.)

ANN: Can we still be in business together?

CYNTHIA: I hope so.

ANN: I could take my vacation.

CYNTHIA: Perhaps you should.

ANN: We ought to be able to work together.

CYNTHIA: I should think so.

ANN: I still care for you.

(A pause.)

ANN: I'm really not an extremist, you know. I won't do anything to embarrass the business.

CYNTHIA: I hope not.

ANN: I think you're quite safe. There may be a few suspicions at first, since we live together and all, but you're very good at creating whatever impression you want.

CYNTHIA: It's a present nuisance but, yes, I'm sure I'm safe.

ANN: You're a very good actress.

CYNTHIA: The keys are in my purse. In the livingroom.

ANN: Thanks.

CYNTHIA: You'll have to step over Todd.

ANN: Perhaps.

CYNTHIA: You two seem to have hit it off.

ANN: Better than I would have thought.

CYNTHIA: I didn't know you could dance so well.

ANN: I haven't danced in years. I like dancing again.

CYNTHIA: Will you be taking a vacation then?

ANN: To San Francisco, I think.

CYNTHIA: Of course.

ANN: Sure you can handle the load alone?

CYNTHIA: Summer's our slow time.

ANN: Then I'll leave Monday.

CYNTHIA: Fine.

ANN: I understand you a little better now, I think.

CYNTHIA: Then something's been accomplished.

ANN: Being who I am, I understand better who you are. Can't you say the same?

(A pause.)

ANN: Cynthia? Can't you say the same?

(They embrace. They are still embraced when OLSON enters.)

OLSON: Hubby needs a lobotomy.

(The women move apart.)

OLSON: What is it about marriage that fights become the excuse for making up? I mean, you two might as well be married, right?

CYNTHIA: *(to Ann)* The keys are in my purse. If you see anyone in San Francisco . . .

ANN: I'll give them your best. See you back at the office.

OLSON: You're leaving?

ANN: Keep writing plays. Bye.

(She exits.)

OLSON: Where's she going?

CYNTHIA: Home.

OLSON: Alone?

CYNTHIA: I think I'll go lie down.

OLSON: Wait a minute. Listen, I know I turn into some kind of a halfass loudmouth when I'm drinking but, seriously, is there anything I can do?

CYNTHIA: I don't think so.

OLSON: You're breaking up, aren't you? Well, I have prior service. A real vet at breaking up. Not only you, I've lived with three ladies since us and broke up with every one of them. I've got experience. Know what I learned?

CYNTHIA: What did you learn?

OLSON: If you're the one being left, it's best to leave town. If you're the one moving out, it's best to throw the whole damn mess, I mean the actual labor of moving, into the lap of a good friend. Which are you?

CYNTHIA: I've been wanting to move closer in for some time now.

OLSON: How much furniture do you have? I'll help you move out.

CYNTHIA: Be serious.

OLSON: I am serious. I'll rent a damn truck and move you wherever you want to go. Into storage if you have no place to stay.

CYNTHIA: I thought you were flying right back.

OLSON: I'll get a later flight. Two hours sleep and I'm raring to go. What do you say? I'm one hell of a truck driver.

CYNTHIA: Why do you want to get involved?

OLSON: We used to be married, for Christ's sake. We had some good times.

CYNTHIA: Yes, there were some good times.

(A car drives away below, ANN going home alone. CYNTHIA is about to lose it..)

OLSON: Don't worry about it. Ann has to live her life. You have to live yours. Discretion has its place.

CYNTHIA: *(bittersweet)* Discretion . . .

OLSON: It's the best I can do on such short notice. I also think it's the truth.

CYNTHIA: I hated it in San Francisco. Every time we went into a gay bar, I sat in terror, worrying that one of our clients would walk in. Then one night one did — a woman whose PR we handled. The way she looked at me, so . . . so knowingly. I didn't want her to know anything about me. I didn't want to make a statement about my sexuality. Why does sexuality have to be political? It's so — personal. Maybe sex belongs in the closet, like a special part of the wardrobe saved for special occasions.

(A pause.)

OLSON: Ann told me about how "Half-Life" got done. I appreciate your support when it counted.

CYNTHIA: I'm sorry you had to find out.

162

OLSON: "The truth shall set us free" and so on. So what do you say? Let me rent a truck. I love driving truck! It's so goddamn macho I can't stand it. I'll turn up some country music on the radio and haul your furniture all goddamn day.

CYNTHIA: Let's talk about it when I can think straight.

OLSON: I'm staying at the hotel, the what's-it's-name. Joe knows. Give me a buzz when you're ready.

CYNTHIA: I'm going to lie down.

OLSON: I have to get a taxi.

CYNTHIA: I'll call one. Let's have a late breakfast and talk about moving me out.

OLSON: I'm one hell of a macho truck driver, lady.

CYNTHIA: I'm sure you are. Goodnight, Todd.

OLSON: Sshh! Mum's the word.

CYNTHIA: Mum's the word.

(She exits. OLSON stares out at the skyline. Then he looks higher, to the stars in a clear sky.)

OLSON: Twinkle, twinkle,
Little star,
How I wonder,
What you are ...

(JOE enters.)

JOE: Taxi shouldn't be long.

OLSON: You goddamn stud.

JOE: Pardon me?

OLSON: I heard about the number you're doing with Willow.

JOE: Oh that. That ended a while back.

OLSON: How so?

JOE: You know — variety's the spice of life. Time to move on to better things.

OLSON: Better than Willow?

JOE: Surely you're not a one-woman man. Not in Hollywood.

OLSON: For me to know and you to find out.

JOE: Or maybe you're gay. Every time you turn around these days, somebody you know turns out to be gay.

OLSON: If I was a woman, I'd be gay.

JOE: That's a little convoluted . . .

OLSON: You and Willow. I think I'm jealous.

JOE: We got together when we played the leads in "Barefoot in the Park." You know how those things happen. The play ended and, well, frankly she bores me now.

OLSON: You played the newscaster, you can always fuck the radio.

JOE: I'm doing quite well, thank you.

OLSON: A real stud.

JOE: No complaints.

OLSON: View like this ought to get them in the mood.

JOE: It doesn't hurt.

OLSON: You ever make it with Willow out here on the deck?

JOE: For me to know and you to find out. Will I be seeing you again before you leave?

OLSON: I'm having breakfast with Cynthia. Then I think I'm going to drive truck.

JOE: Drive truck?

OLSON: What the hell's wrong with driving truck?

(OLSON begins to make the sounds of driving truck — the engine roaring, shifting gears.)

JOE: You'll be able to see the taxi from here. Goodnight.

(OLSON still plays driving truck. JOE exits. OLSON suddenly gestures toward the stars, his voice trailing off as if he's sending his truck out into the universe.)

OLSON: Twinkle, twinkle,
Little star,
How I wonder . . .

(OLSON stares out at the skyline.)

OLSON: How I wonder . . .

(Suddenly OLSON makes the noise of a great explosion and his arms reach forward, then trace the rising outline of a mushroom cloud. The gesture is almost sensuous, as if he were tracing a woman's figure. When the cloud has risen, OLSON is looking up at the stars.)

OLSON: And it came to pass that all the stars in the firmament had ceased to shine. But how was anyone to know?

164

(OLSON looks up at the stars. Slow fade to BLACKOUT. THE PLAY IS OVER.)

For royalties information:
contact Charles Deemer
1-800-294-7176
cdeemer@teleport.com

1985

Waitresses
a play in two acts

First performed at the Cubiculo Theatre in Portland, Oregon, on October 11, 1985. Directed by Peter Fornara.

THE CAST:
Ruby, *late 30s, a waitress and closet country songwriter*
Jill, *21, her daughter*
Duncan, *40s, a wannabe country singer*

THE SET:
Ruby's trailer. Kitchen. Living area.

THE TIME:
The 1980s. Central Oregon.

ACT ONE

1/ day

(AT RISE: RUBY is in the kitchen drinking coffee. DUNCAN'S SONG, "Stale Beer In The Morning, Stale Lovin' At Night," plays on a tape deck. Packed boxes are stacked everywhere. DUNCAN enters, exchanges a silent glance with Ruby, then exits to bedroom. Ruby turns off the tape deck.)

JILL *(off-stage)*: Duncan, hon? I'm listening to that!
RUBY: You know the trouble with being a daughter? You make the same mistakes your mother did!

(RUBY laughs.)

RUBY *(louder, to get a reaction)*: Every daughter makes the same mistakes her mother did!

(JILL enters, carrying a box, setting it down near the others at the door.)

JILL: What?
RUBY: Cheers.

(She sips her coffee.)

JILL: Mother, I'm not going to feel guilty, so you can just quit trying to make me feel like I'm doing something wrong.
RUBY: Every daughter makes the same mistakes her mother made — that's a law of nature.
JILL: If you'd gone to Nashville twenty years ago, instead of feeling sorry for yourself—
RUBY: I couldn't go anywhere — I was taking care of you.
JILL: When I was old enough for someone else to look after me, if you'd taken your songs to Nashville—
RUBY: I never wrote a decent song in my life til I was 25.
JILL: You wrote "The Ballad of a Teenage Mother" while you were carrying me.
RUBY: That wasn't a song — it's the story of my life.

167

JILL: It's a good song, and if you'd taken it to Nashville—
RUBY: My life story isn't for sale.
JILL: If you'd taken any of your songs to Nashville, maybe you wouldn't still be waiting tables in Rimrock.
RUBY: Right. I'd be waiting tables in Nashville.

(JILL starts out for another box.)

RUBY *(after her)*: I don't want to live in Nashville. I hate tourists. It's bad enough here, during hunting season.

(DUNCAN enters for another load.)

DUNCAN *(to JILL)*: I'm gonna get a coke. You want one?
RUBY: No thank you.
DUNCAN: Jill?
JILL: No thanks, hon.
RUBY: How sweet of you to ask.
DUNCAN *(to JILL)*: You getting close?
JILL: Just the kitchen and my clothes.

(DUNCAN exits.)

RUBY *(after him)*: What's your hurry? If you're so goddamned talented, what's the big rush?

(JILL exits upstage and RUBY follows behind, to the doorway.)

RUBY: Reno. Couldn't you at least make it Winnemucca? Nobody in the family ever got married in Winnemucca. I don't know anybody got married in Winnemucca.

(JILL is back with another box.)

RUBY: Or Las Vegas? He shoulda checked out Las Vegas — he probably expects to be singing there some day. You might as well start at the top — big Las Vegas wedding — they'll probably give you free drinks and the honeymoon suite and a stack of quarters to gamble with.

(RUBY moves to fill her coffee cup.)

168

RUBY *(as she's walking)*: But if you got your heart set on Reno — then by God nobody's gonna change it. Nobody coulda changed mine. I thought a Reno wedding was romantic, that's how goddamn stupid I was. I hope to Christ you don't think it's gonna be romantic.

JILL: I told you, Reno's on the way to Nashville.

RUBY: So's Boise — and you hit the Interstate quicker. Nobody in my family ever got married in Boise. You can become a Mormon while you're at it.

JILL: Mother — there's no reason why this should be so hard on you. I'm an adult.

RUBY: You're right. It's not like last time.

JILL: Is that what this is about? Jesus . . .

RUBY: Reno's better than Tiajuana and twenty-one's better than seventeen. I've been a hell of a mother, haven't I? Daughter learns the facts of life just like that.

JILL: I don't believe you. He's trying to make something of himself. You'd think you'd support that — for my sake.

RUBY: Who's buying the gas? Who's paying for the ticket at the wedding factory?

JILL: Duncan is, as a matter of fact.

RUBY: You taking your savings?

(JILL doesn't reply.)

RUBY: You left the receipt on the table yesterday. He hasn't been working, so who's footing the bills when his last unemployment check runs out? You think it's cheap to cut a demo in Nashville?

JILL: What would you know about Nashville? Nothing!

RUBY: I read about Nashville every month.

JILL: In a magazine.

RUBY: Articles written behind the scenes by people in the business. They'll eat that poor boy alive.

JILL: So what? At least he's trying. At least he doesn't sit around and bitch and cry in his beer. At least he's gonna try.

(Now it's RUBY's turn to be quiet. Pause.)

JILL: I was hoping I could get your best wishes.

(No reply.)

JILL: Is that too much to ask?

(No reply. Jill pours herself a coffee.)

RUBY: You're too goddamn much like me, is the problem.
JILL: There's lots of differences, too.
RUBY: Not in what matters. You're too gullible, just like me. A man can sweet-talk you into anything.
JILL: Nobody's sweet-talked me into a baby yet.

(This has stung a little.)

JILL: That didn't come out like I meant it.
RUBY: No, you're right. I was sweet-talked into having you.
JILL: And I've ruined your life . . .?

(This is the signal. Ruby gets up and they embrace. And for the next few moments, they are genuinely close.)

RUBY: Oh, baby . . .
JILL: I'm gonna be okay, mama . . .
RUBY: I just don't want you to get hurt.
JILL: I got to live my own life. I'm too young to hibernate.
RUBY: Is that what I do?
JILL: You don't date anyone any more.
RUBY: Hell, I know the dirt on every asshole in the county . . .
JILL: Duncan's different. He really is. He knows staying here is death.
RUBY: A would-be country singer...just like somebody I'd fall for at your age.
JILL: Then you should give him a chance.
RUBY: I wanted life to be easier for you.
JILL: It's never easy, mama. Everybody's got to do it their own way, according to their own desires.
RUBY: This is your desire, taking your savings and going to Nashville to get eaten alive by—
JILL: Now hush. I won't have talk like that.
RUBY: I just don't want him using you.
JILL: Nashville's my idea anyway. I swear to God, Duncan's just like you — he thinks there's nobody in Nashville but crooked promoters and song thieves. Well, I read those magazines every month, too, and every now and then a dream comes true.

RUBY: But the odds — he shoulda started slow, maybe send them a tape first and see if anybody likes it.

JILL: Nobody can sell you like you yourself can. That's exactly what I told him.

RUBY: Nashville's your idea?

JILL: Duncan's scared. I don't think he'd even try without me. So I gotta stand beside him because I think he's really got it.

RUBY: But what have you got?

JILL: Faith in him.

RUBY: But what have you got inside yourself that's yours no matter what, that you can lean back on no matter what, that nobody can take away from you?

JILL: I've got you.

RUBY: Oh, sugar...

(They embrace again.)

JILL *(breaking it)*: Help me pack?

RUBY: Sure.

(Together they'll pack a box of dishes and glasses from cupboards.)

JILL: Mother, I do know what I'm doing.

(RUBY doesn't reply. A beat, as they pack.)

JILL: What do you hear from Wayne?

RUBY: You know how Wayne is, always talking through his hat.

JILL: You said he was going to record your new song.

RUBY: This weekend, he wants to—

JILL: Mama, that's wonderful!

RUBY: You know nothing's gonna come of it.

JILL: At least you'll hear it. Have a copy of it for yourself.

RUBY: I heard it at the tavern Saturday night.

JILL: Well, then — don't you want a copy for yourself?

RUBY: What am I supposed to do, listen to my own song all day?

JILL: If it's good, why not?

RUBY: That'd make me feel funny. Like I got a swelled head.

JILL: You write good songs.

RUBY: It takes more than talent. I hope Duncan knows that.

JILL: It takes taking a chance — which is just what we're doing.

RUBY: In more ways than one.

JILL: Will you stop worrying about me for one minute?

RUBY: Promise you'll come right home if something happens?

JILL: I'm too old to run home to mama.

RUBY: You're never too old. That's what I'm here for. If something happens and you need help, you call me collect. Promise me.

JILL: Nothing's gonna happen.

RUBY: You just know you can, in case of emergency.

JILL: I know I can.

RUBY: Good. You keep that in the back of your mind and I'll sleep better.

JILL: Aren't you never gonna let go, mama?

RUBY: You're all I've got . . .

(JILL hugs her.)

JILL: You need to get out more. You need more friends.

RUBY: I'm doing fine.

JILL: Wayne's been wanting to take you out, you know he has.

RUBY: Wayne drinks too much.

JILL: Maybe he needs a good woman.

RUBY: A man that needs a woman to keep from drinking is no man to waste time worrying about.

JILL: I've seen the way Rod McNeill looks at you.

RUBY: Will you let me be? The day I want a man, I'm perfectly capable of finding my own.

JILL: Are you ever gonna want a man again? That's what I'm asking.

RUBY: Why should I need a man anyway? I'm doing perfectly fine.

JILL: Don't you get lonely at night, in that big bed all alone?

RUBY: Not that lonely.

JILL: Don't you miss cuddling?

RUBY: Not with someone keeping me awake with his snoring. You got enough worries ahead of you, girl, without fretting about my lovelife. I'll get me one of those vibrators before I hook up with—

JILL: What are you doing thinking about vibrators? They give me the creeps, all plastic and cold...

RUBY: Betty Hale swears by hers.

JILL: Betty Hale has a vibrator? She doesn't!

RUBY: Swears by it. It's pink and has three speeds.

JILL: Three speeds! Speeds — how?

RUBY: What do you mean, how?

JILL: You mean speeds like in and out?

RUBY: Heavens, no! I mean vibrating speeds. She says it beats any man and then some. Always there when you need it and lasts forever, with three speeds for variety.

JILL: That's unnatural.

RUBY: You get my age, having experienced what I have, and you wonder how natural the male half of the race is.

JILL: You know your problem? You never found a man after daddy.

RUBY: They don't come down the pike like him too often.

JILL: I wish I'd known him.

RUBY: He worshipped you, little he got to see you before going to the hospital. His last days, he lived for me bringing you in so he could hold you.

JILL: It's not fair, him dying so young.

RUBY: Nobody ever said life is fair.

JILL: But twenty years, and you're still not over it.

RUBY: Oh, I can barely remember him myself. I look at his picture in the bedroom and it's like something I clipped from a magazine. Like he's a movie star, and I'm some dopey-eyed teenager, fantasizing about what life shoulda been. He wasn't perfect, to tell the truth. He'd get moody and wouldn't talk to me for days at a time.

JILL: Don't, mama. Just remember the good things.

(The dishes are packed now. Jill carries the box to the doorway, Ruby following behind.)

RUBY: More coffee?

JILL: Just half a cup.

(RUBY pours coffee.)

RUBY: You get your last check from Frank?

JILL: Yesterday.

RUBY: You should've given him more notice than you did.

JILL: I don't owe that man nothing.

RUBY: He didn't have to give you a job.

JILL: You got me the job.

RUBY: He's still the boss, he had to go along with it. You don't give people notice, he won't be so obliging next time.

JILL: Won't be a next time.

RUBY: When you talk like that, that's when there's a next time.

JILL: I have faith in Duncan, I really do. I think he's gonna get himself a recording contract.

RUBY: Oh my word.

JILL: He's good enough.

RUBY: Talent has nothing to do with it.

JILL: He has more than talent, he's taking the trouble to get there, to fight for what he believes in.

RUBY: Listen to her!

JILL: You *should* listen to me. When he gets his contract, he'll be looking for new songs besides his own. If you'd write something a man could sing—

RUBY: I can't write about what I don't understand.

JILL: Men are people, too.

RUBY: Then they should act like people.

JILL: Honestly, you get worse every time we have this conversation.

RUBY: I can't help how I feel.

JILL: Well, I'm sure we'll meet some female singers. You can send your songs to them.

(DUNCAN enters, carrying a coke.)

DUNCAN: So you about ready?

JILL: Just my suitcase to finish.

DUNCAN: Let's hit it.

JILL: It won't take but a minute . . .

(JILL exits upstage, to her bedroom.)

(A pause.)

DUNCAN: Let's get it over with, Rube.

RUBY: You son-of-a-bitch.

DUNCAN: I know how you must feel. I don't know what to tell you.

RUBY: That girl's happiness has been my life.

DUNCAN: She's happy.

RUBY: She can't see a thing but all your sweet-talking and dreams of Nashville.

DUNCAN: Look, I gotta go for it, okay? I'm not getting any younger.

RUBY: You don't have to trample her in the process.

DUNCAN: As hard as it may be for you to believe, I love her.

RUBY: I been watching you a long time over the years, Duncan. You even tried sweet-talking me once.

DUNCAN: I love her. I don't know what else to tell you.

RUBY: You don't go trampling over someone you love.

DUNCAN: Nashville's her idea, anyway.

RUBY: And closing her savings account, whose idea is that?

DUNCAN: We're getting married. We're in this together.

RUBY: What happens in Nashville when you can't find work? Hell, you can't even hold a steady job in Rimrock. You expect to nickel and dime playing music in some tavern in Nashville — well, good luck. There's a hundred fools just like you, and all of them ahead of you in line.

DUNCAN: You do what you got to do.

RUBY: There's nothing that says you got to put that girl through this — except your own fear. You're too chickenshit to go to Nashville alone.

DUNCAN: I don't know what to tell you, Rube. I love her and I'm going for it. It's something I should've done years ago.

RUBY: Years ago they would've called it child molesting.

(JILL enters, carrying her suitcase.)

JILL: Well. I guess I'm ready.

(A pause.)

DUNCAN: I'll wait in the car.

(He exits, taking her suitcase.)

RUBY: He's not right for you, honey — he just can't be.

JILL: That's my decision, not yours.

RUBY: Don't you let him use you.

JILL: I love him, mama. Tomorrow at this time, I'll be his wife.

RUBY: Maybe if you just went to Nashville first. You don't have to rush into marrying him.

JILL: I love him. I'm sorry, mama — but that's the way it is. I'm a big girl now. You're gonna have to let go.

RUBY: I don't want to let go.

JILL: You're gonna have to. Bye, mama.

RUBY: You come right home if there's trouble. Call me collect anytime.

(JILL hugs RUBY.)

JILL: Bye, mama.
RUBY: Call me as soon as you get to Nashville.
JILL: I was gonna call you from Reno. After the wedding.
RUBY: I don't want you to make the mistakes I did.
JILL: Marrying daddy wasn't a mistake.
RUBY: Only thing I ever did that wasn't a mistake.
JILL: This is my turn, mama. I'll call you tomorrow.

(They embrace again.)

JILL: Bye.

(And she is gone.)

(RUBY pours another coffee. She stares into space. Then she goes to the phone, dials and waits.)

RUBY *(on phone)*: Sandy? This is Ruby. Listen, hon, I woke up with the beginning of that virus that's been going around and my temperature is one-oh-one. I'm just gonna spend the day and night in bed, so would you tell Frank I won't be in tonight?...He can call Trudy, she told me she needs the extra hours....Thanks, hon, I will. Bye.

(She hangs up. She goes to the cupboard, fetches a bottle of brandy, and pours some into her coffee. She drinks. LIGHTS FADE TO BLACKOUT.)

2/ evening, a month later

(AT RISE: Ruby is putting flowers in a vase for the dinner table. She's been sipping champagne. The table is set for two.)

(There's a knock on the kitchen door. Ruby goes to the door — and it's Jill.)

RUBY: Since when do you have to knock?
JILL: I don't have my key.
RUBY: Where's your key?
JILL: I threw it away.
RUBY: What?

JILL: It's a long story.
RUBY: Don't I even get a hug?
JILL: I'm sorry, I'm beat.

(They embrace.)

JILL: I hate Greyhounds. I just hate them. Welfare mothers and their brats, and alcoholics.
RUBY: Look, I fixed dinner special.
JILL: You didn't have to do that.
RUBY: Of course I didn't. I did it cause I wanted to.
JILL: You don't work tonight?
RUBY: Trudy's taking my shift.
JILL: What's that, champagne?
RUBY: Of course it's champagne. I'll get you one.

(She'll pour one for Jill and top her own glass.)

JILL: The last week's been hell.
RUBY: Don't think about it. You're home now.
JILL: You wouldn't believe what I've been putting up with.
RUBY: I've been there myself.
JILL: How can a man change like that? It was like I was living with this total stranger.
RUBY: Tell me about it.
JILL: And this producer woman — I'd like to get her alone in a dark alley.
RUBY: It's a cut-throat business.
JILL: I thought he was scared of Nashville. He ate it up. He's perfectly capable of playing all their little games. He's probably in bed with her right this minute.
RUBY: I talked to a friend of Wayne's brother, a lawyer, and considering how little time you've been married, he thinks an annulment should be possible.
JILL: I have to think about it.
RUBY: You caught him red-handed, you said.
JILL: Not that way.
RUBY: You said—
JILL: I have to think about what I'm gonna do, is all.
RUBY: The sooner you act—
JILL: Let me do it my way, please!

(Pause.)

JILL: I'm sorry. I'm exhausted. You have more of this?

RUBY: Two bottles.

JILL: You knew it was that bad?

RUBY: Like mother, like daughter. I remember what I went through.

JILL: Please don't condescend.

RUBY: Condescend?

JILL: You act like you have a patent on anything that can happen.

RUBY: I thought I was being sympathetic.

JILL: I don't want sympathy.

RUBY: I know what you're going through, I mean. Cause I've been there myself.

JILL: You have not been there!

RUBY: Honey, I—

JILL: You cannot compare your life to mine! I'm an individual!

RUBY: Of course you are, hon. I didn't mean you weren't an individual.

JILL: Well, I am.

RUBY: You had a miserable trip. I can't stand buses myself.

JILL: I love buses.

RUBY: What?

JILL: I love Greyhound! It's the only way to travel.

(Pause.)

RUBY: Lasagna's in the oven.

JILL: I'm not hungry.

RUBY: It gets better with age. So when you're hungry, it'll be even better.

JILL: You said you had more of this?

RUBY: Two bottles. I bought Scotch, too.

JILL: You have Scotch?

RUBY: Tonight's special. I bought champagne and Scotch. Name your poison.

JILL: You can't afford Scotch.

RUBY: I bought it, didn't I? You want to switch?

JILL: I feel like something strong.

RUBY: How do you want it?

JILL: Neat.

RUBY: Neat — listen to her. Where'd you pick that up, neat?

178

JILL: I can't believe I said that. It's what Duncan says. That son-of-a-bitch, he'd kiss anybody's ass, do anything, to get on the right side of a record producer.

RUBY: It's a world all its own, Nashville.

JILL: It's not like you think, mama. It's not like you read about. It's worse. It's the people that are worse — they're callous, is what they are — they've been away from real people so long they don't know how to behave around them.

RUBY: Well, you're home now. What about your things?

JILL: The suitcase is all I brought.

RUBY: All your dishes and—

JILL: I'll get them later, if it comes to that.

RUBY: If? I thought you made up your mind. You said on the phone—

JILL: I was thinking on the bus ride. Nothing else to do, unless you get a thrill listening to welfare mothers screaming at their little brats.

RUBY: Did you leave him or not?

JILL: I'm here, aren't I?

RUBY: Are you?

JILL: For now.

RUBY: I hope you're not thinking of going back.

JILL: I'm not sure what I'm gonna do. Depends on what Duncan does, I guess.

RUBY: I should think that man already influenced you enough, without depending on what he's gonna do.

JILL: I haven't made any decisions, is all. I just had to get away and have time to think.

RUBY: On the phone, your mind sounded made up.

JILL: It isn't made up. Can you accept that? Does that meet with your approval or should I find someplace else to stay?

RUBY: Your bed's here. You know that.

JILL: I just want time to think.

RUBY: Of course you have time to think. I go on days next week — you can have all day to think.

JILL: Good. That's all I want.

(RUBY pours two scotches, neat.)

JILL: He's gonna cut a record. That's one thing that came out of it. I thought he would and he is. That woman producer is falling all over herself to bring out his record.

RUBY: What you said about him going to bed with her...

JILL: I caught them kissing. I don't know what else they've done.

RUBY: You deserve better. I thought that from the beginning.

JILL: I didn't come here to listen to you bad mouthing my husband, okay? I mean it. I'll go somewhere else before I listen to this.

RUBY: You're hard to follow. You call me like the world's coming to an end and now that you're here you sound like you want to be back in Nashville. Did you catch him kissing another woman or not?

JILL: Maybe he wasn't kissing back. I don't know. I don't know what I think. I walked into the office and he was kissing her. Or she was kissing him. Maybe that's the way they do business in Nashville. Everybody's pretty weird. Not that I met a lot of people. I spent most my time in that goddamn motel room, waiting for the phone to ring.

RUBY: What do you want to happen?

JILL: I don't know what I want. Time to think.

RUBY: You'd better take time to think. You're talking in circles.

JILL: I have a right to talk in circles!

RUBY: Well, you *are* talking in circles!

JILL: Good! I like talking in circles!

RUBY: Congratulations!

(A beat: then they both start laughing.)

JILL: Oh shit. What do men want, anyway?

RUBY: If I knew the answer to that, I'd patent it and get rich selling it to every woman in the country.

JILL: I wasn't asking all that much of him.

RUBY: Asking anything is too much.

JILL: I thought I'd be busy, helping him get appointments and stuff. I thought I'd be his business manager. He said it looked bad, having a woman run his affairs. So instead he lets that woman producer start running his life. He was gonna go to her house for dinner — to her house! I wasn't even invited.

RUBY: Did he go?

JILL: I don't know. That's when I left. It was the last straw. I mean, if he's kissing her in her office, I didn't want to think about what they'd be up to at her home.

RUBY: I don't blame you.

JILL: He hasn't phoned here, has he?

RUBY: No.

JILL: Course, you've been working nights. He'd wait til cheap rates.

RUBY: It's Saturday, been cheap rates all day.

JILL: She's forty if she's a day. Probably older. She wears so much makeup, it's hard to tell.

RUBY: She owns a record company or what?

JILL: She works for her father. I think he balls the women and she balls the men.

RUBY: It's the way they do business out there.

JILL: I knew it'd be tough. And different. Hell, any place is different than Rimrock. But I wanted to help. I wanted to participate. I was supposed to sit in the motel room and wait for things to happen. Two days and I was going stir crazy.

RUBY: You think he's gonna do a record?

JILL: Yes. Oh, I don't know. I just know what he told me and he only knows what they, that woman, was telling him. Maybe she was just putting him on, to get what she was after.

RUBY: Do you think she did? Get what she was after?

JILL: I don't want to think about it.

RUBY: You don't have to do anything you don't want to. As far as I'm concerned, you're on vacation.

JILL: At least I still have some savings left. You were right there, I was gonna be waiting tables and he was gonna be rubbing elbows with the stars.

RUBY: No need for you to wait tables in Nashville.

JILL: It would beat waiting in that motel room. God, I hated that. Just waiting for something to happen.

RUBY: That's what they expect — their women to wait. I spent the best years of my life waiting. I sure got the right profession, being a waitress. "Wait" is my middle name.

JILL: I was gonna be his manager, make things happen. He was embarrassed to be seen with me.

(The phone starts to ring.)

JILL: Oh my God—

RUBY: I don't have to answer it.

JILL: No. I should talk to him. If it's him.

RUBY: It may not be.

JILL: Answer it. He'd call during cheap rates.

RUBY: You sure?

(Jill goes quickly to the phone and answers it.)

JILL: Hello?...I thought it'd be you....You think——...I wasn't going to spend the rest of my life waiting in that motel room, that's why....Duncan, it wasn't fair, that's why....I don't know....Did you go to dinner?...You know damn well who I'm talking about....I'm not sure. Where are you now?...You do what you have to do. I'm gonna do what I have to do....It's a little late, don't you think?...I don't know what....I don't know, I said....I have a lot of thinking to do....Listen, I'm about to sit down for dinner....*(To Ruby)* He hung up on me! That goddamn son-of-a-bitch, who does he think he is?

RUBY: Men are all the same.

JILL: The nerve of him! He makes me so goddamn mad.

RUBY: Here, have a drink and be thankful it's over.

(She tops their drinks.)

JILL: I supported everything he was trying to do. I would've waited tables if it came to that — so he could have time to meet with record producers. All I asked is that I get treated with respect. He was embarrassed to walk into an office with me. He said it looked bad. I was too pushy. He didn't want people to think he was pussy-whipped.

RUBY: God, I haven't heard that expression in years.

JILL: I thought of using it myself — the way that woman producer was tying him around her finger. She was starting with the finger anyway. You know, he went to dinner to her home. It didn't matter if I left or not. I don't exist as far as he's concerned.

RUBY: You hush — he's not worth the worry you're giving him.

JILL: He makes me so mad!

(There's a knock on the kitchen door.)

(Ruby goes to the door, opens it — and Duncan walks in.)

RUBY: No one invited you in.

DUNCAN: I'm here to speak to my wife.

RUBY: This is my house and you're not invited inside.

DUNCAN *(to Jill)*: Where can we go to talk?

JILL: I suppose you think this is funny, calling me like that? Making me think you're in Nashville?

DUNCAN: I didn't say I was in Nashville.

JILL: You didn't say you were at the corner either.

RUBY: You still haven't been invited in.

JILL: It's okay, mama.

DUNCAN: Where can we talk?

JILL: Right here.

DUNCAN: Talk alone.

JILL: I have no secrets.

DUNCAN: You pouring those?

JILL: You've had enough, I'm sure.

DUNCAN: Look, I've been driving all day.

JILL: Driving across the desert without a beer between your legs? Don't make me laugh.

DUNCAN: I didn't come here to listen to you get cute.

JILL: Well, what in hell did you come here for? That's what I'd like to know.

DUNCAN: Because you're my wife.

JILL: Am I now?

DUNCAN: Yes.

JILL: Funny, I don't feel like a wife. Wives participate in lives of their husbands. They're like partners.

DUNCAN: I'm sorry the way things worked out. I really am.

JILL: I'm sorry, too, Duncan, because you lost yourself one hell of a support system. I'd've done anything to help you.

DUNCAN: I had to do things my way.

JILL: Why didn't you just go out there alone?

DUNCAN: I needed you.

JILL: For what? All I did is sit alone in that goddamn motel room.

DUNCAN: I still need you.

JILL: What about Miss Lady Record Producer? Abilene, whatever the hell her name is.

DUNCAN: Abililly.

JILL: Jesus, what the hell kind of a name is that? Abililly.

DUNCAN: It's her name.

JILL: Who could trust a bitch with a name like that?

DUNCAN: I don't trust her. She wasn't interested in my career at all, to tell the truth.

JILL: Then what was she interested in?

DUNCAN: Use your imagination.

JILL: You son-of-a-bitch!

DUNCAN: She played me for a fool, okay? That's all I'm saying.

(He starts laughing.)

JILL: I fail to see anything humorous . . .

183

DUNCAN: You should've seen her. Sick. She wanted me to ball her on camera. She had this video camera in her bedroom and—

JILL: What in hell were you doing in her bedroom?

DUNCAN: It's the center of her goddamn existence. She eats there, works there—

JILL: I'll bet she works there.

DUNCAN: Look, she's a middle-aged lady scared of growing old, who gets her kicks balling in front of a camera. When I found out, I left, okay? Chalk it up to experience.

JILL: You didn't ball her, after making out with her in the office?

DUNCAN: I wasn't making out with her. Give me a break.

JILL: I'd like to know what you call it.

DUNCAN: I told you a hundred times, she just started kissing me. The lady's crazy.

JILL: Right, you didn't enjoy it at all.

DUNCAN: Why settle for pork when I got T-bone at home?

JILL: I am not a piece of meat!

DUNCAN: It's a saying, for Christ's sake!

JILL: You don't even say it right. It's why settle for hamburger if you got steak at home.

DUNCAN: Fine, steak at home. T-bone, pork, steak, what's the difference? The point is, I'm not in the market, if you know what I mean. I'm a happily married man.

(A beat, as JILL assesses the situation.)

JILL: You want a Scotch?

DUNCAN: I'd love a Scotch.

RUBY: Don't mind me, I just own the bottle.

JILL: I don't want us fighting, okay? We're all mature enough to be civil.

RUBY: I just don't like seeing you hurt.

DUNCAN: I'm sorry I hurt you, hon. I was so damn nervous, meeting those record producers.

JILL: I know, that's why I wanted to do the foot-work for you.

DUNCAN: I had to do it myself, is what I'm saying. Hard as it was, it was something I had to do alone.

RUBY: Men.

DUNCAN: Yeah, that's part of it. We're talking Nashville. The country capital of the world. The macho capital. It's all cowboys and independence, that's the myth of it, and it just wouldn't look right, a dude like me having his wife doing all the dirty work for him.

184

JILL: There's more powerful women in Nashville than you think.

DUNCAN: I'm sure there are. I don't think poor Abililly is one of them.

JILL: What's this poor Abililly shit? You sure you didn't ball her?

DUNCAN: Give me a break.

JILL: She sure don't need pity, least of all from you.

DUNCAN: How can you not pity a woman like that?

JILL: So you're not cutting a record or what?

DUNCAN: Yeah, I am.

JILL: You did ball her!

DUNCAN: Different company. Mustang Records wants to do "Stale Beer in the Morning, Stale Love in the Night."

JILL: You're serious?

DUNCAN: Course I'm serious. I haven't signed a contract yet but it looks certain. They're trying to decide on the flip side. I'm supposed to check in with them tomorrow.

JILL: Well, you deserve it.

DUNCAN: Thanks, hon. That means a lot.

JILL: Does it?

DUNCAN: You know it does.

JILL: Duncan, I've been so mad at you!

DUNCAN: I know. I deserved it.

JILL: You sure as hell did.

DUNCAN: So let me make it up to you.

JILL: Oh, honey...

(They embrace. Ruby is beside herself, seeing that once again she is losing her daughter. She pours another Scotch.)

DUNCAN (*breaking the embrace*): I'm starving. Why don't I take us out to dinner?

JILL: On what?

DUNCAN: Let me borrow twenty — against my advance.

JILL: Well, we can eat right here. Mama made lasagna. Is there enough for three?

RUBY: I guess there has to be.

JILL: You don't mind, do you?

RUBY: Would it make a difference if I did?

JILL: Don't be that way. We're celebrating Duncan's record contract.

DUNCAN: I'll be recording your songs one day.

185

JILL *(quickly)*: You didn't tell me about Wayne — did he record you?

RUBY: Just on tape.

JILL: Do you have it? I want to hear it.

RUBY: It's really not record quality — we did it in his garage.

DUNCAN: Buddy Holly recorded in his garage, and he wasn't the first.

RUBY: I'd better set another place for dinner.

(She moves to do so.)

JILL: Did you put on clean sheets?

RRUB: Same clean ones was on the bed when you left.

JILL: It's only a double, honey.

DUNCAN: I plan to spend a lot of time on top of you.

JILL: Oh, you...

(DUNCAN embraces her again.)

JILL: Stop it! *(To RUBY:)* Mama, put on your song.

(And the LIGHTS FADE TO BLACKOUT.)

3/ the next morning

(AT RISE: Ruby is in her robe, drinking coffee in the kitchen. Jill enters from the bedroom, dressed.)

JILL: Morning.

RUBY: Good morning. You ready for coffee?

JILL: I need something . . .

(RUBY will pour her a cup.)

JILL: I didn't sleep well at all.

RUBY: You weren't none too quiet about it either.

JILL: Did we keep you awake?

RUBY: That bed's too old for a workout like that.

JILL: Mother!

RUBY: Well, it's the truth. You want to carry on like a bitch in heat, next time get a motel.

JILL: Well, pardon me. We happen to be married.

RUBY: So you're gonna follow him back to Nashville, aren't you? That's what all that spring action was about?

JILL: You're disgusting.

RUBY: I've been around men a long time. I know how they think.

JILL: He's my husband. I go where he goes.

RUBY: That's what I mean.

JILL: I don't want to fight this morning.

RUBY: I didn't know we were fighting.

JILL: You sound like you're trying to start an argument.

RUBY: I'm just making an observation. Men use loving to get their own way.

JILL: Oh, you just mistrust men on principle.

RUBY: Principles learned from experience.

(DUNCAN enters.)

DUNCAN: Morning.

JILL: You ready for coffee, honey?

DUNCAN: First Nashville, then coffee. Got to see what they want for the flip side.

(He goes to the phone.)

RUBY *(after him)*: Help yourself.

JILL *(a reprimand)*: Mama!

(DUNCAN has dialed the number.)

DUNCAN *(on phone)*: Mr. Conners, please. This is Duncan Jeffries....Thanks....Mr. Conners?...Duncan here....Duncan Jeffries. Thought I'd check in about that flip side....I'm calling long distance from Oregon....Just personal business. I'll be back in a few days....Anyway, I was wondering if you'd reached a decision yet....I just, I had the impression, you know....Sure. Yeah....Well, I don't understand actually. I had the impression—...I thought you liked the song....Yeah, right....Right....Bye.

(He hangs up.)

DUNCAN: Goddamn it!

JILL: Duncan?

DUNCAN: They changed their mind. They're not doing the record.

JILL: Oh, honey...

DUNCAN: Goddamn it anyway — if he didn't want to do it, why lead me on?

RUBY: There's an answer to that.

DUNCAN: Look, I don't need any lip from you, okay?

RUBY: In my house, I say anything I want.

DUNCAN: Just don't push your luck—

JILL: Stop it! Both of you.

(Duncan heads for the door.)

JILL: Where are you going?

DUNCAN: Away from her.

JILL: No, we're gonna act like adults here—

DUNCAN: I'm going out, okay? I'm gonna get breakfast. So how about loaning me five?

JILL: We can all have breakfast here.

DUNCAN: Look, I'm not gonna put up with her lip.

RUBY: Nobody's telling me what I can and can't say in my own house.

JILL: This is insane!

DUNCAN: Give me five.

JILL: I'm not giving you a cent.

DUNCAN: Fine.

(He heads for the door.)

JILL: Don't you go out that door.

DUNCAN: What?

JILL: You heard me.

DUNCAN: I want to hear it again.

JILL: You walk out that door, there's no use coming back.

DUNCAN: So that's the way it is?

JILL: We can all act like adults here. We can have breakfast and be civil.

DUNCAN: You call her being civil?

JILL: We kept her awake. She's a bitch when she doesn't get her sleep.

RUBY: I'm a bitch? I'm trying to have a quiet cup of coffee—

JILL: I don't want to argue! Not with you, not with Duncan.

DUNCAN: You want to come to breakfast with me?

JILL: Damn it, this is childish. There's eggs in the refrigerator.

DUNCAN: I asked you a question.

JILL: I told you how I feel.

DUNCAN: I'm walking out the door to go to breakfast. You want to come or not?

JILL: If you go, don't come back.

DUNCAN: You sure you know what you're saying?

JILL: No! Nobody knows what they're saying this morning. That's the point. So let's just start over. Get yourself a cup of coffee.

DUNCAN: I'm serious. You coming with me or not?

JILL: You're just being stubborn.

DUNCAN: Her or me, which is it?

JILL: I will not be put on the spot like that!

DUNCAN: Her or me?

RUBY: Men...

DUNCAN: Shut your lip!

RUBY: Men! You're all crazy egomaniacs!

DUNCAN: I'm not asking again — her or me?

JILL: I just want some peace and quiet.

(A beat: and DUNCAN walks out.)

JILL *(after him)*: Duncan! Goddamn you! You're acting like a child!

RUBY: Let him go.

JILL: He is so stubborn!

RUBY: They all are.

JILL: Stop it. Stop making pronouncements.

RUBY: He's acting like a child, just like you said.

JILL: He's disappointed. So am I.

RUBY: Defend him all you want, he's still acting like a child.

JILL: Of course I'll defend him. He's my husband.

RUBY: For one who doesn't want an argument—

JILL: Stop it! Let's just be calm a minute. I'm sorry I got bitchy. I hate Nashville. All they do is use people.

(Duncan comes back into the kitchen.)

DUNCAN: This doesn't feel right. I'm pissed at Nashville, not you.

JILL: It doesn't feel right to me either.

(She embraces him.)

DUNCAN *(to RUBY)*: I'm sorry I snapped at you.

RUBY: What do you two want for breakfast?

189

DUNCAN: I don't think my stomach could hold anything.

JILL: Nashville's nothing. We know that now.

DUNCAN: Hell, it is. It's the nut you got to crack. I'm going back and you're coming with me.

JILL: I can't go through that again.

DUNCAN: They liked my song. I know they did. I don't know what happened but I know they liked it. There's more than one producer in Nashville. As a matter of fact, there's nothing but producers. I'll find an honest one somewhere.

JILL: Mail them your tapes.

DUNCAN: It's not the same thing.

JILL: I mean it, hon. I hate it there. I didn't know what it was like. I never dreamed it would—

DUNCAN: Hey, listen to me. I'm going back there. You're my wife, I want you beside me on this.

JILL: Don't do this, Duncan.

DUNCAN: You do what you want, hon, but I'm going back. Today.

JILL: You're broke, aren't you?

DUNCAN: I got enough to get back.

JILL: What is the point of going back there? A woman wants you to ball her on private TV., you get lied to—

DUNCAN: My mind's made up. Now are you coming with me or what?

RUBY: Excuse me, this is where I came in.

(And she exits to the living room.)

JILL: I don't see the point of it when you can mail them your tapes and spare all that shit they dish out.

DUNCAN: Because it's who you know. I learned that much.

JILL: And look who you have to know! What're you gonna do, be a TV star with Abillady wherever her name is. Is that what you're gonna do?

DUNCAN: Give me a break.

JILL: I will not go back to Nashville. I hate it.

DUNCAN: I'm your husband, remember? Nashville was your idea in the first place.

JILL: I was wrong.

DUNCAN: It's the only way to go. I didn't make the rules of the business but that's what they are.

JILL: If you go, you go.

DUNCAN: Are you my wife or not?

JILL: I'm not your slave.

DUNCAN: Answer the question — are you my wife?

JILL: Presently, yes, I am.

DUNCAN: Presently — what's that supposed to mean?

JILL: I'm not going to Nashville, that's all there is to it.

DUNCAN: And if I go?

JILL: If you go, you go.

DUNCAN: What kind of marriage is it, me in Nashville and you here?

JILL: Obviously it's not much of a marriage at all.

DUNCAN: Is that what you want?

JILL: I want to live someplace that's sane. That's all I'm saying. That's all I want. I want to live where I'm treated like a human being and where bitches aren't trying to get my husband to ball them on TV and—

DUNCAN: Is that what's bothering you?

JILL: Everything's bothering me! Nashville is bothering me.

DUNCAN: Well, that's where I'm going, to Nashville. And I'm gonna make it, too, don't think I'm not. I'd like to share that with my wife.

JILL: I don't want to live in Nashville.

DUNCAN: You were there a month.

JILL: That was plenty.

DUNCAN: You didn't see a thing in a month.

JILL: No, you're right, I didn't. Because you kept me in that goddamn motel room.

DUNCAN: You could've gone out any time you wanted.

JILL: And do what?

DUNCAN: See the sights, whatever you wanted.

JILL: I was waiting for the phone to ring.

DUNCAN: So who's fault is it you didn't see Nashville?

JILL: There is no point in this discussion, Duncan. I don't like the kind of people you have to deal with in Nashville and I refuse to have anything to do with them. I know that if you want a musical career, you have to deal with those people but that doesn't mean you have to live there. Lots of country singers live away from Nashville.

DUNCAN: To get started, you got to be in Nashville.

JILL: Then go to Nashville.

DUNCAN: What about you?

JILL: For the millionth time, I made a mistake. I belong here. I'm a Rimrock girl.

DUNCAN: A Rimrock girl?

JILL: I was born here and I like it here. If you can't handle it, shove it.

DUNCAN: A Rimrock girl — you got to be kidding me.

JILL: Yes, a Rimrock girl. *(She goes into a pompom routine from high school.)* Give me a Rim, give me a Rock! Rimrock! Rimrock! Rimmmmmm! Rockkkkk!

(During the above, Ruby has returned to stand in the doorway.)

DUNCAN: Well, Rimrock girl, I'll be in Nashville. I love you, despite this little period of insanity you're having, and I'd like you to join me. So I'll give you a call later, okay?

(A beat: both RUBY and DUNCAN stare at JILL.)

JILL: I will not be stared at!

(She quickly exits to the bedroom.)

RUBY: I think you should go.

DUNCAN: Yeah, you like that a lot, don't you? Makes you feel like a mother.

RUBY: I'm not asking you again . . .

DUNCAN: You don't have to, Rube. But I'll tell you something. I'm not like you. This town ain't enough for me, playing in a goddamn tavern. You got a talent and you're wasting it. I'm not making that mistake, not no more. I'm not over the hill yet and this dude is going for it.

RUBY: Just go for it without my daughter.

DUNCAN: Not your daughter, Rube. My wife.

RUBY: Get the hell out of here.

DUNCAN: You're small town all the way, aren't you?

(A pause: and he exits.)

RUBY *(quietly)*: Men...

(She fetches the garbage from under the sink and exits to empty it.)

(JILL returns from the bedroom.)

JILL: Mama?

192

(When there is no reply, Jill goes to the phone, looks up a number in the yellow pages, and dials.)

JILL *(on phone)*: Hello, Sally? This is Jill. I got back yesterday....It's a long story. Listen, I need an appointment with Dr. Thomas. Do you think you could fit me in later this week?...I'm sure it's nothing but I'm three weeks late and—...*(She hears Ruby and hangs up.)*

(RUBY returns.)

JILL *(to explain herself)*: I was going to call Frank and see if I can get my job back.
RUBY: I hope you didn't burn too many bridges.
JILL: I got the wrong number.
RUBY: Want me to call?
JILL: That'd be sweet, mama.

(Ruby begins to dial the number and Jill moves away, troubled. And the LIGHTS FADE TO BLACKOUT. End of Act One.)

ACT TWO

1/ Late morning, two months later

(AT RISE: Ruby is skimming through a magazine, a cup of coffee at hand, when there's a knock on the kitchen door. She answers it — and it's Duncan. He is dirtier than we've seen him before, tired from two days of hitch-hiking. He enters quickly, carrying an old overnight bag, without waiting to be asked.)

DUNCAN: Where's Jill?

RUBY: I sure get tired of you busting in here without an invitation.

(Duncan exits upstage, going through the house, calling for Jill.)

DUNCAN *(off-stage)*: Jill!...Jill!...Jill!

(He returns to the kitchen.)

RUBY: She's at work.

DUNCAN: Where's she working?

RUBY: Where do you think? At the cafe.

DUNCAN: Call her.

RUBY: I'm not your slave, much as you think all women are.

DUNCAN: What's the number?

RUBY: You can't leave her be, can you? She finally starts getting you out of her system and you have to come back and cause trouble.

DUNCAN: I have to talk to her.

RUBY: It takes two to have a conversation and—

DUNCAN: Just cut the crap and give me the number. Please. Look, I wouldn't be here unless I had reasons. Did she tell you she's pregnant?

RUBY: What are you talking about?

DUNCAN: She's pregnant.

RUBY: I don't believe you.

DUNCAN: Call her and ask her yourself.

RUBY: Who told you she's pregnant?

DUNCAN: A buddy, you don't know him. His girl was at the doctor's the same time Jill was. She thought she was gonna get an abortion.

RUBY: If it's true, I should hope so.

DUNCAN: You have nothing to do with that. That's between her and me.

(RUBY goes to the phone and will dial.)

RUBY: I can't believe she wouldn't tell me.

DUNCAN: Why should she?

RUBY: I'm her mother.

DUNCAN: Yeah — and I'm her husband. I'm the father of the kid and nobody told me. I'd better be the father.

RUBY: Don't you dare talk about her like that... *(on phone)* Trudy?...This is Ruby. Can I speak to Jill?...What? She left for work this morning....Well, thanks, hon.

194

(She hangs up.)

DUNCAN: What's the matter?
RUBY: She didn't go to work this morning.
DUNCAN: Where is she, if she's not at work?
RUBY: I don't know.
DUNCAN: She told you she was going to work?
RUBY: She's on days. She should've been at work. She must've gotten somebody to pull her shift.
DUNCAN: Then where is she?
RUBY: I don't know.
DUNCAN: She mention an abortion to you?
RUBY: No.
DUNCAN: Can she do that here in Rimrock, get an abortion?
RUBY: I don't think so.
DUNCAN: Closest would be Bend, wouldn't it?
RUBY: How's she gonna afford an abortion?
DUNCAN: They got a clinic in Bend?
RUBY: Medical clinic? Sure, they must.
DUNCAN: One of those clinics for poor people. They'd give abortions. Poor people are always getting abortions.
RUBY: She'd talk something like that over with me first.
DUNCAN: What for?
RUBY: Cause that's the way she is. We're close.
DUNCAN: She knows you hate me. She knows what your opinion would be. She don't have to talk to you to know how you feel about it.
RUBY: What'd you do, come here to try and talk her out of it?
DUNCAN: If I'm not too late, yeah.

(Pause.)

RUBY: You don't have a shower in Nashville?
DUNCAN: I've been on the road — I hitch-hiked.
RUBY: What happened to your car?
DUNCAN: I sold it. Look, if she's not at work, where she's supposed to be, then she's probably in Bend, right?
RUBY: You're still assuming she's pregnant.
DUNCAN: She's pregnant, believe me. My buddy's girl heard it from Jill herself. She was pretty upset.
RUBY: Do you blame her?
DUNCAN: It's my kid, too. I have a say here.

RUBY: What kind of say — to have her keep the kid and then raise it alone while you're God knows where doing God knows what? Is that what you mean by having a say?

DUNCAN: I mean the kid's mine as much as hers.

RUBY: If it's yours.

DUNCAN: What do you mean?

RUBY: You said it yourself.

DUNCAN: She seeing somebody else? Is she?

RUBY: No.

DUNCAN: Then it's got to be mine.

RUBY: If it's a baby we're talking about, then it's *hers*.

DUNCAN: Both of ours.

RUBY: I still don't think she's pregnant.

DUNCAN: Then why'd she tell my buddy's girl she is? Why ain't she at work where she's supposed to be? Face it, you don't know what the hell's going on with her.

RUBY: She'd tell me if she was pregnant.

DUNCAN: Well, we'll find out soon enough.

(He sits down at the kitchen table, putting his feet up on the table.)

RUBY: What do you think you're doing?

DUNCAN: Waiting for Jill.

RUBY: Well, don't get comfortable. You're not even invited in yet.

DUNCAN: I came here to see Jill and I'm gonna see Jill. You just better get used to the idea.

RUBY: She'll take one look at you and wonder what the cat drug in.

(DUNCAN gets up.)

DUNCAN: I'm gonna shower.

RUBY: You can't just come in here and say you're gonna use my shower.

DUNCAN: Be nice. You're my mother-in-law.

RUBY: You have no right.

DUNCAN: I look like hell, you said so yourself.

RUBY: No wonder, you have to resort to hitch-hiking.

DUNCAN: You do what you gotta do.

RUBY: Thought you'd have a limousine by now.

DUNCAN: No, you don't. You've been hoping I'd fall flat on my face so you could say "I told you so" to Jill.

RUBY: You got a record out?

DUNCAN: You listen to the radio. What do you think?

RUBY: I'll tell you what I think. You come walking in here uninvited with some cock-and-bull story about Jill being pregnant and off to some clinic to get an abortion and you have to sell your car and hitch-hike to get here — and for what?, I ask myself — unless it's to cause more trouble for my daughter than you've caused her already, which isn't something I'm about to stand here and let happen. I don't know where Jill is but wherever she is and whatever she's doing, I'm sure she's got her reasons and it's not for me and especially not for you to stand here thinking you're gonna tell that girl what she should and shouldn't do.

(A beat: DUNCAN doesn't respond.)

RUBY: I think you should go.
DUNCAN: Don't lift a hand, okay? I'll find a towel myself.

(He exits to bathroom for his shower.)

(Ruby watches him leave. LIGHTS FADE TO BLACKOUT.)

2/ an hour later

(AT RISE: Ruby has been making work for herself in the kitchen. Duncan, freshly showered, enters and sits down at the table. A pause.)

RUBY: How long is this going to go on?
DUNCAN: How do I know? I'm here to see my wife.
RUBY: I'll grant you this much — I don't know where she is. Don't know why she didn't go to work. I guess there may be things she wants to keep from me.

(Pause.)

RUBY: Well?
DUNCAN: Well what?
RUBY: I made a concession.
DUNCAN: Not to me, you didn't. That much was obvious. That and more.
RUBY: More how?
DUNCAN: Do you really want to get into this? Let's just say we can't stand each other and let it go at that.

RUBY: We used to get along.

DUNCAN: That's ancient history.

RUBY: You know what's weird about us? We both want the best for Jill.

DUNCAN: What?

RUBY: We both want the best for Jill.

DUNCAN: I know what you said. I can't believe you're saying it. You think I want the best for her?

RUBY: Sure, because you think what s best for her is being the "woman of the house" — your house.

DUNCAN: I married her for her savings account.

RUBY: You son-of-a-bitch, I knew you were—

DUNCAN: See there? You had me worried for a minute. Thought you were getting senile.

(Pause. Then Ruby goes to the phone and dials a number.)

RUBY *(on phone)*: Sally? This is Ruby. Is Jill there?...You wouldn't know where she is?

DUNCAN *(interrupting loudly)*: You might try the abortion clinic in Bend!

RUBY (on phone): No, it's nothing. Thanks, hon.

(She hangs up.)

RUBY: She wouldn't do that without telling me.

DUNCAN: I thought you were making concessions.

RUBY: Not about that. She must be up to something, but not something like that.

DUNCAN: You said you wanted her to have it.

RUBY: If she needs one.

DUNCAN: What's the big deal then?

RUBY: It's a very big deal.

DUNCAN: You got that right.

RUBY: Just don't count your chickens. I'm sure it must be something else that's bothering her.

DUNCAN: I know what I know.

RUBY: You just don't start in on her, not until you know what's going on. She probably needed a day to get off by herself. She probably took a drive. It hasn't been easy for that girl.

DUNCAN: Nashville's no piece of cake.

RUBY: Nobody said you had to go to Nashville.

DUNCAN: It's where the market is. If you want to cut records, you go to Nashville.

RUBY: There's other ways.

DUNCAN: Sitting in Rimrock, for instance? Getting your songs sung in a dump by a band that can barely tune up?

RUBY: Look who used to play in that band.

DUNCAN: It drove me crazy playing with those guys. I'm better than that and so are you.

RUBY: Don't pick on me, I don't have those kinds of pretensions.

DUNCAN: Look, I'm not gonna argue about my career with you, okay? I'm doing the best I can and I'm hanging in and I'm gonna make it. Persistence is half the battle.

(The door opens and JILL walks in.)

JILL *(seeing him)*: Oh shit.

DUNCAN *(quickly)*: How come you weren't at work?

JILL: That is none of your business.

RUBY: He just barged in and won't leave.

JILL: It's all right, mama. We might as well get this over with.

DUNCAN: You know Annette somebody, who goes with Ted Renner?

JILL: No, am I supposed to?

DUNCAN: You met her in the doctor's office. She knows you.

JILL: Christ.

DUNCAN: Got her in your mind now?

JILL: What are you doing here? How'd you get here, crawl? Your clothes are filthy.

RUBY: He hitch-hiked. He had to sell his car.

DUNCAN: Let's cut the crap. You been to the clinic in Bend, right?

JILL: Wrong.

DUNCAN: Don't lie to me, babe, not about something like this.

JILL: I wasn't in Bend.

DUNCAN: Where were you then?

JILL: That's none of your business.

DUNCAN: Now you listen to me — that baby you're carrying inside you is very much my business, you understand? It's my genes and my toes and my brain cells, so you just stop thinking this has nothing to do with me!

RUBY: I'm not afraid to call the police.

JILL: It's okay. Maybe Duncan and I should discuss this alone.

DUNCAN: Let's go somewhere.

RUBY: No, if it's privacy you want, you can get it right here. *(To Jill:)* I'll just be in the living room, hon.

(She exits upstage.)

JILL: What'd you say her name was? Your friend's girl?
DUNCAN: Annette.
JILL: She was pregnant herself.
DUNCAN: We're talking about you.
JILL: Yes, I'm pregnant.
DUNCAN: And what else?
JILL: There's nothing else.
DUNCAN: Where were you when you should've been at work?
JILL: None of your business.
DUNCAN: I'm not gonna tell you again — this is my business.
JILL: Today has nothing to do with you.
DUNCAN: You're carrying my kid, everything you do has to do with me.

(Jill moves away from him, in retreat.)

DUNCAN: Don't you avoid me. Where were you?

(Jill moves around the room, Duncan in pursuit.)

DUNCAN: You were in Bend, weren't you? Getting an abortion? Killing my kid? If you did that, lady, you're gonna be losing one hell of a lot of sleep in the nights ahead—
JILL: Stop it! I wasn't in Bend. I haven't had an abortion.
DUNCAN: That's the truth?
JILL: It's the truth.

(Pause.)
DUNCAN: So why weren't you at work?
JILL: Duncan, that doesn't concern you.
DUNCAN: Everything concerns me.
JILL: Okay, it does concern you. I was seeing a lawyer. I wrote you I was going to.
DUNCAN: I thought you'd already seen him. You wrote you'd already seen him.
JILL: I was seeing him again.

DUNCAN: For what? I told you I agreed to the terms. What do you mean you saw him again? You changing the terms without consulting me, is that it?

JILL: No.

DUNCAN: You see this lawyer again, after I already agreed to the terms.

JILL: I saw him — socially.

DUNCAN: What?

JILL: It wasn't a professional visit. It was a date.

DUNCAN: You skipped work to have a date with your lawyer?

(JILL doesn't respond.)

DUNCAN: I asked you a question. Are you dating your lawyer?

JILL: I'm seeing him socially, yes.

DUNCAN: And you skip work for this? And here you write what a tough time you're having . . .

JILL: What I do or don't do in my personal life is none of your business.

DUNCAN: I don't want to have to say this again — from here out, everything you do is my business. Okay? What you eat, how much sleep you get, whether you're depressed or feeling good about yourself, how late you stay out, whether you take care of yourself — this is my business because it's gonna affect the health of my child you're carrying — you understand me?

JILL: I find it hard to believe you came here, hitch-hiked here, to make sure I'm feeling good.

DUNCAN: To see about my kid.

JILL: *Our kid.* I have something to do with this.

DUNCAN: Just don't go doing something without consulting me.

JJIL: I'm consulting you now . . . I'm going to get an abortion.

DUNCAN: Over my dead body.

JILL: You can't stop me.

DUNCAN: I can make life miserable for you, you know I can do that.

JILL: Our marriage is over, Duncan.

DUNCAN: We're talking about a kid, not the marriage.

JILL: I'm in no position to raise a kid right now.

DUNCAN: We can work something out.

JILL: Okay, you tell me how you want it to be. I have the kid. Then what?

DUNCAN: What do you mean, then what? You nurse it, you raise it, like a mother's supposed to.

JILL: Okay...

(She pretends to be cradling a baby.)

JILL: I'm nursing the baby. Where are you?

DUNCAN: What do you mean, where am I?

JILL: Where the fuck are you while I'm nursing the baby!?

DUNCAN: I don't know that. It depends.

JILL: Let's say you're in Nashville.

(Jill starts "coughing," patting the "baby" on the back.)

JILL: Poor baby, poor baby. She's got the croup. But how am I gonna afford a visit to the doctor? Ding a ling a ling. Hello, Duncan? Your kid has the croup and I can't afford a doctor on waitress tips, can you send me a couple hundred right away?

(DUNCAN is staring at her.)

JILL: What about that? You gonna send me a couple hundred just like that, with no notice? You ready to be a father to your kid like that?

DUNCAN: If people thought that way, no kid would ever get born. You take care of emergencies when they happen.

JILL: How?

DUNCAN: You just deal with it. Something comes up.

JILL: That's not the way I want to raise a kid. When I have a kid, she's gonna be brought into a loving, secure family.

DUNCAN: What do you mean "she"?

JILL: It was a figure of speech.

DUNCAN: You can't just say "she" and not mean nothing by it. You don't want a son?

JILL: It's a figure of speech! Men are saying, everyone says, "he" all the time, no matter what sex is indicated. I'm trying to teach myself to say "she" instead.

DUNCAN: What for?

JILL: For the hell of it!

(Pause.)

DUNCAN: This lawyer, what's his name?

JILL: That's none of your business.
DUNCAN: I still got the letter.
JILL: Then you can look it up, can't you?
DUNCAN: You talk to him about the abortion?

(She doesn't respond.)

DUNCAN: You two planning this little murder together, are you?
JILL: Stop it! Don't think this has been an easy decision for me.
DUNCAN: Yeah, you've been worrying over it since I got here.
JILL: Why'd you really come here?
DUNCAN: To protect my kid. You could've written me about that, you know.
JILL: Why'd you go to the trouble of hitch-hiking? Why didn't you just call?
DUNCAN: Because I didn't want to give you the opportunity to hang up on me. You had a moral obligation to tell me about this. You had no right to keep it from me. It's my kid, too.
JILL: I didn't think you'd feel so strongly about it.
DUNCAN: My kid...!
JILL: Most men would want me to have an abortion.
DUNCAN: I'm not most men.

(Pause.)

DUNCAN: He wants you to have the abortion, right? This lawyer?
JILL: Don't get down on him, Duncan. He's been very supportive.
DUNCAN: I'll bet he has. Who wants a girlfriend with somebody else's kid?
JILL: Tim is—
DUNCAN: Tim, yeah, I remember now.
JILL: He's a very considerate man. He's not selfish.
DUNCAN: Then he gives you advice?
JILL: He listens while I work things out for myself.
DUNCAN: And you worked out killing my kid. How come you never asked how I felt about it?
JILL: Because it's my body.
DUNCAN: You don't think I had anything to do with the baby inside your body now?

(Ruby returns to the kitchen.)

RUBY: Jill, are you all right?

JILL: I'm fine.

DUNCAN: We're not done.

JILL: I think we are.

DUNCAN: If you have that abortion, you're gonna regret it.

JILL: You're just bastard enough, aren't you?

DUNCAN: It ain't me. It's just the way it is. It's your conscience. I know you, Jill. You're not a murderer. You don't have a violent bone in your body — except for getting mad at me. You do this and you're gonna regret it because your conscience ain't gonna let you rest, hon. A part of you knows better.

RUBY: Get out of my house.

DUNCAN: You think about it a little harder. How can that fetus not be alive and wiggling and growing every day in there? It's part of the biggest miracle you'll ever—

RUBY: Get out!

DUNCAN: I'm gonna call you later and we're gonna talk some more about this. You think about it.

(He exits.)

(Pause.)

RUBY: Then it's true? You're pregnant?

JILL: Yes.

RUBY: I can't believe you didn't tell me.

JILL: I've been trying to sort it out myself.

RUBY: That's hard, alone, with no one to talk to.

JILL: I've had someone. Tim, the lawyer I saw for the divorce, has been a pillar of strength.

RUBY: You have a new boyfriend?

JILL: I guess you could say that.

RUBY: My God, do we ever learn?

JILL: I know — you're hurt because I didn't come to you, mama, but I had to sort some things out first.

RUBY: Depending on a man — is that sorting things out?

JILL: I'm not depending on him. I think I've fallen in love with him.

RUBY: We live in a zoo, don't we? Except none of the animals ever learn any new tricks.

JILL: I'm sorry you've had your feelings hurt.

RUBY: It's not my feelings on the line, believe me.

204

JILL: Mama, please understand that this is something I just had to deal with myself.

RUBY: I thought you said your new boyfriend helped you.

JILL: He just listened.

RUBY: I couldn't've done that?

JILL: Frankly, no. I don't mean that harshly — you know it's true. We're too much alike. You know we are. You'd be comparing my situation with what you went through.

RUBY: If we can't share experiences, how can we ever improve how things are?

JILL: Well, we're sharing now, how's that? I'm pregnant and I'm gonna get an abortion.

RUBY: You've thought it over carefully?

JILL: You don't think I should?

RUBY: I'm just asking if you've done a lot of thinking about it.

JILL: You can't imagine how many sleepless nights I've thought about it.

RUBY: Who's the father?

JILL: Duncan is. You don't think . . .?

RUBY: I was just asking.

JILL: Tim and I aren't that close yet. I'm still a little gun shy.

RUBY: Good, you should be.

JILL: Anyway, they have a clinic in Bend.

RUBY: You can afford it?

JILL: Tim's gonna help me. I can pay him back a little every month.

RUBY: What's it cost?

JILL: I don't want you helping, mama, you have a hard enough time as it is.

RUBY: You're gonna get yourself in debt to that man. You know what that means.

JILL: It's just a loan. You'll like Tim. He's completely different from Duncan. He's very well educated. He says he's a feminist.

RUBY: Oh my God. You sure he isn't queer as well?

JILL: It's gay. And he isn't. Honestly, mama—

RUBY: I mean, if he hasn't even tried to get you in bed yet—

JILL: He has tried.

RUBY: Well, then. And now you're gonna be in debt to him.

JILL: It's a small loan, that's all it is. I'll have it paid off in four or five months. I wouldn't even need it if the clinic would've given me credit.

RUBY: When do you go in?

JILL: Next week.

205

RUBY: What are you gonna do about Duncan?

JILL: What do you mean?

RUBY: He's gonna cause all the trouble he can.

JILL: It's not his decision.

RUBY: That won't stop him.

JILL: Well, he can't cause too much trouble from Nashville.

RUBY: Don't look to me like he's long for Nashville.

JILL: He say how his career's doing?

RUBY: You saw how he looked. Had to sell his car. Looking like a bum.

JILL: Prospects, I mean. He still trying to get a recording contract?

RUBY: He didn't say. If I was him, I'd be concentrating on the next meal.

JILL: He didn't look very good, did he?

RUBY: If he doesn't get his head on straight, he's gonna find himself on a doorstep with nothing but a wine bottle and his dead dreams.

JILL: Duncan's too serious about his music to end up like that.

RUBY: That's what Nashville does. You only read about the stars. For every star, there's a whole city full of men sitting on doorsteps.

JILL: And the women with dead dreams? Where do they sit?

RUBY: Women never sit, you ought to know that. They wait tables. Nashville is full of would-be country singers, song writers, you name it, slinging hash and pouring coffee. Just waiting for their star to come in. Oh God, it's a repeatable world, ain't it? Men on doorsteps and women waiting tables. You ready for a brandy in that?

JILL: Don't you have to work tonight?

RUBY: Lots of daylight yet. I can take a nap later.

JILL: Sure, mama . . .

(And Ruby brings out the brandy bottle as the LIGHTS FADE TO BLACKOUT.)

3/ six months later, morning

(AT RISE: a soft country song is playing on the radio. Ruby, in her robe, sits at the kitchen table, listening to the music and sometimes humming along. She's filing her nails.)

(JILL enters, also in her robe.)

RUBY: How you feeling, hon?

206

JILL: Terrible.

RUBY: It was a big bottle of Scotch you were pouring from.

JILL: Never again.

RUBY: Well, it was good for you, given the circumstances.

JILL: I got really drunk, didn't I?

RUBY: You sure did.

JILL: Did I talk a lot?

RUBY: Sure did.

JILL: I can't remember what I said.

RUBY: Not a lot that made sense. Except some feelings. Some of your feelings made sense.

JILL: I talk about Tim?

RUBY: Sure did.

JILL: You want some coffee?

RUBY: Brandy might help your head. Hair of the dog . . .

JILL: The thought makes me want to puke . . .

RUBY: I can vouch that it works. Once you get over the first couple sips, you're home free. A raw egg in a shot of brandy — sounds putrid, doesn't it? — but I swear to God it works.

JILL: Mama, my stomach isn't going to put up with talk like that.

RUBY: Well, if your head hangs on, you give it a try.

JILL: What did I say about Tim?

RUBY: Pretty much what any woman's gonna say. That he's selfish, thoughtless, he was using you, he's only after one thing, he took unfair advantage of your situation, he's devious, he was seeing another woman all along—

JILL: He's still married!

RUBY: That, too.

JILL: I feel like such an idiot.

RUBY: You don't have to feel bad about it with me.

JILL: I said all those things? Then it's not true, what they say about booze, that it makes you say the truth.

RUBY: You weren't telling the truth?

JILL: No. He's not any of those things. He's a very sweet man.

RUBY: What are you talking about? He dumps you at the ski resort, you have to take a bus back—

JILL: I dumped myself, because I felt so humiliated.

RUBY: You said he dumped you, he used you, he—

JILL: Hush up a minute and I'll tell you.

RUBY: I'm dying to hear.

JILL: It's so embarrassing . . .

RUBY: What happened?

JILL: Well, originally we were gonna just spend the day and drive back Saturday night. But when it got snowing so bad, I suggested we get a room in the lodge.

RUBY: You made the first move?

JILL: Well, I thought he was so shy. How long've we been dating — and he doesn't even make a move? I thought he wasn't making any moves on me because he was shy.

RUBY: I thought you said he tried to get you in bed once.

JILL: Months ago. He'd had too much to drink. He never tried after that, so I thought maybe he was shy and couldn't stand being rejected again. Ends up he wasn't even interested.

RUBY: He must be gay. A man who calls himself a feminist—

JILL: Just hush and let me tell the story. So I practically have to convince him that it's okay to get a room together. I mean, he thought we should get separate rooms, at sixty a throw. It was ridiculous to pay that much. Anyway we get the room and we ski some more and have the most marvelous dinner by candlelight in front of a roaring fire. It was just the most romantic evening you can imagine.

RUBY: And he didn't respond? He's gay.

JILL: So afterwards, when we're back in the room, which has twin beds, he says do I want the bathroom first or second, so I decide, Let's go for it, and take it first and go in and take off my clothes and walk back out naked as a jaybird and give him a big hug and start rubbing all over him — and that's when he tells me he's married. Separated. They have two kids, he still loves her, you name it. I couldn't even get him interested in a one-night stand. The desk said a bus was coming through late if it could make it, so I just took my chances and here I am, humiliated and feeling like the biggest fool in Juniper County.

RUBY: Well, it's lucky you didn't get no one-night stand, if you ask me. You might find yourself pregnant again.

JILL: I didn't know there were any men that moral.

RUBY: I never did think that man was right for you.

JILL: Standing there naked as a jaybird, well, I sure wasn't looking for Mr. Right. I was looking for Mr. Right Now.

RUBY: Why'd you tell me all that other last night?

JILL: Cause I felt humiliated, I guess. I didn't know you could lie like that when you were drunk.

(The doorbell rings. It's from the front door this time.)

RUBY: This lawyer somebody to hound you, like Duncan was?

JILL: No.

208

(Ruby goes to answer the door, exiting upstage. A beat.)

DUNCAN *(off-stage)*: Well, do I get invited in?

(Duncan and Ruby return. We see a different man now. He is dressed to the teeth in the most fashionable western superstar style. Cowboy hat, books, bright fancy shirt.)

DUNCAN : Seeing is believing, right? I got a little time to kill, so I thought I'd drop by. My pilot thought he heard something funny in the engine. It's being checked out at the Bend airport. I borrowed a car and drove on over.
JILL: You came here in an airplane?
DUNCAN: Well, we're headed for L.A. actually. I couldn't resist getting him to go out of his way so I could show off a little bit of God's country.
JILL: Maybe I'd better get dressed . . .
DUNCAN: I don't mind. I mean, I ain't got much time. Engine checked out, so they're just servicing it.
JILL: Well — how've you been?
DUNCAN: Good, good. How about yourself?
JILL: Just fine. Real good, actually. Real good.
DUNCAN: That's good to hear.

(Pause.)

DUNCAN: Well, can I use your phone a minute?
RUBY: Help yourself.

(Duncan goes to the phone and dials. A beat.)

DUNCAN *(on phone)*: Let her rip.

(He hangs up.)

DUNCAN: Mind if I turn on the radio?

(Without waiting for a reply, he turns it on and we hear the end of a country classic.)
DUNCAN: I'll tell you, it's a funny world. Til a couple months ago, I was beginning to believe I was ready for skid row. You wouldn't believe

some of the dives I was living in. Washing dishes in a goddamn truck stop.

(And now the radio plays "Stale Beer in the Morning, Stale Love in the Night". The song will continue as background below.)

DUNCAN: I dropped a record off at the station. Sneak preview. We don't get the official release til next week.

JILL: Jesus, Duncan, you did it, didn't you?

DUNCAN: So far, so good. Looks real good. I couldn't afford all this image-making if it didn't. "Stale Beer in the Morning, Stale Love in the Night." It's gonna be the title of the first album, too. Nashtone picked it up. I had to change it around a little bit but it's basically the same song.

JILL: I'm really glad for you, Duncan.

DUNCAN: I worked for it. Paid my dues and all that. You wouldn't believe some of the holes I was living in toward the end.

JILL: I can imagine. Well, you want anything? A cup of coffee, a beer, or anything?

DUNCAN: I quit drinking, and I'm coffeed out. On a diet, to tell the truth. Want that photo on the album cover to look good. Always was a little vain.

JILL: Yeah, you were.

DUNCAN: So how're you and the lawyer doing?

JILL: Fine. I mean, we're good friends. That's all it's ever been, just being good friends. He's fine. A good friend.

DUNCAN: Well, I teamed up with someone myself. You remember the name Carey Winchester — she's gonna be a bigger star than me, or I don't know talent. I'll probably end up carrying her guitar case and maybe writing her a song or two. Patsy Cline, reborn. You're gonna hear about Carey Winchester.

JILL: She's got a record out, too?

DUNCAN: She's gonna debut with an album. They got a whole campaign worked out. It's gonna be a big splash, even for Nashville.

JILL: She must be something.

DUNCAN: One talented lady.

JILL: And you're good friends with her?

DUNCAN: Well, I hope so. We're engaged.

JILL: That's really great, Duncan. You deserve all the happiness there is.

DUNCAN: Actually Carey's part of the reason I dropped by. She's looking for album material and I was wondering if Rube still had her songs on tape.

JILL: Mama...?

(Ruby, very quite until now, doesn't respond at first. Finally she shuts the radio off.)

RUBY: You love every goddamn minute of this, don't you? You son-of-a-bitch, who do you think you are, busting in here looking like a drugstore cowboy and throwing all this bullshit around? I wasn't born yesterday.

DUNCAN: Don't you get tired of hating men?

JILL: He's making a genuine offer, mama. I know he is. He didn't have to come here.

RUBY: Course he did, to show off his new clown suit and play that demo on the radio.

DUNCAN: This outfit's something, isn't it? When my agent picked it out, I told him, I can't wear shit like that. Do you want to be a star or not, he asked me. So here I am. It's something, Nashville. I think the music is the least important part of it...the musicians, the people that make the music in the first place. Nashville is run by accountants and agents and producers. It's really something.

RUBY: You're not telling me anything I don't know.

DUNCAN: Well, I guess I'll be on my way then. Good to see you, Jill. Glad things are working out for you.

JILL: Wait. This girlfriend of yours, what's her name—

DUNCAN: Carey Winchester. A few months, nobody's gonna have to ask.

JILL: Tell me straight — is she really looking for material?

DUNCAN: I wouldn't say so if she wasn't. I can't promise anything, of course, but she's looking hard, especially for, you know, songs with special meaning to women.

JILL: Give him the tape, mama.

RUBY: Nope.

JILL: It's an opportunity.

RUBY: I don't think so.

DUNCAN: All I can promise you is that Carey will listen to it. I've already told her about you.

JILL: You've told her about mama's songs, really?

DUNCAN: You're a damn good song writer, Rube. I always thought so.

RUBY: Somebody give me a shovel...

JILL: Just give him the tape.

RUBY: It's my only copy and I'm not letting it out of the house.

JILL: Mama, be reasonable.

DUNCAN: I can understand that. Listen, let me give you my card. You make a copy and send it to me. Directly to me, so I can make sure it doesn't get lost in the shuffle. A lot of songwriters' tapes out there — you wouldn't believe how many people write songs. I bet if you picked out five random people in Nashville, four of them write country songs.

(Duncan offers his card to Ruby, who doesn't make a move to take it. So Jill takes it.)

JILL: Thanks. I'll get her to send you a tape.

DUNCAN: Carey'll listen to it, that's all I can promise.

JILL: We appreciate it.

DUNCAN: Well, they're probably wondering what happened to me.

JILL: You look good, Duncan. I'm glad you stopped by.

DUNCAN: You look good, too. You happy?

JILL: Sure.

DUNCAN: That's the important thing.

(Pause.)

DUNCAN: Well, hell, I might as well say what I came here to say. I'm sorry about being so hard on you. I see now that you'd've ended up with all the hassles, raising a kid while I was out on the road most of the time and the kid never knowing its father really anyway. Carey and me, we expect to have one soon as the timing's right. You were right, it's important a kid grows up with both parents there, you know? I came down pretty hard on you at the time and I'm sorry about that.

JILL: Well, thanks doesn't sound like the right thing to say somehow — but, thanks.

DUNCAN: *(to Ruby)* I hope you send that tape. Personally I think you got a pretty good shot at it. See you all.

JILL: Bye. You fly careful now.

DUNCAN: I got a pilot flew helicopter in Nam. He don't even call it flying unless someone's shooting at him.

(And he's out the upstage door. RUBY starts laughing.)

RUBY: My God, that outfit . . .!

JILL: You copy that tape and send it to him. You hear me?

RUBY: There's no point in sending it.

JILL: He's not a liar, mama, it's not in his personality. That lady's looking for material.

RUBY: I'm not gonna send the tape. That's the end of it. I don't want to hear no more about it.

JILL: But why not? What can you lose?

RUBY: Sleep.

JILL: What're you talking about?

RUBY: You asked what I'd lose sending it — I'd lose sleep. I'd be so worried, I wouldn't be able to shut off my mind. Scotch wouldn't even shut it off. I'd keep worrying whether they liked it, whether it was getting played or being stuck in somebody's drawer or maybe they were laughing and thinking how stupid it was for some lady in nowheresville to think she could write a song they'd want to buy in Nashville.

JILL: You are your own worst enemy, that's just what you are. You lack confidence.

RUBY: No. I just accept reality.

JILL: You won't know how good your songs are until you try.

RUBY: I have tried. You keep talking like I never tried before. I just write these songs and keep them hidden in the tavern or something. Well, that's not how it is. I tried sending tapes to Nashville. I tried for a year.

JILL: When did you ever try?

RUBY: You were too little to remember but I tried, believe me. I was going with a guy named Ron then — he sang country himself, of course. Curse of my existence, country singers. Anyway, Ron found this ad in a country magazine, "songs needed immediately," so we put together a tape of my songs and sent it off to Nashville. It was the worst experience of my life.

JILL: You have to keep trying, mama.

RUBY: I wouldn't've minded if they'd just sent the tape back. I wouldn't've minded them saying I had no talent or whatever, but I couldn't deal with what they ended up doing. They stole my songs. Three of them. Oh, they changed them around a bit, but they stole them, free and simple. They never did return the tape. Said they didn't know what happened to it. Said I didn't enclose return postage, but I did. They kept changing their story. I called the studio myself, and they just gave me the run around. A couple months later, maybe longer, maybe six months, seven, and boom — there was my song right on the radio, hardly disguised at all. I phoned the studio again, madder than hell, but their number was disconnected. That's my experience with Nashville.

JILL: I didn't know you went through that. I'm really sorry.

RUBY: School of hard knocks, they call to.

JILL: Hardest school there is.

RUBY: You'd better believe it.

JILL: But this ain't really the same thing, mama.

RUBY: What do I know about his new lady or what kind of studio and recording company she's involved with? They're as likely taking him for a ride as not.

JILL: He paid his dues, you know he has.

RUBY: I'm not sending my songs, that's all there is to it. I'm too old to go through anything like that again.

JILL: You're not old . . .

RUBY: Old enough. And older in experience than in years, believe me.

JILL: I still say you're making a mistake.

RUBY: Well, fine, you just give me that right, okay?

JILL: I don't know why I'm trying to tell you what to do. You never listen to advice.

RUBY: Got a right to make my own mistakes.

JILL: Me, too, mama.

RUBY: Right. It's a free country.

(Pause.)

JILL: I'm moving out. I'm gonna find me an apartment.

RUBY: What're you talking about, moving out?

JILL: I decided last week.

RUBY: That don't make a bit of sense, paying two rents when we could be paying one.

JILL: I got a right to make my own mistakes, just like you.

RUBY: How you gonna afford your own apartment?

JILL: They got some cheap studios in that new complex near the park. I already looked into it.

RUBY: You mad at me or something?

JILL: Course not. But I think I should live alone, mama. I think it'd be good for both of us.

RUBY: I don't give you enough freedom here?

JILL: That has nothing to do with it.

RUBY: It's men, isn't it? You worry you can't bring a man here. I never said you couldn't.

JILL: It has nothing to do with men.

RUBY: Everything has to do with men. That's the goddamn problem with this world, you can't keep the son-of-a-bitches out of anything.

Can't even share a house with your daughter without men botching it up.

JILL: Damn it, mama, it ain't men at all! It's me. I need my own place. And it's you, too. You depend too much on me.

RUBY: What?

JILL: On me being here. On being able to help me.

RUBY: I shouldn't help you?

JILL: I'm twenty-one years old, it's time I lived on my own and got myself out of my own jams and learned from my own mistakes.

RUBY: We work different shifts most of the time. You get lots of time to yourself.

JILL: It ain't the same thing. This is your home. You signed the lease. It's decorated the way you want it, it's—

RUBY: You want to change the drapes or something? Hell, go ahead, hon. I don't care what you want to do around here. Redecorate to your heart's content.

JILL: That's not it. Mama, you're not listening to me.

RUBY: I'm listening to you. I did something wrong.

JILL: No. I just need to be alone. I just need to be alone — can you understand that?

RUBY: It's what happened to you at the ski lodge. You're still feeling bad, humiliated about that.

JILL: Yes, I am, but that's not the topic of conversation now. I'm talking about learning to live alone. You got to learn to live with yourself, too, mama.

RUBY: You think I don't do that?

JILL: Not when you depend on me so much.

RUBY: When do I depend on you?

JILL: On me getting in trouble or making a mistake, so you can play mother and get me out of it, comfort me, tell me how much we're alike.

RUBY: We *are* alike.

JILL: Yes, in many ways we are. That's why I need my own place, to learn how we're different, to learn how I'm my own person.

RUBY: If you want to leave me, you want to leave me.

JILL: Now don't pout. I hate it when you pout.

RUBY: Well, my feelings are hurt. I don't know what I've done.

JILL: You haven't done a thing, damn it.

RUBY: You just don't move out on your mother for no reason.

JILL: The reason is, you're my mother.

RUBY: I give you lots of room, now you know I do.

JILL: I need to have my own apartment. If you can't understand that, then I'm sorry. You'd better learn to understand it because you need your own space as much as I do.

RUBY: Don't you tell me what I need, young lady. You have no idea what I need.

JILL: You need me.

RUBY: I can't help it. It's hard to let go.

JILL: I know. I can feel how it is.

RUBY: You have no idea how it is.

JILL: I think I do. There was life inside me, mama, and I had to let it go.

RUBY: You did the only thing you could do.

JILL: That didn't make it any easier. I'm not even sure I did the right thing.

RUBY: Of course, you did the right thing.

JILL: Well, it's too late to change my mind.

RUBY: You can change your mind about moving out.

JILL: I'll still be close. It's not like I'm moving away.

RUBY: You will, some day. I can feel it in my bones.

JILL: Rimrock ain't the world. It's a little tiny spot on it.

RUBY: There's nothing to hold you here. Not me. Not the town. Certainly not the café.

JILL: I'm moving out, mama, not away.

RUBY: It's the first step, though.

JILL: We'll have to see.

RUBY: First, it's getting off by yourself. Then you meet some man who's looking for a better job in a bigger city—

JILL: It's gonna be a while before I find a man. It won't be anybody in Rimrock.

RUBY: Which is why you'll move away. One of the reasons.

JILL: There's more to life than Rimrock.

RUBY: See there? You're already gone.

JILL: Maybe you're right. Maybe I am already gone.

RUBY: Barely said goodbye.

JILL: I guess this is what this is all about now, isn't it? I'm saying goodbye.

RUBY: Might as well just move to Portland and be done with it.

JILL: Portland's too big. I don't know where it'll be. That's still in the future.

RUBY: What are you waiting for?

JILL: I'm not waiting, mama. That's the point. I'm trying to learn how to make things happen for myself. Like Duncan did. He suffered a lot, I know he did. It was terrible for him, living like such a failure when he has so much talent and he knows it and still it ain't giving him a goddamn thing, not one tiny reward for being so talented, just sweating and trying it make something happen in this world for yourself, something you want and can be proud of , and so you just have to go for it, mama, you can't sit around and wait for it to come because it's never gonna come, not without you going after it. It's gotta be chased. It's gotta be pursued. It don't beckon to no waiting.

(Pause.)

RUBY: So what is it you're after, what're you gonna make happen?
JILL: I don't know. I'm just trying to do first things first. That means learning how to live alone.
RUBY: Well, I'm gonna miss you.
JILL: We'll be seeing each other practically every day.
RUBY: It won't seem the same.
JILL: It's not supposed to be the same. You can use a change in your life, too.
RUBY: Sure.
JILL: Sending Duncan that tape, for example. It'd be good for you to do that.
RUBY: I been through that once. Waiting on pins and needles . . .
JILL: At least you're waiting for something. It beats waiting for nothing. Waiting for nothing at all.

(Pause.)

RUBY: You think his record's really gonna be released? And that stuff about his new girlfriend?
JILL: Yes, I do. And I think you should send him your tape.
RUBY: Maybe I'm just afraid it isn't good enough.
JILL: Play it, mama. You can hear for yourself how good it is. You play it and then I want to show you my studio. I already put down a deposit on it.
RUBY: When did you do that?
JILL: Last week. I've been trying to get the nerve to tell you.
RUBY: You are making things happen for yourself, aren't you?
JILL: I'm trying, mama. I'm sure trying.
RUBY: You think I should send the whole tape, or just a few songs? Make a new tape of the best ones?
JILL: Let's listen and decide.

(RUBY will fetch the tape.)

217

RUBY: I still think this is a perfect waste of time, sending it.
JILL: It sure beats waiting around for nothing.
RUBY: You think so?
JILL: Waiting for something is better than waiting for nothing.
RUBY: It's still waiting, though.

(And "Ruby's Song" starts to play. Jill goes to her mother. They hold one another, listening to the song. LIGHTS BEGIN SLOW FADE TO BLACKOUT. The play is over.)

For royalties information:
contact Charles Deemer
1-800-294-7176
cdeemer@teleport.com

1989

Varmints
A tragi-comedy of the Old West in two acts

First performed at the Firehouse Theatre in Portland, Oregon, on April 28, 1989. Directed by Gary O'Brien.

THE CAST (4M, 2W):
Patrick McGuinness, *a detective, an Irishman*
Ruby, *proprietor of the Canyon City Room & Board, who wears a patch over one eye*
Lester, *her black cook*
Stump, *a miner, who has a wooden leg*
Cincinnatus Hiner Miller, *lawyer, miner, Indian fighter and poet, who wears buckskin*
Miss Lee (Rose), *a woman of mystery*

TIME AND PLACE:
Canyon City in Eastern Oregon, near the end of the gold rush in 1865

THE SET:
Interior of Canyon City Room & Board. Check-in desk upstage, with entrance into kitchen and access to basement. Tables for dining downstage. Left, a main entrance and exit. Also a neutral area. Entrance to rooms, right, with staircase leading to upper levels: upstairs is a hallway, a door, Miss Lee's Room.

ACT ONE

1/ a summer evening

(AT RISE: LIGHTS UP on MCGUINNESS, who addresses the audience.)

MCGUINNESS: So I'm standing on a corner in the windy city of Chicago, puffing on my pipe and looking every bit of the Pinkerton operative that I am, when I'm struck my lightning. There's no other way to put it. I'm electrified to my toes by the flashing clarity of sudden insight. I dare say, Sir Isaac Newton himself couldn't't've been more overwhelmed, being beaned by an apple and having the secrets of the Universe open suddenly before him.

How can I describe the consequences of such sudden insight? My life changed in an instant. Immediately I knew what I must do. So I tapped the ashes of my pipe against the heel of a boot, and returned straightaway to the office, where I resigned. They couldn't believe it: Patrick McGuinness resign! But why? What would I do? "I'm leaving Chicago for business ventures elsewhere," I told them. And then I hurried away to make my plans.

With sudden insight before me, there was no choice but to follow the clues of justice to their conclusion, even though it meant going to the godawful wilds of the new state of Oregon. I shuddered to think what strange beasts and lizards would be waiting for me, so far from the trappings of civilization. But the chameleon I was after would be under one of those same Oregon rocks, I was sure of it — somewhere in that godforsaken territory was my former colleague, Thomas O'Reilly himself, and his beautiful bride Rose, each congratulating the other for pulling off the crime of the century. I could hardly wait to see their expressions when I walked up and, with a tip of my hat, ordered the first round. It would be worth a celebration to be sure, for after solving this crime I would have the reputation to start my own agency. I'd never have to work for another man again.

So I bought my ticket and headed west, in search of gold and lizards. Little did I know how vast that godforsaken Oregon wilderness is and how many cold and sleepless nights I would spend before finding the lizards I was after — or at least finding the prettiest one. I must admit that by this time I was wondering if that flash of lightning hadn't been discharged by the Devil himself, so weary was I in my journey and so hungry for a bowl of Mary Killarney's stew and a mug of stout. Then I walked into Canyon City Room & Board, looking only for a bed and whatever "vittles" — to use a new word I'd learned in the west — whatever vittles would stay put on the table . . . I walked in and soon found myself struck by lightning again . . .

(LIGHTS OFF McGuinness and UP FULL on the interior of Canyon City Room & Board. MILLER is at a table, working on a poem. He recites aloud.)

MILLER: "Here lifts the land of clouds!
Fierce mountain forms,
Made white with everlasting snow,
look down
Through mists of many canyons,
mighty storms
That stretch from Autumn's purple,
drench and drown
The yellow hem of Spring."

(LISTER has entered with Miller's coffee.)

MILLER: What do you think, Lester, my boy?
LESTER: You tell me, Hiner. If this coffee isn't strong enough for you, you can always go to Susie's down the street.
MILLER: Abandon Canyon City's center of culture! Never! I was wondering what you thought of my new poem:
"Tall cedars frown
Dark-brow'd, through banner'd
clouds that stretch and stream
Above the sea from snowy mountain crown.
The heavens roll, and all things drift or seem
To drift about and drive like some majestic dream."
Well?
LESTER: It'll never play at the dance hall.
MILLER: What dance hall recognizes genius? With this poem — number forty-three, my boy — I'm only seven shy of my first book. Mark my word, Lester, I'll be taking the manuscript to Portland before fall.
LESTER: So how's the coffee?
MILLER: Better.
LESTER: There's always Susie's.

MILLER: You know I'm ruthlessly loyal to my friends. As I expect they'll be to me, when my book appears.

LESTER: You name it yet?

MILLER: Don't name the baby before it's born, my boy.

LESTER: You want anything else before I go back to my dishes?

MILLER: I was hoping to meet Miss Lee for coffee.

LESTER: I haven't seen her yet this morning.

MILLER: She spends most of the day in her room, painting, does she not?

LESTER: Ruby would know better than me.

(RUBY has entered from the kitchen and hears this.)

RUBY: I'd know what better?

MILLER: I was wondering when Miss Lee would be down.

RUBY: Miller, I knew it wasn't my food or coffee that had you hanging around here lately. You should be out trying to make a living like the rest of the men.

MILLER: The rest of the men don't have my gift.

RUBY: They don't have something you got, I'll grant you that.

(Lester has started away and will exit.)

MILLER: Lester! Thanks for strengthening the coffee. It's now quite adequate.

RUBY: You ain't in San Francisco, Hiner. Around here, you take what you get.

MILLER: A man takes his sensibilities with him, wherever he may go.

RUBY: How's your book coming?

MILLER: I finished number forty-three only a moment ago:
"I stood where thunderbolts were wont
To smite they Titan-fashioned front,
And heard dark mountains rock and roll;
I saw the lightning's gleaming rod
Reach forth and write on Heaven's scroll
The awful autograph of God!"

(As Miller recites the poem, McGuinness enters, carrying a bag. He looks travel weary. He stands just inside the doorway, leaving the door open behind him.)

RUBY: Help you?

MCGUINNESS: Do you have a spare room?

RUBY: Dollar a night without meals, dollar and a half with.

MCGUINNESS: With.

RUBY: Just sign in.

(Ruby has a pistol in her belt and quickly draws it now, shooting at something on the floor near the door.)

RUBY: And close the door behind you, before the lizards get the run of the place.

(He does so, then cautiously approaches the front desk to sign in.)

RUBY: We stop serving breakfast at eight. Dinner is noon til one-thirty, and supper five to seven.

MCGUINNESS: That's fine. I'd like to pay a week in advance.

RUBY: Let's see, that'd come to ...

MCGUINNESS: Ten-fifty.

RUBY: Right.

(McGuinness pays her.)

RUBY: We got beef stew for dinner.

MCGUINNESS: I've been dreaming of a good stew for weeks.

RUBY: Your room's up the stairs and all the way down the hall.

MCGUINNESS: Thank you.

(He starts to leave, right.)

(As McGuinness approaches the stairway, MISS LEE comes down and enters: he nods as she passes. He starts up the stairs and near the top will eavesdrop for a bit, hearing Miller's poem below.)

(Miss Lee takes the table farthest from Miller's table.)

RUBY: Tea or coffee, Miss Lee?

MISS LEA: Tea. My stomach's unsettled this morning.

RUBY: Not from supper last night, I hope.

MISS LEE: I think not.

RUBY: Be a few minutes.

(She leaves to make the tea.)

(A beat, as Miller decides on his plan of action. He recites from a poem:)

MILLER: "I am sitting alone in the moonlight,
In the moonlight soft and clear,
And a thousand thoughts steal o'er me,
While penciling, sitting here."

(The LIGHTS FADE as a spot comes up on McGuinness on the stairs.)

MCGUINNESS: So I'm listening in to the most godawful poem I've heard in all my days, but grinning all the same, for the young lady downstairs is Rose O'Reilly herself, Chicago's most famous painter and the bride of the biggest lizard this side of hell. She doesn't know me but I surely know her from all the pictures in the Chicago papers when Thomas took her hand in marriage. At last, my journey into this godforsaken Oregon wilderness was nearing its end ...

(LIGHTS OFF McGuinness and back UP FULL in the boarding house.)

MILLER: "By unnamed rivers of the Oregon north,
That roll dark-heaved into the turbulent hills,
I have made my home. The wild heart thrills
With memories fierce, and a world storms forth."

(A beat. Miller moves to Miss Lee's table, standing by it.)

MILLER: Allow me to introduce myself. Cincinnatus Hiner Miller — lawyer, Indian fighter, poet and man of culture. And you are ... ?

(No reply.)

MILLER: Miss Lee, I've heard you called. I understand that you paint. You're an artist. I'd consider it an honor to see your work, Miss Lee.

(No reply.)

224

MILLER: As a poet myself, I well understand the shyness of the sensitive soul. I used to be shy as well. Then it occurred to me, if I don't face the cruel world head-on and let it know that genius has appeared on its philistine shores, then who will play my trumpet for me? No one. No one! Oh, I assure you, it wasn't easy to toot my own horn at first. Humility is my very breath. But it had to be done. Genius is a gift and my choice was to reject it — or to embrace it. I chose the latter.

(No reply.)

MILLER *(reciting)*: "I move among the frowning firs;
Black bats wheel by in rippled whirs!"

(He sits down at the table.)

MILLER: It's from my first book. What do you think?
MISS LEE: Mister ... ?
MILLER: Cincinnatus Hiner Miller — most folks call me Hiner.
MISS LEE: Mr. Miller, I do not recall inviting you to join me.
MILLER: I'm guilty of inviting myself, madam.
MISS LEE: If you don't mind, I prefer to be alone.
MILLER: I like spunk in a woman. Especially in an artist.
MISS LEE: I'm not an artist.
MILLER: I've heard that you paint.
MISS LEE: I dabble. It's — recreation.
MILLER: How many years I resisted admitting my own genius! Thinking I was a mere dabbler, a poet for recreation! I resisted the images that flashed before me, I denied their brilliance. Perhaps you do the same. May I see your paintings?
MISS LEE: I'm waiting for my tea.
MILLER: After your tea, of course.
MISS LEE: Mr. Miller —
MILLER: Hiner.
MISS LEE: Mr. Miller, I'm accustomed to drinking my tea in solitude.
MILLER: Solitude! I have my first pipe in solitude each morning myself. As a poet, I certainly understand solitude. Shall I meet you in your room after tea?
MISS LEE: No.
MILLER: Madam, if I may be permitted to share an instinctive thought — I think you are resisting your own genius.

(Ruby returns with the tea.)

RUBY: If he's bothering you, ma'am, just give a holler.
MILLER: I was just returning to my table. Thank you, Miss Lee, for the charming company.

(He goes back to his table.)

RUBY: Hiner don't usually hang around here in the morning. He usually hangs around his office, waiting for somebody who needs a lawyer. He bother you?
MISS LEE: It's all right. I just needed to stretch before getting back to work. I'll take my tea upstairs.

(She gets up to leave.)

RUBY: You want a refill brought up to your room, just holler.

(As Miss Lee passes, Miller stands up, bowing as she leaves. She exits upstairs.)

RUBY: Don't disturb the guests, Hiner.
MILLER: If you saw in her soul what I see ...
RUBY: I'm not talking about her soul, I'm talking about you leaving her alone.
MILLER: I am a perfect gentleman, as you well know.
RUBY: Just act like one.
MILLER: I cannot do otherwise.
RUBY: You don't fool me, Hiner. You got smitten by that lady, and I'm telling you to leave her be — at least in my place. She came here with a gentleman, and I'm sure she's not available for the likes of you.
MILLER: The gentleman left town, is what I hear.
RUBY: He still might be her husband.
MILLER: Don't vulgarize my attraction, Ruby. It's her artistic soul that interests me. She's painting art up there.
RUBY: Maybe she is, maybe she ain't.

(McGuinness enters from upstairs.)

RUBY: Everything all right?
MCGUINNESS: Beyond my wildest dreams.
RUBY: If you need anything, holler ...

226

MCGUINNESS: A cup of coffee, perhaps?
RUBY: Coming right up.

(She exits.)

MILLER: You look like a weary traveler — perhaps you'd like to join me.
MCGUINNESS: Thank you.

(He sits down at Miller's table.)

MILLER: Cincinnatus Hiner Miller — lawyer, Indian fighter, poet and man of culture.
MCGUINNESS: Pleased to meet you. They call me Paddy.
MILLER: And what brings you to Canyon City, Paddy? Need I ask? The lure of gold! Am I right? The challenge and temptation of instant wealth. Gold, gold! Yes, I can see the obsession in your eyes. Somewhere out there is a vein of gold as rich as an Irishman's blood — and who but an Irishman has the luck to find it? Am I right?
MCGUINNESS: A very close guess, you're making.
MILLER: Gold, gold!
MCGUINNESS: And are you prospecting for gold as well?
MILLER: I settle the legal difficulties that greed for gold engenders — at least until my first book of poems appears. Then I expect to live off my art. And where are you from, Paddy?
MCGUINNESS: Chicago.
MILLER: The windy city!
MCGUINNESS: The windy city, it is.
MILLER: Never been there. I expect to include Chicago on my first tour, however. How do they like poetry there?
MCGUINNESS: In the pubs, fine.
MILLER: I'm not settling for pubs, Paddy. Give me the auditoriums! The concert halls!

(Lester enters with the coffee.)

LESTER: You put anything in your coffee?
MCGUINNESS: A touch of Irish, but seldom this early.
MILLER: Another gold-seeker, Lester. Paddy, this is the best cook in Canyon City, though he sometimes makes the coffee weak.
MCGUINNESS: Pleased to meet you.

LESTER: Don't let Hiner pull your ear. He's always taking artistic license.

MILLER: I didn't know you were familiar with the term, my boy.

LESTER: I'm not your boy, Hiner.

(He exits.)

MILLER: Lester is an enigma. He's wiser than you'd expect a cook to be — not to mention wiser than you'd expect a Negro to be.

MCGUINNESS: I'm surprised to find a Negro in the west. I thought the country would be full of Indians.

MILLER: They've been laying low since I negotiated a treaty.

MCGUINNESS: You had trouble before?

MILLER: It was very bad for a while. It seems the gold strike was on land the Paiutes, in their quaint primitive way, regarded as sacred. Miners were digging up ancestral bones right along with the nuggets. Fortunately, I know the simple needs of the Paiutes and managed to pacify them. Not even the United States Army has been able to get them to sign a treaty, Paddy, but yours truly managed it straightaway. You'll never guess how.

MCGUINNESS: I can't imagine.

MILLER: With a few cases of whiskey.

MCGUINNESS: That's all it took?

MILLER: A trade secret, Paddy. In Canyon City, I'm regarded as a political negotiator of remarkable skill — but there's nothing to it. It's no more than a matter of knowing the enemy's weakness. When I gave them whiskey, they scurried off like lizards.

MCGUINNESS: But what happens when the whiskey's gone?

MILLER: I explained to them that the white man was after Oro Oregono, not a bunch of bones. And the Oro Oregono is almost gone. They'll have the desert back to themselves soon enough.

MCGUINNESS: Oro ... ?

MILLER: Oro Oregono — it's Spanish for "Oregon gold." It also happens to be the title of the epic poem I'm planning for my second book. It'll be the "Iliad" of its day, Paddy! You know the "Iliad," of course.

MCGUINNESS: It rings a bell.

MILLER: It's Greek, written by the blind poet Homer. A masterpiece in its day. About the Trojan War — nation against nation. But out here, Paddy, in the west, it's man against gold, man against his own lust for wealth. This is a theme that outlives nations. Except for the beautiful Helen, would we even remember Troy today? We remember the face that launched a thousand ships but little else. The Trojan horse. Homer, for all his talent, picked too small a theme. Nations die, Paddy, but gold is eternal. And why? Because man's nature is greed. Greed! So that's why, right here in Canyon City, in these dry and barren hills unseen by most of the world, the greatest eternal struggle known to man is happening right before our eyes. Man's lust for gold! Paddy, I'm not ashamed to admit that this work, my second book, will be superior to anything an American has ever written before. Oro Oregono! I already have it whole in my mind.

MCGUINNESS: I never expected to find a poet in the Oregon wilderness.

(The entrance door swings open and a knife comes flying in, crashing on the floor. McGuinness dives under the table. Behind the knife enters STUMP.)

STUMP: Goddamn varmints, stay outside where you belong!

(He'll fetch his knife and sheath it on his wooden leg, which he drags heavily alongside him.)

MILLER: The lizards don't bite, Stump.
STUMP: They still give me the creeps.

(McGuinness gets to his feet.)

MCGUINNESS: They give me the creeps as well.
MILLER: Don't let them bother you, Paddy, or you'll be bothered eternally.
MCGUINNESS: It's been nice talking to you, Hiner.
MILLER: Anytime, lad. Always good to chat with a man from the big city.
MCGUINNESS: I'm sure I'll see you later.

(McGuinness starts to exit upstairs.)

MILLER: Paddy!
MCGUINNESS: Yes?
MILLER: "I sing of the West and I sing of the greed that makes a man act outlandish.
    And all for the lure of Oregon gold — that's Oro Oregono in Spanish!"

It's the opening couplet of my epic!

(McGuinness just looks at him. CROSS FADE TO:)

2/ a moment later

(McGuinness knocks on the door to Miss Lee's room. In the room, Miss Lee is painting on a canvas which we cannot see. The room is filled with canvases.)

MISS LEE: Who is it?
MCGUINNESS: Your new neighbor!
MISS LEE: I'm busy.
MCGUINNESS: I just need a minute of your time.

(Miss Lee opens the door.)

MCGUINNESS: When I passed you earlier, I was thinking, Haven't we met before?
MISS LEE: I don't believe so.
MCGUINNESS: In Chicago.
MISS LEE: You're from — Chicago?
MCGUINNESS: Born and bred. May I come in?
MISS LEE: Yes, of course.

(McGuinness enters.)

MISS LEE: Please excuse the mess.
MCGUINNESS: Quite a painter, I see.
MISS LEE: It's a hobby. You say you're from Chicago?
MCGUINNESS: For a fact.
MISS LEE: I didn't get your name.
MCGUINNESS: Because I didn't give it.
MISS LEE: I'm — Shirley Lee.
MCGUINNESS: Are you now? Then you must not be the one I'm thinking of because her name is Rose. If you'll excuse me ...
MISS LEE: Wait — you haven't told me your name.
MCGUINNESS: People call me Paddy.
MISS LEE: I have been called Rose. It's a nickname.
MCGUINNESS: But you don't think we've met before?
MISS LEE: I'm sure not.

230

MCGUINNESS: Then if you'll excuse me ...

MISS LEE: But I am from Chicago.

MCGUINNESS: Another Rose from Chicago. Surely this is quite a coincidence, meeting in this godforsaken Oregon wilderness.

MISS LEE: What's your last name, Paddy?

MCGUINNESS: McGuinness. Named after the stout I drink like mother's milk itself.

MISS LEE: I've met no Paddy McGuinness, but ...

MCGUINNESS: What is it?

MISS LEE: *(with sudden urgency)* You have to help me, Paddy. I'm in terrible trouble.

MCGUINNESS: But did we meet in Chicago or not?

MISS LEE: No, we didn't — but I know who you are. You work for Pinkerton's.

MCGUINNESS: Formerly, yes. To be honest, it wasn't paying me in the manner in which I'd like to become accustomed — so I came west to seek my fortune.

MISS LEE: You don't have to lie to me, Paddy. You're here to find Thomas O'Reilly, and I'll be more than happy to tell you where he is.

MCGUINNESS: O'Reilly is here? I thought he transferred to the New York office.

MISS LEE: Don't play games with me, Paddy.

MCGUINNESS: And where do you know Thomas O'Reilly from?

MISS LEE: I married him in Chicago. I take it you were at the wedding.

MCGUINNESS: I did hear about Thomas' wedding but I'm sorry to say I was on duty at the time and couldn't attend, not even the marriage of a colleague. The boys tell me the champagne was flowing like Niagara Falls.

MISS LEE: Can we dump the charade? I need your help.

MCGUINNESS: I'd be honored to help a lady of such charm — if I can, of course.

MISS LEE: I think my husband is a criminal.

MCGUINNESS: Thomas O'Reilly a criminal! May I never drink another stout if it's true.

MISS LEE: It is true. I can't prove it — but I feel it. Something is wrong.

MCGUINNESS: And where is Thomas now?

MISS LEE: In the gold fields.

MCGUINNESS: One thing confuses me. You introduced yourself as Miss Lee.

MISS LEE: It wouldn't be safe to use my real name.

MCGUINNESS: I suppose everyone has heard of Rose Mulligan, Chicago's famous painter. But Rose O'Reilly?

MISS LEE: Paddy, Thomas deserted me in Portland. I followed him here.

MCGUINNESS: Deserted a lovely lady like yourself and so soon after the honeymoon! This is not the Thomas I remember, who put away stout with the best of us, and was a gentleman besides.

MISS LEE: He only married me because my father knows this country like the back of his hand. When Thomas found out what he wanted to know, he left me. He assumed I wouldn't have the courage to follow him.

MCGUINNESS: And tell me more about your father.

MISS LEE: Father's been following the gold strikes ever since California in forty-nine.

MCGUINNESS: I cannot imagine it, spending a lifetime in this wilderness, so far from the trappings of civilization.

MISS LEE: It was father who discovered the richest vein in Canyon City, which started the rush here. He sent me a map to it for my wedding present.

MCGUINNESS: A strange gift.

MISS LEE: He invited Thomas to join him while the gold was still there to be taken. In six months, father wrote, Thomas would have enough to buy us a home in Chicago and to start his own agency. I hadn't seen father in years and insisted on coming west as well. Thomas didn't approve but I wouldn't take no for an answer.

MCGUINNESS: A lady of spunk, you are.

MISS LEE: When he abandoned me in Portland, I feared the worst. I think he plans to steal father's claim.

MCGUINNESS: To rob his own father-in-law! May stout turn sour if it's true.

MISS LEE: I need help, Paddy. I can't go into the fields looking for Thomas myself.

MCGUINNESS: You'd have me go into the gold fields in search of your husband?

MISS LEE: Would you?

MCGUINNESS: And me a man who shivers at the mere thought of a lizard crossing my path.

MISS LEE: Thomas is after father's claim, I'm sure of it. Father's life may be in danger.

MCGUINNESS: To be sure, gold makes men behave strangely.

MISS LEE: Will you help me?

MCGUINNESS: I have to think about it.

MISS LEE: Why are you really here? And don't give me any of that nonsense about seeking your fortune.

MCGUINNESS: What a spunky tongue you have. Poor Thomas O'Reilly, to have inspired your ire.

MISS LEE: What are you doing in Canyon City, Paddy?

MCGUINNESS: Let's just say I smelled a rat as far away as Chicago.

MISS LEE: What kind of rat?

MCGUINNESS: I'm not sure. I'm here to find out.

MISS LEE: Perhaps our problems are related.

MCGUINNESS: It's too soon to say.

MISS LEE: But you'll help me?

MCGUINNESS: I'd prefer to help you without actually going into the fields. I have to think about it. I arrived a weary traveler, long overdue for a bath and a full night's rest. As it happens, I get my best ideas in bed.

(STUMP is at the door and knocks.)

STUMP: It's me!

MISS LEE: Just a minute! We'll have to talk later ...

MCGUINNESS: And who might that be?

MISS LEE: Stump — he's an old prospector who likes to tell me mining stories, to help me get into the mood to paint. I'm painting his portrait, part of a series on the mining camp. It's all that keeps me going...

(She lets Stump in.)

STUMP: I'm sure getting tired of — *(He sees McGuinness.)* What the hell you doing here?

MCGUINNESS: I was admiring the lady's work. Thanks for showing me, madam.

(He exits down the hallway. Stump enters the room, Miss Lee quickly closing the door behind him. He'll take off his wooden leg and empty gold dust out of it into a bucket. Then he'll quickly put the leg back on.)

MISS LEE: We've got to talk. That was a Pinkerton detective, Paddy McGuinness — he was asking about Thomas.

STUMP: What?

MISS LEE: He said he could smell a rat as far away as Chicago.

STUMP: I told you your husband wasn't too smart.

MISS LEE: I told him Thomas abandoned me in Portland.

STUMP: Are you crazy?

MISS LEE: I had to tell him something. I told him my father was in the fields with a rich claim and Thomas was out to get it for himself.

STUMP: Did he buy it?

MISS LEE: I'm not sure. I think so. He couldn't possibly have a clue about us.

STUMP: He's here, so he must've suspected Thomas.

MISS LEE: We have to get him into the fields so you can take care of him.

STUMP: You think you can get him out there?

MISS LEE: He's the city type — but yes, I think I can probably sweet-talk him into it.

STUMP: The sooner, the better.

MISS LEE: I'll try to get him out there tomorrow.

(Lester knocks on the door.)

STUMP: Just let me know.

(Miss Lee opens the door. Lester has a tray of tea.)

LESTER: Ruby asked me to bring this up for you.

MISS LEE: That's very nice of her.

STUMP: Well, I hope that ol' mining story inspires you ...

MISS LEE: I'm sure it will. Please visit anytime.

(Stump leaves, and Lester enters. Miss Lee closes the door.)

LESTER: Well, I've been thinking about your offer.

MISS LEE: And ... ?

LESTER: I can't think of a prettier lady to skip town with.

MISS LEE: Understand one thing: after we — take care of business — after we arrive in San Francisco, then that's the end of your employment.

LESTER: Look, once I get paid, I don't care where you go or what you do. Only I want twice the money.

MISS LEE: That's outrageous!

LESTER: You want protection traveling through this country, then you got it. You think you can manage alone, be my guest.

MISS LEE: I'm only asking for a valet since I'll be taking so much — luggage.

LESTER: Valet, right. Indians don't worry you at all.

MISS LEE: Between here and Portland, of course they do.

LESTER: If Hiner hadn't made that treaty, you'd be on your own. As it is, once they sober up, we may all be in trouble. I'm ready to get out of here myself, and twice what you offered is just about right for a grubstake.

MISS LEE: I won't pay it.

LESTER: Then you're on your own, lady.

MISS LEE: I can't afford that much.

LESTER: Course you can. You're a famous Chicago artist, right?

MISS LEE: Who told you that?

LESTER: Word gets around. I got no idea what you plan to paint but if you're as famous as your reputation, and all these here canvasses are getting pictures, then I'm thinking you must have one big show lined up. Probably scenes of the mining camp, am I right? I hear those eastern bigshots just eat up scenes from the West. I figure you'll probably get rich on this show. Famous artist like yourself wouldn't be wasting her time in a hell-hole like Canyon City for nothing. You want me to go on?

MISS LEE: You made your point.

LESTER: Good.

MISS LEE: I'll only pay it because I have no choice. I can't handle all these canvasses myself.

LESTER: You can always try somebody else.

MISS LEE: If the word's out about me, I'm sure anyone else would be as greedy as you are.

LESTER: Hey, you'll be getting your money's worth.

MISS LEE: I'm going to make sure that I do.

LESTER: So when are you going to start painting? I thought you were in a hurry.

MISS LEE: Preparing the canvasses is the hardest part.

LESTER: Harder than painting a picture? Looks to me like you just splatter gold paint on the canvas.

MISS LEE: Are you an art critic, too?

LESTER: My, aren't we touchy?

MISS LEE: I don't appreciate being taken advantage of.

LESTER: You're the one who tried to screw me, lady. We both know you got a big fancy show lined up.

MISS LEE: If you don't mind, I'd like to get back to work.

LESTER: Touchy and pushy, too.

MISS LEE: Good day, Lester.

LESTER: Hey, don't treat me like I'm not grateful or anything. Cooking for Ruby, I'd be here forever trying to save up a grubstake. Now, thanks to you, I can almost smell that ol' breeze coming off the San Francisco Bay. I was a fool to leave, to tell you the truth. That's what I get for thinking I could strike it rich. When I get back to San-fran, I'm going back to the stage where I belong.

MISS LEE: *(sarcastic)* How did I miss it? You're an actor!

LESTER: A Shakespearean actor, as a matter of fact. You ought to see me do Othello.

MISS LEE: Don't make me laugh.

LESTER: You be careful with the sarcasm, lady. Remember that you need me more than I need you.

MISS LEE: Do I?

LESTER: Course you do. All those Paiutes out there; all these canvasses to move. Hey, don't look so upset. You got nothing to cry over. You're a famous artist, you got a big show lined up. You're probably the richest bitch west of the Mississippi. See you at dinner.

(He smiles and exits. Miss Lee closes the door behind him and leans against it, thinking. BLACKOUT.)

3/ two hours later

(SPOT UP on McGuinness.)

MCGUINNESS: So I wake up from my fretful nap with no more enlightenment than when I first hit the pillow. But I also wake up with an appetite fit for an Irish cop and descend the stairs with my stomach full of nostalgia for Mary Killarney's stew ...

(UP FULL as he enters the boarding house. Miller sits at a table.)

MILLER: Join me for dinner, Paddy?

MCGUINNESS: Don't mind if I do.

MILLER: Hope you're not starving. Lester had trouble with the stove and the stew's late.

MCGUINNESS: A lament to my ears, for I'm hungry indeed.

MILLER: I have some deer jerky.

MCGUINNESS: You saved my life.

(Miller gives McGuinness a small stick of jerky.)

236

MILLER: I wonder if I could run an idea past you, as one man of culture to another.

MCGUINNESS: Culture, I'm weak on.

MILLER: I value the opinion of a man from Chicago nonetheless. I've been thinking of ways to liven up the dull life we live here. Unless you like dancing girls and fights, not to mention an occasional duel in the streets, there's no entertainment to be had. Recently we can't even amuse ourselves fighting the Paiutes. Certainly there's no culture. I've been thinking of ways to liven the place up and've hit upon an idea. Shakespeare! I'd produce the Bard right here in Canyon City!

MCGUINNESS: An ambitious plan, indeed. Where would you find the actors?

MILLER: I'd do excerpts. The soliloquies, which I could do myself. "To be or not to be...?" What do you think?

MCGUINNESS: Shakespeare would be culture, for a fact.

MILLER: Of course, if I could find someone else to perform as well — have you ever been on stage, Paddy?

MCGUINNESS: Never in my life.

MILLER: You have a natural thespian presence. Perhaps you'd be willing to join me in a scene or two.

MCGUINNESS: I'm busy on other matters — but the idea's a good one, I can see that. Your enthusiasm is a wonder to behold.

MILLER: Thank you. I'm glad you recognize genius.

(Lester enters.)

LESTER: We'll be ready pretty soon now.

MILLER: Lester, my boy, I've just shared a brilliant idea with Paddy here — I'm going to perform Shakespeare in Canyon City!

LESTER: I didn't know you were an actor.

MILLER: Poetic genius knows no artistic limitations.

LESTER: What play are you going to do?

MILLER: Scenes, my boy. Famous passages. "To be or not to be, that is the question!"

LESTER: "Whether tis nobler in the mind to suffer
The stings and arrows of outrageous fortune,
Or to take arms against a sea of troubles,
And by opposing end them."

(A stunned silence. Then:)

MILLER: My word, where did you learn that?

LESTER: I read as good as you, Hiner. You're serious about doing Shakespeare?

MILLER: I am.

LESTER: Where're you going to do it?

MILLER: Anywhere. Perhaps right here. I'd bring Ruby a good deal of business.

LESTER: Unless you're talking through your hat, how about letting me do something from Othello?

MILLER: You never cease to amaze me. I didn't know you could read.

LESTER: Read, shit. I can act, Hiner. I've been on stage in San Francisco.

MILLER: I sit dumbfounded.

LESTER: If you're not just breaking wind, you've got yourself an Othello — boy.

(He exits.)

MILLER: Extraordinary. Where on earth did he learn Shakespeare?

(Stump enters.)

STUMP: Howdy, Hiner.

MILLER: Afternoon, Stump. Good diggings today?

STUMP: Them days are gone and you know it.

MILLER: You remember my friend, Paddy ... ?

STUMP: Nice to see you again.

MCGUINNESS: The pleasure's mine.

STUMP: Where you hail from?

MCGUINNESS: Chicago.

STUMP: Long way from home. The stew ain't ready?

MILLER: The stove broke down again.

STUMP: I'll eat at Susie's.

(He exits.)

MILLER: He has Canyon City's richest claim. About the only one still bringing in a day's wages.

MCGUINNESS: Where's Susie's?

MILLER: Just down the road.

MCGUINNESS: Decent food?

MILLER: Not bad.

MCGUINNESS: Then I think I'll try Susie's myself before I faint from hunger.

MILLER: I think I'll wait for the stew.

MCGUINNESS: Be seeing you then.

(He exits.)

(Miller begins working on a poem.)

MILLER: "The day is dark and cloudy too
And the mist is eddying round
My toes they ache, you bet they do
As I hear the chill wind sound."

(Miss Lee enters.)

MISS LEE: Mister Miller ...

MILLER: Hiner.

MISS LEE: May I join you?

MILLER: The pleasure is mine.

MILL LEE: *(sitting)* Thank you. We're the only ones having dinner?

MILLER: The stove broke down again. Didn't you smell the smoke?

MISS LEE: I thought something was wrong.

MILLER: Exhaust pipe fell off again. But Lester's got it back on and the stew's brewing.

MISS LEE: You must forgive my earlier rudeness, Hiner.

MILLER: I knew you'd come to your senses. One artistic temperament should recognize another.

MISS LEE: Yes, I do feel I can trust you.

MILLER: We speak the same language — the language of the soul.

MISS LEE: I need help, Hiner. How desperately I need help.

MILLER: I'd be glad to offer my opinion of your paintings.

MISS LEE: Personal help. I find myself in a dreadful dilemma.

MILLER: What dilemma is that?

MISS LEE: I'm ashamed to say.

MILLER: Don't forget I drove the savages out of Canyon City. Other problems shrink in comparison. What's bothering you?

MISS LEE: My problem is Lester.

MILLER: Lester? Our Lester?

MISS LEE: Yes.

MILLER: He's made an uncouth advance? I'm shocked.

MISS LEE: Not exactly.

MILLER: Then what is it?

MISS LEE: You must promise to tell no one.

MILLER: A poet's word is his honor, madam.

MISS LEE: It concerns my reasons for being here.

MILLER: I thought you came to Canyon City to paint.

MISS LEE: Painting is only a hobby.

MILLER: Ah, I once thought of myself as a hobbyist as well! How we resist the genius that stares at us from the mirror each morning.

MISS LEE: I came here because ... well, there's this organization in Chicago ... they arrange marriages. Through them I began a correspondence with a Mr. Lester Brown. He sounded so intelligent in his letters. He's widely read, articulate, kind, his letters always quoted Shakespeare, he seemed so thoughtful and caring ...

MILLER: Madam, are you telling me you came to Canyon City to marry Lester?

MISS LEE: But of course I can't! It's shocking he never told me. Even though his name was Brown, I never dreamed he wasn't white.

MILLER: Obviously you can't and won't marry him.

MISS LEE: He says he loves me and if I don't marry him he'll write my family in Chicago that I came west to marry a Negro. The scandal would kill mother, I know it would.

MILLER: Lester threatened that?

MISS LEE: Hiner, what can I do?

MILLER: I'll confront him immediately.

MISS LEE: No! You don't know his temper. He'd know I told you and would do something even worse than writing my family.

MILLER: I don't fear Lester, madam.

MISS LEE: I was hoping there'd be some way you could occupy him while I escaped to Portland. He keeps an eye on me day and night. He frightens me.

MILLER: You want to go to Portland?

MISS LEE: There's no reason for me to stay here.

MILLER: Then I can take care of Lester for you. When do you want to leave?

MISS LEE: Next week — I do want to finish my paintings on the mining camp.

MILLER: The mining camp is the world in miniature — it's your duty as an artist to finish the paintings. I myself am about to begin an epic poem on the same theme. Oro Oregono! One of your paintings may serve to illustrate the book when it appears.

MISS LEE: Oh dear ...

MILLER: Madam?

MISS LEE: I'll need to get my paintings to Portland.

MILLER: There's no problem there.

MISS LEE: They're too heavy for me to manage alone.

MILLER: Of course, I'll help. They can be loaded atop the stage.

MISS LEE: I was wondering if I might rent my own wagon.

MILLER: Instead of the stage?

MISS LEE: The trip here was so unpleasant. I know how to drive a team — if you think it's safe, of course.

MILLER: Well, yes, you could rent one. If you wait until after the Shakespeare performance, I could accompany you.

MISS LEE: The Shakespeare performance?

MILLER: I'm bringing culture to Canyon City.

MISS LEE: How nice.

MILLER: If you rented a wagon, it would save me a stage ride as well. I have business in Portland. My new book needs a publisher.

MISS LEE: But I need to get out of town without Lester knowing. And to get my paintings out as well. I fear Lester wants to steal them — it'd be something else to blackmail me with. I might even have to sneak out of town at night.

(She seems very upset now.)

MILLER: *(soothing)* Don't worry about a thing, madam. I'll take care of everything.

MISS LEE: What a relief. Perhaps I can sleep now — suddenly I'm so tired ... I think I'll skip dinner.

MILLER: You do look tired, madam. I suggest a nap.

MISS LEE: Yes. And thank you again.

(She exits.)

(Miller goes back to working on a poem.)

MILLER: "O how I wish I was again at home
In the valley of the old Willamette
And never again I'd wish to roam
I'll seal the assertion with 'Damn it!'"

(Lester enters.)

LESTER: Everybody go to Susie's?

MILLER: Variety is good for the stomach, my boy.

LESTER: What's it take for you to stop calling me your boy, Hiner?

MILLER: My apologies for a bad habit. Sit down a minute. I'm curious about how you happen to be a student of Shakespeare.

LESTER: You think you've got the only brain in town?

MILLER: I'm just not used to finding a cook who —

LESTER: Listen, Hiner, look at yourself in the mirror one time. We come from the same backwater stock, boy.

MILLER: There's a major difference.

LESTER: You're a white man, Hiner. That's the difference.

MILLER: We remain brothers under the skin. The difference I was

—

LESTER: We're not fighting the Civil War for what's under the skin.

MILLER: Lester, I was very impressed with your reading of Hamlet. It just seems strange that a man of your talent would end up in Canyon City.

LESTER: You're here yourself, Hiner.

MILLER: Because where there's gold, there's greed — and a lawyer thrives on greed.

LESTER: You're not thriving much that I can see.

MILLER: We both arrived too late to thrive — you're stuck in the kitchen, I'm stuck in my office. We should've hit the fields six months ago.

(A beat.)

MILLER: May I ask you a personal question?

LESTER: Depends.

MILLER: Have you ever been married?

LESTER: Not my predilection.

MILLER: "Predilection" — my word!

LESTER: Look, Hiner, I may be an African savage to some folks but my father happened to be an educated man and he passed it on to his son. So cut the surprise crap. You ever want to challenge me to a spelling bee, boy, you're on.

MILLER: Lester, I think you're just the man to help me with the Shakespeare show.

LESTER: I told you I want to do Othello.

MILLER: I haven't decided exactly what scenes I'll do but I'm glad you're interested.

LESTER: You just let me know. You want some stew?

MILLER: My mind is racing ahead of my stomach at the moment. I have a good deal of planning to do.

(Ruby enters.)

RUBY: Where the hell's my dinner crowd?
MILLER: They went to Susie's. I'm sure you'll have them back for supper.
RUBY: You ain't having dinner?
MILLER: Too much on my mind. Ruby, I'm bringing Shakespeare to Canyon City!

(He exits.)

RUBY: You sure you got that pipe on good? I can't afford to lose my supper crowd as well.
LESTER: It's fixed.
RUBY: I hope so.
LESTER: Now all we need is customers.
RUBY: We'll serve the stew for supper.

(McGuinness enters.)

MCGUINNESS: Madam, I just had dinner at Susie's and promise never to make that mistake again.
RUBY: You live and learn around here.

(She starts away, stops and sees that Lester isn't following her.)

RUBY: You taking the day off?
LESTER: Don't I wish.
MCGUINNESS: I wonder if I might borrow him for a moment.
RUBY: You need something done in your room?
MCGUINNESS: It's a private matter, madam. It won't take a minute.
RUBY: That screen door needs fixing.
LESTER: I know.
RUBY: Five minutes.

(She exits.)

LESTER: What's on your mind?
MCGUINNESS: Miss Lee.

LESTER: What's that got to do with me?

MCGUINNESS: I suspect that you know more about what's going on in Canyon City than anyone. If you want the facts behind the facade, ask the working man.

LESTER: So what are you asking me?

MCGUINNESS: Is Miss Lee married? Has a man ever come around to see her?

LESTER: If I know, why should I tell you?

MCGUINNESS: Because we're brothers under the skin.

LESTER: You don't know a thing about me.

MCGUINNESS: "No Irish Need Apply." I know the pains of prejudice, too. You'd be as odd a sight out in the gold fields as I'd be with my accent. We both have to keep up our guard. Am I right?

LESTER: Guard up, hell, it's keeping my life that worries me. I came up here because I heard Oregon had outlawed slavery and entered the Union a free state. Nobody told me they outlawed residency for free Negroes at the same time. I just want to get a grubstake and out of here before anybody starts enforcing the law.

MCGUINNESS: If you help me, Lester, I can make it worth your while.

LESTER: Why are you so interested in Miss Lee?

MCGUINNESS: Because I happen to know that your Miss Lee is in reality the most famous painter in Chicago and the wife of a rat named Thomas O'Reilly.

LESTER: Who's he?

MCGUINNESS: He's a former colleague of mine at Pinkerton's Detective Agency.

LESTER: You're a detective?

MCGUINNESS: Freelance at the moment.

LESTER: So are you interested in Miss Lee or her husband?

MCGUINNESS: Her husband. According to the lady, he ditched her in Portland in order to come here and steal her father's gold claim.

LESTER: There's not a claim worth a hill of beans out there except for Stump's.

MCGUINNESS: He was terribly nervous when I sat with him at Susie's. Could he be her father?

LESTER: Crazier things have happened around here.

MCGUINNESS: Or perhaps she's lying, covering up for her husband. Perhaps Thomas O'Reilly has committed the crime of the century.

LESTER: What crime is that?

MCGUINNESS: A certain gold heist in Chicago remains un-solved. A train was carrying gold ore from the west to New York. Only when the train got to New York, seven sacks of ore were missing. As it happens, the train had only one stop, to switch engines in Chicago. Whatever happened, must have happened in Chicago. So I'm thinking that maybe Thomas O'Reilly, who left town right after the train passed through, managed to get those missing sacks of ore onto his own train coming west.

LESTER: I don't see what that's got to do with Canyon City.

MGUINNESS: What do you do with stolen gold ore? If you want to make legitimate claim to it, I mean. You do this: you put it back in the gold fields from which it came and then bring it out as if you're mining it.

LESTER: That's what you think Miss Lee and her husband are doing?

MCGUINNESS: I do. I worked with him. He was very ambitious — and very smart. And, of course, he left just after the ore passed through Chicago.

LESTER: Man, you've sure got a complicated way of thinking.

MCGUINNESS: Back to Rose — your Miss Lee. Has she had visitors?

LESTER: As far as I know, she doesn't do anything but sit in her room and paint.

MCGUINNESS: And only Stump is still bringing gold out of the fields?

LESTER: He's the only one still making a living on it.

MCGUINNESS: He's old enough to be her father.

LESTER: Miss Lee doesn't seem like the criminal type to me.

MCGUINNESS: You'd be surprised who turns out to be dishonest, Lester. There's no way to foresee it.

LESTER: I never have been able to figure out white folks, I'll grant you that.

MCGUINNESS: Will you keep your eyes and ears open?

LESTER: Sure, if I find out anything about a father or a husband, I'll let you know. I'd better get back to work.

(He exits. McGuinness heads for the stairway and meets Miss Lee coming in.)

MCGUINNESS: Miss Lee — do you have a moment?

MISS LEE: I was just coming to look for you. Have you thought about what I said?

MCGUINNESS: I have. Shall we sit down?

(They sit.)

MCGUINNESS: I've decided to help you.
MISS LEE: Thank God.
MCGUINNESS: As much as I detest the thought of entering that godforsaken desert with its lizards and strange creatures, it's the only way to find the rock that Thomas O'Reilly is hiding under. It will be a difficult search.
MISS LEE: I can give you a copy of the map to father's claim.
MCGUINNESS: That would make the chase easier, to be sure.
MISS LEE: But the map is — hidden. I couldn't give it to you before tomorrow.
MCGUINNESS: The sooner the better, so tomorrow it is.

(Ruby enters. She draws her pistol and shoots at a lizard on the floor. McGuinness, in response, again dives under the table.)

RUBY: It's all right, that's one lizard that won't be inviting his friends in. Anybody need coffee?
(McGuinness will crawl out and get to his feet to leave.)

MISS LEE: Nothing for me, thanks.
MCGUINNESS: I still have Susie's indigestion, not to mention being frightened out of my wits.
RUBY: Sorry about that, Paddy. It's the way we keep house around here.
MCGUINNESS: So I'm beginning to understand. It's been nice talking to you, Miss Lee.

(He exits upstairs.)

(Ruby sits down across the table from Miss Lee.)

RUBY: He's not snooping, is he?
MISS LEE: Just a lonely stranger, looking for company.
RUBY: You look a little upset.
MISS LEE: Do I? I guess I'm tired. I've been painting such long hours.
RUBY: You're sure I can't help with some of the painting myself?
MISS LEE: It's too complicated a process. I'll be fine, really.

RUBY: Well, it won't be long now.

(LIGHTS FADE, SPOT UP on McGuinness upstairs.)

MCGUINNESS: So I am face to face with a considerable dilemma —
is she telling me the truth or not? If she can produce a map to her
father's claim, then surely this is a clue worth pursuing. Yet it may be a
ploy to lure me into those godforsaken gold fields. Kill a man out there
and his family surely will miss the funeral. I'd hate to be known as the
misguided soul who went west for his fortune and was never heard from
again. More than ever, the burden of sudden insight was heavy on my
heart and I almost wished that apple of knowledge had not beaned me
so squarely on a distant windy day in Chicago when I thought I was
doing nothing more than puffing on my pipe.

(LIGHTS OFF McGuinness and BACK UP in the boardinghouse.)

RUBY: Have you decided where you're going?
MISS LEE: No.
RUBY: I'm going to open my own place in San Francisco.
MISS LEE: That sounds nice.
RUBY: It'll be the fanciest saloon in the city. Maybe you'd want to
join me.
MISS LEE: No, I couldn't do that ...
RUBY: You probably have other plans.
MISS LEE: Well, several possibilities — I haven't really made up
my mind yet.
RUBY: Probably have some man waiting for you ...
MISS LEE: Certainly not that.
RUBY: Then maybe you'd reconsider.
MISS LEE: I don't have a head for business.
RUBY: I do. You wouldn't have to do a thing but sit around looking
pretty.
MISS LEE: I don't think I understand.
RUBY: I've been noticing you don't seem to have much use for
men. It's more than killing your husband in cold blood. You've been
rejecting Hiner's advances. I noticed that, too.
MISS LEE: What are you trying to say?
RUBY: I been watching you closely.
MISS LEE: And ... ?
RUBY: Well, I don't know how to explain it exactly. I'm not so good
with words. But, well, I have a present for you.

MISS LEE: A present?

RUBY: I was gonna save it til we got out of town but, hell, I'm all unsettled to tell you the truth. I don't know if you'll appreciate it or not.

MISS LEE: That's very sweet of you. Where is it?

RUBY: I got it behind the counter. I'll fetch it. Might as well get it over with.

(She gets a box from behind the counter and returns, setting it in front of Miss Lee.)

RUBY: I'm not used to giving presents to somebody so refined, is the thing. But I liked you right off. I really did.

MISS LEE: Why, thank you, Ruby, that's a very sweet thing to say.

RUBY: And the way you got Stump to murder your husband, I admire a woman who can wrap a man around her finger like that. Men are so goddamn stupid. So I'm thinking, this is a very special kind of woman. Not to mention being beautiful to boot. And she ain't no sucker for a sweet-talking gent like Hiner, maybe that's what I like about you best of all. So I wanted to do something sweet for you but I don't know you that well, of course, and never have gotten a present for a lady of class, which you definitely are — so, anyway, it's just something that came from the heart, you might say, and something that I wouldn't be without myself — so maybe you can appreciate it, too.

MISS LEE: May I open it?

RUBY: Might as well.

(Miss Lee takes the top off the box and looks inside — but she's not sure what she's found and brings it out, holding it up. It's a dildo made from an elk horn.)

RUBY: I shot that damn elk myself, and made one out of each horn. I got the other, of course. We got matches.

(Miss Lee drops the dildo back into the box in horror and rises.)

RUBY: Don't you know what it is?

MISS LEE: I most certainly do know what it is.

(She's hurrying to go up the stairs.)

RUBY: *(after her)* I had a Paiute chief say some magic over it. It's got mighty powerful medicine, if you know what I mean.

(Miss Lee doesn't reply, hurrying to get away.)

RUBY: It's a damn sight better than a man!

(Miss Lee is gone.)

RUBY: Goddamn it, anyway.

(She sees a lizard, draws her pistol and fires at the floor several times.)

RUBY: Goddamn varmints!

(BLACKOUT. End of Act One.)

ACT TWO

1/ two days later

(AT RISE: Miller and Lester are rehearsing a scene from Shakespeare, each with a script in hand.)

MILLER: *(as Othello)* "Ay, let her rot and perish
Tis a thing I would cherish
My heart is turned to stone
As hard as any bone
Yet it hurts my hand
Do you understand?"
LESTER: Hiner—
MILLER: "O the world hath no one sweeter
Even if she is a cheater

She might — "
LESTER: Hiner!
MILLER: Yes?
LESTER: What the hell is that?
MILLER: "Othello", of course.
LESTER: It's not Shakespeare's "Othello."
MILLER: It most certainly is.
LESTER: The Bard didn't write doggerel.
MILLER: Doggerel!? This is the Bard adapted by yours truly for the mentality of the mining camp. You don't think miners would understand Elizabethan English, do you? You have to adapt the Bard to suit the occasion at hand.
LESTER: I thought I was going to play Othello.
MILLER: Don't be jealous, my boy, you can learn much by working with a more experienced thespian like yours truly.
"She might lie by an emperor's side
And give him orders or skin his hide."

(A pause.)

MILLER: Your line, my boy.
LESTER: Hey boy, yourself. I played Othello on the stage in San Francisco, Hiner.
MILLER: It's still your line.
LESTER: So I want to play Othello.
MILLER: This is not San Francisco! We are in a mining camp, we are playing to a very unusual and unique audience. I have experience with this audience and you do not. Your line.
LESTER: What're you going to do, wear dark makeup?
MILLER: If you're such an experienced thespian, you shouldn't have to ask such an elementary question. I'm still waiting.
LESTER: This is sick. I used to think any part's better than none. Now I'm not so sure.
MILLER: *(re-cueing)* "She might lie by an emperor's side
And give him orders or skin his hide"
LESTER: Jesus ... *(finally, without enthusiasm)* "Othello, this is not your way."
MILLER: "Iago, it is today."
LESTER: "O beware, my lord, of jealousy:
It is much, much worse than leprosy.
It's a green-eyed monster that mocks
Everything within the ticks of clocks."

250

Jesus, Hiner!

MILLER: Continue, you're doing very well.

LESTER: "The cuckold may live in bliss
When the husband doesn't see the kiss."

MILLER: "Hark, Iago, I must see before I doubt
And with sober eyes devoid of stout.
I need very clear proof
Before going through the roof."

LESTER: "This I am most glad to hear,
Especially since you've drunk no beer.
For now I can warn you as a friend:
Never to Cassio your wife lend,
Permit no moment of the two alone,
Or Cassio would take her as his own."
This is babbling doggerel, Hiner.

MILLER: The miners will love it. Trust me, my boy.

LESTER: I'm not your boy.

MILLER: I'm sorry — but I repeat: we cannot present the Bard in Elizabethan glory to an audience whose common tongue is in the gutter. We must make it easy for them. So I offer rhyme and music!

LESTER: We'll be laughed off the stage.

MILLER: This translation worked in the mountains of California. I'm sure it will work in the desert of Oregon as well.

(Ruby enters from the kitchen.)

RUBY: Lester, you plan to fix supper today?

LESTER: Right away.

RUBY: I wouldn't want to interrupt your new career.

LESTER: I've got no career with this material ...

(He starts off toward the kitchen.)

MILLER: Put it to memory, my boy!

(Lester is gone.)

MILLER: I'm sorry to have kept him for so long.

RUBY: It's a free country, he can cook or he can quit.

MILLER: Not exactly a free country — not for a Negro.

RUBY: If he can avoid getting lynched, he's as free as any of us.

MILLER: Which worries me.

RUBY: What do you mean?

MILLER: He'd be free to quit, for example.

RUBY: He won't quit til he gets a grubstake to move on.

MILLER: Unless he had reason.

RUBY: What reason is that?

MILLER: Ruby, I need your help. Lester is not the man he appears to be.

RUBY: Looks like any other down-and-out miner to me — except for the color of his skin. He arrived too late for the best diggings, same as you did. When he gets his grubstake, he'll be off to Alaska, trying his luck again.

MILLER: He's here for a wife, not a fortune.

RUBY: What're you talking about?

MILLER: He's hoping to marry Miss Lee.

RUBY: Who told you that?

MILLER: Miss Lee herself. They were matched by a social service. She's a mail order bride, you might say. Only he neglected to tell her that he was a Negro. The poor woman is beside herself. It's a wonder she's getting any painting done at all.

RUBY: Miss Lee told you she came here to marry Lester?

MILLER: That's right. Which is why I cast him in the play, to keep him occupied. She wants to sneak away to Portland without him following her. Only I can't keep him in rehearsal day and night, Ruby — which is why I'm asking you to keep an eye on him as well.

RUBY: Miss Lee plans to sneak away to Portland?

MILLER: The very day of our performance. I hope to meet her there later.

RUBY: What've you, taken a liking to her, Hiner?

MILLER: I sense that we possess kindred artistic souls.

RUBY: Answer me this: why did she come out to a hell-hole like Canyon City to get married?

MILLER: She came because the groom invited her. Surely he thought he'd strike it rich. Greed is not negated by love; the groom is as greedy as any man.

RUBY: Lester's not gonna like it if he finds out you're helping her escape.

MILLER: But he won't find out. Surely you won't ... ?

RUBY: Not me, Hiner. Your secret's good as gold with me.

MILLER: I wouldn't have told you if I didn't know that.

RUBY: I'll watch him like a hawk, Hiner. Miss Lee won't get no trouble from Lester.

MILLER: Very good. Well, then, if you'll excuse me, I have lines to memorize myself.

252

RUBY: You're doing this shindig on Saturday?

MILLER: Indeed. Which gives me only two days to put a considerable amount of poetry to memory. To which end, I beg my departure.

(He leaves, running into Stump as he enters.)

STUMP: Hiner.

MILLER: No time to chat, my friend.

(Miller is gone.)

RUBY: You're out of the fields early today.

STUMP: Those Indians are sending smoke signals something fierce. They're beginning to worry me.

RUBY: You expect trouble?

STUMP: I think we should get out of here sooner rather than later.

RUBY: When you got in mind?

STUMP: On the stage to Portland — a week from Saturday.

RUBY: But you're still bringing gold out.

STUMP: I want to make sure I get my skin out of here.

RUBY: She's still got a lot of paintings to do.

STUMP: We'll take what we can.

(He heads for the stairway.)

RUBY: Where're you going?

STUMP: Empty my goddamn leg — you think it's easy dragging all this weight around?

(He drags his leg to the staircase. Before reaching it, he quickly turns, drawing his knife, but does not throw it: the lizard has scurried away.)

STUMP: Goddamn varmints ...

(He starts up the stairway to CROSSFADE:)

2/ a moment later

(Miss Lee is painting as Stump knocks on her door.)

STUMP: It's me!

(Miss Lee lets him in.)

STUMP: My leg's killing me ...
MISS LEE: Sit down and relax.

(He'll sit on the bed, his back to the audience: Miss Lee will remove his wooden leg and dump its contents into a bucket, which she puts back under the bed.)

STUMP: I've been thinking. What's our goddamn hurry? My leg's always killing me — I'm gonna start carrying out less at one time.
MISS LEE: Don't avoid the subject.
STUMP: You nervous or something?
MISS LEE: I want to know if it's taken care of.
STUMP: Of course, it's taken care of.
MISS LEE: You're sure?
STUMP: You want the gory details?
MISS LEE: No. I just want to make sure you got it done.
STUMP: That Irishman's coyote-meat by now. Was easier than your husband.
MISS LEE: As long as it's done.
STUMP: I been thinking: we're gonna need excuses when the time comes to leave. Might as well start planting the seeds now. I'm gonna tell Ruby I'm opening a cigar store in Portland.
MISS LEE: A cigar store?
STUMP: I need a reason for leaving, don't I?
MISS LEE: I suppose so.
STUMP: What'll she think, seeing me all packed up and waiting for the stage without any explanation? This way, she has it set in her mind what I'm doing. You need an excuse, too.
MISS LEE: I hadn't thought of that — but perhaps I do.
STUMP: How're you coming with the paintings?
MISS LEE: Slowly but surely.
STUMP: How come you ain't painted no scenes yet?
MISS LEE: I told you before, it's easier to prime all the canvases first.
STUMP: But nothing's ready to take.
MISS LEE: They'll be ready.
STUMP: Well, we got nothing but time.
MISS LEE: I'm working as fast as I can.

STUMP: Thing is, this leg is killing me. I'm not gonna bring out so much at a time. Take us a little longer to haul it all out but —
MISS LEE: We've got nothing but time.

(He's putting his leg back on.)

MISS LEE: Will you be bringing in another load today?
STUMP: I'm sure sore — but yeah, I got time for one more.
MISS LEE: Where did you — leave him?
STUMP: You sure you don't want the gory details?

(Ruby has come up with a tray of tea and knocks on the door.)

RUBY: Anybody home? I brought you tea ...
MISS LEE: Just a minute!

(Stump gets up from the bed. Ruby enters and Stump moves to leave.)

RUBY: Why if I'd known you were here, Stump, I'd've brought an extra cup.
STUMP: Just leaving.

(He does. Miss Lee closes the door behind him.)

RUBY: Anything the matter?
MISS LEE: Of course not.
RUBY: He was up here so long I got nervous.
MISS LEE: He was just making small talk. I think he gets lonely.
RUBY: Well, we got something serious to talk about. Stump wants to get out of here a week from Saturday. He saw smoke signals and is worried about the Paiutes. Wants to take the stage to Portland.
MISS LEE: That complicates everything.
RUBY: You got that right. Can we be ready this weekend?
MISS LEE: That would really be rushing it. You're sure he wants to leave that soon?
RUBY: Guess them Paiutes changed his mind. Last thing we need is more trouble with them.
MISS LEE: I'm not sure what our next move should be.
RUBY: Would you have time to paint some dummies before he leaves? You know, some mining scenes without the gold primer on the canvas?

MISS LEE: I'm barely keeping up preparing the real canvases.

RUBY: At least if he left with dummies, we'd still have the gold.

MISS LEE: Doesn't he expect you to go with him?

RUBY: Not necessarily. I could think of a reason for staying.

MISS LEE: It might make him suspicious, especially if he's worried about Indians.

RUBY: Well, he's planning to go to Portland next week is all I know. I could leave with him and the dummies and wait for you in Portland.

MISS LEE: That might work.

RUBY: That'd give you time to finish up the real ones.

MISS LEE: Actually that's quite a good idea.

RUBY: Course, I'll have to trust you to show up.

MISS LEE: Of course I'll show up. I owe everything to you.

RUBY: Do you?

MISS LEE: When Stump came to you to double-cross me, you could've gone along with him. I wouldn't have anything without you.

RUBY: Between you and Stump, it was an easy choice.

MISS LEE: Then you should trust me.

RUBY: Goddamn it, I do. Maybe I just like you too much.

MISS LEE: I like you, too, Ruby — as a friend. I'm sorry if I'm not ...

RUBY: Well, I been rejected before.

(A beat.)

RUBY: What if I take my share of the real paintings, and Stump takes the dummies? That'd leave you behind with your share.

MISS LEE: That's more painting than I have time to do.

RUBY: Then I have to trust you with the real ones.

MISS LEE: Of course, you have to trust me. And I trust you as well.

RUBY: Trust me for what?

MISS LEE: For being my partner in this.

RUBY: I'd better think of a reason to stay behind. Stump can leave with the dummies alone.

MISS LEE: As long as it doesn't make him suspicious.

RUBY: That way I don't have to wait for you in Portland — or come back here and find you're already gone.

MISS LEE: Ruby, I don't understand this sudden suspicion. I thought we were partners in this. You came to me about Stump. I've trusted your honesty all along.

RUBY: Well, I guess all this change of plans is making me nervous.

MISS LEE: I think your idea about the dummies is quite brilliant. But I'd better get started on them. I certainly don't want you to lose

sleep over me.
RUBY: I lose lots of sleep because of you.

(She starts to leave. Miss Lee watches her carefully.)

RUBY: *(turning at doorway)* I know I'm not much to look at and probably don't have proper manners for a city lady like yourself, but I swear I care for you one hell of a lot.
MISS LEE: Then trust me.
RUBY: I got no choice. You know why? Cause love's a goddamn disease. I wish you'd never come to town.
MISS LEE: When we're out of this, you'll be glad I did.
RUBY: We'll see about that, won't we?

(Ruby is in the doorway; Miss Lee in the room: they regard one another as LIGHTS FADE TO BLACKOUT.)

3/ two days later

(AT RISE: A SPOT on McGuinness. He wears a bloody head bandage and his clothes are a mess. He's obviously been through hell.)

MCGUINNESS: And so I took the map and headed out into the godforsaken Oregon wilderness. And if lizards and other varmints weren't frightening enough, the Indians were getting ready to go on the warpath — or so I imagined, from all the smoke signals on the horizon, smoke as thick as fumes over a Chicago factory. What does it mean, I wondered, and the more I worried about the smoke signals, the more reckless I got in letting down my guard. When I finally found the ore crusher out in the desert, looking dilapidated and deserted, and right where Rose's map said it would be, I entered with more fear of the Indians than of the lizard I'd come to find. You can see the price I paid for being so reckless: Thomas surprised me from behind and put a two-by-four on my head with all the free swing of a Chicago butcher at the meat rack. Surely he was proud of that swing, as I fell down an embankment with the blood of my skull flowing behind. Surely he thought I was a goner, and well I might have been, had a couple of stray miners not wandered into my burial ground and thereby interrupted my journey on the bleeding river to the end. They even were kind enough to put me astride a mule and to lead me back to this semblance of civilization

257

called Canyon City, where I was going to surprise sweet Rose like the Ghost of Christmas Past itself.

(LIGHTS UP FULL on McGuinness and Lester. Lester, in dress rehearsal for the play, is in white face and wearing a rather inept attempt at suggesting Elizabethan costume.)

LESTER: You just sit down and take it easy ...

(He'll help McGuinness to a chair.)

MCGUINNESS: You look as white as a ghost ... am I alive?
LESTER: You're gonna be okay ...
MCGUINNESS: Did I frighten you, lad?
LESTER: What the hell happened to you?
MCGUINNESS: You look so pale ...
LESTER: This? It's Hiner's theatrical makeup. We're doing our scene later on.
MCGUINNESS: Are you a clown?
LESTER: I'm supposed to be Iago. Between you and me, Paddy, the Bard will be fertilizing his grave as soon as I start speaking. Now what trouble did you get into out there?
MCGUINNESS: Is Miss Lee still here?
LESTER: I think she's upstairs painting.
MCGUINNESS: You have to help me, Lester. Her husband did this to me. He's out in the fields with a shipment of heisted gold. At least I think the gold must be out there. He used a two-by-four like a butcher his blade, leaving me for buzzard meat. A couple of wandering miners ruined his plan.
LESTER: Is he still out there?
MCGUINNESS: Unless he's here.
LESTER: I sure haven't seen any strangers around here.

(Miller enters. He wears the same inept Elizabethan costume and is in black face.)

MILLER: "I sing of the west and I sing of the greed that makes a man act outlandish." I see you've learned the first lesson of the mines, Paddy.
LESTER: He had a two-by-four put to his skull. He's lucky he's still alive.

MILLER: It was for greed, am I right? You stumbled across someone else's claim and this is your reward. Greed is the very blood of our lives.

LESTER: He says Miss Lee's husband did this.

MILLER: Her husband?

MCGUINNESS: Thomas O'Reilly is his name. I knew him in Chicago.

MILLER: She has a husband — here?

MCGUINNESS: They're in cahoots together in the crime of the century. I mention it because I'm going to need all the help I can get. Especially here in the wilderness, where I have no more sense of being accepted than in the House of Lords. Will you help me, gentlemen?

MILLER: *(to Lester)* Did you know she had a husband?

LESTER: It's news to me.

MILLER: *(to McGuinness)* And you're sure?

MCGUINNESS: I followed them from Chicago, of course I'm sure.

MILLER: Miss Lee is married? But —

MCGUINNESS: Her name is Rose Mulligan and now O'Reilly.

MILLER: *(to Lester)* I thought you were hoping to marry her.

LESTER: What're you talking about?

MILLER: You met her through a social club. You corresponded and then you proposed, and she came west to marry you.

LESTER: What've you been drinking, Hiner? I'm not about to get married, especially not to no white woman and double especially to no white woman here in Oregon. Last thing I need is to be guest of honor at a necktie party.

MILLER: This is all very strange.

MCGUINNESS: Not so strange, if you knew the mind of Thomas O'Reilly. His plan is ingenious if I say so myself.

LESTER: What plan?

MCGUINNESS: It's a complicated story. Suffice it to say that there was a gold heist in Chicago, and the gold and Thomas O'Reilly disappeared together. I think he's bringing the gold out of the fields as if he's mining it himself.

MILLER: How are they going to bring gold into town without anyone knowing about it?

MCGUINNESS: A piece of the puzzle that troubles me as well.

MILLER: I never read about any gold heist in Chicago.

MCGUINNESS: And where is the newspaper you could read it in? In the east, the heist is called the crime of the century. All the civilized world is talking about it.

LESTER: There's greed for you, Hiner.

MCGUINNESS: Greed, it is.

MILLER: I believe I know Miss Lee well enough to say that criminal activity is nothing she would have a part of.

LESTER: Nobody knows Miss Lee. All she does is sit up in her room and paint.

MILLER: One artist can recognize another. Their souls speak in harmony.

MCGUINNESS: If you know her so well, perhaps you could find out what she's really up to in her room.

MILLER: She paints.

MCGUINNESS: I have a feeling there's more to it than that.

MILLER: If her soul were less than pure, I would see it immediately.

MCGUINNESS: I was hoping you would help me. But if you can't get by that pretty face of hers ...

LESTER: He's got you pegged right, Hiner.

MILLER: I'll talk to her, if that will convince you. I'll ask her if she's married. She wouldn't lie to me.

MCGUINNESS: If you talk to her in her room, I could listen at the door.

MILLER: Spy on us?

MCGUINNESS: To weigh the evidence for myself.

MILLER: That would not be fair to Miss Lee.

MCGUINNESS: I hope you're not worried that you're wrong about her.

MILLER: I'm not wrong at all. If it takes a small deceit to prove her purity to you, then yes, I'll do it.

MCGUINNESS: Give me time to get to my room.

MILLER: You soon will owe me an apology, Paddy.

MCGUINNESS: If an apology is due, then surely you'll be getting it.

(He leaves and goes upstairs.)

LESTER: What if he's right?

MILLER: He can't be.

LESTER: Does this change of plan mean I can wash my face?

MILLER: Certainly not. This won't take a minute, and then we can rehearse as planned.

(Miller starts for the stairway.)

LESTER: I think we both look like fools.

MILLER: It's called theatricality. The miners will love it.

LESTER: *(after him)* You going to put on a dress and be Desdemona, too?

(Miller exits upstairs. Lester heads for the kitchen. CROSSFADE to upstairs.)

4/ a moment later

(Miss Lee is painting. Miller knocks on the door.)

MILLER: Madam, it is I!

MISS LEE: Just a minute.

(She opens the door — and is startled by his appearance.)

MISS LEE: Aaa!

(Miller comes in and closes the door. McGuinness comes out and positions himself outside the door to listen.)

MILLER: It's just theatrical makeup, madam. I am about to rehearse as Othello.

MISS LEE: Really? Then have you come up with a plan?

(Miller, knowing that McGuinness is listening, makes a gesture for her to stop this direction of talk.)

MISS LEE: Hiner, did you think of something or not?

MILLER: *(changing the subject)* What magnificent paintings!

(He will hold up a canvas: this is the first time we've seen one, and it's nothing but a gold-primed canvas.)

MILLER: I knew you had genius! It captures the very soul of the mining camp. Gold, gold!

(He looks at the many other canvases in the room, all of them the same.)

MILLER: And this one ... the same. And ... the same. But of course! Scenes from a mining camp, each one reduced to its essence, to its bare essentials ... each one reduced to gold! "I sing of the west and I sing of the greed that makes a man act outlandish ..." Yes, yes, these paintings will illustrate my epic poem beautifully. You paint nothing but gold! Only a genius could have conceived of such simplicity.

MISS LEE: Hiner, quit beating around the bush. Do you have a plan to help me or not?

MILLER: *(clears his throat)* Madam, I've been talking with Paddy McGuinness, and he —

MISS LEE: McGuinness? When?

MILLER: Just a moment ago, and —

MISS LEE: A moment ago? Here?

MILLER: Yes, ma'am. He had a terrible accident and, well, madam, he has a rather bizarre explanation of what transpired.

MISS LEE: *(a step ahead of him)* He's upset you, hasn't he? With talk of my poor husband, Thomas. They were very good friends back in Chicago.

MILLER: You admit having a husband?

MISS LEE: He died last winter. I fear it was a widow's vulnerability that made me such an easy target for that horrid Mr. Brown.

MILLER: You were married to Thomas O'Reilly?

MISS LEE: Why, yes. Very happily so. My life has become such a tragedy since his untimely departure.

MILLER: Your art will be made stronger for it.

MISS LEE: I do hope so.

MILLER: If your husband is deceased, then Paddy must be wrong about who beaned him with a two-by-four.

MISS LEE: Of course, he's wrong, and ... oh no, I pray it isn't true!

MILLER: What isn't true, madam?

MISS LEE: But that would be just like William!

MILLER: William, madam?

MISS LEE: Thomas' twin brother. You see, for an anniversary present, just before Thomas took ill, my father gave us a map to a gold mine out here. Thomas planned a leave of absence so we might come out and take advantage of it. Then the illness struck and, well, to make a long story brief, somewhere along the way, the map disappeared. I never thought too much about it because frankly my father is a wee bit senile and one is never sure whether he knows what he's talking about. I didn't even look for it until just before I came west to — well, to get married.

(She begins to cry.)

MILLER: Please, madam, use this.

(He offers her a handkerchief.)

MISS LEE: You're too kind.

MILLER: I'm honored to grace it with your tears. Please go on.

MISS LEE: There's not much more to tell. The map was missing, or at least I couldn't find it. Perhaps Thomas had a secret hiding place for it. But if you're implying that there's someone in town who looks like Thomas, well, it does make one wonder, doesn't it?

MILLER: You think your brother-in-law found the map?

MISS LEE: It's a definite possibility, I should think. Oh, Mr. Miller —

MILLER: Please call me Joaquin.

MISS LEE: Joaquin.

MILLER: It's my new pen name. After the heroic Mexican, Joaquin Murietta. You're the first to have permission to use it.

MISS LEE: I'm so honored. *Joaquin*: I just want to get out of here. Soon.

MILLER: I can understand why, madam. All of this surely interferes with your calling.

MISS LEE: It most certainly does.

MILLER: Madam, you are a lady of great integrity!

MISS LEE: Why, thank you.

(McGuinness enters the room, his gun drawn. Lester will come up the stairs below and listen at the door. And Ruby will soon come up behind him, gun drawn on Lester, to listen in as well.)

MCGUINNESS: Integrity, indeed! Rose, I must hand it to you, you are a wife to do Thomas proud, almost as brilliant in your conniving as he.

MILLER: Madam, let me handle this. Put away that pistol, Paddy!

MCGUINNESS: There's no twin, Hiner.

MILLER: The lady says there is.

MCGUINNESS: She and Thomas are in this scheme together.

MILLER: You're pushing your luck, Paddy.

MCGUINNESS: Stay out of this, Hiner. Why don't you go practice your lines somewhere?

MILLER: I will not abandon the lady.

MCGUINNESS: There's no twin.

MISS LEE: *(to Miller)* He and William must be in this together.

MCGUINNESS: Then who tried to kill me in the gold fields?

MILLER: I am an artist of the theater, Paddy. Your melodramatic exaggeration does not convince me. You are, in a word — acting!

MCGUINNESS: Get the hell out of here before I lose my patience.

MILLER: We both play to our audience. I put on black face, you put on a bloody bandage.

MCGUINNESS: Where is he, Rose?

MISS LEE: Where is who?

MCGUINNESS: You know who I mean. Thomas.

MISS LEE: You were at the funeral! A fine friend of the family you turned out to be!

MCGUINNESS: You won't get away with this, Rose. You might as well make it easy on yourself. I have more against Thomas than you.

MISS LEE: You should have nothing at all against me, Paddy.

MCGUINNESS: Where is he?

MILLER: Don't let him frighten you, madam.

MCGUINNESS: What're you going to do, Joaquin Hiner —

MILLER: You don't have permission to call me Joaquin.

MCGUINNESS: — take the gun away from me? Then come on, let's get on with it, if I have to shoot you in the leg I'd rather be done with it.

MILLER: You're threatening an attorney of law, in case you've forgotten.

MCGUINNESS: You'll bleed like a dog catcher if you come one step closer.

MISS LEE: Listen to him, Joaquin.

MILLER: He doesn't scare me, madam!

MISS LEE: Paddy, if it's only Thomas you're after, perhaps I can be of help.

MCGUINNESS: I'm sure you can.

MISS LEE: As long as it's worth my while.

MCGUINNESS: And what would make it worth your while?

MISS LEE: Joaquin, please go. I need to talk to Paddy alone.

MILLER: I'm a little confused about —

MCGUINNESS: Get out of here, Hiner! Now!

MILLER: *(to Miss Lee)* Is your husband dead or not?

(He regards Miss Lee, who just looks at him.)

MILLER: I'm stunned.

MISS LEE: Please go — Joaquin, I'll explain later.

MILLER: Very well, then. I'll leave you two alone, but I shan't be far, Paddy, and if you lift a hand to harm her —

264

MCGUINNESS: Just go, Hiner.

(Lester and Ruby move up the hallway before Miller turns and exits, going down the stairs and out the main exit. When he passes, they take their places at the door again, eavesdropping, Ruby still with the gun drawn on Lester.)

MCGUINNESS: Well, Rose, now it's just the two of us.

MISS LEE: If I help you get Thomas, naturally I want something in return.

MCGUINNESS: And what would that be? The paintings, am I right? Because this gold paint is worth a fortune. Thomas hauled the ore into the fields and crushed it, and you mixed it in the paint. You're a very clever lady, Rose, but I need the paintings as evidence.

MISS LEE: Let me leave with four of the paintings. That will still leave you with plenty to collect the reward with. I presume that's what you're after.

MCGUINNESS: The reward will be nice, to be sure. But matching wits with you and Thomas has its pleasures as well. If I solve this case, everyone in the crime business will know about Paddy McGuinness. There's just one problem. Why should I trust you?

MISS LEE: Because I knew I was going to double-cross Thomas from the moment I married him. Why else would I marry a common detective?

MCGUINNESS: I was curious what you saw in him, being famous and all.

MISS LEE: Let's just say that the plan for the gold heist was part of the proposal.

MCGUINNESS: So how were you going to double-cross him?

MISS LEE: I had a plan for when we got out of Canyon City — which is now obsolete, obviously. I can double-cross him and help you at the same time. You can get the reward and the glory, and I can escape with a modest income.

MCGUINNESS: Somehow this sounds too good to be true.

MISS LEE: Don't forget that I have to trust you as well. You could double-cross me and turn me in.

MCGUINNESS: Then if we have a deal, it's built on mutual trust.

MISS LEE: That's right.

MCGUINNESS: So where is he?

MISS LEE: In the fields, as far as I know.

MCGUINNESS: Why don't I believe you?

MISS LEE: I was to meet him here later this afternoon, during the performance of the play, when the town would be deserted. He must be arranging for the horses.

MCGUINNESS: You were making your getaway this afternoon?

MISS LEE: Yes.

MCGUINNESS: Where were you going to meet him?

MISS LEE: Why, right here — just before the play began. He wanted people to see us first, so they wouldn't be missing us until later. They'd think we were somewhere in the crowd, watching the play.

MCGUINNESS: Then we'll find out if you're telling the truth soon enough.

MISS LEE: Of course I'm telling you the truth!

MCGUINNESS: We'll surely see, won't we?

MISS LEE: Will you let me go after you have Thomas?

MCGUINNESS: It depends.

MISS LEE: On what?

MCGUINNESS: I can't predict the future.

MISS LEE: You don't trust me.

MCGUINNESS: I'm reserving judgment. Make yourself comfortable, Rose. Paint if you like. We have a lizard to catch.

(LIGHTS FADE in room and COME UP in main area as Ruby hustles Lester downstairs.)

RUBY: That double-crossing scumbag! Well, she's not getting away with this. You're gonna help me double-cross her back, Lester.

LESTER: If it's all the same to you —

RUBY: It ain't. You do what I tell you to do.

LESTER: You don't need me to double-cross her.

RUBY: I need someone to do the heavy lifting, and that's you.

LESTER: There's lots of strong bodies around here — and white ones to boot.

RUBY: You'll travel to Portland as my valet.

LESTER: Your slave.

RUBY: Whatever you want to call yourself.

LESTER: I don't want anything to do with any of this.

RUBY: All I have to do is yell "rape" and your ass is grass, boy.

LESTER: *(giving in)* So what's the plan?

RUBY: First, we've got to get the paintings out of her room.

LESTER: How do we do that?

RUBY: I'm not sure. Maybe when they're down here before the play, you can move them to the upstairs storage room.

LESTER: What happens when Paddy discovers they're gone?

RUBY: I'll say I saw somebody take them. Hiner maybe. No, he's too stupid. Her husband. He'd be perfect.

LESTER: If I'm moving them before the play, Hiner will be wondering where I am.

RUBY: I'll tell him I had an emergency. You're fixing the stove. After the play, when they discover the paintings are missing, I'll say you didn't fix it after all, you disappeared yourself.

LESTER: How much is my life worth then?

MISS LEE: I'll say I saw you take off with a wagon, heading west. Actually the paintings will be locked up in the storage room, and you'll be hiding out in the fields. We'll get back together later.

LESTER: I just got one more question. What if you double-cross me?

RUBY: I need you. I can't move all those paintings myself.

LESTER: You're a pretty tough bird, Ruby, I think you could handle it.

RUBY: And being alone on the trail to Portland, with the Paiutes sending smoke signals out there? No thanks.

LESTER: The Paiutes are acting up again?

RUBY: That's what I hear.

LESTER: Just what we need.

RUBY: We'll be long gone before the Paiutes do anything. In the meantime, pretend you're getting ready for the play.

LESTER: Damn, you white folks sure have a thing about double-crosses. Wearing this makeup, I almost feel like double-crossing someone myself.

RUBY: You be careful, boy.

LESTER: Hey, that's just a figure of speech, Ruby. Just a figure of speech, okay?

(LIGHTS FADE to BLACKOUT.)

5/ an hour later

(LIGHTS UP in Miss Lee's room. She is painting, the canvas invisible to the audience. McGuinness watches her carefully.)

MISS LEE: So what do you think?

MCGUINNESS: I don't know anything about art.

MISS LEE: But you recognize the nude female body, don't you?

267

(He doesn't reply.)

MISS LEE: Do you think she's beautiful?

MCGUINNESS: I don't know why you're painting a naked lady.

MISS LEE: For your enjoyment.

MCGUINNESS: I don't know what you're getting at.

MISS LEE: Then I'll try to explain.

(She slowly disrobes down to her slip during the speech below.)

MISS LEE: It doesn't bother me that you know nothing about art, by the way. You're honest to admit it. Thomas was exactly the opposite. He was a buffoon, as a matter of fact. Apparently he'd been studying art history in the encyclopedia in order to impress me. I even painted purposely awful once, just to hear his praise. I really can't tell you why he chose me, what the origin of his infatuation was. Who can figure out the male mind? Can you tell me something about the male mind, Paddy?

MCGUINNESS: What are you doing there?

MISS LEE: *(ignoring this, continuing)* Whatever the reason, Thomas became infatuated with me, hopelessly so. He'd come to my openings and make an utter fool of himself. Then he came up with his plan. I was astounded the first time he told me. I could have gone and told the police right then. But I didn't, Paddy. Do you want to know why? ... I said, do you want to know why?

MCGUINNESS: You're making me very nervous, Rose.

MISS LEE: Because I'm not as successful as everyone thinks. Financially speaking, I mean. Just because your photograph appears in the newspaper, just because many people recognize your name, just because you're noted for being "a great artist" — do you realize that I sometimes water-color Christmas cards in order to make ends meet? I said, did you know that?

MCGUINNESS: No, I didn't.

MISS LEE: Touch my breasts.

MCGUINNESS: I'll do no such thing. Get dressed.

MISS LEE: Let's double-cross Thomas together. What kind of a reward will you get, compared to all the gold we can share? And some things money can't buy, Paddy. I like you much better than Thomas. There's an earthy honesty about you. I find it very exciting. I'll bet you would make love to me outdoors, on the ground in a rainstorm, surrounded by Indians sending up their smoke signals, the howl of coyotes —

MCGUINNESS: Stop this nonsense!
MISS LEE: Make love to me, Paddy.

(During the above, Miller has entered the room behind
McGuinness. He carries a huge law book, which he crashes over
McGuinness' head. McGuinness falls to the floor. Miller quickly covers
his eyes so as not to see Miss Lee in her slip.)

MISS LEE: Joaquin, I was so afraid he heard you come in.
MILLER: Dress yourself, madam. I'll wait for you downstairs.
MISS LEE: How can I repay you, Joaquin?
MILLER: We'll worry about that later. Don't waste time, he'll be
back on his feet soon.
MISS LEE: I'll be right down.

(Miller leaves, stumbling about with his eyes still covered. In the
room, Miss Lee will take McGuinness' gun and head downstairs,
LIGHTS FADING behind her. LIGHTS UP in the main area as Miller
comes downstairs. Lester is still in white face and costume, going over
his lines. Ruby is behind the desk, guarding Lester, as Miller enters the
area.)

MILLER: *(quick composure)* Well — how are the lines coming?
LESTER: Don't worry about me.
MILLER: I confess to a case of mild jitters. Miss Lee is on her way
down — I thought maybe a mid-day stroll would calm me down.
RUBY: You've sure gotten interested in her.
MILLER: We're kindred souls.
RUBY: You just watch yourself. A woman like that has broken many
a heart.
MILLER: I can watch out for myself.

(Stump enters. He is a little drunk.)

STUMP: When's this damn play start? Hiner, you look silly as a
goat. You, too, Lester.
MILLER: You're quite early, Stump.
STUMP: Any more whiskey and I'd miss the play entirely.
RUBY: You want some coffee?
STUMP: I think I need it.
RUBY: Go in the kitchen and help yourself.
LESTER: I'll get it.

RUBY: He can get it himself.
STUMP: What the hell happened to the service around here?

(He exits to the kitchen.)

MILLER: Well. Perhaps I'll get some fresh air.

(Ruby draws her gun on Miller.)

RUBY: Sorry, nobody's going nowhere.
MILLER: *(uncertain)* I beg your pardon?

(Miss Lee enters, her pistol drawn: she and Ruby draw a bead on one another simultaneously, a stalemate.)

MISS LEE: You can put away the gun — we're in this together.
RUBY: Then you put yours away first.

(Stump enters: he'll distract Ruby and Miss Lee, giving time for Lester to draw a small pistol he has hidden on his person, which he'll point at Miss Lee, then Ruby, back and forth, unsure who his number one enemy is.)

STUMP: What the hell?
LESTER: Everybody relax!

(This distraction gives Stump time to draw a small weapon as well. A circle forms: Lester has his gun on Ruby, who has her gun on Miss Lee, who has her gun on Stump, who has his gun on Lester.)

STUMP: Now what the hell's going on around here? Get that damn gun off me. I thought we were in this together.
MISS LEE: Sorry, Stump.
STUMP: You double-crossing me?
MISS LEE: You should talk.
STUMP: So that's it? If I didn't have to keep Lester covered, I'd blow you to smithereens.
MISS LEE: Sorry, but I've already got you covered, Stump.
STUMP: Well, if I go, Lester goes — not that it matters none.
LESTER: Hey, it sure does matter! If I go, Ruby goes.
RUBY: And if I go, she goes.
MISS LEE: If I go, Stump goes.

(A beat: Miller has been watching this with a certain fascination.)

MILLER: Perhaps I can help.
RUBY: Shut up, Hiner. Lester, take your gun off me.
LESTER: I don't trust you.
MILLER: As you may recall from my work with the Paiutes, I am a negotiator of considerable skill.
STUMP: If you're so good, how come they've been sending smoke signals out there?
MILLER: Smoke signals don't mean there's danger. They're merely practicing their oral tradition.
LESTER: Hiner, if you think you can reach a compromise here, I'm all for it.
STUMP: Shut up.
MISS LEE: Lester, why don't you go upstairs and get the paintings?
LESTER: Because if I move I'm a dead man.
MISS LEE: Stump? If you let him go, I'll take my gun off you and you can get out of here.
RUBY: You let Stump go and you're buzzard meat. Nobody's going nowhere.
MILLER: Am I to understand Paddy was right? There's been a gold heist?

(Everyone ignores him.)

LESTER: Look, we're all in this together, whether we like it or not. Why not share the wealth four ways?
MISS LEE: When McGuinness comes to, there won't be any wealth to share.
STUMP: What are you talking about? That Irishman is buzzard meat.
MISS LEE: He's right upstairs, Stump.
MILLER: And there's gold upstairs as well? I thought this was all some kind of joke. Well, then — all of you just relax. I'll go upstairs and see if McGuinness has come to.
RUBY: Don't you go anywhere, Hiner.
MILLER: Who's going to stop me? Who would dare to turn his gun on me and lose one's position of power in the stalemate?

(Miller starts for the stairs.)

MISS LEE: Someone stop him!

LESTER: I've got a better idea — Stump, how about I walk out of here and you put your gun on Ruby instead? Be one less compromise to make in the end.

STUMP: I'm not letting you get away with the paintings.

MISS LEE: Unless we stop him, Hiner will, goddamn it!

STUMP: Hiner!

MILLER: *(at the foot of the stairs)* Yes?

STUMP: What're you going to do up there?

MILLER: I'm not sure. Depends if Paddy has come to or not, I suppose. I wouldn't mind sharing with a man from the city like himself.

MISS LEE: I'll stop him, Ruby, okay? But when I put my gun on Hiner, you have to move yours to Stump or he'll shoot me for sure.

STUMP: Damn right, I will.

RUBY: But then you'll be free to go as you please.

MISS LEE: Trust me, goddamn it!

RUBY: I already made that mistake.

MILLER: Well, it appears that you all have a good deal more to discuss before reaching an agreement. So if you'll excuse me ...

(Just as Miller heads up the stairs, McGuinness staggers in from the main entrance with an arrow in his shoulder.)

MCGUINNESS: If only the apple of insight had missed my head in Chicago ...

RUBY: What the hell happened to you?

MCGUINNESS: As near as I can surmise from such a short and unpleasant gander, after crawling down the drain pipe to make my getaway, I do believe the Indians are starting to burn down the town ...

MILLER: Impossible — I made peace with the Paiutes!

MCGUINNESS: Where's Thomas, Rose?

RUBY: She got Stump to kill him for her.

STUMP: I was willing to split with you, Ruby.

RUBY: I made the mistake of listening to my heart.

STUMP: What the hell's that mean?

RUBY: I double-crossed you and she double-crossed me right back. She was going to leave town with Hiner.

LESTER: She was supposed to be leaving town with me.

MISS LEE: I would have, if you hadn't been so greedy about your price.

RUBY: But Hiner didn't even know what he was getting in on.

LESTER: Don't think I did. I thought she was an artist.

MISS LEE: I am an artist!

MILLER: If that is true, madam, then I fail to see how you can —

RUBY: Goddamn it, there's Paiutes out there! Are we gonna defend ourselves or stand around squabbling over who double-crossed who?

MCGUINNESS: She has a point.

RUBY: I say we lower weapons at three. Agreed?

(All nod or mumble agreement.)

RUBY: One, two, three.

(All lower their guns.)

STUMP: I'm getting the hell out of here!

(He exits.)

MISS LEE: Joaquin, maybe you can talk to their chief.

MILLER: There must have been a change in command. New chiefs don't always respect the treaties of their predecessors.

(Stump staggers back in with an arrow in his stomach. He falls to the floor, dead.)

RUBY: We'd better get ready to fight!

MISS LEE: Lester, get the paintings!

LESTER: Your gold ain't worth Hiner's doggerel now, lady.

RUBY: Take positions at the windows ...

MCGUINNESS: You can't be serious? The few of us can't stand them off. There's too many of them out there.

RUBY: You got a better idea?

MILLER: I do, as a matter of fact.

(Miller starts away.)

RUBY: Where the hell you going?

MILLER: I'm going down to the cellar where I can think in solitude.

RUBY: Fine goddamn peacemaker you are.

MILLER: Give me time, I'll think of something.

(He exits. The others prepare to defend the boarding house. They face the audience, as if placing themselves at windows at the front of the building, waiting. The sounds of TRADITIONAL INDIAN DRUM-MING AND CHANTING are faintly heard.)

RUBY: Half the town must be on fire.
MCGUINNESS: Why are they so angry?
RUBY: They're savages.
LESTER: I think they're pissed because the bones of their ances-tors got dug up.
MCGUINNESS: I wonder if you might reason with them?
LESTER: Me?
MCGUINNESS: Being of dark skin — maybe they'll listen to you. As I recall from the journal of Lewis and Clark, the Indians were quite taken by a man with black skin.
LESTER: You're serious?
MCGUINNESS: A Negro valet, I believe he was. The Indians were utterly taken with him. They adored him. If you'd remove the makeup, they might think of you as a dark brother.

(He tosses Lester a cloth napkin from one of the tables. Lester will wipe off his makeup.)

MCGUINNESS: Perhaps it's a long shot — but on the other hand, I'd say our chances are so slim that anything's worth a try.
LESTER: I hope you know what you're talking about.
MCGUINNESS: Historical fact, in the journal of Lewis and Clark. I don't think the times have changed all that much since then. Do you think it's worth a try?
LESTER: Like you say, our options are limited.
MCGUINNESS: You're a good man, Lester.

(Lester grabs another white napkin and starts toward the door, waving it as a peace offering.)

RUBY: Lester?
LESTER: Yeah?
RUBY: If you make it, don't forget about us.

(Lester laughs, shakes his head and exits.)

RUBY: He's sure waving that napkin to beat hell ...

274

MCGUINNESS: I think he's going to make it. One of the braves is riding toward him. Look, he's smiling!

RUBY: My God, I believe he is at that ... a grin as bright as gold on his face ...

MCGUINNESS: I think the Indian's going to talk to him ... oops ...

(They look out in horror. Lester staggers back in, an arrow in his stomach.)

LESTER: Paddy, you can take your Lewis and Clark and shove it ...

(He falls dead.)

RUBY: Looks like we got no choice but to go down fighting.

MCGUINNESS: Perhaps Hiner's right, and the cellar is safer.

RUBY: Not if they burn down the building, it ain't.

MCGUINNESS: That's a decision each must make for himself. Ladies, if you'll excuse me, I wish our circumstances of parting were different ... and dear Rose, do you really think you'd have gotten away with it?

RUBY: *(answering first)* If she'd trusted me, and if them Paiutes was behaving ...

MCGUINNESS: I do admire your genius, Rose. An inspired plan, painting the gold dust on canvas.

RUBY: Her stupid husband was going to bring it out like he mined it, drawing attention to himself.

(Miss Lee, who's been in shock and helpless, now loses it.)

MISS LEE: Somebody has to get the paintings ...

(She heads for the stairs.)

RUBY: Where the hell you going?

(No reply.)

RUBY: *(after her)* I'd get ready to defend yourself if I was you.

(Miss Lee is gone, upstairs.)

RUBY: *(after her)* The top floors will be the first to go!

MCGUINNESS: You coming with me to the cellar?

RUBY: I'm fighting it out til the end.

MCGUINNESS: There's more Indians out there than varmints in the desert.

RUBY: Indians and varmints don't scare me, neither one.

MCGUINNESS: When I saw smoke signals, I started shaking in my boots. I wish somebody here had done the same. Gold is blinding, isn't it?

RUBY: You gonna give me a hand?

MCGUINNESS: The way I'm shaking, I couldn't hit the side of a barn. Good luck to you.

(No reply. McGuinness turns and heads for the cellar.)

MCGUINNESS: *(on his way)* What I'd give for a pint of stout about now ...

(He exits.)

(Ruby is alone. She waits, gun ready, for the final attack. The sound of DRUMMING rises.)

(LIGHTS FADE TO BLACKOUT. A SPOT comes up on McGuinness. The LIGHTING IS RED and suggests surrounding fire, a vision of hell.)

MCGUINNESS: Never have I seen such a massacre. Never have I smelled such a stench of burning flesh.

(ANOTHER SPOT on Miller, in WHITE LIGHT, a vision of heaven.)

MILLER: *(reciting from "Oro Oregono")* "I sing of the West and I sing of the greed that makes a man act outlandish
And all for the lure of Oregon gold — that's Oro Oregono in Spanish."

MCGUINNESS: For what seemed like days I waited in the charred rubble of the cellar, wondering what my fate would be. Never has the luck of the Irish been more wondrous than on the day I crawled out into the sunshine, realizing I was still alive, with no Indians to be found.

MILLER: "Into the deserts and mountains they come, like hornets swarming to honey.

They sacrifice home and family and friends, and all for the greed for money.

They dig for days and weeks and months til blisters turn to stone.

As hard as ore their hands become, and muscles 'round their bones.

A nugget here! A nugget there! Nature lures them well,

And so they dig and dig again, how long we cannot tell."

MCGUINNESS: And who had survived as well but Hiner, whom I found weeping uncontrollably under a fallen building, babbling no language I could understand. It was all I could do to keep him from running into the desert like a madman. He babbled nonstop right up to the blessed arrival of our rescuers, who looked like white angels as they rode through the charred remains of Canyon City, looking for survivors and finding only two.

I returned to Chicago and back to work for Pinkerton. Never would I have given thought to the nightmare of the Oregon wilderness again had I not found a piece in the Tribune about Hiner himself, complete with photograph, Hiner who was in London and calling himself Joaquin Miller now, decked out in buckskin like Buffalo Bill and plugging a book of poems called "Oro Oregono." In London they were calling him the Lord Byron of the West. Far across the sea, he'd become an American hero.

MILLER: "They found his bones in a deep long hole across the desert sand.

His hand clutched 'round a sterile stone, a pick ax in his hand.

But here's the telling mark, my friend — though the stench was strong and vile,

This miner felt no grief or pain — his lips were in a smile!"

MCGUINNESS: Well, he was famous enough now, I suppose, but the Hiner I remember is still the whimpering fool in the charred remains of Canyon City, and when the U.S. Army finally rose up to chase the Indians and get sweet revenge with massacres of their own, there was no Hiner heeding the call of the bugle, he was safe across the sea in buckskin.

And as for me, I was safe as well, enjoying a glass of Guinness in Chicago, and being very careful now where I smoked my pipe on a windy afternoon — for there is no temptation more treacherous than the lure of sudden insight, when knowledge comes clear in whole cloth. When such clarity happens, my friend, run from it! Run from knowledge and insight!

MILLER: "And in the desert sand beside the grave wherein he sprawled,

in careful printed hand, this very message had been scrawled:

'Yes, a sinner rotted here, whose greedy smile has vanished,

Who lusted after Oregon gold!' — that's Oro Oregono in Spanish."

MCGUINNESS: Run from the truth! — or you may find yourself drawn into a godforsaken Oregon wilderness, where anything at all can happen...

(The LIGHTS INTENSIFY, FIERY RED, the RED washing over Miller now as well: DRUMMING RISES, we hear the sounds of plaintive CHANTING AND DRUMMING, the Native American Blues, as both men are washed in RED LIGHT. Hold: and BLACKOUT. The play is over.)

For royalties information:
Charles Deemer
1-800-294-7176
cdeemer@teleport.com

1998

Famililly
a play in two acts

First produced at the Wharf Rat Theatre in Salem, Massachusetts, on August 7, 1998. Directed by Laney Roberts.

Winner of the 1997 "Crossing Borders" international new play competition and the 1998 Buckham Alley Theatre Playwrights Competition. Also the highest ranking stage play in the 1998 New Century Writer Awards and a finalist for the 1998 Oregon Book Award.

THE CAST:
George, *patriarch of the Wellington clan, retired*
Martha, *his wife*
Thomas, *their oldest son, an accountant, 30s*
Vincent, *Thomas' lifemate, an architect, 30s-40s*
Emily, *their daughter, college professor, 30s*
June, *Thomas' ex-wife, budding jazz singer, 30s*

SETTING:
The Wellington condo in San Francisco. Living room. Stairs lead to bedroom. Upstage exits to kitchen and den. Front door.

TIME:
July 4, 1976. *Act II, scene ii*: one year later, July 4, 1977.

ACT ONE

(AT RISE: The living room of a luxurious condominium in San Francisco. Stairs lead to bedrooms. Hallway leads to kitchen, den, bathroom. Front door. It is morning, July 4, 1976.)

(VINCENT, 30s, is in the room, dressed in 18th century costume, suggesting Benjamin Franklin. EMILY, 30s, is on the divan, a body under a blanket. Vincent is reading a typed script, "going over lines," preparing for a one-man show he is doing tonight. Finally he puts down the script, stands up and begins "a dry run." In the beginning, his tone is casual, matter-of-fact; he is doing this primarily for lines.)

VINCENT: "When in the course of human events, it becomes necessary for a people to change the institutions which have nurtured them since birth, and to assume among the powers of the earth, the redefinition of such institutions to which the Laws of Nature entitle them, a decent respect to the opinions of humankind requires that they should declare the causes which impel them to such changes."

(Emily coughs, gets up and obliviously wanders out of the room, on her way to the bathroom. Vincent watches her, amused, but says nothing until she is gone. Then he turns to the audience.)

VINCENT:*(to audience)* Emily, the brightest Wellington of them all. Tenured professor of history at Columbia University. Younger sister of Thomas, who is my — my what? I refuse to say "significant other." Significant other what? My lover. My partner in life. It is not like Emily to come home to a family reunion. Apparently the last time, years before Thomas and I got together, she and her father really got into it. You'll get the details later.

(He looks at the spot where Emily exited, then turns back to the audience. Now he'll play his show directly to the audience at performance level.)

VINCENT: *(to audience)* "We hold these truths to be self-evident, that all children are created equal, that they are endowed by their Creator with certain unalienable rights, that among these are Life, Shelter, Security, Education, and Nurturing. That to secure these rights,

280

Families are instituted among men and women, deriving their definition and social acceptance from the consent of the people. That when any definition of Family becomes destructive of these ends, it is the Right of the people to abolish or redefine it, and to institute a new kind of Family, laying its foundation on such principles and organizing its authority in such form, as to them seem most likely to effect the Safety and Welfare of the children."

(Emily returns.)

EMILY: Vincent, why are you dressed like that?
VINCENT: Emily! And good morning to you, too! Are we feeling a bit woozy this morning?
EMILY: Please don't tell me there's a costume party.
VINCENT: "There's a costume party." Close, but no cigarillo. *(Modeling his costume)* Who do you think I am?
EMILY: I haven't a clue.
VINCENT: You don't recognize gentle Ben, the scatological connoisseur of the Revolution?
EMILY: Of course. What do you mean, "close" to a costume party?
VINCENT: We, my dear, are riding a float in the parade. And later I'm doing a one-man show. You won't believe how I've rewritten the Declaration of Independence! Want to hear it?
EMILY: It's too early to concentrate. I couldn't find any coffee.
VINCENT: The coffee pot is in the den, not the kitchen. Be right back.
EMILY: You're a dearheart.
VINCENT: Dearheart! Is that what you academics say to one another now? Gag me!

(He leaves.)

(Emily speaks to the audience.)

EMILY: Just before every holiday I get the same phone call: "When are we going to see you?," Mom asks. I try to explain how busy I am, but my parents understand little about the demands of an academic life. This year Thomas was the first to call, reminding me that it was the Bicentennial. Hence a bigger family ta-do than usual. So I decided on a compromise. My plan was to make an appearance, spend the holiday in San Francisco, and then visit my girlfriend Sharon in Santa Barbara for a few days. Then I'd return to New York and get back to work on my biography of Mercy Otis Warren. I'll tell you more about her later.

(Vincent quickly returns with a mug of coffee.)

VINCENT: Bottom of the pot. Hope you run on 40-weight.

EMILY: Thanks. Where is everybody?

VINCENT: At the Gala Bicentennial Breakfast.

EMILY: You weren't invited?

VINCENT: I told them I had to rehearse for my show tonight. You know how your father and I are.

EMILY: I'm amazed he let you in the house.

VINCENT: A grand gesture for the Patriotism of the occasion! Something like that.

EMILY: So we're all staying here?

VINCENT: Absolutely. The family that sleeps together and all that — well, not literally. They gave Thomas and I separate bedrooms, which is why you're on the couch. I thought of sneaking across the hallway for a visit last night, but I was afraid I'd activate your father's trip wire.

EMILY: Thomas was supposed to get me a hotel room.

VINCENT: A little late now. The Bicentennial is the biggest thing to hit town since the Pope. *(Quick aside to audience)* Did the Pope ever come to San Francisco?

EMILY: I can't wait til it's over.

VINCENT: You don't like parades and costume parties?

EMILY: I don't like history according to Disney.

VINCENT: I'm glad you made the effort to come. This may be the last time everybody's together. Your father doesn't look well.

EMILY *(changing the subject)*: So you and Thomas must be doing great.

VINCENT: Splendidly. You didn't hear, I take it?

EMILY: Hear what?

VINCENT: We're getting Billy.

EMILY: Are you serious?

VINCENT: Very soon now. I'm going to be a mother!

(He moves quickly to speak to the audience.)

VINCENT: A little background. Thomas married June when they were still in college. He told me he already was attracted to men but felt guilty and sinful about it. How could he not, given a father like he had? Marriage was supposed to be his moral salvation. Of course, it wasn't.

282

Thomas and I met when June was pregnant, and I think we fell in love the very day his son, Billy, was born. At least I did. After that, things got hairy in a real hurry, and pretty ugly, too, as I'm sure you can imagine.

(He moves quickly back into the scene.)

EMILY: What about June?

VINCENT: Are you ready for this? It was her idea.

EMILY: Impossible. June's homophobic.

VINCENT: She must have matured to mere fascism.

EMILY: Why would she want to give up Billy?

VINCENT: She says she's a lousy parent. Yours truly, on the other hand, will be spectacular at it! I'm so excited.

EMILY: June's a born-to-breed, traditional, wide-hipped, all-American mother. She must be losing it.

VINCENT: That, too — but Thomas and I are just thrilled. Well, Thomas comes and goes. And we're both so nervous! I haven't been this nervous since high school when I went to my first bathhouse.

EMILY: You, I can see as a great parent. My brother, I'm not so sure about.

VINCENT: It's such a responsibility! I've been reading Dr. Spock.

(Emily has to smile.)

VINCENT: Don't poke fun if you've never read him. Dr. Spock is a real page-turner. "Will the baby gag on his first solid food?" *(To audience)* "Will he throw up in front of company?"

(Thomas rushes in. He is dressed like Thomas Jefferson, complete with wig.)

THOMAS *(to Emily)*: Good, you're up.

VINCENT *(to audience)*: The love of my life!

THOMAS *(quickly going on)*: What a goddamn mess breakfast was. We ran into June in the lobby.

VINCENT: With Billy?

THOMAS: She was with some asshole with tattoos wearing a baseball cap. Can you imagine a baseball cap at the Hilton? It was very awkward.

EMILY: I always thought blue collar was more her type. Vincent told me you're getting Billy.

THOMAS: It's not supposed to be public knowledge.

VINCENT: My, now we don't even trust our sister. *(To Emily)* Seeing June always makes him irrational. It's such a turn on.

THOMAS: I don't want to deal with the parents about getting Billy yet.

EMILY: So how are they?

THOMAS: I don't know. The same. Dad talks, mother talks, nobody listens.

VINCENT: Tell her about the cruise.

THOMAS: They're going on a cruise.

VINCENT *(to audience)*: Scheduled to leave next week.

THOMAS: I'll believe it when I see it.

EMILY: Mom's been after him for years.

THOMAS: What about you? You able to get any sleep?

EMILY: I expected a hotel room.

THOMAS: Mom wanted us all to stay here.

EMILY: I'm just teasing you. Hey, give me a hug. It's great to see you.

(They hug.)

THOMAS: Good to see you, too. I'm really glad you came.

EMILY: I reserve judgment.

VINCENT: Are your parents still planning on coffee and dessert?

THOMAS: Worse. They invited June.

VINCENT: Forewarned is forearmed. I'll flirt with her tattooed hunk. That ought to piss her off. *(To audience)* June and I go way back.

THOMAS: I think she has to give him a ride somewhere, then come here. I can't believe they invited her.

EMILY: Of course, they would. Dad adores her, and Mom believes the world is a lovely place where everyone adores everybody.

THOMAS: I couldn't stop them, Vincent.

VINCENT: Don't worry about it. Where's my son?, is what I want to know.

THOMAS: With a sitter.

VINCENT: You don't leave a two-year old boy with a sitter on the Fourth of July. Do you? I don't remember reading anything about that in Dr. Spock.

THOMAS: He's reading Dr. Spock.

EMILY: He told me.

VINCENT: She's so irresponsible. The sooner we get Billy, the better for everybody.

EMILY: I can't believe June isn't a Model Mother.

THOMAS: She's got some heavy problems.

EMILY: I knew that. But when did mental imbalance ever discourage a parent? Of course, I only know about my own family.

THOMAS: Who is due here any minute for coffee. Do you plan to be here? Or are you saving actually talking to them for later?

EMILY: I don't think I'm up for it yet. Maybe I'll go for a walk.

VINCENT: And you're the one who wanted to be "a famililly" when you grew up. *(To audience)* One of the family stories.

EMILY: You saw the home movies?

VINCENT: More than once.

EMILY: Dad really does hate you.

VINCENT: He didn't show them to me. Thomas borrowed the projector.

THOMAS: At your insistence.

VINCENT: I think family history is important.

EMILY: Don't get me started, Vincent.

THOMAS *(changing the subject)*: We've got to get you a costume. You are coming to the parade, right? They'd expect you to be on the float.

EMILY: I wasn't told about a parade. Or a costume party. Or whatever else is planned. I was told to be here and that all the arrangements were made. You didn't tell me everybody would be staying here together either.

THOMAS: Vincent, can you manage the costume?

EMILY: I'm not up for this, Thomas.

THOMAS: Dad's counting on having all of us on the float. You don't have to do anything but stand there in your costume.

VINCENT: Smile and do the windshield wiper routine.

EMILY: You didn't warn me I was walking into this.

THOMAS: Listen, if you don't want to be here, you'd better get going. You can go out the back way just in case.

EMILY: I'm not ready to belong to this family again!

VINCENT: Calm down, "dearheart". Meet you back here then?

THOMAS: Sure.

VINCENT: Follow the leader.

(He turns to the audience before leaving:)

VINCENT *(to audience)*: Enjoy meeting "the famililly!"

(Vincent and Emily exit as Thomas moves to speak to the audience.)

THOMAS: My dad and sister refight the sixties every time they get together, which fortunately hasn't been very often. She's so much like him, is the thing. Stubborn as hell. They both devour history, disagree on the meaning of it all, and neither will give an inch. Listening to them makes me glad I'm an accountant: either the books balance or they don't.

(GEORGE and MARTHA WELLINGTON enter, dressed as their namesakes, the Washingtons, the Father and Mother of the Country. George wears a wig. Martha is helping George, who looks very tired. When he speaks, we can hear the physical pain in his voice.)

MARTHA: Thomas! Your father needs to lie down.
THOMAS: What happened?
GEORGE: It's nothing.

(Martha leads George to the divan, Thomas coming forward to help, and they get George stretched out and comfortable.)

MARTHA: He got very dizzy after you left, and he has pains.
GEORGE: A little light-headed, is all.
MARTHA: Where's Emily?
THOMAS: Vincent took her to get a costume.
GEORGE: She doesn't even have her costume yet?
MARTHA: Now don't you get upset. I'm sure everything is taken care of. *(To Thomas)* There's some place open?
GEORGE: Chinese don't celebrate the Fourth, mother. Chinese tailors will get filthy rich today.
THOMAS: I was about to put on coffee. Dad, can I get you anything?
GEORGE: Your mother won't let me have a fizz yet.
THOMAS: I'll make a fresh pot of coffee.

(He leaves, moving as if he is eager to get out of there.)

GEORGE: Don't hover over me like that, mother. I got a little dizzy, is all.
MARTHA: Where does it hurt?
GEORGE: Where doesn't it?
MARTHA: Maybe you shouldn't ride on the float.
GEORGE: Let me get my second wind.
MARTHA: Okay, we'll see how you feel later.

GEORGE: I'd feel better if you stopped hovering over me.

(Martha moves away, speaking to the audience.)

MARTHA *(to audience)*: You can't do anything for him. He thinks it's a weakness to ask for help.
(Thomas sticks his head in the room.)

THOMAS: Anybody going to want pastries?
GEORGE: Nothing for me, son.
MARTHA: I'm so full, I'll probably skip lunch.

(Thomas exits.)

GEORGE: He seem okay to you?
MARTHA: Yes.
GEORGE: He acts like he's upset about something.
MARTHA: I don't think he's ever been happier.
GEORGE: I'm sure Jack the Ripper was happy, too.
MARTHA: George, don't.
GEORGE: Happiness doesn't really have much to do with anything, does it? As far as right and wrong are concerned?
MARTHA: George, please don't start a row, today of all days.
GEORGE: Every time I see June, I think of Billy having no father in the house.
MARTHA: As many children grow up today with one parent as two. Billy will be fine.
GEORGE: Kids need both parents. The downfall of the family is going to be the downfall of the country, mark my word. I'm glad I won't be around to see it.
MARTHA: What has made you so morbid today?
GEORGE: You ever wonder if we live up to our roots? I mean, look at us. What would our Founding Fathers think if they were alive today? I shudder to imagine.
MARTHA: When you feel bad, it touches everything you think about.
GEORGE: You don't believe the world's going to hell in a hand-basket?
MARTHA: I think when you get your second wind, you won't be talking like that. *(Changing the subject)* What a surprise running into June. How did she look to you?
GEORGE: Tired.

MARTHA: I thought she looked ill. I bet she's not eating right. *(To audience)* Thomas always did most of the cooking.

GEORGE: I think she's just tired, mother. Of course she'd be tired, raising a son by herself. I worry about her and Billy all alone in that big house.

MARTHA: I'm sure they do fine.

GEORGE: You don't worry about her?

MARTHA: Not really. You know who I worry about.

GEORGE: And you know what I have to say about it.

MARTHA: Emily's as much a part of my flesh as Thomas is. I can't dismiss her.

(Thomas enters with coffee.)

THOMAS: Here we are.

MARTHA: I was just telling George that June didn't look well. Didn't you think so?

THOMAS: How so?

GEORGE: She's got to be exhausted. Not easy being a single parent.

THOMAS: She left Billy with a sitter, Dad. Not too much fatigue in that.

MARTHA: She always did drive herself too hard.

GEORGE: And now she has no help.

THOMAS *(ignoring this)*: She still blames herself for not finishing school. She blames herself for not being more than a housewife. She even blames herself — you know, for how we turned out.

MARTHA: She once told me she always wanted to be a singer. A vocalist, she called it. She used to stop by a piano bar and sing along when she was single, always brought down the house. The pianist told her she reminded him of young Peggy Lee. Imagine telling that to an impressionable young woman.

THOMAS: She does have a good voice, actually. But I can't picture her with the gumption to pay the dues it would take.

MARTHA: Well, she has Billy to think about now.

GEORGE: Not easy being a single parent. Not easy at all.

THOMAS: Will you excuse me a minute?

(He moves away and speaks to the audience.)

THOMAS: I felt like I was suffocating. Obviously I was the Fallen Son in Dad's eyes, but I'd learned to let his little digs go in one ear and out the other. Now, what with the stress of Emily being here, and everybody wondering when she and Dad would get into it; and June on her way over, which I considered the worst timing because Dad was bound to bring up Billy — I needed a couple of deep breaths and a battery charge, like immediately.

(Thomas quickly exits.)

MARTHA: Why must you torment him? He doesn't want to talk about June.

GEORGE: I'm not forcing him to talk about her.

MARTHA: You keep bringing her up.

GEORGE: You brought her up!

MARTHA: I think he still cares for her.

GEORGE: Mother, he's a homosexual. It isn't a passing phase he's in.

MARTHA: I'm perfectly aware of that.

GEORGE: So he doesn't still hold a torch for June. Never did. She's not his element, so to speak.

MARTHA: He can still care for her, and I think he does. This is all much harder on him than he admits. Or than you admit.

GEORGE: I doubt that very seriously.

MARTHA: Why can't you give him the benefit of the doubt?

GEORGE: Why should I? They kept me awake all night.

MARTHA: Who?

GEORGE: The two of them. I kept expecting to hear someone sneak across the hall.

MARTHA: What a thing to lose sleep over!

GEORGE: I wouldn't put it past them.

MARTHA: Serves you right, making them use separate bedrooms. Long as they've been living together now.

GEORGE: I'm not running a cat house.

MARTHA: You're just itching for a fight with Vincent, aren't you?

GEORGE: I can be polite to him. It doesn't mean I approve of him or encourage what they do.

MARTHA: You've never appreciated how difficult it was for Thomas to come out.

GEORGE: Since when is lust difficult? It's doing the right thing that's hard.

MARTHA: That's not fair. He loves Vincent.

GEORGE: We'll never agree, mother.

MARTHA: You don't want to talk about Emily — well, I don't want to talk about this. I would like this to be a special day. We may not have everybody together again.

(The doorbell rings. George sits up.)

MARTHA: You don't have to get up.

(Thomas rushes in and to the door.)

THOMAS: I'll get it.
(Thomas answers the door. JUNE walks in. She's pretty but doesn't take advantage of it and looks, in fact, like she could use some sleep.)

THOMAS: Hello. Come in.
JUNE: They said it would be all right to come over.
THOMAS: Of course, it's all right. Coffee?
JUNE: Yes, thanks. I love your costume.
THOMAS: Still sugar and cream?

(June smiles and nods. Thomas leaves to fetch coffee.)

MARTHA: I'm so glad you could stop by.
GEORGE: Wish you had Billy.
JUNE: To be honest, it's nice to have some time to myself.
MARTHA: We'll have you to dinner soon. Right after we get back from our cruise.
JUNE: A cruise!
MARTHA: We leave next week. It only took me thirty years to get him to take me.
GEORGE: We're not on the high seas yet, mother.
MARTHA: No backing out on me!
GEORGE: I may get hit by a truck tomorrow.
MARTHA: Listen to him.
JUNE: Where are you going?
MARTHA: The Bahamas. We'll be gone 10 days.
GEORGE: Probably seasick the whole time.
MARTHA: He's been in one of his moods all morning.
GEORGE (ignoring this): So how's the Billy boy doing?
JUNE: He's great.
GEORGE: I thought of taking him on the cruise. Of course, I knew you wouldn't give him up for that long.

(June moves to speak to the audience:)

JUNE *(to audience)*: So they didn't know yet. I guessed as much since they hadn't said anything about it at the Hilton. It was just like Thomas to put off something important to the last possible moment. Thomas is the great procrastinator.

MARTHA: What an interesting young man you were with.

JUNE *(moving back into scene)*: Joey? He's in my jazz improv class.

GEORGE: Your what?

JUNE: I'm taking some music classes at night.

GEORGE: I didn't know that.

MARTHA: Oh, you did so. His memory's going.

JUNE: I don't think I told either of you.

GEORGE: That keeps you pretty busy, doesn't it?

JUNE: Too busy, I'm afraid.

GEORGE: Keeping care of Billy is a full-time job in itself.

JUNE *(wanting to get out of this)*: It can be, that's for sure. I wonder if Thomas needs any help.

(But he is just now entering.)

MARTHA: June is taking a music class!

THOMAS: Really? You finally bit the bullet.

JUNE: Yep.

THOMAS: I didn't ask if you wanted a pastry.

JUNE: No thanks.

MARTHA: Does anyone mind if I take my coffee upstairs? I want to freshen up.

THOMAS: Of course not.

MARTHA: George? I want to touch up your wig. You probably are ready to get out from under it.

GEORGE: What she's trying to say is, You two probably want some time alone.

MARTHA: Now that you mention it, I'm sure they do. George?

(Martha and George start upstairs to their bedroom. Martha tries to help him but he pushes her away.)

GEORGE: Quit hovering over me.

(George starts upstairs. On her way out behind him, Martha speaks to the audience.)

MARTHA *(to audience)*: I gave up trying to change him long ago. The glass on the table is never full, and whether it's half-empty or half-full is completely up to you.

(She exits behind George.)

JUNE: Where's Vincent?
THOMAS: He's helping Emily get a costume.
JUNE: So she finally broke down and came home.
THOMAS: Only in a manner of speaking. I think she's already ready to leave.
JUNE: She still teaching at Columbia?
THOMAS: Oh, yes. Tenure and everything.
JUNE: I'm sorry I missed her.
THOMAS: June, I don't want Dad to find out what's coming down sooner than he has to. Especially not today. Everybody's looking at this like it's the Last Family Reunion.
JUNE: I certainly don't plan on telling him.
THOMAS: I just wanted to touch bases with you. I'll tell Mom first and let her break the news to him.

(A pause.)

THOMAS: Not getting cold feet are you?
JUNE: I don't think so.
THOMAS: That's not very encouraging.
JUNE: I'm fine. It's just going to be quite a change.
THOMAS: You're doing the right thing.
JUNE: The only part that worries me is Vincent. He and I need to reach an understanding.
THOMAS: I've wanted you two to be friends from the start.
JUNE: I'm not sure that can happen. But we can be civil, for Billy's sake. Where do you think Vincent's at with all this?
THOMAS: You said some pretty vicious things about him.
JUNE: All of us said things we regret.
THOMAS: True enough.
JUNE: Billy will pick up on any animosity between us.
THOMAS: I'll talk to Vincent and test the waters. Maybe we can sit down together.

JUNE: Thanks, Thomas.

THOMAS: What's your schedule?

JUNE: I'm only in the city for the day, so later would be great if you have time.

THOMAS: We have a party tonight but there's a break after the parade. You could come by around four, and we could all go out for a drink.

JUNE: If Vincent's up to it, that would be perfect.

THOMAS: So you're studying music again.

(June moves forward to speak to the audience:)

JUNE *(to audience)*: I hate it when he pretends to be interested in what I'm doing. Especially about something as important to me as music. Money was never a problem with us — but would he buy me a piano? I'm a musician, for God's sake, I need a piano as much as he needs a calculator. But he never took — he still doesn't take — my music seriously. It's just my hobby, as far as he's concerned. So when he starts pretending he's interested in what I'm doing, I just turn him off, I might as well be wearing a hearing aid and flipping the switch.

(The door opens and Vincent enters.)

VINCENT: Oops — didn't mean to interrupt.

(He starts out.)

THOMAS: Vincent, wait a minute. We need to talk.

VINCENT: Emily won't come in unless the coast is clear. Where are your parents?

THOMAS: Upstairs.

(Vincent calls into the hallway.)

VINCENT: The coast is clear! *(To the audience)* Tenure at Columbia, and she's afraid to face her parents.

(He moves into the room, leaving the door open.)

JUNE: I like your costume. Ben Franklin, right?

VINCENT: A kind word? What are you setting me up for?

JUNE: I'd better be going.

THOMAS: Vincent, I was thinking later the three of us could get together for a drink. We need to find a way to all work together — for Billy's sake.

(Emily enters. She is dressed in a period costume.)

EMILY: Hi, June.
JUNE: What a surprise. I hear you got tenure.
EMILY: A couple years ago, actually.
JUNE: Congratulations. So, Thomas, I'll call later.
THOMAS: Great.
JUNE: Nice seeing you, Emily.

(June starts out.)

VINCENT: Farewell to you, too! *(To the audience)* She can't stand to be in the same room with me.

(June moves quickly to speak to the audience.)

JUNE: No, that's not true. I've never hated Vincent the way I think I'd hate "the other woman," if Thomas had left me for one. That's what I was afraid was going to happen. After Billy was born, nothing was the same between us, and I thought Thomas was having an affair. With a woman, I mean. But when you lose your spouse, the person you love, the person you expect to spend the rest of your life with, the father of your child — when you lose him to another man — I don't know how to describe the feeling. I was shocked. I hadn't seen it coming, not that way, not a clue. It's like waking up on another planet. Well, I flipped out, is what happened.

(Thomas quickly moves forward.)

FLASHBACK:

THOMAS: June, I can only be who I am.
JUNE: But you knew all along! You've been lying to me since the day we met!
THOMAS: No, it's much more complicated than that.
JUNE: You married me when you knew what you were!
THOMAS: Don't say "what" like I'm some kind of insect.

JUNE: "What" is being a liar! Why? Did you think I was going to cure you? Did you need me so people at work wouldn't suspect what you are?

THOMAS: I married you because I love you.

JUNE: How can you say that?

THOMAS: It's true. I still love you. I've just stopped desiring you.

JUNE: Get the fuck out of my house. Go to your queer friend and do your faggot sex together.

THOMAS: You don't use words like that.

JUNE: At least you found somebody who'll let you fuck them in the ass.

THOMAS: That's not what this is about.

JUNE: Thomas, what the hell do you want from me? Approval?

THOMAS: No. Understanding.

JUNE: What I understand is that you've been living a lie with me, Thomas. You're a goddamn liar!

(She quickly exits, as Thomas watches her go. Vincent brings Thomas back into the scene.)

VINCENT: What do you think?

THOMAS: I'm worried about her.

VINCENT: About the costume! We didn't have much of a selection.

THOMAS: Looks fine.

VINCENT: Now what persona will you use?

EMILY: Vincent, for Christ's sake—

VINCENT: You have to *be* someone, "dearheart."

EMILY: Fine. I'm Mercy Otis Warren.

THOMAS: Who the hell is that?

EMILY: America's first playwright. Younger sister of James Otis.

THOMAS: That explains everything. Who's James Otis?

EMILY: Are you kidding me? Vincent, tell him.

VINCENT: I'm just a dirty old man, what do I know? I write clever one-liners for Poor Richard's Almanac. *(To audience)* Benjamin Franklin also had the best collection of scatological literature in the colonies. Definitely our most anal Founding Father.

EMILY: Otis is the man who first said, "No taxation without representation!"

THOMAS: I thought that was Patrick Henry.

VINCENT: That's "Give me puberty or give me death!"

EMILY: Otis is one of the more fascinating characters in the revolution. He was a conservative — he didn't want a revolution, he wanted American representation in the British Parliament.

VINCENT: Really? So tell me, who was the first American drag queen? *(To audience)* This should be interesting.

EMILY: Not my area of specialization, Vincent.

VINCENT: If it ain't Mom and Apple Pie, it ain't in the history books. Same old story.

EMILY: You get no argument from me. History is what the winners tell the losers.

(CROSS FADE to upstairs bedroom. George is out of his wig, stretched out on the bed, talking to Martha off-stage.)

GEORGE: I wonder if your life really passes before your eyes just before you die.

MARTHA *(O.S.):* Please don't talk like that.

GEORGE: I hope so. Hope I remember things I haven't been able to recall for years. There are so many memories I have just bits and pieces of, like maybe I remember just a small thing that happened, but I can't remember what went before or after. It would be nice to have a complete memory of something again. If that's what it's going to be like—.

(Martha enters from the bathroom.)

MARTHA: You're getting beyond morbid, George.

GEORGE: Aren't you curious about it?

MARTHA: No.

GEORGE: Well, I am.

MARTHA: You worry me. You really don't feel well, do you?

GEORGE: I haven't felt well in years.

MARTHA: I mean right now. Promise me you'll see the doctor before we leave on the cruise.

GEORGE: Pretty short notice.

MARTHA: It's an emergency. He'll let you in.

GEORGE: I'm getting old, mother. Doctors can't do a thing about it.

MARTHA: You're not that old.

GEORGE: I feel older every day.

MARTHA: Wait til we get to sea. The salt air will do wonders for you.

GEORGE: Probably spend the whole trip barfing.

MARTHA: You're just determined to be miserable today, aren't you? Well, I'm not letting you bring me down to your level. If you want to feel sorry for yourself, be my guest. I'm going to enjoy the family being together again..

GEORGE: Is that what we are? A family?

MARTHA: Of course we're a family. What a thing to say.

GEORGE: Not a family the way it used to be. How many homosexuals were in your parents' family?

MARTHA: Things were different then.

GEORGE: You can say that again.

MARTHA: There probably were more homosexuals than we knew about, George, only they kept to themselves.

GEORGE: That's exactly what I mean. It was unthinkable to flaunt your sex life in public. A disgrace.

MARTHA: Thomas is not a disgrace. He can't help the way he is.

GEORGE: Does that give them license to keep everybody awake all night?

MARTHA: You kept yourself awake, worrying about them! I'm going downstairs. Please try to relax. You have time for a little nap.

GEORGE: I'm not sleepy.

MARTHA: You want to come downstairs with me?

GEORGE: I'll be down directly, mother.

MARTHA: You're sure you're up to being on the float?

GEORGE: I'll be fine. Just give me a minute to get my second wind.

(George watches Martha leave. Then he goes to a closet and takes out a blue canvas bag. He stares at it. CROSS FADE to downstairs.)

EMILY: I'm amazed at the change in June's attitude.

THOMAS: She just hates the responsibility of being a parent. Apparently she's going to try and do something with her music.

(Vincent is the first to see Martha coming down the stairs.)

VINCENT: All hail the Mother of Our Country!

(He moves to her, taking her arm.)

VINCENT: What can I get you? Coffee? A drink?

MARTHA: Emily!

EMILY: Hi, Mom.

(They embrace a bit stiffly.)

MARTHA: I'm so happy you were able to come. I know how busy you are.

EMILY: Well, here I am. *(Modeling her costume:)* I didn't know exactly what I was getting into.

THOMAS: She's America's first playwright. What was her name?

EMILY: Mercy Otis Warren.

MARTHA: Really? Isn't that marvelous?

EMILY: You look good, Mom. How's Dad doing?

MARTHA: I'm worried about him. He had a dizzy spell this morning, and you know how stubborn he can be about seeing a doctor. We're leaving on a cruise next week.

EMILY: So I hear.

MARTHA: I want him to get a checkup before we go.

THOMAS: Is he feeling well enough to do the parade?

MARTHA: We'll see how he feels after his nap.

VINCENT: I'm sure we can find a stool for him on the float. At least he won't have to be on his feet.

MARTHA: How thoughtful.

EMILY: I'm nervous about seeing him. We got in such a brawl the last time.

THOMAS: Don't talk about college and the sixties, and you'll be fine.

VINCENT: Try peaceful coexistence. Look at me. I know he doesn't approve of me — but here I am!

MARTHA: That's not true, Vincent. Of course he likes you.

THOMAS: Mother, please.

VINCENT: I'm a guest in his house, at any rate. There's definite signs of progress there.

MARTHA: It's not you two so much. He worries more about Billy not having a father in the house.

(Thomas and Vincent exchange a knowing glance.)

THOMAS: Billy has a father.

MARTHA: I know that. George is old-fashioned. He thinks children need two parents in the home.

(A pause.)

THOMAS: Mom, there's something I should tell you. *(To Vincent)* Unless you object.

VINCENT: Your decision. *(To audience)* I'm not touching that with a ten-foot you-know-what.

THOMAS *(to Vincent)*: Maybe Mom can break it to him on the cruise.

EMILY: I think it's a good idea, Thomas.

MARTHA: What are you talking about?

THOMAS: Vincent and I are getting Billy.

(Martha just looks at him, puzzled.)

THOMAS: We're getting official custody. We'll be raising him, starting next week, right after you leave on the cruise. It's something we've been working on for a while now.

MARTHA: Billy will be living with you?

THOMAS: Yes. It was June's idea, actually.

MARTHA: She doesn't want him any more?

THOMAS: She says she's not a very good parent. And I guess she wants to pursue her music. Of course, she can spend all the time with Billy she wants.

MARTHA: I don't know what to say. I didn't know something like that was allowed.

THOMAS: We both know Dad's going to flip out when he hears. I'm hoping you can be a buffer for that by breaking the news to him on the cruise.

VINCENT: May I say something? Martha, you and I get along pretty well, I think, and I want you to know that we've all given this a good deal of thought. The primary reason we're doing this is for Billy. With two of us in the home, he'll always have someone to be there for him.

THOMAS: I'm sure June will be over for dinner and visiting a lot. He'll have three parents, is what it amounts, too. We're all very excited about this. We know it's best for Billy.

VINCENT: I've been reading Dr. Spock.

EMILY: Change the subject, he's coming down.

(George comes downstairs.)

GEORGE: Emily! Come give your old man a hug.

(Emily is taken aback by the greeting.)

EMILY: Hi, Dad.

GEORGE: You heard me.

(She moves to him, and they awkwardly embrace.)

GEORGE: I know how busy you are — thanks for being here.

EMILY: Thomas wouldn't take no for an answer.

GEORGE: Good for you, son. Family wouldn't be complete without you. What is it you used to say? "I want to be a famililly when I grow up!"

(Emily speaks to the audience.)

EMILY *(to audience)*: Something pops out of your mouth when you're seven, and it follows you to your grave.

MARTHA: Weren't you able to sleep, dear?

GEORGE: Don't want to sleep through the most important holiday of my lifetime! I can stay in bed all day tomorrow if it comes to that. I like your costume.

MARTHA: She's America's first playwright.

GEORGE: Mercy Otis Warren. Sister of James Otis.

EMILY: I'm impressed.

GEORGE: "No taxation without representation!" His law clerk, Samuel Adams, took that little proposition considerably farther than Otis intended. If I remember correctly, Otis went crazy when the fighting started, and they had to carry him out of Boston in a strait jacket.

EMILY: A bit exaggerated, perhaps.

GEORGE *(ignoring this)*: Otis spent the entire revolution in exile. He burned his life's work, he was so depressed about the violence. That's why we know so little about him. John Adams called him the First Patriot. You're not the only historian in the family, young lady.

EMILY: Very good.

GEORGE: After the revolution, they threw a James Otis Day for him in Boston, and at the celebration Otis saw Hamilton and others dancing the minuet. He thought they were behaving like a bunch of English aristocrats! Depressed him all over again. I think that's when he decided to burn all his papers. Mercy was editing them at the time.

EMILY: There's some controversy about some of that.

(Martha senses potential conflict and intervenes.)

MARTHA: Emily, let me give you the grand tour.

300

GEORGE: Now mother, just relax. There's lots of time for grand tours.

MARTHA: You're not going to start an argument about history, are you?

GEORGE: No, I'm not starting an argument about anything. Emily, tell her.

EMILY *(tentatively)*: We're fine, Mom.

GEORGE *(to Emily)*: Now come with me.

(He takes her hand and starts toward the stairs. Emily isn't sure what is going on — and neither is anyone else.)

MARTHA: George?

GEORGE: We'll be back before it's time to go. I'm sure you all can amuse yourselves.

THOMAS: Dad, what's going on?

GEORGE: Will everyone just relax, for God's sake?

(They have started up the stairs.)

EMILY: Mom, it's okay.

(Everyone watches them move up the stairs and out of sight.)

VINCENT *(to the audience)*: I love it when people act unpredictably! We all get in such ruts, don't you think?

THOMAS: What's he doing?

MARTHA: I have no idea.

THOMAS: This is really weird, Mom.

VINCENT: I think he's on a roll, and we should all just go along with it.

THOMAS: You haven't been around him long enough to know what you're talking about.

MARTHA: Maybe he just needs to talk to her alone.

VINCENT: Exactly. Why do you always have to think the worst?

THOMAS: Because those two are stubborn as hell and have the same argument every time they get together.

MARTHA: And I for one refuse to sit here and get upset by it.

(She starts away.)

THOMAS: Where are you going?

MARTHA: I'm getting a head start on dinner.

(She moves toward the kitchen, speaking to the audience:)

MARTHA *(to audience)*: The glass is half-empty or it's half-full. It's completely up to you.

(She exits.)

THOMAS: You don't know their history. This is definitely out of character.

VINCENT: So what are you going to do? Sit here and wait for blood to come flowing down the stairs?

THOMAS: That's not funny.

VINCENT: I do detect something of a self-fulfilling prophecy in this family.

THOMAS: You don't have any foundation for what you're saying. Let's change the subject.

VINCENT: Okay. How about doing me a favor?

THOMAS: What?

VINCENT: Listen to my monologue. I need an audience.

(CROSS FADE to bedroom upstairs.)

GEORGE: I need to lie down a minute.

(He stretches out on the bed.)

EMILY: Dad, are you all right?

GEORGE: Not exactly.

EMILY: What's the problem?

GEORGE: That's what I want to talk to you about.

EMILY: Okay.

GEORGE: We've had our differences, I realize, ever since you went to Berkeley. Before, I suppose — since high school. I just want you to know there's something I respect about you very much.

EMILY *(on her guard)* And what's that?

GEORGE: Your intellect.

EMILY: You think I'm a stupid bleeding-heart liberal.

GEORGE: That has more to do with values than intellect.

EMILY: I'm not sure I understand the distinction in this case.

GEORGE: Your values make you ask the wrong questions.

302

EMILY: I see. Dad, if you brought me up here to try and change my value system—

GEORGE: I didn't.

EMILY: I almost didn't come here, to avoid this very conversation. I don't know why you can't just leave it alone.

GEORGE: Have I said anything about Berkeley?

EMILY: Surely you think that's where my values went wrong.

GEORGE: Of course I do. Because they did. But I didn't bring it up, you did.

EMILY: What kind of bullshit is that?

GEORGE: All that education and you talk like a longshoreman. Excuse me, longshore *person*.

(She starts for the stairs.)

EMILY: I'm not doing this, Dad.

(George sits up, which takes some effort.)

GEORGE: Wait a minute.

EMILY: I don't want to fight with you about college or the sixties or anything else. End of conversation.

(She's heading out when she is stopped by what he says next.)

GEORGE: Damn it, Emily, I'm sick!

(She turns to him.)

GEORGE: It's serious. I don't want your mother to know.

(Emily slowly comes back into the room.)

EMILY: What's wrong with you?

GEORGE: I have cancer.

EMILY: Oh, Dad...

GEORGE: It's getting worse. Sometimes I think I can feel it getting worse by the hour.

EMILY: You're not having any kind of treatment?

GEORGE: You saw what happened to your Uncle Henry. The cure is worse than the disease. Three months ago, they gave me six months. I think it's going to be less.

EMILY: You haven't told anyone?

GEORGE: No.

EMILY: Why me?

GEORGE: Because you're the only one in the family who can keep your head. I'm not going through what Henry went through, I can promise you that. I'm doing it myself first. I've been reading up on how to do that.

EMILY: Dad, I'm so sorry.

GEORGE: No tears, Emily. That's another reason I'm telling you. I haven't seen you cry since the fourth or fifth grade.

EMILY: First time someone's complimented me on that particular character defect.

GEORGE: Keeping control of your emotions is not a character defect.

EMILY: So what you're telling me is — you're going to do it yourself?

GEORGE: Yes.

EMILY: How?

GEORGE: With pills, liquor and a bag. It's as painless and clean as it gets.

EMILY: Have you talked to your doctor about this?

GEORGE: Of course not. He'd try to talk me out of it, if he didn't report me to the police. You fail at something like this, and they throw you in jail.

EMILY: I see. So when is this going to happen?

GEORGE: I was planning it right after the cruise. Only now I'm not sure I have that long.

EMILY: Jesus, Dad, you should get to a doctor. If you're in pain, at least they can give you something for it.

GEORGE: They already have. I skip the pills now and again so I can monitor myself.

EMILY: There must be an easier way.

GEORGE: Believe me, I've thought a lot about the best way to do it. Do I do it alone and let someone discover me? Do I do it here — or would that make it unbearable for your mother to keep living here? So then do I get a motel room or what? And the more I think about it, the more I get angry that it has to be so complicated. A man dies, for Christ's sake. It's inevitable. It's the most natural thing in the world. So why can't this be as natural an event as a birth?

EMILY: If it could happen any way you want, how would it be?

GEORGE: I've thought about that, too. I'd have all of you around me. You'd respect my decision to do it this way. It would be like a celebration — like a wake, I suppose, and then we'd all say goodnight, goodbye, and I'd fall asleep and that would be that.

EMILY: Dad, that's beautiful.

GEORGE: Can you imagine your mother going along with that? Thomas would be even worse.

EMILY: Have you thought about telling them what you want? Maybe they'll surprise you.

GEORGE: I wouldn't know where to begin.

EMILY: Just tell them what you told me. And tell them how you would like it to be.

(A pause.)

EMILY: I could tell them, if you'd like.

GEORGE: You'd do that, wouldn't you?

EMILY: Of course I would.

GEORGE: They say Indian chiefs would just walk into the woods and die when it was time. I think they had the right idea.

EMILY: Talk to Mom. She needs to know what you're going through.

GEORGE: I don't want a hysterical woman on my hands.

EMILY: Give her the chance to surprise you. She's a very strong woman. And a very practical one. She saw what Uncle Henry went through, the same as you. She'll understand why you're doing this.

(CROSS FADE to downstairs. Vincent is rehearsing his show, as Thomas listens.)

VINCENT: "...to institute a new kind of Family, laying its foundation on such principles and organizing its authority in such form, as to them seem most likely to effect the Safety and Welfare of the children. Such has been the patient sufferance of many men and women today, and such is now the necessity that constrains them to alter their former concept of Family."

(He moves his focus from Thomas to the audience.)

VINCENT: "Prudence, indeed, would dictate that a definition of Family long established should not be changed for light and transient causes; and accordingly all experience hath shewn that humankind are more disposed to suffer, while evils are sufferable, than to right themselves by abolishing the forms of Family to which they are accustomed. But when a long train of atrocities and dysfunctions, pursuing invariably the same result, evinces a pattern to expose the children to unbearable suffering and insecurity, it is their right, it is their duty, to throw off such a definition of Family, and to provide new kinds of families for the well-being of the children."

(George and Emily come downstairs.)

GEORGE: What the hell are you babbling about, Vincent?
VINCENT: *(quickly, to audience)* To be continued.
EMILY: Where's Mom?
THOMAS: In the kitchen.

(Emily exits to fetch Martha.)

GEORGE: New kinds of families? Seriously, what was that about?
THOMAS: Vincent was rehearsing for his little skit tonight.
VINCENT *(to audience)*: "His little skit"!
GEORGE: About family values?
THOMAS: Dad, it's nothing. I think we'd better get going.
GEORGE: We've got lots of time.
THOMAS: I'm sure traffic will be a nightmare.

(Emily and Martha return.)

EMILY: Dad wants to have a family meeting.
THOMAS: A what?
EMILY: Family meeting. He has something to tell us.
MARTHA: George?
GEORGE: She's right, mother.
VINCENT: In that case, if you will excuse me...
THOMAS: You can stay.

(There is a silence, while everyone looks to see what George will do.)

GEORGE: Sit down and relax, Vincent. All of you. This won't take long.

(Everyone gets comfortable. There is tension in the room: George has never called "a family meeting" before.)

GEORGE: Well. This isn't going to be as easy as I thought.

EMILY: You're doing fine.

MARTHA: Emily, do you know what's going on here?

GEORGE: Yes, she does, mother. I told her because I knew she's the only one in the family who wouldn't go into hysterics.

MARTHA: What on earth are you talking about? I know you've been keeping something from me. What is it? George?

GEORGE: Just calm down.

MARTHA: I want to know what's going on here!

GEORGE: I can't tell you while you're talking!

EMILY: Dad, take it easy.

MARTHA: George?

EMILY: Mom, let him tell it his way.

(A pause.)

GEORGE: Christ, what a mess.

EMILY: Take your time.

(A pause.)

GEORGE: I have cancer. Three months ago, they gave me six months to live.

(Martha puts a hand over her mouth. Thomas stares in disbelief. Vincent is calm.)

GEORGE: I think that assessment was optimistic.

MARTHA: Why didn't you tell me?

GEORGE: I didn't want to upset you sooner than necessary. Any of you.

(A silence.)

GEORGE: Look, this isn't any easier for me than it is for you. But I'm not going through what Henry went through. I'm not taking radiation or chemo. In other words, I'm taking care of the situation myself.

(A pause. No one knows what to say.)

THOMAS: Are you saying what I think you're saying?

GEORGE: Yes, I am. And that part's been decided. No discussion.
VINCENT: I think what you're doing is very brave.
EMILY: So do I.

(Martha and Thomas, on the other hand, look horrified.)

GEORGE: Upstairs, Emily asked me how it would happen if I could have my way. I told her I'd like all of you around me, that we'd have a kind of wake, and then I'd take the pills and liquor, and put the bag over my head, and go to sleep.

(Martha suddenly gets up.)

MARTHA: Well, that's just fine for you, isn't it? You don't have to watch yourself twitch and groan and throw up and whatever else it is that happens!

(She moves for the stairway.)

GEORGE: Mother!

(Martha exits to the bedroom upstairs.)

GEORGE *(to Emily)*: I told you this would happen.
EMILY: Excuse me.

(Emily goes upstairs to comfort Martha.)

GEORGE: Why the hell can't a man die as he pleases?
THOMAS: Because it's selfish.
VINCENT: Really?
THOMAS: He's thinking only of himself.
VINCENT: And who are you thinking of? I'm on your side, George, I think a man has the right to die any way he chooses.
THOMAS: If you're determined to do that, why didn't you just go somewhere and do it? Why do you have to drag everyone else through the gory details?

(Thomas gets up and goes to the bedroom upstairs. An awkward silence.)

VINCENT: Here's an unlikely coalition.

GEORGE: What?

VINCENT: I'm sorry. It struck me as funny.

GEORGE: What did?

VINCENT: The two of us. Being on the same side here.

GEORGE: Our Founding Fathers would be so ashamed. We don't have the moral character to carry their boots.

VINCENT: I don't think that's true.

GEORGE: Good God, man. Look around you.

VINCENT: I thought you were going to say, Look in the mirror.

GEORGE: Yes. That, too.

VINCENT: I don't think I have the energy for this. If you'll excuse me.

(He starts away.)

GEORGE: What do you have against family values?

VINCENT: I have nothing against family values. Quite the contrary.

GEORGE: What the hell do you know about it?

VINCENT: More than you imagine.

GEORGE: You'll never raise children. You don't know the first thing about it.

VINCENT: Don't be so sure of that.

GEORGE: You made a choice of lifestyle that goes completely against the notion of family.

VINCENT: Then we need new notions, don't we?

GEORGE: We need a return to the values of the past.

VINCENT: Not going to happen.

GEORGE: If you're right, it's the downfall of the country.

VINCENT: A little revolution is a good thing. Jefferson said so.

GEORGE: Don't patronize me. You have that completely out of context.

VINCENT: I don't think so.

GEORGE: The kind of revolution you're talking about, the kind of revolution you are living, is against marriage and against family and against everything that made this country great.

VINCENT: Thomas and I are as good as married.

GEORGE: That's absurd. Marriage is at the foundation of raising a family, a man and woman in holy bonding.

VINCENT: We can do that, too.

GEORGE: Not until science has men bearing children. The way this country's going, it'll probably happen. But that doesn't make it right.

VINCENT: We can raise a child who's already been born.

GEORGE: Adopt? They let you do that now?

VINCENT: You're trying my patience here.

GEORGE: Maybe they do. Wouldn't surprise me.

VINCENT: Maybe you should just crawl off into the bushes and take care of business.

GEORGE: You'd like that, I'm sure.

VINCENT: That was uncalled for. I apologize. I truly do.

(The stress has finally gotten to George. He sits with his head in his hands. A pause.)

VINCENT: I wish we could get along.

(No response from George.)

VINCENT: I'd like to be a part of this family. I don't have one of my own. My parents are gone. My brother won't speak to me.

(No reply.)

VINCENT: "I want to be a famililly when I grow up."

(George looks up.)

VINCENT: It's a charming story. Thomas can't remember how old Emily was when she said it.

GEORGE: Seven. Eight maybe. Thomas was always talking about how he wanted to be a policeman—

VINCENT: A policeman! He never told me that part.

GEORGE: —and so Emily started saying, "I want to be a famililly when I grow up." She said it so often it could drive you crazy.

VINCENT: I like it. "I want to be a famililly when I grow up."

GEORGE: Your connection to this family, such as it is, is through lust.

VINCENT: Why do straight people think gay people are sex fiends?

GEORGE: I'll grant you one thing: I don't understand much of anything any more.

VINCENT: I don't understand all that much myself. But I do understand this. That what happens between consenting adults in a bedroom doesn't have the earth-shattering influence on the state of the nation that some people think it does.

(A pause.)

GEORGE: This isn't the way I wanted it to be.
VINCENT: May I ask you a personal question?

(No reply.)

VINCENT: What are you going to miss the most?
GEORGE: What?
VINCENT: What are you going to miss the most?
GEORGE: Watching Billy grow up. But maybe that would end up being too painful. A boy needs two parents.
VINCENT: Billy has two parents.
GEORGE: I mean living together. A father, a mother — a family.
VINCENT: He's getting two parents living together.

(George stares at him.)

GEORGE: June's getting remarried?
VINCENT: No.
GEORGE: I don't understand.
VINCENT: June doesn't think she's a good parent.
GEORGE: No wonder, trying to raise a boy by herself. Going to a job, going to school. I have no idea why she decided to go to night school.
VINCENT: She wants to be a musician. A jazz vocalist, piano player, something like that. It's so important to her that she's giving up Billy.
GEORGE: What are you talking about?
VINCENT: She's giving him to Thomas and I to raise. We're going to be the primary providers, the parents, for Billy. Of course, she'll be able to visit as often as she likes.
GEORGE: You're getting Billy?

(Vincent nods.)

GEORGE: You and Thomas?

(Vincent nods.)

VINCENT: We're going to be a famililly.

(George stares at him. BLACKOUT. Act One is over.)

ACT TWO

Scene One

(AT RISE: SPOT up on George, who talks to the audience.)

GEORGE: You get to be my age, you look back for what went wrong. What happened to the traditional American values? You used to go out and work hard for what you wanted. You used to get married for life.

Well, I fault ourselves. I fault the kind of parents we became. We tried to save our kids from going through all the hardships we went through, and that was a mistake. We had the experience of standing in soup lines during the Great Depression, of being bombed by the Japanese at Pearl Harbor — you don't forget experiences like that. They become rooted in the fabric of your being. Because those experiences are clear, they are without ambiguity.

When a foreign country makes a surprise attack and sinks your navy, you don't get lost in rhetoric about whether war is right or wrong — you roll up your sleeves and get to work. You do what has to be done to defend your country. Everybody pitches in and works together as one big American family.

Maybe you have to suffer to learn these things, and when parents of my generation started protecting their children from going through the hard times that we went through, we ended up doing them a disservice. We spoiled them, is what it amounts to. We gave them the idea you could get what you wanted without working for it, that the world was some kind of play thing for their personal and selfish amusement. Our children never learned how to pitch in and work together, all they looked out for is number one.

When's the last time you heard of a marriage staying together for the sake of the children? Something like that is unthinkable today. Community and family values have gone down the drain.

(A pause.)

GEORGE: Well, there's nothing I can do about it. It's not my world any more. The thing is — and this is sad in a way — it makes it a hell of a lot easier for me to think about throwing in the towel. Because I just don't understand America any more.

(LIGHTS UP FULL to reveal: the same moment that ended Act One.)
GEORGE: You and Thomas?

(Vincent nods.)

VINCENT: We're going to be a famililly.

(George stares at him.)

VINCENT: I think we'll be excellent parents.
GEORGE: But it's not quite the same as being husband and wife and a real family, is it?
VINCENT: No, it's not the same — it's better. Because Thomas and I can give Billy a stable home.

(A pause.)

VINCENT: I admit I'm nervous. I've been reading Dr. Spock.
GEORGE: Dr. Spock. Maybe that's what happened. A whole generation of mothers took a pinko's advice on raising their children.

(George stands up. He wearily starts for the kitchen.)

VINCENT: Billy still needs his grandfather.

(George stops and turns to Vincent.)

VINCENT: That's true no matter who raises him. I think the loss of grandparents, the loss of the extended family, is a great tragedy in American life.

313

GEORGE: You do?

VINCENT: Absolutely. You look surprised.

GEORGE: I'm shocked, to be honest. Were you close to your grandparents?

VINCENT: Very. To both of them. My grandfather told me things about my dad that I'd never have learned otherwise. It's a valuable perspective to have. Billy needs you in his life.

(A pause. George is studying him.)

GEORGE: I'm having a Ramos fizz. Care to join me?

VINCENT: Normally it's early for me — but under the circumstances, yes. Nice of you to ask.

GEORGE: I have the original recipe. I'll make a pitcher.

(He exits, as Thomas comes downstairs.)

VINCENT (to audience): That turned out much better than I expected.

THOMAS: What's going on?

VINCENT: He's making Ramos fizzes. I told him. Thomas, I had to. He's so worried about Billy. We have to convince him this is the right thing to do.

THOMAS: You'll never convince him of that.

VINCENT: I think he's more reasonable than you think.

THOMAS: On what evidence do you say that?

VINCENT: His world is changing. It's ending actually. That must be a terrible thing to go through. Maybe we'll feel the same way when we're his age.

THOMAS: The man is a homophobe.

VINCENT: He's also dying.

THOMAS: Don't lecture me on dying. I watched one of my best friends die, moment by moment.

VINCENT: I know you did, Thomas.

THOMAS: Frank fought back to his last breath, he found joy beyond my comprehension in what life was left to him. He was so brave!

(Emily comes downstairs.)

EMILY: Mom's taking a nap. Where's Dad?

THOMAS: Finally making his Ramos fizzes.

EMILY: Are we having a wake?

THOMAS: Ask Vincent. He and Dad have become bosom buddies. *(To Vincent)* I can't believe you told him.

VINCENT: It was spontaneous. A gut feeling it was the right thing to do. Maybe you had to be there.

THOMAS: When he gets some liquor in him, we'll never hear the end of it.

VINCENT: Lighten up. Give your old man a break — I think he's going to surprise you. I'll see if he needs any help. *(To audience, on his way out)* Familillies!

(Vincent exits.)

THOMAS: I don't believe this.

EMILY: Try to go with the flow. It's all you can do.

THOMAS: How can you defend him?

EMILY: I think it's his right to choose how he dies.

THOMAS: At our expense?

EMILY: He's been keeping it from everyone, as a matter of fact. I'm the one who suggested telling you. I thought you had a right to know. If I knew how you were going to handle it...

THOMAS: Mom's not taking it any better than I am.

EMILY: She was shocked — but she's stronger than any of us. Mom will be fine.

THOMAS: So what are we supposed to do now? Get drunk with him and call it a wake?

EMILY: We're going with the flow.

THOMAS: What about the parade?

EMILY: I guess we play it by ear.

(George and Vincent return with a pitcher of Ramos fizzes and glasses.)

VINCENT: Who's ready for a Ramos fizz?

THOMAS: It's a little early, isn't it?

VINCENT: It is the Bicentennial.

GEORGE: Who am I pouring for?

EMILY: I'll have one.

GEORGE: Thomas?

THOMAS: Too early for me.

VINCENT *("party pooper")*: You sure?

THOMAS: Positive.

GEORGE: Where's Martha?

EMILY: Upstairs napping.

GEORGE: I shouldn't have told her.

THOMAS: I don't think you should've told any of us.

GEORGE: *(to Emily)* See there? *(To Thomas)* Why not?

THOMAS: I was expressing my opinion. I don't want to start an argument.

EMILY: Good idea.

GEORGE: What's wrong with a debate? If you don't have the courage of your convictions, where are you?

THOMAS: We have never had a debate in this family. We have arguments, and this doesn't seem like the time or place.

GEORGE: Better take advantage of me while you can.

THOMAS: Dad, for Christ's sake—

GEORGE: What? I'm dying, goddamn it! You think I like doing this?

THOMAS: I think you like...

(A pause.)

GEORGE: Say it.

THOMAS: *(to audience)* He's determined to pick a fight with me.

GEORGE: Say it!

THOMAS: I think you like the notoriety of this.

GEORGE: Notoriety.

EMILY: *("don't do this")* Thomas...

GEORGE *(to audience)*: You raise a child, and what the hell happens? You try to give a child a sense of how the world works. If you stick your hand in fire, you get burned. If you cross the street without looking, you have a chance of getting hit. But that's about all you can accomplish.

VINCENT: For the record, I don't think any of this has anything to do with wanting notoriety.

THOMAS: What do you know about it?

VINCENT: I know the man isn't doing this in order to amuse us with some kind of holiday fireworks.

THOMAS: What're you talking about? You don't plan on doing this today, do you? Jesus Christ!

GEORGE: No, I wasn't planning to.

VINCENT: I'm talking about the context of what he's going through. You said his motive was notoriety.

THOMAS: I was angry, okay? I didn't mean it the way it came out.

GEORGE: I know you didn't mean it, son.

(A pause.)

316

GEORGE: But why not today?

EMILY: Dad?

GEORGE: I feel like my own body has become a time bomb. So what the hell am I supposed to do about it? I sure as hell don't want to get stuck out in the middle of the ocean feeling like this. So — why not today?

THOMAS: Great, Vincent — you and your big mouth.

VINCENT: Whoa, Silver! Are you blaming me for something?

THOMAS: You put the idea in his head.

GEORGE: And not a bad one either.

EMILY: Dad, don't pursue this unless you really mean it.

GEORGE: I do mean it. I feel better having said so.

THOMAS: You don't know what you're saying.

GEORGE: I've been walking around like a deflated balloon. I feel like I've just gotten a jolt of helium.

(A pause. Everyone just looks at him.)

GEORGE: The problem will be getting your mother to go along. I could use some help with that.

EMILY: You're really serious about this?

GEORGE: All of you are already here. That's the way I've wanted it to be ever since I decided. I just worry about Martha.

EMILY: I can talk to her.

GEORGE: I'd appreciate that. The sooner the better.

EMILY: She's napping.

GEORGE: Are you sure? I think she's escaping. Check on her, would you? I think she needs to be down here now.

EMILY: Excuse me.

(She starts away, speaking to the audience.)

EMILY: I have no doubts that he's serious.

(She exits upstairs.)

VINCENT: You're a remarkable man.

GEORGE: Not much choice when you have to face facts.

THOMAS: Oh, please.

(Moving to the stairs, he speaks to the audience.)

THOMAS: I think the cancer's spread to his brain.

(Thomas goes upstairs.)

VINCENT: This is a side of Thomas I've never seen before.
GEORGE: He's so damn thin-skinned.

(CROSS FADE to upstairs. Emily sits on the edge of the bed.)

MARTHA: Is it time to go to the parade?
EMILY: Not yet.
MARTHA: Where's George?
EMILY: Downstairs. How are you feeling?
MARTHA: Worried about George. He won't go to a doctor.
EMILY: He's afraid to. He saw what happened to Uncle Henry.
MARTHA: I know. I don't blame him. Who would want to go through that?
EMILY: Mom, he's not feeling well at all. I mean today, right now. Since all of us are already here — well, he's thinking maybe now is the time.
MARTHA: The time?
THOMAS (entering): We can't let him go through with it.
EMILY: Don't meddle in what you don't understand.
THOMAS: Don't lecture me about "understanding!" I buried my oldest friend last year.
MARTHA: Please don't fight.
EMILY: I'm sorry. I just think Dad has the right to choose how he leaves us.
THOMAS: Not when he's putting us through this.
MARTHA: What would you do?
THOMAS: I'd call the police.
EMILY: Don't be ridiculous.
THOMAS: He's a danger to himself. That's obvious, isn't it? He doesn't know what he's saying.
MARTHA: I think he knows perfectly well.
THOMAS: Mom, this is not like him. He's never been a coward.
EMILY: He's not being a coward now.
MARTHA: We don't feel how much pain he's in.
THOMAS: You want to talk about pain? When Frank died last winter, that was pain. But he never gave up.
EMILY: Thomas, it's not the same thing.
MARTHA: I'd better see how he's doing.

(She'll start downstairs.)

THOMAS: Frank faced death with so much courage. Why is Dad giving up? Why won't he fight it?
EMILY: I don't know. But I think it's his right to.

(CROSS FADE to downstairs, as Martha enters.)

MARTHA: George, how are you feeling?
GEORGE: Better, under the circumstances. Did Emily talk to you?
MARTHA: Yes, she did. This isn't one of your sick jokes, is it?
GEORGE: No joke. I feel good about making a decision. I think maybe the uncertainty was the worst part. Now I feel like I have a purpose again.
MARTHA: What about the parade?
GEORGE: They'll have to get along without us.
MARTHA: You were looking forward to it.
GEORGE: I've been looking forward to lots of things, mother. I know how much you were looking forward to the cruise.
MARTHA: George, the cruise doesn't matter now.
GEORGE: I need to know I'm in control — and that feeling is going fast. I have it right now, but I can't tell you if I'll have it tomorrow. I've always wanted everyone around me for this. And here you are.

(Emily and Thomas have entered above.)

THOMAS: Am I the only one who is against this?

(There is a silence. Vincent nods at him.)

THOMAS: Dad, for the last time — please see a doctor. Let me call an ambulance.
GEORGE: I'm not going through what Henry went through.
THOMAS: They're making progress in medical research all the time! Just because Uncle Henry went through hell doesn't mean you have to. They're always coming up with something new.
GEORGE: Maybe you're right — but it's not a gamble I'm willing to take.
THOMAS: Why won't you fight this, for God's sake?
GEORGE: Maybe I'm just too tired. Not just my health. Any of it. What America's become. It's not my world any more. I don't belong

here.

(A pause.)

GEORGE: Mother, you want a fizz?
MARTHA: Yes, thank you.
GEORGE: Thomas?
THOMAS: No.
GEORGE: *(mustering all the energy he can)* I thought we were having a wake here. Everyone looks so glum.

(Everyone just looks at him.)

GEORGE: I think we should be celebrating the good times we've had. There were many of them, as I remember.
EMILY: I remember lots of good times, too.
VINCENT: "I want to be a famililly when I grow up."
MARTHA: You were so adorable when you came up with that.
EMILY: Went downhill from there, didn't I?
MARTHA: What do you mean?
EMILY: I never quite reached that level of adoration again.
THOMAS: That's ridiculous.
EMILY: When was I the apple of anyone's eye again?
THOMAS: When you got the scholarship to U Mass. I was damn proud of you then.
EMILY: I don't think we want to get into that, Thomas.
GEORGE: Why not?
EMILY: Isn't it obvious?
MARTHA: George, Emily's right.
GEORGE: For God's sake, why is everybody so worried about everything? We still have freedom of speech in this family, same as in the country.
VINCENT *(to audience)*: More or less.
MARTHA: Please, let's not talk about politics.
THOMAS: I was just pointing out that Emily's life didn't end when she was seven, as far as being admired is concerned.
GEORGE: U Mass was a hell of a lot better than Berkeley, I'll grant you that. At least she started going to classes again.
EMILY: You stopped paying my bills at Berkeley. What choice did I have?
GEORGE: I offered you the option of returning to class.
EMILY: How could I attend class when there was a strike going on?

320

GEORGE: You could have ignored it.
EMILY: Strike-breaking was not an option.
GEORGE: See there? I rest my case.
MARTHA: Stop it! Both of you.

(She moves forward to speak to the audience.)

MARTHA *(to audience)*: If George was going to change his mind, it was going to have to come from within. The more we disagreed with him, the more stubborn he was going to get.

(Martha moves quickly back into the scene.)

MARTHA: So how can we help out, George? Are you doing it down here or upstairs?
GEORGE: I haven't gotten that far.
MARTHA: If you're doing it, don't you think it's time to get ready? You're not going to be much use if you get drunk.
THOMAS *(taking Martha aside)*: What are you doing? If he gets drunk, we can call the police.
GEORGE: No conspiracies, Thomas!

(He gets to his feet, and Emily goes to him.)

EMILY: Are you all right?
GEORGE: Mother's right. I have to get my bag upstairs.
EMILY: I'll get it. Tell me where.
GEORGE: A blue canvas bag in the back of my closet.

(Emily exits.)

VINCENT: Is there anything I can do?
GEORGE: Keep Thomas from pestering me.
THOMAS: Don't worry. It's obvious I can't stop you.
GEORGE: Thank you. It's not the same as getting my family behind me — but it's better than nothing.
VINCENT: You have a lot of support here.
GEORGE: You surprise me, Vincent.
VINCENT: Well, you've surprised me, too.
GEORGE: I'm not condoning homosexuality.
VINCENT: I'm not condoning Republicans.

MARTHA: I don't want to hear anything about politics. George, you said you wanted to remember the good times. Maybe we should show some movies.

GEORGE: I've got a better idea. We can tell stories.

VINCENT: I love family stories.

GEORGE: We have our share.

THOMAS: Everyone's heard them a zillion times.

VINCENT: I haven't. I'm sure there's many I've never heard.

(CROSS FADE to Emily upstairs. She has the blue bag on the bed and has unzipped it. She is looking through its contents.)

EMILY *(to audience)*: He'd done his homework. There was a pamphlet with instructions on how to use the pills, which would be crushed and mixed in apple sauce; and the liquor, mixed with fruit concentrate; and a large bag to fit over the head; and a large rubber band to secure it — all items of which were in the bag. There was a spoon, other utensils. No doubt about his making preparations for this. But looking at the contents in the bag, understanding how much thought and work had already gone into this, suddenly my father's suicide became something more than an idea, a theory, and I felt myself having a change of heart.

(CROSS FADE downstairs.)

GEORGE: We shouldn't begin until Emily gets here. Maybe she's having trouble up there.

VINCENT: I'll check.

(He starts for the stairs but meets Emily as she comes down and enters the room, carrying the blue bag.)

EMILY: Here it is.

(She gives the bag to George.)

MARTHA: We thought we'd tell family stories.

EMILY: Dad, I'm having second thoughts about this.

THOMAS: Thank God!

GEORGE: Don't disappoint me here.

EMILY: So much can go wrong that would be painful for you.

GEORGE: Nothing will go wrong. I have a pamphlet you can read.

EMILY: I glanced at it.

GEORGE: You snooped in my bag? Can't I trust anybody around here?

THOMAS: Emily's right. A lot can go wrong here, Dad.

GEORGE: Then I'll do the goddamn thing by myself.

(He starts unsteadily for the stairs.)

MARTHA: George, we're going to tell family stories.

GEORGE: You have to have a goddamn family to do that.

(The doorbell rings. For a moment, everyone stops and looks at the door. No one is expected.)

THOMAS: I'll get it.

(He opens the door and June steps in.)

JUNE: Sorry to come without calling first. Can we go somewhere and talk?

(But George has seen her.)

GEORGE: June! Get yourself in here!

MARTHA: George, don't start something.

GEORGE: What's this I hear about you abandoning motherhood?

JUNE: What's going on?

THOMAS: Bad timing, really bad timing.

GEORGE: Tell me I heard wrong!

JUNE: Is he all right?

THOMAS: Not by a long shot.

GEORGE: Will you get in here?

(June moves into the room, with Thomas following.)

JUNE: If I'm interrupting something—

VINCENT: June, would you like a Ramos fizz? Believe me, it will help.

JUNE: I can't stay. I just need to talk to Thomas a minute.

GEORGE: You're avoiding the question. Are you giving up Billy or not?

(Everyone is waiting for her answer.)

JUNE: I'm not sure.

THOMAS: Jesus Christ.

JUNE: Thomas, I need more time to think about it.

VINCENT: This isn't fair.

JUNE: I'm not backing out necessarily. I think maybe we should wait at least til fall.

GEORGE: You know in your heart it's wrong to give up your child. I'm proud of you.

JUNE *(to Thomas)*: Can we go somewhere and talk?

THOMAS: We damn well better. Vincent?

VINCENT *(to Martha)*: Are you going to be okay?

MARTHA: I'll be fine.

GEORGE: People can't move their children around like real estate. What the hell happened to this country?

THOMAS *(to Martha)*: We'll be back as soon as we can.

(Thomas, Vincent and June exit.)

GEORGE: She doesn't want to do this. They're twisting her arm. I'm ashamed to have a son who'd do a thing like that.

EMILY: I think it really was her idea, Dad.

GEORGE: Sounds to me like she's changed her mind.

EMILY: I'm sure it's not an easy decision for her.

(George starts again for the stairs, moving unsteadily, and Martha hurries to support him.)

MARTHA: What do you think you're doing?

GEORGE: You know damn well what I'm doing.

MARTHA: You can't do something like this out of spite.

GEORGE: I can do it any goddamn way I choose to do it. Get out of my way.

MARTHA: George, please—!

GEORGE: Leave me alone!

(Martha, close to losing it, sits down.)

EMILY: Dad, you're not being fair. You don't have to cause this much hurt.

(George stops and turns into the room. We sense he knows she's right but is too proud to admit it.)

EMILY: Do it bravely, not cruelly.

GEORGE: Who's being cruel here? Is it too much to ask for the support of my family?

(Vincent steps out to address the audience, continuing his one-man show.)

VINCENT *(to audience)*: "The history of the present Family in the United States is a history of repeated injuries and usurpations, all having in direct object the establishment of absolute Disregard for the well-being and security of children. To prove this, let Facts be submitted to a candid world."

GEORGE: I wanted family support and didn't get it. You turned on me yourself.

EMILY: I apologize for that. Seeing what was in the bag made it seem more real to me than before. I panicked for a minute.

VINCENT *(to audience)*: "Over half the marriages in the United States end in divorce; almost one in three divorced adults cite abuse as the reason for termination;"

EMILY: This isn't easy for any of us, Dad.

VINCENT *(to audience)*: "one-quarter of the violent crimes in the U.S. is wife assault;"

GEORGE: Please don't cry, mother. I need you to be strong now.

MARTHA: I don't think I have any strength left.

(George moves to Martha.)

VINCENT *(to audience)*: "A woman is physically abused in this country every nine seconds;"

GEORGE: Give me your hand.

(Martha does. George helps her to her feet.)

VINCENT *(to audience)*: "Two-thirds of the attacks are by some-one she knows, often a husband or boyfriend;"

GEORGE: I'm asking you to come upstairs with me.

MARTHA: Are you sure this is the only way?

GEORGE: Positive.

VINCENT *(to audience)*: "Sixty percent of battered women are beaten while they are pregnant;"

MARTHA: Don't you want to wait and see if June changes her mind?

GEORGE: I wish I could wait for a lot of things. But I can't.

VINCENT *(to audience)*: "Forty-two percent of murdered women are killed by their intimate male partners;"

GEORGE: There're no good choices here, mother. This is the best one we have.

VINCENT *(to audience)*: "One in six female rape victims is under the age of 12; one-fifth of these have been raped by their fathers;"

GEORGE: Will you come upstairs with me?

MARTHA: Of course, I will.

(They start upstairs together, moving slowly.)

VINCENT *(to audience)*: "By conservative estimates, one in three girls is sexually abused by age 18, one in four by age 14;"

EMILY: Can't I come?

VINCENT *(to audience)*: "Approximately one in six boys is sexually abused by age 16;"

GEORGE: I thought you didn't approve.

EMILY: I was scared for a minute, Dad. Don't hold it against me.

GEORGE: Then come along if you like.

(They head slowly for the stairs, the pace determined by George, who is in clear physical pain.)

VINCENT *(to audience)*: "The average age of entry into prostitution is 13; there are half a million adolescent prostitutes in the United States;"

MARTHA: Are you sure you can make it up the stairs? We can do it down here.

GEORGE: I think I'd like to be in my own bed. Unless you don't approve. I can see how you wouldn't.

MARTHA: I'd rather do it down here, George.

GEORGE: Then down here it is.

(They will move slowly back to the divan.)

VINCENT *(to audience)*: "So destructive are these oppressions to the welfare of children, and so linked are they to the assumptions of traditional family values, that we must now declare a new and independent kind of Family for the raising and nurturing of our children;"

GEORGE: I've already crushed up the pills. I just have to mix them in the apple sauce. And pour the concentrate in the vodka. Maybe you could do that for me, Emily.

EMILY: Of course.

(She'll go to the divan, open the bag and begin the preparations.)

VINCENT *(to audience)*: "In behalf of our children, we therefore and hereby publish and declare that we hold no further allegiance to traditional family values and replace them with more stable values stemming from a broader concept of Family, in which parents may be any two adults committed and pledged to the rearing of children;"

MARTHA: Here we are.

(She helps George onto the divan. Emily is preparing the food and drink.)

GEORGE: I should've done this yesterday.

MARTHA: I'm glad you waited.

EMILY: I wouldn't have seen you if you'd done that.

VINCENT *(to audience)*: "That the biological mother need not be one of these nurturing parents;"

GEORGE: How's it coming?

EMILY: Almost ready.

GEORGE: The head bag should be in there. With a rubber band.

EMILY: I found it.

MARTHA: I hate seeing you in pain.

GEORGE: This is going to be a great relief, mother. Emily?

EMILY: Okay. What do you do first?

GEORGE: The apple sauce.

(Emily hands George the jar of applesauce into which she has mixed the crushed pills. She hands him a spoon. He eats the applesauce.)

VINCENT *(to audience)*: "That these parents may include homo-sexual couples and lesbian couples, whether ritually married or not;"

MARTHA: A part of me wants to do this with you.

GEORGE: Don't be ridiculous. You'll live to be ninety.

(George finishes the apple sauce.)

GEORGE: Now the other.

(Emily gives him the bottle of vodka, into which the concentrate has been poured. George drinks it.)

VINCENT *(to audience)*: "And that no criteria for parenthood is appropriate except commitment to the welfare of the children and to learning the skills necessary for securing same;"
GEORGE: The bag.

(Emily helps put the bag over George's head, securing it with a rubber band. Both women help him stretch out on the divan.)

MARTHA: I'm taking your hand, George. You give me a yank if something goes wrong and you want the bag removed. Do you understand me?

(George shakes his head and speaks through the bag, "I hear you!" Then he stretches out, getting comfortable.)

VINCENT *(to audience)*: "Signed under oath, July 4, 1976."

(Vincent exits.)

(A pause. Both women sit with George, Martha holding his hand.)

EMILY: Dad, I need to tell you something I should've said a long time ago. Remember when you were on the road, how you used to take me on business trips sometimes? I must've been 9 or 10. I especially remember a trip we took to Phoenix, and afterwards we drove to the Grand Canyon. We always stopped at the historical markers and you'd read them to me and explain more about the history. You seemed to know everything about the history of where we were, no matter where we went. I think it was those trips that turned me into an historian.

Those are wonderful memories. What I'm trying to say is, it wasn't easy for us during the sixties, it wasn't an easy time for anybody, and somehow we built this wall between us, we found differences that we had as adults that were irrelevant when I was Daddy's Girl, going on business trips with you, worshipping you, really — we just got off track and somehow our differences began to outweigh the rest.

I just want you to know that I cherish those memories. I always have. I always will. I love you, Dad.

(George lifts his free hand, and Emily takes it. Now Martha holds one hand, Emily the other. George is motionless on the divan, the bag over his head. LIGHTS FADE TO BLACKOUT.)

Scene Two

(LIGHTS UP. Living room. A YEAR LATER, July 4, 1977.)

(Thomas and June face the audience, looking out a window to the front yard. Thomas, and everyone else, wear street clothes now.)

JUNE: He's grown so much!
THOMAS: Tell me about it.
JUNE: He really likes Vincent, doesn't he?
THOMAS: Vincent is incredible. He's like a natural mother and an ideal dad combined. You know what he's doing? Learning to play softball. He's not naturally athletic at all, but he wants to be able to play catch with the kid and all the rest, so he enrolled in this softball class at the Y, and he's on a team and everything. He's so bad at it! But he doesn't quit, I'll hand that to him.
JUNE: He's so devoted to being a parent.
THOMAS: Totally. He quit his job.
JUNE: Can you two afford that?
THOMAS: He's consulting out of the house. He has as much work as he wants.
JUNE: I'm glad things are turning out so well for you.
THOMAS: How about you? How'd you like being on the road?
JUNE: It was grueling, and I certainly don't plan on singing with the band the rest of my life, but I look at it as paying dues. I think we'll be putting out an album. I want to hang around for that, then I'll probably go back to school. I still have so much to learn.
THOMAS: Things are working out for you, too, then.
JUNE: He sees us. (She waves) Hi, Billy! (She blows him a kiss) Well, I guess we'd better get going.
THOMAS: You can have him a day longer if you like.
JUNE: We'll see how it goes. Can I give you a call?
THOMAS: Of course.

(They embrace.)

JUNE: We did something great having Billy, didn't we?

329

THOMAS: Yes, we did.
JUNE: What time are you going to the cemetery?
THOMAS: Twoish.
JUNE: We'll meet you there.
THOMAS: That'd be great.
JUNE: Thanks again — for everything.

(She kisses him on the cheek and exits out the front door.)

(Martha comes downstairs from the bedroom.)

MARTHA: Has June left yet?
THOMAS: She's just leaving. You can catch her if you hurry.

(Martha hurries out the front door, as Emily enters from the den.)

EMILY: June take Billy?
THOMAS: They're just leaving.
EMILY: How long before we go to the cemetery?
THOMAS: A couple hours. Two, I think Mom said.
EMILY: It seems like more than a year to me.
THOMAS: I know what you mean.
EMILY: He would've liked how Billy is turning out.
THOMAS: No, he wouldn't have been able to see it.
EMILY: I think you're wrong, Thomas.

(Vincent enters through the front door.)

VINCENT: Did you try to convince her to take him another day?
THOMAS: I did. She's going to call later. And meet us at the
cemetery, too.
VINCENT *(to Emily)*: We need a break.
EMILY: I can imagine.
VINCENT: Not that being a mother isn't the most delightful
experience of my life. I just need the battery recharged now and then.
EMILY: We were just talking about how it seems longer than a year
ago.
VINCENT: I've lost all concept of time in terms of days and
weeks and months. I think only in shoe sizes now.
EMILY: You two are great with him. I think Dad would have seen it
and been proud.
VINCENT: I think he would have, too.

THOMAS: It's nice to think so, but I don't know.

VINCENT: Ever the pessimist. *(He gives Thomas a hug.)* I love you anyway.

THOMAS: I don't feel like there's closure. I leave, scared to death we're not getting Billy after all — and when I come home, he's dead.

EMILY: Maybe it couldn't have happened if you were there.

(Martha enters the front door.)

MARTHA: Now that that's taken care of, I have an announcement to make.

(The others exchange surprised glances, wondering what's up.)

MARTHA: I'm leaving on a cruise next week.

THOMAS: Mom, that's great.

EMILY: How long will you be gone?

MARTHA: A year.

THOMAS: A year!

EMILY: Where on earth are you going?

MARTHA: Around the world. I'm taking my time. George planned the whole itinerary for me.

(George enters, beaming at her.)

MARTHA: After touring the Caribbean, I go to England and spend three months in London. Then Paris, Rome.

EMILY: Dad planned everything out?

GEORGE *(to audience)*: I think I always knew I wouldn't last long enough for the cruise. In subtle ways, your body tells you things like that. And she's far more interested in that sort of thing than I am anyway, so I decided the best thing I could do under the circumstances was to make all the arrangements for a cruise that would end all cruises — a trip around the world!

THOMAS: Why didn't you tell us before?

MARTHA: I hadn't made up my mind whether to do it. It took me a year to decide.

EMILY: Is someone renting the condo?

MARTHA: I'm selling it.

GEORGE *(to audience)*: I thought she'd've done it before now, to tell the truth.

MARTHA: It's so much more room than I need.

VINCENT: Do you know where you're moving?

MARTHA: I'll worry about that when I get back.

VINCENT: I have a suggestion. We talked about it, Thomas.

THOMAS: You tell her. *(To audience)* Vincent feels much stronger about this than I do.

VINCENT: We need a larger place as well — so why don't you move in with us?

MARTHA: Heavens, I couldn't do that.

VINCENT: Please think about it.

(Vincent stares at Thomas.)

VINCENT *(to audience)*: I was going to stare at him until he spoke up!

(He stares at Thomas some more.)

THOMAS: We were thinking of looking for a house with a cottage behind it, or maybe an apartment attached. Something like that. You wouldn't have to be under foot.

VINCENT *(to audience)*: A point on which he would not compromise.

MARTHA: At least that wouldn't be like living in the same house. I need my space as much as you do.

VINCENT: Billy would love having you so close.

EMILY: What a great idea.

GEORGE *(to audience)*: She took the words right out of my mouth.

EMILY: Good for you guys.

VINCENT *(to audience)*: "Guys!" Isn't she sweet?

THOMAS: No need to decide now.

VINCENT: You can think about it in London, Rome, Paris! I'm already jealous.

MARTHA: And I will think about it. So who's ready for lunch?

(Everyone exits to the kitchen, and George speaks to the audience.)

GEORGE *(to audience)*: There was this moment, almost one year ago to the hour, just before I lost consciousness, when I wanted to change my mind. Maybe it was a reflex. Maybe it was something else, something I misunderstood for wanting to change my mind — I was running on so much adrenaline and nerves and fear, I can't say I was thinking very clearly. Maybe it was my life passing before my eyes. I suddenly felt so full of mental energy, so full of life, I was sure I was

332

going to explode! But somewhere in all that was a nagging thought, like a thorn under a fingernail, asking, What the hell am I doing here? What the hell is this bag doing over my head, why is it getting so hard to breathe? And in the next instant, nothing.

(He moves to the divan, where he will stretch out.)

GEORGE: Do I regret doing it? Under the circumstances, no. I wish I'd been lucky, like James Otis. When his world changed beyond his comprehension, and he couldn't take it any more, he got struck by lightning and died on the spot. A true story, that not even Emily can argue with. Incredible, isn't it? I didn't get that luxury. *(He gets comfortable.)* The point is, I'd do it again, the same way, all things being equal. I'll tell you something else. The hard part isn't death. The hard part is life. The hard part is getting there. Once you pass the threshold, it's a piece of cake.

(He is lying on the divan. He closes his eyes. The LIGHTS SLOWLY FADE as we hear:)

VINCENT (recorded voice): "When in the course of human events, it becomes necessary for a people to change the institutions which have nurtured them since birth, and to assume among the powers of the earth, the redefinition of such institutions to which the Laws of Nature entitle them, a decent respect to the opinions of humankind requires that they should declare the causes which impel them to such changes. We hold these truths to be self-evident, that all children are created equal, that they are endowed by their Creator with certain unalienable rights, that among these are Life, Shelter, Security, Education, and Nurturing. That to secure these rights, Families are instituted among men and women..."

(The lights have faded slowly to BLACKOUT. The play is over.)

For royalties information:
contact Charles Deemer
1-800-294-7176
cdeemer@teleport.com

1999, 1984

Sad Laughter
a play in two acts

First performed at Clark College in Vancouver, Washington, on April 2, 1999. Directed by Charles Deemer. A different, three-act version under the title The Comedian In Spite of Himself *was first performed at the New Rose Theatre on May 10, 1984. Directed by Gary O'Brien.*

THE CAST:
Moliere, *the great French playwright*
Armande, *his young wife, an actress*
Madeleine, *his former mistress, an actress*
La Grange, *Moliere's friend and an actor, the narrator, who plays many roles*

THE SET:
A unit set, for quick changes of place.

THE TIME AND PLACE:
Paris and elsewhere, 1658-1673

(Excerpts from Moliere's work in verse translations by Richard Wilbur. Used with permission. Adaptations from Moliere's work in prose by Charles Deemer.)

(ACTOR'S NOTE: Moliere has a slight stutter when he is upset. This is only occasionally noted in the text but the actor should be aware of this and use it to effect.)

ACT ONE

prologue/

(A DARK STAGE: and we hear the voice of LA GRANGE in the darkness:)

LA GRANGE *(V.O.)*: In darkness is the proper place to start
Our play, for darkness holds the human heart
In profound mystery. Who can look
Into the heart of man and find the hook
On which to hang a life? —Naked, stark:
A piece of meat called man. But the mark
Of man is not so easily drawn.

(And a SPOT comes up on LA GRANGE on stage, as narrator.)

LA GRANGE: —Moliere:
Jean-Baptiste Poquelin, my friend: but where
To start? He suffered, yes; so do we all.
He laughed. He . . . laughed. I think he'd be appalled
To hear me say he cried. I saw him once
And, catching him, I saw him play the dunce
He knew so well on stage. It was as if
No pain, no grief, no agony or rift
Was worth a tear except to shed on stage
For all to see, in this way to assuage
What, privately, he could not share. This man
I loved, who taught me all I understand
About the stage, I hardly knew. Begin
In darkness, then:

(And the LIGHTS begin a SLOW FADE:)

LA GRANGE: What clarity we win
Will rise between the darkness we see now
And the certain night that gets us anyhow.

(It is DARK.)

LA GRANGE *(V.O.)*: Begin in darkness:
sixteen sixty-three:
In Paris, two players rehearse a scene.

1/ at the theater

(THE LIGHTS RISE ON ARMANDE AND MADELEINE, who are rehearsing the opening scene from "The Critique of the School for Wives." ARMANDE is six months pregnant.)

MADELEINE: "Cousin, has no one called on you?"
ARMANDE: "Not a soul."
MADELEINE: "Then we've both been alone all day — which surprises me."
ARMANDE: "I'm surprised as well. Ordinarily all the court loafers would be dropping by your house."
MADELEINE: "I miss them; it's made the afternoon very long."

(LA GRANGE quickly enters. He is visibly upset about something.)

LA GRANGE: Where's Jean?
ARMANDE: Isn't he at his desk?
LA GRANGE: He wasn't a moment ago.
MADELEINE: Is something the matter?
LA GRANGE: The Hotel players are starting to play dirty.
MADELEINE: I heard that they're preparing a play to answer "The Critique."
ARMANDE: Jean's already working on a reply to their reply.
MADELEINE: The box office will love it.
LA GRANGE: I'm not sure the King will.
MADELEINE: Of course he will — why else would he call our rivalry a "war of comedy"? The Hotel de Bourgogne can write all the plays they want, Jean is going to get the last word.
LA GRANGE: On stage, he will — but they're changing the rules and getting personal. Listen, when you see Jean, tell him I have to see him right away.

(He quickly exits.)

MADELEINE: He's already working on a reply to their reply?
ARMANDE: He began as soon as he heard rumor of it.

336

MADELEINE: They'll regret the night they ridiculed "The School for Wives" on stage. You don't win that kind of a fight with Jean.

ARMANDE: He's been working like he's possessed.

MADELEINE: I'd like to learn the lines to this one before we begin another. From the beginning? . . . "Cousin, has no one called on you?"

ARMANDE: "Not a soul."

MADELEINE: "Then we've both been alone all day — which surprises me."

ARMANDE: "I'm surprised as well. Ordinarily all the court loafers would be dropping by your house."

MADELEINE: "I miss them; it's made the afternoon very long."

ARMANDE: "I've found it short enough."

MADELEINE: "That's because you're clever enough to appreciate solitude."

ARMANDE: "That's kind of you to say — but I don't think I'm clever at all."

MADELEINE: "At any rate, I always appreciate company."

(MOLIERE suddenly enters: he wears an exaggerated costume of a pregnant woman, waddling in like a duck: pure slapstick.)

MOLIERE: Quack, quack! Quack, quack, quack!

(ARMANDE can't help but laugh; MADELEINE, on the other hand, is not amused.)

MOLIERE: It's going to be an elephant! I'm carrying an elephant! Quack, quack!

ARMANDE *(laughing)*: Stop it!

MOLIERE: Oh, my feet are so sore! Oh my poor feet!

(He plops down onto the floor.)

MOLIERE: But now how will I ever get up?

(He struggles to get up but can't.)

MADELEINE: Since we can't rehearse, excuse me . . .

(She leaves. MOLIERE is still struggling to get up.)

ARMANDE: You've upset Madeleine.

MOLIERE *(ignoring this)*: Get a horse and rope, will you? It's the only way I'll ever get up!
ARMANDE: It's not that hard, silly.
MOLIERE: Come help me!

(ARMANDE goes to him to help but MOLIERE pulls her down onto the floor with him.)

MOLIERE: Quack, quack, quack! Quack, quack, quack, quack, quack!
ARMANDE: Jean, stop it . . .!

(Playful wrestling on the floor. Then, suddenly:)

MOLIERE: Sshh! Oh my God . . .
ARMANDE: What is it?
MOLIERE: Hear it? Sshh . . .!

(MOLIERE is trying to find the source of the sound he hears.)

ARMANDE: Jean . . .?
MOLIERE: Aha!

(He finds what he's looking for. He puts his ear to Armande's belly.)

MOLIERE: He speaks! He's begging for an early release! *(Speaking to her womb:)* You have to do nine months like everyone else! No special favors, understand?

(And he's playfully wrestling with Armande again, when LA GRANGE enters.)

(LA GRANGE clears his throat, trying to get their attention. No luck. Finally:)

LA GRANGE: Jean?

(Still no luck. He approaches the pair and taps Moliere on the shoulder.)

MOLIERE *(in response)*: Quack, quack, quack!
LA GRANGE: The King wants to see you immediately.

338

MOLIERE: Quack, quack—!

LA GRANGE: *The King!*

MOLIERE: The King?

LA GRANGE: Urgently. As soon as you can get there. Now!

(Moliere gets up, leaving Armande on the floor, a completely different mood now.)

MOLIERE: What about?

LA GRANGE: I'll explain on the way.

(They hurry off, leaving a bewildered Armande on the floor, as the LIGHTS FADE TO BLACKOUT.)

2/ at Court

(LIGHTS up on LA GRANGE as narrator:)

LA GRANGE: Moliere was not a stranger to the Court:
His father built the royal chairs, the sort
Of honor passed father to son. But Jean
Abandoned family honor and took none
But his own advice. Would such a will
Before the King be haughty — or be still?

(LA GRANGE puts on a crown to become the King, as MOLIERE enters.)

LA GRANGE: Moliere...

MOLIERE *(bowing)*: You wish to see me, my liege?

LA GRANGE: Yes.

(A beat. The King is not sure how to begin.)

LA GRANGE: So how's the new play coming?

MOLIERE: We have our first read-through tonight.

LA GRANGE: So soon? What do you call it?

MOLIERE: "The Versailles Impromptu."

LA GRANGE: And its subject is the Bourgogne Players, of course.

MOLIERE: In a manner of speaking.

LA GRANGE: A manner of speaking, indeed! If you weren't so clever, Jean, and your father in Court, I'd think twice about letting you turn your wit loose on the Crown's own company.

MOLIERE: I merely reply to their own "wit," my liege.

LA GRANGE: They make fun of your plays because they are jealous.

MOLIERE: I don't see why. They do tragedy so much better than we do. The trifling success of "The School for Wives" did not threaten their own reputation. There was no need for them to ridicule my play on stage.

LA GRANGE: But how clever of you to respond with your own "Critique"! I found it very enjoyable.

MOLIERE: Thank you, my liege.

(A beat.)

MOLIERE: Is that all, my liege?

LA GRANGE: No. How's your father?

MOLIERE: Busy.

LA GRANGE: Decorating the new palace is no small chore. But he finally accepts your acting?

MOLIERE: Better now than when I acted in the provinces.

LA GRANGE: You decorate Court life as much as he, in your way.

MOLIERE: Thank you, my liege.

(A beat.)

LA GRANGE: And how's Armande?

MOLIERE: Very well.

LA GRANGE: When's the baby due?

MOLIERE: After the first of the year.

LA GRANGE: You must be very excited.

MOLIERE: Indeed, I am, my liege.

LA GRANGE *(beginning to get to it now)*: And you've been married for how long?

MOLIERE: Almost two years.

LA GRANGE: But Armande's been a member of your troupe considerably longer, hasn't she?

MOLIERE: Madeleine began caring for her sister about ten years ago, as we were getting residency in Lyons.

LA GRANGE: Then you've known Armande since she was . . .

340

MOLIERE: Since she was ten, my liege. I think I know what you really want to ask: who am I to win the heart of a beautiful young woman twenty years my junior? I can only reply, a most fortunate man indeed.

LA GRANGE: Others wonder about that.

MOLIERE: I've heard the rumors about me, my liege. This is why you summoned me, I presume. The Players are saying that I am like Arnolphe in "The School for Wives," aren't they? Since I play the role, and wrote it myself, therefore it must be Jean-Baptiste Moliere himself on stage — and since Arnolphe is a cuckold, so am I. Which means the child Armande carries is not my own. I know how they talk.

LA GRANGE: People say far worse, I'm afraid.

MOLIERE: What can be worse than to be cuckolded by a beautiful young wife?

LA GRANGE: Does the name Montfleury mean anything to you?

MOLIERE: An actor with the Players, I believe.

LA GRANGE: He also has connections with the Society of the Holy Sacrament. Those zealots are forever trying to tell the King how to run France. I received a letter from Montfleury in which he claims that years ago, when your company was wandering through the provinces, you were the lover of Madeleine Bejart.

MOLIERE: I don't deny that, my liege. Madeleine and I remain close friends or I wouldn't trust her as our business manager.

LA GRANGE: The letter goes on to say that she left the company for a spell.

MOLIERE: Yes.

LA GRANGE: Having a child and then rejoining the troupe later, with the child in tow.

MOLIERE: When Madeleine rejoined the company, it was with Armande, her younger sister.

LA GRANGE: Can you be sure Armande isn't her child?

(MOLIERE is stunned and not sure how to reply.)

LA GRANGE: And yours.

MOLIERE: Mine, my liege? He's saying that I married my own...? That's a scandalous lie!

LA GRANGE: Would you like to see the letter?

MOLIERE: Of course!

(The King gives him the letter, as:)

LA GRANGE: Don't think I believe the accusation for a minute. In fact, I've been waiting for the Society of the Holy Sacrament to come up with something as outrageous as this. I'm sorry the Crown's Players are implicated, of course.

MOLIERE: If they put such scandal on stage, my liege—!

LA GRANGE: They won't. I've already dismissed Montfleury from the company. I'm sure it's the Society's doing. The more outrageous the accusation, the better, in the eyes of those fanatics.

MOLIERE: I must deny these charges at once.

LA GRANGE: Not yet. I want to give them a little more rope. All the better to hang themselves.

MOLIERE: My liege, I'm accused of marrying my own daughter! You know how rumors spread...if Armande were to learn of this, in her condition...

LA GRANGE: You'd make their case if you complain too loudly. When the time comes, your best attack will be through your work.

MOLIERE: But my liege—

LA GRANGE: Your work can be of great use to the Crown. For now, say nothing of this. I look forward to your new play.

MOLIERE: Very well, my liege.

(He bows and starts away.)

LA GRANGE: Jean...?

MOLIERE: My liege?

LA GRANGE: When can I see the next installment in the "war of comedy"?

MOLIERE: We'll be ready in a week, my liege.

LA GRANGE: Then don't look so glum. The Crown will not let these rumors go unchallenged. I'll tell the Players to ignore Montfleury and start matching their wits with your own.

MOLIERE: Thank you, my liege.

(He bows and exits. LA GRANGE removes the crown and addresses the audience:)

LA GRANGE: Moliere obeyed the King and held his tongue
Against this slander, even though it stung
Worse than all before. But keeping still
Was difficult for such a man of will.

(BLACKOUT.)

342

3/ at the theater

(LIGHTS UP on MADELEINE, who is working on the theater's books, when MOLIERE enters.)

MOLIERE: We have to talk.

MADELEINE: I was just about to look for you. I want to double ticket prices for the "Impromptu."

MOLIERE: But why?

MADELEINE: Because the public's willing to pay and we can use the income. The "war of comedy" won't last forever. We must take advantage of it while we can.

MOLIERE: You think it's about to end?

MADELEINE: They'll resign eventually. You're certainly going to have the last word.

MOLIERE: On stage, perhaps.

MADELEINE: On stage, where it counts.

MOLIERE: The salons, I think, draw more influence than the stage.

MADELEINE: And what do they say about you in the salons?

MOLIERE: You haven't heard?

MADELEINE: I don't pay attention to gossip.

MOLIERE: When the King beckoned me, he wanted to know if I was Armande's father.

MADELEINE: My God, Jean—

MOLIERE: One of the Crown's players made the accusation. That when you left us, it was to have a child — our child. And you returned with her, claiming Armande was your little sister.

MADELEINE: The King believes this?

MOLIERE: No. Neither do I.

MADELEINE: Thank God!

MOLIERE: The whole thing is amusing in a way.

MADELEINE: I'd call it vicious.

MOLIERE: When I'm called a cuckold, they suppose I'm not the father. Now they suppose I am!

MADELEINE: Of course, you're the father. Armande has no lovers.

MOLIERE: Armande's father, I mean. If I'm her father, and the baby's father — a double father . . .

MADELEINE: It's groundless, vicious gossip. Thank God Armande hasn't gotten wind of it.

MOLIERE: The King won't let me deny it.

MADELEINE: You shouldn't stoop to their level by even acknowledging something so ridiculous.

MOLIERE: You didn't have a child, did you?

MADELEINE: Of course not!

MOLIERE: I wanted to hear it from you.

MADELEINE: The salons are gutters.

MOLIERE: And we're entertainers — off stage as well as on,
whether we want to be or not..

(LIGHTS FADE on Moliere and Madeleine as LA GRANGE as
narrator comes forward:)

LA GRANGE: Montfleury's accusation did not rest
But rather caused a flutter in the breast
Of all the salon wits and courtly stout
(The very ones that Moliere wrote about).
How little time it takes gossip to find
A home in vengeful hearts and tiny minds.

4/ at the salon

(LIGHTS UP on a "caricature prop," a flat on which are painted two
aristocratic women with fans. In the "head holes" appear the faces of
the actresses playing Madeleine and Armande. Each has an arm
through an "arm hole," holding a fan.)

ARMANDE: He married his own daughter?

MADELEINE: His own daughter.

ARMANDE: But that's so — unthinkable.

MADELEINE: Why, he even flaunts the sin on stage, portraying
the very crime he commits. Surely Satan owns his soul. There can't be a
more evil man in France.

ARMANDE: More evil than the King?

MADELEINE: Yes, more evil than the King.

ARMANDE: And he continues to flaunt this sin in his new play as
well?

MADELEINE: His new play, the "Impromptu" — well, I wouldn't
even call it a play. They portray themselves, rehearsing a play.

ARMANDE: To what point?

MADELEINE: To continue their jealous mockery of the Crown's
players. It's all become a bore, really.

344

ARMANDE: People are flocking to see the play nonetheless.

MADELEINE: People have no capacity for keeping their wanton passions in check. This is precisely what he plays to.

ARMANDE: One would expect him to run out of material.

MADELEINE: A perverse mind can indulge itself indefinitely.

(Now MOLIERE comes forward, playing to the audience, in a scene from the "Impromptu":)

MOLIERE: "Run out of material? My dear Marquis, we'll always furnish Moliere with plenty of material since we're hardly changing our ways, despite his satires. Even without going outside the court, he still has twenty types of people who have been spared his pen. For example, consider those in court who show one another the greatest friendship — until backs are turned. Then the entertainment is tearing each other apart! Or consider those who are positively sickening with the sweetness of their flattery, or those who make no distinction between the various court regulars they adore. Moliere will always have more material than he needs. Indeed, all that he has satirized to date is a mere trifle compared to what is yet to come."

(He moves off. Focus returns to the "caricature prop.")

MADELEINE: I saw Louise de La Valliere leaving the palace the other day.

ARMANDE: The King's whore! How can you bear to set eyes on her?

MADELEINE: I had no choice: she simply passed before my view. I noticed that she's putting on weight.

ARMANDE: And no wonder, the time she spends at the King's table.

MADELEINE: It occurred to me that the King's bed might be the cause.

ARMANDE: Are you suggesting that the King's whore is...pregnant?

MADELEINE: Pregnant!

ARMANDE: How scandalous!

(The women begin to fan themselves furiously. And BLACKOUT.)

5/ at the theater

(LIGHTS UP on LA GRANGE:)

LA GRANGE: Indeed, the lady favored by the King
Was pregnant. A ball was planned, the hottest thing
To hit the court in months. As the day
Approached, Moliere was asked to write a play...

(He moves off as MOLIERE and ARMANDE enter. ARMANDE is very pregnant now.)

MOLIERE: They'll be royalty from England, Spain. The King is eager to show off the new palace.

ARMANDE: I heard that's not all he wants to show off. Louise de La Valliere is pregnant.

MOLIERE: Do I hear right? My own wife gives credence to gossip.

ARMANDE: I haven't heard any gossip. I saw her the other day and she's as pregnant as I am.

MOLIERE: What's important is that the King is very happy.

ARMANDE: I'm so proud that you received a commission.

MOLIERE: Be proud for all of us. It will be the most respected audience ever gathered in a theater.

ARMANDE: Do you know what you're going to write?

MOLIERE: I've been working on two ideas. One's based on a story by Moreto — about a princess who vows never to fall in love, only to fall for a prince who has pretended to make the same vow. I want you to play the princess. It's the female lead.

ARMANDE: If it's the lead, then Madeleine should play it.

MOLIERE: She's too old. Besides, the public is ready for someone new. They're ready for you.

ARMANDE: Jean, I'm not ready for a lead role.

MOLIERE: You were wonderful in the "Critique."

ARMANDE: Not a large part. Nor in the "Impromptu."

MOLIERE: Haven't I been training you for this moment ever since you were a child?

ARMANDE: I don't know — have you?

MOLIERE: The time's right, Armande. I'm saving the role for you. You'll be ready as soon as you recuperate, I should think.

ARMANDE: But if I'm not, promise me you'll offer the part to someone else. You don't want to disappoint the King.

MOLIERE: I can give the King the other play. The princess belongs to you.

(MOLIERE approaches to kiss her but is stopped by:)

ARMANDE: Oh!
MOLIERE: My dear?
ARMANDE: Jean—!
MOLIERE: What is it?
ARMANDE: I think it's time . . .
MOLIERE: Time?...Time!
ARMANDE: Get the doctor . . .
MOLIERE *(calling off)*: Madeleine! Madeleine!
ARMANDE: I need the doctor . . .
MOLIERE: SHE'S READY IN HERE! MADELEINE!

(MADELEINE enters, will quickly move Armande off as Moliere is no help at all.)

MOLIERE; She's ready! We have to do something!...I'll find the doctor! Everything's going to be fine. Yes, take her home, that's the idea — and don't panic! Nobody panic! Everything's going to be fine . . .

(BLACKOUT.)

6/ at home

(LIGHTS UP on LA GRANGE.)

LA GRANGE: At home, Armande lets nature take its course. The husband in the hall's a different horse.

(LA GRANGE puts on spectacles and a hat and becomes the doctor.)

LA GRANGE: Relax — you can't bring this new life to birth by pacing the floor.

(A YELP from ARMANDE off stage.)

MOLIERE: What's going on in there?

LA GRANGE: The miracle of birth.

MOLIERE: She sounds in pain.

LA GRANGE: Nothing is wrong, Jean. She's having a baby. It happens all the time.

(Another YELP.)

MOLIERE: Not like that!

LA GRANGE: You've upset yourself. I hate to think what noxious humors you're spreading through your system. I want to cleanse you before damage is done to your liver. Come with me.

MOLIERE: I'm not leaving this spot.

LA GRANGE: Very well. We'll do it here.

(He exits. More YELPS and GROANS.)

MOLIERE: Armande, my sweet! I love you in there!

(A LOUD YELP as if in reply.)

(LA GRANGE returns with a chamber pot, a folding screen and his bag.)

LA GRANGE: Here we go.

MOLIERE: She needs one more than I do.

LA GRANGE: Behind the screen and drop your pants.

MOLIERE *(doing so)*: I don't know why you're always giving me these damn things.

LA GRANGE: Because you have a very volatile system. You work too hard and you worry too much. You don't get enough sleep. As a result, noxious humors build up in your body and if we don't expel them, you'll damage your liver, fill your blood with impurities—

MOLIERE: I know the speech! I'm going to put the damn thing in a play some day.

LA GRANGE: If you can't trust your doctor, Jean...

MOLIERE: I just never feel different afterwards — except in my coin purse.

LA GRANGE: Here we go...

(He takes the enema device from his bag and goes behind the screen.)

LA GRANGE: Bend over.

(A beat.)

MOLIERE: Oooooo!
LA GRANGE: That wasn't so bad, was it?
MOLIERE: Average. Better than this morning.
LA GRANGE: We'll rest a minute . . .

(A beat. And MADELEINE enters.)

MADELEINE: It's a boy! A healthy boy . . .!

(And she's just as quickly gone, rejoining Armande off stage.)

MOLIERE *(behind the screen)*: A healthy boy? Did you hear that? I have a son! I—...*(as the enema takes effect:)*...a son! It's ...ooo! ...oh!... it's a ...ooooooo! . . .

(As LIGHTS FADE TO BLACKOUT.)

7/ at the salon

(LIGHTS UP on the "caricature prop.")

MADELEINE: A son. Whom Moliere named Louis, after the King.
ARMANDE: Shocking.
MADELEINE: To have living proof of such a sin.
ARMANDE: The child should be sacrificed. The Romans would have done it.
MADELEINE: We're more modern today. But be sure of this: the Lord will deliver retribution.
ARMANDE: I think the King gets in the Lord's line of sight.
MADELEINE: If the King saw Moliere clearly, then he'd have to turn clear vision into his own house — and then he'd find a whore in his bed!

(They cackle and fan, as the LIGHTS FADE TO BLACKOUT.)

8/ at the theater

(LIGHTS UP on LA GRANGE.)

LA GRANGE: But how the leading ladies were distressed
When young Armande was cast as the princess.

(LIGHTS UP FULL as LA GRANGE turns to MOLIERE.)

LA GRANGE: You'd better talk to Madeleine yourself.
MOLIERE: She didn't seem upset at the read-through.
LA GRANGE: I'm telling you because I think we have to clear the
air. We don't have that much rehearsal time and considering the
importance of the performance . . .
MOLIERE: Get her, I'll talk to her.

(LA GRANGE exits. MOLIERE returns to working on a new script.
He tries out a speech aloud, from "Tartuffe":)

MOLIERE: "Brother, I don't pretend to be a sage,
Nor have I all the wisdom of the age.
There's just one insight I would dare to claim:
I know that true and false are not the same;
And just as there is nothing I more revere
Than a soul whose faith is steadfast and sincere,
Nothing that I more cherish and admire
Than honest zeal and true religious fire,
So there is nothing that I find more base
Than specious piety's dishonest face."

(MADELEINE has entered.)

MADELEINE: You want to see me?
MOLIERE: I thought it was you who wanted to see me.

(A beat.)

MOLIERE: Charles tells me you're upset about something.
MADELEINE: I'm surprised you had to be told.
MOLIERE: Don't complain behind my back, Madeleine. We've
been through too much together for that.

MADELEINE: Jean, my sister has learned a good deal in a very short time, thanks to your excellent coaching. But—

MOLIERE: But you think you should play the princess yourself.

MADELEINE: She's had very little experience on stage and considering the extraordinary nature of the occasion, and the royalty from around the world who'll be in the audience—

MOLIERE: Therefore, you should play the princess yourself.

MADELEINE: Not necessarily. But someone with experience. If not me, Therese or Catherine.

MOLIERE: My three leading ladies worry that their province is being taken over by a newcomer: my wife.

MADELEINE: My sister.

MOLIERE: You should have more faith in her talent.

MADELEINE: I'm not worried about her talent but her experience. None of us have performed before such royalty before.

MOLIERE: We're presenting a play and a half, remember. I've given you the best role in the fragment from "Tartuffe."

MADELEINE: I'm delighted with the part.

MOLIERE: Then why the jealousy of Armande?

MADELEINE: I don't think she can handle the pressure.

MOLIERE: And I believe she can. If you'll excuse me, I have work to do.

(BLACKOUT.)

9/ at the theater

(LIGHTS UP on ARMANDE as the Princess of Elis. In fact, she is not a very good actress:)

ARMANDE: "I love to be alone here — no room in the palace matches the simple beauty of nature, these trees, these rocks and the river, the fresh air: I never tire of coming here. Why do they demand my presence at the chariot races? I think they want to win my heart but my heart belongs here. They want love — but love is a great weakness and I'll never give my heart to anyone. They act like my slaves now, wooing me, but if I gave one of them my heart, he'd soon enough become my tyrant."

(LIGHTS UP FULL as LA GRANGE comes forward as a courtier. He applauds madly, then will pursue ARMANDE, representing a flock of male admirers.)

LA GRANGE *(courtier #1)*: Bravo, bravo! I've never seen such a performance on any stage in France — ever!

LA GRANGE *(#2)*: Theater has reached a new grandeur!

LA GRANGE *(#3)*: Madam, if you might give me a private moment so I could—

LA GRANGE *(#4)*: I've written you a poem, madam, and—

LA GRANGE *(#5)*: Bravo, madam! Bravo and bravo and bravo! My carriage is—

(ARMANDE is gone. LA GRANGE turns to the audience as narrator:)

10/ outside the theater

LA GRANGE: Indeed, the courtiers came from near and far
To woo the heart of France's bright new star.

(MOLIERE enters.)

MOLIERE: Have you seen Armande?

LA GRANGE: I believe she went to watch the fireworks.

MOLIERE: Alone?

LA GRANGE: Who can be alone in this throng? When the King throws a party, he throws a party!

MOLIERE: I mean was she — with anyone?

LA GRANGE: About a half a dozen went off together.

MOLIERE: Half a dozen — an even number then? Not an odd number?

LA GRANGE: I don't know precisely, Jean. I didn't count them.

MOLIERE: Were they divided into couples?

LA GRANGE: Perhaps they were, yes.

MOLIERE: Then Armande left with an escort?

LA GRANGE: Yes, I suppose she did.

MOLIERE: Who?

LA GRANGE: I wasn't paying all that much attention.

MOLIERE: One of the visiting courtiers?

LA GRANGE: Yes, perhaps so.

MOLIERE: What nationality?

LA GRANGE: English, I think.

MOLIERE: Sycophants, the lot of them! English sycophants, Spanish sycophants, even French sycophants — don't you think so?

LA GRANGE: What's a sycophant?

MOLIERE: A boot-licker! A flattering hypocrite! I should've foreseen that this would happen. Armande's performance was satisfactory, considering her inexperience, but the way these royal toadies line up to praise her...I hope it doesn't go to her head.

LA GRANGE: The damn sycophants.

MOLIERE: It's everywhere you look: false flattery, hypocritical boot-licking, the braggadocio of imbeciles. Putting up "Tartuffe" tomorrow night will be perfectly timed, Charles.

LA GRANGE: You finished the script?

MOLIERE: No, we'll just do the first three acts. The King thinks the "Princess" is good — wait until he sees "Tartuffe."

(MADELEINE enters.)

MADELEINE: Jean, you and Armande must come quickly. Something's wrong with little Louis. The doctor's with him now.

MOLIERE: What happened?

MADELEINE: The doctor says it's serious.

LA GRANGE: I'll find Armande.

(BLACKOUT.)

11/ at the salon

(LIGHTS UP on the "caricature prop":)

MADELEINE: Providential retribution, there can be no doubt about it.

ARMANDE: Providential retribution.

MADELEINE: Just rewards for the sin of incest.

ARMANDE: There can be no doubt about it.

MADELEINE: The King's bastard will be next.

ARMANDE: Providential retribution.

(They fan as lights FADE TO BLACKOUT.)

12/ at Court

(LIGHTS UP on LA GRANGE:)

LA GRANGE: Three days after little Louis died,
"Tartuffe" had stunned a crowd that didn't hide
Its anger and dismay. Even the King
Was stunned: guests had fled the royal fling.

(He puts on the crown to become the King, as MOLIERE enters.)

MOLIERE *(bowing)*: My liege ...
LA GRANGE: My mother has left Versailles.
MOLIERE: So I was told, my liege.
LA GRANGE: I received a communication from the Archbishop of Paris. Would you like to hear it?
MOLIERE: If you think I—
LA GRANGE: "This new play by Moliere is wholly injurious to religion. It can only have the most dangerous effects. Moreover—"
MOLIERE: I get the drift, my liege.
LA GRANGE: I'm sorry to have to bring this up. I know how badly you feel about little Louis.
MOLIERE *(bitter)*: Providence, my liege.
LA GRANGE: Yes. How is Armande taking it?
MOLIERE: Guiltily, as well she should.
LA GRANGE: You shouldn't be too hard on her.
MOLIERE: She was watching fireworks instead of her child.
LA GRANGE: Perhaps there was nothing she could've done.
MOLIERE: Perhaps. What did you think of the play yourself, my liege?
LA GRANGE: Tartuffe reminded me of some of our holier-than-thou rascals in the Society of the Holy Sacrament. I'd like to see you finish it.
MOLIERE: There's no question about finishing it, my liege. But what about the Archbishop of Paris?
LA GRANGE: He wants me to ban further performances.
MOLIERE: But why?
LA GRANGE: Because he thinks the play attacks religion.
MOLIERE: Nothing could be farther from the truth.
LA GRANGE: He has a point. You put a man of God on stage and then make him the greatest scoundrel imaginable, betraying the man who most believes in him, trying to seduce his wife—

354

MOLIERE: A false man of God, my liege. A hypocrite.

LA GRANGE: Many people couldn't distinguish between true and false piety in the play. They think you're attacking religion outright, and I have no choice but to ban further performances.

MOLIERE: But my liege—!

LA GRANGE: I don't approve of mother leaving in a huff! She doesn't approve of my child, let alone my taste in women. She can make my life particularly miserable when she's angry. Like hounding me to marry.

MOLIERE: My liege, I do not attack religion. I merely attack the vices of my day by ridiculing them.

LA GRANGE: When you finish the play, I'll look at it again. Until then, I'm banning "Tartuffe" from public performance. You may go.

MOLIERE: Good day, my liege.

LA GRANGE (coyly): You can still perform it privately. As a matter of fact, I'd like Cardinal Chigi to see it. He's a kinsman of the Pope and is coming to Paris on other matters. Can a performance be arranged for him?

MOLIERE: Certainly.

LA GRANGE: Good day, Jean.

(MOLIERE bows and exits. LA GRANGE removes the crown:)

LA GRANGE: With "Tartuffe" banned, the season's incomplete;
A new play must be found within the week.

13/ at the theater

(MOLIERE storms in to join LA GRANGE.)

MOLIERE: What the hell kind of rehearsal change is this?

LA GRANGE: I'm not sure which one you mean.

MOLIERE: This one I am looking at, in your own hand.

LA GRANGE: Jean, I made several—

MOLIERE: This one! Canceling rehearsal of Act Four of "Tartuffe."

LA GRANGE: I assumed we're performing only the first three acts for the Cardinal.

MOLIERE: What's that got to do with it?

LA GRANGE: I assumed you hadn't finished Act Four yet.

MOLIERE: So what?

LA GRANGE: Fine, I'll restore the rehearsal immediately.

MOLIERE: Get Armande.
LA GRANGE *(half-mocking)*: Yes, sir!

(He exits.)

(MOLIERE paces. He has a passage from a new play and he tries it out, aloud, from "Don Juan":)

MOLIERE: ". . . hypocrisy is a fashionable vice and therefore passes for virtue. This gives many advantages to the hypocrite's profession. He's always respected. When all other views are exposed, men attack them freely, but hypocrisy is immune to criticism — surely no one can find a better role to play than the role of a good man."

(ARMANDE enters.)

ARMANDE: Charles says that you wish to see me.
MOLIERE: I've heard a rumor that you're taking diction lessons.
ARMANDE: Yes, I am.
MOLIERE: I give the d-diction lessons in this company!
ARMANDE: But you've been so busy that—
MOLIERE: Who is he?
ARMANDE: His name is Pierre.
MOLIERE: What are his qualifications?
ARMANDE: He's a poet.
MOLIERE: A poet! Really?
ARMANDE: Yes.
MOLIERE: What makes you think you need diction lessons?
ARMANDE: He kindly offered them and I—
MOLIERE: Offered them!
ARMANDE: Yes.
MOLIERE: Then he admires you?
ARMANDE: He saw me in the "Princess" and "Tartuffe."
MOLIERE: And he flattered you?
ARMANDE: He said I need work on my diction and he kindly offered to give me lessons.
MOLIERE: And you have time on your hands, with "Tartuffe" and soon "Don Juan" in rehearsal?
ARMANDE: What's "Don Juan"?
MOLIERE: What I'm replacing "Tartuffe" with. I wrote you a major part.
ARMANDE: I see Pierre only once a week.

356

MOLIERE: But you'd prefer to see him more often...?

ARMANDE: I'd prefer that you say what's really on your mind. *(A beat.)* Jean, I have no interest in Pierre beyond diction lessons. *(A beat.)* Don't you believe me?

MOLIERE: I'm not sure.

ARMANDE: It's the truth.

MOLIERE: He sent you a poem. I had to bribe the boy who delivered it. *(Offering the poem:)* Here, I'd like you to read it.

ARMANDE *(not accepting it)*: Jean, I've given him no encouragement.

MOLIERE: Read it! *(A beat.)* Very well. I'll read it myself:
"Armande, these lines are not meant to embarrass
But I'm quite mad about your mons veneris."

ARMANDE: Jean!—

MOLIERE: "And though I am not noted for my wit,
I am a man who appreciates good tits."

ARMANDE: Stop it! What are you accusing me of? Taking him for a lover?

MOLIERE: You said it, I didn't.

ARMANDE: There's no point in talking about something so ridiculous. I'll see you at rehearsal.

MOLIERE: Now that the cat's out of the bag, look who doesn't want to talk about it.

ARMANDE: I don't see what's wrong with taking diction lessons from Pierre — or I didn't, until he wrote that awful poem. I didn't know he was going to do that.

MOLIERE: And the others?

ARMANDE: There are no others.

MOLIERE: The courtiers have been following you around like cats in heat.

ARMANDE: That's not my fault! What's happened to you? You accuse me of causing little Louis's death, you—

MOLIERE: I said he needed his mother.

ARMANDE: When do I have time to be a mother? And I don't have a string of lovers, no matter what you think. I have no one. I have you. But when do we even see one another any more? You're always writing a play or directing rehearsals. I'm always learning lines or rehearsing. Our life together has turned into one long rehearsal.

MOLIERE: Plays don't write themselves.

ARMANDE: You don't even seem to enjoy what little time we do have alone together. I haven't been unfaithful...

MOLIERE: Please don't cry. *(A beat.)* You know I can't stand it when you cry! *(A beat.)* Listen — all right, maybe I have been working too hard.

ARMANDE: How can you think such things about me?

MOLIERE: I often play the cuckold on stage, don't I? So maybe I'm just practicing. That's what we live for, isn't it? Perfecting our parts? Fine-tuning our roles? I know I haven't given you much attention lately. I mean, you're right, our life is a rehearsal. My life is a dress rehearsal for a play. Even now, as I hear myself talking, I wonder where I'll be putting this, in what future scene in what future play I'll be standing before someone like you, perhaps before you yourself, the actress, and I'll be the actor, and we'll be talking — in some play, some day — much as we are talking here now. Because that's what my life seems to be, a dress rehearsal for a play. Which, strictly speaking, doesn't really make my life much of a life at all, does it?

ARMANDE: What especially hurts about your lack of trust in me is that I'm pregnant again.

MOLIERE: What?

ARMANDE: But if you imagine such things about me—

MOLIERE: You're pregnant?

ARMANDE: Yes.

MOLIERE: But this is wonderful!

ARMANDE: It is?

MOLIERE: Of course!

ARMANDE: I thought so, until you started accusing me of—

MOLIERE: I wasn't accusing you of anything. I was just babbling. I probably need an enema! Come on, let's tell the others. Charles! Madeleine!

ARMANDE: Please don't make a scene.

MOLIERE: When the child is born, I want you to quit the stage.

ARMANDE: Jean, I feel too tired to celebrate.

MOLIERE: You rest — in fact, I'm going to replace you in "Don Juan."

ARMANDE: Please don't.

MOLIERE *(ignoring this)*: You go home and rest.

(ARMANDE exits.)

MOLIERE: Charles! Madeleine! Where the hell is everybody?

(MADELEINE enters.)

358

MADELEINE: Is Armande all right? She looks upset.
MOLIERE: She's pregnant. Isn't that wonderful?

(No response: Madeleine is upset at the news but trying to hide it.)

MOLIERE: I'm replacing her in "Don Juan." She's going to leave the stage.

(LA GRANGE enters.)

LA GRANGE: What's going on?
MOLIERE: Armande is pregnant.
LA GRANGE: Congratulations. Where is she?
MOLIERE: Going home to rest. She's quitting the stage.
LA GRANGE: Really?
MADELEINE *(sudden agitation)*: Jean, I have to talk to you. Alone. Charles, do you mind?
MOLIERE: I want to celebrate.
MADELEINE: Jean, please.

(She stares at Charles.)

LA GRANGE: Well, anyway, congratulations . . .

(He exits, puzzled.)

MOLIERE: What's the matter with you? Charles is as much a part of the family as we are.
MADELEINE: Don't say that.
MOLIERE: He's been with the company almost as long as you have. Longer, counting the time you were gone.
MADELEINE: That's what we have to talk about, Jean.

(A beat: she is having a hard time starting, getting to the real subject.)

MOLIERE: Let me guess. You don't like "Don Juan."
MADELEINE: Those whom "Tartuffe" upset, "Don Juan" will upset twice over.
MOLIERE: Don Juan is a hypocrite.
MADELEINE: So is Tartuffe but few recognize the fact. I think you want trouble. You want scandal. And that troubles me very much.

MOLIERE: I merely satirize the vices I see—

MADELEINE: I know the explanation, Jean. You recite it like a litany. But I didn't come here to talk about "Don Juan."

MOLIERE: Then what is it? What's bothering you?

MADELEINE: My soul is bothering me.

(Moliere laughs. When he sees that Madeleine is sincerely upset, he stops. He is confused.)

MOLIERE: Sorry. I didn't mean to interrupt.

MADELEINE: When I returned to the troupe in the provinces, bringing Armande with me, I came under false pretenses.

MOLIERE: I don't recall any pretenses at all. Theater's in your blood and you wanted to return. We welcomed you with open arms.

MADELEINE: I shouldn't have brought Armande.

(Moliere thinks he understands what is going on.)

MOLIERE: So that's it! For all the women I put on stage, I'll never understand where female jealousy comes from. I'm surprised at you. The love we shared, Madeleine, the love I still feel for you — it's a spiritual love, not physical. Don't be jealous of Armande because she's having my child.

MADELEINE: Not jealous. Afraid, for all of us.

MOLIERE: You're not making sense.

MADELEINE: I shouldn't have returned with Armande because she isn't my sister. She's my daughter.

(It takes Moliere a moment to comprehend what she is saying.)

MOLIERE: I don't believe it.

MADELEINE: It's true, Jean, I swear it is.

MOLIERE: You're telling me I married my own daughter?

MADELEINE: I don't know.

MOLIERE: Is she your daughter or not?

MADELEINE: You may not be the father. There were others.

MOLIERE: You never told me that.

(She doesn't respond. Moliere will become furious.)

MOLIERE: Why didn't you tell me that?

MADELEINE: Jean, I—...I didn't think it was any of your business.

MOLIERE: Who my lover sleeps with is not my business?!

MADELEINE: We were so young.

MOLIERE: Not you, apparently, oh no, not sweet innocent Madeleine. Well, if I'm not the father, then who is? Did you sleep through the whole goddamn company or what? Is Charles the father? *(Calling off:)* Charles!

MADELEINE: Jean, for God's sake, don't you understand what I'm saying?

MOLIERE: Very well. Charles!

(LA GRANGE hurries in.)

LA GRANGE: Yes?

MADELEINE: Jean, please...don't do this...

(A beat: LA GRANGE is tense, wondering what is going on.)

MOLIERE: Have you ever gone to bed with Madeleine?

(LA GRANGE is confused by the question. He turns to Madeleine:)

LA GRANGE: Is he serious?

MOLIERE: I do not ask questions unless I mean them! Have you or not?

MADELEINE: He has — but he is not a candidate.

LA GRANGE: A candidate? For what?

MADELEINE: Let him go, Jean.

MOLIERE: You may go.

(LA GRANGE, puzzled, hesitates.)

MOLIERE: I said, you may go!

LA GRANGE: Yes, sir!

(And he hurries off.)

MOLIERE: Then who are the "candidates"?

MADELEINE: It doesn't matter. The point is, you are one, in fact the most probable one. I think that's why little Louis was taken from you. I think—

MOLIERE: Providential retribution?

MADELEINE: For the sake of your own soul, Jean, don't ridicule the possibility.

MOLIERE: Louis died because the doctors couldn't save him! Because all they know how to do is drain blood and give enemas! Children are dying all the time!

MADELEINE: I'm her mother. And you may be her father. I swear it's true.

MOLIERE: I can't believe you never told me.

MADELEINE: It didn't matter at first. I never dreamed you'd one day marry her. When you did, I knew it was wrong, I knew it was sinful, but when I tried to tell you—

MOLIERE: We don't know that! That I'm actually the father. How many candidates are there?

MADELEINE: Including you, three.

MOLIERE: Three!

MADELEINE: I would think you'd wish there were dozens.

MOLIERE: I don't know what to think.

MADELEINE: I pray you're not her father.

MOLIERE: I can only be sure of what I absolutely know. One, that I'm her husband. Two, that I'm the father of her... Christ, I don't even know if I can be sure of that. If you can lie to me so easily, live a charade so easily, perhaps she can as well.

MADELEINE: After so many years, I didn't know how to tell you.

MOLIERE: In words that speak the truth!

MADELEINE: I know I should have. I know I'll pay the consequences for not telling you. But all that's past and can't be changed. The only thing I can change now is the present, my life now and in the future. Which is why I'm quitting the company.

MOLIERE: Don't be ridiculous. What else could you do?

MADELEINE: I can pray for my soul.

(Moliere just stares at her.)

MOLIERE: I don't know whether to laugh or cry.

MADELEINE: I think you should pray as well.

MOLIERE: Have you told anyone else about this?

MADELEINE: Of course not.

MOLIERE: You must not, ever. You must promise me that.

MADELEINE: I shall tell a priest, I think.

MOLIERE: Where it will remain in confidence. But no one else. Ever. You must promise me.

MADELEINE: I barely had the strength to tell you.

MOLIERE: You don't have to leave the company. You can still attend to the books. You don't have to go on stage.

MADELEINE: No, I have to listen to my spirit, Jean, troubled as it may be.

(A beat. Moliere is at a loss for words.)

MADELEINE: Will you tell Armande?

MOLIERE: No. And you won't either.

MADELEINE: I'll pray for both of you.

MOLIERE: I'm sure you will.

MADELEINE: I can't save your soul, Jean. Or Armande's. I can only save my own — if it's not too late.

MOLIERE: Then save it, Madeleine. Get out of here and save your soul.

(A beat: and Madeleine turns and leaves. Moliere kicks a chair, and LIGHTS FADE TO BLACKOUT.)

(END OF ACT ONE)

ACT TWO

14/ at the salon

(LIGHTS UP on the "caricature prop.")

ARMANDE: A private performance before the Cardinal from Rome? And what did he say about "Tartuffe"?

MADELEINE: He liked it.

ARMANDE: I don't believe it!

MADELEINE: He said he found nothing offensive to religion in it at all.

ARMANDE: No!

MADELEINE: The Cardinal's no fool. He's setting a trap for the King. He well knows that if it weren't for the pressure we ourselves put on the King, Moliere's blasphemy would still be on stage today. By pretending to give approval now, the Cardinal is giving the King rope to hang himself. He'll see what kind of moral fiber the King really has.

ARMANDE: If he's righteous enough to continue the ban, despite approval?

MADELEINE: Exactly.

ARMANDE: What a delicious trap!

(They fan to BLACKOUT.)

15/ at the theater

(LIGHTS UP on LA GRANGE:)

LA GRANGE: A stubborn man who became even more
Stubborn when Madeleine was gone: Jean swore
Revenge on one and all, though who can say
Just what the ghosts were he would chase away.

(LIGHTS UP FULL on Moliere, asleep at his desk, as La Grange approaches him. Several empty bottles of wine clutter the desk.)

(La Grange goes to the desk and gently shakes Moliere, waking him.)

LA GRANGE: Jean? Come on, time to go home.

MOLIERE: What time is it?

LA GRANGE: After two.

MOLIERE: What are you doing here?

LA GRANGE: I could ask you the same thing. I've been working lines with Therese.

MOLIERE: How's she doing?

LA GRANGE: She's not Madeleine but she'll do fine. You ready to go?

MOLIERE: No, go on. I have a scene I want to finish.

LA GRANGE: For "Don Juan"?

MOLIERE: Yes. What do you think?

364

(He hands La Grange a speech.)

LA GRANGE *(reading)*: "Hereon I'll be the censor of everyone, judging all but myself harshly. I'll not forget the slightest disfavor toward me but patiently seek my inevitable revenge...." *(He stops reading:)* It's a long one, Jean. You can't rewrite indefinitely.
MOLIERE *(ignoring this)*: You want a drink?
LA GRANGE: Sure, thanks.

(Moliere will pour two glasses of wine.)

MOLIERE: So Therese will work out?
LA GRANGE: I think so.

(A beat: Moliere passes La Grange his glass of wine.)

LA GRANGE: You want to talk about it?
MOLIERE: About what?
LA GRANGE: Madeleine leaving the company.
MOLIERE: What's there to say?
LA GRANGE: It surprised the hell out of me, Jean. She must've given you a reason.
MOLIERE: She said she wants to save her soul.
LA GRANGE: I didn't know her soul was in jeopardy.
MOLIERE: Don't ask me what she's doing. I don't understand her.
LA GRANGE: I thought you might know.
MOLIERE: Well, I don't.
LA GRANGE: Or do and don't want to talk about it.
MOLIERE: Don't pry, Charles.
LA GRANGE: What are friends for, if not to pry? We've been friends for almost twenty years, you and I. Last week, when you asked if I'd ever been to bed with Madeleine, it was obvious that something was going on. I hope you didn't let her go without an argument.
MOLIERE: I can't save her soul for her.
LA GRANGE: What's she feeling so guilty about? *(A beat.)* Having too many lovers?
MOLIERE: You tell me.
LA GRANGE: The short time I was her lover, Jean, was long after you and her had gone separate ways. It was about a year after she returned to the company.
MOLIERE: It was after she returned with Armande?

LA GRANGE: Yes. I didn't think there was anything still going on between you two.

MOLIERE: There wasn't.

LA GRANGE: You almost seemed — well, jealous.

(A beat: Moliere ignores this.)

MOLIERE: Another drink?

LA GRANGE: No thanks. Can I walk you home?

MOLIERE: I'll be fine.

LA GRANGE: Jean, it's probably none of my business, but I have noticed that you've been staying all night at the theater recently. It's upset Armande.

MOLIERE: I have a new play to finish!

LA GRANGE: It's affecting her performance as well.

MOLIERE: Plays don't write themselves.

LA GRANGE: I don't think she understands what's going on. Correction: I know she doesn't. Because she asked me what's going on. I didn't know what to tell her.

MOLIERE: Tell her that when "Don Juan" closes, we'll need a new play to replace it. It's time I got started on one.

LA GRANGE: We used to put in a couple of revivals each season, Jean. Do you plan to fill the season with new plays?

MOLIERE: Perhaps I do.

LA GRANGE: But why? The revivals always do well.

MOLIERE: I didn't know you wanted to take over the company, Charles.

LA GRANGE: You know better than that.

MOLIERE: Then stop telling me how to select our plays.

LA GRANGE: I'm worried about you, is all.

MOLIERE: Don't be.

LA GRANGE: I can't help it.

(No reply.)

LA GRANGE: You're like a brother to me. I hate to see you this way. I'd like to help if I could.

(No reply.)

LA GRANGE: Well, good night.

(He exits.)

366

(A beat: Moliere tries to work but can't concentrate. ARMANDE
enters. She is visibly pregnant.)

ARMANDE: Jean?
MOLIERE: What are you doing here?
ARMANDE: Aren't you ever coming home?
MOLIERE: Armande, I have work to do. I'm doing the best I can.
ARMANDE: Do you spend the night here?
MOLIERE: If necessary, yes!
ARMANDE: You don't have to shout at me.

(A beat.)

ARMANDE: Have I done something wrong?
MOLIERE: Of course not.
ARMANDE: Since Madeleine left, you'd think I have leprosy.
MOLIERE: I'm trying to finish a new scene.
ARMANDE: Are you going to be adding new scenes right up to
curtain?
MOLIERE: Please go home. You need your sleep.
ARMANDE: So do you. You haven't been home all week.

(A beat.)

ARMANDE: If you're sleeping here at the theater, so am I.

(She looks for a spot to make a bed, will start to prepare one on the
floor.)

MOLIERE: What are you doing?
ARMANDE: Spending the night with my husband.
MOLIERE: You can't sleep on the floor.
ARMANDE: We used to always sleep on the floor. Or the ground.
MOLIERE: Not in your condition.
ARMANDE: It can't be helped. I'm spending the night with my
husband.

(A beat.)

MOLIERE: You win. We'll go home. But I have to put in another
hour or so. I'll make my bed in the ante-room.

ARMANDE: You don't have to do that.

MOLIERE: You need your sleep. I don't want to wake you when I come to bed.

ARMANDE: But you will come home?

MOLIERE: Yes.

(She hurries into his arms. Moliere is uncomfortable, at a loss of what to do.)

ARMANDE: I was so afraid you were angry at me for something. You can't believe what thoughts went through my head. Since everything seemed to change after Madeleine left, I even worried that you and she were lovers.

MOLIERE: That's not true.

ARMANDE: I know.

MOLIERE: Madeleine left because of — personal problems.

ARMANDE: I think she's seeking God.

(A beat, as they embrace.)

ARMANDE: Hold me tight, Jean.

(They embrace, Moliere is worried, as LIGHTS FADE TO BLACK-OUT.)

(LIGHTS UP on LA GRANGE:)

LA GRANGE: February, sixteen sixty-five:
"Don Juan" premieres and instantly the cry
Goes up again to ban such blasphemy.
The King summons Moliere — an old story.

(He puts on the crown to become the King, as Moliere enters.)

16/ at court

MOLIERE *(bowing)*: My liege...

LA GRANGE: You've seen the articles about your play, I trust.

MOLIERE: I don't have time to read opinions that are so predictable.

LA GRANGE: I think they've quite outdone themselves. The critic Rochemont would throw you to wild beasts, after the Romans.

MOLIERE: How fortunate for me he doesn't wear the crown.

LA GRANGE: Another would merely have you struck down by lightning.

MOLIERE: It's not the season for thunderstorms.

LA GRANGE: And Prince Conti writes, "The problem is that a dunce is left to defend religion while the witty Don Juan himself pronounces scandalous criticism on everything holy. How can the fool prevail?"

MOLIERE: I played the so-called dunce myself and feel I held my own. It's Don Juan, not I, who's struck down by lightning in the end.

LA GRANGE: An ending that satisfies no one.

MOLIERE: Did you enjoy the beginning of the play, my liege? Or perhaps the middle?

LA GRANGE: Much of it, yes. But you do put me in a very difficult position.

MOLIERE: When the Papal agent approved "Tartuffe," I thought you might remove the ban.

LA GRANGE: The climate wasn't right to do that. Nor can I let "Don Juan" continue.

MOLIERE: Because the Society of the Holy Sacrament disapproves?

LA GRANGE: I dislike the Society as much as you do, Jean. More! They've never supported my reign. But I'll be honest with you: the Spanish King is dying. Do you have any idea what that means?

MOLIERE: I pay little attention to such things, my liege.

LA GRANGE: The King's daughter has a legitimate hereditary right to the Spanish possessions in the Netherlands. Mother has pointed out that if I were to marry her, that claim would rightly come to France.

MOLIERE: We were discussing my banned plays, my liege.

LA GRANGE: If we go to war — and I must assume that Spain would challenge our rightful claim — if we go to war, the religious climate here at home must be without controversy. The world must see and understand the righteousness of our cause. Do you understand what I'm saying?

MOLIERE: No, my liege.

LA GRANGE: This is no time to draw divisions in our ranks!

MOLIERE: I merely satirize the vices—

LA GRANGE: Stop satirizing religion!

MOLIERE: I have never satirized religion.

LA GRANGE: "Don Juan" is banned from further performance.

MOLIERE: Then good day, my liege.

LA GRANGE: Wait a minute! Damn it, Jean, you're too stubborn for your own good. Maybe you should've followed your father and become the Crown's upholsterer.

MOLIERE: My father always thought so.

LA GRANGE: But then I wouldn't have reason to offer my personal patronage.

MOLIERE: Patronage, my liege?

LA GRANGE: You have another mouth to feed. I forget her name.

MOLIERE: Esprit-Madeleine.

LA GRANGE: I'm sure you can use the added income. Henceforth, you'll be known as the King's Players of the Palais Royal. You'll receive an annual allowance of six thousand livres.

MOLIERE: I don't understand...

LA GRANGE: I'm sure you'll be very busy finding a play to substitute for "Don Juan." Perhaps this will give you a little added incentive.

MOLIERE: I'm astounded and honored, my liege.

LA GRANGE: I expect you to wear the honor well, Jean. In fact, I demand it.

(BLACKOUT.)

17/ at the theater

(LIGHTS UP on LA GRANGE.)

LA GRANGE: In sixteen sixty-seven, with the King
At war, Moliere again unfurls his wings.

(LIGHTS UP FULL on theater.)

LA GRANGE: This is madness, Jean. There's no other way to put it.

MOLIERE: I've made major revisions. It's not the same play at all.

LA GRANGE: It reads like the same play to me.

MOLIERE: I've even changed the title. I call it "The Impostor."

LA GRANGE: "The Impostor," "Tartuffe," what's the difference? The focus of the play remains virtually unchanged.

MOLIERE: The play is about an impostor! Doesn't the language mean anything? The man is a pious hypocrite.

LA GRANGE: Jean, with the country at war, and considering the King's clear position on "Tartuffe"—

MOLIERE: This play is "The Impostor." I-m-p-o-s-t-o-r!

LA GRANGE: Jean, that's a cheap attempt to—

MOLIERE: I don't want to talk about it. I'm expecting Armande, we have a private matter to discuss.

LA GRANGE: You're too damn stubborn for your own good. Ever since Madeleine left, you've been acting strangely even for you.

MOLIERE: Charles, you may go.

LA GRANGE: I don't like watching you dig your own grave.

(ARMANDE enters.)

MOLIERE: You may go, Charles.

(LA GRANGE leaves.)

ARMANDE: You wished to see me?

MOLIERE: Yes. I'm moving out. I'm taking my daughter with me.

(A beat.)

MOLIERE: You don't object?

ARMANDE: Getting away might be good for you.

MOLIERE: I thought you might insist on keeping the child.

ARMANDE: Neither of us has time for her.

MOLIERE: Lately all your spare time goes to Michel Baron.

ARMANDE: I don't know what to tell you, Jean.

MOLIERE: You might try the truth for a change.

ARMANDE: I don't love him.

MOLIERE: You prefer his bed to mine.

ARMANDE: That's not true — what is true is that you no longer sleep in our bed. You haven't since Madeliene left. I got tired of sleeping alone.

MOLIERE: I asked you to leave the stage, to spend time with Esprit.

ARMANDE: This is why you won't sleep with me? Because I became the actress you trained me to become? I thought it was because your real love is for my sister.

MOLIERE: That's ridiculous. You know how busy I am.

ARMANDE: I can only try and make sense out of your actions, Jean. You never talk to me. I never know what you want. One day you say I should leave the stage, the next you offer me a great part. I don't think I really know you at all.

MOLIERE: Everybody knows me — I reveal myself to the world!

ARMANDE: Only on stage.

MOLIERE: All it takes is the price of a ticket to know me.

ARMANDE: I'm talking about my husband, not the playwright and actor. We play roles on stage, not ourselves.

MOLIERE: I don't always distinguish the difference.

ARMANDE: I'm not the naive girl you married. I have a life apart from the roles you write for me.

MOLIERE: So I've noticed.

ARMANDE: I'm not going to fight with you, Jean. Do what you have to do. I wish you well, whatever it is. You've been a good teacher.

MOLIERE: Why, with a recommendation like that, I could open "a school for wives"!

(ARMANDE just looks at him.)

MOLIERE: "A school for wives . . ."?

ARMANDE: I get the reference, Jean — I just don't think it's funny.

MOLIERE: Then you're not as good a student as you think.

ARMANDE: I think it's sad. You use your wit to keep anyone from getting close to you. Except, perhaps, Madeleine. And that's why you've changed since she's gone.

(A beat. MOLIERE starts coughing.)

ARMANDE: Goodbye, Jean.

(She turns and leaves. MOLIERE continues coughing to BLACK-OUT.)

18/ at Court

(LIGHTS UP on LA GRANDE.)

LA GRANDE: Sixteen sixty-nine: the war is won,
The King is home. Moliere, who swore he's done
With Paris, now comes to the city still
Again, to see the King and heed his will.

(He puts on the crown as MOLIERE enters and bows.)

MOLIERE: My liege — my belated congratulations on your victory.
LA GRANGE: The glory belongs to France.
MOLIERE: But of course.
LA GRANGE: You've taken up residence in Auteuil. And Armande
remains in Paris.
MOLIERE: My doctor thinks Paris is bad for my health, my liege.
LA GRANGE: I see. I've been catching up on what's transpired
during my absence, and I just learned that you presented a revised
version of "Tartuffe" — called "The Impostor" now, I believe?
MOLIERE: It's a new play, my liege.
LA GRANGE: Which the Archbishop immediately banned — it
played only a single night.
MOLIERE: Yes, my liege.
LA GRANGE: However, several in Court who saw it tell me that you
changed the ending considerably. Something about an officer from the
King appearing...?
MOLIERE: I can recite the passage if you wish, my liege.
LA GRANGE: Just give me the gist.
MOLIERE: Tartuffe, you recall—
LA GRANGE: You still call him Tartuffe?
MOLIERE: Yes, my liege. Though it's a different play, I wanted to
suggest a certain continuity.
LA GRANGE: Go on.
MOLIERE: The hypocrite has swindled Orgon out of all his
property, even though Orgon believed in him. But he doesn't get away
with it because an officer from the King appears in the nick of time, and
everything is set right. So there is no doubt that Tartuffe is a hypocrite,
my liege.
LA GRANGE: I never disliked the play but you left me no choice
but to ban it. National unity was at stake, with certain war on the
horizon. Now, of course, the situation is different.

(MOLIERE begins to cough violently.)

LA GRANGE: Have you seen a doctor about that cough?
MOLIERE: I'm fine, my liege.
LA GRANGE: I want you to perform the play publicly. And go
ahead and call it "Tartuffe."
MOLIERE: My liege?

LA GRANGE: There are those in the Society who think they ran the country in my absence. It's time to put them in their place.

(LA GRANGE takes off the crown and speaks to the audience.)

LA GRANGE: Needless to say, "Tartuffe" was such a hit
That everyone in Paris rushed to it.

19/ at the salon

(LIGHTS UP on the caricature prop.)

ARMANDE: They say Paris has never seen such a popular theatrical event.
MADELEINE: Because the people have no will to resist temptation. We must be stronger than ever.
ARMANDE: But membership in the Society is falling.
MADELEINE: If we have fewer eyes, so may we see more clearly that we have a King who panders to popular taste. And an author who adds the sin of impiety to his sin of the flesh.
ARMANDE: They say his wife has taken a young lover.
MADELEINE: Being a cuckold is the least of his worries.

(BLACKOUT.)

20/ at a convent

(LIGHTS UP on LA GRANGE.)

LA GRANGE: How fast the years pass in the heat of work:
But who could know that Madeleine would look
So deeply in her Bible and her soul
And find so much that she thinks must be told.
Sixteen seventy-two: and time, at last,
To meet her God unburdened by the past.

(MOLIERE and ARMANDE are visiting MADELEINE on her deathbed.)

374

MOLIERE: Don't try to talk.
MADELEINE *(very weak)*: I must...
MOLIERE: Please, try to get some rest...
MADELEINE: Armande...?
ARMANDE: I'm right here.
MADELEINE: Armande...closer...

(ARMANDE moves her head close to MADELEINE's.)

MOLIERE: I think she's becoming delirious.
MADELEINE: Closer, Armande... I have something I must...
ARMANDE: Madeleine?

(MOLIERE pulls ARMANDE back away from MADELEINE.)

MOLIERE: Let the poor woman rest.

(Now MADELEINE will struggle to sit up.)

MOLIERE: I think you'd better get the priest.
MADELEINE: Armande...I must tell you...
ARMANDE: I hate to see her like this.
MOLIERE: It won't be long — get the priest!

(ARMANDE exits. MADELEINE struggles to sit up, finally succeeding.)

MADELEINE: Armande...you must pray for your soul...Jean won't listen...but you, Armande, you must save your soul...my dear daughter...

(The strain has been too much for her. She drops back down onto the bed. ARMANDE enters with LA GRANGE as the priest. Understanding that the end is very near now, ARMANDE embraces MADELEINE.)

ARMANDE: My dear, sweet sister...
LA GRANGE: Absolve, Domine, animae omnium fidelium defunctorum ab omni vinculo delictorus. Et gratia tua illis succurente mereantur evadere judicium ultionis. Et lucis aeternae beatitudine perfrui.

(During the rites above, MOLIERE stands and moves away from the others, distraught. And BLACKOUT.)

21/ at the theater

(LIGHTS UP on LA GRANGE.)

LA GRANGE: Moliere mourned — and then picked up his pen
To ridicule doctors and medicine.
An afternoon in sixteen seventy-three:
In Paris, two players rehearse a scene.

(UP FULL to include MOLIERE. They are rehearsing a scene from "The Imaginary Invalid".)

MOLIERE: "Then tell me this: what does one do when one is sick?"
LA GRANGE: "Not a thing."
MOLIERE: "Nothing?"
LA GRANGE: "Nothing. Get some rest. Left to her own devices, Nature cures her own illnesses. It's we who can get in the way; indeed, most men die of the cure, not of the disease."
MOLIERE: "But certainly we can help Nature along?"
LA GRANGE: "We like to think so — just as in every age we believe what we wish could be true. Today doctors are quick to recite the litany of medicine, claiming many benefits from their methods, but all this is just rhetoric."
MOLIERE: "Well, listen to you! If a doctor were here, he'd certainly have something to say about that."
LA GRANGE: "Each man must deal with medicine as he prefers — but at his own risk. I'm not on a crusade, merely hoping to enlighten you. We really should go together to see one of Moliere's comedies on the subject."
MOLIERE: "From what I've heard about Moliere, he's an insolent fool! What does a playwright know about medicine? In fact, I think he's quite rude to put doctors on his stage. If I were a doctor, I'd get even with this Moliere fellow. The minute he got sick, I'd let him suffer! I'd make no prescription, do no bloodletting, administer no enema — I'd tell him, 'Croak, you old fool, if you think medicine is so useless!'"
LA GRANGE: "I doubt if Moliere would even call a doctor if he got sick. I've heard he detests them."
MOLIERE: "All the worse for him. Let him croak!"

(They are done. A beat.)

MOLIERE: Well?
LA GRANGE: To be honest, I don't like it.
MOLIERE: Could you be more specific?
LA GRANGE: It sounds a little defensive. A little self-indulgent.
MOLIERE: Will the audience laugh?
LA GRANGE: Perhaps — but with you or at you?
MOLIERE: As long as they laugh, Charles, we have them where we want them.

(A beat.)

MOLIERE: That's all I have for now.
LA GRANGE: Jean, there's something I have to talk to you about.
MOLIERE: Very well. Wine?
LA GRANGE: Please.

(MOLIERE will pour them wine.)

MOLIERE: Let me guess what's on your mind. Armande is leaving the stage.
LA GRANGE: Why on earth do you say that?
MOLIERE: I've been waiting for it. Since I begged her to retire for years, I've been expecting her to ever since we separated. One of life's little jokes.
LA GRANGE: It does involve Armande, actually.
MOLIERE: Oh? You mean — you and Armande...?
LA GRANGE: You don't think—?
MOLIERE: You took up with Madeleine — now you want to take up with Armande, am I right?
LA GRANGE: No!
MOLIERE: Wouldn't bother me, actually. To your health.

(But only MOLIERE drinks.)

LA GRANGE: I have a serious matter to discuss with you, Jean.
MOLIERE: I'm all ears.
LA GRANGE: I don't know how to begin.
MOLIERE: At the beginning, of course.

LA GRANGE: Very well. I want you to look at a certain sequence of events with me.

MOLIERE: A history lesson, Charles?

LA GRANGE: In a sense, yes. We form a company, we go into the provinces, you and Madeleine become lovers, Madeleine suddenly leaves the company, she returns with a young girl whom she says is her sister.

MOLIERE: And Charles ends up in Madeleine's bed.

LA GRANGE: Has it ever occurred to you that Armande is exactly the right age to have been born within a year of Madeleine's leaving the company?

MOLIERE: If it just now occurred to you, Charles, you're years behind everyone else! We've already had that little scandal, please don't revive it.

LA GRANGE: I've been thinking about Madeleine's sudden desire to save her soul. What would drive her to that?

MOLIERE: She had to do something. She was past her prime as a leading lady.

LA GRANGE: There's more to it than that. I've also been thinking about this sudden hatred of medicine you have, all because little Louis died so young, because you say Madeleine became delirious on her death bed—

MOLIERE: Doctors are fools! They know nothing, they do nothing! Weren't you paying attention to the scene we just did?

LA GRANGE: Yes. And I ask myself, why is the greatest playwright on the Continent, who can write about anything, making so much out of so little?

MOLIETE: So little!?

LA GRANGE: None of us likes getting an enema, Jean. But few use it as a reason to ban medical science.

MOLIERE: Their methods accomplish nothing! They make everything worse!

LA GRANGE: Can we discuss this calmly?

MOLIERE: I am calm!

(A beat.)

MOLIERE: I am calm.

(MOLIERE pours more wine.)

LA GRANGE: Have you heard of Pascal's Wager?

378

MOLIERE: You've taken up gambling?

LA GRANGE: It's an argument for the existence of God.

MOLIERE: I'm not an atheist, Charles.

LA GRANGE: Bear me out, Jean, please. Pascal argues this way: he asks us to imagine belief in God as a kind of wager. If one believes in God but God does not exist, what is lost? Nothing, really, except that one has held a false belief. And if God does exist, then, of course one has held a true belief. But look at the opposite: disbelief in God. Again, nothing is lost if God does not exist, one simply has a true belief. But if God exists, what happens to the disbeliever then? He burns in hell!

(A beat.)

LA GRANGE: Do you understand the argument?

MOLIERE: I'm not sure.

LA GRANGE: Pascal defends belief in God because it's opposite provides the only set of circumstances in which something truly unfortunate can happen.

MOLIERE: But I already told you that I believe in God. Everyone I know believes in God.

LA GRANGE: What about belief or disbelief that Armande is Madeleine's daughter?

MOLIERE: Charles, it's getting late and you're much more interested in philosophy than I am. I'm afraid that—

LA GRANGE: Don't run away from the logic of my argument. Listen to me: if, in fact, Armande is Madeleine's daughter, then you may well be the father. So it is possible that you are guilty of the sin of incest. To prepare yourself for the worst possibility, by the logic of Pascal's Wager, you should believe that this is so.

MOLIERE: Believe that I married my own daughter?

LA GRANGE: So you can pray for forgiveness. It's the safest alternative.

(MOLIERE starts laughing.)

LA GRANGE: You don't fool me by laughing, Jean. Laughter has always been your mask. I think you already have reached the same conclusion. I think this is behind your exaggerated attack on medicine. You don't like what you see in the mirror.

MOLIERE: This is madness.

LA GRANGE: In a way, yes, it certainly is. But you have to protect yourself against the worst thing that can happen, Jean. I think the same logic applies to Armande.

MOLIERE: You've played this Pascal's Wager game with Armande?

LA GRANGE: No. But I shall. I must.

MOLIERE: You read too much philosophy! You're an actor, not a thinker.

LA GRANGE: I try to be both.

MOLIERE: You think too much, Charles.

LA GRANGE: And you don't think enough.

(ARMANDE enters.)

ARMANDE: If I'm interrupting something . . .

MOLIERE: Not at all — we just rehearsed a scene from "The Imaginary Invalid." Charles hates it.

LA GRANDE: I think it needs a lot of work.

ARMANDE: May I see it?

(MOLIERE hands ARMANDE the script and she starts reading. MOLIERE and LA GRANGE exchange glances. Finally:)

LA GRANGE: Well — I have work to do.

MOLIERE: I hope you change your mind, Charles. About the script.

LA GRANGE: After I see more, perhaps.

(He exits. ARMANDE looks up from her reading.)

ARMANDE: This sounds just like you, Jean. Everything you write is so personal.

(She continues reading to BLACKOUT.)

(LIGHTS UP on LA GRANGE.)

LA GRANGE: February seventeenth: one year
To the day since Madeleine, from fear
Or piety, tried to tie the knot.
On stage, Moliere's new play unfolds its plot.

380

(LIGHTS UP on a performance of "The Imaginary Invalid." MOLIERE plays the lead and is very sick. ARMANDE plays his maid disguised as a doctor. There is considerable slapstick here, despite MOLIERE's eventual coughing up of blood.)

ARMANDE: "Who's your doctor?"
MOLIERE: "Monsieur Purgon."
ARMANDE: "Never heard of him. What's his diagnosis?"
MOLIERE *(losing his place)*: "I get pains in my chest."
ARMANDE *(taking over)*: "And you eat chicken?"
MOLIERE: "Yes."
ARMANDE: "Imbecile."
MOLIERE *(finding his place)*: "Veal."
ARMANDE: "Ignoramus."
MOLIERE: "Sometimes only broth . . ."
ARMANDE: "Jackass."
MOLIERE: "Eggs."
ARMANDE: "Moron!"
MOLIERE: "A few prunes——"

(He starts coughing violently.)

ARMANDE *(moving ahead again)*: "What in the world are you doing with that arm?"
MOLIERE: "My arm?"
ARMANDE: "It's completely useless. I'd have it cut off immediately."
MOLIERE: "My arm?"
ARMANDE: "It draws nourishment to itself and stunts the health of that entire side of the body."
MOLIERE: "But—I need my arm . . ."
ARMANDE: "I'd also get rid of that right eye if I were you . . ."

(MOLIERE is coughing violently again.)

ARMANDE: "It stunts the health of your left eye . . ."

(MOLIERE has lost control, but the audience is howling, thinking it all part of the play. ARMANDE looks for a way to get off stage.)

ARMANDE: "Well, I wish I could stay but I have an important meeting about a recent death. I have to recommend what could've been done to save the patient. Goodbye."

(She rushes off stage, MOLIERE coughs violently, BLACKOUT and QUICKLY UP ON:)

23/ backstage

(ARMANDE rushes to LA GRANGE.)

LA GRANGE: Is he still coughing up blood?
ARMANDE: Yes. I don't see how he can finish.
LA GRANGE: I'll go out and cancel the performance.
ARMANDE: Maybe I could cut straight to the finale. Did anyone find a doctor?
LA GRANGE: None will come.
ARMANDE: I'm going back on to finish up.
LA GRANGE: I'll have to lead you into it — let's go!

(LIGHT CHANGE again to:)

24/ on stage

(LA GRANGE takes over.)

LA GRANGE: "Novus Doctor Ignoramus
Omni regimentus
Sui powerfulble
Et sui monitarble
Et alles be riches"
CHORUS *(LA GRANGE, ARMANDE, MOLIERE)*: "Bene, bene, bene
Omna spenda the money
Enemarissimus comprehende
Enemarissimus omni bene
Et bleedet humanee
Et killet humanee"
MOLIERE *(with difficulty)*: "Omni anni, omni anni
Novus Doctor omni bene
Mille poxas
Mille feveras

Pleurisias et dysenterias
Et sui rigor mortis"
CHORUS: "Bene, bene, bene
Omna spenda the money
Enemarissimus comprehende
Enemarissimus omni bene
Et bleedet humanee
Et killet humanee"

(LAUGHTER and APPLAUSE at play's end, as ARMANDE and LA GRANGE all but carry MOLIERE off stage, as LIGHTS CHANGE to:)

25/ backstage

(MOLIERE sinks to the floor, coughing.)

ARMANDE: We need a doctor. We need a priest.
LA GRANGE: Armande, listen to me, it's too late for Jean. It's not too late for you.
ARMANDE: We have to find—...
LA GRANGE: He wouldn't listen to me. He wouldn't bet Pascal's Wager.

(MOLIERE comes out of it a little.)

MOLIERE: "Bene, bene, bene
Omna spenda the money—"
ARMANDE: Don't try to speak, Jean. The doctor will be here soon.
LA GRANGE: They won't come, Armande. You know that. He made his choice. But it's not too late for you.
ARMANDE: What are you talking about?
LA GRANGE: What if this is providential retribution?
ARMANDE: I don't understand what you mean.
LA GRANGE: If he married his own daughter. And you your own father.
ARMANDE: Charles, this is no time to talk crazy.
LA GRANGE: Please go to a priest.
ARMANDE: Charles, my husband...Jean is dying.
MOLIERE: "Omna spenda the money
Enemarissimus comprehende
Enemarissimus omni bene"

ARMANDE: Sshh, Jean. Sshh.

LA GRANGE: Don't you understand what I'm saying?

ARMANDE *(ignoring him)*: The doctor will be here soon, Jean. The doctor and the priest are on their way.

MOLIERE: "Et bleedet humanee"

LA GRANDE: Armande?

ARMANDE: Sshh.

MOLIERE: "Et killet humanee"

ARMANDE: Soon, Jean, soon. Sshh.

(SLOW FADE TO BLACKOUT.)

26/ at Court

(LIGHTS UP on LA GRANGE.)

LA GRANGE: Moliere—
Jean-Baptiste Poquelin, my friend: but where
To end? This man I loved, who would not heed
His friends no more than God: Moliere could feed
His own misery like no man I've known.
So when he died, my dear friend died alone.

(LIGHTS UP FULL on LA GRANGE as King and ARMANDE in mourning.)

LA GRANGE: He'd hardly endeared himself to the medical profession.

ARMANDE: A priest finally came but it was too late. I doubt if Jean would have talked to him anyway.

LA GRANGE: No, I suppose not. Not that he didn't believe. He was — stubborn.

ARMANDE: My liege, I don't know what to do with his body.

LA GRANGE: The Archbishop has made it quite clear that holy law is holy law, and he can't be buried in consecrated ground.

ARMANDE: Am I to bury him out of town, along some roadside?

LA GRANGE: I found a technicality we can take advantage of. Consecrated ground extends only four feet deep. We'll bury him five. But we must do it at night — at St. Joseph's.

ARMANDE: St. Joseph's — with the suicides and unbaptized children.

384

LA GRANGE: It's the best I can do.
ARMANDE: I'm grateful for your help, my liege.
LA GRANGE: Then you'll bury him tonight?
ARMANDE: Yes, my liege.
LA GRANGE: It would be inappropriate, under the circumstances,
for me to attend...
ARMANDE: I understand, my liege.

(BLACKOUT.)
27/ at Moliere's casket

(LIGHTS UP on LA GRANDE, watching over MOLIERE'S casket.)

LA GRANDE: Who can look
Into the heart of man and find the hook
On which to hang a life? —Naked, stark:
A piece of meat called man. But the mark
Of man is not so easily drawn.

(ARMANDE enters in mourning.)

ARMANDE: A priest will see me right after he's buried.
LA GRANGE: Good.
ARMANDE: Do you think it could be true?
LA GRANGE: The genius of Pascal's Wager is that it covers all
bets.
ARMANDE: He was tormented by the possibility, wasn't he?
LA GRANGE: Perhaps. He was a hard man to know very well. I
loved him but I never really understood him.
ARMANDE: "All it takes is a ticket to my play to know me."
LA GRANGE: "Plays don't write themselves."

(A beat.)

ARMANDE: I'm going to revive "Tartuffe."
LA GRANGE: Really?
ARMANDE: You under-studied Orgon. If we get right to work, we
could have it up in a week. Jean wouldn't want the theater to go dark.
LA GRANGE: No, he wouldn't. "Busy, busy."
ARMANDE: Then you'll do it?
LA GRANGE: I have no choice — Pascal's Wager, you know? I'll
let you have a moment alone . . .

ARMANDE: No — I've had quite enough time alone.

(They exit.)

(LIGHTS INTENSIFY on the casket.)

(Then LIGHTS BEGIN SLOW FADE as we hear:)

LA GRANGE *(V.O.)*: End
In darkness, then: what clarity we win
Will rise between the darkness we see now
And the certain night that gets us anyhow.
End in darkness, then . . .

(LIGHTS continue to FADE: until SUDDENLY: A SHOCKING
CHANGE OF FOCUS:)

(LIGHTS UP on MOLIERE, as he rises up out of the casket.)

28/ epilogue

MOLIERE: Shed no tears! You rot in one grave as another;
If you don't believe that, don't ever have a mother.
The luck that gets us all got me—
Though I'm better off than most, you must agree.
Consider this: though I am dust, you're glad to pay
Right through the nose to see my plays!
Without me, Montfleury's just a name;
Because of me, he has a kind of fame.
The Archbishop of Paris is no concern of yours
Except for me — I give him the notoriety he deserves.
In other words, why shed a tear for me?
My plays live on until eternity!
Oh, I know — in your age the time is getting short,
Everywhere there's war, famine, a great environmental wart.
Yet you insist your own age is unique:
"Never has civilization reached such a peak!"
But I question this wisdom found on TV and in "Forbes,"
Though maybe that's presumptuous, coming from a corpse.
Still, I don't see our times as different, I confess,
Since in your age, as in mine, it's all a mess.

386

Though you've reached the moon, discovered strange galactic gasses,

Three hundred years later, the world's still full of asses!

(LA GRANGE enters.)

LA GRANGE: So we hope we've moved you and given you a little fun; In truth,—

MOLIERE & LA GRANGE: — there's not a damn thing new beneath the sun.

(MUSIC FANFARE AND CURTAIN CALL: THE PLAY IS OVER.)

For royalties information:
Charles Deemer
1-800-294-7176
cdeemer@teleport.com

1998

Bedrooms & Bars
a play in two acts

*First performed at the Raindog Playwrights' Project in Portland, Oregon, on
February 13, 1998. Directed by Charles Deemer.*

Finalist for the 1998 Oregon Book Award.

THE CAST:
Quinn, *a barfly, ex-teacher, 30s*
Deadra, *a barfly, 30s*
Megan, *Deadra's twin sister (played by same actress)*

THE SETTING:
Table in a bar. Quinn's small studio apartment. A hospital bed. A
ferry deck.

THE TIME:
The 1980s.

ACT ONE

1/ The Bar, Saturday Night. Early 1980's.

(AT RISE: QUINN and DEADRA sit at a table. Each has a fresh drink.)

QUINN: Thanks for the drink.
DEADRA: You're very welcome.
QUINN: I'm Quinn.
DEADRA: I know. Deadra
QUINN: I know. Cheers.
DEADRA: Cheers.

(They drink.)

QUINN: Where's what's-his-name?
DEADRA: I'm not sure who you mean.
QUINN: The guy I always see you with.
DEADRA: You'd think someone like that would ring a bell, wouldn't you? I have no idea who you mean.
QUINN: The guy you go with.
DEADRA: I don't go with anyone.
QUINN: You're in here a lot together. He's always betting on games.
DEADRA: George?
QUINN: George, right.
DEADRA: He left town last week. He got a new job.
QUINN: You two aren't an item?
DEADRA: Heavens, no. We're just buddies.
QUINN: That's encouraging.
DEADRA: In what way?
QUINN: When you make your move on me, I can say yes without a guilty conscience.
DEADRA: You don't beat around the bush.
QUINN: Bullshit's not part of my nature.
DEADRA: Sorry to disappoint you, Quinn, but I won't be making a move on you.
QUINN: Win a few, lose a few.
DEADRA: Are you always so direct?

QUINN: Always.

DEADRA: At least you're not "a secretive Scorpio." I have this thing about meeting Scorpio men. It always gets me in trouble.

QUINN: Bingo.

DEADRA: No.

QUINN: November 1st.

DEADRA: Please tell me you're kidding.

QUINN: Would I kid about being the sign of the genitals? What about you?

DEADRA: Guess.

QUINN: Actually, I've never asked anyone their sign before.

DEADRA: Don't ask — guess.

QUINN: Not a clue.

DEADRA: You've seen me in here a lot. You should have some impression about me.

QUINN: We've never talked before.

DEADRA: Why is that? Are you shy?

QUINN: You're usually in here with George. And now suddenly you're foot loose and fancy free.

DEADRA: I've always been that. The question is, how come you never talked to me before?

QUINN: We never ended up on adjacent barstools.

DEADRA: Which is surprising since whenever I walk in the door, you're here.

QUINN: Isn't that the pot calling the kettle black?

DEADRA: I see you have a great affection for clichés.

QUINN: Only great writing becomes a cliché. Otherwise we forget it as soon as we hear it.

DEADRA: And you're a student of great writing.

QUINN: I'm a writer of bad verse, which gives me great appreciation for the good stuff.

DEADRA: Do you publish?

QUINN: I don't even send anything out.

DEADRA: That sounds like fear of rejection.

QUINN: I write for myself. It's a very noble tradition.

DEADRA: But you deprive the public of enjoying your work.

QUINN: If you'd read my stuff, you wouldn't say that. I write for an audience of one.

DEADRA: Too bad. If you had a book out, I could take it home to bed.

QUINN: Why take the poetry when you can take the poet?

DEADRA: I'm not picking you up, Quinn.

QUINN: The night's still young.

(A pause.)

QUINN: You never told me what sign you are.
DEADRA: Scorpio.
QUINN: Scorpio?
DEADRA: November 5th.
QUINN: Sex and death meets sex and death. I think we're on a roll.
DEADRA: There are variations to that theme. A lot depends on what's in your various houses.
QUINN: And in your house is — let me guess. A live-in boyfriend who hasn't shown up yet.
DEADRA: I have an apartment.
QUINN: Same question.
DEADRA: No live-in boyfriend. No boyfriend, period.
QUINN: This gets better all the time.
DEADRA: Are you hard of hearing? I am not, repeat not, picking you up.
QUINN: Why did you suggest we get a table?
DEADRA: Because I see you in here all the time, and we never talk.
QUINN: We could talk at the bar. I think you wanted to get a table because you have an ulterior motive.
DEADRA: Actually, I do. But it's not what you think. I need a favor.
QUINN: Bingo.
DEADRA: I can't stay at my apartment tonight.
QUINN: Why not?
DEADRA: Let's just say I need a break.
QUINN: From what?
DEADRA: This is where it gets complicated. If you were a gentleman, you wouldn't make me explain. You'd say, "I have a sofa you can crash on."
QUINN: Unfortunately, my very small apartment has only one double-bed. So unless we sleep together, one of us will have to sleep on the floor.
DEADRA: I have no problem with sleeping on the floor.
QUINN: I may want to be chivalrous. What do you need a break from?
DEADRA: House guests. They're driving me crazy.
QUINN: Then kick them out.
DEADRA: I can't just yet.
QUINN: Why not?

DEADRA: One of them hurt his foot. I think it's infected.
QUINN: How many are there?
DEADRA: Two.
QUINN: Sex?
DEADRA: No, I'm not sleeping with them — and I wouldn't tell you if I was.
QUINN: I meant, are they both male or what?
DEADRA: They're a couple.
QUINN: So tell them to go home.
DEADRA: I don't think John should be moved just yet. I've been trying to get him to see a doctor.
QUINN: I'm impressed you're so worried about him. Are you sure you're a Scorpio? You don't seem selfish enough.
DEADRA: Not every Scorpio is fixated on sex and death.
QUINN: Then what's the point of astrology?
DEADRA: It's about acting in accordance with natural energies.
QUINN *(Theme from Twilight Zone)*: Dee-dee-dee-dee dee-dee-dee-dee.
DEADRA: Energies are very real.
QUINN: Whatever. Anyway, sure.
DEADRA: Sure what?
QUINN: You can crash at my place. I'll spend the night with a lady friend.
DEADRA: Thank you, Quinn.
QUINN: No problem. Let me make a phone call. You ready for another drink?
DEADRA: Absolutely.
QUINN: My kind of girl.

(He exits. Deadra watches him go. BLACKOUT.)

2/ The Bar, Ten Minutes Later.

(LIGHTS UP: ten minutes later, Quinn returns with drinks.)

DEADRA: I bet she was glad to hear from you.
QUINN: She wasn't home. I'll try later.
DEADRA: Your girlfriend?
QUINN: Not really.
DEADRA: But you sleep with her?
QUINN: Now and again.

392

DEADRA: How convenient.

QUINN: We think so. You have a problem with that?

DEADRA: Why should I care what you do?

QUINN: I mean, in general. Do you have a problem with casual sex?

DEADRA: It's not my style, but no, I don't.

(Quinn just looks at her.)

DEADRA: You look like you don't believe me.

QUINN: Let's just say I know a couple of your ex-boyfriends.

DEADRA: Who?

QUINN: I don't want to get them in trouble.

DEADRA: I don't know what you think you know about me, Quinn, but I hope you don't believe everything you hear in bars.

QUINN: I know a couple of guys you've taken home. I'm surprised to hear you say it isn't your style.

DEADRA: So you're sitting here because you expect me to take you home?

QUINN: I'm sitting here because you invited me. Not vice-versa.

DEADRA: Because I need a place to crash tonight. Under the circumstances, I don't think I should accept your offer

QUINN: You don't have to get uptight about it.

DEADRA: You don't have to insult me.

QUINN: I'm sorry. I had you pegged as a woman waiting for Mr. Right Now. But you're absolutely correct — I know nothing about you. Maybe you're waiting for Mr. Right after all.

DEADRA: Hardly.

QUINN: Spoken like a graduate from the school of hard knocks.

DEADRA: Aren't we all?

QUINN: How many times have you been married?

DEADRA: Once.

QUINN: Only once, I'm impressed. Children?

DEADRA: No.

QUINN: So what happened?

DEADRA: This is getting a little personal, Quinn.

QUINN: Then I retract the question. Read any good books lately?

DEADRA: Fuck you..

QUINN: I assume you don't mean that literally.

DEADRA: You're insulting me again.

QUINN: How do you come up with that?

DEADRA: The subtext is that since I won't talk about anything personal, let's talk about something trivial.

QUINN: I don't think books are trivial.

DEADRA: I'm talking about the context.

QUINN: Context up your ass.

DEADRA: Maybe you could call your girlfriend again.

QUINN: She's not my girlfriend.

DEADRA: Whoever she is, maybe she's back.

(A pause.)

QUINN: I've been married three times.

DEADRA: Three!

QUINN: And lived to tell the tale. Actually it's not as bad as it sounds.

DEADRA: You can spare me the details.

(He ignores this.)

QUINN: The first wasn't supposed to happen. I was barely twenty-one and home on leave from the Army. My girlfriend and I were at a fraternity party when her roommate said she's running off to Reno with her fiancee. They wanted us to come along to stand up for them.

DEADRA: My God — and you ended up doing it yourself.

QUINN: You got it.

DEADRA: That's terrible. And number two?

QUINN: I'm not done with number one. You ever been to a wedding chapel in Reno?

DEADRA: Hardly.

QUINN: There is no better cathedral for exhibiting the America genius for marketing. We went to the Little Chapel of Roses. You walk into something that's part mail order house and part convention booth. Brochures and display ads are everywhere. Suddenly this "facilitator" drops on you like flies on garbage and the next thing you know, you're sitting down looking at page after page of photos illustrating your options. Do you want the Simple Podium Ceremony or the Stained-Glass-and-Organ Model? A love sonnet by Shakespeare? An aria from *Tristan and Isolde*? Ten or twenty or thirty invited guests, performed by the best actors in the region?

DEADRA: So what did you choose?

QUINN: The Pinkie and Blue Boy Special.

DEADRA: What was that?

QUINN: I don't remember exactly.

DEADRA: And you ended up having a double wedding?

QUINN: Exactly.

DEADRA: How did that happen?

394

QUINN: I don't remember.

DEADRA: You don't remember anything?

QUINN: My memory ends with picking out Pinkie and Blue Boy. I think it may have had to do with the actors who stood up for us. Maybe they wore pink and blue.

DEADRA: I remember my wedding perfectly.

QUINN: Not I. Don't you ever have blackouts?

DEADRA: Never. Do you have them often?

QUINN: Comes with the territory.

DEADRA: That's not a good sign, Quinn.

QUINN: You see any good signs in the world today?

DEADRA: I'm referring to your health. So what happened after the double wedding?

QUINN: We all drove home. I went back to the Army, and everybody else went back to school.

DEADRA: You didn't even have a honeymoon?

QUINN: Didn't have a marriage. Back in Germany, where I was stationed, I sobered up long enough to realize the horror of what we'd done. Fortunately the feeling was mutual. We were able to get the marriage annulled.

DEADRA: So it doesn't count.

QUINN: Not legally. But in the heart, believe me, it was a true mistake.

DEADRA: One down, two to go.

QUINN: Two was the one that counted.

DEADRA: But it didn't last either.

QUINN: Not my fault. Not entirely, anyway. She left me for another woman.

DEADRA: Ouch. How did that make you feel?

QUINN: Like a prickless piece of shit. Actually, it probably would have ended anyway.

DEADRA: How did you meet her?

QUINN: I went back to school after the Army. She was my philosophy professor.

DEADRA: The plot thickens.

QUINN: We didn't get involved until after I finished her class. We ran into each another in a bar one night, and it was love at last gulp. I was the first man she met who could out-drink her.

DEADRA: Was she older?

QUINN: I had a few months on her. I was a returning student and she was a recent Ph.D.

DEADRA: A very bright woman.

QUINN: Bright as they come.

DEADRA: You think bright is sexy?

QUINN: Absolutely. Don't you?

DEADRA: Depends who's wearing the intelligence. How long were you married?

QUINN: Five years. And we lived together four before that.

DEADRA: Nine years is a long time.

QUINN: Tell me about it.

DEADRA: You had no clues she liked women?

QUINN: Sure, I did. But I thought it was all in the realm of fantasy. Apparently she tried it out and decided that's where she belonged.

DEADRA: I'm sorry.

QUINN: The Greeks, Aeschylus and the like, said suffering leads to wisdom. I should've sent her a thank you card for the extra lessons.

DEADRA: Which brings us to marriage number three.

QUINN: The worst of all. Absolute insanity.

DEADRA: What happened?

QUINN: I don't remember.

DEADRA: Quinn, these blackouts should worry you.

QUINN: She was someone at the high school, another teacher, and I think she went on a mission to save me. You know the type?

DEADRA: Addicted do-gooder? Butts into everybody's life but their own?

QUINN: Exactly. I gave her a ride home after a faculty party, she invited me in for a drink, and I ended up staying the three-day weekend. We were married a month later.

DEADRA: You do move fast.

QUINN: It was quickly obvious we didn't belong together. One night I found my belongings boxed up on the front porch. I took the hint.

DEADRA: That's quite a history.

QUINN: I haven't been married in five years. I'm on a roll.

(A pause.)

DEADRA: George told me you teach high school. What subject?

QUINN: History. You?

DEADRA: I'm a phlebotomist.

QUINN: Fantastic. What the hell's that?

DEADRA: I draw blood.

QUINN: I thought that was a vampire.

DEADRA: Cute, Quinn.

QUINN: You mean, that's it? You draw blood all day?

DEADRA: Mostly. I also do a little research, which I prefer. But unfortunately drawing blood keeps me busy.

QUINN: Did you know "vamp" comes from vampire? Are you a vamp, Deadra?

DEADRA: Weren't you going to call your sex partner again?

QUINN: You're trying to get rid of me.

DEADRA: I'm tired of being insulted.

QUINN: I wasn't insulting you. You're overly sensitive.

DEADRA: You're patronizing me, Quinn.

QUINN: Hey, lighten up. You call yourself a Scorpio? Where's the thick skin?

DEADRA: You'd better make your phone call.

QUINN: I think I'm changing my mind.

DEADRA: About what?

QUINN: I'll sleep on the floor.

DEADRA: Under the circumstances, maybe that's not such a good idea.

QUINN: You think I'll be in danger?

DEADRA: I'm wondering if I will.

QUINN: From what?

DEADRA: The question is, from who?

QUINN: From me? You think you're dealing with the King of the Date Rape here?

DEADRA: I didn't say that.

QUINN: Fuck you didn't. No pun intended.

DEADRA: I wouldn't be comfortable with you there.

QUINN: Look, lady, I can go pull peter in the bathroom if worst comes to worst.

DEADRA: What a colorful way to put it.

QUINN: Whatever turns you on.

DEADRA: Are you always this vulgar?

QUINN: You think I'm being vulgar?

DEADRA: What would you call it?

QUINN: Being pissed.

DEADRA: Then I owe you an apology.

QUINN: Damn right.

DEADRA: Some people change personality completely when they drink. I don't really know you, Quinn.

QUINN: The only way I change is that booze loosens me up.

DEADRA: Is that why you drink?

QUINN: What kind of question is that?

DEADRA: I'm just curious. I drink for the social life.

QQUIN: You can find a social life in church.

DEADRA: Not any more. I'm more or less a defrocked Catholic.

QUINN: I figured.

DEADRA: You did?

QUINN: You reek Catholicism, Deadra. You ever think about entering a nunnery?

DEADRA: As a matter of fact, I did. When I was in junior high.

QUINN: What changed your mind?

DEADRA: Smoking cigarettes. I loved to smoke cigarettes.

QUINN: I've never seen you smoke.

DEADRA: I quit. It killed both my parents. Are your parents living?

QUINN: Just my dad. He's in a retirement center in Seattle.

DEADRA: Any brothers or sisters?

QUINN: No.

DEADRA: I have a twin sister.

QUINN: Really? I can't imagine what it would be like to be a twin.

DEADRA: We're not close.

QUINN: You never dressed up alike and the rest?

DEADRA: Sure, in grade school. When we started junior high, my parents divorced and I went with Dad and Megan went with Mom. They were dead before we graduated.

QUINN: Where is she now?

DEADRA: She's the success story of the family. She teaches biology at Harvard. We exchange Christmas cards, and that's about it.

(She notices that Quinn is staring at her in a funny way.)

DEADRA: What's the matter?

QUINN: I'm trying to imagine two of you. It's a little mind-boggling. Is your twin married?

DEADRA: Happily so, as near as I can tell.

QUINN: How come you never remarried?

DEADRA: I'd settle for meeting someone who keeps my interest.

QUINN: Like George.

DEADRA: George is a good buddy, yes.

QUINN: What about a romantic interest?

DEADRA: Guys seem to want more than I can deliver.

QUINN: Like what, for example?

DEADRA: Like marriage or something just as serious.

QUINN: And you're not the marrying kind.

DEADRA: Definitely not.

398

QUINN: A real heart-breaker.

DEADRA: You, of all people, should respect the avoidance of marriage.

QUINN: Touché. I'm losing points here, aren't I?

DEADRA: You're trying much too hard, Quinn.

QUINN: Ah. You like men who play hard to get. I can do that.

DEADRA: Maybe you should make that phone call.

QUINN: Tell you what. If she's not home, I got a buddy where I can crash. Either way, you'll have my pad to yourself.

DEADRA: You're too young to use a word like "pad".

QUINN: My dad raised me on Kerouac and Ginsberg. Here's the key. Let me write down the address.

(He'll scribble the address on a bar napkin.)

DEADRA: I feel guilty kicking you out of your own apartment.

QUINN: But think how safe you'll be from my crazed Scorpio rapist hormones.

DEADRA: Okay, you win. Sleep on the floor.

QUINN: I don't want to sleep on the floor.

DEADRA: You're sure?

QUINN: Of course I'm sure. If Melinda's not home, I'll head for the Dandelion Pub. I'll find a lonely lady to take me home.

DEADRA: You do that often?

QUINN: Not often enough. So make yourself at home. I think I have leftover pizza in the refrig. Watch TV, play tapes, whatever you want.

DEADRA: What kind of music do you like?

QUINN: I find myself playing the same music my dad listened to. I think I was brain-washed as a kid.

DEADRA: Like for instance?

QUINN: You ever hear of Gerry Mulligan?

DEADRA: Of course. I love him.

QUINN: You ever hear Mulligan with Chet Baker playing trumpet behind him? Like on "My Funny Valentine"?

DEADRA: I love the way they do that.

QUINN: You'll dig my tapes then.

DEADRA: It'll be a treat to hear some decent music. I just have an old radio at home.

QUINN: Shame on you.

DEADRA: I might treat myself to a CD player for Christmas.

QUINN: I've been meaning to upgrade myself. If I go CD before you do, I'll give you my cassette player.

DEADRA: That's sweet of you.

QUINN: I'm a sweet guy now and again.

DEADRA: I can see that. Maybe we could listen to a little music before you go over to your friend's.

QUINN: Some other time.

DEADRA: I should crash early anyway.

QUINN: Don't let me keep you up.

DEADRA: I can't thank you enough for this.

QUINN: What would you have done if I'd said no? Or put down conditions, like sleeping with me?

DEADRA: I don't know. Ask somebody else. I can always stay with my friend Annie, but I'd have to put up with whatever guy she drags home tonight.

QUINN: I need to meet Annie.

DEADRA: No, you don't.

QUINN: May I ask you something else before you go?

DEADRA: Of course.

QUINN: Why me?

DEADRA: Actually it was spontaneous.

QUINN: How do you mean?

DEADRA: If you remember, I was sitting at the end of the bar when you came in, and there was a stool next to me but you didn't take it.

QUINN: True.

DEADRA: Why not?

QUINN: Seemed a little forward.

DEADRA: You really are shy.

QUINN: I hadn't filled my tank yet. I sat down at the bar, and you bought me a drink. Then you suggested we get a table. I assumed you were hustling me.

DEADRA: Really?

QUINN: You don't see why?

DEADRA: I just wanted to talk to you. I see you in here all the time but we never talk.

QUINN: Well, tonight we broke the ice.

DEADRA: That we did, Quinn.

QUINN: Deadra. Did you know the name means sexy?

DEADRA: And what does Quinn mean?

QUINN: Intelligent.

DEADRA: Which you seem to be.

QUINN: Ditto, you. Sexy.

DEADRA: Thank you.

QUINN: I'd better make that phone call. Take care.

DEADRA: Thanks again.
QUINN: No problem.

(He leaves. Deadra watches him go. BLACKOUT.)

3/ The Bedroom. The Next Morning

(AT RISE: Deadra is in bed. She's partially dressed with a cover over her. Quinn enters. He sees that she is still asleep. He moves slowly into the room, grabs a towel that is on the floor, and exits to bathroom. BLACKOUT.)

4/ The Bedroom. Fifteen Minutes Later.

(LIGHTS UP: we hear a shower running. Deadra wakes, sits up. She hears the shower and is confused. She gets out of bed and moves closer to listen to the shower. Suddenly it goes off. She hurries back to bed and under the covers. Quinn enters wearing a robe.)

DEADRA: Good morning.
QUINN: Good morning. How'd you sleep?
DEADRA: Wonderfully. Have you been here long?

(Quinn studies her.)

QUINN: All night. You don't remember?
DEADRA: Of course I remember.
QUINN: It was incredible, wasn't it?

(She doesn't reply.)

QUINN: Maybe just for me.
DEADRA: No. I mean, yes, of course it was. I sure slept soundly.
QUINN: That you did.
DEADRA: I'm feeling just great.

(Quinn starts laughing.)

DEADRA: I don't see what's so amusing.
QUINN: You don't even remember our wild sex, do you? Be honest.

DEADRA: No, I don't.

QUINN: That's really terrific, Deadra. Cosmic sex and you can't even remember it.

DEADRA: I'm sorry. I'm sure it was wonderful.

(Quinn smiles and shakes his head.)

DEADRA: I guess I had too much to drink.

QUINN: No shit, Dick Tracy. I'm putting you on, Deadra. Sexy Lady of the Blackouts. You got on my case about having them, and you have them yourself.

DEADRA: You didn't spend the night?

QUINN: I said I wouldn't, and I didn't. I'm a gentleman and a scholar, in case you haven't noticed.

DEADRA: You found your lady friend?

QUINN: Unfortunately, no.

DEADRA: You picked up somebody at the Dandelion?

QUINN: I slept in the car.

DEADRA: In the car!

QUINN: In the car. I don't recommend it.

DEADRA: Why?

QUINN: I didn't want you to stay awake all night waiting for me to rape you.

DEADRA: I wouldn't've done that.

QUINN: We'll never know.

DEADRA: I'm really sorry.

QUINN: I'll recover.

DEADRA: Let me make it up to you. Buy you breakfast?

QUINN: I'll think about it.

DEADRA: It's the least I can do. Let me shower first. If you don't mind.

QUINN: Be my guest.

(She gets out of bed.)

QUINN: Where shall we eat?

DEADRA: You decide.

(She grabs the rest of her clothes and exits to the bathroom. Quinn watches her go. BLACKOUT.)

402

5/ Bedroom. Half An Hour Later.

(LIGHTS UP. Quinn is dressed. Deadra enters from the bathroom, dressed.)

QUINN: Did you listen to Mulligan last night?
DEADRA: I was so tired I went straight to bed.
QUINN: So what about today? Going back home to face the guests?
DEADRA: I'm going to put my foot down. I've got to get John to go to the hospital.
QUINN: Or at least to go home.
DEADRA: He doesn't have a home.
QUINN: He's just visiting?
DEADRA: He and Maggie have been living under a bridge.
QUINN: You put up homeless people? That's remarkable.
DEADRA: I wish I had a bigger place, so I could put up more.
QUINN: Isn't it dangerous?
DEADRA: Life is dangerous.
QUINN: There's a bit of Mother Teresa in you, isn't there?
DEADRA: I can sympathize with them. I lived on the streets myself once.
QUINN: Seriously?
DEADRA: Just to see what it was like. It was horrible, even knowing I could quit and go home whenever I wanted. It's one thing to have an intellectual understanding of what they go through, but try living it yourself.
QUINN: How long were you out there?
DEADRA: Three days. That's all I could take.
QUINN: I'm impressed. How often do you put these homeless people up?
DEADRA: Usually only in emergencies. Or when I feel too guilty about having an empty sofa. I know John and Maggie from the neighborhood, I'm sure you've seen them around. I ran into them during the rainy spell last week, and John had hurt his foot, so I let them get out of the weather. When it stopped raining, they didn't leave.
QUINN: Because you don't have the heart to evict them.
DEADRA: Well, I have to put my foot down.
QUINN: Damn right you do. Deadra, you can't save the world. I hope you know that.
DEADRA: I'm not trying to save the world. I was just letting them get out of the weather for a while.

QUINN: I was going to say you're a person who can't say "No" —
except you said no often enough last night.

DEADRA: That's because you quit too soon.

QUINN: I did?

DEADRA: Couldn't you tell I wanted us to come here together? I
suggested we listen to music.

QUINN: I thought that was just to listen to music.

DEADRA: I was warming up to you.

QUINN: Now you tell me.

DEADRA: You were in too much of a hurry. Not a good part of your
personality, Quinn.

QUINN: I'll work on it.

DEADRA: It's just as well. We wouldn't have gotten any sleep.

QUINN: Probably not.

DEADRA: And I really needed a good night's sleep.

QUINN: Which you got.

DEADRA: Thanks to you.

QUINN: Which I didn't. Thanks to you.

DEADRA: Now you're making me feel guilty.

QUINN: You do that a lot. Would a Bloody Mary make you feel
better?

DEADRA: You're having one?

QUINN: My Sunday luxury.

DEADRA: I'd love one.

QUINN: Not here. The Gypsy's open this early. They also serve
breakfast.

DEADRA: Then the Gypsy it is.

(BLACKOUT.)

6/ Bedroom. Two Hours Later.

(LIGHTS UP. Quinn and Deadra return after breakfast.)

DEADRA: I know I left it here somewhere.

(She's looking for something.)

DEADRA: Maybe in the bathroom.

(She exits — and quickly returns, holding her lipstick.)

DEADRA: Tah-dah!

QUINN: Great.

DEADRA: So. Thank you for the good company.

QUINN: Do you have to run off?

DEADRA: I'm dreading it — but I do. I have to tell them to go.

QUINN: So do it.

DEADRA: I will. I really will.

QUINN: You want help?

DEADRA: How do you mean?

QUINN: Moral support. I'll tag along. Make sure you do it.

DEADRA: You don't have anything better to do today?

QUINN: Go to the bar and watch football.

DEADRA: Isn't that what you like to do?

QUINN: It's what I do because there's nothing else to do. So when do we leave?

DEADRA: They sleep even later than me. That's another problem. I have to creep around in my own apartment.

QUINN: Not good, Deadra.

DEADRA: I know.

QUINN: So we'll give them thirty minutes, an hour, and then we drag their asses to the emergency room. Sound good?

DEADRA: Perfect. We'll do it.

QUINN: Absolutely.

(A pause: they look at one another.)

DEADRA: What's the matter?

QUINN: I have this sudden urge to kiss you.

DEADRA: I know.

QUINN: How do you feel about that?

DEADRA: I think you talk too much.

(They kiss. And again. BLACKOUT.)

7/ Bedroom. Two Hours Later.

(LIGHTS UP. Quinn and Deadra are dressing after lovemaking.)

DEADRA: I feel so damn good.

QUINN: Two of us.

DEADRA: Unfortunately I still have guests at home.

QUINN: We're supposed to take them to the hospital.

DEADRA: Right.

QUINN: So tell me something. Is this a one-time deal or do we have something worth pursuing here?

DEADRA: Don't move too fast for me, Quinn.

QUINN: Okay.

(A pause.)

DEADRA: Yes.

QUINN: Yes — as in ...yes?

DEADRA: I want to do this again.

QUINN: Good. Me, too.

DEADRA: But don't push it, okay?

QUINN: One moment of erotic ecstasy at a time.

DEADRA: Don't try to verbalize everything.

QUINN: What I meant is, you're a free spirit. I respect that.

DEADRA: Good.

QUINN: And I'll promise you something. I won't ask you to marry me.

DEADRA: Good!

(A pause.)

DEADRA: It's always so great in the beginning, isn't it?

QUINN: Beginnings are better than endings.

DEADRA: What happens? Why can't people maintain?

QUINN: The beginning is simple. Man, woman, chemistry, lust, satisfaction. Now we have to get up and go out there and take your guests to the hospital, and who the hell knows what's waiting for us, all ready to pounce on this wonderful biological simplicity and turn it into some complicated head trip. The mind defeats the body every time.

DEADRA: You know what usually ruins it for me? The guy goes out and picks somebody up. We have a great sex life, and he still messes around. Why do guys always do that?

QUINN: Why did my wife ruin a perfectly wonderful marriage by going out and having an affair with a woman?

DEADRA: Because it wasn't so perfect for her after all.

QUINN: So maybe the sex with these guys isn't as perfect as you think.

DEADRA: At least we don't have that problem. Do we?

QUINN: Definitely not.

DEADRA: I want what I'm feeling now to last as long as it can.

QUINN: We can do that.

DEADRA: I hope so.

QUINN: You don't sound very secure about it.

DEADRA: I guess not.

QUINN: What happens if you go out on a limb and trust me not to mess around behind your back?

DEADRA: Trust a man? There's a leap of faith.

QUINN: Trust me. I'm a one-woman kind of guy, Deadra.

DEADRA: With three ex-wives.

QUINN: I married them one at a time, okay? I'm a serial monogamist.

(A pause.)

QUINN: And I can trust you, too, right?

DEADRA: When I'm happy, I don't sleep around.

QUINN: I believe you.

DEADRA: Good, because I'll never lie to you. Not even when, you know ...

QUINN: When...?

DEADRA: Everything turns to crap.

QUINN: As it has to, right?

DEADRA: As it always has. With you, too, Quinn. Three marriages, for God's sake. Did you expect to get divorced when you said, "I do"?

QUINN: Of course not.

DEADRA: I rest my case.

(A pause.)

DEADRA: You know what I really like? You're so easy to talk to.

QUINN: Good.

DEADRA: You're different than I imagined. You're so quiet, I thought you'd be boring. Do you realize how many boring people there are in the world?

QUINN: Most of them on a barstool.

DEADRA: Which is where I usually find you.

QUINN: Touché.

DEADRA: You're interesting, Quinn. That's a gift.

QUINN: I like talking to you, too.

DEADRA: That's going to help us, isn't it?

QUINN: It can't hurt.

DEADRA: I didn't think you liked me.

QUINN: Why?

DEADRA: Because you never talked to me.

QUINN: We never ended up on adjacent barstools.

DEADRA: I thought you dismissed me as just another stupid chick at the bar, like I never read a book in my life.

QUINN: So what have you read lately?

DEADRA: "I'm dysfunctional, you're dysfunctional."

QUINN: Don't change the subject.

DEADRA: That's the name of the book.

QUINN: Great title!

DEADRA: It's an expose of the self-help industry.

QUINN: Long overdue.

DEADRA: Today it's "in" to be an addict or a victim — or both.

QUINN: With a tortured inner child.

DEADRA: And abusive parents.

QUINN: Incest victim.

DEADRA: Date raped in junior high.

QUINN: Can't express feelings.

DEADRA: Especially men.

QUINN: That's who I meant.

DEADRA: Poor self-image.

QUINN: Post-menstrual Stress Disorder.

DEADRA: Shrinking-dick Disorder.

QUINN: Like, shit happens, right? I hate whiners. Why can't people stop wallowing in the past and get on with their lives?

DEADRA: Exactly.

QUINN: Of course, everybody on the goddamn planet is in denial about something.

DEADRA: Usually about being in denial!

QUINN: Absolutely.

DEADRA: What are you in denial about?

QUINN: You don't want to know.

DEADRA: Yes, I do.

QUINN: No, you don't.

DEADRA: Do.

QUINN: Don't.

DEADRA: Tell me!

(She starts tickling him.)

DEADRA: Tell me!

408

QUINN: Okay! Stop it!

DEADRA: What are you in denial about?

QUINN: You tell me first.

DEADRA: I asked you first.

QUINN: But mine's heavier than yours.

DEADRA: Okay. I'm in denial about — how afraid I am that this is going to end sooner than I want it to.

QUINN: Maybe you'll be surprised.

DEADRA: What are you in denial about?

QUINN: Falling in love with you.

DEADRA: No.

QUINN: That I'm bound to eventually

DEADRA: No! Goddamn it, Quinn! Why do you have to go and ruin everything?

QUINN: I knew you wouldn't like it.

DEADRA: Then why didn't you just keep it to yourself?

QUINN: Because it's the truth.

DEADRA: I don't want to hear it.

QUINN: You'd rather I lie?

DEADRA: I'd rather enjoy what we have!

QUINN: Please don't do this.

DEADRA: You did it, Quinn.

QUINN: I'm not in love with you yet, okay? I was only talking about future possibilities.

DEADRA: I would never marry you, Quinn. Just get that idea out of your head entirely.

QUINN: I never asked you! I told you, I never will ask you. I mean it. Deadra, for Christ's sake, you're making a—

TOGETHER: Mountain out of a molehill!

DEADRA: You and your goddamn clichés.

QUINN: I didn't think you'd get so upset.

DEADRA: Because you don't know me at all.

QUINN: True. But I want to.

DEADRA: Don't push any of that Valentine's Day crap at me, okay? No flowers, no candy—

QUINN: Deadra, slow down! Just relax a minute. A moment ago you were marveling at how good you felt.

DEADRA: You ruined it.

QUINN: We can get back to where we were.

DEADRA: The context is different now.

QUINN: It doesn't have to be.

DEADRA: I'm not the marrying kind. That's the first thing you
have to know about me.

QUINN: You're a free spirit. Got it.

DEADRA: I don't want you to lay any expectations on me, okay? If
we do this, we do it one day at a time.

QUINN: I can do that.

DEADRA: Just don't lay some marriage or commitment trip on me,
okay?

QUINN: I promise.

DEADRA: You start doing that, Quinn, you just set yourself up for
heartbreak. Look at your own life, with three marriages. Three times you
thought it was for eternity, three times it got shoved back in your face.
Who needs it?

QUINN: We don't need that, Deadra. You're right.

DEADRA: I just want to go slow with this.

QUINN: We will. We are.

DEADRA: I just want to feel happy for as long as I can.

QUINN: In the present tense.

DEADRA: Exactly. In the present tense.

QUINN: No talking about the future.

DEADRA: Exactly.

QUINN: One present tense day at a time.

DEADRA: Right.

QUINN: I can do that.

DEADRA: I hope so.

QUINN: Deadra?

(He kisses her. At first she resists. Then she gives in, and they
enjoy a long, passionate kiss.)

DEADRA: Don't do that again, Quinn.

QUINN: Promise. I want you to hear something.

(Quinn puts on the Mulligan-Baker version of "My Funny
Valentine." It will begin playing softly in the background.)

QUINN: Can you remember the first time you heard this?

DEADRA: Not really.

QUINN: I can, like it was yesterday. I was in the Army. I'm one of
the lucky few who had a great military experience. I mean it. When I look
at what other guys went through, even if they didn't go to Nam, I really

410

had it made. They sent me to the Army Language School in Monterey; I became a Russian linguist.

DEADRA: That's impressive.

QUINN: It wasn't the job that was so great but the guys I was with. Most of them had degrees in history or literature or philosophy. They joined the Army Security Agency to escape the war and bide time and try to figure out what to do with their lives. It was like having a hundred big brothers, all of them giving me great books to read.

DEADRA: I never heard of the Army being like that.

QUINN: One night after we'd made it back just before curfew — we were stationed in Germany, and it really pissed everybody off that the Army had curfew but the Air Force didn't. This particular night, we came back to the billets just before curfew and, as we usually did, we drank a few beers that somebody had snuck in from the NCO Club, and we listened to records. That's when a buddy of mine, Donovan, put on Mulligan-Baker doing "My Funny Valentine." Man, it really hit me. I'd just figured out what a stupid thing it was to get married and had sent her — this woman who was my wife, for God's sake! — a letter about it. I'd get her letter the next day, saying that we needed to annul the marriage, the same thing I'd written. Our letters crossed in the mail.

DEADRA: You were on the same wavelength.

QUINN: Donovan put on "My Funny Valentine," and I just started weeping. Bawling like a baby. It was so goddamn beautiful, so incredibly lyrical, fragile, delicate — everything that my life wasn't.

(Deadra embraces him. Then Quinn pulls back, and they start dancing to the music.)

QUINN: Today my life feels very simple and very beautiful.

(A pause.)

QUINN: May I ask you something?

DEADRA: Don't talk, Quinn. Don't ask anything, and don't say anything. Just hold me close. Just dance.

QUINN: I can do that.

DEADRA: Then shut up.

QUINN: I can do that, too.

(Deadra stops dancing.)

DEADRA: Quinn? Please don't ruin it.

(Quinn raises both hands, a gesture of surrender. He takes her in his arms again. They start dancing.)

(FADE TO BLACKOUT as they dance.)

8/ The Bedroom. The Next Morning, 3 A.M.

(Dim lights. Deadra is in bed, asleep. Quinn is sitting up at the bedside table, eating something)

DEADRA: Quinn?
QUINN: Hmm?
DEADRA: What are you doing?
QUINN: Umm-hmm!
DEADRA: Is something wrong?
QUINN: Umm-UMM! It's great!

(Deadra slides over beside him.)

DEADRA: What're you eating?
QUINN: Peanut butter and pickles.
DEADRA: What?
QUINN: Peanut butter pickles! Want to try one?

(He prepares a peanut-buttered pickle for her.)

DEADRA: Couldn't you sleep?
QUINN: I'm famished. This is fantastic, here.

(He shoves the pickle at her.)

DEADRA: Quinn! What is it?
QUINN: I told you. A dill pickle with peanut butter spread on it.
DEADRA: It looks sickening.
QUINN: Don't judge it. Try it. Open up.
DEADRA: No!

(He grabs her face, playfully trying to open her mouth with one hand in order to shove in the pickle with the other.)

QUINN: Where's your spirit of adventure?
DEADRA: It'll make me sick!
QUINN: Just try one bite.
DEADRA: Stop it! I'll try, stop, I promise I'll try.

(Quinn stops.)

QUINN: One bite.
DEADRA: Just one.

(He holds out the pickle for her to bite.)

DEADRA: Let me hold it.
QUINN: You don't trust me. I'm crushed.

(He gives her the pickle.)

DEADRA: Just one bite ...

(She takes a small bite. She tastes it,)

DEADRA: Oh my God ...

(She takes another bite.)

QUINN: Good, right?
DEADRA: Umm-hmm!
QUINN: I'll make more.
DEADRA: Quinn, this is amazing!
QUINN: Stick with me, babe. Your taste buds will go places they've never been before.
DEADRA: This is incredible! Why haven't I ever heard of it?
QUINN: You hang around with the wrong crowd. Ready for another?
DEADRA: Yes!
QUINN: Come and get it.

(He holds the pickle in his teeth, half of it sticking out for Deadra to take. She comes to him and takes the exposed end into her mouth. They start chewing their own end of the pickle, their lips moving closer, until they touch in a kiss. Suddenly they are kissing passionately and falling back onto the bed — as the LIGHTS FADE TO BLACKOUT.)

9/ The Bedroom. Morning, 11 A.M.

(Quinn sits up in bed, writing.)

QUINN: You're witnessing history here. I wrote my first sonnet.
DEADRA: Congratulations.
QUINN: That's not the historical part. I may actually read it to you.
DEADRA: Please do!
QUINN: I think it's kind of fun.
DEADRA: I'd love to hear it.
QUINN: Sonnet for an audience of two:

(He reads the sonnet with much energy:)

QUINN: To take my heart, please take my warts as well!
I'm not a perfect man — but still I grow
when most men at my age freeze what they know,
and growth leads where not you or I can tell.
Sometimes I belch! Sometimes I fart and smell!
Sometimes I wake you up before the dawn
and lead you to the kitchen arm-in-arm,
where peanut-buttered pickles ring our bell.
I don't mean all the stuff in marriage vows.
I mean the human truth from A to Z,
and if you find, my dear, that your heart bows
this way — then I'm for you, and you're for me.
What is life without a little fun?
Let me know if you think you're the one.

(Quinn grins.. Deadra looks at him seriously. BLACKOUT.)

(END OF ACT ONE)

414

ACT TWO

1/ The Bar. A Month Later.

(AT RISE: Quinn joins Deadra at a table in the bar. He carries a drink. She already has hers.)

QUINN: Sorry I'm late.
DEADRA: Quinn, I think we should talk about tomorrow.
QUINN: You're not getting cold feet on me?
DEADRA: Yes, I am.
QUINN: Deadra, we've been through this a million times.
DEADRA: Three or four.
QUINN: It's not a big deal. You don't have to meet him if you don't want to.
DEADRA: It would look rude not to.
QUINN: Then meet him.
DEADRA: It feels like you're taking me home to meet the family. That you want your father to approve of me.
QUINN: Okay, I'll cancel.
DEADRA: Why can't you just go see him alone?
QUINN: We go together, or we don't go.
DEADRA: I don't like that attitude at all.
QUINN: It's not about seeing dad anyway. It's about getting away together. It's about enjoying Seattle. Going to the public market and taking a ferry ride.
DEADRA: You know you have to see him if you're there.
QUINN: I can see him alone! Jesus Christ, Deadra, why does this have to be such a big issue with you?
DEADRA: Because you're going too fast for me. I'm not ready to meet your family.
QUINN: So screw it. We won't go.
DEADRA: You're not listening to me.
QUINN: The point is to enjoy Seattle together. I can't do that if I'm up there alone.
DEADRA: Why don't you go see your father? I have some things I want to do this weekend anyway.
QUINN: What things?
DEADRA: Does it matter?

415

(No reply.)

DEADRA: You don't own me, Quinn.

QUINN: I never said I owned you. Jesus.

DEADRA: You have expectations of me.

QUINN: You have expectations of me, too.

DEADRA: I'm beginning to feel...

QUINN: What?

DEADRA: Pressured.

QUINN: Pressured. Great.

DEADRA: It's how I feel.

QUINN: Deadra, you'd fuck up a wet dream.

DEADRA: That's a wonderful thing to tell me. Why in the world do you want to spend any time with me if all I do is fuck up your wet dreams?

(She gets up to leave.)

QUINN: Sit down. Please. I regret saying that.

(She sits back down.)

DEADRA: You damn well should regret saying it.

QUINN: Deadra, I'm aware of the fact that you need one hell of a lot more space than I do. I'm trying to give you that. I really am. Please try to give me a little slack here. I'm not a tyrant. I'm not into owning you in any way. I'm certainly not your husband and never will be.

DEADRA: Then you'll go to Seattle alone?

QUINN: Is that what you want?

DEADRA: I know you're looking forward to seeing your father. Admit it.

QUINN: Admitted.

DEADRA: Then go see him.

QUINN: I just thought we could kill two birds with one stone and make a weekend of it. I didn't know you were busy. If you'd've told me, I never would have suggested the trip.

DEADRA: It's not something I have to do. Just something I need to take care of sooner rather than later.

QUINN: Fine.

DEADRA: What I have to do is clean my apartment. Even though I spend most of my time in your apartment lately, I still pay rent and it's beginning to look like a pig pen over there. I need a day to clean it. I'm going to let some people stay there for a while.

QUINN: Homeless people?

DEADRA: Don't look at me like I'm crazy. Maggie's pregnant. She can't sleep under a bridge in her condition.

QUINN: What's this Mother Teresa complex about?

DEADRA: Pardon me if I care about people.

QUINN: The homeless problem is much bigger than your ability to solve it, Deadra.

DEADRA: I don't think in grandiose terms like that. I'm simple-minded — the rent's paid on an apartment nobody is using, and other people desperately need a roof over their heads. I don't find that very complicated.

QUINN: But why do you have to clean it? It can't be worse than living under a bridge, no matter how dirty it is.

DEADRA: I would never invite guests into a dirty apartment!

QUINN: Deadra, I don't want to argue about it with you. I was looking forward to showing you Seattle, okay? I'm as simple-minded as you are.

DEADRA: And I'd love to go to Seattle with you sometime.

QUINN: Right.

DEADRA: Why don't you believe me?

QUINN: If you wanted to see Seattle so badly, I think you'd jump at a chance to go.

DEADRA: I have to have a certain order in my life, Quinn. I can't drop everything and play house with you every weekend. Especially after spending all week with you.

QUINN: Then clean it tomorrow.

DEADRA: I will.

QUINN: I probably should clean mine, too.

DEADRA: I wasn't going to bring it up.

QUINN: Thanks a lot.

DEADRA: What about visiting your father?

QUINN: It can wait.

DEADRA: Then may I make a suggestion?

QUINN: Why the fuck not?

DEADRA: God, you get bummed out easily.

QUINN: Who's bummed out?

DEADRA: You are! I thought this weekend was special, like it was your father's birthday or something. If it isn't, then how about this? We do Seattle next weekend instead.

QUINN: You'd come with me?

DEADRA: Of course. But I'm not sure I want to meet your father yet. We'll play that one by ear when we get there.

QUINN: That's fair.

DEADRA: You don't mind waiting a week?

QUINN: Of course not. Why the hell didn't you say this in the beginning?

DEADRA: Your energy was in charge, Quinn.

QUINN: Week after next it is. Toast.

(They clink glasses.)

QUINN: And tomorrow we'll clean our apartments. Meet for dinner?

DEADRA: Sounds good.

QUINN: Amazing.

DEADRA: What is?

QUINN: I thought we were having a fight.

DEADRA: Well, we were getting in the neighborhood.

QUINN: If you'd've just asked if we could wait a week, we wouldn't't've had to go through all that.

DEADRA: I told you as soon as I could get a word in.

QUINN: Not true.

DEADRA: Quinn, you were on your little hurt-feelings trip and I was trying to change the subject.

QUINN: Deadra...forget it.

DEADRA: What?

QUINN: It's not worth pursuing.

DEADRA: If we start letting something fester, Quinn, we're headed for trouble. What were you going to say?

QUINN: I was going to say, I now am going to say, that you and I are too much alike sometimes. Both bull-headed as hell. That's Scorpios again, isn't it?

DEADRA: No doubt.

QUINN: I'm sure glad we have great sex. I can put up with almost anything.

DEADRA: I hope you don't think that's a compliment. Because I hate it when you say things like that

QUINN: Let's change the subject.

(A pause.)

QUINN: How'd your day go?

DEADRA: You don't want to know.

QUINN: Now I really want to know.

DEADRA: I got fired.

QUINN: What?

DEADRA: I got canned.

QUINN: That's terrible. What happened?

DEADRA: First, it's not terrible. It's probably a blessing in disguise. The hospital belongs in the Middle Ages. This saves me from quitting.

QUINN: What was their reason?

DEADRA: They pulled a surprise drug test a week ago. I flunked

QUINN: Then challenge the results.

DEADRA: I flunked it, Quinn. Fair and square. They found marijuana. I usually have a joint in the can every morning.

QUINN: You smoke pot at work?

DEADRA: Don't look at me like the Moral Crusader. I know you drink at lunch because I've been there.

QUINN: It's not the same thing.

DEADRA: Pot's better for you than booze is.

QUINN: Pot's illegal.

DEADRA: So's oral sex in many parts of this wonderful country. Does it stop anybody? Does it stop you?

QUINN: So what are you going to do?

DEADRA: I can't believe you asked that.

QUINN: I'm trying to be supportive here.

DEADRA: By treating me like an idiot? I'm going to get another job, Quinn. I have two interviews Monday.

QUINN: I didn't mean to imply you weren't going to get another job.

DEADRA: And you're not going to support me financially, ever, so don't even ask.

QUINN: Never crossed my mind.

DEADRA: One interview's with a clinic I really, really want to work for. Cross your fingers for me.

QUINN: I will.

(A pause.)

DEADRA: What is it? You're dying to ask me something.

QUINN: You really smoke pot every morning?

DEADRA: Most mornings. You have a problem with that?

QUINN: No. I just didn't know.

DEADRA: Do I know everything about you? Of course not.

QUINN: It doesn't affect you at work?

DEADRA: Of course it does. That's why I do it. It calms me down. It helps me get through the day. You disapprove, don't you?

QUINN: Not really. I'm just surprised.

DEADRA: Shocked.

QUINN: Yes, a little shocked.

DEADRA: A whole lot shocked.

QUINN: Not a whole lot. Just — shocked.

DEADRA: Do two martinis at lunch affect how you teach in the afternoon?

QUINN: No.

DEADRA: You're sure about that?

QUINN: I don't teach, Deadra. I sell magazines.

(Deadra is shocked to hear this. She waits for more but none is coming.)

DEADRA: What're you talking about?

QUINN: I lost my teaching job two years ago.

DEADRA: George said you're a teacher.

QUINN: Everybody in here thinks I still teach. I never got around to telling anybody.

DEADRA: What happened?

QUINN: They found a pint of vodka in my desk. Actually they were pretty nice about it. I resigned, and it stayed out of the papers.

DEADRA: Why didn't you tell me?

QUINN: I just did.

DEADRA: Why didn't you tell me before?

QUINN: I didn't want to disappoint you. Who wants to go with a guy who sells *Sports Illustrated* and *Better Homes & Gardens*?

DEADRA: Oh, Quinn...I bet you're a great teacher.

QUINN: Killer teacher.

DEADRA: You can find another position.

QUINN: Probably. Just haven't had the energy to look yet. You really don't want to stay at the hospital?

DEADRA: No way. Ever since it was sold, they run it like a business. To hell with the patients. I'm glad to get out. I should be celebrating.

QUINN: To your getting the job at the clinic.

DEADRA: To you finding another teaching job.

QUINN: When I'm ready.

(They clink glasses and drink.)

QUINN: To going to Seattle in two weeks.

(They clink glasses and drink.)

DEADRA: To us. May we always be able to talk openly to one another.
QUINN: To telling the truth.
DEADRA: All of it.
QUINN: And nothing but.
DEADRA: No matter how much it hurts.
QUINN: No matter how much.

(They clink glasses. BLACKOUT.)

2/ The Bar. 10 Days Later.

(AT RISE: Deadra sits at a table. Quinn stands behind her, his hands over her eyes.)

QUINN: Guess who?
DEADRA: Someone with warm hands.
QUINN: Animal, mineral or vegetable?
DEADRA: Animal. Very.
QUINN: Masculine or feminine?
DEADRA: Definitely masculine.
QUINN: Species?
DEADRA: Homo sexappealinus.
QUINN: Very good.
DEADRA: Homo sounds wrong. Macho sexappealinus.
QUINN: Macho? Give me a break.
DEADRA: You're right. Mascu-sexappealinus.
QUINN: -ah, -um.
DEADRA: What?
QUINN: I was declining it. Mascu-sexappealinus, mascu-sexappealina, mascu-sexappealinum.
DEADRA: Where did you learn Latin?
QUINN: In college.
DEADRA: I learn something new about you every day, Quinn.

QUINN: Quinn! You know who it is!

(He removes his hands, bends over and kisses her.)

QUINN: Happy birthday.

(He sits down.)

DEADRA: You remembered.
QUINN: I can do that sometimes..
DEADRA: I've never been big on birthdays.
QUINN: There's a first time for everything.

(He takes a present out of his sportscoat pocket, a ring box.)

QUINN: Happy birthday, Deadra.

(He holds out the ring box but Deadra doesn't reach for it. Quinn puts it on the table in front of her.)

QUINN: Open it.
DEADRA: I don't want a present.
QUINN: Come on. I went to a lot of trouble to do this.
DEADRA: This is not a good surprise, Quinn.
QUINN: What's the matter with you?
DEADRA: I can tell what's going on here, and I don't like it one bit.
QQUIN: You have no idea what's in the box.
DEADRA: A ring.
QUINN: Deadra—
DEADRA: Goddamn you, you have no right giving me a ring!
QUINN: It's not a ring, okay?
DEADRA: You always have to screw everything up!
QUINN: Hello? It's not a ring!
DEADRA: You always make everything so complicated!
QUINN: Calling Deadra! There is no ring in that box. Repeat, there is no ring in that box.
DEADRA: It looks like a ring.
QUINN: It's a box I found in a dumpster, for God's sake.
DEADRA: It's a ring box, Quinn.
QUINN: Fine, it's a ring box — but it is *not* a ring! Now will you open the goddamn thing so we can move on with our lives here?
DEADRA: You shouldn't have gotten me a present.

422

QUINN: I'm sorry, but I did. It will never happen again. Will you open it, please?

(A pause. Then Deadra opens the box. She takes out a folded sheet of paper. She looks at it.)

DEADRA: You wrote me a poem?
QUINN: Another sonnet.
DEADRA: I'm sorry I got angry. Do I get to hear it?
QUINN: Of course. It's your birthday present.

(She hands the paper back and Quinn prepares to read:)

QUINN: It's not as good as the other one.
DEADRA: Quinn...
QUINN: The skyline hangs above the bay, a mist
of mystery as in a dream, and we
stand close upon the ferry's deck and kiss,
and I feel all the world as it should be.
These are moments that my heart holds dear.
When you are near, somehow I am alive
more than I've been, and everything is clear
to me: I know for what I want to strive.
Yet I don't want my love to burden you,
a chain around your heart, presumption of
your time. The things that I would hope to do
for us are full of caring and my love.
I love you for each moment that I have
and ask from you such love as you can give.

(A pause. Deadra is very moved.)

QUINN: What do you think?
DEADRA: No one ever wrote me poetry before.
QUINN: I kept thinking of our ferry ride in Seattle, and this what came out.
DEADRA: It's beautiful. Goddamn it.
QUINN: "Goddamn it"?
DEADRA: Yes! You have no right to give me something so beautiful.
QUINN: Holy Christ.

DEADRA: Quinn, when you do this, it makes me feel like I'm supposed to do something in return.

QUINN: That's your problem, Deadra. I'm making no demands here.

DEADRA: That's not true.

QUINN: I'm not!

DEADRA: You want romance, Quinn.

QUINN: Doesn't everybody?

DEADRA: No! I don't.

QUINN: Come on.

DEADRA: I'm serious. You write this, and I'm expected to live up to some romantic image of how it was in Seattle, for just a moment, on a ferry ride.

QUINN: Deadra, listen to what I wrote: "I love you for each moment that I have, and ask from you such love as you can give." Get it? "Such love as you can give." That is not a demand. That leaves you a free spirit, Deadra, so get off this fixation of being pressured to do something, okay?

DEADRA: You're asking me to love you. Isn't that what you wrote? "Such love..." You want me to love you.

QUINN: Of course I want you to love me.

DEADRA: I told you how I feel about that.

QUINN: That the word "love" is hugely misused. We agreed about that.

DEADRA: So we weren't going to use it, remember?

QUINN: I was writing a love poem, Deadra. The word "love" is usually included.

DEADRA: You had no right to write me a love poem. It puts me on the spot.

QUINN: Well, excuse me!

(He tears up the poem and drops the pieces on the table.)

QUINN: There. Happy birthday anyway. How about a different present? How about a triple vodka collins?

DEADRA: Every time I'm honest with you, you get mad.

QUINN: Deadra, did you enjoy Seattle?

DEADRA: Of course I did.

QUINN: And the ferry ride?

DEADRA: It was a really magical night.

QUINN: Then what's wrong with trying to commemorate it in a sonnet? It's a very old tradition.

DEADRA: Quinn...

424

QUINN: You know what I think? You, my dear, are afraid to be happy. You're afraid of how good I make you feel. You're afraid of all this.

DEADRA: Don't do it, Quinn.

QUINN: But why? Why would somebody be afraid of happiness? Man, I have been asking myself that for a few weeks now. Why is Deadra so afraid of happiness? Because she's been hurt. Because she's been hurt really badly. So badly that she's spending all of her energy making sure she never gets hurt again, and one way to do that is not to let anyone get too close to her because if they can't get too close, then they can't touch her, and if they can't touch her in her most intimate places, in her heart of hearts, then that means they really can't hurt her. You've got a bullet-proof shield around your heart, Deadra. And when I get too close, when my love starts bouncing off the shield, then you panic and lash out at me.

(A pause.)

QUINN: Am I close?

DEADRA: No, you're not.

QUINN: Bullshit.

DEADRA: I didn't want to have to tell you this, Quinn. You're forcing my hand here.

QUINN: Good. No secrets, Scorpio. Put all the cards on the table.

DEADRA: I hate doing this. It's going to sound so goddamn maudlin.

QUINN: I'll bear that in mind.

DEADRA: You bastard.

QUINN: Whatever, Deadra. Are you going to level with me or not?

DEADRA: It didn't have to be this way. If you'd just respect my space and stop trying to go so fast.

QUINN: Deadra, I love you. Everything that you're about concerns me.

DEADRA: I don't want you to love me.

QUINN: That's clear enough. Do you have something new to add?

DEADRA: Yes — but it's going to sound like a soap opera.

QUINN: Life is a soap opera, Deadra. Where have you been?

DEADRA: Promise not to interrupt til I'm done.

QUINN: Promise.

DEADRA: This is going to sound so goddamn sappy.

QUINN: I won't laugh, okay?

DEADRA: About five months ago I went in for my routine physical and they found some things that weren't good. Don't ask for details because I'm not going to tell you. I shouldn't be telling you this much. The point is, there's really nothing they can do for me, so they figure I have six months to a year...I'm like a ticking time bomb here, Quinn. That's why I can't be in a serious relationship with you. When I explode, I don't want to take anyone with me.

QUINN: Deadra...

DEADRA: I'm sure this is much harder for you than it is for me. I just got dealt a bad biological deck or something. It happens to people all the time.

QUINN: Is it cancer or what? There must be some kind of treatment.

DEADRA: I said there's nothing they can do.

QUINN: I wish you'd've told me earlier.

DEADRA: We shouldn't have gotten involved. I'm just going to hurt you.

QUINN: Hurt happens. I'm going to take time off from work.

DEADRA: Quinn, don't.

QUINN: I can get a loan, I can borrow money. We'll take a trip. Go to Mexico or someplace.

DEADRA: Listen to you.

QUINN: I'm serious.

DEADRA: I know you are. That's the problem.

QUINN: Goddamn it, I love you! I want as much of you as time will let me have.

DEADRA: Where were you five or ten years ago?

QUINN: In this bar, Deadra. Where were you?

DEADRA: In Nebraska.

QUINN: Does your sister know?

DEADRA: No.

QUINN: I'm glad you told me.

DEADRA: How can you say that?

QUINN: How do you think I'd've felt learning this after you're gone? Worse than now, believe me.

DEADRA: I hate this conversation.

QUINN: This is reality. It's not a soap opera, Deadra. It's what is happening with you, and that affects what is happening with me.

DEADRA: Which is exactly what I didn't want to happen.

QUINN: I'm glad you told me.

DEADRA: Nothing can ever stay simple, can it?

QUINN: This is getting very simple, Deadra. We're down to the nitty-gritty here.

426

DEADRA: We don't have to decide anything right now, do we?
QUINN: Of course not.
DEADRA: Good. I've had enough of this for one night.
QUINN: No problem.
DEADRA: What time is it?
QUINN: Eightish.
DEADRA: I told Annie I'd stop by.
QUINN: Meet you here later?
DEADRA: Sure.
QUINN: How long will you be?
DEADRA: I don't know. Not long. See you later then.

(She gets up to go. Quinn stands.)

QUINN: Deadra? We'll do the best we can, okay?

(Deadra looks at him. BLACKOUT.)

3/ The Bedroom. Later That Night.

(AT RISE: Quinn is finishing dialing a number on the phone.)

QUINN: Annie?...This is Quinn. Is Deadra there?...She said she was coming to see you....Hours ago. Around eight. ...Listen — do you know where else she might be? Some other girlfriend's or something? ... Thanks...No, I'm all right. Talk to you later.

(He hangs up. He stares across the room. BLACKOUT.)

4/ The Bedroom. The Next Afternoon.

(AT RISE: Deadra is putting clothes she's left at Quinn's apartment into a large, plastic garbage bag. She carries it out of the apartment. BLACKOUT.)

5/ The Bedroom. A Week Later.

(AT RISE: Quinn is on the phone.)

427

QUINN: Seattle?...Did she give you her return address?...Annie, I have to get in touch with her....I'm worried about her, Annie—...Annie, listen to me. I just want to get in touch with her, okay? Just to see how she's doing.....Because I'm worried about her!.....I didn't know you knew....What do you mean?... No.... No fucking way. She wouldn't do something like that to me....I don't believe you....Annie, I don't know what trip you're on here, but that's bullshit. Deadra would never lie to me....No way! She'd get an Oscar if that was true....Bullshit!

(He slams down the phone. BLACKOUT.)

6/ The Bar. Four Months Later

(AT RISE: Deadra sits at a table, sipping a drink. Quinn appears behind her. He looks at her, trying to gain his composure. He comes to the table and sits down.)

QUINN: Deadra.
DEADRA: Hello, Quinn.
QUINN: Long time, no see and all that. What's it been? Three, four months?
DEADRA: Too long.
QUINN: I'm surprised you let me know you were in town.
DEADRA: I wanted to talk to you.
QUINN: Well, I'd suggest picking up where we left off, but I don't exactly remember our last conversation. Something about you stopping by Annie's and meeting me later.
DEADRA: Don't make this harder than it has to be.
QUINN: You never showed. Worse, you disappeared. I stop by your apartment, it's being lived in by your homeless friends. Next thing I know, Annie tells me you moved to Seattle. No explanation, no goodbye, nothing.
DEADRA: I'm so sorry.
QUINN: Pardon me if I take that with a grain of salt.

(A pause.)

DEADRA: Can I buy you a drink?
QUINN: No thanks.
DEADRA: You're turning down a drink?
QUINN: I haven't had a drink in three weeks.

428

DEADRA: That's hard to believe.

QUINN: My doctor didn't give me much choice.

DEADRA: What's the matter with you?

QUINN: I have cancer of the liver. Oh, I'm sorry. You control the market on that one, don't you?

DEADRA: Quinn, please.

QUINN: We're not here to talk about my health.

DEADRA: You're right, we're not.

QUINN: So why the phone call?

DEADRA: I wanted to see you.

QUINN: Why?

DEADRA: I thought we should talk.

QUINN: Why?

DEADRA: Quinn — I hardly know where to begin. It's so good to see you. It really is.

QUINN: Cut the crap, Deadra.

DEADRA: You're still angry at me.

(He just looks at her.)

DEADRA: You really hate me, don't you?

QUINN: No. I'd like to, believe me. But I don't. I marvel at you.

DEADRA: I can't live with myself, thinking you hate me. I want to explain why I had to do it that way.

QUINN: This ought to be good.

DEADRA: I was falling in love with you.

QUINN: Was that so terrible?

DEADRA: Yes, it was. For you, who can't remember getting married, maybe that's hard to understand. Loss of memory is a wonderful gift sometimes. Unfortunately, I don't have it. I remember what it was like being in love, and I promised myself never to go through that again.

QUINN: You got hurt, so you're gun shy. Is that it?

DEADRA: You make it sound so commonplace.

QUINN: You're not the first person to get hurt in a relationship, Deadra.

DEADRA: Don't patronize me. I was happily married, and I remember it. I remember my wedding, which was everything I imagined it should be, which was straight out of my little girl's dreams. We honeymooned in Hawaii, in Maui, and it was more romantic than I thought possible.

QUINN: So what happened?

DEADRA: I need you to know this, Quinn. Maybe it will help you understand a few things.

QUINN: You've got the floor.

DEADRA: I was doing part-time work for the Red Cross then, which put me on the road sometimes. Tim taught at the University in Eugene, in the English Department. We gave the most incredible parties, filled with bright and interesting people. My job occasionally took me out of town, and I was going to be on the road for our fifth anniversary. It didn't seem to bother Tim, but it bothered me. So I made arrangements to get home early, surprise him. I had about a three hour drive to get back and I left after work, expecting to get home in time to take him to dinner, maybe go out dancing afterwards. But I had car trouble on the way, and to make a long story short, it was past midnight before I got home. But now I was determined to surprise him more than ever, so I went to an all-night supermarket and bought champagne and flowers, and I let myself in and tiptoed into our bedroom and lit a candle — and that's when I saw her. She must've been one of his students, she looked so young. She was on my side of the bed, asleep in his arms, and he had his mouth open but for some reason wasn't snoring, together they looked like the happiest couple on the face of the earth. Quinn, I didn't know what to do. I just stared at them for the longest time. Then I leaned forward and blew out the candle and walked out of the bedroom. I never went back.

QUINN: Jesus.

DEADRA: I got in my car and drove back to southern Oregon. I filed for divorce the next day.

QUINN: You didn't talk to him first?

DEADRA: I didn't see the point. I was lifeless, Quinn. I had nothing to say to him. I had nothing to say to anyone.

(A pause.)

QUINN: How do I know you're telling me the truth now?

DEADRA: You can't imagine how much it hurts me to hear you say that.

QUINN: Why should I believe you?

DEADRA: No reason, I guess.

QUINN: Look at the line you gave me, Deadra. An incurable illness, of all things. It proves the old saw, doesn't it? If you're going to lie, go the whole hog. Nobody will believe you could possibly make up something that extreme.

DEADRA: You were going much too fast for me.

(A pause.)

DEADRA: So what do we do now?
QUINN: That depends on where we are. And I have no idea where we are.
DEADRA: Can we start over?
QUINN: Deadra, you live in Seattle now. Don't you?
DEADRA: No.
QUINN: Jesus.
DEADRA: I told Annie to say that so you wouldn't come looking for me. I moved across the river. I got the position I wanted at the clinic.
QUINN: Well, fucking congratulations.
DEADRA: I was hoping we could start seeing each other again. I miss you.
QUINN: Where the hell are you coming from now?
DEADRA: Desperation.
QUINN: You're something else.
DEADRA: I want you back in my life.
QUINN: I don't know if I can do that.
DEADRA: Can you think about it?

(A pause.)

DEADRA: Please?
QUINN: I can think about it.
DEADRA: Can we talk on the phone?
QUINN: Maybe.
DEADRA: Here's my number.

(She'll write it down on a bar napkin.)

DEADRA: I'd like to have you over for dinner.
QUINN: You're moving too fast for me, Deadra.
DEADRA: Now you know what it feels like.
QUINN: Is that what you're trying to do?
DEADRA: I'm trying to get you back in my life. I'm trying to tell you I made a mistake.

(A pause.)

DEADRA: I was afraid you wouldn't meet me.

QUINN: I almost didn't.

DEADRA: So do you feel like a movie or something tonight?

QUINN: I have other plans.

DEADRA: I see. Is she anyone I know?

QUINN: I'm having dinner with a buddy.

DEADRA: And afterwards?

QUINN: I'm going home.

DEADRA: I must sound as desperate as I feel.

QUINN: You do.

DEADRA: I can't help it.

QUINN: I'm flattered. Puzzled but flattered.

DEADRA: Why should you be puzzled?

QUINN: You rejected me, Deadra.

DEADRA: No. I never did that. I ran from you. It's not the same thing.

QUINN: It felt like rejection.

DEADRA: I want to make it up to you.

QUINN: I have to think about all this.

(A pause.)

QUINN: I've got to get going.

DEADRA: It's wonderful seeing you again. Please call me.

QUINN: I phoned every hospital in Seattle looking for you.

DEADRA: Lucky you, it's only a local call after all.

(He stands up. She stands up. Quinn offers his hand. Deadra embraces him.)

DEADRA: I love you, Quinn.

(He breaks the embrace and leaves. She watches him go. BLACK-OUT.)

7/ The Bedroom. Deadra's Birthday.

(AT RISE: Deadra is in bed, sleeping. Quinn is surreptitiously dressing. Deadra opens her eyes.)

DEADRA: Quinn? What're you doing?

QUINN: I'm going for a walk.

432

(She turns on the light. She wears a night gown.)

DEADRA: Why?

QUINN: I'm not sure.

DEADRA: Is something the matter?

QUINN: It's not working, Deadra.

DEADRA: How can you say that? I had a wonderful birthday. Wonderful dinner, we made wonderful love.

QUINN: I don't trust you.

DEADRA: About what?

QUINN: About this. About what's happening here. I don't exactly know what's happening here, is the problem. The past few months have been — weird. I don't know how else to put it.

DEADRA: Weird? You could've fooled me.

QUINN: We can't recapture the past.

DEADRA: I thought we were doing a pretty good job at it.

QUINN: I've been thinking a lot about what I want, Deadra. The first thing I want to do is get healthy. That requires a lot of change, and sitting in a bar watching you get drunk isn't cutting it. Maybe the person I'm becoming isn't someone you want to be around.

DEADRA: That should be my decision.

QUINN: I can't party the way I used to.

DEADRA: I can't either.

QUINN: You did a pretty good job last night.

DEADRA: It's my birthday, for Christ's sake. So what are you saying? Suddenly you don't want to be around me because I drink?

QUINN: That's part of it.

DEADRA: Then I'll quit.

QUINN: Don't be ridiculous.

DEADRA: I'm willing to make sacrifices here, Quinn. Accommodations. It would be nice to see you do a little of that in my direction.

QUINN: You don't really want to quit drinking, Deadra.

DEADRA: Quit telling me what I want.

(A pause.)

DEADRA: What a terrific birthday. The scarf you gave me didn't mean anything to you?

QUINN: It's not what I planned to give you.

DEADRA: Great. And what was that?

QUINN: It doesn't matter.

DEADRA: Of course not. Apparently nothing about me matters any more.

QUINN: I planned to give you another sonnet. I've been writing a lot of them lately.

DEADRA: Why didn't you give it to me?

QUINN: Because it says goodbye.

DEADRA: I see. You wanted to make sure you got laid first. So let's hear it. Read the goddamn thing to me.

QUINN: I didn't bring you here to get laid.

DEADRA: Read the sonnet, Quinn. You owe me that goddamn much.

(He takes a folded piece of paper out of his pocket, unfolds it and reads:)

QUINN: If our lips should never meet again;
if your arms should not around me wrap
in such a way to tell me of your ken;

(He stops and crumples up the poem.)

QUINN: You drink too damn much.

DEADRA: Spare me the sermon, Quinn!

QUINN: We're alike, Deadra — a couple of barflies. It's like a prolonged suicide.

DEADRA: Don't lecture me about dying. I think I know a hell of a lot more about the subject than you do.

QUINN: Whatever you say.

DEADRA: Quinn, look at this.

(She takes her purse from the bedside table, opens it and takes out bottles of pills.)

DEADRA: Here's all the crap I have to take to get through the day.

QUINN: What's all this?

DEADRA: They're supposed to make my last few months more comfortable.

QUINN: What are you talking about?

DEADRA: I told you the truth the first time, Quinn. I'm a time-bomb.

QUINN: Bullshit.

DEADRA: Think what you want.

434

(He's reading the bottles of pills.)

QUINN: I never heard of this stuff.
DEADRA: I can't imagine how I'd get by without them.
QUINN: What the fuck are you talking about?
DEADRA: I'm trying to tell you how it is with me.
QUINN: That you're dying?

(She nods her head, yes.)

QUINN: Christ. Don't you know Annie told me the whole story? You give guys that line to keep them from getting too close.
DEADRA: Annie told you exactly what I asked her to tell you.
QUINN: Bullshit.
DEADRA: Believe what you believe, Quinn. All I can do is tell the truth.
QUINN: Why would you tell me and then change your mind?
DEADRA: I told you because I wanted you to know me. To know me truly. But I wasn't prepared for your reaction, Quinn, and I panicked. The only way I knew how to change your energy was to make you believe I was lying to you. So that's what I did.
QUINN: I don't believe you.
DEADRA: As soon as I fled you, as soon as I got as far away from you as I could, I knew I'd made a mistake. I couldn't do what you wanted, I couldn't ride into the sunset with you for a few months — but I learned that I couldn't live without you either. I wanted you in my life. So this time, I hadn't planned to tell you the truth at all. I was going to enjoy you as much as I could in the time I had left.
QUINN: You're a total fruit cake.
DEADRA: Don't hate me for telling you the truth.
QUINN: I'll be back tomorrow morning at ten. I want you out of here. I want you out of my life.

(He turns to leave.)

DEADRA: How did it go? "If our lips should never meet again..." I bet it was a beautiful sonnet.

(Quinn doesn't respond. BLACKOUT.)

435

8/ The Bedroom. Five Weeks Later.

(AT RISE: Quinn is on the phone.)

QUINN: Annie, listen to me. I'll say it again as clearly as I can. I don't give a shit. She's not a part of my life any more. I don't want to know what you're telling me. Do I make myself clear?....Is this like before, you're just saying what she wants me to believe?... Okay, then, what's the name of her doctor?....Do you have his phone number?....

(He writes down a telephone number.)

QUINN: I don't know what I'm going to do. I'll think about it.

(He hangs up. He stares at the phone. He picks up the phone number he wrote down and stares at it. He starts dialing. BLACKOUT.)

9/ Hospital Room. Three Days Later.

(AT RISE: Deadra is in bed, napping. Quinn sits in a chair nearby. Deadra stirs.)

DEADRA: Was I sleeping long?
QUINN: Half an hour.
DEADRA: And you stayed. You're sweet.
QUINN: I'm here for the duration, Deadra.
DEADRA: I may last longer than everybody thinks.
QUINN: Good.
DEADRA: And maybe not.
QUINN: We'll take it one moment at a time. I brought goodies.

(He'll get up and go to his backpack on the floor. He'll take out a small bottle of vodka, a can of mix, and a glass. He'll mix Deadra a drink.)

DEADRA: You spoil me.
QUINN: That's the idea. I probably shouldn't be doing this, but I figure a couple more won't phase your liver one way or the other. One vodka collins coming up.
DEADRA: What if the nurse comes in?
QUINN: What's she going to do? Kill you?
DEADRA: I love you.

QUINN: Here we go.
DEADRA: Aren't you joining me?
QUINN: I think I quit.
DEADRA: Good for you.
QUINN: Let me rephrase that. I hope I quit.
DEADRA: I hope so, too. Cheers.

(She drinks.)

QUINN: Okay?
DEADRA: Perfect.
QUINN: We aim to please.
DEADRA: Quinn, you're incredible.
QUINN: I have my moments.
DEADRA: I like to imagine what you'll be like as an old man. Very distinguished looking, I bet.
QUINN: I imagine things, too. What it would've been like to meet you five, ten years ago.
DEADRA: You wouldn't've liked me then. I was a mess. More than now, as hard as that is to believe.
QUINN: Being a mess is part of your charm.
DEADRA: Messes aren't pretty, Quinn.
QUINN: In your case, messy is sexy.
DEADRA: Only you would think that.
QUINN: You look beautiful.
DEADRA: I'm so tired.
QUINN: Go back to sleep if you want.
DEADRA: Will you hold my hand?
QUINN: With pleasure.
DEADRA: Can I save the rest of this for later?
QUINN: Of course.

(Deadra gives him the glass, which he puts beside the bed. He takes her hand.)

DEADRA: Quinn, I want you to do something for me.
QUINN: Name it.
DEADRA: I want to be cremated. I want you to take my ashes on that ferry and put me in the Sound. Don't let Megan do anything else. It's really important to me. Will you do that?
QUINN: Promise.
DEADRA: Whenever you take the ferry, you can say hello.

QUINN: I'll be taking it often.
DEADRA: I'm glad....I'm so tired.
QUINN: Take a nap. I'll be right here.
DEADRA: I love you, Quinn.
QUINN: I love you, Deadra.

(She closes her eyes. Quinn holds her hand. BLACKOUT.)

10/ Ferry Boat Deck. A Week Later.

(AT RISE: Quinn has just finished dumping Deadra's ashes into the Sound. Her twin sister, MEGAN, looks on.)

QUINN: What do I do with the box?
MEGAN: May I have it?
QUINN: Thanks.

(He gives the box that held the ashes to Megan.)

MEGAN: Are you okay?
QUINN: Not really.
MEGAN: I don't know how I feel. She brought so much destruction to herself. I think I stopped having feelings about that a long time ago.
QUINN: She did the best she could under the circumstances.
MEGAN: You really think so?
QUINN: Of course I do. She was a remarkable woman.
MEGAN: Had you been together long?
QUINN: No.
MEGAN: When you told me where she wanted her ashes spread, I was surprised. I didn't realize Seattle was so special to her.
QUINN: We had an unforgettable time here. We took this very ferry.
MEGAN: I see.
QUINN: I wrote her a poem about it, a sonnet. "The skyline hangs above the bay, a mist of mystery as in a dream..."
MEGAN: The skyline is beautiful, isn't it?
QUINN: The weather was different. There was a layer of fog on the ground, making the skyline look like it was hanging above the water.
MEGAN: May I ask you a personal question?
QUINN: I'm getting vibes here that I'm going to have to defend her. I don't think this is the time or place for that.

MEGAN: Everything that happened to Deadra, she brought on herself.

QUINN: I don't think that's true.

MEGAN: She started abusing her body in junior high and never stopped.

QUINN: What are you getting at?

MEGAN: She was an alcoholic, and she died an alcoholic's death

QUINN: Deadra had a lot of pain to cover up.

MEGAN: She gave me that same crap for years. It was one of her many excuses to drink.

QUINN: You never caught your husband in bed with another woman

MEGAN: She told you that happened to her?

QUINN: I'm sure she never confided in you. She told me you two weren't close.

MEGAN: She brought on the destruction of her marriage just like she brought on everything else.

QUINN: I don't believe you.

MEGAN: Her husband and I were very close. As a matter of fact, for a while I was a little jealous that she'd met him first. He told me everything

QUINN: Like what?

MEGAN: He'd gone out of town to a conference to deliver a paper. He was scheduled to be gone for their anniversary, but was able to move himself up on the program so he could come home and surprise her. He walked into the house with champagne and flowers and found her with one of his students, both half-naked and passed out on the sofa. That was the beginning of the end.

QUINN: She told me she was the one with champagne and flowers. She found him in bed with one of his students.

MEGAN: Deadra lived in her own little fantasy world. She'd say whatever it took to feed it and keep it alive. I'm sorry to be the one to tell you.

QUINN: No, you're not. You're enjoying this.

MEGAN: I can see you loved her very much.

QUINN: That doesn't change anything, you know. That she screwed up the marriage. That all happened in the past. It has nothing to do with us.

MEGAN: You two were good drinking buddies, I take it.

QUINN: Yes, I'm a drunk. That's what you want me to say, isn't it?

MEGAN: Alcohol doesn't encourage clear perception, Quinn. That's all I'm trying to point out here.

QUINN: I'll tell you how clear Deadra's perception was. She let homeless people stay in her apartment. She couldn't stand the thought of them living under bridges, especially in bad weather, especially when she learned a homeless woman was pregnant. So she opened her door for them, no questions asked, and gave them a dry, warm place to stay. If it takes a drunk to do that, then we need more goddamn drunks in the world.

MEGAN: She really did that?

QUINN: Yes, she really did that. Have you ever done something that noble? Or come even close?

MEGAN: I can't solve the world's problems.

QUINN: That's exactly what I told her. And she went ahead and invited them in anyway. Which is more than you and I have done. So who the hell are we to criticize her?

MEGAN: You have no idea what causes I support.

(No reply.)

MEGAN: This isn't easy for either of us.

(No reply.)

MEGAN: Will you be going right back to Portland?

QUINN: I have to be at work tomorrow.

MEGAN: What do you do?

QUINN: Does it matter?

MEGAN: I'm just curious.

QUINN: I teach.

MEGAN: Really?

(A pause.)

MEGAN: Elementary school?...High school?

QUINN: No, I teach in a goddamn university, just like you do. I have a Ph.D. and I teach American literature. I'm also writing a book on the history of the sonnet. Anything else you want to know?

MEGAN: I didn't mean to make you angry.

(A pause.)

MEGAN: Very well then. Have a safe trip home.

440

(She starts away.)

QUINN: Megan?
MEGAN: Yes?
QUINN: Give her some slack. She did the best she could.
MEGAN: Deadra never did the best she could.
QUINN: She wanted the world to be a much better place than it was. She suffered that it wasn't.
MEGAN: You're a hopeless romantic if you believe that.
QUINN: What's wrong with being a romantic?
MEGAN: Goodbye, Quinn.

(She starts away again. Quinn calls after her.)

QUINN: Wait a minute.

(Megan ignores him.)

QUINN: I said, what the hell's wrong with being a romantic?

(Megan is gone. Quinn turns and stares out at the audience. BLACKOUT. The play is over.)

For royalties information:
Charles Deemer
1-800-294-7176
cdeemer@teleport.com

1975

The Stiff
a farce in one act

THE CAST (4M, 2W):
President John Jones, *the leader of the people*
Mrs. Eunice Jones, *his wife*
Chi Chi, *his mistress*
Neck, *the mortician*
Charles, *his assistant*
Dr. Alberts, *the doctor*

THE TIME:
Any time

THE PLACE:
A back room in the Public Hall in a foreign country.

THE SET:
Upstage center is a table on which is a casket. A window, upstage left, looks out upon the square. Entrance into the room is stage right. Modest furnishings: this is the room in which the corpses of public figures are kept before being put on display to the people.

442

(AT RISE: DR. ALBERTS has his back to the audience, inspecting a body in the casket. Waiting expectantly are MRS. JONES, NECK and CHARLES. Mrs. Jones, who is in mourning, is dressed in black. She holds a black lace handkerchief over her sobs. The doctor turns and moves away from the casket.)

NECK: Well, doctor?
DR. ALBERTS: Your suspicions are correct. I find the organ to be tumescent.

(Mrs. Jones breaks into tears.)

CHARLES: Please, Mrs. Jones.
MRS. JONES: *(struggling)* It's sca— ... scan— ... it's scanda—
CHARLES: Now, now.
NECK: Perhaps you could give her something.
DR. ALBERTS: Comes, Mrs. Jones. You must try to relax.

(The doctor and Mrs. Jones start out.)

NECK: Thank you, doctor.
DR. ALBERTS: I feel I should be the one thanking you. In my long career I've never seen anything like this before.
MRS. JONES: *(sobbing)* It's scandalous ...
DR. ALBERTS: Come with me. I'll administer a sedative.

(The doctor escorts her off.)

CHARLES: What do we do now?
NECK: I'm not sure.
CHARLES: You could display only half the body. The upper half.
NECK: And compromise my reputation? I didn't get where I am by displaying only half the body. People expect a full deck.
CHARLES: They've been waiting out there for hours. The lines are

———

NECK: I know how long the lines are. Let them wait. We can't display the body as it is.
CHARLES: Of course not.
NECK: We've got to get rid of it.
CHARLES: Perhaps if ...
NECK: If what?
CHARLES: If we dismembered ... it was just a thought.

NECK: I do not mutilate bodies. The entire body will be viewed intact or not at all. I have my reputation to think of.

CHARLES: It was just a suggestion.

(A pause.)

CHARLES: Perhaps it will go away.

NECK: Perhaps.

CHARLES: We can wait and hope. We can pray.

NECK: Yes, we can pray.

(They pray. Then they approach the casket and look at the body.)

NECK: No luck.

CHARLES: They must be getting impatient out there. The lines started forming as soon as his death was announced.

NECK: I know, I know.

CHARLES: He certainly is popular. Even dead. I suppose because he was so average. According to the polls, there was never a more average man.

NECK: We have to think of something.

CHARLES: At least Mrs. Jones noticed the problem before the doors were opened. If the people had been let in before anyone noticed

...

NECK: If you want to thank Mrs. Jones, send her flowers.

CHARLES: I'm sorry.

NECK: We have to think of something.

CHARLES: Yes.

NECK: I must have done something wrong.

CHARLES: Do you think so?

NECK: Perhaps I was nervous without knowing it. I've never prepared a President before. Something inconsequential could have slipped my notice, and consequently have become — consequential. If I had somehow erred in draining all the blood, for example. Perhaps such an error would explain it.

CHARLES: That might be an explanation.

NECK: On the other hand, the blood measured five point three quarts, which is average.

CHARLES: Then that must not be it.

NECK: Perhaps it has even happened before. I'm much too busy to read all of the literature. New findings are always popping up. A premature ossification, for example. I've heard rumors of such a thing.

CHARLES: That might be an explanation.

NECK: On the other hand, then one would presume that the organ would ossify in its normal state.

CHARLES: Then that must not be it.

NECK: Unless, of course, he died while the organ was ...?

CHARLES: You don't think he died like that?

NECK: Suppose he did. Followed by premature ossification ...

CHARLES: Sounds unlikely to me.

NECK: There's one way to find out. I'll question his wife.

CHARLES: About that?

NECK: It's a delicate matter, I know. But we must find out. It could be the explanation. Get Mrs. Jones.

CHARLES: But the doctor was going to give her a sedative. She'll be resting.

NECK: A sedative will make the matter less delicate. Get Mrs. Jones.

CHARLES: Yes, sir.

(Charles exits. Neck moves to stare at the body. Mrs. Jones and Charles enter.)

MRS. JONES: You wanted to see me?

NECK: Yes, ma'am. Please sit down.

MRS. JONES: The doctor suggested I nap until the matter is settled.

NECK: This will only take a minute. Charles, perhaps you would leave us alone.

CHARLES: Of course.

(He exits.)

NECK: Madam, I don't want you to think that I'm being overly personal. But this matter is highly unusual, as you know. I have never seen anything like it in all my years as Public Mortician. Nor has Dr. Alberts seen anything like it, as you heard for yourself. So the explanation, which we must find before correcting the difficulty, is likely to come from unexpected directions. Therefore, we must follow every clue. However delicate.

MRS. JONES: What is it you want to know? I'll help in any way I can.

NECK: Very good. You are standing up admirably.

MRS. JONES: Please be quick. I'm very tired.

NECK: Certainly. Mrs. Jones, were you near your husband when he died?

MRS. JONES: Yes.

NECK: How near?

MRS. JONES: Pardon me?

NECK: Did he die, by chance, in bed?

MRS. JONES: Yes. How did you know?

NECK: A wild guess. Now madam, this will seem to be none of my business, but there is something else I must ask you.

MRS. JONES: Simply ask it.

NECK: When your husband was in bed, just before he died ... were you by chance ... making love?

(Mrs. Jones breaks into tears.)

NECK: I know the matter is very personal, madam. But it might be the clue we need. If you were making love, you see, and if he died with ... the way he is now, madam ... and if premature ossification occurred, which is not unheard of ... then, you see ...

MRS. JONES: We haven't made love in ten years.

NECK: Oh.

MRS. JONES: We've had separate bedrooms for fifteen.

NECK: I see.

MRS. JONES: I tried to get him interested. God knows, I tried. But always without success. Always without ... that happening. And now for him to respond while dead ... is God so cruel?

NECK: Take your nap, Mrs. Jones. You've been helpful.

MRS. JONES: How can we show the body?

NECK: We'll think of something.

(Mrs. Jones exits. Charles enters.)

CHARLES: Well?

NECK: They haven't slept together in years. As far as she's concerned, he was impotent.

CHARLES: Without meaning to sound crude, sir, if that's impotence, many a man would embrace it.

(Dr. Alberts enters.)

DR. ALBERTS: What did you say to her? She's more upset than ever.

NECK: We're trying to find out the cause of this, doctor.

DR. ALBERTS: Yes, I can see why you'd want to.

NECK: Perhaps you have an explanation.

DR. ALBERTS: If I did, it would revolutionize medical theory.

NECK: We have to get rid of it before we show the body.

DR. ALBERTS: I suppose you do.

NECK: Not only would it be highly irregular to show him like this, I would be held personally accountable for an utter disregard of decorum. The people would eat me alive.

DR. ALBERTS: Perhaps you exaggerate.

NECK: Never under-estimate the seriousness of a breach of decorum.

DR. ALBERTS: I wish I could be of more assistance. Unfortunately, the reproductive system is not my area of specialty. And I do have to get back to the hospital.

NECK: We appreciate your coming. A second opinion is always useful in a case like this.

DR. ALBERTS: I can report without qualification that the corpse has an erection.

NECK: Thank you very much, Dr. Alberts.

DR. ALBERTS: Glad to be of help. Oh yes — Mrs. Jones is resting in the lounge.

(He exits.)

CHARLES: What do we do now?

NECK: We think of something.

(Charles goes to the window.)

CHARLES: They don't look very patient to me.

NECK: I can well imagine.

CHARLES: You don't have to imagine — you can come see for yourself.

NECK: I prefer to imagine!

(A pause.)

CHARLES: Perhaps if ... ?

NECK: Well? If what?

CHARLES: We covered it with flowers.

NECK: I have never heard of displaying flowers in the crotch.

447

CHARLES: But it would cover it up.

NECK: Only as a last resort. Flowers in such a place would be too irregular. What would the reviewers think?

CHARLES: It was just a suggestion.

NECK: On the other hand, if we folded his hands over it ...

CHARLES: I don't think so, sir. Without meaning to sound crude, if I saw such a thing, I'd think he had been playing with himself.

NECK: But you think flowers would work? I wonder.

(Chi Chi enters, dressed as a nun.)

NECK: May I help you?

CHI CHI: Is that him?

NECK: If you mean the body of the President, it is. The services will begin directly, sister. Please wait in the auditorium.

CHI CHI: Oh. I'm ... Miss Jones. His sister.

NECK: I didn't realize.

(She starts toward the casket but is intercepted by Charles.)

CHARLES: Maybe you shouldn't look just yet.

NECK: The viewing comes later, Sister Jones.

CHI CHI: But I want to look now.

NECK: If you looked now, consider how anticlimactic the formal viewing would be. All that inspiring oratory for nothing. We'll be starting very soon — please.

CHI CHI: Oh, all right. But I wish you'd hurry.

(She exits.)

CHARLES: I didn't know he had a sister.

NECK: Nor did I.

CHARLES: Do you smell something?

NECK: Sweet?

CHARLES: Sort of.

NECK: I can't put my finger on it.

CHARLES: Did she strike you as peculiar?

NECK: Not as peculiar as our friend. Our responsibility, I'm sorry to say.

(Mrs. Jones enters.)

MRS. JONES: Did the nun perform the rites already?

NECK: No, ma'am.

MRS. JONES: Where's Dr. Alberts?

NECK: He returned to the hospital. You shouldn't be up, madam.

MRS. JONES: I was lying down in the lounge when I felt as if someone was staring at me. When I opened my eyes, the doctor was there. Then he vanished. I thought perhaps he wanted to see me about something. Or was it all my imagination?

NECK: Your imagination, I think.

MRS. JONES: I can't sleep.

NECK: It would be difficult, yes.

MRS. JONES: But I do feel better. I'm very much in control of myself now.

NECK: I'm pleased to hear that.

MRS. JONES: I've even found an amusing side to everything. This is exactly something John would do. He was always trying to be different. I suppose because he was so average. Lately he had taken to fads. Mysticism. Meditation. Trying to control his heartbeat with his mind.

NECK: Trying to control his heartbeat?

MRS. JONES: Mind over matter, and all that. He would get in this ridiculous position, what do you call it? With his legs crossed, the way they do in the East. Japan, I suppose it is. He had taken to talking about Japan in his sleep.

NECK: You heard him?

MRS. JONES: Now and then, when I would stop by his bedroom to see if ... yes, sometimes I'd catch him talking about Japan in his sleep. His next vacation, perhaps. I take it everyone sits cross-legged over there, with blank expressions on their faces. He would sit that way for hours and not say a word, hardly seeming to breathe. He claimed it improved his circulation.

NECK: Mrs. Jones, we've thought of a way to display the body.

MRS. JONES: You can get rid of it?

NECK: We can hide it. We can cover it up with an arrangement of flowers.

MRS. JONES: Flowers? There?

NECK: Yes. Especially if you publicly arrange them yourself. The people would regard it as erotic tenderness. They'd grant you a certain flair for intimacy. They would love you for it. And then they would pass by the body and see only the flowers, nothing else.

MRS. JONES: You know how that must hurt me.

NECK: I'm sorry, madam. This is no time for delicacy.

MRS. JONES: If there's no other way ...

NECK: There's no other way.

MRS. JONES: Then it must be done.

NECK: Bravo, madam. Come. You have bouquets without end to choose from. The people have mourned your loss with an unprecedented run on floral shops. You pick the flowers, and Charles and I will do the rest.

(They all exit. A beat.)

(In the casket, Jones sits up and looks around. He wiggles a bit, stretching, getting comfortable. Hearing someone, he gets back down.)

(Chi Chi enters and approaches the casket.)

CHI CHI: *(seeing his erection)* Boopy, shame on you!

(She giggles. Jones sits up.)

JONES: What are you doing here?

CHI CHI: I wanted to see how you look as a corpse. And really, boopy.

JONES: Nothing's going as planned.

CHI CHI: I can see that.

JONES: I couldn't help it. I keep thinking about you.

(He grabs for her.)

CHI CHI: Hands off. You're supposed to be dead.

JONES: Lock the door. It will solve everyone's problem.

CHI CHI: You're supposed to be on display.

JONES: They refused to show me like this.

(Chi Chi giggles.)

JONES: It isn't funny.

CHI CHI: I think it's cute.

(Dr. Alberts enters. Hearing him, Jones starts to get back down in the casket, then sees who it is.)

DR. ALBERTS: It's only me. *(To Chi Chi)* What are you doing here in that ridiculous outfit?

CHI CHI: I wanted to see how he looked as a corpse. No one stops a nun from going where she pleases.

DR. ALBERTS: You haven't helped matters, Mr. President.

JONES: I tried my best.

CHI CHI: He couldn't take his nasty mind off me.

DR. ALBERTS: They're getting flowers. This plan is to ... of course, you already know about that. You were here.

CHI CHI: I don't know.

DR. ALBERTS: You shouldn't be here in the first place.

JONES: Leave her alone. There's nothing to be done about it now.

DR. ALBERTS: You and your powers of meditation. I thought you could control your bodily processes. You're lucky another doctor didn't get the case and pronounce you alive.

JONES: My blood pressure would have fooled them.

DR. ALBERTS: Your erection wouldn't!

CHI CHI: You really should be ashamed of yourself, boopy. Having those thoughts in a coffin ... I'm not sure I appreciate that.

DR. ALBERTS: Get back down before they come in with the flowers.

CHI CHI: What are the flowers for?

JONES: They're hiding my problem with a bouquet.

CHI CHI: How darling!

DR. ALBERTS: Get down! *(Jones does)* And you get out of here. We don't have all —

(Neck and Charles enter with a large bouquet of mums.)

NECK: Doctor, Sister Jones. Is something the matter?

DR. ALBERTS: Not at all.

NECK: I thought you had to return to the hospital.

DR. ALBERTS: I phoned in. They don't need me, so I thought I might be of use here.

CHARLES: We solved the problem.

DR. ALBERTS: Mrs. Jones told me. I ran into her in the lounge. I congratulate you.

CHARLES: My idea.

DR. ALBERTS: I think it will work.

NECK: I'm sorry you had to be exposed to this, sister. It is highly irregular, I assure you.

CHI CHI: I think it's a cute idea.

NECK: You do?

DR. ALBERTS: *(to get Chi Chi out)* We'll leave you to your business ...

CHI CHI: Only I think roses would be more romantic.

(The doctor exits, getting Chi Chi out of there.)

CHARLES: She's right.

NECK: Be grateful we talked her out of skunkweed.

CHARLES: It's remarkable, isn't it?

NECK: What?

CHARLES: The whole idea of it. I mean, one doesn't think of such a thing happening to the President. At least, I never have. As average as he was, I still put him up on a pedestal. Can you imagine the President going to the john with the Sunday paper on the morning after? Imagine having to use the toilet next and having the place stink to high heaven — by the President! He always seemed above all that. Even though I knew he was average.

NECK: If you ask me, he's one of a kind. Let's give him the flowers and move him out.

CHARLES: I can't imagine him being impotent. It must have just happened with his wife.

NECK: The flowers.

(Charles approaches the casket with the bouquet.)

CHARLES: Well, old sport, we have to hide you from the public.

(He playfully flicks the hidden erection with an index finger and Jones immediately sits up, grabbing his crotch in pain.)

JONES: AARGH!

CHARLES: Be Jesus!

NECK: Mister President!

CHARLES: *(falling to his knees)* Hallowed be thy name, thy kingdom come, thy will be done —

JONES: Stop that! I've not risen from the dead. I'm quite alive.

NECK: I was led to believe ... I myself prepared the body ...

JONES: It wasn't me.

NECK: I would have sworn it was.

JONES: That's only because I'm so average I look like anyone else. How do you suppose I got elected President? Everyone thought they were voting for themselves.

CHARLES: I always said you were a regular chap.

JONES: Too regular.

NECK: But the lines outside, Mr. President. Dr. Alberts pronounced you dead. It was in the papers. The public is waiting outside to view the body.

JONES: Don't worry, they'll get to see the body. Just give me a minute. Why on earth did you do that?

CHARLES: I'm sorry, I did it without thinking. I was overcome that even the President, even the corpse of the President —

NECK: Imbecile!

JONES: It doesn't matter now. Only, gentlemen, I'm afraid you're going to have to be sworn to secrecy about this.

NECK: I'm a man of ethics, Mr. President.

JONES: How much?

NECK: Half a million.

JONES: Split between the two of you. No bargaining. Remember, I'm still Commander-in-Chief.

NECK: *(to Charles)* Seventy-thirty.

CHARLES: Forty-sixty.

NECK: Sold.

JONES: Dr. Alberts will make the arrangements.

NECK: He also knows?

JONES: He's in love with my wife. He expects to marry her. Unfortunately, he's not her type. But he won't know that til I'm long gone.

NECK: The matter appears to be very complicated.

JONES: All you have to know is that I'm dead. Now put those flowers on me and ...

CHARLES: It's gone, Mr. President.

NECK: It must have been the blow.

JONES: Do we still need the flowers?

NECK: I'm not sure. Your wife —

JONES: Please — the widow Jones.

NECK: She will be expecting flowers.

JONES: Then we'll have flowers. Let's get moving, the people have been waiting for me long enough.

NECK: There was nothing we could do, Mr. President.

JONES: I'm not blaming you.

DR. ALBERTS: *(off stage)* It's the wife's prerogative to choose the flowers!

CHARLES: Someone's coming!

(Jones gets down in the casket. Chi Chi enters, carrying a bouquet of roses, followed by Dr. Alberts.)

CHI CHI: The President deserves the best. Roses.
DR. ALBERTS: You are being difficult.
NECK: Doctor? Sister Jones?
CHI CHI: Use these.
DR. ALBERTS: Mrs. Jones would not approve.
JONES: *(sitting up)* Chi Chi, what is it now?
NECK: Chi Chi?
CHI CHI: I'm not going to let you have less than roses. Especially down there. It's gone!
DR. ALBERTS: I've had enough of your go-go dancer, Jones. It was quite satisfactory to go along with this so you could run off to Japan with her, but when she begins getting in the way, ruining our cover, that's another matter entirely. I pronounced you dead. My reputation is at stake.
JONES: Chi Chi, please. Let the Widow Jones have her way. She's in mourning.
DR. ALBERTS: You'd better straighten this out, and quickly. The people won't put up with waiting out there much longer. They'll be storming the hall.

(He exits.)

NECK: Can he be trusted?
JONES: Of course. If I'm not dead, my wife is not a widow. Let's dispense with the flowers and get moving.
CHI CHI: But flowers is a darling idea. It just should be roses.

(The doctor hurries in.)

DR. ALBERTS: Your wife is coming!
JONES: Please. The Widow Jones.

(He gets down. Mrs. Jones enters with a bouquet of skunkweed.)

MRS. JONES: Are we ready?
NECK: We found a way to correct the matter after all, madam, and flowers won't be necessary.
MRS. JONES: But I want flowers. I want these.
NECK: Skunkweed, madam?

MRS. JONES: I've changed my mind about mums. They suggest mummies.

DR. ALBERTS: But skunkweed is hardly appropriate.

MRS. JONES: On the contrary. Where did the roses come from?

DR. ALBERTS: The sister was paying her respects.

MRS. JONES: Is it the roses I smell?

CHI CHI: It's called Burning Desire. You like it?

MRS. JONES: Who are you?

CHI CHI: Oh. His sister.

DR. ALBERTS: She means the Lord's sister, of course. I believe it's time to open the doors ...

MRS. JONES: I want a moment alone with my husband.

NECK: We are pressed for time, madam.

MRS. JONES: I won't be long. I have that small right, don't I?

NECK: Of course.

MRS. JONES: *(to Chi Chi)* Perhaps you would stay.

DR. ALBERTS: I'm sure the sister has urgent business elsewhere.

MRS. JONES: I would find it comforting if she stayed for just a moment.

CHI CHI: Okay.

NECK: Please be quick, madam. The people have been waiting for so long to pay their respects.

(All exit but the women and Jones down in the casket.)

MRS. JONES: I feel I must make a confession.

CHI CHI: Sure.

MRS. JONES: Are you really wearing perfume? I didn't think it was allowed.

CHI CHI: Oh. Well, only on special occasions. I mean, since he was President and all. What is it you want to confess about?

MRS. JONES: I have been unfaithful to my husband.

CHI CHI: Really?

MRS. JONES: Many times.

CHI CHI: I guess only the first time's the rough one.

MRS. JONES: Sometimes in this very room.

CHI CHI: Far out.

MRS. JONES: With Charles, the mortician's assistant. We've been seeing each other for years. In this very room.

CHI CHI: Sounds pretty kinky.

Were dead bodies in here?

MRS. JONES: *(ignoring this)* I want to be alone with my husband now.

CHI CHI: What for?

MRS. JONES: To pray, of course.

CHI CHI: Oh. Well, sure. But I think they're in a hurry.

(She exits. Mrs. Jones speaks to the casket.)

MRS. JONES: And so we are alone at last, my darling. Do you know how long it's been? How long I've had to share you — first with them, the people, your constituency? Who elected you because you are so average. And later sharing you with your fads, your beloved meditations and mysticisms. And all along I still loved you. Charles is nothing. Charles is itching a scratch. I still love you, and this is why I must kill you. Even though you're already dead, I must kill you. For once, you must not get the last word. The coda will belong to me.

(She removes a knife from her person and approaches the casket.)

MRS. JONES: You'll never know I'm doing this. But I'll know. God, if he cares, will know. The final rejection belongs to me.

(She raises the knife and looks down at the body. Dr. Alberts enters.)

MRS. JONES: You've lost your erection!

DR. ALBERTS: Eunice, don't!

(The knife starts down as Jones grabs her hand. There is a struggle and the doctor joins in. Breaking free, Mrs. Jones thrusts wildly and stabs the doctor. He falls. Mrs. Jones thinks she has stabbed her husband.)

MRS. JONES: John, forgive me! Forgive me!

(Neck, Charles and Chi Chi enter.)

NECK: What happened?

MRS. JONES: I murdered my husb –

(She sees Jones sitting up, quite alive.)

456

JONES: Hello, Eunice.

MRS. JONES: But I thought —

JONES: Dr. Alberts looks dead to me.

NECK: The doors have been opened! The people expect oratory and a view of the body!

JONES: Then let's put the doctor in the casket.

NECK: It won't work, Mr. President. They expect you.

JONES: But who am I? The man who the polls called more average than anyone. Help me with the body.

NECK: There's too much blood. It will compromise my reputation.

JONES: We'll cover him with flowers. Everywhere but the face. They'll want to see the face.

NECK: Your face.

JONES: An average face. One is as good as another.

NECK: But what about you?

JONES: I am dead. This is my body.

NECK: But our arrangement ... ?

(Jones begins to scribble a note.)

CHARLES: What about my forty percent?

JONES: I'll give you something for the bank.

CHI CHI: Is it still to Japan, boopy?

MRS. JONES: Boopy? You and my husband? With a nun, John?

JONES: She dances. I'm sorry, Eunice. I tried to make it as painless as possible.

CHI CHI: He kept thinking about me in the coffin. You think you're kinky.

MRS. JONES: I would call it something else.

JONES: *(handing the note)* Take this to the bank.

NECK: Very good, Mr. President.

JONES: Come on, Chi Chi.

MRS. JONES: Chi Chi?

CHI CHI: Sayonara!

(Jones and Chi Chi exit.)

NECK: Well, Charles, let's give the people their body.

CHARLES: I hope they don't notice the difference.

NECK: Perhaps we should cover the face as well. Just to be on the safe side. The eyes should suffice. Easy now ...

(The doctor is put into the casket.)

MRS. JONES: Charles?
CHARLES: Yes, ma'am?

(They regard one another. A beat.)

CHARLES: Do you want me to come back?
MRS. JONES: No. We can come back later. First I must make my
appearance. I must show my grief.
NECK: The people would expect grief, madam.
MRS. JONES: What the people expect, they deserve. What they
deserve, they get. Always.

(All exit and BLACKOUT.)

For royalties information:
Charles Deemer
cdeemer@teleport.com
1-800-294-7176

458

1981

Country Northwestern
a play in two acts

First performed at Theatre Workshop in Portland, Oregon, on November 6, 1981. Directed by Steve Smith.

THE CAST (in order of appearance; 4M, 4W):
Michelle, *a young filmmaker*
Rick, *her cameraman*
Red, *owner of the Rapids Restaurant & Lounge*
Dotty, *bartender at the Lounge, who is blind*
Buck Timber, *an itinerant country singer*
Gayle Goodwyn, *a country superstar*
Mrs. Ames, *a resident of Harvest Acres, a retirement center*
Mr. Fredericks, *manager of Harvest Acres*

THE PLACE:
Rapids, Oregon, on the Umpqua River out of Roseburg

THE TIME:
Spring, 1972

THE SET:
The lounge at the restaurant in Rapids. Upstage right is a bar, off of which is the entrance-exit. Another entrance-exit stage left leads to the restaurant. Downstage from the bar are several tables.
Still farther downstage is a neutral playing area.

Songs: "Thank Heaven For You", "Country Northwestern", and "Hangin' In" by Lynne Fuqua. "Your Cheatin' Fart" and "Great Speckled Fraulein" by Charles Deemer.

ACT ONE

(AT RISE: a dark stage. SPOTS come up on MICHELLE and RICK, who stand some distance apart in the neutral area.)

MICHELLE: Crazy Rick. At least once a month he phones me at some weird hour of the morning, stoned and babbling, probably horny, expecting me to hijack a plane up to see him.

RICK: Michelle, you will not believe this country. It's the end of the earth. After Oregon, there's no place else to go.

MICHELLE: Unless you're a filmmaker. Then you live in Southern California.

RICK: You can make a movie anywhere. I find lots of work up here.

MICHELLE: I have to pay the rent, Rick.

RICK: So do a documentary on the Blazers. I'll shoot it and when they win the championship in a year or two, you'll have a gold mine to market.

MICHELLE: I had to ask to find out he was talking about the local professional basketball team. Real good, Rick. Real macho.

RICK: So do a documentary on Ken Kesey. He lives in Oregon.

MICHELLE: Better — but a little too obvious. Rick, it's seventy-two. The sixties are quite dead.

RICH: This country is a cinematographer's dream. Make a film and I'll shoot it. Everything is so green here.

MICHELLE: Like money?

(A third SPOT comes up on RED in the lounge area.)

RED: The dam would be expensive, we all knew that. Fact is, for a while I was hoping it would be too expensive to build. Or if they were set on building it, that they would go down river, where they could put up the sonofabitch without putting the town under water. Wouldn't lose nothing that way but a few Federal campgrounds. But flooding the town — where the hell are folks supposed to go? Especially Dotty, blind like she is. But you know the government — between the town and those Federal picnic tables, they set their mind on flooding the town. Wasn't a damn thing we could do about it.

(SPOT off Red.)

460

RICK: *(sleepily now)* Hello?

MICHELLE: Hi, Rick.

RICK: Michelle?

MICHELLE: I know, it's about time I called you for a change.

RICK: Are you in Oregon?

MICHELLE: I'm home. I called to find out what you can tell me about Rapids.

RICK: Rapids? It's when a river —

MICHELLE: Not what, where. The town of Rapids. Do you know where it is?

RICK: Yeah, I think it's out the Umpqua from Roseburg.

MICHELLE: Where's that from Portland?

RICK: Less than 200 miles south. What's with the sudden interest in Rapids?

MICHELLE: I've been following a series of articles in the paper. They've built this dam on the river and in a few months the town of Rapids is going to be flooded out of existence. I want to do a documentary on the final days in the town. I'm looking for a good cameraman. You interested?

RICK: Of course I'm interested. Tell me more.

(LIGHTS UP FULL on the lounge. Rick gets behind a camera with portable sound equipment and is filming Red, who sits at the bar. DOTTY, the blind bartender, is behind the bar. Michelle stands off to the side, interviewing Red.)

MICHELLE: Interview with Red Mitchell, take one. Action.

RICK: Rolling.

(A beat.)

MICHELLE: Action, Red.

RED: I start now?

MICHELLE: Right, whenever I say "action."

RED: Okay. Well, let's see. I came here in, oh, it must have been ... I'd say around 1946. After the war. I knew Skeeter Davis in the Army — he's Dotty's ex and got killed. So when I brung her the news and some things he wanted her to have — course, she knew he was killed by then — anyway, she had the place up for sale. So I bought it and kept her on behind the bar. Been here ever since.

MICHELLE: What was business like in those days?

RED: The town had seen better days for sure. Hills was pretty well logged out by then, and the loggers were moving up river. Down river belonged to the government. So I was taking a chance buying a restaurant.

MICHELLE: Did you get any tourists up here then?

DOTTY: We always had good fishing.

RED: More tourists were coming all the time. The boom was in the sixties. More retired folks moved in, too, mostly from California. Got to where we'd have a pretty lively summer, especially after we built the motel and had live music in here. And we always did have the best restaurant in town. The only one for about the last five years.

MICHELLE: What was a Saturday night like in the good old days? When it got pretty lively ... ?

RED: After we added the motel and the campground, we'd have a real busy summer, year after year. Didn't make any difference if it was Saturday night or Wednesday night really — on vacation, it's all the same. Course, things got even livelier on weekends with the music.

MICHELLE: What kind of music did you have?

RED: Country.

DOTTY: Gayle Goodwyn sang here. This is her home town.

RED: I don't think they want to hear about that.

MICHELLE: Who did you say?

DOTTY: Gayle Goodwyn. She sang in here a hundred times if she sang once. She grew up in Rapids.

RICK: *The* Gayle Goodwyn?

RED: Yeah, but she ain't been back for years.

DOTTY: Her first hit was about growing up here. And, of course, last year she was given that award on television. She used to sing right in here, all the time.

RED: That was ten years ago. She went to Nashville about '61 or '62, I guess. When did she leave Buck?

DOTTY: Summer '61, I think.

RED: They used to be married. His real name's Henry Lancaster but he got to calling himself Buck Timber. He was quite a country singer himself in those days.

DOTTY: Gayle's real name ain't Goodwyn either. It's Miller. She didn't marry a Goodwyn, the record company give her the name. I heard so on the radio.

MICHELLE: And Buck Timber is a country singer, too?

RED: Yeah, but nobody ever heard of him like they know Gayle Goodwyn. He may be dead for all I know.

DOTTY: For my money, neither sings alone as good as they used to sing together. That was right in here. Course, I ain't heard Buck sing for years. Don't know if he's even singing any more.

RED: Buck and Gayle could pack them in on a weekend, that's for sure.

(ACTION FREEZES in lounge and LIGHTS COME DOWN HALF. GAYLE and BUCK move into LIGHTED neutral area, each with a guitar, and sing like in the good old days.)

BUCK: *(singing)* I've always been a rambler
I never settled down
I took the road to be my own best friend
But lately I've been finding
All my roads lead back to you
I've found my home
You are my journey's end
BUCK AND GAYLE: *(singing)* Thank heaven for you
You've always seen me through
You know the ways to ease my troubled mind
Thank heaven for you
For the love that's been so true
You are the one I never thought I'd find
GAYLE: *(singing)* I wake up in the morning
To find you close to me
And the love I feel is much too strong to hide
You are the one I've waited for
You are my dreams made real
Come take my hand
I need you by my side
BUCK AND GAYLE: *(singing)* Thank heaven for you
You've always seen me through
You know the way to ease my troubled mind
Thank heaven for you
For the love that's been so true
You are the one I never thought I'd find
MICHELLE: Cut!

(BLACKOUT. A beat. LIGHTS COME UP on lounge, where Gayle is alone, strumming her guitar. She is in the process of writing a new song. Stuck, she cusses under her breath and exits left.)

(Buck enters right, carrying his guitar case. He looks around. He goes to the bar and pours himself a shot. Seeing the guitar Gayle left behind at a table, he goes to it, sits down and starts strumming the guitar.)

(Gayle returns, entering left. Seeing Buck, she stops in her tracks. They regard one another for a moment.)

BUCK: I'll be damned.

GAYLE: Hello, Buck.

BUCK: Great minds think alike or what?

GAYLE: Perhaps.

BUCK: *(about using the guitar)* Hope you don't mind ...

GAYLE: Help yourself. It's a present from my new manager.

BUCK: I would've expected him to buy you something fancier.

GAYLE: Her. It's my traveling guitar, not my concert one.

BUCK: Where is everybody?

GAYLE: A young couple's here to make a movie of some kind. Red's taken them down to the river.

BUCK: I read where you're making a movie yourself.

GAYLE: My agent's negotiating something like that. Nothing definite yet.

BUCK: Expect him to pull it off?

GAYLE: Yes, I think *she* will come up with something.

BUCK: Sounds like you got a full house working for you.

GAYLE: I try to be associated with the best. How about yourself? You still playing?

BUCK: Of course I'm still playing. Jesus.

GAYLE: I didn't mean it like it sounded. You should know I'm a fan.

BUCK: Yeah, I'm still beating the strings. Have a gig next week in Portland, as a matter of fact. Then up to Renton the following week.

GAYLE: And so you stopped on your way to see Rapids one more time before it ... what's the word? Sinks?

BUCK: Gets flooded, sinks, same difference.

GAYLE: I knew I was sentimental. I didn't know you were.

BUCK: Oh, I just came by to see what was going on. What's your excuse?

GAYLE: My excuse — the one I gave my manager — is that I have the flu and I'm in Palm Springs to recuperate. I wanted to get up here before I go on tour.

(Dotty enters left. Though blind, she knows her way around very well. Buck quickly gestures "sshh" to Gayle, in order to surprise Dotty.)

464

DOTTY: Red?

GAYLE: He took that couple down to the river. They wanted to film him down there.

DOTTY: I still don't understand what this movie business is all about.

GAYLE: Just the story of the town, I guess.

DOTTY: What town? They should've come before folks moved out.

(Buck has moved behind Dotty and now puts his hands over her eyes.)

DOTTY: Who's that?

BUCK: *(disguising his voice)* Three guesses.

DOTTY: It ain't Red. Hands are too warm.

BUCK: No, it ain't Red.

DOTTY: Let me feel.

(Buck removes his hands. Dotty turns and with both hands feels the contours of his face.)

DOTTY: I don't know you.

BUCK: *(in normal voice)* Oh yes, you do.

DOTTY: *(still feeling)* It can't be.

BUCK: Sure as hell is, though.

DOTTY: Buck!

(They embrace.)

BUCK: Hello, Dotty babe. How come you ain't made me one of your specials yet?

DOTTY: Buck, you son of a gun ... it's getting to be like old home week around here.

BUCK: *(breaking the embrace)* Then mix some specials, damn it. How about one of Dotty's specials, Gayle?

DOTTY: If a Blind Dotty don't do it, nothing will.

GAYLE: I think I'll pass.

BUCK: Come on. You don't want to celebrate old home week?

GAYLE: Pass.

(Blackout.)

MICHELE'S VOICE IN DARKNESS: Interview with Buck Timber, take one.

RICK'S VOICE IN DARKNESS: Rolling.

(A SPOT comes up on Buck.)

BUCK: I have a gig in Portland next week and this is on the way. I'd heard about it going under water because of the dam but wasn't sure when — didn't know if it was already under water actually. So I just came by to see what was going on. I got a lot of memories here. Had some good times here. Let me tell you something — I'm not bragging, it's the plain truth. Red and Dotty will tell you. So will Gayle, if she's honest about it. In 1960 Buck Timber was a name that brought folks in the door. I could play any club from Renton to Bakersfield. Hell, there was even a record promoter in California who was trying to get me to cut a record. You remember that, Red? One summer he pestered me no end, trying to get me down to California to cut a record. It must have been 1961 or so. He'd phone me right here at the bar, begging me to come down to California. Remember, Red?

(LIGHTS UP FULL in lounge, with Buck, Red, Dotty and Gayle. It is 1961.)

RED: *(at phone)* Buck, for Christ's sake, won't you just talk to the man?

BUCK: Ain't got a thing to say to him.

RED: So tell him that yourself. It's the third time he's called today.

GAYLE: Maybe it's not like you think.

BUCK: Like hell. If you've seen one record promoter, you've seen them all. They're like vultures.

DOTTY: When did you ever meet a record promoter?

BUCK: I know more than you think about record promoters.

RED: What do I tell him, Buck?

GAYLE: I don't see the harm in just talking to him.

BUCK: Because he wants me to change my style.

RED: How do you know he's even heard you?

BUCK: Why's he calling, if he ain't heard me?

RED: You got a reputation in Bakersfield, don't you? He probably wants to hear for himself what all the talk is about.

BUCK: Then he can drive his ass up here and catch my show.

RED: He's not going to wait all day, Buck.

GAYLE: Can I talk to him?

466

BUCK: I'll talk to him. Christ.

(He goes to the phone.)

BUCK: This is Buck Timber. ... Not so fast, partner. I want to make something clear.
RED: Jesus, Buck.
BUCK: I don't sing Hollywood western, and I don't sing rockabilly, and I don't sing popular. I sing Woody Guthrie and Jimmie Rodgers, mainly. ... Woody Guthrie.
RED: Sometimes I think he's afraid of success.
BUCK: If you don't know, I can't tell you.

(He hangs up.)

BUCK: He never heard of Woody Guthrie!
RED: Damn, but you're afraid of success.
BUCK: Depends on what you mean by success.
RED: Do you realize all it would take is one hit record? Then you could record any damn thing you want. Your name would sell it.
BUCK: Sure, that's why Hank Thompson has to cut a record about the jungle. "Rockin' in the congo, rockin' in the congo." You can have it.
GAYLE: He called because he heard about you, and you only sing what you want to, don't you? You should've listened to what he had to say.
BUCK: They have a way of changing you, believe me. Look what happened to Woody at the Rainbow Room.
RED: I don't see it hurt his reputation any.
BUCK: Because he had the balls to walk out. They wanted to turn him into Gene Autry or somedamnbody. Woody Guthrie, America's Ramblin' Cowboy, they were billing him. They even had a costume made up for him — chaps, fancy boots, the works. Woody says he's ashamed he lasted two verses of his first song. He shouldn't have gone on stage at all. The damn tables had white tablecloths, for Christ's sake. People were sipping champagne like it was New Year's eve. Woody says he felt like he was in a zoo.
RED: I still say you can write your own ticket once you make a name for yourself.
BUCK: I got a name, from Renton to Bakersfield. I can get a gig anywhere on the west coast.

RED: In the clubs, sure. Because you're good, you're damn good. But until you cut a record, you're nothing. You should be writing your own ticket, anywhere you want to be.

BUCK: What's wrong with being right here? We're not doing all that bad, are we, babe?

GAYLE: We're doing fine.

BUCK: Damn right, we are.

(LIGHTS DOWN HALF as Gayle moves forward into SPOT in neutral area.)

GAYLE: Buck was running the show in those days, and I trusted him to do right by us. The truth is, I wouldn't be singing at all if it wasn't for him. He kept pushing me on, telling me I had a voice as pure as Patsy Cline. And we weren't doing bad at the time, playing clubs along the west coast. We'd spend summer and fall in Rapids, then go to California for the winter. But I always wished Buck wasn't so stubborn. Whenever a record promoter took interest, he'd almost run to get away. He said he didn't like the way country music was changing, he'd have nothing to do with helping it along. Rock and roll was ruining country, Buck said, and popularity would ruin it even more. So more and more we got requests on stage for songs that we didn't know. The times were changing, and we weren't changing with them. The fact is, many of the new songs were songs I wouldn't mind singing at all, but Buck would have nothing to do with them.

MICHELLE: Cut!

(LIGHTS UP FULL in lounge. It is 1972.)

BUCK: That all you need?

MICHELLE: For the time being. We want to do some shooting outside while the sun's up.

RICK: Is there a bridge across the river somewhere?

RED: About five miles down river. Go to the highway and turn left. If the Corps' already closed it, you're going to have to go into Roseburg.

MICHELLE: Thanks.

RICK: Catch you all later.

(Michelle and Rick exit right.)

BUCK: Do you think they know what they're doing?

RED: Appears to me they do.

BUCK: They don't have much when it comes to equipment.

GAYLE: They can make do with what they have. My manager's brother did a real nice documentary on country fiddling, using a smaller camera than what they got. It was on educational television. Looked real nice, real professional.

BUCK: A movie with you in it will be commercial easy. They stumbled across a real golden egg in their nest.

GAYLE: I hope they do a good job. Be a nice tribute to the town.

BUCK: I'm surprised CBS isn't here doing it.

RED: CBS ain't interested in Rapids, Oregon.

DOTTY: Seems to me the folks who lived here weren't interested in Rapids either.

RED: Everyone signed the petitions. What else could we do?

DOTTY: Raise a stink.

BUCK: Damn right. Just refuse to move, refuse to budge.

RED: Face it, this town was already dying. When news of the dam leaked out, folks just moved away faster than normal.

GAYLE: You didn't.

RED: Us and a few others. Been here too long to move fast, I guess.

GAYLE: It's still about as pretty country as you can find.

DOTTY: I remember your song about Rapids. Can I twist your arm to sing it?

GAYLE: Maybe later. Right now I feel like taking a walk and enjoying some of that scenery out there.

BUCK: Want company?

GAYLE: To be honest, no.

BUCK: Didn't think so.

GAYLE: Nothing personal.

BUCK: Course not. Don't fall in.

GAYLE: I'll try not to.

(She exits right, taking her guitar.)

BUCK: I think I'm ready for another special.

DOTTY: One Blind Dotty, coming up.

BUCK: You joining me, Red?

RED: Sure.

DOTTY: Then let's make it three.

BUCK: When I try to explain about a Blind Dotty, folks don't believe me.

RED: It's one of a kind.

DOTTY: You know, Skeeter actually discovered it. He had it in the Army and sent me the recipe. In the Army they called it Artillery Punch. Gin, whiskey, rum, white wine, soda and grapefruit juice.

BUCK: Sure as hell tastes better than it sounds.

DOTTY: I wonder how folks will take to it in Yakima.

BUCK: You're heading up to Yakima?

DOTTY: Red's brother has a bar there.

RED: It's not much but he's thinking of expanding.

BUCK: To make room for you?

RED: His business has always been pretty good.

DOTTY: I always wanted to see Yakima.

BUCK: Yakima's all right. I played there a couple times.

DOTTY: Red says his brother has a real nice spread. Built it himself.

BUCK: So when are you taking off?

DOTTY: They want everybody out of town by next Monday.

RED: We might hang around Roseburg for a while.

DOTTY: What for?

RED: Just to relax. We've been in such a god awful rush lately.

DOTTY: You never told me about relaxing in Roseburg. We can rest when we get to Yakima.

RED: I expect Fred'd put us right to work.

DOTTY: We can take our time driving up.

RED: That, too, I guess.

DOTTY: *(delivering the drinks)* Three Blind Dotties.

BUCK: Well, cheers, all.

DOTTY: Seems like somebody ought to make a toast.

BUCK: Red?

RED: Go ahead.

BUCK: To the obvious, I guess — to a fine little town that's going under water. Got a lot of memories here. *(They drink.)* Damn, that's good.

DOTTY: Don't forget it'll sneak up on you.

BUCK: I'm counting on it.

DOTTY: You old son of a gun — I wasn't sure I'd ever see you again.

BUCK: You ought to know better than that.

DOTTY: I'm just glad you came before we headed for Yakima. Gayle, too. It means a lot.

RED: Gayle says she had to cancel a concert to come. I imagine that cost her a pretty penny.

BUCK: She can make it up easy enough.

RED: How do you mean?

BUCK: I'm not saying she's here for a publicity stunt or anything, but it can't hurt her image, visiting the home town before it's flooded.

RED: She seems to be keeping mighty quiet about it, out there looking at the scenery. Where's the publicity in that?

BUCK: We'll find out, I guess.

DOTTY: When did you get so damn suspicious?

BUCK: Ever since I heard that first record of hers. It didn't strike me like she was quite telling the truth on that song, even if she did get a gold record. I've been suspicious of Gayle Goodwyn ever since.

(LIGHTS DOWN in bar and UP on Gayle in neutral area. She has her guitar.)

GAYLE: *(singing)* I was born in a place where the sky was always clear
Where you took the trees for granted in a forest live with deer
Where every face was friendly and every voice was kind
And that country northwestern soothed your mind

(Chorus) I've been through Kentucky, Oklahoma, Tennessee
But my home in the west won't let me be
Where the clean sparklin' river comes flowin' through the pines
Got that country northwestern on my mind

(She plays a guitar lick.)

GAYLE: *(singing)* I headed down to Nashville, left behind my rollin' hills
I found a world of glitter, spotlights and fancy frills
But sometimes in my dreams my way back home I find
And feel that country northwestern in my mind

(Chorus repeats.)

(BLACKOUT. LIGHTS UP in neutral area, where Rick and Michelle are filming.)

MICHELLE: Action.

RICK: Rolling.

MICHELLE: Sweep and zoom in on her.

RICK: And we zoom ... she's writing something.

471

MICHELLE: Okay, pull back. I want to end with the bend in the river.

RICK: Can I hold on her a minute? She looks involved.

MICHELLE: A beat of six.

RICK: One, two, three —

MICHELLE: Then back to where the river bends.

RICK: Six. And we're at the bend in the river.

MICHELLE: Hold a sec ... and cut.

RICK: Cut. I wonder what she's writing.

MICHELLE: Her tax return.

RICK: Very funny. Want to check out that bridge now?

MICHELLE: Will you let me call the shots, please?

RICK: I thought you wanted to shoot from across the river.

MICHELLE: Eventually. I also want to shoot with a sense of continuity. I'm still working some concepts out.

RICK: You know, she could be writing her next gold record down there. A million dollar song. Incredible.

MICHELLE: Not really. What's more smaltzy and commercial than your home town being flooded by a dam? Country fans ought to eat it up.

RICK: You think she's writing a song about that?

MICHELLE: It's probably why she came.

RICK: You get tough skin down there in L.A.

MICHELLE: I'm a survivor. Obviously she is, too.

RICK: You sure got a break, though. If she can sell a song, she can sell your film.

MICHELLE: If she's in it, I suppose she can.

RICK: What do you mean, if she's in it?

MICHELLE: If my concept includes using her.

RICK: How can you not use her? Gayle Goodwyn is down there scribbling her next hit record and you have it on film. You have her talking about growing up here on film. You'd leave that on the editing room floor when every country fan in the world would pay to see it?

MICHELLE: Rick, do you know what it's like to work on Hollywood fluff? Do you have any idea?

RICK: Not too hot, right?

MICHELLE: Frustrating. It's filming by computer, by consumer analysis, by market demand, by the most intricate attention to every detail but one — what are you trying to mean? On this one, I want to please myself. I want to say something I really mean.

RICK: A lady of such integrity.

MICHELLE: I'm serious.

RICK: So am I.

(He embraces her but Michelle resists.)

MICHELLE: I want to get more shooting in.

RICK: Okay. What's going on anyway?

MICHELLE: Nothing. I want to get more shooting in while the sun's right.

RICK: I got the impression you really weren't participating last night. You have a steady guy in L.A.?

MICHELLE: I don't have to answer that.

RICK: You spoiled me long ago. Something was wrong last night.

MICHELLE: I guess I'm preoccupied with what's happening here. I don't understand it.

RICK: Dams are built every day.

MICHELLE: But the consequences — everyone is taking it so calmly.

RICK: Can't fight city hall.

MICHELLE: I suppose I'm still looking for my point of view. I haven't decided what kind of film I'm making.

RICK: How about making it a comic love story? Gracing the hillside with passion as a gesture to the sea from which we came.

MICHELLE: Rick, you're nuts.

(They embrace. Buck enters and sees them. He backs off to announce his arrival with a song.)

BUCK: *(singing)* There's lots of mean women on almost every street

Lots of mean women on almost every street

But I've got the meanest woman ever walked on two feet

(Buck "notices" them.)

BUCK: Well, howdy. Shooting scenery for the movie?

RICK: Gayle's down along the river, if you're looking for her.

BUCK: Is that a fact? Damned if she ain't.

MICHELLE: Let's check out the bridge, Rick.

RICK: You're the boss.

BUCK: Guess you've got a real winner, with the great Gayle Goodwyn in your movie. What a break.

MICHELLE: It's not the kind of film that depends on a star.

BUCK: Sure as hell can't hurt, though. She'll probably make all the difference in the world at the box office.

MICHELLE: I'm not necessarily making this for whatever money it may earn. I work in Hollywood, so I know about the commercial market. This project is something different.

BUCK: You don't want it to be a success?

MICHELLE: I would be pleased if it was a success. But making money isn't my motivation.

BUCK: But you still have to cover expenses. Like royalties, for instance. Funny I haven't been asked to sign a release or contract yet.

RICK: My fault. I haven't gotten to it yet.

BUCK: I imagine Gayle will ask a pretty penny to sign.

MICHELLE: Dotty and Red have signed releases. If you don't want to sign one, fine. I can shoot around you. I can shoot around the great Gayle Goodwyn, too.

BUCK: No offense. I was just curious about your budget. If you can't pay royalties, that's fine with me. I'll still sign a release.

MICHELLE: We have more shooting to do.

BUCK: I hope you make one hell of a movie. I like your attitude. I'd love to be included.

RICK: You used to be married to Gayle, didn't you?

BUCK: Six years. Between you and me, she wouldn't ever have climbed onto a stage without a boot in the butt from me. Then later, after we were separated, she changed her style and became famous. So where are you?

RICK: You don't like her style?

BUCK: Do you like making movies in Hollywood?

MICHELLE: It pays the rent.

BUCK: Let me put it this way. I don't buy her records.

RICK: What records do you buy?

BUCK: Ernest Tubb. Hank Snow, Hank Williams. Ramblin' Jack Elliott and Woody Guthrie. Patsy Cline. Gayle used to remind me of Patsy Cline.

MICHELLE: Would you talk about country music on film?

BUCK: Sure, what do you want to know? I'd better warn you, I'm old-fashioned. Buck Timber, the Ramblin' Dinosaur ...

MICHELLE: Roll it, Rick.

RICK: Rolling ...

(BLACKOUT. SPOT UP on Gayle in the neutral area, right.)

474

GAYLE: I've never understood how a song gets written. Bits and pieces of a tune come to mind, usually while I'm just fiddling around on the guitar. I don't play much in concerts any more, that's what the band is for, to give the fuller sound people want today. But alone, fiddling around on the guitar, sometimes fragments of a tune will begin to catch my ear, and then sometimes words attach themselves to the pieces of tune, and somehow a song begins to take shape. It's always struck me as an irrational and mysterious process. A moment ago, sitting watching the river, trying to imagine that all of this would soon be under water, these hillsides where I played as a girl would be flooded, the swimming hold near the bridge would be lost forever — thinking this way while fiddling on the guitar, I felt a song was beginning to break through, a song about what was happening to my home town. But this feeling came too quickly, too consciously, and before words attached themselves to the fragments of a tune, I stopped. Suddenly it was very quiet, moreso than I've been used to. It was as if silence itself was a song.

(Buck enters as LIGHTS COME UP in the area.)

BUCK: You've been on candid camera. Up there — the movie makers have been snooping on you.
GAYLE: It's okay with me.
BUCK: Long as you get your royalties, right?
GAYLE: I don't think this will be a commercial film. Probably something they'll show at festivals.
BUCK: All the same, somebody in your position, being a superstar and all —
GAYLE: I don't want to argue about it, Buck.
BUCK: What do you want to argue about then?
GAYLE: I don't want to argue, period. I'm heading back.
BUCK: Wait a minute. You know, you could put a stop to all this if you had a mind to.
GAYLE: How?
BUCK: For instance — what if you called the TV station in Roseburg and told them you were up here and didn't plan to leave? If they flood Rapids, they have to put the great Gayle Goodwyn under water as well. The networks would pick up a story like that, you know damn well they would. And then the Corps of Engineers would have a controversy on their hands. They wouldn't dare flood the town.
GAYLE: That's a very romantic notion. However, I'm a realist.
BUCK: You think they could flood the town with the country singer of the year up here? No way.

GAYLE: You're still a dreamer. That's charming, in a way. But I'm not a dreamer, Buck.

(She exits.)

(Buck watches her go. Then he looks up to where Rick and Michelle have been filming.)

BUCK: Hey, Rick, Michelle! You ever see a Ramblin' Dinosaur piss across the Umpqua? Start the camera rolling ...

(BLACKOUT. A SPOT comes up on Dotty in the lounge.)

DOTTY: At first, I thought, well, there's no way they can get away with this. You can't just decide to put a town on the map under water. You can't just move everybody out. Not without a vote, and nobody here wanted to move, those of us left had lived here all our lives. So when the meetings were called I thought, we'll just all go to the meetings and tell them we don't like this idea at all, and that'll be the end of it.
(A SPOT comes up on Red in the lounge.)

RED: You take one man, and he's free; two, and pretty soon you got an argument; add a third and you've got government, and then you're really in a mess. I knew we didn't have a chance in hell as soon as the proposal for the dam came out in the Roseburg paper. The government had the choice of flooding the town or flooding their picnic tables. Which do you think they're going to do?
DOTTY: When it became clear to me that there wasn't going to be anything like a vote, that their minds were made up and we had nothing to say about it, the only thing they were really interested in was how much they were going to have to shell up to buy us off from lynching them, then I thought to myself, Lord have mercy, who are these men, what do they look like? I never wanted to have eyesight so much in my life. I wanted to see for myself what men like that looked like.
RED: They had their argument, of course. The town was dying anyway, which was true enough. Young folks had moved out til there weren't any to speak of. The mill had closed long ago, the hills had been logged out long ago. They were going to give the area a new life, they said, by making a big recreation area. What did the opinions of a few sentimental old-timers matter?

(LIGHTS UP FULL in lounge as Gayle enters.)

DOTTY: Gayle, is that you?

GAYLE: You have a sixth sense.

DOTTY: Sounded like your walk.

RED: Buck went out looking for you.

GAYLE: He found me.

DOTTY: You keep Red from getting bored with himself, I've got chores to do.

RED: What chores you talking about?

DOTTY: Packing, for one.

RED: We don't have to leave til Monday.

DOTTY: Seeing how I'll end up packing for both of us, I need a head start.

(She exits.)

RED: Hell, I can pack myself in half an hour.

GAYLE: It's so quiet out there. I'd forgotten. I think I'm overdue for a vacation.

RED: I've always been partial to this country.

GAYLE: I've never been to Yakima. Is it pretty?

RED: It's all right.

GAYLE: Moving is harder on Dotty than you, isn't it? It's incredible the way she gets around here. She must have every nook and cranny memorized.

RED: She gets around as good as any of us.

GAYLE: Now she'll have to memorize a whole new territory. Or is it really a sixth sense?

RED: Gayle, maybe you can help me out a little. Something just between you and me.

GAYLE: What is it?

RED: You see, Dotty and me have had separate bedrooms upstairs for years now.

GAYLE: That's no business of mine.

RED: It's not like she's my wife, is what I'm saying. It's not like I have that kind of responsibility. We're more like good friends.

GAYLE: What are you trying to say?

RED: I want to go to Yakima alone. I know it must sound awful of me to say so. But it's the truth. I'm too old to be a caretaker. Because it's like you say, she'll have to learn a whole new territory.

GAYLE: You said you wanted help. Sounds to me like you've got your mind made up.

RED: Help to talk sense to her. You see, I called this fellow I heard about and he sent me this brochure about the place he runs. It's in the hills outside of Roseburg, overlooking the river, just like here. Dotty's always talking about how much she loves the sound of the river. So I thought, maybe she's better off staying there. They have nurses who are trained special and —

(Buck enters, interrupting him.)

BUCK: You know what I think? I think that lady knows more about making movies than I figured. I'm not saying she'll have a hit on her hands but I wouldn't be surprised if that movie turns out to be pretty interesting.

GAYLE: If you'll excuse me, I'll give Dotty a hand.

BUCK: Go ahead, desert me.

(She exits.)

BUCK: She's avoiding me like the plague.

RED: What do you expect, married like you was?

BUCK: I expect a little civilized nostalgia.

RED: She's acting civilized to me.

(Gayle has left behind her guitar and Buck will go to it, pick it up.)

BUCK: Go head, gang up on me.

RED: That's not what I meant.

BUCK: You have any idea what a guitar like this costs?

RED: Plenty.

BUCK: And this is just her traveling guitar. She saves the diamond-studded one for concerts.

RED: She earned it.

BUCK: You don't earn a goddamn thing in the music business, Red. You either kiss ass or you don't kiss ass.

RED: Gayle's done all right with herself.

BUCK: I wish this was her concert guitar. I'd be inspired to play something obscene on it.

RED: What's the point in that?

BUCK: What's the point in anything? Because if this was her concert guitar, I'd feel like playing an obscene song. On principle, partner.

RED: So if you feel like playing a dirty song, sing a dirty song.

BUCK: I get it — you want to hear a dirty song.

RED: I didn't say that. Jesus Christ, I can't open my mouth without you changing everything around. You sure as hell used to be easier to get along with.

BUCK: Here you go, Red. Dedicated to you.

(He sings, to the tune of "Your Cheatin' Heart".)

BUCK: *(singing)* Your cheatin' fart
Will make you reek
You'll smell so bad
For weeks and weeks
Relief won't come
Until you bathe
I'll throw some soap
Into your grave

The stench spreads 'round
Like clouds of smog
I'd rather live
With fifty hogs
You try to hide
Behind perfume
But your cheatin' fart
Still smells on you

(He lifts a leg to fart. Nothing.)

BUCK: I'm getting old, partner. Lost the touch. I used to be able to sound off at will and light them with firecrackers.

RED: Where the hell did you find that song?

BUCK: Picked it up in a bottle on the beach.

RED: Like hell you did.

BUCK: I wrote the son-of-a-bitch myself. Give me a little credit. Written a hundred others like it, too.

RED: I enjoyed it.

BUCK: Think it'll play in Nashville?

RED: You got to be dreaming.

BUCK: Red, you hit it on the nose. I'm dreaming. I'd like to see country music raise a little hell again, where I could get up on the bandstand at Grand Ol' Opry and sing about something as natural as passing wind.

RED: They ain't never sung about that on the Opry. You're as crazy as ever.

BUCK: I sure as hell hope so! I'm so crazy I'd like to stop them from flooding the town, partner. If I had Gayle's clout, I'd stage a sit-in, just like the college kids. I wouldn't budge. I'd grab that shotgun off the wall and fend them off if I had to. I'd phone Walter Cronkite person-to-person and give him an exclusive interview. The Corps would have to back down once Uncle Walter got into the act.

RED: Like hell they would. The army drags the college kids off, don't it? They'd drag you off as well.

BUCK: Maybe they would and maybe they wouldn't. But let me tell you something, buddy. The only way to find out is to try it and see what happens.

(Michelle and Rick enter.)

BUCK: Out of film already?
MICHELLE: We have lots of film.
BUCK: If you're taking a break, how about a drink?
RICK: Sure. Scotch and water for me.
MICHELLE: Do you have white wine?
RED: Umpqua's finest.
BUCK: I'll get Dotty to make you one of her specials later.
MICHELLE: What are the chances of having a party here?
BUCK: There you go.
MICHELLE: I'm serious. I'd like to film a party going on.
RED: Don't know where you'd find the folks to come, unless you want to invite the Corps of Engineers.
MICHELLE: A private party's fine.
BUCK: *(going to exit, left, to yell)* Hey, Dotty, we're going to have a party!
MICHELLE: It'll be like a wake.
RICK: Far out.
MICHELLE: Maybe we can all loosen up and talk about the good old days some more. Send the town out in style.
BUCK: You going to join the party or just film it?
RICK: Pull a Hitchcock and appear in a scene yourself.
MICHELLE: Makes no difference.

480

BUCK: So when do we start?

(Dotty and Gayle enter.)

DOTTY: What're you yelling about?
BUCK: The lady wants to have a party. Like a wake.
DOTTY: You Catholic?
MICHELLE: I want something festive and final for the film. A wake, going away party, whatever you want to call it.
GAYLE: Sounds interesting.
MICHELLE: I don't want it to be interesting. I want it to be sincere. Let's start drinking and see what happens.
BUCK: My kind of girl. Make a bucket of specials, Dotty.
MICHELLE: Start rolling, Rick. Just forget about the camera, everybody. Let's just toast the town for a while.
RICK: Rolling...

(A long beat. No one is partying.)

BUCK: Hey, come on now, we're supposed to be having a party! Make a mess of specials, Dotty.
GAYLE: None for me.
BUCK: No sobers allowed at a wake.
DOTTY: Why don't you sing while I'm mixing drinks?
GAYLE: Maybe later.
BUCK: Hell, I'll sing. *(Singing)* "Your cheatin' fart / Will make you reek."
GAYLE: I hate that song.
RED: This is all on film, Buck.
BUCK: If you don't like it, you can cut it out later, right, Michelle? (Singing) "You'll smell so bad / For weeks and weeks"
DOTTY: They don't want to hear that. Do *(singing)* "Hey, good lookin' ... "
DOTTY AND BUCK: *(singing)* "Whatcha got cookin' / How's about cookin' something up with me?"
BUCK: Remember this one? *(Singing)* "There stands the glass / Fill it up to the brim"
BUCK AND DOTTY: *(singing)* "Til my troubles grow dim / It's my first one today"
BUCK: *(singing)* "Detour, there's a muddy road ahead"
BUCK AND DOTTY: *(singing)* "Detour, I paid no mind to what it said"

BUCK: Here's one I bet you forgot. *(Singing)* "Way down yonder in the Indian nation / I ride my pony on the reservation"

BUCK AND DOTTY: *(singing)* "In those Oklahoma hills where I was born"

BUCK, DOTTY AND GAYLE: *(singing)* "Way down yonder in the Indian nation / A cowboy's life is my occupation / In those Oklahoma hills where I belong"

GAYLE: *(singing, with guitar)* I was born in a place where the sky was always clear
Where you took the trees for granted in a forest live with deer
Where every face was friendly and every voice was kind
And that country northwestern soothed your mind

I've been through Kentucky, Oklahoma, Tennessee
But my home in the west won't let me be
Where the clean sparklin' river comes flowin' through the pines
Got that country northwestern on my mind"

(Near the end of the song, Buck fetches the shotgun on the wall.)

BUCK: *(with the shotgun)* That's a bullshit song, Gayle.

GAYLE: Buck ... ?

RED: It's not loaded.

BUCK: Like hell it ain't. I loaded it myself this morning. Found the shells in the drawer, Red.

RED: Then what the hell?

DOTTY: What's going on?

BUCK: Red, I want you to get some rope. Don't ask no questions, just get it.

RED: They're still filming.

BUCK: You keep on filming, too. I'm going to give you something to make a movie about.

DOTTY: You quit this fool nonsense, and let's get on with the party.

BUCK: Oh, we'll have ourselves a party, don't worry about that.

GAYLE: Perhaps you can share what's going on with the rest of us.

BUCK: Damn it, Red!

RED: Be right back.

(He exits for the rope.)

BUCK: Remember this one, Dotty?

BUCK: *(singing)* "There's lotsa mean women
On almost any street
Lotsa mean women
On almost any street
But I got the meanest woman
Ever walked on two feet"
DOTTY: Jimmie Rodgers.
BUCK: Bull's-eye.
GAYLE: *(singing)* "It wasn't God who made honky tonk angels — "
RED: *(returning)* Here's your rope. I hope I'm wrong about what
you plan to do with it.
BUCK: Tie her to a chair.
GAYLE: That isn't very funny.
BUCK: Tie her up, Red.
GAYLE: Listen here, goddamn it — !
RED: Buck, why don't you just put away the rifle?
BUCK: You ever know me to back down, partner?
RED: Gayle, we'd better do like he says.
GAYLE: I'll help you.

(She sits obediently in a chair while Red ties her up.)

BUCK: If you behave yourself, I won't gag you. Do I make myself
clear?
GAYLE: Yes sir, Mr. Timber. Talk about being phony. Mr. Henry
Lancaster.
DOTTY: This doesn't make any sense, Buck.
BUCK: It will in a minute.
MICHELLE: What's going on, Buck? Tell the camera.
BUCK: I'll talk to the camera later. Just keep the film rolling. There's
a TV station in Roseburg. Do you think they can develop your film?
MICHELLE: They should have a lab.
BUCK: You take the film to Roseburg when I'm finished and get it
developed and show it to them. Tell them there's a crazed Ramblin'
Dinosaur up here who's holding superstar Gayle Goodwyn hostage.
He'll let her go if they don't flood the town. Otherwise she gets a
number right between the eyes.
RED: Jesus, Buck — !
BUCK: I'm not going to murder anyone. But they don't know that.
Shit, that's on film.
MICHELLE: We'll put in a new roll when you're ready. But I don't
think it'll work, Buck.

BUCK: It's worth a try. That's the trouble with people today, they don't try.

RED: All you'll do is draw the police up here.

BUCK: We got a real army of confidence here, don't we? All right. Screw it. Let the town sink, it's not my home any more. Hell with it.

RED: Then I can untie her?

BUCK: Hell no. I'll do something else with her. She's too good a trade not to bargain with for something.

DOTTY: You fool, let her go.

BUCK: You tell the station in Roseburg that there's a raving Ramblin' Dinosaur pervert up here who's liable to rape the great Gayle Goodwyn unless they put my little film on the tube. I want prime time on the news.

MICHELLE: I'm not sure what film you're talking about now.

BUCK: I'm going to sing a song and you're going to film it. I want it shown on prime time.

DOTTY: You don't have to tie Gayle up to get on television. Just go down there and audition like everybody else.

BUCK: I've got a special song in mind, Dotty. They won't touch it unless I bargain from a position of strength.

MICHELLE: What song's that?

BUCK: *(singing)* "Your cheatin' fart
Will make you reek"

RED: They won't put that on TV! I don't care who you tie up.

BUCK: Don't know unless you try. Assholes.

MICHELLE: Pretty bizarre, Buck.

GAYLE: There's kids who watch TV at prime time.

BUCK: Did I ask your opinion? Gag her, Red.

GAYLE: I'm sorry. I'll keep quiet.

BUCK: Children fart. Then they have the good sense to laugh about it. It's only adults who get uptight about it.

RICK: This is all so anal.

BUCK: What's so anal about a fart? It's perfectly natural. So what's wrong with singing about it then?

MICHELLE: We'll do it, Buck. Let me know when you're ready.

RICK: This is better than a wake.

(MRS. AMES enters.)

MRS. AMES: Excuse me. I'm looking for Dorothy Davis.

DOTTY: That's me.

MRS. AMES: I'm Mrs. Ames from Harvest Acres.

RED: *(to get Dotty away)* I've got to take Dotty back to the kitchen, Buck.

DOTTY: *(being hustled away)* What are you doing?

RED: I'll explain everything in a minute ...

(They exit.)

MRS. AMES: I'm sure Dorothy will like Harvest Acres very much. We spoil everyone rotten. We really do. It's a privilege to be able to be a part of it. It's actually like being in a country club. A country club for seniors, you might say. Everybody gets spoiled rotten. We're just terrible that way.

MICHELLE: Keep it rolling, Rick ...

RICK: Not missing a thing ...

MRS. AMES: Dorothy will love it there. Is she packed and ready to go?

BUCK: Jesus Christ.

(LIGHTS FADE TO BLACKOUT. End of Act I.)

ACT TWO

(AT RISE: both Gayle and Mrs. Ames are tied to chairs, Mrs. Ames gagged as well. Buck is fiddling with Gayle's guitar. Mrs. Ames looks scared out of her wits.)

GAYLE: How long is this going to go on?

BUCK: Til Roseburg puts me on the tube.

GAYLE: How do you know they're not on their way to California?

BUCK: They haven't finished their movie.

GAYLE: They may have given up on it. I'm sure they weren't expecting this.

BUCK: This will make a better movie than the other.

GAYLE: Am I to understand my singing inspired all this? Why do you dislike "Country Northwestern" so much?

BUCK: Because it's a bullshit song.

GAYLE: I'm all ears if you care to tell me why.

BUCK: "A forest full of deer" — when's the last time you seen a deer within ten miles of Rapids? They cleared out a step ahead of the loggers.

GAYLE: I meant it more as an image.

BUCK: Red's right — this town started dying long ago. Of course, once that Hollywood promoter decided he'd rather make you famous than me, I guess he needed a bullshit song to fit your new style.

GAYLE: He had nothing to do with the song.

BUCK: But he helped you, didn't he? You seemed pretty interested in him when he came up here. Don't tell me you didn't look him up after you left me.

GAYLE: Only because I didn't know anyone else in the recording business. He seemed interested in my career.

BUCK: That ain't all he was interested in.

GAYLE: That's why we didn't get along, finally.

BUCK: Congratulations.

GAYLE: I know I was young and naive. But I survived and I made it on my own.

BUCK: It's kind of humorous actually. A guy comes up from California in order to discover me and a month later you're running down there so he can discover you. Don't tell me he didn't help your career — and for a price, right?

GAYLE: He got me my first gig, yes. I don't have to answer the rest.

BUCK: He change your style?

GAYLE: No.

BUCK: Who changed your style?

GAYLE: I did.

BUCK: Bullshit. You don't have that much of a business sense.

GAYLE: I did after going hungry for three years. I changed my style to sound like myself. It wasn't natural for me to try and sound like Patsy Cline.

BUCK: Sometimes you sounded better. It wasn't like you were imitating her. You were extending her, the way Ramblin' Jack extends Woody.

486

GAYLE: I had to sing in a style comfortable for me.

BUCK: Sure got comfortable financially.

GAYLE: Buck, I know you're a purist. I actually admire that in a way. You keep the rest of us aware of our roots.

BUCK: Jesus Christ. *(Singing, to the tune of "The Great Speckled Bird")* "What a beautiful thought I am thinking
Concerning a great speckled fraulein"

GAYLE: You're your own worst enemy.

BUCK: *(singing)* "She is rolling around and is naked
'Cept for fifty tattoos on her behind
(Chorus) Fraulein, fraulein
Tattoos on her behind
The initials of those who've come and gone
Fraulein, fraulein
Lives on white wine
And the soup of one large chicken bone"

(He grins at Gayle.)

BUCK: *(singing)* "I tattooed an M just for mother
I tattooed a G for God's grace"

DOTTY: *(entering)* Why did everybody decide to go over the deep end at once?

BUCK: "I tattooed a D just for Dotty —"

DOTTY: No, you didn't either, you crazy fool. Now you untie Gayle right this minute, unless you already have.

GAYLE: He hasn't.

DOTTY: Buck Timber, you untie Gayle this minute before I do it myself.

BUCK: She's being held hostage.

DOTTY: That don't mean she has to be tied up.

(Dotty finds Gayle and begins to untie her.)

BUCK: Go ahead, she can't go anywhere. I have her distributor cap.

GAYLE: I didn't realize all this was premeditated.

BUCK: Oh, this part isn't. But I figured something interesting was bound to happen sooner or later and I didn't want you getting away before the dust settled.

(Gayle is free.)

GAYLE: Thanks, Dotty.
DOTTY: Now if you still have that shotgun —

(She stumbles into the chair with Mrs. Ames.)

DOTTY: Who the hell is this?

(Mrs. Ames makes noises through her gag.)

BUCK: I think she escaped from some asylum.
DOTTY: I'll have you loose in a second.
BUCK: At least keep the gag on.
GAYLE: Must I ask permission to use the facilities?
BUCK: Go ahead. You ain't going anywhere.
GAYLE: You're such a gentleman.

(She exits.)

DOTTY: There we go.
MRS. AMES: My word! I didn't expect that. Of course, Lester uses me in one of his magic tricks now and then. I kept waiting for the trick to happen.
BUCK: What did I tell you?
MRS. AMES: Lester does his tricks after the movies. Every Sunday afternoon there's old movies in the recreation center. We have such a good time! Cary Grant and Spencer Tracy. Mr. Fredericks gives a little pep talk and we get free popcorn.
BUCK: I think that's terrific, lady. Free popcorn.
MRS. AMES: Sometimes we have a talent show. Arnold plays his accordion. Samuel and Marie sing a duet. That's when Lester will do his magic show, and sometimes he uses me as an assistant.
BUCK: You like tricks?
MRS. AMES: I thought that's why you tied me up!
BUCK: I know some tricks. I can turn a glass into a peach.
DOTTY: Lord, that trick's older than I am.
MRS. AMES: Lester can have you pick a card from a deck and put it back and then when he shuffles, the card just flies up into the air!

(Buck moves to the bar for a glass and a bar towel.)

BUCK: What we have here is an ordinary glass, am I right? And here you see one ordinary bar towel.

488

DOTTY: There can't be anybody who ever knew a logger who doesn't know that trick.

BUCK: You ever seen a glass turned into a peach, lady?

MRS. AMES: Oh no, but it sounds wonderful!

BUCK: Great. I'm going to turn this here glass into a peach. But I need your help. We drape the towel over the glass like this ... and say a few magic words, abra-cadabra ... and now I want you to hold onto the glass through the towel while I take the other end. There you go.

(Mrs. Ames holds the glass through the towel and Buck will begin to twist the other end of the towel.)

BUCK: A few more magic words ... abra ... cadabra ... shazam!

(The towel is twisted and Buck suddenly moves his end to his crotch: a huge phallus is suggested, with Mrs. Ames holding its head.)

BUCK: Now ain't that a peach!

MRS. AMES: Oh my!

(Buck laughs his head off and lets go of his end of the towel. Mrs. Ames removes the towel from the glass.)

DOTTY: I didn't know there were any suckers left in Oregon.

BUCK: Ain't that a peach!

MRS. AMES: *(puzzled)* But it's still a glass.

BUCK: Jesus Christ.

RED: *(entering with a portable TV set)* Where do you want this?

BUCK: On the bar, buddy.

RED: I still say it's a waste of time even watching for it.

MRS. AMES: Am I missing something?

BUCK: I ain't got the strength to explain, lady.

MRS. AMES: You should see Lester's tricks at Harvest Acres! Is Dorothy packed and ready to go?

DOTTY: Just where is it you think I'm going?

MRS. AMES: You're Dorothy?

DOTTY: Everybody calls me Dotty.

RED: She ain't the right Dorothy because you're at the wrong address. This here is a kind of family reunion. So maybe you'd better be on your way ...

MRS. AMES: But I have this letter ...

(She brings it out.)

DOTTY: Give it to me.
RED: Let me see that.
MRS. AMES: My word!

(Dotty gets the letter first.)

DOTTY: Buck! Read it to me.
RED: Dotty, that letter's got nothing to do with nothing.
DOTTY: Then why are you so interested in it? Buck ...

(Buck takes the letter and will read it silently.)

DOTTY: What's it say?
RED: You can tell she's nuttier than a fruit cake.
MRS. AMES: Harvest Acres is so nice. We spoil everyone rotten.
BUCK: This letter don't make a bit of sense, Dotty.
RED: See there?
BUCK: You got the wrong Dorothy, lady. Better go back to where you come from.
MRS. AMES: I got a lift from a soldier. He was so nice. He said his uncle's at Harvest Acres, only I don't think I've met the gentleman. I don't know everyone by name. I have to be careful because so many men propose to me as soon as they meet me.
RED: Lady, this here is a private family gathering. If you need a ride somewhere —
BUCK: Not so fast, Red. There's a quicker way to get her out of the way.

(Buck will tie her back to the chair and gag her again.)

RED: I'll be glad to take her where she wants to go.
DOTTY: What's going on? What's Buck doing?
BUCK: Nothing you wouldn't do yourself under the circumstances.
MRS. AMES: Is this another trick?
BUCK: Sure is, lady.
MRS. AMES: I didn't understand the other one.
BUCK: (gagging her) You know how it is with us amateurs. Sorry we're not as good as your friend.
MRS. AMES: (cut short by the gag) Les —
GAYLE: (returning) Not again.

RED: You're not doing Gayle again, too, are you?

BUCK: Nope. Time to turn on the tube and see how much of a trade the great Gayle Goodwyn is really worth.

RED: They won't put on that song, I can promise you that.

DOTTY: This foolishness has gone on long enough. Can I speak to you private, Gayle?

GAYLE: Buck?

BUCK: Sure, go ahead.

DOTTY: Let's go in the kitchen ...

(Dotty and Gayle exit.)

BUCK: *(still with the letter)* You ought to be ashamed of yourself, partner.

RED: I was just asking for information.

BUCK: You'd actually put Dotty away in a place like that?

RED: I didn't know what it was like, except for what this brochure said. It looked real nice in the brochure. It's on the river, and Dotty's always talking about how much she likes to hear the river.

BUCK: So why do you want to ditch her?

RED: I'm not ditching her. It's not like we're married, for Christ's sake. Sure, she has no trouble here, knowing her way around like she does. But someplace else it'll be different. She'll need somebody to watch after her.

BUCK: Then Yakima's just a crock?

RED: My brother has a tavern there. He don't know about Dotty.

BUCK: But she sure knows about Yakima.

RED: I had to tell her something. Jesus, I don't know what to do now. We ain't married.

BUCK: Sounds to me like you've got yourself a problem.

(He goes to the TV and turns it on. It's positioned so the audience doesn't see the picture.)

RED: I'm not trained to be a nurse.

BUCK: You gonna watch the news?

RED: You're wasting your time. They won't show something like that on television, I don't care if you kidnap the President.

BUCK: Just between you and me, partner, I think you're right.

RED: What?

BUCK: I think I could have Nixon tied up in here and they still wouldn't mention farting on TV.

RED: Then why the hell did you tie Gayle up? What the hell's the point of all this?

BUCK: To see what happens. I'm not betting on me winning but you never know. Don't know unless you try, I do know that. Besides, it was worth it to get Gayle riled up.

RED: You're not the easiest fellow in the world to understand. Do you mind if I put the shotgun away? It makes me nervous.

BUCK: Go ahead. It's not loaded.

RED: You said you found the shells in the drawer.

BUCK: I did. I was looking for a match.

RED: You get crazier all the time.

BUCK: I hope so. The news is coming on.

(LIGHTS FADE, as SPOTS UP on Michelle and Rick in the neutral area. They each will play a double role.)

MICHELLE: KPIC-TV, Roseburg.

RICK: In the news tonight, country superstar Gayle Goodwyn is being held hostage in Rapids by a man identifying himself as her ex-husband. With the story is Doris Fletcher. Doris.

MICHELLE: Thanks, Arthur. A man who calls himself Buck Timber, the former husband of country singer Gayle Goodwyn, is holding the superstar hostage in the lounge area of the Rapids Restaurant. Rapids, of course, is the small town that will be flooded by the new Umpqua Dam, beginning next week. The story comes to us from two filmmakers who have been in Rapids for several days now. They are in the studio with us — Rick Olds and Michelle Cadbury. Rick, is Buck Timber asking for a ransom of some kind?

RICK: Not exactly. He had us film a song that he wants to be telecast on the news tonight.

MICHELLE: We've seen that film, Arthur, and I guess you could be generous and call it a ribald satire of the country classic, "Your Cheatin' Heart." Is it your impression that Gayle Goodwyn's life is in danger?

RICK: Not really. He's been drinking. I think it's more like a practical joke.

MICHELLE: Do you have any questions, Arthur?

RICK: Yes. Michelle, you are directing a film on location in Rapids. Does Gayle Goodwyn have a role in the movie?

MICHELLE: No.

RICK: No role at all?

MICHELLE: Perhaps a cameo. I'm undecided. The film is not about her, it's about the town.

492

RICK: More on country singer Gayle Goodwyn on the news at eleven. "The Dating Game" is next.

(BLACKOUT. LIGHTS UP on lounge area as before. Buck turns off the TV.)

RED: If that don't bring the cops up here, I don't know what will.
BUCK: Want to bet how long it takes them?
RED: Damn it, Buck, this isn't funny any more.
BUCK: I didn't know you thought it was funny before.

(Dotty and Gayle enter. Dotty is carrying a suitcase.)

BUCK: We got on the news after all, Dotty.
DOTTY: Give Gayle her distributor cap. She's giving me a lift.
RED: Where do you think you're going?
DOTTY: To the Roseburg Hotel.
RED: Like hell you are.
DOTTY: Give her the cap, Buck.
BUCK: I think Red can explain himself. Partner?
RED: Well, hell ...
DOTTY: If you've got something to say, then say it.
RED: I ran across the brochure and —
DOTTY: — and figured it was as good a place as any to dump me on your way out of town. The cap, damn it!
BUCK: *(fetching it)* If you want to hide something from Gayle Goodwyn, hide it in the vicinity of a liquor bottle. She never goes near the stuff. Catch, superstar.

(He tosses the distributor cap, retrieved behind the bar, to Gayle. She catches it.)

RED: It doesn't make a bit of sense to go to Roseburg. You can stay here, even if you don't want to talk to me. And if you want to come along to Yakima, that's fine, too.
DOTTY: Sure, you can say that now. Just don't expect me to believe it.
RED: You're always talking about how you like to hear the river close by. I was just finding out what they had to offer. I didn't ask for no lady off her trolley to come up here.
DOTTY: I can take care of myself, and don't you forget it.

BUCK: You'll miss the fireworks if you leave. The cops should be on their way up here right now.

RED: I'll take you to Roseburg tomorrow myself, if that's what you want.

DOTTY: That's what I want.

RED: There's nothing in Roseburg.

DOTTY: There's nothing here either.

BUCK: Now that you two have kissed and made up, how about mixing some specials, Dotty?

GAYLE: Don't you think you've had enough?

BUCK: Make mine a double.

RED: You shouldn't be drinking when the cops come.

DOTTY: Why are the police coming?

BUCK: We were on the news. They said a superstar was being held hostage up here. If you leave, they'll be disappointed.

GAYLE: You've outdone yourself this time.

BUCK: Why thank you, ma'am.

GAYLE: Now maybe you'll put my distributor cap back where you found it.

RED: I'll do it.

GAYLE: I appreciate it.

RED: No trouble.

(He takes the cap and exits.)

GAYLE: You'd better think of what you're going to tell the police.

(He yodels.)

BUCK: Yodel-lay-he-oh, a-lay-he-oh, a-lay-he.

DOTTY: You're not talking to the police. Gayle can talk to them herself and explain that it's all a big misunderstanding.

GAYLE: They'll wonder why she's tied up.

DOTTY: They don't even have to come in here. You can explain everything outside and send them on their way.

BUCK: Still the peace-maker, Dotty.

RED: *(entering)* Patrol car's heading this way. What do we do now?

DOTTY: Go out there and talk to them, Gayle.

GAYLE: I've half a mind to let them lock you up.

BUCK: What do you have against Ramblin' Dinosaurs?

494

DOTTY: You won't either. One practical joker around here is enough.

BUCK: I can explain everything myself.

DOTTY: You stay right here.

BUCK: Let them hear it from the dinosaur's mouth.

(He exits.)

DOTTY: *(after him)* Damn it, Buck, you fool ... !

GAYLE: I'll talk to them.

(She exits behind Buck.)

(A beat.)

RED: Dotty, I can explain.

DOTTY: If that's all you think of me after all these years ...

RED: You know as well as I do that a change won't be easy for you. I was checking out other possibilities.

DOTTY: I can take care of myself.

RED: I know that as well as anyone. Better.

DOTTY: If I'm such a burden to you —

RED: You ain't a burden. I just thought maybe you'd want to stay near the river.

(A beat.)

RED: So come with me to Yakima.

DOTTY: I don't need sympathy.

RED: The tavern's doing real fine, my brother says. You can tend bar and it'll be like it used to be here, with enough customers to make the day go fast. You can convert a whole new crowd to your specials.

DOTTY: I can find a bartending job in Roseburg.

RED: Roseburg's not the town that Yakima is.

DOTTY: I don't owe you nothing. It's not like we was married.

RED: No, it ain't. But that doesn't mean I don't care for you.

DOTTY: Hell of a way to show it, fixing to put me away.

RED: Damn it, that's a lie. I was just finding out about it so you could make up your own mind. I didn't know nuts like her had anything to do with it.

DOTTY: Why do you want me to go to Yakima with you?

RED: Because I'm used to you, damn it.

DOTTY: Your brother know about me?

RED: Course he does.

DOTTY: He know about Harvest Acres?

RED: I didn't tell anybody about it. I shouldn't have even written them.

DOTTY: That's the first sensible thing you've said.

(A beat.)

DOTTY: What are the police doing?

(Red goes to a window to see.)

RED: Gayle seems to be doing the talking.

DOTTY: *(Regarding Mrs. Ames)* Maybe we should turn her over to the police.

RED: That would just take more explaining. I'll drive her back to Harvest Acres when this is over.

DOTTY: Buck behaving himself?

RED: Seems to be.

DOTTY: He's crazier than ever.

RED: One of a kind. Rick and Michelle just drove up.

DOTTY: You'd better go out there and make sure they don't speak out of turn.

RED: Buck worries me more than they do.

(Red exits.)

(Dotty comes forward to speak to the audience.)

DOTTY: It was during the hearings, and I'd put my name down to give my opinion as to why I thought they shouldn't build the dam where it would flood the town. They had this microphone set up where you spoke and when my name got called I carefully made my way to the microphone to give my opinion. Getting there without tripping was the easy part because I could feel myself shaking once I was there. I'd never given a speech before in my life. I stood there shaking a minute, then took a deep breath and just blurted out what was on my mind.

I said, Well, I've been listening to a lot of folks talk about how pretty this country is and how it won't be the same once the dam is in. I've never seen the countryside, of course, or any other scenery for that matter, so I guess 'pretty' isn't the word for me to use here. I'll use the word 'lovely' instead.

I'm here to tell you that the Umpqua River through Rapids has a lovely voice. If you put in that dam, you're going to change the river's voice, just as sure as you're going to ruin the scenery for those others who spoke. But it's not only the voice of the river that's going to change — the voices of waterfowl will be lost, too, and the voice of the rain when it touches the river's shallows. The splashes in the swimming hole when grandkids are playing in the summertime will be gone. All of these sounds and more are going to vanish if you change the voice of the river because the river's voice was lovely enough to attract those other voices in the first place. When you ruin a river, you see, you just don't ruin one thing. You ruin the big family of other things that depend on the river.

Thank you, that's all I have to say.

Well, I'd been so nervous to speak that I tripped on my way back to my seat and fell flat on my fanny. A few people rushed to my side but I told them to go away, I could manage by myself. But, hell, I felt foolish falling like I did.

Later Red told me that I was wasting my time speaking out like that, they'd already made up their minds. It wasn't the voice of the river they were ignoring, he said, but the voice of the people.

(Entering are Rick, Michelle, Buck, Red and Gayle.)

RICK: *(seeing Mrs. Ames)* Far out, you still have her tied up.

BUCK: Only way to shut her up.

RED: They're on their way, Dotty. Gayle explained everything.

BUCK: And don't think I don't appreciate it.

GAYLE: No comment.

RED: I guess I'd better drive her back to Harvest Acres.

BUCK: What's your rush? We're supposed to be having a wake. Where's the camera?

RICK: I left everything in the car.

BUCK: By the way, thanks a hell of a lot for getting my song on the tube.

RICK: They wouldn't show it.

BUCK: Of course they wouldn't. What makes you so stupid to take the film to Roseburg in the first place? You should've headed straight back to California.

RICK: I live in Portland.

BUCK: You act like you live in California.

MICHELLE: We went to Roseburg because we weren't sure whether you were kidding or not.

BUCK: You thought I'd shoot her? I admit it was a temptation, but only because I used to be married to her.

RICK: We showed them the film. A couple people cracked up at your song. They really liked it. They just couldn't put it on.

GAYLE: I guess there's a market for everything.

RICK: There's definitely a market for this story. Especially if Gayle refuses to leave. They'd never flood the town then.

GAYLE: What?

RICK: There's a lot of reporters on their way up here. You can give them something to write about.

DOTTY: And we'll send them on their way, just like we did the police.

RICK: I think you should think about it, Gayle.

BUCK: How about that?

RED: Why are you on Buck's side all of a sudden?

MICHELLE: He thinks he's doing me a favor by getting publicity for the film.

RICK: Sure it will help the film. But that's not all it will do. It will raise an important issue here. That's what Buck was really getting at. Right?

BUCK: A dinosaur ahead of my time.

GAYLE: I have a concert in Atlanta on Saturday night.

BUCK: So much for saving the town. Who's ready for a special?

RED: Besides, the dam's built, ain't it? It's a done deal.

RICK: You can bargain to have them move the buildings to higher ground.

MICHELLE: Stop doing this, Rick. They went through bargaining long ago.

DOTTY: Wasn't much bargaining to it.

RICK: You can make them bargain now. Right, Buck?

BUCK: This is your show. I retired.

GAYLE: Just let it be, Rick. What's done is done.

DOTTY: If you're still going into Roseburg, Gayle, I can use a lift.

RED: I thought we settled that you're coming with me to Yakima.

DOTTY: I want to think about it.

RICK: Am I the only one who wants to try and salvage something here?

MICHELLE: Yes, so just get off it, okay?

RICK: I don't believe this.

RED: It's too late to change anything.

GAYLE: Let me get my bag, Dotty.
(She exits.)

RED: It don't make sense to go to Roseburg.

DOTTY: I'll be at the hotel. I need a little time to think.

BUCK: Looks like the reporters are going to have to settle for you and me, partner.

RED: I might as well go into Roseburg myself.

DOTTY: Suit yourself.

BUCK: Somebody better drop off ding-a-ling here.

RED: I have room.

DOTTY: If you think I'm riding with you, I'm not. I'm riding with Gayle.

RED: Fine. But I'm coming by the Roseburg Hotel tomorrow afternoon and if you want to come along to Yakima, you'd better be ready to travel. I'm tired of trying to talk sense into you.

DOTTY: If I want to go, I'll be ready.

RED: Fine and dandy.

(Gayle returns with her bag.)

GAYLE: The guitar and I'm ready.

BUCK: Allow me.

RED: Go ahead and take Dotty with you. I'm coming by the hotel tomorrow afternoon.

GAYLE: I'll be heading south in the morning. So I'll say goodbye now. I wish the circumstances could have been different — but it's been great to see you again.

RICK: You can make the circumstances different.

GAYLE: If I actually believed that, maybe I'd try. But I don't believe it. This is all a lot bigger than us.

BUCK: One traveling guitar ready to travel.

GAYLE: Thanks, Buck. Good to see you again.

BUCK: No need exaggerating on my account.

GAYLE: If I can ever help you out in any way, you can write me through the record company. They forward everything.

BUCK: Sure enough.

DOTTY: If you come into Roseburg tomorrow morning, I'll let you buy me breakfast.

BUCK: Damn, that sounds too good to pass up. I'll be there.

GAYLE: Good luck with the movie. It's an important story.

RICK: Just not important enough to change the ending.

MICHELLE: The ending is the only ending possible. It's nice meeting you, Gayle. I'll be listening for your records.

GAYLE: Is somebody going to do something about her?

RED: I'll take her to Harvest Acres.

DOTTY: Gayle, I'm ready when you are.

RED: Tomorrow afternoon at two. You're welcome to come to Yakima and tend bar in my brother's tavern.

DOTTY: I said I'll think about it.

BUCK: I'll tell the reporters you're on your way to Portland. Maybe that will throw them off.

GAYLE: We'll probably pass them on the road.

RED: Two in the afternoon, Dotty!

(Gayle and Dotty exit.)

MICHELLE: I want to get some night shooting in. The moon is full tonight.

RICK: You're the boss.

MICHELLE: Tomorrow I want to get Red packing and leaving. I want to interview someone from the Corps of Engineers, too.

BUCK: What're you trying to do, tell both sides of the story?

MICHELLE: I expect he may add a fine irony.

RED: I'd better get this lady back.

BUCK: Keep the gag on.

RICK: You want this on film?

MICHELLE: No.

RED: Here we go, lady. I'm taking you home.

(Untied, Mrs. Ames removes her gag.)

MRS. AMES: Why did Dorothy leave without me?

BUCK: Red, put the gag back on.

(MR. FREDERICKS enters.)

FREDERICKS: Good evening.

MRS. AMES: Mr. Fredericks!

FREDERICKS: Hello, Abigail. I'm Horace Fredericks from Harvest Acres. She's one of ours.

BUCK: So she told us.

FREDERICKS: I hope she hasn't been too much trouble. Her enthusiasm gets the best of her sometimes, and she tries to recruit for us. Not always with the best PR, if you know what I mean. Time to come home, Abigail.

MRS. AMES: Dorothy just left.

FREDERICKS: I met her outside. We don't want to miss your late snack, do we?

MRS. AMES: I certainly don't!

FREDERICKS: This is where the dam is going to flood, isn't it? A shame. The moon rising over the river now is just gorgeous. But you can't fight progress, can you? Goodnight.

MRS. AMES: Goodnight, everyone!

(Fredericks and Mrs. Ames exit.)

BUCK: Ain't that a peach.

MICHELLE: Let's get the moon over the river.

RICK: You got it.

BUCK: If you want more of me, I'm taking off in the morning.

MICHELLE: We'll be back later.

(Michelle and Rick exit.)

BUCK: Ain't nobody here but us dinosaurs.

RED: I don't know why she wants to spend the night in Roseburg.

BUCK: Dotty will manage, wherever she is.

RED: I think I'll go upstairs and do a little packing. I sure don't want to talk to no reporters.

(He exits. Buck is alone.)

BUCK: And that left me to handle the reporters by myself. I had a fine time with them. I told them how Gayle was sneaking out the back way, driving twenty miles of dirt road before hooking up with the freeway on her way to Portland. She was off to do a concert in London, I told them. When they asked about her ex-husband, well, I couldn't resist telling them that he was going to London as well. They were having a trial reconciliation and were going to have a kind of second honeymoon in Europe after the concert. I wish I'd been around when Gayle read that in the paper.

The next morning I took Dotty to breakfast and damned if she and Red didn't catch my gig in Portland that weekend, on their way to Yakima together.

I kept listening to the radio for Gayle's song about the dam and all, but her next song turned out to be about a woman needing a man like a fish needs a bicycle, which somebody told me is a pretty well known saying among certain kinds of ladies. When Gayle didn't write a song about the dam, I thought maybe I'd try one myself.

I kept thinking of all the songs Woody Guthrie wrote about dams on the Columbia — *(singing)* "That Bonneville Dam is a sight to see, makes that e-lek-a tricity" — and, anyway, this here's what I ended up with.

(Singing) I read the news about my home town
A dam washed it away
No one yelled and no one cried
They just packed and left one day
They said that nothing could be done
Though they never said just why
I guess you can't fight city hall
But I would've liked to try

(Chorus) Hangin' in
Hangin' on
Another drink, my friend, and another song
Hangin' on
Hangin' in
If life is just a game, my friend, then few folks are playin' to win

(Next verse:)

BUCK: *(singing)* Folks tell me that I drink too much
When I step out at night
They tell me that I talk too loud
The way I fuss and fight
But they're just doing what they're told
While I do as I please
I ain't got much but I ain't sold out
You won't find me on my knees

(Chorus.)

(As Buck plays a guitar solo, Rick and Michelle appear in the neutral area.)

RICK: *(sleepily)* Hello?

MICHELLE: It's Michelle. Are you awake?

RICK: I am now. What time is it?

MICHELLE: Midnight. Two. I lost track.

RICK: You sound bombed.

MICHELLE: I finished the film.

RICK: Hey, that's great.

MICHELLE: I goddamn finished editing the film ...

RICK: How'd it turn out?

MICHELLE: I think it's good, Rick. I really do.

RICK: Did you end up using Gayle?

MICHELLE: A little. It's all very low key. It's very quiet and it's very menacing at the same time.

RICK: In what way?

MICHELLE: It's all so inevitable. And it's all so very sad.

RICK: I'm anxious to see it.

MICHELLE: Oh Rick, it's all so inevitable and so very, very sad.

(FOCUS returns to Buck, singing his song.)

BUCK: *(singing)* Well, I once met an agent
He said he liked my song
Said he'd make me famous
But my image was all wrong
He was talking about a sequined suit
As I headed for the door
I guess you just can't make a star
From a ramblin' dinosaur

(Chorus) Hangin' in
Hangin' on
Another drink, my friend, and another song
Hangin' on
Hangin' in
If life is just a game, my friend, then few folks are playin' to win

(FADE TO BLACKOUT. The play is over.)

For royalties information:
Charles Deemer
1-800-294-7176
cdeemer@teleport.com)

1979

The Pardon
a play in two acts

First performed at Theatre Workshop in Portland, Oregon, on March 16, 1979.
Directed by Steve Smith.

THE CAST (4M, 4W):
Frank, *the narrator*
Horace, *his father*
Evelyn, *his mother*
Sheri, *his sister*
Carl, *his brother-in-law*
Les, *his uncle*
Harriet, *his high school sweetheart*
Jocelyn, *his Canadian lover*

THE TIME:
Spring, 1977; and other events, before and after.

THE PLACE:
Rutherford, on Maryland's Eastern Shore; and in the mind of the
narrator

ACT ONE

(We are in the landscape of the conscience, where time and space are awash. The stage area is open and free: boundaries flutter, actors move through time and space in an instant, sometimes "presenting" the action, sometimes "representing" it, often quickly moving back and forth between the two forms.

The actors never leave the stage. When not "in" the action, they sit in chairs or on stools — or, in Horace's case, in a wheelchair.

These areas must be defined: a radio station; a living area; a podium area, with an open area adjacent to it.)

(AT RISE: all the actors are in their chairs. Then FRANK gets up and moves forward to speak to the audience.)

FRANK: There was a war. Perhaps you remember. There was a war but there were no heroes.

I assumed I'd never return. Who could have foreseen a Presidential pardon? So I'd learned to live with it. At least, after ten years, a few things were going my way again. I found a job in my profession, which is radio. And I met someone. You'll meet Jocelyn later. I really don't know where I'd be without her. Not that a sense of debt is the best foundation, if you know what I mean.

(Frank moves toward the radio station area.)

FRANK: When I arrived I didn't phone my parents. I wasn't sure whether they wanted to see me. Father hadn't approved of my leaving and mother ... perhaps she didn't either. I think I understand Dad's reasons: like many of his generation, he had sacrificed much to his war. A pair of functioning legs, in Dad's case, and his sex. This gave a certain coloring to his opinion about me. He'd returned home a hero. His medals and chevrons and discharge couldn't be missed in our home, they were hung where some families hang Jesus. Like father, like son, was his notion.

(Frank is in the radio station area. SHERI moves into the living area.)

SHERI: *("answering the phone")* Hello?

FRANK: I was speechless. After ten years it came to this: an automatic, straight-forward "hello".

SHERI: Hello? ... Who is this, please? ... Hello! Will you at least breathe heavy or something? ... Creep!

FRANK: So I stiffened my courage with a few drinks and called back. Sheri told me that she and Carl had been thinking about me ever since Carter offered the pardon.

SHERI: Are you at Dad's?

FRANK: At the Greyhound depot. Can you pick me up?

SHERI: Of course. We'll be there in ten minutes.

(LIGHTS OFF living area.)

FRANK: Sheri's older by a year, and there are just the two of us. We used to be very close.

When I went to the radio station, I found it hadn't changed at all. I shouldn't have been surprised. Uncle Les would never risk upsetting his advertisers. Middle-of-the-road pap: something for everyone, and everything for no one. There were a few exceptions, however, to keep the FCC off his back. I became one of the exceptions.

(He sits down "at the board.")

FRANK: The same antiques. The studio was obsolete ten years ago. Walter Winchell's hand-me-down mic ... and these pots, they always gave me the feeling I was flying a World War II bomber. ... Well, here goes ...

(And he is "on in the air" as in the past.)

FRANK: Yes indeedy! This is Lovin' Dan the Sixty-Minute Man! Bringing you the very best in rhythm-n-blues, from bebop to boogie, from blues to ballads, the Golden Hits and the Silver Also Rans. We got the gamut, we got it all! The sound of the 1950s! And it's all for you, baby, on WRUT radio! In rah-rah-Rutherford, Maryland!

(MUSIC: Sh-Boom by The Chords, preferably. Otherwise another classic 50s R&B song: it need only be vintage, black and up-tempo. Sheri enters the radio station area.)

SHERI: Want to dance?

506

FRANK: *(getting up)* The advantage of having an older sister was that I could bop as well as any guy in high school.

(They dance, doing the bop: lights come up on HORACE and EVELYN in the living area. Evelyn is working on the books of the family business; Horace is in his wheelchair.)

HORACE: Frank! You turn that off and get down here!

EVELYN: Horace, I'm going to order another two thousand brooders next quarter.

HORACE: I've told him a hundred times about playing nigger music. Frank!

EVELYN: Do you approve, dear?

HORACE: What?

FRANK: Oh brother ... what do we do now?

SHERI: He's calling you, not me.

(She moves off.)

FRANK: Sheri! ... I thought Dad was outside where he wouldn't hear us. He raises broilers.

EVELYN: It will help pay for the extension and we can make room by storing the feed in the barn.

HORACE: The feed arrived this morning. It has to be stacked. Frank!

EVELYN: What I'm suggesting is —

HORACE: How can you think with that racket going on? Frank!

FRANK: I'm coming! — hold your horses ...

(The music stops. Frank moves into the living area.)

EVELYN: It's what the kids are listening to.

HORACE: Not in this house.

FRANK: *(entering)* You wanted me? ... I'm sorry about the volume. I thought you were outside. I was studying when Sheri —

HORACE: Was she playing that record or were you?

FRANK: I was.

HORACE: I thought we'd reached an understanding last month.

EVELYN: Frank, do you think if we moved the feed to the barn we could handle another two thousand chicks?

FRANK: Sure, I guess so.

HORACE: If you don't mind, I am settling something here.

FRANK: Dad, I haven't been playing those records. *(To the audience)* Well, that wasn't true.

HORACE: *(to audience)* I always knew when he was lying.

FRANK: *(to audience)* Sometimes late at night, after everyone had gone to bed, I'd listen to the records he wouldn't let me play. I was supposed to have taken them to the dump because the records were obscene, he thought. Incredible records ... Work With Me, Annie, by The Midnighters, The Dominoes' Sixty-Minute Man, The Clovers' One Mint Julep ... you could get the records across the river in colored town.

HORACE: That's exactly why I disapproved.

EVELYN: Horace was the disciplinarian of the family but it was only Frank he picked on. Sheri could get away with murder.

FRANK: The music had so much energy, it made you want to explode, to pop right out of your skin. And some of the songs, the ones we liked best — well, they sounded kind of wicked actually. Dirty. I have to admit that was an attraction.

HORACE: *(back to Frank)* I trusted you to destroy those nigger records yourself.

FRANK: But Dad —

HORACE: There's plenty of decent music in this house.

EVELYN: *(to audience)* Benny Goodman and Spike Jones.

HORACE: If you can't listen to decent music —

EVELYN: Didn't you want Frank to stack the feed, dear?

HORACE: I haven't finished, if you don't mind.

EVELYN: *(starting another sequence to audience)* The harsh words that passed through this house about that music. The more parents got upset about rock-n-roll, the more the kids wanted to listen to it.

HORACE: I'm not talking about Elvis. At least he's white. I'm talking about nigger music.

FRANK: Rhythm-n-blues.

HORACE: The Supreme Court decision about schools was bad enough. Mingling had to stop somewhere. Social mingling, I mean, because I've worked with Negroes all my life. But playing their music went too far.

(And back to Frank.)

HORACE: Can I trust you to destroy those nigger records or do I have to do it myself?

FRANK: What difference does it make?

HORACE: I think you'd learn more by doing it yourself.

(A Benny Goodman record begins to play.)

EVELYN: How can you argue to the King of Swing?

(She moves Horace's wheelchair around, dancing.)
EVELYN: *(to Frank)* You should have seen us when they had dances on the pier.
FRANK: I bet you were great.
HORACE: *(stopping "the dance")* That was a long time ago.
FRANK: You could bop to this.
EVELYN: The bop, I'll have you know, is nothing but the jitterbug.

(She and Frank begin to dance, as Horace moves off.)

EVELYN: What do you think, dear? Wouldn't you say this is —

(She sees that Horace is gone. The music stops.)

(The phone rings.)

FRANK: It's probably Harriet.

(He moves "toward the phone".)

EVELYN: *(to audience)* What died in Horace after the war was not a part of his body but a part of his spirit. He couldn't have fun, and that's what I missed most of all — just having fun.

(She moves off.)

(LIGHTS UP on JOCELYN in the open area; Frank remains in the living area.)

FRANK: *("on the phone")* One step at a time, Jocelyn. At least I made it here.
JOCELYN: Where are you staying?
FRANK: With Sheri and her husband.
JOCELYN: When will you be seeing your parents?
FRANK: Tomorrow, I guess.
JOCELYN: You're doing the right thing. There was no other way, Morris.

FRANK: *(to audience)* Morris Appleway. It had been the first name to pop into my head. In Ontario they had a regular factory going, almost all the new parts anyone would need — a phony driver's license, draft card, social security, you name it. They had everything you needed except a new head. A new memory. So I told them I'd try being Morris Appleway this time around, and I swear to God that over a year went by before it hit me that Morris rhymed with Horace.

JOCELYN: I think you should stay as long as it takes.

FRANK: I'm due back on the air Monday.

JOCELYN: Someone can fill in for you. You're doing something very important. Will you call me as soon as you've seen your parents?

(Sheri and CARL enter the living area.)

FRANK: One step at a time, okay? Listen, I'm running up Sis's phone bill.

JCOELYN: Call me tomorrow, Morris.

(Frank hangs up.)

FRANK: *(to Sheri and Carl)* She's fine. She misses me already.

JOCELYN: *(to audience)* As soon as he left for the States, I told myself that when he called I'd tell him that it wasn't working out. I was going to get my own apartment. I needed time alone, to think. Then he phoned, I heard his voice, and I didn't have the heart to say it. It wasn't that I was afraid of hurting him. I was afraid of breaking him.

(LIGHTS OFF Jocelyn.)

SHERI: I'd like to meet her.

FRANK: She's very Canadian. People are different up there, you know.

CARL: In what way?

FRANK: They don't start wars.

SHERI: *(to audience)* Well, it wasn't going at all as I'd imagined it would. I expected a homecoming, a grand reunion. He was so bitter.

CARL: Who can blame him?

SHERI: So I got out our best dope and tried to loosen everybody up.

CARL: *(back to Frank)* How long will you be in town?

FRANK: I'm not sure.

("The joint" is passed around during the conversation below.)

CARL: You know, Frank, I really admire what you did.

FRANK: Leaving or coming back?

CARL: Leaving. They should pass out medals of honor with the pardon.

FRANK: I saw enough medals on the wall growing up.

SHERI: You must feel like you've been in a time warp.

FRANK: Why did you ask me if I was at Dad's? You singled him out. Have they split up?

SHERI: Frank ... Mother's dead.

CARL: It's been six or seven years.

SHERI: 1970. Dad moved to Oyster Island.

FRANK: I see.

SHERI: *(to audience)* I couldn't handle it at all. He has no contact with the family for ten years and returns to learn that Mother's been dead like forever. I just wanted to change the subject. I just wanted to deal with something I could handle.

(Back to the others: she laughs.)

CARL: What's so funny?

SHERI: I was thinking of the first time I offered Frank dope. God, was I loaded. Carl was speaking in the park.

CARL: 1966: the war had just been escalated.

(They move into the podium area.)

SHERI: *(to audience)* I think it must have been the first time anyone had protested anything in Rutherford. Not that anybody showed up to listen. A few of Carl's students were there, and every now and then someone would pass by, listen a minute, and hurry on.

FRANK: I was on my way to work at the radio station.

CARL: *(behind the podium)* Even if we believe that only military targets at Hanoi and Haiphong were bombed, who can believe for a minute that we will stop there?

FRANK: Uncle Les had given me a job at WRUT as soon as I graduated from college. He also sat on my draft board. This was no small advantage in 1966.

CARL: Who can believe for a minute that we are not setting loose a military arsenal aimed at no less than genocide in Southeast Asia?

FRANK: I'm sure I'd never heard the term "genocide" before. But it was Sheri who interested me most, sitting in the middle of Rutherford Park, sharing a joint with college students. I couldn't believe it.

SHERI: Hey, Frank! Want a toke?

FRANK: Do you know how obvious you are?

SHERI: Take some literature. Read it on the air!

FRANK: *(to audience)* And with the pamphlets she handed me a small flag. I didn't know at the time it was North Vietnamese.

SHERI: Are you going to share this with me or not?

FRANK: I'm late for work.

(Frank moves toward the radio station area as LIGHTS COME DOWN. And LIGHTS UP on LES at the station, "on the phone," talking to EVELYN in the living area.)

LES: Evey, a day wouldn't be complete without flirting with you. You know you love it.

EVELYN: I appreciate the compliments. I didn't know it was flirting.

LES: Damn right, it's flirting. You married the wrong brother.

EVELYN: I don't remember you asking me.

LES: Regrets! I love it. Let's fly to Reno.

EVELYN: If there's one place I've never had a desire to see —

LES: The Rutherford courthouse, then. That would raise some eyebrows.

EVELYN: *(laughing)* Les, you're an absolute tonic.

LES: Is that good or bad?

EVELYN: Good! You make me laugh. But I do have to run.

LES: Will you settle for an affair?

EVELYN: Goodbye, Les. Thank you for cheering up a very dreary day.

(LIGHTS OFF Evelyn.)

LES: *(to audience)* Oh, it was harmless enough in the beginning, flirting with Evey. I could make her laugh but it was a far cry from the way she used to be. As a young woman she'd been the life of the party wherever she went.

(Frank enters the area.)

LES: Frank, do you have a minute?

FRANK: Sure.

LES: We have a little problem. Some busybody's filed a written complaint that we aren't serving the colored community. He's challenging our license renewal. Coloreds are over thirty percent now, he claims, and we don't have any programming for them.

FRANK: *(to audience)* The station wasn't serving my interests, for that matter.

LES: I was speaking to your mother a moment ago and she mentioned that you used to listen to colored music in high school. It occurred to me that maybe you could put together a program for them.

FRANK: I still have a collection of 50s rhythm-n-blues.

LES: Makes no difference what it is, as long as we protect ourselves. What's the flag?

FRANK: They were handing them out in the park.

LES: Looks South American. Anyway, why don't you give it some thought and get back to me at the end of the week.

FRANK: *(to audience)* And that's how I became Lovin' Dan the Sixty-Minute Man. Sixty minutes of pure 50s vintage rhythm-n-blues, every Saturday night. The show went over so well that soon I had three hours. The Saturday show made my week.

LES: Frank, do you have a minute?

FRANK: Whenever Uncle Les had something on his mind, he came to me. Perhaps he thought of it as keeping business in the family.

(And back to Les.)

FRANK: What's up?

LES: On Memorial Day —

FRANK: This would be 1967.

LES: I want to sponsor a dance supporting our boys overseas. Something patriotic to counteract all the protesting.

FRANK: *(to audience)* Protesting in Rutherford was pretty much of a farce.

LES: Something like that can devastate morale over there. I want to do something positive. On TV you hear all this stuff about a Vietnam summer. I want to nip them in the bud.

FRANK: So what's the problem?

LES: None at all. I'm just asking you to emcee the show. I want to honor the real patriots in the community — our boys in Vietnam.

(Carl and Sheri move forward to lead, like cheerleaders, VOICES OFF.)

VOICES OFF: Hey, hey, LBJ, how many kids did you kill today?

(Etc.)

FRANK: *(moving toward the podium area)* On Memorial Day, a small crowd of protesters met us outside the hotel. Sheri, of course, was among them.
VOICES OFF: All we are saying, is give peace a chance.

(Etc.)

(HORACE, Evelyn and Les join Frank in the open area near the podium.)
EVELYN: Horace, ignore them. She doesn't know what she's doing.
HORACE: What the hell do they think they're accomplishing?
VOICES OFF: Ho, Ho, Ho Chi Minh!

(Etc.)

HORACE: Listen to them. They're cheering the Communists. They want a Communist victory.
EVELYN: Ignore them.
HORACE: If you don't like this country, then get the hell out, you goddamn slackers!
FRANK: Dad, you're reacting just how they want you to.
HORACE: What did we fight Hitler for? Love it or leave it!
VOICES OFF: Hey, hey, LBJ, how many kids did you kill today?

(Etc.)

EVELYN: *(to audience)* Sheri was rebellious even as a child. Horace had doted on her and now she was hurting him, screaming her head off out there. Horace and I belonged to a different generation. We had no time for yelling in the streets.
SHERI: *(coming forward, breaking in)* You lived through the depression. There wasn't yelling in the streets going on then? *(To audience)* She was blind to everything that interfered with raising chickens on her safe little sandbar.

(Les moves away from the others as we move toward a new time frame.)

514

EVELYN: You think I liked doing that? We went into the business because it was something Horace could manage after the war.

SHERI: I just wanted to live my own life.

EVELYN: You certainly did that. You wouldn't raise a hand to help us with the business. If it wasn't for Frank, I don't know how we'd have managed.

(Sheri moves off. New time frame.)

HORACE: Now don't you fret, Evelyn. Sheri's dating a good boy. Mrs. Adams told me herself that she would keep an eye on them, no matter how late the party went.

EVELYN: Are you trying to marry her off to that boy?

HORACE: She could do far worse, couldn't she? Relax and come to bed.

EVELYN: I'd be awake anyway.

FRANK: Here're the totals you wanted.

HORACE: The chickens grow by themselves, without all that book work.

EVELYN: Goodnight, dear.

(They peck, and Horace moves off.)

FRANK: What's our taxes?

EVELYN: Oh, I've a ways to go before figuring them.

FRANK: Anything else I can help with?

EVELYN: Maybe your father's right. I am tired.

FRANK: Just tell me what to do.

EVELYN: You could add these receipts.

FRANK: Be glad to.

EVELYN: I don't think we could stay in business without your help.

FRANK: You did fine when I was little.

EVELYN: I was younger then. Would you mind waiting up until Sheri gets home?

FRANK: Sure.

EVELYN: Goodnight.

(Evelyn moves off. Frank turns on "the radio": low rhythm-n-blues from Philadelphia.)

(A beat. Sheri enters.)

SHERI: Everyone in bed?

FRANK: Mom just went.

SHERI: Is she mad?

FRANK: A little, I guess.

SHERI: What're you doing?

FRANK: Helping Mom with taxes.

SHERI: Yuk. Philly's coming in great tonight.

FRANK: Weather must be perfect.

SHERI: I can't wait to see Philly.

FRANK: You sound like you've got plans.

SHERI: I'll see it next year. I'll have my own apartment in College Park and every weekend a bunch of us will go to Philly.

FRANK: You'll probably end up going to Rutherford College and living at home.

SHERI: Oh, I love this song ...

(The R&B music fades into VOICES OFF: "hey, hey, LBJ" etc.)

(Horace, Les and Evelyn move back into the playing area.)

HORACE: I think we should call the police.

LES: They'll get bored with themselves if we ignore them. Let's enjoy ourselves. May I have permission to dance with Evey, brother?

(Carl and Sheri softly sing and hum "We Shall Overcome" as Les and Evelyn dance.)

HORACE: *(watching them, then to audience)* That was the night it occurred to me that she was capable of having an affair. I didn't suspect Les, not yet. It really didn't matter who it would be. But watching her laugh as they danced —

EVELYN: *(laughing)* Oh Les ...

HORACE: — something of the young woman I married returned. She was different before the war. Evelyn had her wild side.

FRANK: Mother, wild?

HORACE: You'd be surprised.

FRANK: She was always working. Who can imagine someone like that being wild? I can't even imagine my parents making love.

HORACE: She was one of a kind ... and dance, boy, did she love to dance. We could out-step any couple on the peninsula.

(Horace gets out of his wheelchair and walks over to cut in on Les. The music becomes something from the big band era. Horace and Evelyn dance to a fast number, and they are quite good together.)

EVELYN: *(stopping)* Come outside for a minute.

(She leads him to another part of the playing area.)

EVELYN: Now close your eyes. I have a surprise.
HORACE: What is it?
EVELYN: Just close your eyes — and no peeking!

(He does. Evelyn "holds a small bottle" under his nose.)

HORACE: *(opening his eyes)* Dandelion wine!
EVELYN: Daddy opened the first bottle this afternoon.
HORACE: And you snitched a little
EVELYN: Well, not much ...
HORACE: Your dandelion wine puts crazy thoughts in my head.
EVELYN: Like what?
HORACE: Oh, like what I might be doing a few years from now.
EVELYN: Don't tell me if I'm not there, too.
HORACE: There's a girl there, all right. She's holding a baby. And I'm just coming up to the dock with enough oysters to want to celebrate a little. I think we should get a baby-sitter. Yep, I think we owe it to ourselves to celebrate tonight.
EVELYN: Who's the girl?
HORACE: The one responsible for putting crazy thoughts in my head.

(Laughing, they embrace. Les moves to them as Frank moves to the podium.)

LES: I think Frank's ready to begin.

(Horace returns to the wheel chair.)

FRANK: *(to the audience)* Uncle Les had written a poem for the occasion. The author was to remain anonymous.
CARL: We'd made our point and I suggested we leave. Several disagreed and elected to stay. I didn't like this division because it was

517

always my notion that we were stronger together than apart. So Sheri and I decided to stay, too.

FRANK: *(reading the poem)* I'm proud to be an American
Of the red, white and blue
In God's own chosen country
I'm free and so are you
For Jefferson and Thomas Paine
And countless others, too
Gave their lives for liberty
Of the red, white and blue
They died, as others die today
In a far-off foreign land
Fighting the hammer and sickle
For the glory of Uncle Sam
(breaking from poem) I think you get the drift. The damn thing went on for over twenty stanzas! I think Uncle Les was born a century too late.

LES: Actually the poem took considerably more skill than most people realize.

SHERI: There was no place to pee and I had to go pretty bad. So I went back into this alley between the hotel and a tavern where I could use the facilities and that's where I heard a couple guys talking about the balloon bombs.

LES: For example, "land" and "Sam" make what is called an off-rhyme. It's a very effective poetic device. English had been my minor in college.

SHERI: They'd filled balloons with chicken blood and were going to throw them inside.

FRANK: And now, ladies and gentlemen, I want to present a very special award.

(Harriet comes forward.)

CARL: As soon as Sheri told me, I knew we had to try and stop it.

FRANK: The man whom we honor next gave as much to his country as a man can be asked to give. He gave his life. Killed in action in December of last year, Daniel Truitt became the first in our community to make the supreme patriotic sacrifice. Accepting this plaque in his memory —

CARL: They must've found another entrance because by the time I explained to the guards at the door what the problem was, they'd had time to get in and throw them.

518

FRANK: — is Daniel's widow, Mrs. Harriet Truitt.

(Harriet screams and Frank ducks, miming reaction to the blood bombs being thrown.)

LES: Grab them!
CARL: *(moving to the podium)* On behalf of the Rutherford Against Genocide Committee —
HORACE: Shut him up!
CARL: — we don't condone violence of any kind!
HORACE: Get them out of here!
SHERI: It was awful, being arrested with Dad there shouting at us. They didn't let us go until one of the guards who'd been at the door explained how we'd warned them and tried to stop it.

(All but Evelyn, Frank and Harriet move off.)

EVELYN: Horace drank himself into oblivion after that. Les had to help me get him into the car. He suggested a nightcap but I didn't want to leave Horace alone. Les was so insistent that we settled on coffee, which we drank in his car parked beside mine in the lot. It was there that Les made his first advances, and there that I realized my rejection of him was without will and that if he chose to pursue me, he would have me.

(She moves off.)

FRANK: We hadn't been hurt but we were drenched in chicken blood.
HARRIET: It was a very unnerving experience.

(Hand in hand, they move forward.)

FRANK: I have a gross analogy: this wasn't the first blood we'd shared.
HARRIET: That's awful.
FRANK: Harriet, you see, married Daniel while I was at the University of Maryland. I thought I was still in love with her then, so it hurt. In 1959, when we were seniors at Rutherford High, our petting had finally, inevitably, reach its (ahem) climax on a spring moon-filled night in the back seat of my '52 Merc convertible. We had the top down.
HARRIET: Were you a virgin? It's not so unfashionable to ask today.

FRANK: I plead guilty.

HARRIET: At the time I thought I was the only virgin over sixteen on the planet.

FRANK: In 1959, genitalia hadn't gone public yet. We didn't have *Penthouse*. We had nudist magazines filled with naked families playing volleyball, and to a person their genitalia were depicted as hairless smudges. This wasn't much help.

HARRIET: Despite this handicap we succeeded — how does one put it? — in lining ourselves up properly. I believe we did.

FRANK: Eventually.

HARRIET: I believe I told you I loved you.

FRANK: And not for the first time.

HARRIET: And did you love me?

FRANK: Of course. This was 1959.

HARRIET: Then what went wrong?

FRANK: I'm not sure. Perhaps it was the special logic of the fifties. Or maybe it was only Rutherford. Or only us. I do know this: that if you slept with a nice girl in 1959 —

HARRIET: And was I a nice girl?

FRANK: I knew no other kind. If you slept with her, then ipso facto you were in love with her.

HARRIET: Ipso facto.

FRANK: The times knew no other moral possibility. And if you loved her, ipso facto you married her. One's sense of moral responsibility was strongly syllogistic in those days.

HARRIET: Shoo-be-do-be: we were in love, therefore we made love.

FRANK: Sha-na-na: we made love, therefore we were in love.

HARRIET: Ipso ...

FRANK: ... facto.

HARRIET: Actually I felt like a tramp afterwards. I was sure you'd drop me in a minute.

(A beat: Frank clears his throat.)

FRANK: Will you marry me?

HARRIET: Yes. I believe I said yes.

FRANK: Yes.

HARRIET: What else could I say? There was blood all over his back seat upholstery. He loved that car!

FRANK: So we were engaged, and not thirty minutes after sharing our loss of virginity.

HARRIET: Very secretly engaged.

FRANK: And very secretly rehearsing, continuing to rehearse, for the real thing: the marriage bed.

HARRIET: Four months later I missed my period.

FRANK: But no slinky abortion, folks!

HARRIET: The proverbial false alarm. But it did scare the hell out of us.

FRANK: And she means both of us.

HARRIET: So thereafter we refrained from climbing into the back seat.

FRANK: But not without wall-climbing discipline, certain insatiable appetites having been whetted.

HARRIET: And he means in both of us. Though, of course, a nice girl didn't admit such a thing in 1959.

FRANK: Unsatisfied appetites lead to frustration; frustration to arguments —

HARRIET: And to make a long story short, since we really didn't want to get married quite yet anyway, we did the next best thing.

FRANK: We broke up.

HARRIET: Rationally and only temporarily.

FRANK: We were biding time until we finished college. I went away to the University of Maryland. I would date other girls.

HARRIET: I stayed home and attended Rutherford College and would date other men. Why do you say girls and I say men?

FRANK: The times were chauvinistic all the way around.

HARRIET: Then I met Daniel and was swept off my feet and we were married the summer after my Junior year.

FRANK: So ends the love story of Frank and Harriet. Still friends?

HARRIET: Still friends.

(They peck, and Harriet moves off.)

FRANK: The blood-throwing incident rallied the community behind "our boys overseas", as it was usually put. What was called Vietnam Summer on the mainland became, on our little peninsula, a summer of preparations for Christmas. Sweaters were knitted and vegetables were canned; Rutherford would flood Vietnam with Christmas packages for our boys overseas.

(Behind him now, Horace, Evelyn, Carl and Sheri seat themselves as if around a dinner table. An empty chair waits for Frank.)

HORACE: Let us pray ...

FRANK: But what had impressed me about the incident at the dance was Carl, that he would criticize the blood-throwing even though he led the protesting against the war. I hardly knew him at all. Sheri had met him during summer vacation, shortly after he'd started teaching at the college. They had a whirlwind courtship, married, and kept to themselves.

HORACE: ... for the bounty of food on our table that the less fortune do not share ...

FRANK: Mother was forever trying to bring us all together. One of the few times she succeeded was on Dad's birthday, 1967.

(He takes his seat "at the table.")

HORACE: ... and bless, too, our brave soldiers overseas who fight to preserve our precious freedoms. Amen.

SHERI: I was on my best behavior.

CARL: I was on my best behavior.

EVELYN: We were still a family. Differences of opinion did not change the fact. We were a family and ought to be able to sit around the same table without arguing.

(The sequence below is very fast.)

EVELYN: We've been blessed with good weather.

FRANK: Weather's been perfect.

HORACE: Reminds me of a story General Eisenhower used to tell.

SHERI: The beach crowds are huge.

FRANK: Weather's been great.

HORACE: Ike had this saying about the weather.

EVELYN: But the humidity will be here soon enough.

SHERI: The beach crowds are fantastic.

CARL: Most of them my students.

FRANK: Weather's ideal.

HORACE: If you don't like the weather, Ike used to say, wait a while. He used to tell us that.

(A beat: the doorbell rings.)

EVELYN: (getting up) I'll get it.

LES: (entering) Hi, Evey. Sorry to interrupt your dinner.

HORACE: Grab a chair and dig in.

LES: Can I speak to you for a moment?

HORACE: Sure.

(Les and Horace confer privately.)

CARL: Students would rather sunbathe than study.

SHERI: I'm not sure I blame them.

FRANK: Weather's sure been great.

HORACE: *(with bad news)* Goddamn it!

EVELYN: I thought, My God, Les told him about us!

LES: And seeing the fear on her face, I wished I had phoned.

EVELYN: *(to change the subject)* Does everyone want dessert?

LES: Horace, we need all the persuasion we can get.

EVELYN: What happened?

LES: The war took Tommy Adams. Tom Senior went crazy when he got the news. He's got a gun and is drinking over at the tavern. We've got to get it away from him before someone gets hurt.

CARL: People are dying this very minute in Vietnam.

HORACE: You know what I saw on television the other night? I saw a mock funeral. I saw North Vietnamese flags draped over coffins. Who the hell are you really mourning?

SHERI: I won't sit here and be attacked.

FRANK: Does everyone want dessert?

SHERI: Let's go.

(Carl and Sheri move off with Horace following them.)

HORACE: Tommy Adams has given his life for his country over there, and you have no right to —

SHERI: I didn't marry Tommy Adams, I married Carl! And they are having a civil war over there!

HORACE: A communist takeover is not a civil war!

SHERI: Don't you know that Ho Chi Minh — !

HORACE: Get out of my house!

(Carl and Sheri are gone. A beat: Frank moves off. Horace waits off. Les and Evelyn are alone.)

LES: I have to see you again.

EVELYN: Les—

LES: It was good. You know it was good.

EVELYN: I'm sorry it happened. I had too much to drink.

LES: It was bound to happen sooner or later. I love you, Evey.

EVELYN: Please don't tell me that.

LES: I love you.

EVELYN: I'm so confused, I —

HORACE: *(returning, interrupting)* We'd better get that gun from Tom Senior.

(Frank returns, carrying a birthday cake. Evelyn, under great control, begins to sing.)

EVELYN: Happy birthday to you.

EVELYN & FRANK: Happy birthday to you,
Happy birthday, dear Horace

EVELYN & FRANK & LES: Happy birthday to you.

(Frank moves toward radio station area, others move off. Voices rise.)

VOICES OFF: Ho, Ho, Ho Chi Minh! *etc.*

FRANK: I'm not sure when, during this Vietnam Summer of 1967, that I became a closet critic of the war. It no longer made sense to me to fight a war so far from home, with so little support at home. Television told a story that was not true in Rutherford, that hundreds upon hundreds of young men who were being asked to fight this war, and their sisters and girl friends and wives who were being asked to send them off with blessings, were in open rebellion. In Rutherford what little protest there was continued to be cliquish, with Carl at the center of it. Sheri and Dad had stopped communicating altogether.

EVELYN: *(in living area, with Les)* It was the summer of my adultery.

FRANK: Then, near the end of July, Black Panther Rap Brown came to Cambridge on the bayside of the peninsula, only thirty miles from Rutherford. What began as a speech ended in the smoldering ashes of a race riot. The Vietnam War was a white man's war, Brown had said, a white man's war waged against the non-white peoples of Vietnam. The war was racist.

EVELYN: Oh Les, this is wrong. I know this is wrong.

FRANK: After the riot, everyone seemed on edge. Uncle Les started carrying a gun and he told his employees to do the same. Even as sweaters were knitted and vegetables canned for our boys overseas, there was a new feeling of uncertainty in town. The race riot had struck too close to home.

EVELYN: Poor, poor Horace.

LES: Poor, poor Evelyn ...

FRANK: Then, on a Wednesday in hot, humid August ...

LES: ... she can't admit she loves me.

FRANK: I was doing production work at the station when it happened. We had less than an hour left in our broadcast day, and the DJ and I were the only ones at the studio.

VOICES OFF: Ho, Ho, Ho Chi Minh! *etc.*

FRANK: Students, only a few of whom were local, entered the station, kicked out the DJ and came on the air as People's Liberation Radio. I couldn't believe what I was hearing on the monitor. They hadn't noticed me in the production studio, so I got out while I could and phoned the police from a pay phone. Then I tried to reach Uncle Les. When he didn't answer, I decided to leave him a note on his door.

(LIGHTS DOWN on Frank in the studio area.)

EVELYN: I can't leave Horace.

LES: I haven't asked you to.

EVELYN: One day he'll find out.

LES: Yes.

EVELYN: I want to stop before that happens.

LES: Evey, I love you. I can't give you up now.

(Horace appears outside the living area.)

HORACE: *(he is drunk)* You're goddamn right, I knew. You don't hide much in a small town.

FRANK: *(moving to Horace)* Dad, what are you doing here?

HORACE: I'm not sure yet.

FRANK: I've got to find Uncle Les. Some radicals took over the station.

HORACE: You'll find him right inside.

FRANK: He didn't answer his phone.

HORACE: He doesn't want to be interrupted. Your mother's in there.

FRANK: Dad?

FRANK: Your mother and Les are lovers.

(LIGHTS OFF Horace and Frank.)

LES: We can work something out. Maybe if we level with him, he'll understand.

EVELYN: I don't want anything to be understood. I want to leave you and forget that anything happened.

LES: You know you love me.

EVELYN: No, Les, I don't know.

LES: You still love Horace?

EVELYN: I betray him.

(The door bell rings.)

LES: You'd better get in the bedroom.

EVELYN: Of course, the bedroom.

(She moves off. The bell rings again and Les moves forward to meet Frank.)

LES: Why Frank—

FRANK: Turn on the radio. Some radicals have taken over the station.

LES: What?

FRANK: I phoned the police; maybe they've arrested them by now. They threw Joe off the air and came on as People's Liberation Radio.

LES: I'd better get down there right away.

FRANK: Dad's outside. He said mother's here.

LES: Well, she was here. She brought over an apple pie, the sweetheart.

FRANK: Dad has another explanation.

LES: I'd better get to the station.

HORACE: *(coming forward)* Where is she?

LES: Horace, I don't know what gave you the idea that Evelyn is here. She did come by this afternoon and —

EVELYN: *(coming forward)* I'm here.

LES: Jesus Christ, Evey. Look, I've got to get to the station.

HORACE: I have something to say.

LES: Radicals have overthrown the station, and I intend to do something about it.

FRANK: I already called the police.

EVELYN: Will someone take me home?

HORACE: What makes you think you have a home to go to?

LES: For Christ's sake, Horace, she's not herself, can't you see that? She needed someone to talk to. She's not well.

EVELYN: I am perfectly well. I just don't feel able to drive. Someone take me home.

(Frank starts to move away.)

EVELYN: Frank?
HORACE: Let him go.
EVELYN: Take me home, Frank.
LES: I'll take you home.
HORACE: Don't think I don't know what's been going on.
EVELYN: Frank!?
LES: Horace, you're drunk and making a mountain out of nothing.
HORACE: I know why she's here.
EVELYN: I want to go home. Frank!
HORACE: Maybe this is your home now. It's where your bed is.
LES: Jesus Christ, Horace —
FRANK: Stop it! Just shut up!

(Frank moves off and is met by JOCELYN, in half-lights, dreamlike.)

EVELYN: *(after him)* Frank, don't leave me here!
JOCELYN: Morris, what is it?
EVELYN: Frank!
JOCELYN: Morris!
FRANK: Everything keeps coming back.
JOCELYN: It's Jocelyn. I'm right here.
EVELYN: Frank!
JOCELYN: Morris, I'm right here.
EVELYN: It's not like you think, Frank!
JOCELYN: You have to resolve it, Morris.
FRANK: I'm a coward.
JOCELYN: Morris, listen to me. It's safe to go back now. You have the pardon. Use it. See them again.
FRANK: They wouldn't let me in the house.
JOCELYN: Of course they would.
FRANK: I'm a coward. I ran. He doesn't forget a thing like that.
JOCELYN: Ten years have passed.
EVELYN: Please, Frank ...
FRANK: He'll be living World War II until he dies.
JOCELYN: Are you any different? The past is still speaking to you. You have to resolve it before it eats you alive.
EVELYN: Forgive me, Frank ...
JOCELYN: Maybe going back will be a kind of exorcism. Get rid of the past, Morris. For our sake.

FRANK: I put her on such a pedestal. She ran everything: the business, the home, us, him. How could she betray him?

JOCELYN: Go back. Learn to know them again.

EVELYN: Please forgive me ...

JOCELYN: Go back, Morris.

EVELYN: Frank ...

(Frank moves off alone. A beat.)

FRANK: I left and went back to the radio station. The radicals were gone but the police were still there. I told them what I knew about it. When the police left, instead of closing down the station I pulled out the on-the-air cable and did almost an hour of my Lovin' Dan the Sixty-Minute Man show. I thought it was one of the best sequences I'd ever done but of course no one could hear it. ... We'll have an intermission now.

(LIGHTS DOWN: end of Act One.)

ACT TWO

(AT RISE: Frank is at the phone in the living area. First he speaks to the audience.)

FRANK: The next morning, my first in the States in ten years, I lay in bed staring at the ceiling and asking myself, Morris Appleway, what now, Frank White? Frank White, what next, Morris Appleway? I mean, who the hell was I? When I got up, I went to the phone and called Jocelyn first thing.

(LIGHTS UP on Jocelyn in the radio station area.)

528

JOCELYN: When the phone rang, guessing it was Morris, I hesitated. I knew I should say to him, Morris, I love you, I think I love you, but I can't live with you now because you have no future until you settle with your past. But with Morris, it was always difficult to get to the heart of a matter. He was fragile. Sometimes I felt that it was I alone who was holding his life together. His new life, I mean: it was the old life that kept haunting him.

FRANK: *("on the phone")* I guess I'll look around town this morning.

JOCELYN: Will you be seeing your parents today?

FRANK: Dad's moved to Oyster Island. It's in the Chesapeake.

JOCELYN: Is that far?

FRANK: No. Maybe I'll get out there today. I haven't decided. Maybe I'll catch the first bus out of town.

JOCELYN: Don't run away, Morris. I know it's not easy.

FRANK: Christ, Jocelyn ...

JOCELYN: What is it?

FRANK: Mom's dead.

JOCELYN: Oh Morris, no.

FRANK: She's been dead for years.

JOCELYN: I'm so sorry.

FRANK: At least it's one less thing to resolve. My morbid sense of humor.

JOCELYN: Please see your father today.

FRANK: Don't take any bets.

JOCELYN: You need to. Call me tonight and tell me how it went.

(LIGHTS OFF Jocelyn. Sheri enters the living area.)

SHERI: You're up early. Sleep okay?

FRANK: I slept fine.

SHERI: What's on the agenda for today?

FRANK: I thought I'd look around town and maybe catch the mail boat to see Dad.

SHERI: Does he know you're here?

FRANK: No.

SHERI: He'll be glad to see you. I mean that.

FRANK: Do you see him often?

SHERI: He has us out for dinner.

FRANK: He and Carl get along?

SHERI: Real well in football season.

FRANK: I thought he'd have shamed you out of town.

SHERI: He tried hard enough. You know how stubborn I am.

FRANK: But you've kissed and made up?

SHERI: We just don't talk about those days.

FRANK: Well, that's convenient, isn't it? If you don't talk about it, then none of it really happened. Why didn't I think of that?

SHERI: The country made a mistake. Everyone admits that now.

FRANK: So you grant a pardon, shake hands, and everything is forgotten.

SHERI: I know it hasn't been easy for you. But a pardon's better late than never, isn't it?

FRANK: Good question.

SHERI: What you had to go through is criminal.

FRANK: What the hell do you know about what I've been through?

SHERI: I'm sorry. I just imagine it must've been terrible.

FRANK: Not any more. I'm not washing dishes. I've not digging ditches. I'm not even selling dope. I didn't sell my body to any dirty old men — that's about all I haven't done. I finally got into radio again. It's a beginning.

SHERI: You're going to stay in Canada?

FRANK: *(reacting to her surprise)* You never really realize how obnoxious Americans can be until you live apart from them. The pardon doesn't necessarily change anything. The United States is not the only country on the face of the earth.

CARL: *(entering)* Morning. I'd like you to come to my Ethics class today.

FRANK: I want to catch the mail boat to Oyster Island.

CARL: Day after tomorrow, then. My students can learn one hell of a lot from you, Frank. The Vietnam War is ancient history to them.

FRANK: Only to them?

SHERI: To all of us.

CARL: I swear to God, Carter should've given every one of you the medal of honor.

FRANK: You think so?

CARL: You're the closest that damn war came to having heroes.

(A beat.)

FRANK: Where's mother buried?

CARL: In Rutherford Memorial.

(Frank moves forward, the others move off.)

FRANK: It was like looking for the proverbial needle in a haystack, wandering through the cemetery, going from gravestone to gravestone, looking for my mother's marker. Sheri offered to show me but I wanted to be alone. *(He kneels.)* When I found it, it was stark marble like the others — cold, immaculate, bearing her name and date but no epitaph. Perhaps no one knew what to say.

(Harriet comes forward, as in mourning, and kneels.)

FRANK: *(rising)* I was about to leave when I ran into Harriet. She had come with flowers for Daniel.
HARRIET: *(rising)* It was good seeing you again. I'm not sure why you decided to leave but it was the right thing to do. You're alive.
FRANK: Yeah, I'm that.
HARRIET: I wish Daniel had run to Canada, too.
FRANK: Goodbye, Harriet.

(Frank moves into the radio station as Harriet moves off.)

FRANK: If only Daniel had gone to Canada. It sounded so easy. Go to Canada and save your neck. At least I'm alive, she said. I'd been right all along and ten years never happened and welcome home, American hero.
LES: *(in radio station area)* Frank! Jesus Christ — I didn't know you were in town.
FRANK: I got in yesterday.
LES: Did you now? Well, Jesus. You're looking good.
FRANK: The station looks the same.
LES: We're the Rock of Gibraltar. You worked here long enough to know that.

(Les laughs and slaps Frank on the back.)

FRANK: His laughter was like a release of obligation. In it was the feeling that we no longer had anything of substance to talk about. We were left with the social graces — we'd politely inquire how each had been, I'd take the nostalgic tour of the station, I'd turn down the mandatory invitation to lunch, and I'd leave.
LES: What the hell, he walks in without warning after ten years. I'm supposed to drag out the past?

FRANK: No. I didn't want that either. The first time through was plenty.

(A beat. Time frame changes.)

LES: Frank, do you have a minute?
FRANK: There's nothing to discuss.
LES: You jumped to conclusions last night.
FRANK: Did I?
LES: Your mother and I are dear friends. You had no right to imply the rest.
FRANK: If you'll excuse me, I have production work.
LES: It can wait. I think we'd better clear the air. We do work together.
FRANK: I work for you, not with you.
LES: I think a good deal of your mother. I show her considerably more respect than you did last night.
FRANK: Is that all?
LES: You judge her too harshly. She loves you very much.
FRANK: Look, I have work to do.
LES: I care for her very much.

(Les moves off. Frank sits down at the board.)

FRANK: The next few weeks were like a long downer. I avoided Uncle Les during the day, then went home to stare at the same depressing TV images of students being clubbed by police. I felt drugged and only straightened up on Saturday nights, when for a few hours I was transformed into Lovin' Dan the Sixty-Minute Man.

Oh yes indeedy, The Chords from 1954! Life could be a dream, sh-boom! You get nothing but The True Word from Lovin' Dan. Life could be a dream, sh-boom! Can you dig it? Yes indeedy, we got the Golden Hits and the Silver Also Rans. The sound of the 1950s. And it's the only thing left, my friends. Can you dig it? The only thing left — and it will stand! Yes indeedy! Going way back to 1948 now, back to Baltimore's own Sonny Til and the Orioles, a little tune called It's Too Soon To Know...

(LIGHTS UP on Horace and Evelyn in the living area, while remaining on Frank as Lovin' Dan.)

HORACE: Do you want a divorce?
EVELYN: No.

532

FRANK: And here's The Five Satins, In the Still of the Night ...

HORACE: How long have you been sleeping with him?

EVELYN: My God, does it matter?

HORACE: Has he asked you to marry him?

EVELYN: I don't love him. I've never loved him.

FRANK: It's Lovey Dovey by The Clovers! Honey Love by The Drifters!

HORACE: You go to him.

EVELYN: I've never loved him.

FRANK: Pledging My Love by Johnny Ace!

HORACE: He satisfies you in a way I no longer can.

EVELYN: No, he doesn't even do that.

HORACE: Then why?

EVELYN: I don't know why.

HORACE: *(to audience now)* We were getting nowhere, and I had to get out of the house. If she wanted her freedom, she could have it but she was going to have to ask for it herself.

EVELYN: I just wanted the past to disappear. I wanted to continue on as if nothing had happened.

HORACE: I went out to do chores in the chickenhouse. When I came back inside, I found her on the floor of the bathroom.

FRANK: Altar of Love by The Channels! Goodnight My Love by Jesse Belvin!

EVELYN: I don't even recall doing it.

FRANK: The Ten Commandments of Love by The Moonglows!

HORACE: She'd slashed her wrist. Blood was everywhere.

EVELYN: No — I'd struck at one wrist, once, lightly. Seeing the blood, I must have fainted.

FRANK: Symbol of Love by the G-Clefs!

HORACE: I was sure she'd killed herself.

FRANK: Treasure of Love by Clyde McPhatter! Chapel of Love by the Dixie Cups!

EVELYN: It would always seem like a bad dream to me. If I'd meant to do that, I think I would have succeeded.

HORACE: I was the last thing I'd expected her to do.

FRANK: Ship of Love by The Nutmegs!

(The studio phone rings.)

FRANK: Glory of Love by The Velvatones!

(He "answers the phone")

FRANK: WRUT, Lovin' Dan.
HORACE: *("on the phone")* Frank?
FRANK: Dad?
HORACE: Get here as soon as you can. Something terrible has happened.

(LIGHTS DOWN in living area, up on Les in radio station area.)

LES: *(to audience)* It was the last thing I expected her to do. We had been together for several hours only the night before. She hadn't given me a clue that she was unhappy. She always felt sorry for Horace, of course, but it wasn't the kind of thing that would lead to desperation. When Frank attacked me in the studio, I thought he'd reached the breaking point. It never occurred to me that she was in the hospital. I'd been with her only the night before.

(Frank attacks Les.)

FRANK: You son-of-a-bitch!
LES: What the hell!

(They struggle until Les finally gets Frank in a controlling head-lock.)

LES: What the hell is going on?
FRANK: She tried to kill herself because of you ... You and your fucking respect ...
LES: Where is she? What happened?
FRANK: At the hospital. You goddamn —
LES: You don't understand the first thing about this!
FRANK: I understand what drove her to it.
LES: I'm not going to try to explain it to you. When I let you go, you're going to stay put and shut up. Am I right?
FRANK: Fuck you.

(Les tightens his grip.)

LES: Am I right?

(Frank groans in pain, and Les lets him loose.)

LES: I'll talk to you later.

FRANK: Stay away from her.

LES: This is not your business.

FRANK: If I had a gun, it would be. I'd blow your fucking head off.

LES: The only reason you're not carrying a gun in the jungle over there is because I thought you had something to offer this community. Watch your step, boy. You can fight that war over there yet.

(Frank moves toward the living area.)

LES: Of course, it was an idle threat. Evey would never forgive me for that. I loved her very much.

(LIGHTS OFF Les and up in the living area as Frank meets Carl there.)

CARL: Frank, what's the matter? Are you all right?

FRANK: I need some help ...

CARL: Of course.

FRANK: My whole world is collapsing ...

CARL: What happened?

FRANK: Listen, I've got to get the hell out of here. I have to go somewhere. I think I'm going to be drafted.

CARL: Christ almighty.

FRANK: I don't know what to do.

CARL: I know some people in Canada, Frank. Listen to me: you have options. They'd be glad to help you. It's an honor with them, helping someone who has the moral courage to skip that crap over there.

FRANK: I don't have moral —

CARL: *(quickly, to audience)* He seemed to be on bad acid or something, which wasn't like Frank at all. I phoned Canada and made the arrangements and the next morning we put him on a bus.

SHERI: *(coming forward)* She's resting comfortably.

FRANK: Did you tell her that I ...

SHERI: No.

CARL: No one knows but us.

SHERI: You can write them later.

CARL: I don't think you should let anyone know your return address. Including us.

FRANK: Was Uncle Les with her?

SHERI: Not while I was.

CARL: Keep in touch, Frank. And be careful.

SHERI: I know you're doing the right thing — but God I wish there was another way.

(She moves forward to embrace him but Frank backs away.)

(Jocelyn moves forward.)

JOCELYN: Morris?

SHERI: Frank?

FRANK: Jocelyn ...

JOCELYN: I'm right here.

CARL: *(to audience)* I'd asked him to phone collect when he arrived in Ontario. When he didn't, I phoned my friends to see if he'd made it.

FRANK: I'm a coward, Jocelyn.

JOCELYN: Don't, Morris.

FRANK: I ran.

CARL: He'd arrived all right. He arrived and hit the sack and had been sleeping twelve hours when I called. I was relieved, believe me. Frank seemed so unsure of himself. He was doing a very courageous thing.

FRANK: I ran from everything.

CARL: And we needed him up there — we needed all the moral heroes we could get.

JOCELYN: It was an immoral and terrible war.

FRANK: I didn't run from the war. I ran from myself. How can I be pardoned when I'm a coward?

JCOELYN: You're not a coward. Not if you go back to the States and resolve it. The past is eating you alive, Morris.

SHERI: It occurred to me that I might never see him again.

JOCELYN: Go back, Morris.

(Carl, Sheri and Jocelyn move off.)

FRANK: When I took the mail boat to Oyster Island, I spent the entire trip at the railing on the upper deck. The spring day was the peninsula at its best, the sky flat blue and punctuated by white gulls that followed our wake. I watched alone in the wind and spray of the day, under the flat blue sky filled with gulls, as silent as a sailor on watch, a navigator who reckoned not where he was going but where he had been.

(Horace wheels forward into the living area.)

HORACE: I expected you to come back.

FRANK: Then you know more than I did. The visit is, well, impulsive.

HORACE: What do you do in Canada?

FRANK: I have a radio job. And you? I don't see any chickens.

HORACE: I have my disability and social security. It's enough on the island.

FRANK: I've never been on the island before.

HORACE: More tourists are visiting all the time. Of course, they don't stay but an hour before the mail boat goes back. We've got no facilities for them.

(A beat.)

FRANK: I heard about Mom. Sheri told me how it happened. *(To audience)* She died in an auto wreck. Hit broadside by a drunken driver.

(LIGHTS UP on Les and Evelyn in front of the podium area.)

EVELYN: *(drunk)* I want another.

LES: I think you've had plenty.

HORACE: Les was driving.

FRANK: Sheri didn't tell me that.

HORACE: He got out with hardly a scratch.

LES: Please, Evey. You're already past your limit.

EVELYN: I'm finding a new limit. That's just what I'm doing.

LES: You're a three-drink woman, and you'll always be a three-drink woman.

HORACE: It surprised me. I thought she'd stopped seeing him.

EVELYN: *(to audience, sober)* He was so persistent. I didn't want to hurt him. I didn't want to hurt Horace. I didn't want to hurt anyone.

HORACE: I made her make a choice. She said she wanted to save the marriage.

EVELYN: I did, I did.

LES: I'll drive you home.

EVELYN: *(drunk)* One for the road?

LES: No more, Evey. I mean it. Let's go.

EVELYN: I'm going to call Toronto.

LES: Evey, we tried Toronto. We tried Ontario and Quebec and Vancouver. Don't you remember?

EVELYN: I'm just going to ask if there's a listing.

LES: He wouldn't be using his real name.

EVELYN: I want to talk to Frank!

LES: Come on, goddamn it.

HORACE: I guess she'd been seeing him all along.

EVELYN: *(to audience)* That's not true. This was going to be the last time. I meant to tell him so.

LES: Come on. *(To audience)* We started off. I'd had a few drinks myself but there's nothing I could've done, the fellow ran a red light. All the same, I've never forgiven myself for what happened. I know that it wasn't my fault but it doesn't help. I loved her so much.

(Les and Evelyn move off.)

HORACE: Can you stay overnight?

FRANK: I have to be back on the air Monday.

HORACE: Then you have to head back tomorrow?

FRANK: I'm afraid so.

HORACE: You won't want to miss the boat. You'd be stranded here until tomorrow afternoon.

FRANK: My boss wouldn't appreciate that.

HORACE: I've often wondered how you were making out.

FRANK: No complaints.

HORACE: That's more than most of us can say.

FRANK: Well, I don't want to miss the boat.

HORACE: No, it would be a long swim.

FRANK: I'll write.

HORACE: You don't need no more address than Oyster Island.

FRANK: Dad, I don't know how to say this but there were things you were right about. More right than I was.

HORACE: A lot of folks were wrong. I don't know anybody who was right about that war. It wasn't a time when being right was possible.

FRANK: It wasn't so much the war ... I just shouldn't have gone when I did.

HORACE: There are parents who wish their sons had gone to Canada.

FRANK: In a way it was easier leaving than coming back. I feel so removed from everything here.

HORACE: I felt the same thing, coming home in '45. I had to adjust.

FRANK: Maybe more than I did.

(A beat.)

FRANK: I'd better get that boat.
HORACE: Frank ... son ...
FRANK: Dad?
HORACE: Have a safe trip. And write.
FRANK: I will.

(Horace moves off as Carl and Sheri enter the living area.)

CARL: I told my class about you today. They were only kids when the Vietnam shit was hitting the fan, and it's hard for them to realize how divided the country was then. You have my eternal admiration, Frank.
SHERI: Have a safe trip. And write.
CARL: Hell, visit again. And bring your girl.
SHERI: I'd love to meet her.
FRANK: I'll be in touch.

(Carl and Sheri move off. LIGHTS UP on Jocelyn in the radio station area, to which Frank now heads.)

JOCELYN: I was directing commercials for TV when he came to work as a DJ. He was American and there was a lot of speculation, since his age was about right, that maybe he was in exile from the States. There were so many Americans who had come here that way.
FRANK: I'd seen her a few times in the hallway. I asked someone her name. I looked for a ring but she wore none.
JOCELYN: He asked me to dinner. It was strange — he looked as if he were ready to burst into tears.
FRANK: We dated. And we danced.

(An R&B classic begins to play, an instrumental, perhaps "Honky Tonk" etc.)

JOCELYN: I can't dance to this.
FRANK: Sure you can. You've got a great teacher.
JOCELYN: I'm going to need one.
FRANK: Just copy me.

(They begin to dance.)

FRANK: I'll have you know I was once the best rhythm-n-blues jockey on the Eastern Shore.

JOCELYN: I can believe it.

FRANK: Lovin' Dan the Sixty-Minute Man! From bebop to boogie, from blues to ballads, the sound of the 1950s! It will stand!

JOCELYN: How am I doing?

FRANK: Terrific.

JOCELYN: What do you call this?

FRANK: The bop. Yes, indeedy! We're boppin' in Canada from coast to coast! The dance with the most! Lovin' Dan your host!

JOCELYN: Morris, you're amazing. I thought you were shy.

FRANK: Hey, who's Morris? You're dancing with Lovin' Dan the Sixty-Minute Man.

JOCELYN: *(breaking away)* We danced and danced and danced. I don't know when I'd had so much fun.

FRANK: Then one night we made love.

JOCELYN: It was the best ever for me, on merely a physical level. This was going to keep me with him longer than I might have stayed, once I learned about the rest. Then President Carter granted the pardon, he could return to the States without consequences, and I expected him to jump at the opportunity.

FRANK: Things were finally going well for me again.

JOCELYN: On the surface.

FRANK: I wanted to forget the past. The pardon was a vivid reminder.

JOCELYN: You had to go back.

(A beat. Time shift.)

JOCELYN: How did it go?

FRANK: I told Sheri and Carl about you.

JOCELYN: That's not what I mean.

FRANK: Maybe you'd better ask a direct question.

JOCELYN: How did you and your father get along?

FRANK: We exchanged war stories. I didn't have much to say.

JOCELYN: And your sister?

FRANK: Her husband thinks I'm a goddamn hero. He thinks I deserve a fucking medal.

JOCELYN: Obviously you don't agree.

FRANK: Nobody wants to talk about anything real.

JOCELYN: Is that so surprising?

FRANK: There's nothing for me there any more. No one wants to deal with it. With the family, with the war, nothing. It's like none of it happened. The past is just past. Forgotten. Dead. Silent.

(The others move forward and surround the action, dream-like.)

JOCELYN: Maybe that's necessary. Maybe only then can we live in the present.

EVELYN: Someone please take me home.

FRANK: But so much happened. So goddamn much happened!

CARL: I told my class about you today.

FRANK: Doesn't it mean anything? Doesn't it influence anything?

JOCELYN: You. It influences you, Morris. Still.

LES: I show her considerably more respect than you did last night.

HORACE: It wasn't a time when being right was possible.

FRANK: Jocelyn, I may or may not be a coward. But I know I'm a liar.

JOCELYN: Why are you always so hard on yourself?

FRANK: Listen to me.

JOCELYN: No, Morris, it's time you listen to me.

SHERI: I just wanted to deal with something I could handle.

FRANK: A liar, do you understand?

JOCELYN: Morris, I —

FRANK: There! Right there!

JOCELYN: We have to talk, Morris. About us.

FRANK: My name is Frank.

(A beat.)

FRANK: I said my name isn't Morris, it's Frank. I've been lying to you.

JOCELYN: To yourself, not to me.

HARRIET: I wish Daniel had run to Canada.

FRANK: Doesn't it mean anything to you? My name is Frank White!

JOCELYN: Fine. I'll change my vocabulary. Your name is Frank. I love you, Frank, but I can't live with you just now.

FRANK: What?

HARRIET: You're alive.

JOCELYN: I've taken an apartment. We can still date, Morris. Frank. I'm glad you went back. It's a beginning.

FRANK: Yeah, great. A goddamn moral hero, that's me.

JOCELYN: I'm moving out because I think it's important that you spend time with yourself. You have to learn to be Frank again.

FRANK: My name is Morris Appleway! Frank White's dead. He got killed in the war.

JOCELYN: Frank— ... Morris ... let's have dinner together soon.

FRANK: You think it's easy doing what I did? Killing yourself? Sticking a phony driver's license in your wallet, a social security number you never saw before, you think it's easy to look some well-meaning clerk in the eye who's asking you what goddamn name you want to use, what goddamn name you want to spend the rest of your phony life with, you think it's easy to go through with that?

HARRIET: But you're alive.

FRANK: To have a trade but be afraid of using it because they can trace you that way? To cross the street thinking every son-of-a-bitch you meet is a spy out to blow your cover, you think that's pleasant?

HARRIET, SHERI, CARL: You're alive.

FRANK: It stinks. That whole country stinks. They pretend it never happened, it was just something that's come and gone, like the goddamn seasons, first it's goddamn winter and then it's goddamn summer.

HORACE, EVELYN, LES: But you're alive.

FRANK: Okay, so I went back. I went back because you said I should resolve it.

JOCELYN: And learn to forgive. I still think so.

FRANK: So I resolved it. Want to hear how? I hope the United States disappears from the face of the earth.

JOCELYN: That doesn't solve anything.

FRANK: So what do I get? I come back to learn I'm being jilted by the woman I was going to marry. I was going to become a Canadian citizen. I was going to marry and live happily ever after. I was going to have children and they were going to grow up with accents and never cross the border their entire lives. Carter giving me a pardon? What a joke. What incredible gall! It's me who should be giving out pardons.

JOCELYN: Yes, I agree.

THE ENTIRE CIRCLE: But you're alive, you're alive.

(A beat.)

FRANK: He's been through hell, Jocelyn. He's been through hell.

JOCELYN: Who?

FRANK: His war took his manhood from him. It's a hell of a lot more than I lost. Mom couldn't handle it and ran. I'm my mother's goddamn son, Jocelyn. And my father's goddamn son.

JOCELYN: *(gently)* We'll have dinner soon.

FRANK: I need you, Jocelyn.

JOCELYN: I love you.

SHERI, CARL, HARRIET: You're alive, Morris.

HORACE, EVELYN, LES: You're alive, Frank.

JOCELYN: I'm so glad you're alive.

SHERI: Dear Frank: Dad died peaceably in his sleep last night. I tried to call but you've moved. I assume this will be forwarded and reach you. I enclose your letter to Dad, which arrived in this morning's mail.

(Everyone moves off except Frank.)

FRANK: There was a war. There was a war but there were no heroes. Perhaps you remember. ... Goodnight.

(BLACKOUT. The play is over.)

For royalties information:
Charles Deemer
cdeemer@teleport.com
1-800-294-7176

543

1996

Who Forgives?
a play in two acts

First performed (in a slightly different version) at the Cork Arts Center in Cork, Ireland, on December 9, 1996. Directed by Charles Ruxton.

THE CAST:
Ed, *40s, the boarder, a music teacher*
Cynthia, *40s, the landlord*
Alice, *30s, the neighbor*
Amy, *teens, the girl, a music student*
Heather, *teens, a former student of Ed's (played by same actress who plays Amy)*

THE SET:
The central playing area is the living room of Cynthia's home. A sofa, coffee table, chairs, phone, answering machine, tape deck, books.
Neutral playing areas as indicated; area where Amy plays her violin.

THE TIME:
The present.

/ prologue

(SHADOWY MOOD LIGHTS come up on Amy, playing the violin, part of a string quartet (recorded music), haunting, which becomes the play's THEME. Mendelssohn's String Quartet in A minor, first movement, Adagio. AREA LIGHTS up on Ed, facing the audience, as the music softly continues.)

ED: Mendelssohn's String Quartet in A minor. Opus 13 — "13," which should have been a sign. The first movement. Adagio.

The first time Amy played it, I wept. I'd never had a student evoke such emotion from the piece before. From that moment on, I never doubted her talent. But the rest...the rest is more complicated.

She was 12 or 13 at the time, playing like an angel, evoking emotions she couldn't have been aware of at her age. So I am not ashamed of loving her.

But I did not abuse her. You can think what you want, but that's the truth.

(Ed continues speaking to the audience as he starts moving into the living room.)

ED: I was less than a week out of prison when the trouble started all over again. I think I expected it would. After all, as far as the public was concerned, I was guilty until proven innocent.

/ night

(The same Mendelssohn is playing, now from the tape deck upstage. Ed sits in a chair in the living room and starts meditating. His eyes are closed.)

(The door opens and Cynthia comes in, returning from an AA meeting. She ignores Ed, going straight to the telephone answering machine and looking down at the number of recorded messages. Ed senses someone else is in the room and opens his eyes. He gets up and heads for the tape deck.)

CYNTHIA: Only nine messages.
ED: Nine's plenty.

(He turns off the music.)

CYNTHIA: What did we have yesterday? Almost twenty? Nine's a definite improvement.
ED: One hate call is one too many. I've caused you—
CYNTHIA: We don't know all of them are hate calls, now do we? It's been the media as well. And maybe even a few supporters, for all we know.
ED: Miss Bernstein, if it doesn't stop by the end of the week, I think I should move on.
CYNTHIA: *(ignoring this)* You know what gets me? How the reporters can't take no for an answer. You'd think journalism school would teach them what "no comment" means.
ED: I'm nothing but trouble. I force you to turn off your phone because it rings off the hook. I've created a scandal in the neighborhood. I've—
CYNTHIA: Mr. Ramsey, I believed you were innocent from the beginning.
ED: I am innocent.
CYNTHIA: I wouldn't have rented to you otherwise. We're not going to let this keep us from doing what's right.
ED: I feel like such a burden.
CYNTHIA: You are no burden at all. I'm going to put on coffee. I invited my friend Alice over for dessert.
ED: Then if you'll excuse me.
CYNTHIA: You're invited, too.
ED: Miss Bernstein, I—
CYNTHIA: You've been here almost a week, Mr. Ramsey. You can call me Cynthia.
ED: Only if you call me Ed.
CYNTHIA: Ed — you are perfectly welcome to join us. Alice is like a little sister to me. We don't get to visit often, other than at meetings, so this is something special.
ED: I don't feel very social tonight, I'm afraid.
CYNTHIA: Alice is new in recovery and very determined to turn her life around. She might inspire you.

ED: You think I need inspiration?

CYNTHIA: All of us need inspiration, Ed! Just relax and join us. I'm not taking no for an answer.

ED: I'll stay just a little while. Does she know about...?

CYNTHIA: Of course not. And if she finds out, you're telling her, not me.

ED: I appreciate that.

CYNTHIA: As far as I'm concerned, you're a music teacher looking for a job. Anything else you want her to know is up to you.

ED: Thanks, Cynthia.

CYNTHIA: I did you a favor, you can do me one. Take Alice off my hands while I'm in the kitchen. Ever since I became her sponsor, she's been talking my ear off. I can use a break. All you have to do is listen, she's quite good at doing all the talking.

ED: I suppose I can manage that.

CYNTHIA: Of course you can.

(The doorbell rings. Ed looks disturbed.)

CYNTHIA: Alice doesn't bite, Ed.

(She opens the door and Alice comes into the room.)

CYNTHIA: Alice, this is Ed Ramsey.

ALICE: Hello.

ED: Hi.

(There is an awkward pause.)

CYNTHIA: Everybody sit down. Ed, if you don't like the color of your room, blame Alice. She picked it out — and did most of the painting. I'd never have had the room ready in time without her.

ALICE: I'm a professional volunteer.

ED: That's because you weren't in the Army. You learn *never* to volunteer.

ALICE: You were in the Army?

ED: Only technically. I played in the band. It's not your typical Army life.

CYNTHIA: Ed teaches music.

ALICE: Really? What instrument?

ED: Used to teach music. Violin's my first love.

ALICE: I didn't know the Army had a violin band.

ED: I played clarinet in the Army.

ALICE: How many instruments do you play?

ED: Too many. Jack of all trades, master of none.

CYNTHIA: If you two will excuse me, I'll make coffee. Wait til you taste the cake!

(And she's gone. An awkward pause.)

ED: Have you known Cynthia long?

ALICE: Most of my life. She was my older sister's best friend all through school.

ED: She's a great friend to have, from what I've seen.

ALICE: She saved my life, I can tell you that. Without Cynthia's support, I'd probably still be swilling the sauce. I'm an alcoholic. She's my sponsor.

ED: So she told me. How long have you been sober?

ALICE: Almost a year.

ED: My congratulations.

ALICE: Are you...?

ED: An alcoholic? No. But I've met a lot of them. Even been to a few meetings.

ALICE: Really?

ED: With, ah, friends.

(Ed smiles. A pause.)

ALICE: I don't know why I'm so nervous. Usually you can't shut me up. How did you happen to rent a room here?

ED: I, you know, saw the ad . . .

ALICE: Well, Cynthia's been threatening to do this for months. Not just for the extra income either, but I think for the company as well. Her husband died quite a few years ago now, and she's kept pretty much to herself the last few years, since I've gotten to know her again, I mean. To be honest, I worry about her. I'm glad you're here to keep her company. Of course, I'm a fine one to talk, I've been divorced twice and don't have any more of a social life than she does, other than meetings, of course. I don't know what I'd do without all the people I've met in AA. It's like having a second family. Well, a first family, really — my family isn't all that close. My sister married an Air Force officer and travels around the world. She's the only one I was ever close to. Cynthia's like a big sister to me now, sort of in place of Carol, you know what I mean? Not that we see each other all that often, except at meetings, we live on opposite sides of town.

I'm sorry. I'm doing all the talking.

ED: I don't mind.

ALICE: Actually, I'm shy. I think that's why I drink. I mean, drank! To tell the truth, when I sobered up I expected that my true self would reveal itself as some kind of silent wallflower, maybe even a little mysteriously so, like Greta Garbo — but here I am, talking to beat the band, just like when I was drinking, except that now I make more sense. Well, maybe not more sense but at least what I say is understandable now, I'm not slurring my words and making a total fool of myself. God, the stuff I got into when I was drinking! Thank your stars that you don't have that kind of problem.

ED: I do.

ALICE: And you should. Especially in this culture, where there's so much pressure to drink and have a good time — just look at the ads on television! You'd think you couldn't find a mate or be happy without a bottle in your hand.

(Cynthia returns with a tray of coffee and cake. Ed stands up.)

ED: I'm afraid I'm not feeling very social tonight. It's been very nice meeting you, Alice. I'm sorry I'm not better company.

ALICE: Oh God, I'm driving you away, aren't I?

ED: It's not that at all. I'm just very tired.

CYNTHIA: Ed, you are sitting back down and having your cake. Sit.

(He sits back down.)

ALICE: I talked his ear off.

ED: No, you're very good company. I've had a long day, is all.

CYNTHIA: He's looking for a teaching job.

ED: Anything, really.

CYNTHIA: Don't settle for less. And if there's a problem with rent, you come to me before you do something stupid, you understand me? I can always find something for you to do around here.

ED: That's very kind, but I'm sure I'll find something soon.

(A beat.)

ALICE: Cynthia, this is so yummy!

CYNTHIA: I thought you'd like it. Ed?
ED: Very tasty.

(They eat in silence a moment. Ed suddenly stands up.)

ED: I'm sorry. I just don't feel like good company tonight. It's nice to meet you, Alice.
ALICE: Nice to meet you, too.
ED: Goodnight.
CYNTHIA: Goodnight, Ed.

(The women watch him leave.)

ALICE: I drove him away.
CYNTHIA: I don't think so. He feels under a lot of pressure to find work.
ALICE: He's not from here?
CYNTHIA: He is — but he's been away for a while. I'm sure he'll find something soon.
ALICE: It would be nice to have music in the house. Does he play often?
CYNTHIA: I haven't heard him play yet. He told me his violin is still in storage.
ALICE: That's a shame. I'd love to hear him play.
CYNTHIA: I expect he'll be practicing once he gets settled in.
ALICE: He's very different than the boarder I expected.
CYNTHIA: Who did you expect?
ALICE: Someone much older. Someone retired and living on social security. I suppose once he finds a job and has a steady income again, he'll want his own apartment.
CYNTHIA: Perhaps.
ALICE: So tell me, Cynthia: is it nice to have a man around the house?
CYNTHIA: Get that gleam out of your eye. There is nothing going on between us now or in the future. I can guarantee you.
ALICE: He's a nice looking man. Cultured, easy to talk to—
CYNTHIA: Speak for yourself, Alice. I am not interested in what you have in mind.
ALICE: I think about dating again.
CYNTHIA: You know what the rule is — no relationship during your first year of sobriety.
ALICE: I didn't say relationship. I said dating.

CYNTHIA: One has a way of leading to the other.

ALICE: Joe at the meeting has asked me to a movie a couple times.

CYNTHIA: Joe relapses like clockwork. If you want my advice, stay away from him.

ALICE: I figured that much out on my own.

CYNTHIA: More cake?

ALICE: No. I'd better get going. I start at six tomorrow.

CYNTHIA: I thought you had the late night shift.

ALICE: I finally got them to give me days. All the time I've been at Safeway, it's the least they can do. Thanks for having me over.

(The phone starts ringing.)

ALICE: I can find my way out. I'll call you tomorrow.

(Alice leaves, and Cynthia picks up the phone.)

CYNTHIA: Hello? . . . Just a minute, let me see if he's still up.

(She moves toward Ed's room.)

CYNTHIA: Ed? Telephone! Are you awake?

ED *(O.S.)*: Be right there!

(Cynthia goes back to the phone.)

CYNTHIA: *(on phone)* He's on his way. Who is this? . . . I didn't recognize your voice, dear. . . . No, now is fine. Here he is.

(Ed comes forward and takes the phone.)

ED: Hello? . . . I don't know what to say. . . . If you mean that— . . .Thank you. I really mean that. . . . Yes. And thank you.

(He sets down the receiver.)

ED: It was Amy.

CYNTHIA: What a surprise!

ED: How did she know I was here?

CYNTHIA: Maybe she saw the articles in the paper and looked me up in the phone book. She'd know you're staying here.

ED: She said she just called a TV station and retracted her story. She told them the truth. I can't believe she did that.

(He starts for his bedroom.)

CYNTHIA: She told them what exactly?
ED: That it was her stepfather who abused her. Just as I suspected.
CYNTHIA: She told them you're innocent?
ED: Yes. She's finally telling the truth.
CYNTHIA: Well, this calls for a celebration. Are you going to see her?
ED: Of course not.
CYNTHIA: I thought you'd want to thank her in person.
ED: I don't think it's a good idea for me to see her.

(CROSS FADE TO: Alice on the telephone, that same night.)

ALICE: Mary, I made a total fool of myself. I was actually breaking into a sweat. . . . Yes, he's nice. That's why I was so nervous. I wanted him to like me. . . . I don't know why. It was visceral. .. . No, I'm not ready for a relationship, even if he was interested, which I'm sure he's not. I couldn't shut up. I just babbled and babbled. He got away as soon as he could.

(CROSS FADE TO: Living room. Cynthia has let Amy in. She is carrying her violin case.)

/the next afternoon

AMY: But on the phone you said to be here at two.
CYNTHIA: I forgot he had an appointment with his parole officer this afternoon. But he won't be long, dear. Shall we sit down?

(Amy is hesitant.)

CYNTHIA: He told me to make sure you wait.
AMY: Really?
CYNTHIA: Really.

(Amy sits down on the divan. Cynthia joins her.)

CYNTHIA: What a courageous thing you did. And what a surprise! When I called you the other day, you didn't say anything about it.

AMY: Well, since he wanted to be my teacher again, least I could do is finally tell the truth.

CYNTHIA: Better late than never, I always say.

AMY: My mom doesn't know I came. She'd have a cow if she knew. Not that she ever pays attention to what I'm doing.

CYNTHIA: She doesn't approve of Mr. Ramsey?

AMY: Not after what happened. She never believes anything I say. Her boyfriends are all saints, as far as she's concerned.

CYNTHIA: It hasn't been easy for you, poor dear.

AMY: Not as bad as for him. People have been really awful to him here, haven't they?

CYNTHIA: It could've been worse. And I'm sure everything will be fine now, thanks to you.

AMY: I hope so. I've really been feeling guilty. When you called, I didn't know what to think. The last thing I expected was that he'd want me for a student again. I ruined his life.

CYNTHIA: Whatever you did or he did is over now. It's time for a fresh beginning.

AMY: He didn't do anything, is what I'm saying. When the social worker found out what was going on and everything, I wanted to tell, I really did, but I was too scared to. I told mom once and she didn't even believe me. Then at the police station, they kept talking so much and saying things that got me all confused and everything . . . When I signed the paper, I didn't even know what I was signing.

CYNTHIA: We don't have to talk about the past, Amy.

AMY: I wrote him in prison. I used my girlfriend's name because I didn't know if it was allowed or not. But I said things so he'd know it was me. I wanted him to know what really happened. When he didn't reply, I thought he didn't believe me.

CYNTHIA: I'm sure they wouldn't let him write you.

AMY: I thought he could've found a way if he really wanted to.

(Cynthia wants to change the subject. She looks at her watch.)

CYNTHIA: I don't know what's keeping him. He'll be so happy to see that you're still practicing.

AMY: I don't very much.

CYNTHIA: Mr. Ramsey told me you're the best student he ever had.

AMY: He did?

CYNTHIA: Absolutely. How he raves about your talent!

AMY: Well, I used to be pretty good. I haven't practiced much since, you know, everything happened. I practice but I haven't been taking lessons or anything.

CYNTHIA: All that's about to change, young lady.

AMY: That would be great.

(Cynthia stands up.)

CYNTHIA: I'm going to let you make yourself at home, dear. I have some errands to run. I'm sure he'll be home any minute now.

AMY: I could come back later.

CYNTHIA: Don't be ridiculous. You can watch TV while you're waiting. It's in my bedroom.

AMY: You wouldn't mind?

CYNTHIA: Of course not. Let me show you.

(Amy gets up and Cynthia starts her in the direction of the bedroom. Amy leaves her violin case on the floor by the divan.)

CYNTHIA: It's the first door on the left. I have cable with all the trimmings, a big comfy bed to stretch out on — you just make yourself at home, dear.

AMY: I know you told me your name on the phone, but I forgot.

CYNTHIA: Cynthia.

AMY: This is turning out so much better than I thought. I almost didn't come over. It was all I could do to call him last night.

CYNTHIA: You have nothing to worry about, Amy. Mr. Ramsey talks about you all the time.

AMY: Last night he sounded so surprised to hear from me.

CYNTHIA: It's been so long since he's heard your voice! But he's thrilled to have you back in his life.

AMY: Really?

CYNTHIA: *(ignoring this)* There's pop in the refrigerator if you're thirsty. I should be back before your lesson is over.

(And Cynthia is out the door.)

(Amy can't believe how well everything has turned out. She turns and heads for the bedroom to watch TV.)

(CROSS FADE TO: table in cafe, where Ed and Alice are having coffee.)

ALICE: You're staring.

ED: I'm sorry.

ALICE: I feel like you can see right through me.

ED: You seem tense. I hope it's not the company.

ALICE: That's not it at all. I'm flattered you called. I'm also shocked.

ED: It was pretty short notice. Why are you shocked?

ALICE: I was afraid I talked so much last night you'd never want to see me again.

ED: You were obviously wrong.

ALICE: I was hoping we'd see each other again. I just didn't expect it to happen. Or even if it did, that it would be so soon.

ED: One, I felt like I had to get out of the house; and two, I felt like having company. Cynthia told me you'd started early and would be off in the afternoon. So I rolled the dice and phoned you.

ALIC I'm glad you did. I already said that, didn't I?

(Nervous laughter.)

ED: So you work at Safeway.

ALICE: Not very glamorous, is it?

ED: Do you like it?

ALICE: Actually, I do.

ED: Then that's glamour enough.

ALICE: Are you looking for a music teaching job?

ED: Ideally, but I may have to settle for what I can get.

ALICE: I've never met a music teacher before. That sounds silly, doesn't it?

ED: Well, I've never met someone who rings up my groceries. So we're even.

ALICE: You know, when I started there during high school, I thought it was a temporary job, until I went to college. Then when I finally took a year at the community college, I dropped out and went back to work. I've been there ever since. I keep telling myself I'm going to take night classes but I always forget to register in time. I think it's too late now, I'm too old to go back to school. So I seem to be stuck at Safeway.

ED: But you said you like it.

ALICE: Well, I really do. But a part of me thinks I should do something more with my life than ring up groceries all day.

ED: You don't have children?

ALICE: No. And I've thought of that, too. The old biological clock is getting pretty active lately. Do you have children?

ED: No. I never married.

ALICE: That's unusual.

ED: I'm not gay, if that's what you're thinking.

ALICE: Actually, it is what I was thinking! Thanks for letting me know.

ED: Would you have been disappointed?

ALICE: That sounds like a leading question.

ED: Very leading.

ALICE: Yes, I would have been disappointed.

ED: I'm glad.

ALICE: I'm glad you're glad.

(Another awkward pause.)

ALICE: My palms are sweating.

ED: Does that mean you're going to inherit money?

ALICE: That's itching. Sweaty palms mean I'm nervous as hell and angry at myself for it.

ED: Why are you nervous?

ALICE: I'll tell you some other time.

ED: Fair enough.

ALICE: You, of course, are the Rock of Gibraltar, no doubt.

ED: Hardly. Alice, I get the impression that both of us are a little rusty at this. Am I right?

ALICE: I have coffee out all the time.

ED: You know what I mean.

ALICE: Yes, we are. I mean, I am. Rusty. At this sort of thing. Is this a date?

ED: Yes, I'd call it a date. An afternoon date.

ALICE: Just checking. That's definitely it, then. The sweaty palms. This is my first date in over a year.

ED: Now that surprises me.

ALICE: I'm not supposed to be in a relationship during the first year of sobriety. Not to jump the gun. Oh shit, that really sounded stupid, didn't it? Just forget I said any of that.

ED: What you said was charming.

ALICE: Good, let's quit while we're ahead.

(She stands up.)

ED: Can I call you again?
ALICE: You'd better.
ED: I will.
ALICE: I'll try not to move my bed next to the phone.

(CROSS FADE TO...)

/living room, later that afternoon

(Amy is sitting on the divan, bored. Waiting. Cynthia enters.)

CYNTHIA: Well, how did it go?
AMY: He never showed.
CYNTHIA: Really? I hope there isn't trouble with his parole officer.
AMY: You think he's in trouble?
CYNTHIA: I have no idea. Maybe something came up, he had to do some community service today or something. Can you come back tomorrow?
AMY: You sure he really wants to do this?
CYNTHIA: Of course I am! Same time tomorrow — and you have my word of honor he'll be here.

(CROSS FADE TO Alice on telephone, that night.)

ALICE: We had such a wonderful day! It's a little frightening, actually . . . Because, you know — you've been there yourself, Mary. It's hard to learn to trust a man again. Isn't it?...I'm taking it one day at a time, believe me. But today was wonderful! I can't remember when I felt so in sync with someone...Of course, I am. He's supposed to call tonight...What happens, happens. Right?...I'm taking it slow, and he's just as gun shy as I am. I don't feel pressure at all that we have to, you know, go out every weekend or hop in bed right away or anything like that. It's so damn comfortable, Mary! I love the way this is happening.

(CROSS FADE TO: living room, LIGHTS UP LOW.)

/ that night, late

(The room is dark. Cynthia is sitting in the stuffed chair. The door opens and Ed enters, moving in the darkness through the room. He is limping. Suddenly the light by Cynthia's chair comes on. She's turned on the light, which is still low. Ed, ignoring her, limps by on the way to his room.)

CYNTHIA: What happened to you?
ED: I was recognized. Consequently I got kneed in the balls and kicked in the shins. I had my hair pulled and my stomach punched. I got mistaken for a soccer ball and was kicked around the parking lot. How was your evening?
CYNTHIA: I'm so sorry.
ED: Good for you.

(He starts off again.)

CYNTHIA: I get the impression you're mad at me. I don't understand why.

(Ed stops and turns to her.)

ED: I'm not mad at you.

(A beat.)

ED: I didn't expect to hear from Amy again.
CYNTHIA: But she's done you a favor!
ED: I know, I should be grateful. I am, actually. It was just such a shock to hear from her.
CYNTHIA: Well, you can blame me for that.
ED: What are you talking about?
CYNTHIA: I called her and suggested she ask about getting music lessons again. I think that's what inspired her to tell the truth.
ED: You what? Who the hell do you think you are?
CYNTHIA: Ed, have you been drinking?
ED: You're a drunk, so nobody else can drink, is that it?
CYNTHIA: That was uncalled for.
ED: You have no right to choose my students for me. Assuming I decide to teach again, which is a decision I haven't made yet.
CYNTHIA: Of course you'll teach again. It's your calling.

ED: What business is this of yours?

CYNTHIA: I was just trying to help.

ED: You should mind your own business, Miss Bernstein.

(He turns to go.)

CYNTHIA: I'm sorry you got roughed up.

ED: Not half as sorry as I am.

CYNTHIA: Some people are just that way.

ED: Yes, they are. I could've saved everybody the trouble by going to Seattle. Some place I've never been before. I know you mean well — but, please, don't make any more decisions for me.

CYNTHIA: I already have. I told Amy to come by for a lesson tomorrow.

ED: I'm too rusty to teach.

CYNTHIA: Then begin with Amy. I think she may be as rusty as you are. You both could get back to speed together. However you musicians put it.

ED: I need to move on. It was a mistake to accept your offer and move in here.

CYNTHIA: You can't forgive her, can you? Even now, after she went out on a limb for you.

ED: I don't have to forgive her. I never blamed her in the first place.

CYNTHIA: I'm not sure I understand.

ED: I don't have the energy to explain it. It gets complicated.

CYNTHIA: You might try.

ED: No, I don't want to try. I don't want to bring up the past. I want to forget it and get on with my life.

CYNTHIA: I can understand that. I thought giving Amy lessons would—

ED: No, I can't just pick up the pieces and go on like nothing happened.

CYNTHIA: Then you're still angry at her.

ED: It has nothing to do with anger. I never blamed her. I always knew it was her stepfather who was abusing her. I told the police so — as if they'd take my word for anything.

CYNTHIA: Do this for her. I know you care about her. You should have seen her eyes light up when I told her you wanted to give her lessons again. I assumed it was what you wanted. If giving lessons isn't "getting on with your life," what is?

ED: Okay, I'll think about it.

CYNTHIA: It's a wonderful opportunity for you both.

ED: I'm not making any promises.
CYNTHIA: Goodnight, Ed.

(They move off to their bedrooms. CROSS FADE TO: Alice on the phone, late that night. The phone woke her up.)

ALICE: What time is it? . . . Yes, but that's all right. What's going on? ...That's sweet, Ed...I look forward to it, too....No, I was up reading...I don't mind....Goodnight, Ed... .I'm thinking about you, too.

(CROSS FADE TO: Living room.)

/ the next morning

(Ed lets Amy in. She is carrying her violin.)

ED: Good morning, Amy.
AMY: Hi.
ED: How are you?
AMY: Nervous.
ED: I'm a little nervous myself. You might as well come in and sit down.
AMY: Thank you.

(She slowly enters the room.)

ED: Make yourself at home.

(He gestures for her to sit on a chair. She does, putting the violin case on the floor beside her. Ed moves to the sofa, still limping a little.)

AMY: Did you hurt your leg?
ED: I slipped and fell. Nothing serious.

(He sits down.)

ED: No need to start the lesson right away.
AMY: Good. I think I'm too nervous to play.
ED: To be honest, I haven't played in five years myself. You?
AMY: Not very much.
ED: I'm ashamed of you.

AMY: Things have been really crazy at home.

ED: I'm sorry to hear that. Your stepfather died, didn't he?

AMY: Four years ago. Mom's boyfriends aren't much better. I wrote you about it.

ED: I know.

AMY: You never answered.

ED: They wouldn't let me write to you, Amy.

AMY: I was hoping you'd find a way.

ED: They have pretty tight security in there. It was impossible to write to you.

(A beat.)

ED: I never blamed you, Amy. I always had a suspicion about what was really going on.

AMY: I feel so guilty . . . the police got me so mixed up, I didn't know what I was signing.

ED: I understand.

AMY: And the things they told me about you. Why do they hate you so much?

ED: They were under a lot of pressure to make a conviction.

AMY: I never believed anything they said about you. Because I know you.

ED: I hope so.

AMY: I thought you'd hate me forever.

ED: I could never hate you.

(A beat. Amy looks around.)

AMY: Where's your violin?

ED: It's in storage.

AMY: You haven't even gotten it out of storage yet?

ED: I'm a little afraid to, I think. Maybe I don't want to hear how rusty I am. But I suppose we should find out how rusty you are. That's what we're here for.

AMY: I don't feel like playing all that much.

ED: Some other time, then.

(A beat.)

AMY: I'm almost eighteen. I'm getting my own place as soon as I can, too. Mom's drinking more than ever. It's a nightmare living at home.

ED: I always hoped your gift would break you free from all that. Maybe it will yet.

AMY: I don't know if I'll ever play as well as I used to.

ED: You have an extraordinary gift, Amy. More extraordinary considering how hard it's been for you at home. You have a responsibility to nurture it.

AMY: Then you'll help me?

(A beat.)

AMY: I need a teacher.

ED: Yes, I'll help you.

(Amy smiles and Ed smiles back, more at ease together now that they've settled this.)

AMY: Is Cynthia your girlfriend or something? You live together?

ED: Heavens, no. She wrote me just before I got out, offering to rent me a room. I took her up on it.

(A beat.)

AMY: When are you getting your violin out of storage?

ED: I'll tell you what. How would you like to go on a little errand with me, and we'll get it out of storage right now?

AMY: That'd be great.

ED: We can take the bus, and I'll get my violin, and tomorrow we can start lessons in earnest. How does that sound? Maybe practicing is just what we both need. Every life needs discipline, right?

AMY: Right.

ED: In prison, I'd close my eyes and hear you playing like an angel.

AMY: I don't think I'll play like an angel right away.

ED: Don't worry — I won't be teaching like one either. We can get up to speed together. A deal?

AMY: A deal!

(He gets to his feet, and Amy stands up. For a moment they face one another, standing, and there is a suggestion that they are being drawn together, almost like past lovers — clearly, they share an affection for one another that borders on the physical. Ed breaks the spell.)

ED: Let's get out of here.

(CROSS FADE TO: Alice and Cynthia in a dress shop, where Alice is holding up a new dress in front of a mirror.)

/ **a week later**

ALICE: What do you think? Should I try it on?

CYNTHIA: You really want to know?

ALICE: You don't like it. What's wrong with it?

CYNTHIA: The dress is fine. I can't believe *you.*

ALICE: What do you mean?

CYNTHIA: How many times have you gone out with him the past week? And now this.

ALICE: All "this" is, is buying a new dress!

CYNTHIA: It's like you're picking out a wedding dress.

ALICE: Don't be ridiculous.

CYNTHIA: Are you sure you're doing the right thing?

ALICE: Going out with him? Of course. I haven't felt this alive in years.

CYNTHIA: Are you sleeping with him?

ALICE: Is that my friend or my sponsor asking?

CYNTHIA: Both.

ALICE: You don't pull any punches, do you?

CYNTHIA: Not when the stakes are so high.

ALICE: Cynthia, you're the one jumping the gun here, not me.

CYNTHIA: I asked if you were sleeping with him.

ALICE: No, we haven't slept together. Not because I didn't want to. I'm not sure he's interested in me that way.

CYNTHIA: That doesn't surprise me.

ALICE: He told me he's not gay. I guess I'm not his type or something. I mean, he treats me wonderfully, as a friend. I know, I shouldn't be talking this way.

CYNTHIA: Then why are you?

ALICE: I care for him, Cynthia. Sometimes it scares me how much I care for him.

CYNTHIA: Why are you doing this to yourself?

ALICE: Because I feel in my gut it's the right thing to do. It's like I had, what do you call it?, an epiphany — like when I decided to go into treatment. You wake up one morning, and suddenly there's great clarity in your life.

CYNTHIA: I just don't want to see you get hurt.

ALICE: I'm taking it one day at a time, believe me. But at least I'm willing to take a risk with a man again. Even if he does end up rejecting me.

CYNTHIA: Alice, you hardly know him.

ALICE: Well, how do I get to know him unless I go out with him?

CYNTHIA: You shouldn't get into a relationship during your first year of sobriety.

ALICE: We talked about that, too. Neither of us have "relationship" in mind right now.

CYNTHIA: Boy, are you in denial!

ALICE: I think I'm thinking this through pretty well.

CYNTHIA: Just listen to yourself. Textbook denial.

ALICE: Cynthia — are you jealous? Is that what this is about?

CYNTHIA: Jealous? You can grab a better straw than that.

ALICE: I finally have a reason to get dressed up, is all. And he's such a sweet man — you've seen that yourself.

CYNTHIA: You don't have the slightest idea how I feel about him.

ALICE: You've always spoken well of him — or at least until I started dating him.

CYNTHIA: You don't know the half of what is going on.

ALICE: What do you mean?

CYNTHIA: He's here, Alice, because I wrote and offered to rent him a room. I wrote him — in prison.

ALICE: Ed told me everything. He's innocent. Amy retracted everything.

CYNTHIA: I can prove he's guilty.

ALICE: You're going to have to, Cynthia, because I don't find this little joke of yours funny at all.

CYNTHIA: *(She starts rooting through her purse)* I've been carrying this around for ten years. Here — read it.

(She hands Alice a folded, worn newspaper clipping. Alice starts reading.)

ALICE: I don't understand why you're doing this, Cynthia. It's as if you're jealous that I'm going out with him.

CYNTHIA: Read it. Barbara in the article is my sister. Was. She had a stroke four years ago. Heather is my niece.

ALICE: *(reading to herself)* Oh my God . . .

CYNTHIA: I went through the entire agonizing experience with her. The entire disgusting display of what justice is really about in this country today. How they completely ignore the victim, the rights and the feelings of the victimized. Heather was one of his music students. Just like this girl Amy. Heather could play like a child prodigy. We all expected great things of her.

Then Mr. Ramsey came along. Oh, he had a wonderful reputation as a music teacher, of course, and we certainly had no reason to suspect what he really was. A perpetrator, a pervert.

ALICE: It says here he didn't go to jail .

CYNTHIA: They call it plea-bargaining. They call it wheeling and dealing. They call it everything but what it really is — a travesty of justice, a shameful slap in the face of the victims. Victims have no rights, none. It still disgusts me.

ALICE: What happened to Heather?

CYNTHIA: What do you think happened? Her life was ruined.

(CROSS FADE TO: Heather in neutral area, a street hooker, leering at the audience:)

HEATHER: *(same actress as Amy)* Hey, Mr. Music Man, what the hell you doing with Amy? She's a little old for you, isn't she?

(Ed moves into the area, as if in a dream.)

ED: Heather?

HEATHER: Man, she looks a hell of a lot older than 11 or 12 to me. What's going on with you, chasing the older stuff in your middle years? Thought you liked them young and pre-pubescent, all starry-eyed and full of that crap you tell them about their talent.

ED: You did have talent. You played violin beautifully.

HEATHER: You asshole. I'm not going to buy into that crap any more.

ED: I never lied to you.

HEATHER: Never told me what the fuck you had on your mind either — pun intended. It was all just lies, you fucker, all sweet candy for the seduction.

ED: No! You had genuine talent.

HEATHER: Talent for spreading my legs for you. Talent for sucking your cock, much as it used to choke me. You were right about one thing — I did get used to it. You'd be surprised how good I've gotten.

ED: Stop talking that way.

HEATHER: You want me to suck your cock, Mr. Music Man? Or is Amy taking care of that for you now?

ED: Stop it!

HEATHER: You telling her how good she plays the violin? Lying fucker.

ED: Stop!

(CROSS FADE TO:. . .)

/living room

(. . .where Cynthia and Alice have entered. Cynthia shows Alice a folder of other newspaper articles about the case.)

CYNTHIA: I have everything ever written about Mr. Ed Ramsey. I could write a book about him. He plea-bargained his way into a treatment program, and that was the end of it. What an obscenity. Four years later, look what happened, he did the same thing to Amy.

ALICE: Cynthia, she retracted everything.

CYNTHIA: I don't believe her. The poor girl, I don't think she knows what is real and what isn't. My niece didn't. Heather worshipped that man, which is exactly what they set out to do.

(Alice puts down the articles.)

ALICE: Cynthia, what are you going to do?

CYNTHIA: I'm not sure.

ALICE: I don't know what to think. I feel like I've got creepy-crawlies all up and down my skin.

CYNTHIA: You want to go out to dinner with this man?

(A pause.)

CYNTHIA: It shouldn't be a hard question to answer, Alice.

ALICE: What if Amy is telling the truth?

CYNTHIA: Don't be ridiculous. You see how mixed up she is. She's still infatuated with him, just like Heather was.

ALICE: But what if he never abused her? She says her step-father did it. Ed says the same thing.

CYNTHIA: You can't give any credence to what he says!

ALICE: The girl changed her story.

CYNTHIA: Did you ever ask yourself why?

ALICE: Because she felt guilty.

566

CYNTHIA: Because she's infatuated with him! He's the only one who pays any attention to her.

ALICE: That's not the only explanation, Cynthia. I think Amy is telling the truth now.

CYNTHIA: Then thank God I invited her here. We'll find out soon enough.

ALICE: You invited her?

CYNTHIA I set up lessons again — because I want to catch him at it. Then maybe they'll finally lock him up and throw away the key.

ALICE: That's using her as bait.

CYNTHIA: He's already destroyed her. The important thing now is to get him back in prison.

ALICE: What I'm hearing you tell me, Cynthia, is that you set them up with lessons together, hoping he would seduce her. I just don't understand how you could do something like that.

CYNTHIA: He's a monster. You don't comprehend that yet. The girl is obviously deluded. She'll probably do the seducing herself.

ALICE: Even if that's true, it doesn't justify what you're doing.

CYNTHIA: Who the hell's side are you on here?

ALICE: It's not a matter of sides. You have to face him about this, Cynthia, before it eats you alive inside. We can talk to him together if you like.

CYNTHIA: I can fight my own battles.

ALICE: I'm just asking you not to jump to conclusions.

CYNTHIA: You're blinded by infatuation.

ALICE: Don't sell me short, Cynthia.

CYNTHIA: It certainly feels like you're on his side. I feel like you're betraying me.

ALICE: I know how much pain you're feeling now.

CYNTHIA: You don't know shit about what I'm feeling.

ALICE: I'm shocked, Cynthia. I really am. When I talk to him, when I'm with him, I can't imagine he's capable of something like this. Maybe he's not any more, is all I'm saying — or maybe he has those kinds of urges under control, because treatment is working for him.

CYNTHIA: I won't have obscenity like that spoken in my house!

(The door opens, and Ed and Amy walk in, laughing, looking almost like a couple.)

AMY: We found the best ice cream! I had this huge cone with "Colossal Chocolate" and "Monster Mocha.".

ED: And I settled for a dish of "Marionberry Matinee."

567

AMY: It was awesome.

ED: I'd say we discovered the best ice cream parlor this fair city has to offer. Wouldn't you agree?

AMY: Totally.

(Ed finally notices that Cynthia and Alice are just staring at him.)

ED: Cynthia? Alice? Is something the matter?

(BLACKOUT. END OF ACT ONE.)

ACT TWO

/ continuous action

(AT RISE: the same moment that ended Act One.)

ED: Is something the matter?

(Alice takes charge, speaking on her feet, trying to hustle Cynthia out of there before a spontaneous confrontation erupts.)

(When they leave, the newspaper articles remain on the coffee table.)

ALICE: Actually, we were just on our way to the store. So if you'll excuse us. Oh, Amy, can I talk to you a minute? I'll wait outside. I have a favor to ask.

AMY: Sure.

ED: It was dinner at six, wasn't it?

ALICE: Six, right.

ED: I look forward to it.
ALICE: Right.

(And Alice has Cynthia out of there.)

ED: What was that all about?
AMY: Is she your new girlfriend?
ED: No.
AMY: You're sure seeing her a lot.
ED: Which is no business of yours, is it? I have something to show you.

(Ed takes a letter out and hands it to Amy.)

ED: Does the name Hans Koeller mean anything to you?
AMY: Should it?
ED: Shame on you. I took you to hear him, remember? He's the first violinist with the symphony.
AMY: I don't remember. Are you in love with her?
ED: I have something important to discuss with you. This letter invites you to audition for the Junior Symphony.
AMY: I don't think she's your type.
ED: Did you hear what I said?
AMY: I don't think I'm ready for that.
ED: Not yet. But your progress is remarkable. Not only that —
Koeller will take you on as a student.
AMY: But you're my teacher.
ED: I don't think you realize what an honor this is. He does very little teaching any more. He's highly selective about who he takes on. I sent him one of your old tapes, and he was very impressed. I did tell him you're a little rusty.
AMY: Then I get two teachers?
ED: One. I'll be leaving town.

(Amy is clearly shocked and disappointed by this.)

ED: I have to find a job, Amy. I have an interview next week. It looks very promising.
AMY: So you're dumping me off on him? Great.
ED: This is an extraordinary opportunity for you, young lady.
Koeller is very picky about who he takes on. Not only that, he's a

graduate of Julliard and still has many contacts there. It's the opportunity of a lifetime.

AMY: You're my teacher.

ED: He can do much more for your career than I can.

AMY: I can't afford lessons from some big shot like that.

ED: Don't worry about it. I've already made arrangements with him.

AMY: So where are you moving to?

(Ed hesitates a moment before replying, thinking on his feet.)

ED: Seattle. I have a job interview next Friday.

AMY: You could take me with you.

ED: That's not possible. Even if Koeller wasn't interested, you still have school to finish.

AMY: I can finish school in Seattle.

ED: I'm not taking you to Seattle.

AMY: I can go there on my own.

ED: You wouldn't get far, once you're reported as missing. You're still a minor, young lady.

AMY: Not for long. When I'm 18, I can do anything I want. I'm not staying at home, that's for sure. I can follow you to Seattle and move in next door to you if I want. There's nothing you could do about it either. It's a free country.

ED: Amy, I know this must be very scary for you — opportunities like this always are. They are also very rare. Studying with Koeller can be the most important thing that ever happened to you. He can pull a lot of strings for you.

AMY: If I can't study with you, maybe I won't study with anybody.

ED: You're being a selfish, foolish girl. It's a sin to waste a raw talent like yours.

AMY: I know what sin is.

(A beat.)

ED: Amy, please, let the idea sink in. I can always visit and check on your progress. Your success is very important to me.

AMY: Why can't I have two teachers? Two's better than one. Why can't you find a job here?

ED: I'm still controversial here.

AMY: Then why can't I study with somebody in the Seattle Symphony? Seattle's bigger than here. It's much more important to study in Seattle.

ED: You are not going with me. That's my final word on the matter.

AMY: My final word is you can't stop me.

ED: Why are you doing this?

AMY: You're the one doing it. You get my confidence up again and then abandon me. You're just like my mother — you're only nice when you want something from me.

ED: Amy, I'm not abandoning you.

AMY: That's what it feels like.

ED: It's not like I'm your father. I'm your music teacher — and frankly, Koeller will be much better for you than I am.

AMY: You're the closest I've ever had to a father.

ED: Amy, please . . .

AMY: You think you can just walk out on me, and it won't mean a thing, right? You forgive me, you act like you care about me again . . . and then you just say goodbye . . . like it doesn't matter at all. I'm supposed to just go on like nothing happened, right?

ED: I didn't know you felt that way.

AMY: How couldn't you know?

ED: I need this job, Amy. I'm not abandoning you. I'll be able to come down often and see how you're doing.

(Amy is sulking.)

ED: You don't believe me?

AMY: Why should I believe you?

ED: Because I wouldn't lie to you.

(A beat.)

ED: Because I care about what happens to you.

(A beat.)

ED: Alice is waiting for you.

(Amy starts away.)

ED: Amy?

(She stops and turns.)

ED: I'd never do anything to hurt you.

(She doesn't respond.)

ED: This is the opportunity of a lifetime.
AMY: Then why is this the worst day of my life?

(She leaves.)

(Ed is upset by this turn of events. He goes to the tape deck and turns on music. String Quartet, high energy, frantic: the uptempo section of the THEME.)

(He comes back and sits on the divan. He sees the newspaper articles on the coffee table. He picks one up. He is shocked at what he's found. He quickly looks through them all, in growing panic. He drops them, a few falling to the floor. What to do? He gets to his feet and hurries to his room.)

(The MUSIC plays. Frantic.)

(Alice enters. She sees the articles on the floor. She picks them up, putting them back inside the manila envelope. She goes to the tape deck and turns it off. She turns and waits.)

(Ed enters, reacting to the new silence. They face one another.)
ED: You read the articles.
ALICE: Yes.
ED: That was ten years ago. I haven't been in trouble since.
ALICE: Why's Amy so upset?
ED: I told her I'm leaving town.
ALICE: What are you talking about?
ED: I have a job interview.
ALICE: You were going to go without telling me? You're just full of secrets, aren't you?
ED: Alice, I used to be very sick, but that was a long time ago. I went through treatment. I've been able to keep myself out of trouble since then, no matter what the law thinks.
ALICE: You told me you were innocent.
ED: I went to jail for something I didn't do. I've never touched Amy improperly. I'm in recovery, Alice. Just like you. I take it one day at a time. Just like you.

572

ALICE: Cynthia thinks treatment can't work with you. She thinks Amy is lying.

ED: But Cynthia's the only one who believes in me . . .

ALICE: She's been faking it, Ed. Don't you realize who Cynthia is?

ED: Apparently not. I thought she believed I'm innocent.

ALICE: Cynthia is Heather's aunt. The woman in the paper, the mother, is Cynthia's sister.

(Ed is too shocked to reply.)

ALICE: She set you up. She rented you a room so she could keep an eye on you. She thinks she wants revenge of some kind.

ED: She wouldn't like you telling me this.

ALICE: No, she wouldn't. I don't know who to believe any more. Everything's suddenly so complicated.

ED: It does get complicated. But it's also very simple.

ALICE: I can't picture you that way. I try but I just can't. Ed, is this why . . .?

ED: Ask whatever you want, Alice.

ALICE: Why you've never made a move on me? Only someone as young as Amy can arouse you?

ED: I care for you a lot, Alice.

ALICE: That's not what I asked.

ED: I've never laid a hand on Amy. It's the God's truth. Alice, I haven't been in trouble for ten years! I've learned how to, well, deal with certain thoughts — without acting on them...

ALICE: Then you still have thoughts?

ED: What do you want me to say, Alice? That I lust after young girls, that they're the only ones who get it up for me?

ALICE: It would seem so.

ED: Alice, I— . . . I wanted so much to make love to you. I just couldn't. I was afraid I would fail. I don't know what else to tell you.

(A beat.)

ALICE: I want to believe you, Ed.

ED: I'm telling you the truth.

ALICE: Maybe I can help you. But I need to know the whole truth.

ED: Most people don't want the truth. They want to hear what they expect you to say.

ALICE: What do they expect you to say?

ED: That I was abused as a child myself, how's that? You believe that? That I'm just perpetuating the cycle, that I'm a victim who makes other victims? That's something people expect you to say.

ALICE: I want the truth.

ED: Okay. I'm responsible for having done some horrible things in my life — but I offer no excuses. I alone am responsible. That's what I'm living with, Alice. That's the horror I go to bed with.

ALICE: In AA, I had to admit I am powerless.

ED: Alice, I did those things, and I can't take them back. I'm not powerless. I'm responsible.

(A beat.)

ED: Amy told me I'm the closest thing she's ever had to a father.

ALICE: Cynthia thinks she's infatuated with you.

ED: I'm sure that's part of it.

ALICE: And the rest?

ED: She knows how much I care for her.

ALICE: How much *do* you care for her?

ED: It doesn't matter. I'm leaving town. I have a job interview in San Francisco. I told Amy it was in Seattle. I was afraid she'd threaten to follow me — which, in fact, she did. That's when she told me I'm like a father to her.

ALICE: How'd that make you feel?

ED: Are we in a meeting now, Alice? Sorry. That was uncalled for.

ALICE: Then you're leaving town?

ED: I can't get a teaching job here, Alice. What school would hire me after all the publicity?

(A beat. Ed just looks at her.)

ALICE: I'm confused. Then you still find Amy attractive? Desirable?

ED: Yes.

ALICE: My God . . .

ED: Does it shock you? You can relax. I was more attracted to her when she was 12.

ALICE: Then where's your progress?

ED: My progress is that I'm not acting on my feelings!

(A beat.)

ED: Alice, the thoughts in my head used to drive me mad. I didn't want them there, but there they were, as big as life, thoughts and feelings of... it's hard to describe ...

ALICE: Lust.

ED: No. "Lust" doesn't do it. Not lust. Longing. Incredible longing. For connection to innocence, I think. Amy, Heather: young girls are so — pristine. So — untainted.

ALICE: Jesus ...

ED: Alice, longing for innocence is not a crime. Thoughts are just thoughts. Feelings are just feelings. It's what we do with them that makes us sick — or makes us well.

ALICE: What is "well" about wanting sex with a child?

ED: Nothing at all. That's the horror of it, if you act on such feelings and thoughts, you create the very opposite of the innocence that attracts you in the first place. It's a little like drinking, isn't it? Just because you think of drinking, Alice, doesn't mean you have to take a drink.

ALICE: Raping young girls is not like drinking. And just because you're not drinking doesn't mean you're sober either.

ED: We're talking about obsessive behavior here, Alice. We may have more in common than you think.

ALICE: I read somewhere that sex crimes have more to do with power than desire.

ED: That's one theory. There are others. All are probably partly true. None tell the whole story.

ALICE: You sound like someone in denial.

ED: The wonderful thing about denial is that there's no defense against it. If I say I'm not, if I deny denial, then saying so is used as evidence that I am.

ALICE: I definitely think you are.

ED: I think too much, I'll grant you that.

ALICE: About Amy?

ED: Christ. I'll forget you said that. About everything, Alice. About my life.

ALICE: Stop thinking and do something about it. Get back into treatment.

ED: Please don't patronize me.

ALICE: I thought you were patronizing me.

(A beat.)

ALICE: Ed, I want to understand and I want to help.

ED: Why?

ALICE: Because I've fallen in love with you.

ED: No, Alice . . .

ALICE: I know it's not mutual. I believe what you've told me, that you've stayed out of trouble, but I think you're in danger of relapsing if you don't get help.

ED: You said that already.

ALICE: Please don't push me away.

ED: Alice, I can only work on one thing at a time at the moment. That's why I'm leaving town. That's why I'm not letting Amy know where I'm going. We've been having too much fun this past week; we've been getting too close. I'm feeling things I haven't felt in a long time, things that scare me. I remember how much I used to desire her.

ALICE: You can't run from your feelings, Ed. You have to face them and deal with them.

(A beat.)

ED: I have an interview in San Francisco. It's probably best if I leave as soon as possible.

ALICE: You can't do this alone.

ED: Then I'm sorry because right now it's the way I have to do it.

ALICE: I'm sorry, too.

ED: I'll be out of here first thing in the morning.

ALICE: I thought I meant more to you than this.

ED: What do you want from me, Alice?

(She goes to him, embracing him.)

ALICE: Let me help you.

(Ed pushes her away.)

ED: Alice, please . . . you don't understand what you're getting into.

ALICE: No, I'm sure I don't. But I do understand how much pain you're in. I know how much you need help.

(Ed moves away, changes the subject.)

ED: Where's Cynthia?

ALICE: Next door. I think she should spend the night with me.

ED: I understand.

ALICE: Give what you're doing some thought. You can't run away forever.

(Ed doesn't reply.)

ALICE: If you do decide to leave, please call me first. Ed?
ED: Okay.
ALICE: Call me any time.

(No reply. She leaves.)

(Ed is alone. CROSS FADE, with spot remaining on Ed, to Amy in her area, playing the THEME on her violin. Ed watches her. He turns to the audience:)

ED: Longing for innocence is not a crime.

(CROSS FADE TO: Cynthia in neutral area, a bar, speaking to the audience.)

CYNTHIA: There are times when the ends justify the means, they have to. Look at Hitler. If someone had killed him, had blown Hitler's brains out before he sent another trainload of Jews to their death, would anyone with human feelings feel bad about that? Or we would think, At last! — someone finally had the courage to do what was right, someone had the balls to do what it takes to rid the world of Hitler. We would've given that person a goddamn medal.

(CROSS FADE TO:…)
/ living room, that evening

(The doorbell rings. Ed comes into the room from his bedroom and goes to the door. It's Amy.)

AMY: What's going on?
ED: I'm not feeling well, Amy. I was just about to turn in early.
AMY: Alice didn't say you were sick. She said your date got called off because something came up.
ED: I wouldn't call it a date. We were going to dinner and a concert. What came up is, I'm not feeling well.

AMY: Then later she and Cynthia got in this big fight and Cynthia stormed off and went to town, and now Alice is looking for her, and I don't know what's going on. Why is everybody angry all of a sudden?

ED: Amy, another thing that came up is that I have to leave . . . leave for Seattle . . . first thing in the morning.

AMY: Why?

ED: *(ignoring this)* Have you thought about studying with Koeller?

AMY: I want to go with you. I could live where you're living, just like you were my real dad. I don't take up much space. I'd practice all the time with you around, I know I would.

(Ed goes to the table, where the envelope of articles remains.)

ED: There are some newspaper articles in here. I want you to go next door and read them. Maybe then you'll understand why you can't go with me.

AMY: What are they?

ED: Just read them.

AMY: I'll read them now.

ED: No. I don't want to be around when you do. You'll understand once you've read them.

AMY: Can't you just tell me what they say?

ED: Maybe it's better you hear it from me than from Cynthia.

AMY: Hear what?

ED: What the articles say is that I'm guilty, Amy. What I was sent to prison for — I was guilty of that earlier, before I met you. It's a sickness I have, a deep psychological illness, and I was treated for it, and I'm much better now, mostly, but it's something like cancer, it can lie in remission and then suddenly flair up and become a serious problem again, so it's something I have to be alert about, always, and even though it's been a long time now since I've been sick that way, it never really goes away entirely and . . . just read the articles.

(He hands her the envelope. Amy doesn't know what to do with it. Suddenly she comes forward and embraces him, clutching onto him with a sense of desperation.)

ED: Amy, please . . .

AMY: You're just saying this to make me not want to go to Seattle with you.

(She kisses him passionately. Despite himself, Ed is getting aroused. He starts kissing back. Amy moves them to the divan, where they sit down, still clutched. Ed briefly breaks away.)

AMY: I love you.
ED: Amy, stop . . .
AMY: I want you.
ED: No!

(She stops him with a passionate kiss. The door opens and Alice walks in. She is shocked to see them embraced on the divan. Ed pulls away. Amy sees Alice and quickly stands up, straightening herself up. Then she hurries out of the house.)

ED: Alice . . . she flung herself at me . . .

(Alice just looks at him in shock. He gets up and picks up the articles.)

ED: Look, I gave her the articles to read. I tried to get her to understand. I didn't start anything, Alice. She got so upset when I told her I was leaving right away, she just flipped out and came on to me. I was as shocked as you are. I'm telling you the truth. Talk to her, you'll see how upset she is.
ALICE: I have a more immediate problem. Cynthia's drinking again. We had a fight and she drove to town. I went looking for her — I thought she might be going to a meeting. It took me a while to try the bars. I just missed her in two.
ED: Is there anything I can do to help?
ALICE: Get a motel room for the night.
ED: If I help you look for her, we can cover twice as much territory.
ALICE: I came over to tell you to get out of here.
ED: I appreciate your concern.
(Alice turns to go.)

ED: Alice, I need to know that you believe me. I wasn't kissing her back.
ALICE: I'm sorry. I don't know who to believe any more.

(She exits. Ed turns to the audience.)

ED: I wasn't kissing her back.

(CROSS FADE TO: ...)

/ that night, a bar stool

(Cynthia faces the audience, sitting on a barstool. She is high.)

CYNTHIA: I would torture the sonofabitch. I would peel off his goddamn toenails one by one. I'd hope to God he'd never been circumcised so I could take a razor and slice off the goddamn foreskin myself, and maybe accidentally-on-purpose slip a little and take off an inch or two more while I'm at it.

It would be so goddamn easy. Zip, zip, zip! Cut up his face, make him look uglier than shit, look like the monster he really is. Make him so goddamn ugly anybody, any kid, any young girl, would take off in fright the minute she saw him. If he can't get close to them, he can't do shit, understand what I'm saying? Give him a face to match his morals.

(She is slicing the air with the knife.)

CYNTHIA: Zip, zip, zip!

(CROSS FADE TO: ...)

/ dark living room, that night, past midnight

(Ed is asleep on the divan. Heather appears, dressed like a street hooker, a figure in Ed's nightmare.)

HEATHER: Hey, Mr. Music Man, hello again! You sure got yourself in some deep shit this time. Man follows his cock, no telling where it will lead him.

(Ed sits up abruptly, sweating, waking out of a nightmare.)

ED: Heather?
HEATHER: Bet you thought you could get me out of your mind forever. You trying to forget me, Mr. Music Man?
ED: I'm so sorry.

HEATHER: Doesn't do it, asshole. I'm like a short circuit in the wiring of your brain, and you ain't never getting rid of me!

ED: I never wanted to hurt you.

HEATHER: Then what was I doing in the fucking hospital last week? Some John beat the crap out of me, broke my goddamn jaw. Man, you wouldn't believe the weird shit they want me to do. You'd be shocked — as I remember, you weren't into much that was kinky.

ED: Dear God...

HEATHER: I do draw the line — this John who beat me up wanted to stick a lighted cigar up my pussy, you believe that shit? I told him to go fuck himself. But I get a kick out of some of the weird ones. Especially the Johns who want me to piss on them. There's poetic justice in doing that and believe me, I piss on those assholes real fine!

ED: I'm getting better. I really am.

HEATHER: Save that bullshit for a shrink. I gotta get back to work, Mr. Music Man. Unless, of course, I can do something for you. You need a blow job or something? You want a date?

(Heather exits. Ed collapses back on the divan and closes his eyes. A beat.)

(The living room door opens and Cynthia comes in, drunk. She's carrying a paper sack with a bottle in it. She sees Ed and moves close to him, staring down at him. She moves clumsily to the tape deck and turns on the music THEME.)

(Ed stirs. Cynthia sits and drinks. Ed sits up. He sees Cynthia.)

ED: I'll be leaving in the morning.

CYNTHIA: You sonofabitch. I bet you can talk your way out of anything. Or was it your goddamn lawyer who got you off?

ED: You should get to bed.

CYNTHIA: I'll go to bed when I goddamn feel like it. You want a drink?

ED: No thank you. I'm going to bed myself.

CYNTHIA: Wait a goddamn minute. We need to talk.

ED: Miss Bernstein, I learned who you really are and I know how terrible it must be for you—

CYNTHIA: Cut the crap! You don't know shit.

ED: Ten years ago, I was a very sick man.

CYNTHIA: "Sick."

(She shakes her head in disgust.)

CYNTHIA: How about perverted?
ED: Yes, it's a perversion. But I can't erase the past. I can only deal with and live in the present.
CYNTHIA: They should lock you up and throw away the goddamn key.
ED: I can understand how you might feel that way.
CYNTHIA: You don't understand shit.
ED: I'm going to bed.

(He stands up.)

CYNTHIA: Wait a minute. I have something to say here. Sit down, for Christ's sake. You can give me that goddamn much.

(Ed sits back down. He watches her a moment, then turns away.)

CYNTHIA: So tell me — who was the better student, Heather or Amy?
ED: What?
CYNTHIA: Who was your better student?
ED: That's difficult to say.
CYNTHIA: Heather played like an angel. Everyone said so. People more important than you said so. What do you think? Was Heather any good?
ED: That was so long ago—
CYNTHIA: Everybody expected great things from her. Like Amy, I bet. People expect great things from her, don't they? I bet you have lots of special students like that. You get in all their pants, too, don't you? You sonofabitch . . .
ED: Miss Bernstein, you can't make me feel more guilt or horror at my past than I've already felt.
CYNTHIA: You ruined Heather's life. You ruined my sister, my family, my life . . .
ED: I wish there was a way I could take all that back but I can't. All I can do is make sure I never do anything like that again.
CYNTHIA: You glib sonofabitch.

(The door opens and Alice enters.)

ALICE: Cynthia, thank God you're all right!

CYNTHIA: Who the hell said I'm all right? If I'd murdered this sonofabitch, then I'd be great . . .

ALICE: Ed, please get out.

(Ed stands up.)

CYNTHIA: No! I'm not done with you.

ALICE: Cynthia, I want you to listen to me.

CYNTHIA: I'm going to figure out what the hell to do with you.

ALICE: Cynthia, listen to me!

CYNTHIA: You want a drink?

ALICE: No, and I think you've had plenty. Give me the bottle.

CYNTHIA: Go to hell.

ALICE: Don't do this to yourself.

CYNTHIA: I want to do something to Mr. Ramsey, don't you understand that?

ALICE: I understand how you feel. Ed, please go.

(Ed moves toward the door.)

CYNTHIA: No! You sonofabitch, you're lucky I'm a coward . . .

ED: I don't know what else I can say, Miss Bernstein. I've tried to do what amounts to a Ninth Step with you. Isn't that what you call it when somebody makes amends?

CYNTHIA: Make amends!

ED: We're all in recovery here. Or should be.

CYNTHIA: Coming from you, recovery sounds obscene.

ED: I take it one day at a time, just like you. And whether you like it or not, I've been out of trouble for ten years now.

CYNTHIA: You lying sonofabitch.

ALICE: I believe him, Cynthia.

CYNTHIA: What time is it?

(She moves toward the door.)

ALICE: Where do you think you're going?

CYNTHIA: I need a drink.

ALICE: You most certainly do not! I'm taking you into detox, Cynthia.

CYNTHIA: He wants to do a Ninth Step! You just never quit, do you?

ED: I know forgiveness is hard to give sometimes—
CYNTHIA: Forgiveness!
ED: You can forgive yourself, for starters.
CYNTHIA: Forgive myself for what?
ED: For relapsing. For throwing five years of sobriety down the drain.
ALICE: Ed, just cool it, please.
ED: For letting anger fester in your belly until it explodes into self-destruction.
CYNTHIA: It's you I want to destroy!
ALICE: Stop it!
CYNTHIA: You're so goddamn glib, so goddamn smooth-talking, when you don't know shit about what my family has been through. You have no idea what it's like to be raped. Heather trusted you. Amy trusted you.

(In what follows, Cynthia keeps talking and Ed's lines and Alice's lines overlap until the indicated silence.)

CYNTHIA: They look up to you. You get them to believe that they're special, that they're talented, and the more you bullshit them, the more they trust you.
ED: I don't bullshit them.
CYNTHIA: They'll do anything for you. Because it's inconceivable that you would hurt them, that's how deep the trust goes, that's how much they have come to need you, to need the attention and affection that you give them. I know what the hell I'm talking about. I worshipped him. I worshipped Mr. Baxter from the day I walked into his class.
ALICE: Cynthia?

(During the long speech below, Alice will move to comfort Cynthia, holding her in her arms by the end of the speech.)

CYNTHIA: I didn't understand why he gave me so much attention. Why he let me stay after school and help him. I only knew I felt special when I was with him, he was always telling me how smart I was, how creative I was, how unusual I was, and later how pretty I was and how desirable I was. He'd joke that he wished he was back in Jr. High himself, just so he could go steady with me. And I loved to hear that, I fed on that kind of flattery from him, so when he finally made his move, when finally one of our after-school rides, when he'd usually drive me home, always careful to drop me off a block away so my mother wouldn't notice; when finally we went to his house, not mine, and inside his house and into his bedroom, where he undressed in front of me, as if nothing unusual was going on at all, and then undressed me, like it was the most natural thing in the world, even then I wanted to please him, I wanted him to like me, and it wasn't until later, after several months had gone by, that the bad dreams began and I didn't want to do it with him any more, because I didn't understand it, and sometimes he was mean to me now, he was making demands of me now, and asking me to do things I never heard of anyone doing before, things I didn't want to do even though I still wanted to please him, always, but not by doing things that made me feel sick in my stomach, that tied nauseous knots in my stomach, like a physical gut reaction I had no control over, gagging when he put it in my mouth, screaming when he put it up my ass, I couldn't help it, I wanted to please him but I couldn't help not liking it, not pleasing him, and then he began to slap me, and demand more from me, until I no longer wanted to please him at all, I just wanted it to stop, I wanted to go away, to move away, to go anywhere he wasn't, and I hated him then, I hated him in a way that taught me what hate really was, and if he hadn't moved, if suddenly the new school year started and he was no longer there, no longer teaching, I think I might have killed him.

Or maybe I was already a coward, even then. Like I am now.

(Silence. Cynthia is exhausted in Alice's arms.)

ALICE: We're going to detox.
CYNTHIA: I'm so tired . . .

(Alice starts leading her to the door.)

ALICE: I'm so sorry you went through that. I wish you'd told me before.
CYNTHIA: I need some sleep . . .
ALICE: We'll be there before you know it.

(At the door, she turns to Ed.)

ED: I have a taxi picking me up at six in the morning.
ALICE: Will I talk to you before then?
ED: If you like.
ALICE: What about you? What do you like?
ED: You could come back after you drop her off.

ALICE: Let me think about it.

(She leads Cynthia out. Ed goes to his room. BLACKOUT.)

(KNOCKING on the door in the darkness. LIGHTS UP on: ...)

/the next morning, early

(Ed enters, carrying a suitcase. He answers the door. It's Amy.)

ED: I thought you were my cab.
AMY: Do you hate me?
ED: No.
AMY: I came up with a plan. Will you listen to it?
ED: Amy ...
AMY: You could adopt me.

(This is the last thing Ed expected to hear. He almost has to smile.)

AMY: It would solve everything.
ED: I can't do that, Amy.
AMY: Why are you doing this to me?
ED: Because I care for you very much.
AMY: If you really loved me, you'd take me with you.
ED: Amy, life isn't always as kind and gentle and innocent, as pristine, as it should be. Your stepfather took your childhood away from you. Everyone gets hurt when that happens. All of us.

(Amy is silent and pouting.)

ED: Every time I hear Mendelssohn, I think of you. Because when I hear you play, I see a vision of a world unlike any I've ever known — except in my imagination.

I used to think that when you imagine such a world, you can bring a little piece of it into being by acting on the feelings and thoughts of your imagination. But something horrible happens in the translation, Amy, something goes terribly wrong when you try to bring the imagination into the world with some kind of literal deed ... except, perhaps, when the act is a work of art.

When you play music, Amy, you turn the world into a place I want to be and I'm glad to be alive. I don't know if I'm making any sense.

Amy, what do you feel when you're playing Mendelssohn?
AMY: Peace.
ED: Yes, peace.

(A beat.)

AMY: I love you.
ED: I know.
AMY: If I ask you something, will you tell me the truth?
ED: Of course.
AMY: Did you really do what they said you did?
ED: Yes, Amy, I did.
AMY: How could you?
ED: It's a sickness I have. But I'm getting better, I've been getting better for quite a while now.

(A beat.)

ED: Do you hate me now?

(Amy shakes her head, no.)

ED: I hope not.
AMY: Did you ever think that way about me?
ED: *(lying)* No.

(He quickly stands up.)

ED: I have to get my other bag.

(He starts for the stairs. At the bottom of them he turns to speak to the audience.)

ED: *(to audience)* What the hell did you expect me to tell her?

(He exits.)

(Amy waits. The door opens, and Alice enters.)

ALICE: Amy, are you all right?
AMY: He's getting his other bag.
ALICE: I asked how you were.

AMY: I'm great.

ALICE: No you're not.

AMY: He didn't do anything wrong when you came in before.

ALICE: I know.

(Ed comes back with his bag.)

ED: Cynthia get in detox okay?

ALICE: She'll be fine. I'd like to speak to you a moment, if I may.

ED: Of course.

ALICE: Wait in the car, Amy. I'll give you a ride home.

AMY: (to Ed) Will you write me?

ED: Of course I will.

AMY: I'll write you every day.

(She exits.)

ED: She still may go to Seattle, thinking she's following me. I hope you'll take care of her.

ALICE: I can't keep her here if she's set on going. But I think we're becoming friends. I'll do what I can.

ED: Don't tell her where I really am.

ALICE: Not a chance, believe me.

ED: Say what you mean, Alice. If she found me, you think I'd fuck her brains out, is that it?

ALICE: You said it, I didn't.

ED: You people never quit, do you? You're determined to believe the worst. As if you could loathe me, loathe what I've done, more than I've loathed myself.

Can you imagine how many times I've thought of taking the easy way out? Good riddance, everyone should agree on that. If I killed myself, I'd be doing everybody a favor. But I haven't taken the easy way out because that would only get one perp off the streets, only yours truly, and there are a lot of us, Alice, hundreds and thousands of us, everywhere you look. Getting rid of me may make Cynthia feel good but what does it do to protect the children? Does it shock you that I care about the children? I do, more than you imagine, and getting rid of one perp won't cut it.

But if I change — if I can show others that recovery works, that behavior can change — maybe even "longing" can change, I don't know, I'm not there yet — but if I can show in my own behavior that obsessive, selfish, destructive behavior can be stopped in its tracks — then maybe I can inspire someone else to start treatment and change as well, Alice, and then we have two perps off the streets, and then maybe three and four and five . . .

That's why I haven't taken the easy way out.

(A beat.)

ALICE: God, it's so hard to say what I'm feeling right now. I just want you to understand that I believe you, Ed — about not being improper with Amy. And I think that means you've made an incredible positive step in your life. But it's just a start. You need to be back in a program.

ED: What I've been doing has been working, Alice. Mostly.

ALICE: You can't do it yourself.

ED: I appreciate your concern.

ALICE: I'll be praying for you.

ED: Thank you.

(There's an awkward moment, and then they embrace.)

(CROSS FADE to: . . .)

/ epilogue

(AMY in her area, playing the THEME on the violin. ED moves into his area, looking at her. Then he turns to the audience, and the music will fade out below and Amy disappear in darkness.)

ED: My name's Ed, and I'm a perp.

Cynthia once told me that the whole human race belongs in recovery. I think she has a point. Take denial, for example. The denial that people like me are, in so many ways, just like you.

Last week, when you looked out your kitchen window, that was me mowing the lawn next door. You waved, and I waved back.

Sometimes I bag your groceries at the supermarket. You tell me how your kids are doing in school. You tell me that corny joke you heard earlier in the week.

One summer I coached your boy's Little League team. Over the years, I taught both your daughters how to swim.

I've done many things in my life that I'm proud of. I won a Bronze Star on the battlefield. I was chosen Entrepreneur of the Year. Last Sunday I sang a solo in the church choir. Of course, I've also done things that horrify me. That's why "change" is the most important word in my vocabulary. "Change" is the first thing on my mind in the morning and the last thing on my mind at night. I don't expect you to understand me. I don't expect you to forgive me. I expect you to believe me when I say I'm in recovery, that I'm changing.

My name's Ed, and I'm a perp. Thanks for calling on me. Keep coming back.

(LAUGHTER in the darkness: LIGHTS UP on Heather, the hooker.)

HEATHER: Keep coming back! You got that right, Mr. Music Man — the johns *always* come back!

(Ed looks at her in horror.)

HEATHER: Anybody want a date? Keep coming back!

(The THEME plays, rising. and BLACKOUT. The play is over.)

For royalties information:
Charles Deemer
1-800-294-7176
cdeemer@teleport.com

About the Author

CHARLES DEEMER was raised in Virginia, Texas and Southern California. He received his BA at UCLA (Phi Beta Kappa, Honors English) and his MFA in Playwriting at the University of Oregon.

Deemer has had forty-one plays produced, dozens of short stories and articles published, and six screenplays optioned. His play *Famililly* won the 1997 "Crossing Borders" international new play competition. The public television version of his play *Christmas at the Juniper Tavern* won a regional ACE award. Three of his short stories were selected to the "Roll of Honor" in *Best American Short Stories*.

Deemer is the former editor of *Sweet Reason: a journal of ideas, history and culture* and the former managing editor of *Oregon Business* magazine.

Deemer has received two Oregon Arts Commission fellowships, one for fiction and one for drama. He won the Oregon Arts Foundation theater award and has been both a distinguished-writer-in-residence and a distinguished-scholar-in-residence at the Catlin Gabel School. Several of his plays have been supported by grants from the Oregon Council for the Humanities. Deemer has taught writing workshops at Fishtrap, the Pacific NW Writers Conference, Moonfish, and elsewhere.

Presently Deemer teaches screenwriting at Portland State University and, via the Internet, at Eastern Oregon University, as well as for Writers on the Net and Classical Arts University. Since 1994 he has been the webmaster of the Screenwriters and Playwrights Home Page at *http://www.screenwright.com*.

Charles Deemer lives in Portland, Oregon, with his wife, Harriet, and their dog, Levi.

Sooner or later, the kind of work I do
will be acknowledged.

It's nice to have it happen
while you're still alive.
But when you do this sort of thing,
you have to believe in history
and you have to believe in

the ancestry of art.

You have to believe that
you're filing things in the archives.

Maybe they will be appreciated in your lifetime
and maybe they won't.

It doesn't really matter.

—Paul Shrader